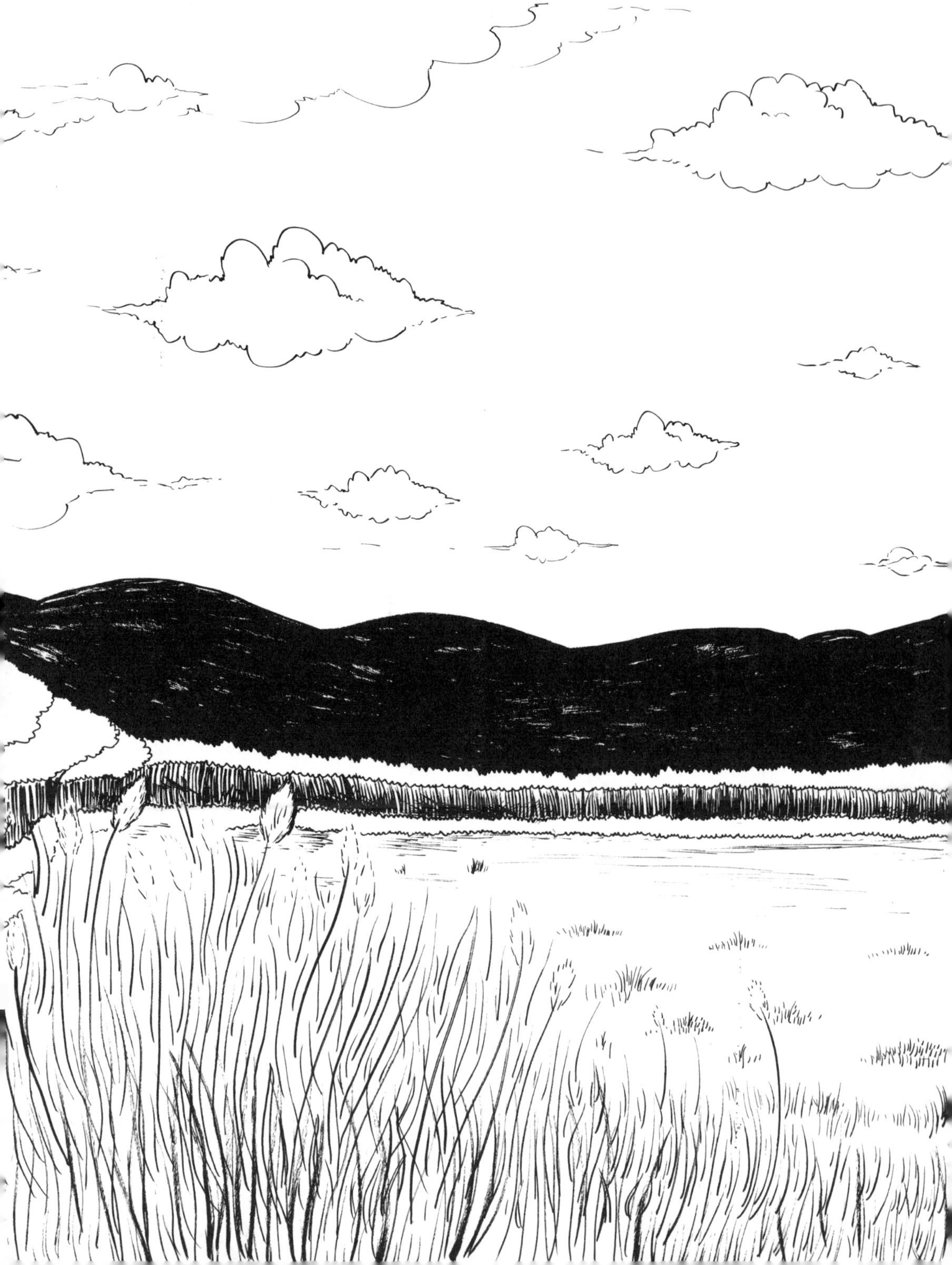

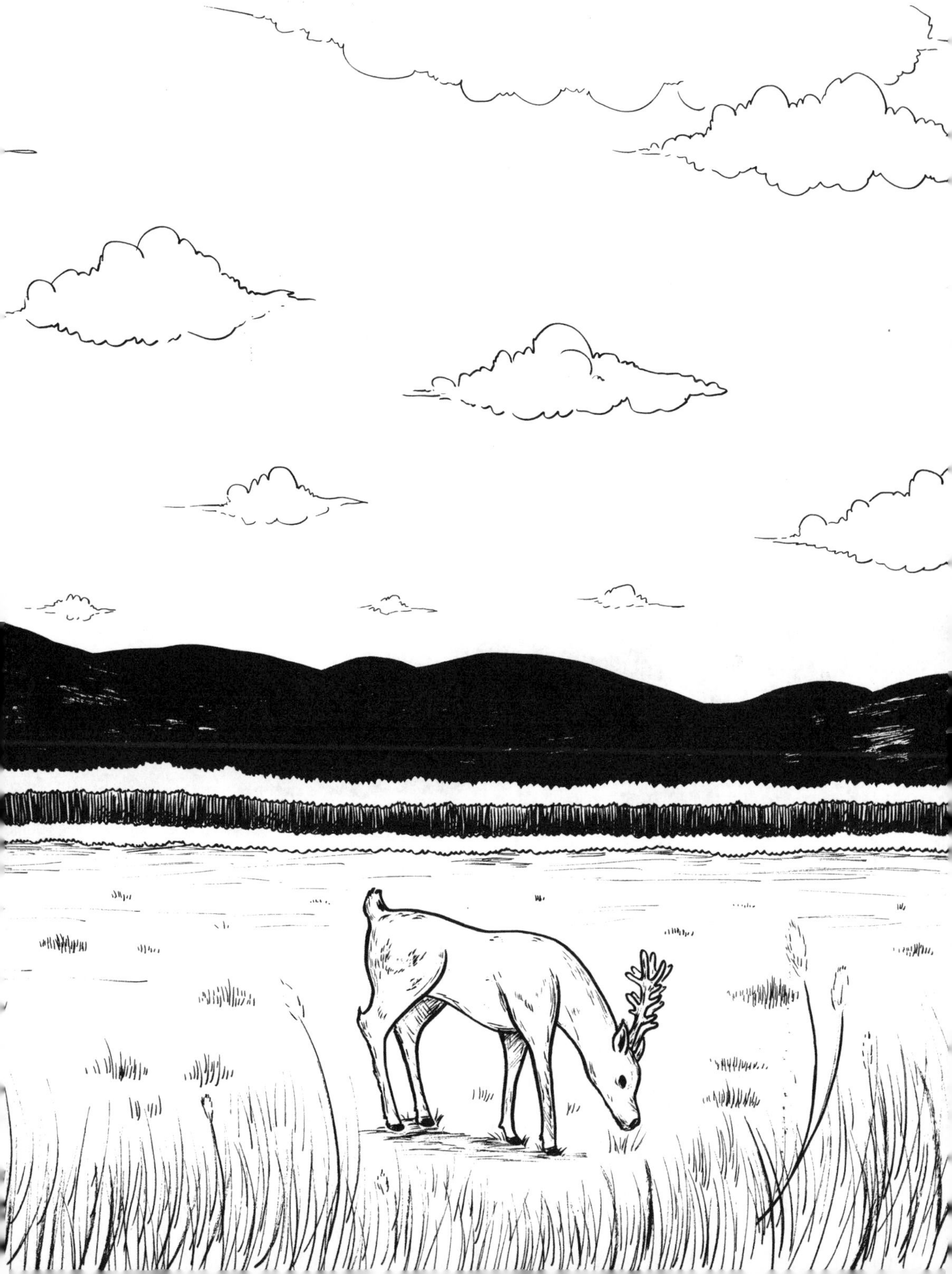

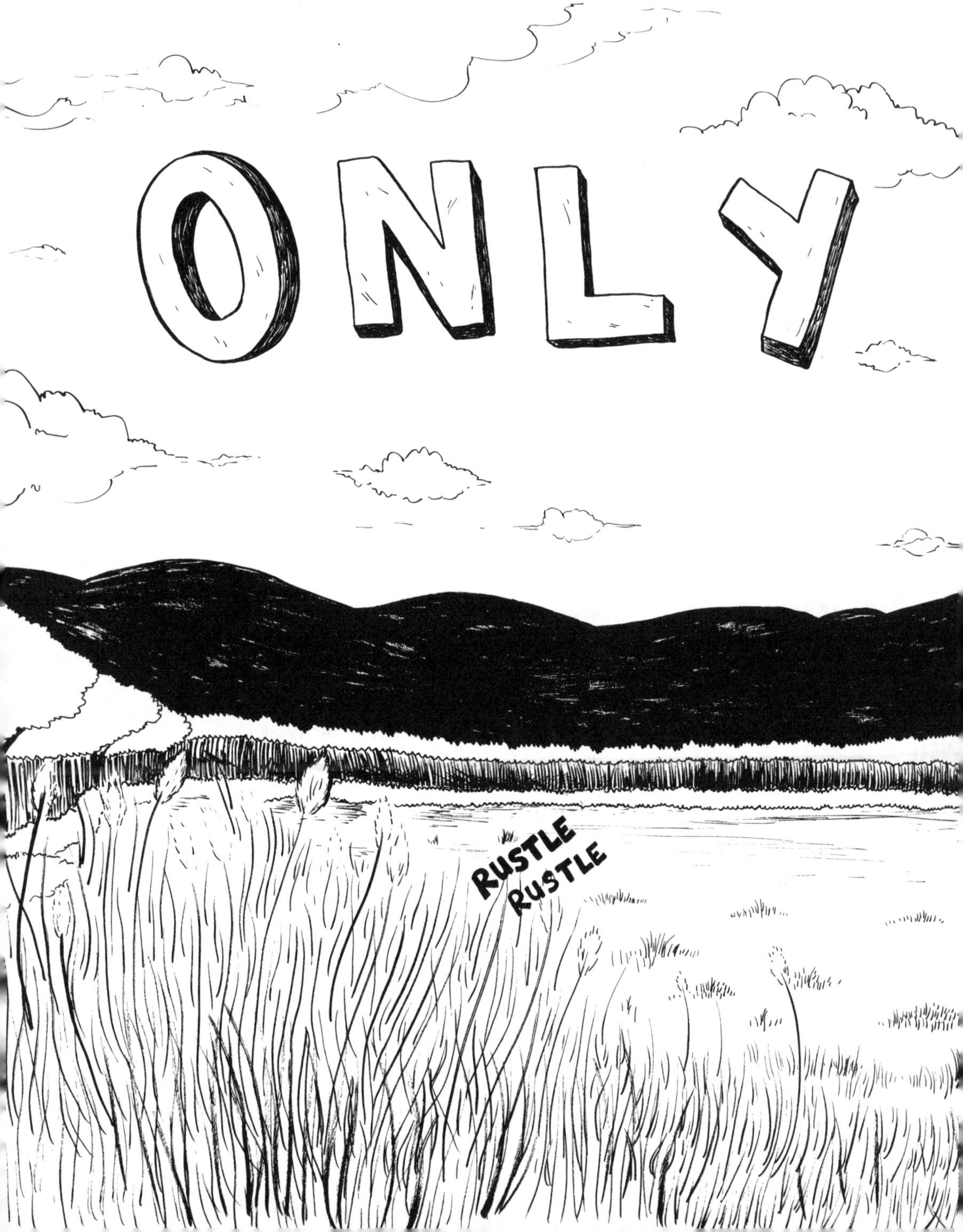
ONLY
RUSTLE
RUSTLE

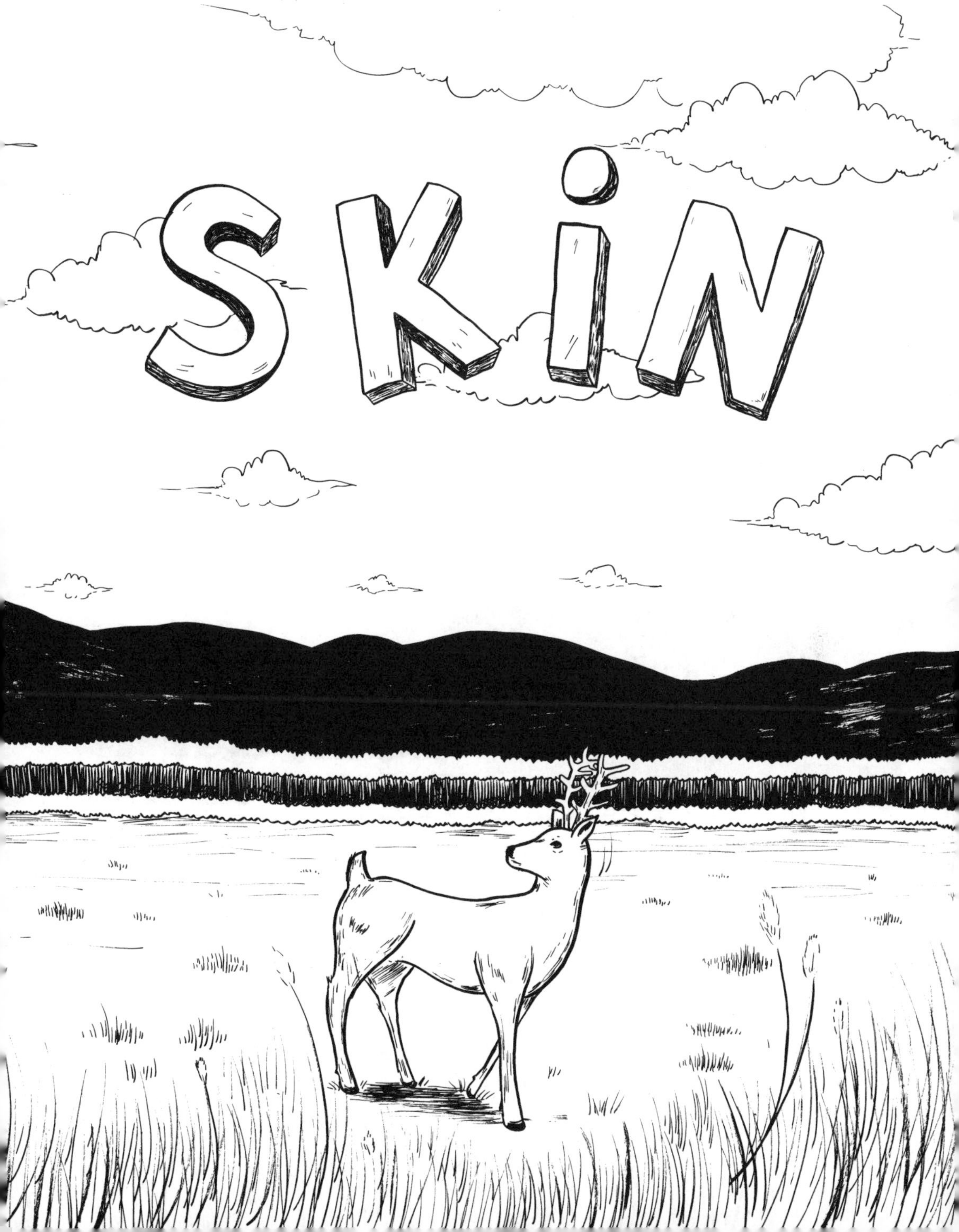
SKIN

PUBLISHED BY SECRET ACRES
DESIGNED BY SEAN FORD

SECRET ACRES
75-22 37th AVENUE, #452
JACKSON HEIGHTS, NY 11372

PRINTED IN THE UNITED STATES

LIBRARY OF CONGRESS PCN: 2011924537

ISBN10: 0-9831662-0-X
ISBN13: 978-0-9831662-0-7

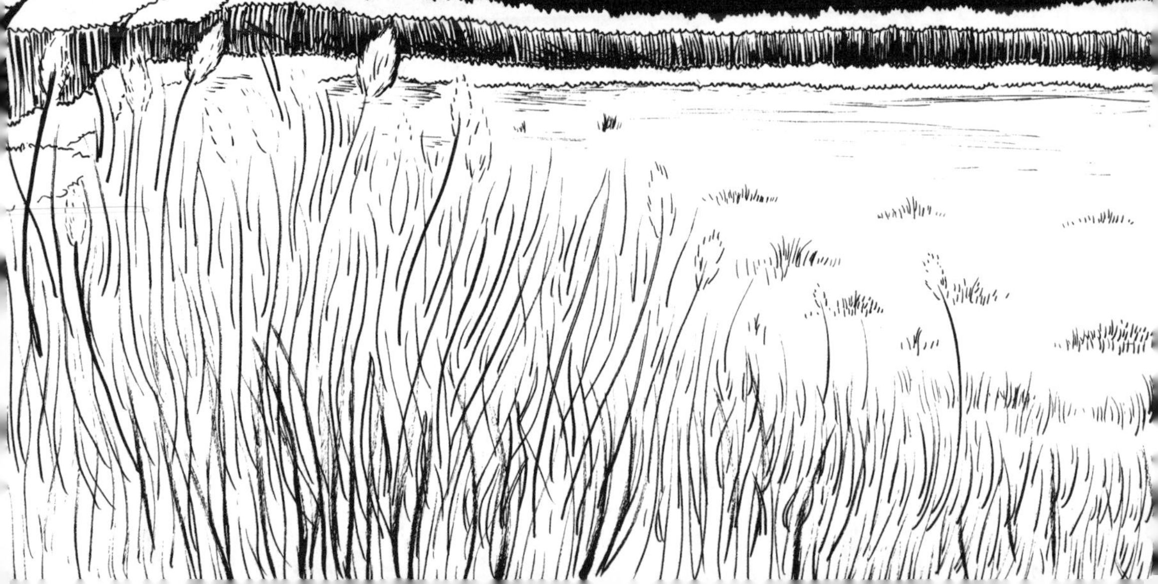

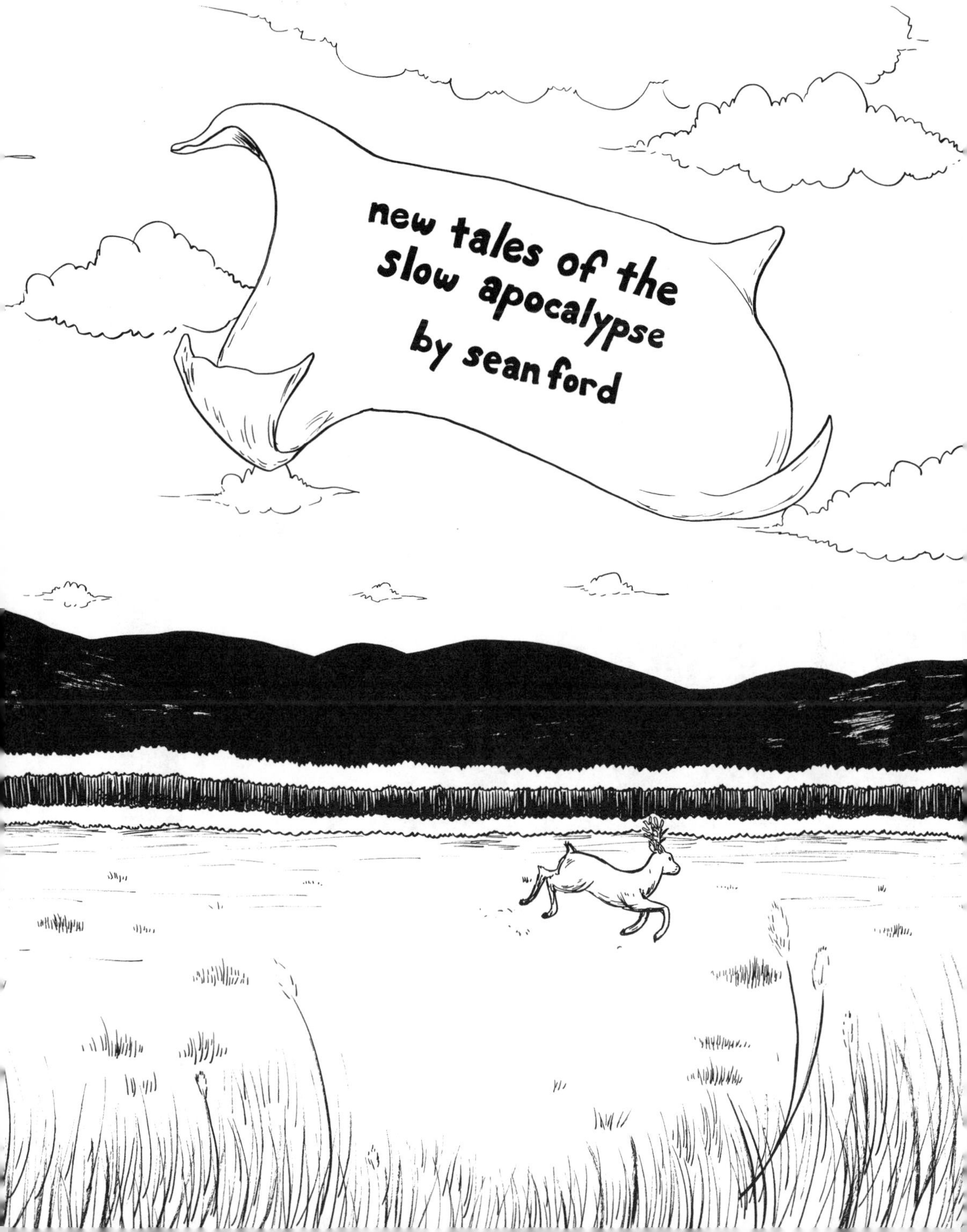
new tales of the
slow apocalypse
by sean ford

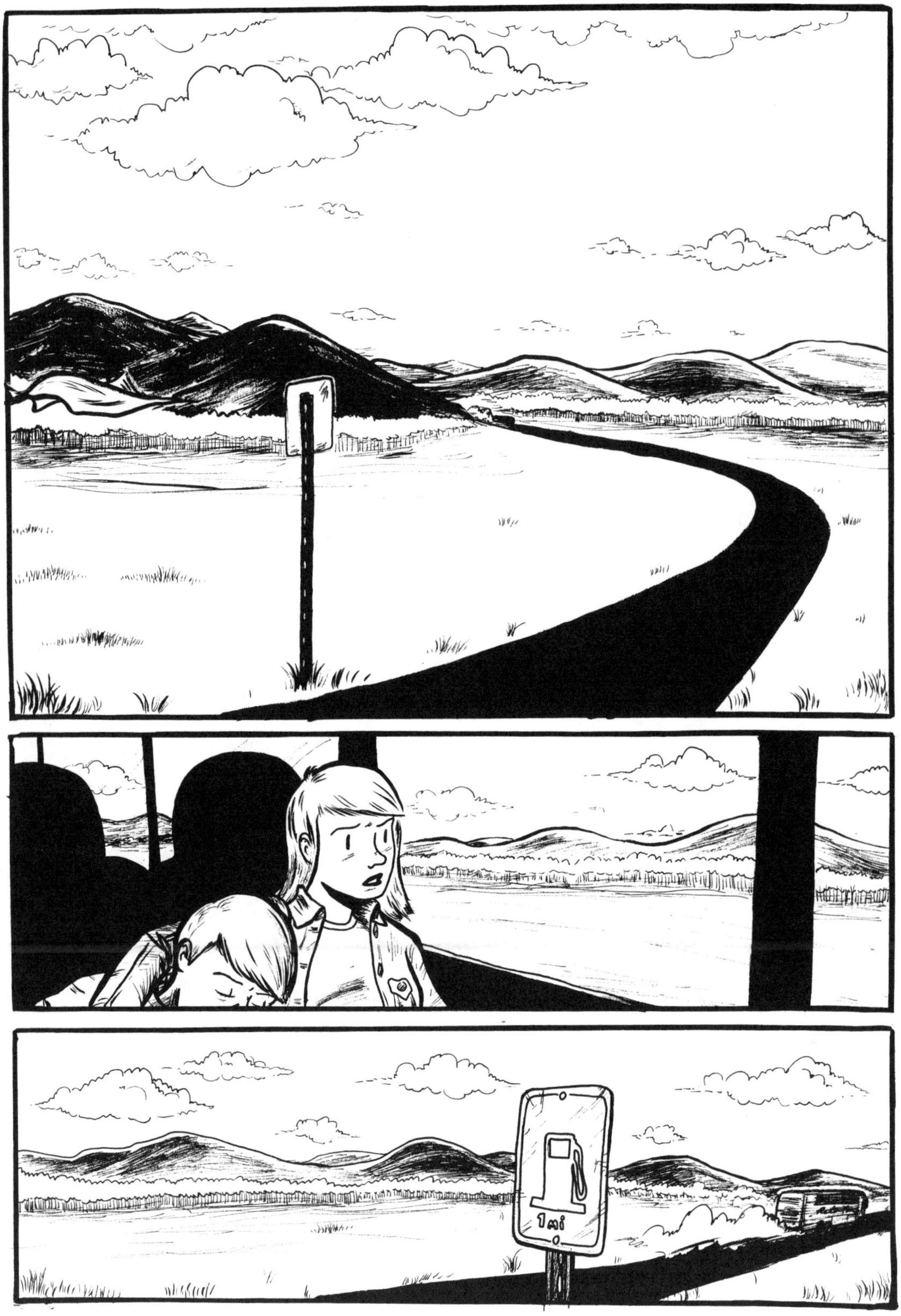
1 mi

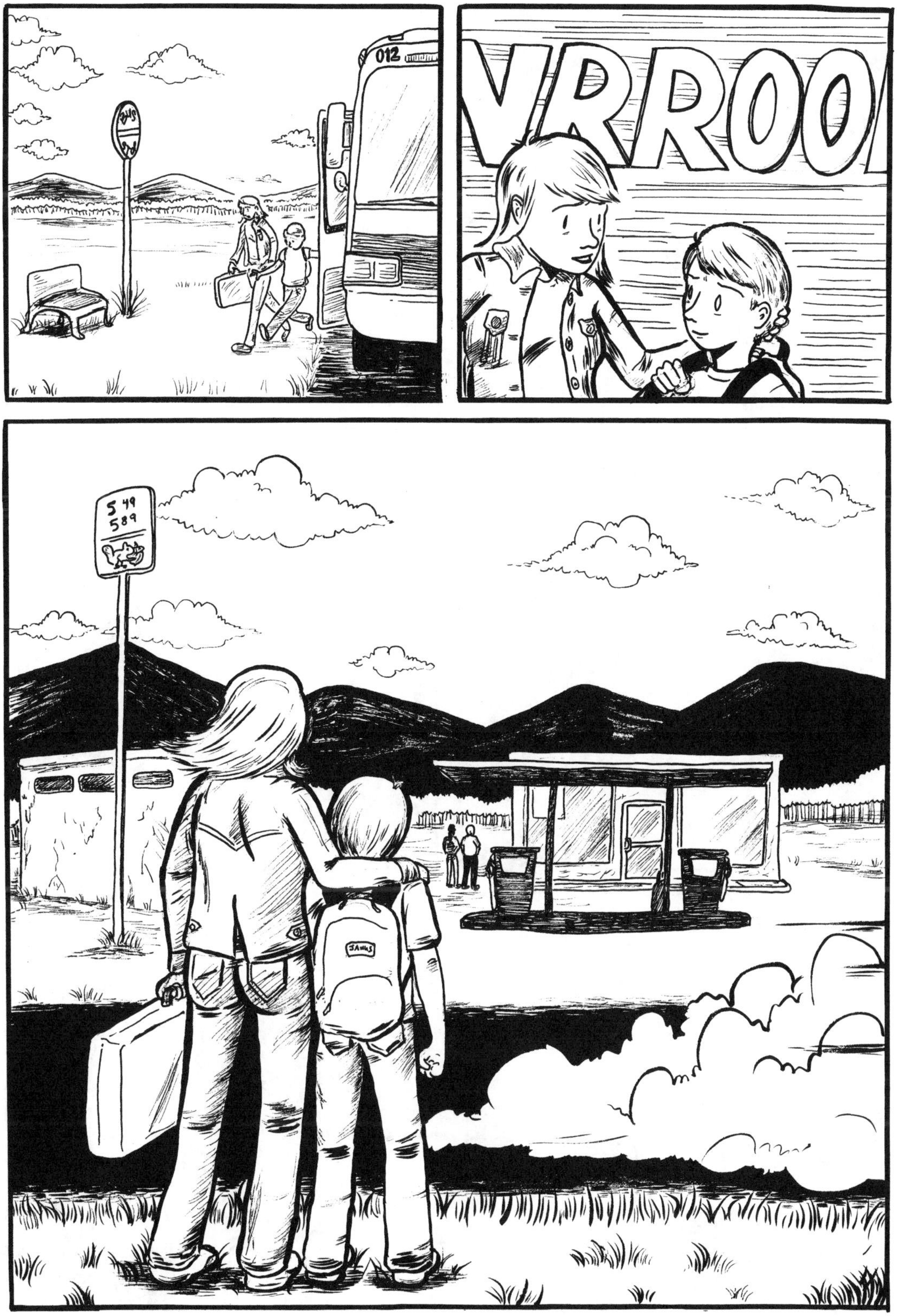
012
VRROO
5 49
589

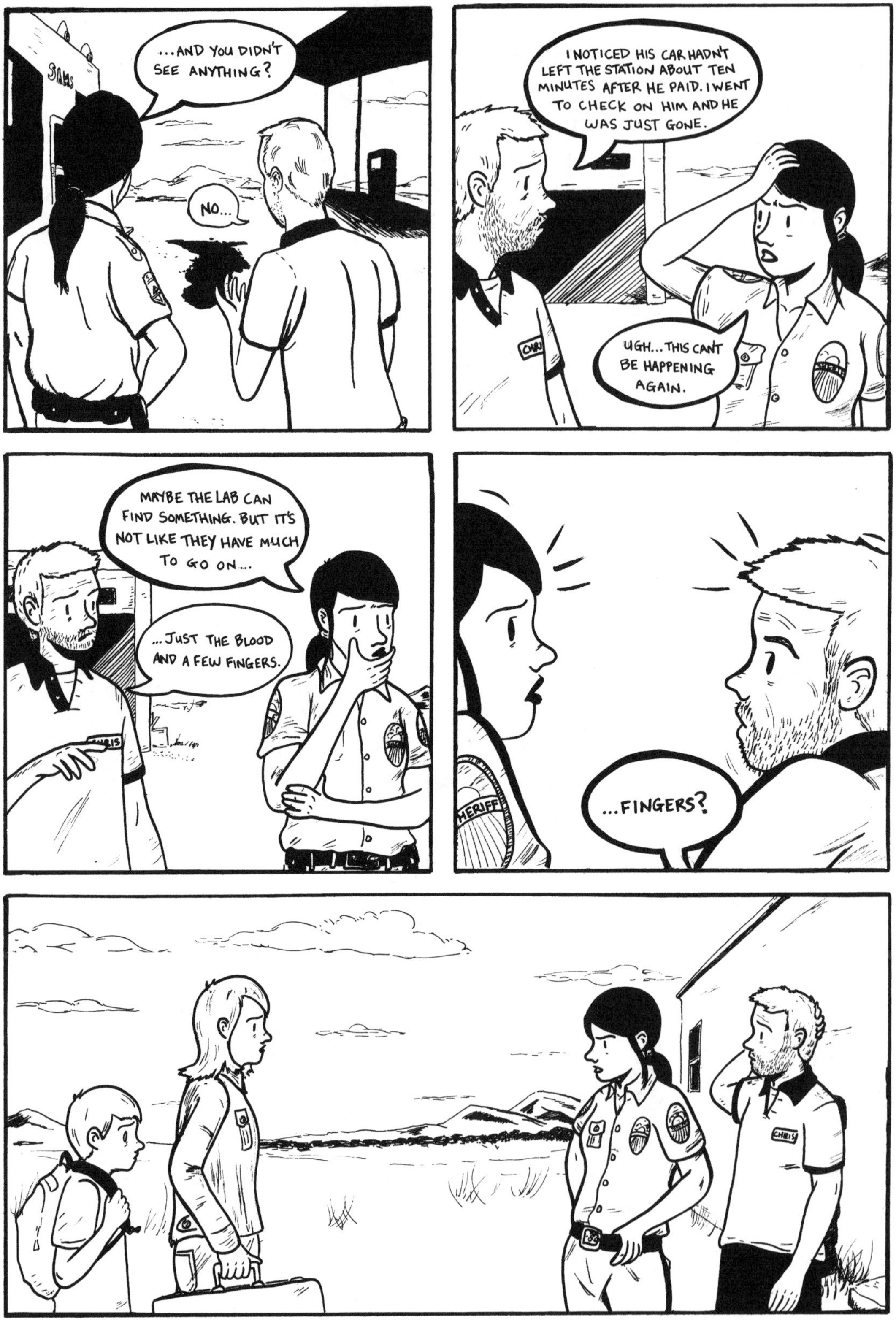
...AND YOU DIDN'T SEE ANYTHING?
NO...
I NOTICED HIS CAR HADN'T LEFT THE STATION ABOUT TEN MINUTES AFTER HE PAID. I WENT TO CHECK ON HIM AND HE WAS JUST GONE.
UGH... THIS CANT BE HAPPENING AGAIN.
MAYBE THE LAB CAN FIND SOMETHING. BUT IT'S NOT LIKE THEY HAVE MUCH TO GO ON....
...JUST THE BLOOD AND A FEW FINGERS.
...FINGERS?
CHRIS

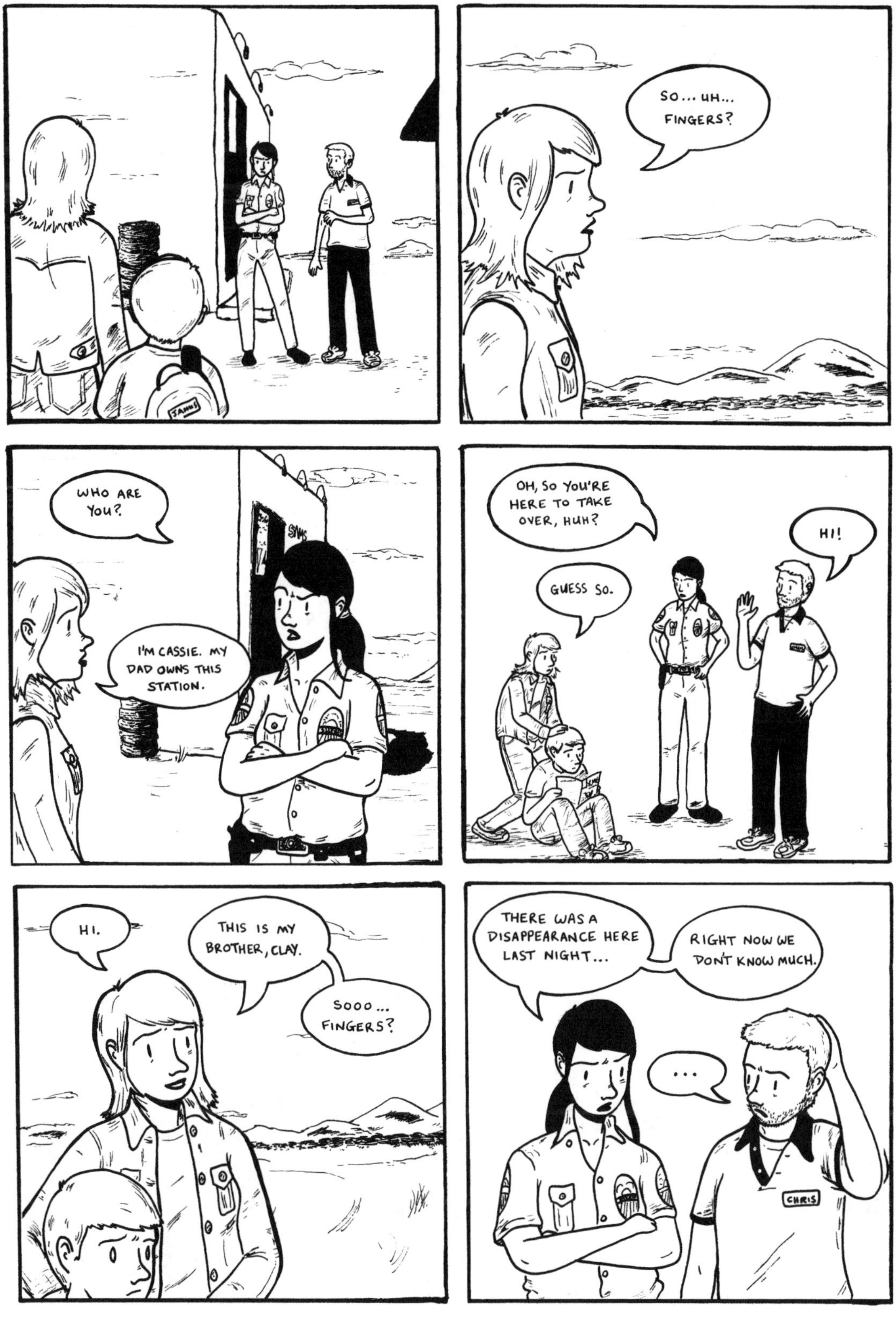
SO... UH... FINGERS?
WHO ARE YOU?
I'M CASSIE. MY DAD OWNS THIS STATION.
OH, SO YOU'RE HERE TO TAKE OVER, HUH?
GUESS SO.
HI!
HI.
THIS IS MY BROTHER, CLAY.
SOOO... FINGERS?
THERE WAS A DISAPPEARANCE HERE LAST NIGHT...
RIGHT NOW WE DON'T KNOW MUCH.
...
CHRIS

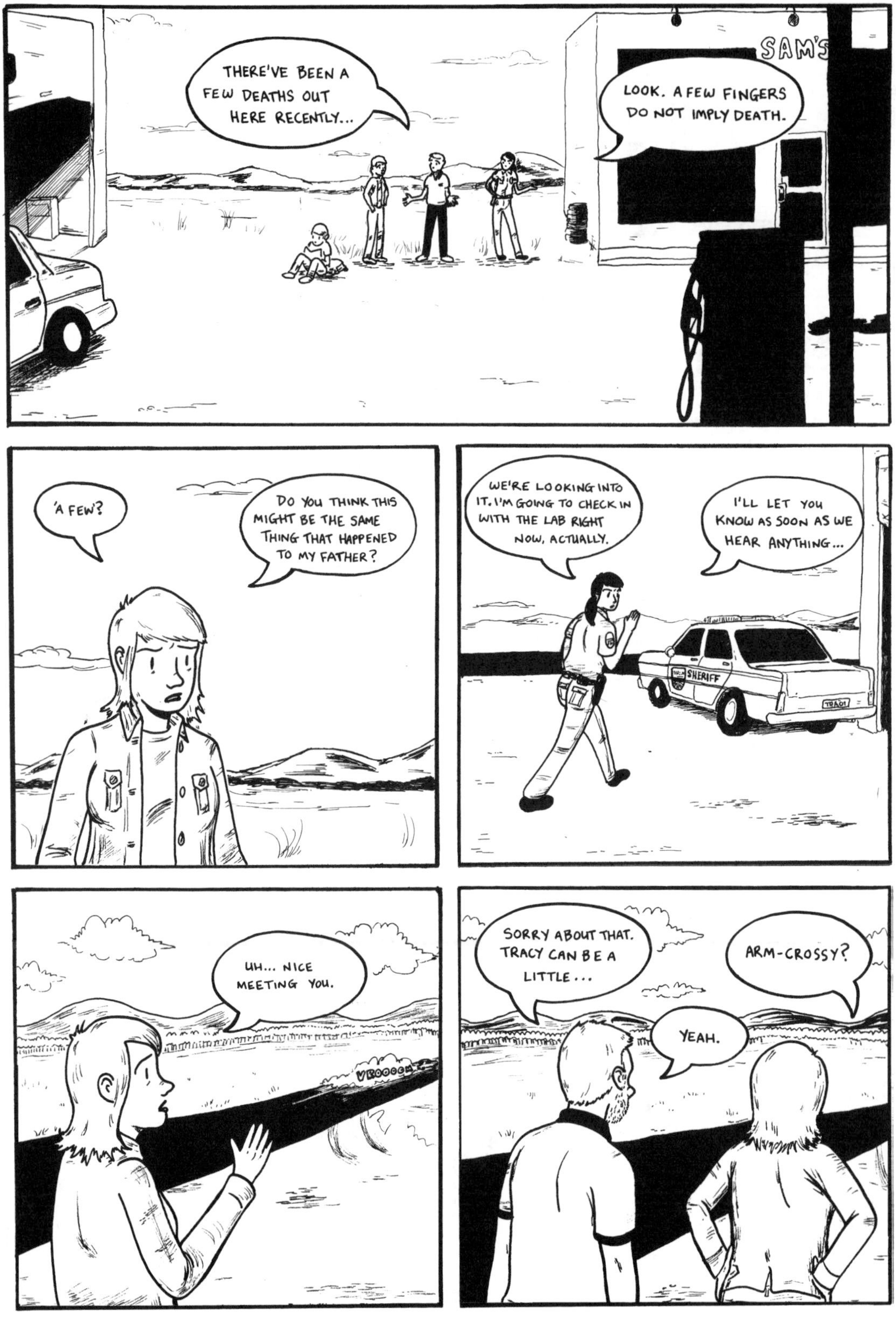

THERE'VE BEEN A FEW DEATHS OUT HERE RECENTLY...
SAM'S
LOOK. A FEW FINGERS DO NOT IMPLY DEATH.
'A FEW'?
DO YOU THINK THIS MIGHT BE THE SAME THING THAT HAPPENED TO MY FATHER?
WE'RE LOOKING INTO IT. I'M GOING TO CHECK IN WITH THE LAB RIGHT NOW, ACTUALLY.
I'LL LET YOU KNOW AS SOON AS WE HEAR ANYTHING...
SHERIFF
UH... NICE MEETING YOU.
SORRY ABOUT THAT. TRACY CAN BE A LITTLE...
ARM-CROSSY?
YEAH.

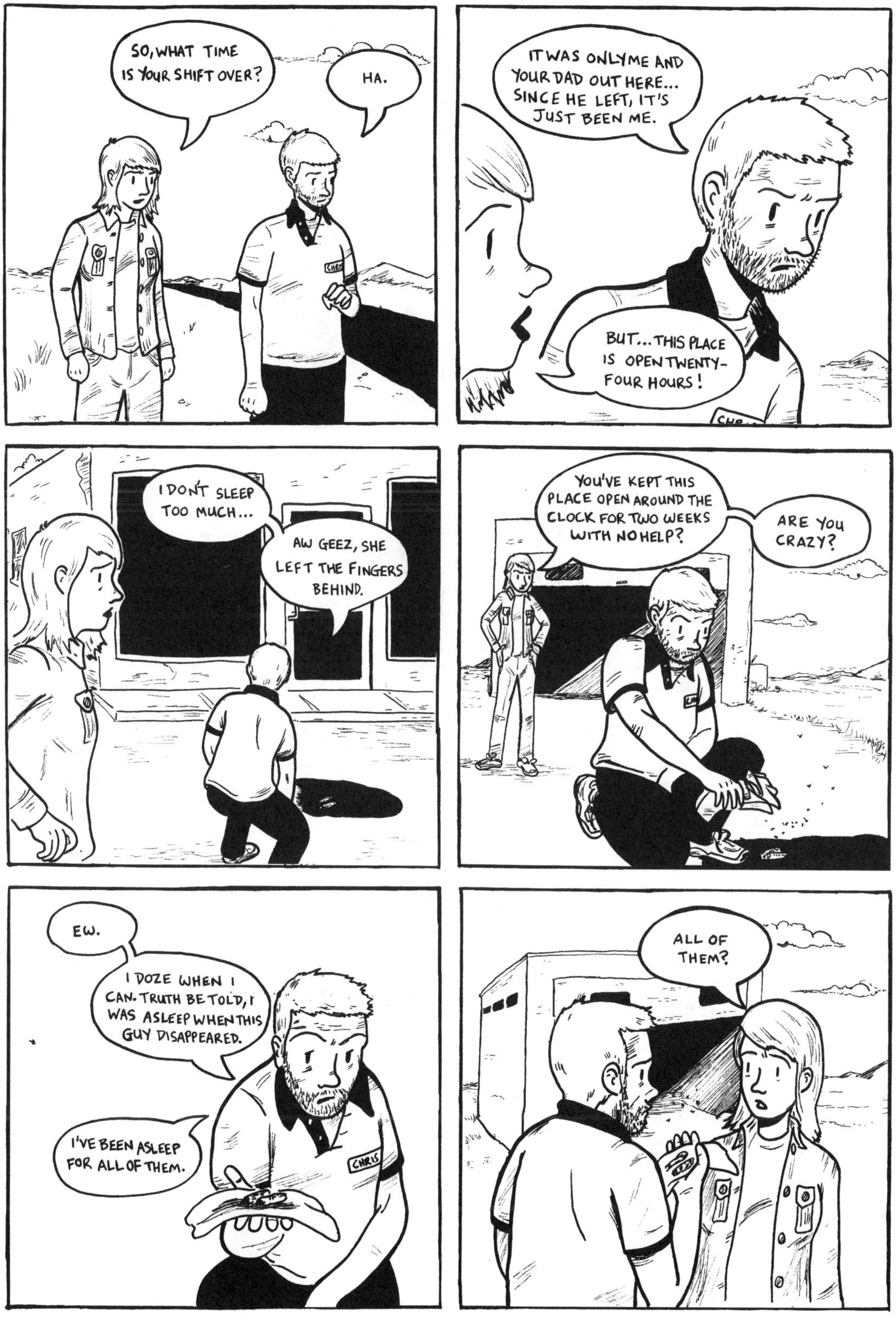
SO, WHAT TIME IS YOUR SHIFT OVER?
HA.
IT WAS ONLY ME AND YOUR DAD OUT HERE... SINCE HE LEFT, IT'S JUST BEEN ME.
BUT... THIS PLACE IS OPEN TWENTY-FOUR HOURS!
I DON'T SLEEP TOO MUCH...
AW GEEZ, SHE LEFT THE FINGERS BEHIND.
YOU'VE KEPT THIS PLACE OPEN AROUND THE CLOCK FOR TWO WEEKS WITH NO HELP?
ARE YOU CRAZY?
EW.
I DOZE WHEN I CAN. TRUTH BE TOLD, I WAS ASLEEP WHEN THIS GUY DISAPPEARED.
I'VE BEEN ASLEEP FOR ALL OF THEM.
ALL OF THEM?

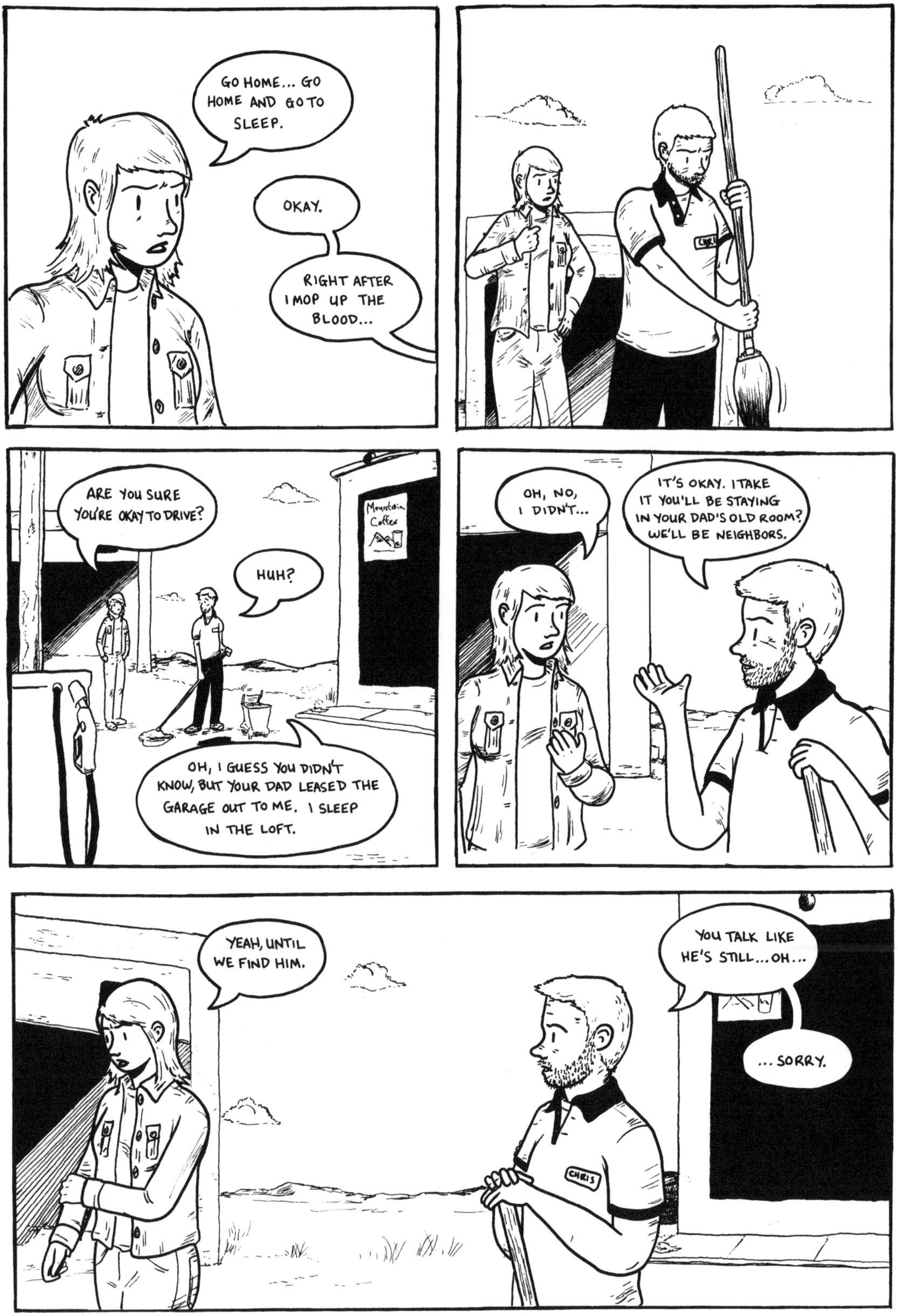
GO HOME... GO HOME AND GO TO SLEEP.
OKAY.
RIGHT AFTER I MOP UP THE BLOOD...
ARE YOU SURE YOU'RE OKAY TO DRIVE?
HUH?
OH, I GUESS YOU DIDN'T KNOW, BUT YOUR DAD LEASED THE GARAGE OUT TO ME. I SLEEP IN THE LOFT.
OH, NO, I DIDN'T...
IT'S OKAY. I TAKE IT YOU'LL BE STAYING IN YOUR DAD'S OLD ROOM? WE'LL BE NEIGHBORS.
YEAH, UNTIL WE FIND HIM.
YOU TALK LIKE HE'S STILL... OH...
... SORRY.
CHRIS

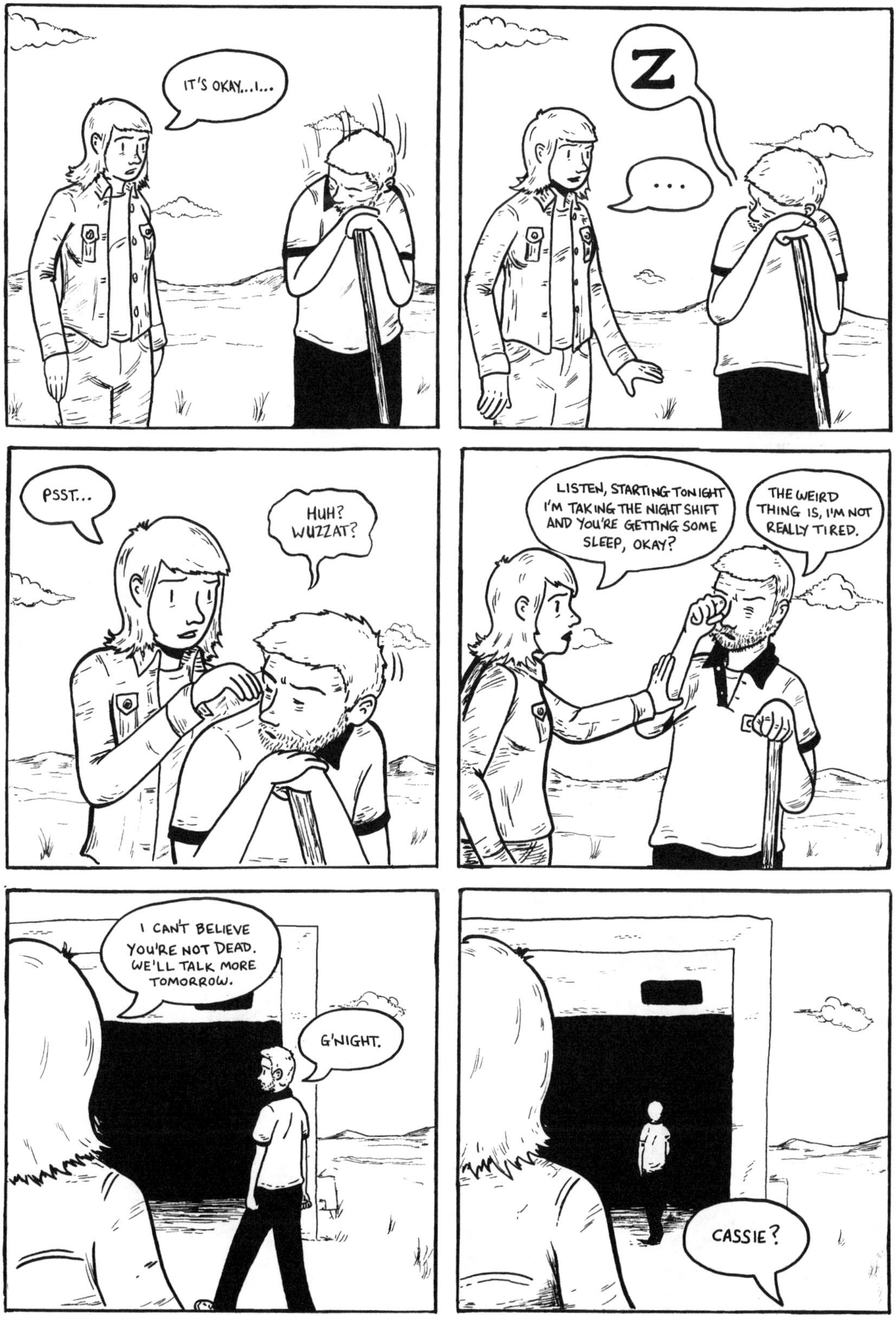
IT'S OKAY...I...
Z
...
PSST...
HUH? WUZZAT?
LISTEN, STARTING TONIGHT I'M TAKING THE NIGHT SHIFT AND YOU'RE GETTING SOME SLEEP, OKAY?
THE WEIRD THING IS, I'M NOT REALLY TIRED.
I CAN'T BELIEVE YOU'RE NOT DEAD. WE'LL TALK MORE TOMORROW.
G'NIGHT.
CASSIE?

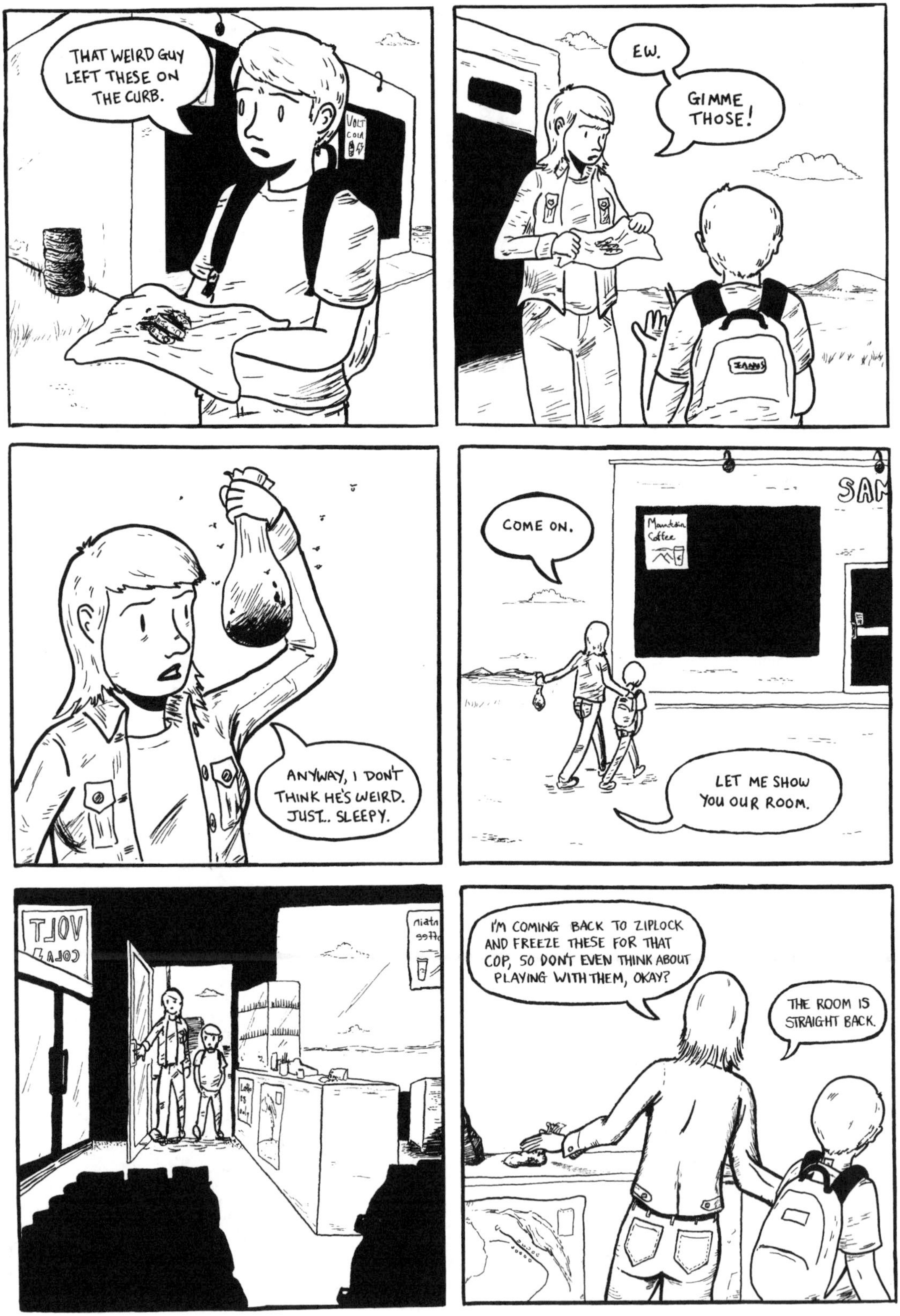
THAT WEIRD GUY LEFT THESE ON THE CURB.
VOLT COLA
EW.
GIMME THOSE!
ANYWAY, I DON'T THINK HE'S WEIRD. JUST.. SLEEPY.
COME ON.
Mountain Coffee
SAM
LET ME SHOW YOU OUR ROOM.
I'M COMING BACK TO ZIPLOCK AND FREEZE THESE FOR THAT COP, SO DON'T EVEN THINK ABOUT PLAYING WITH THEM, OKAY?
THE ROOM IS STRAIGHT BACK.

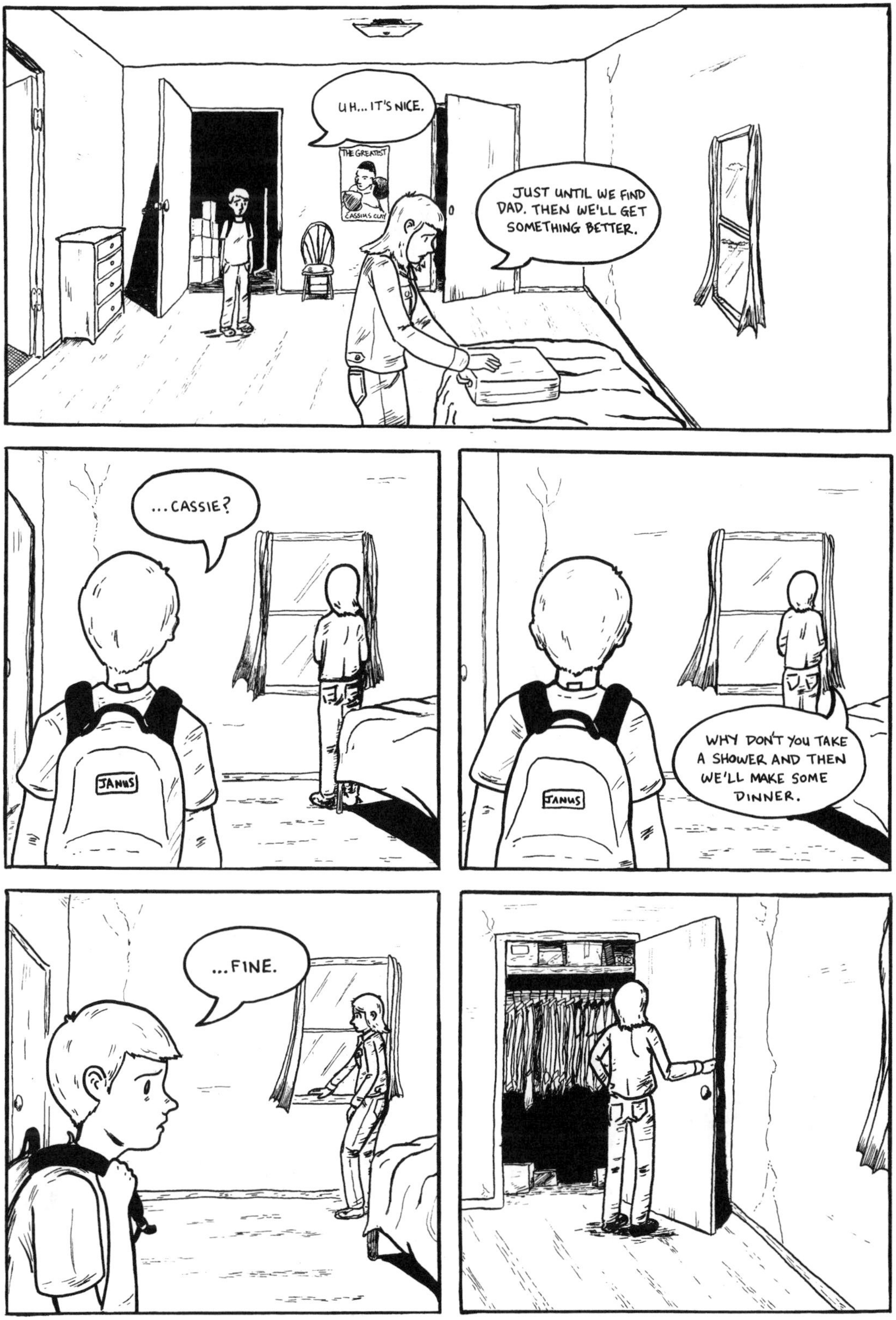
UH... IT'S NICE.
THE GREATEST
CASSIUS CLAY
JUST UNTIL WE FIND DAD. THEN WE'LL GET SOMETHING BETTER.
...CASSIE?
JANUS
JANUS
WHY DON'T YOU TAKE A SHOWER AND THEN WE'LL MAKE SOME DINNER.
...FINE.

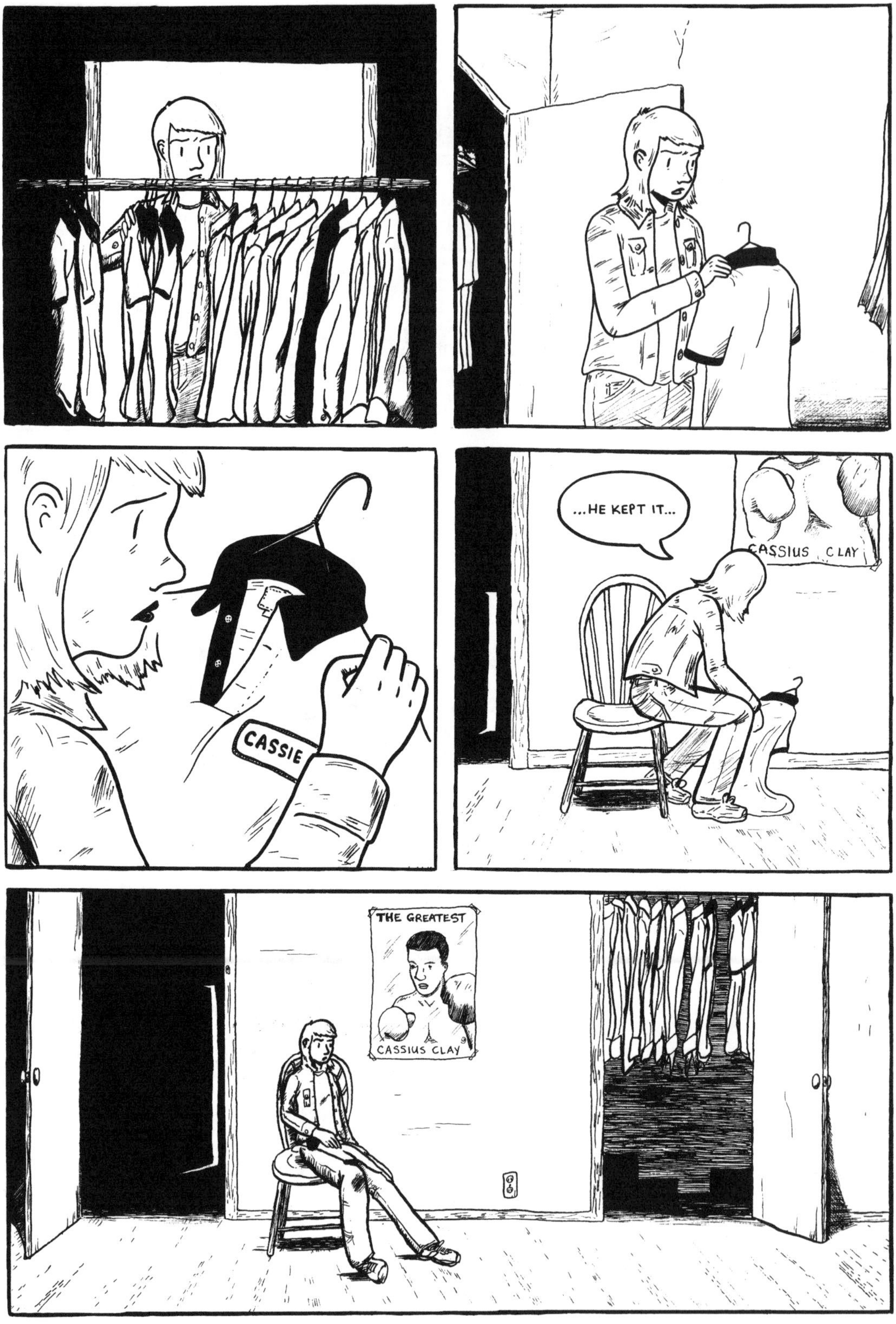
CASSIE
...HE KEPT IT...
CASSIUS CLAY
THE GREATEST
CASSIUS CLAY

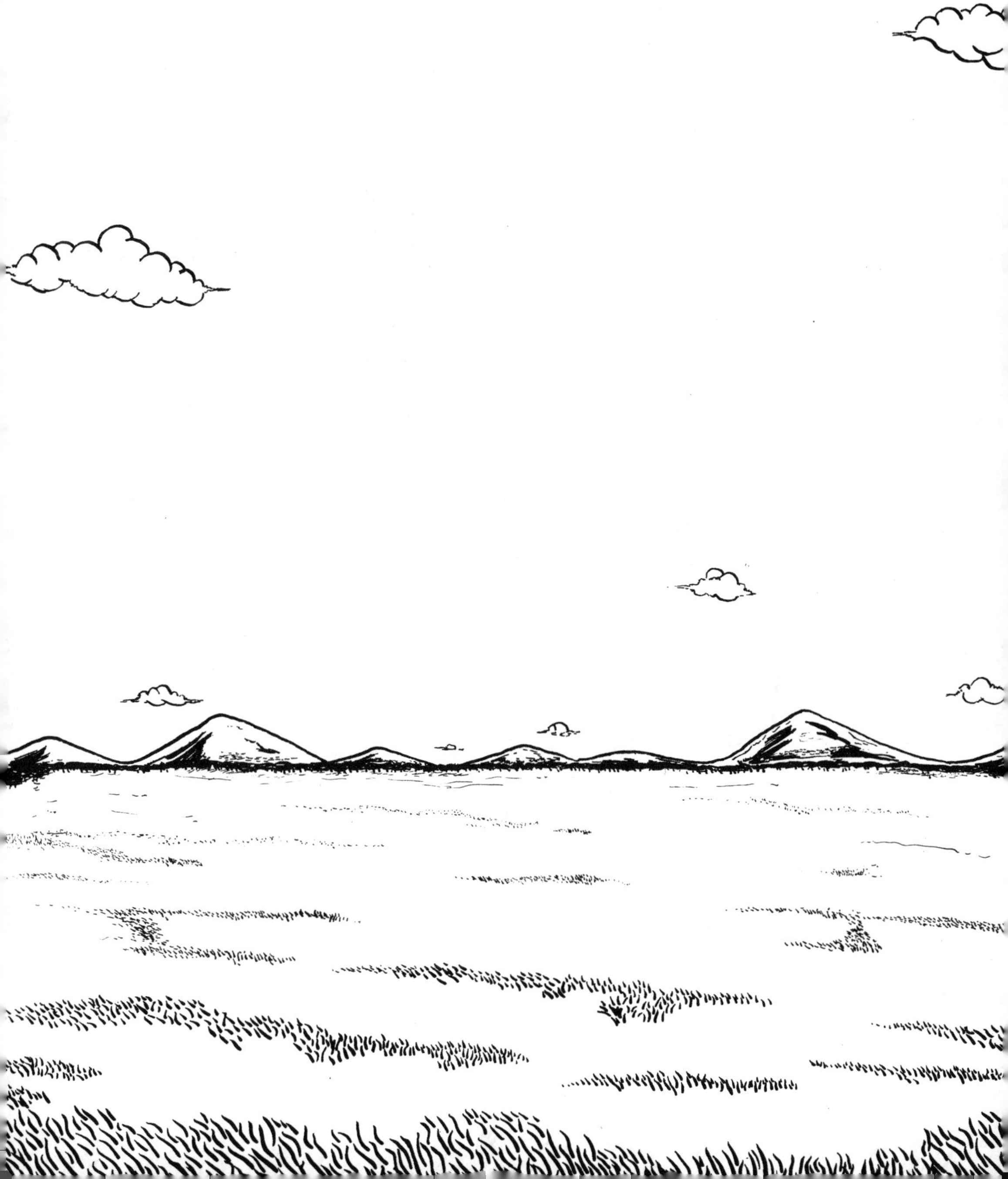

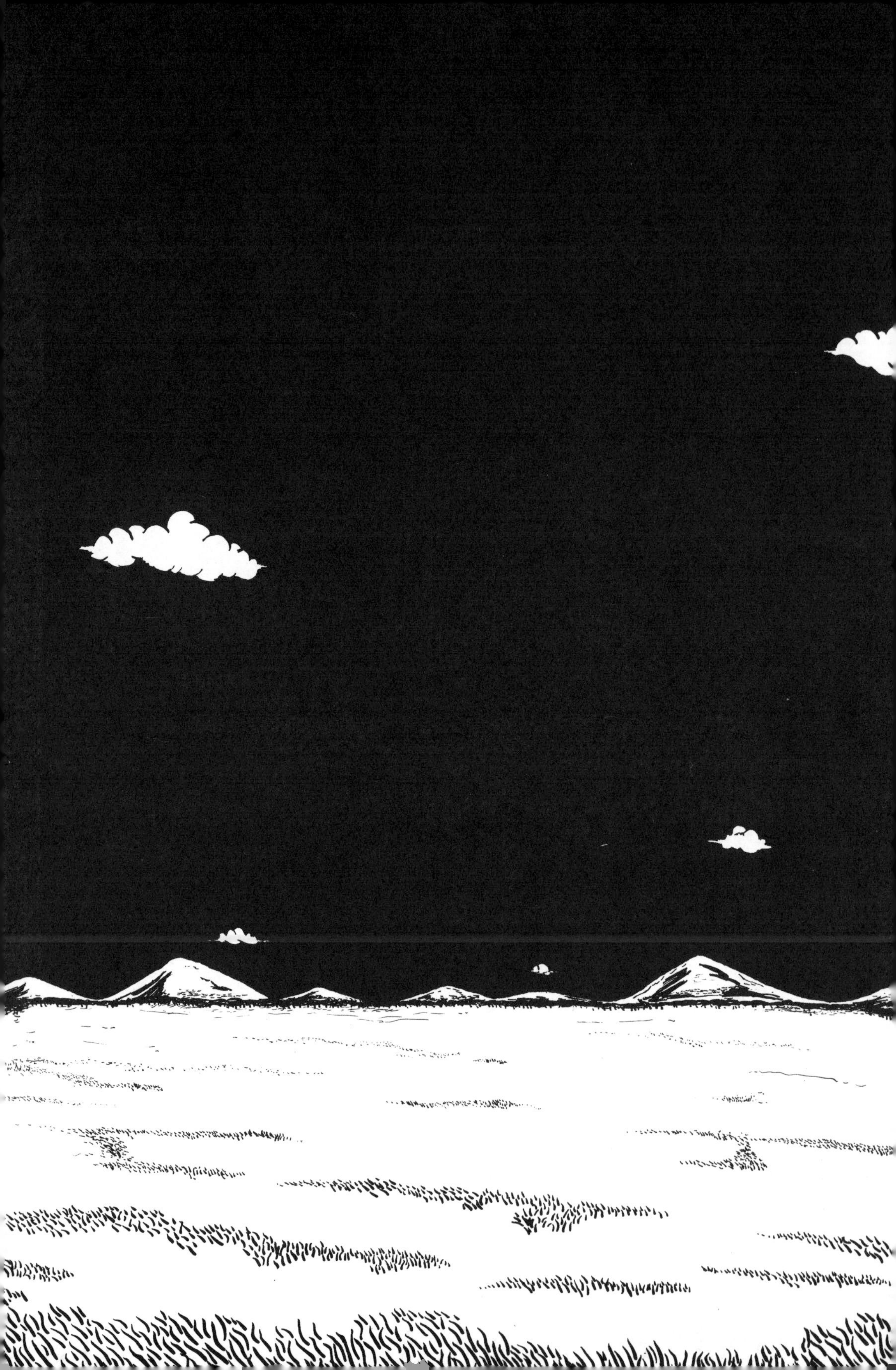

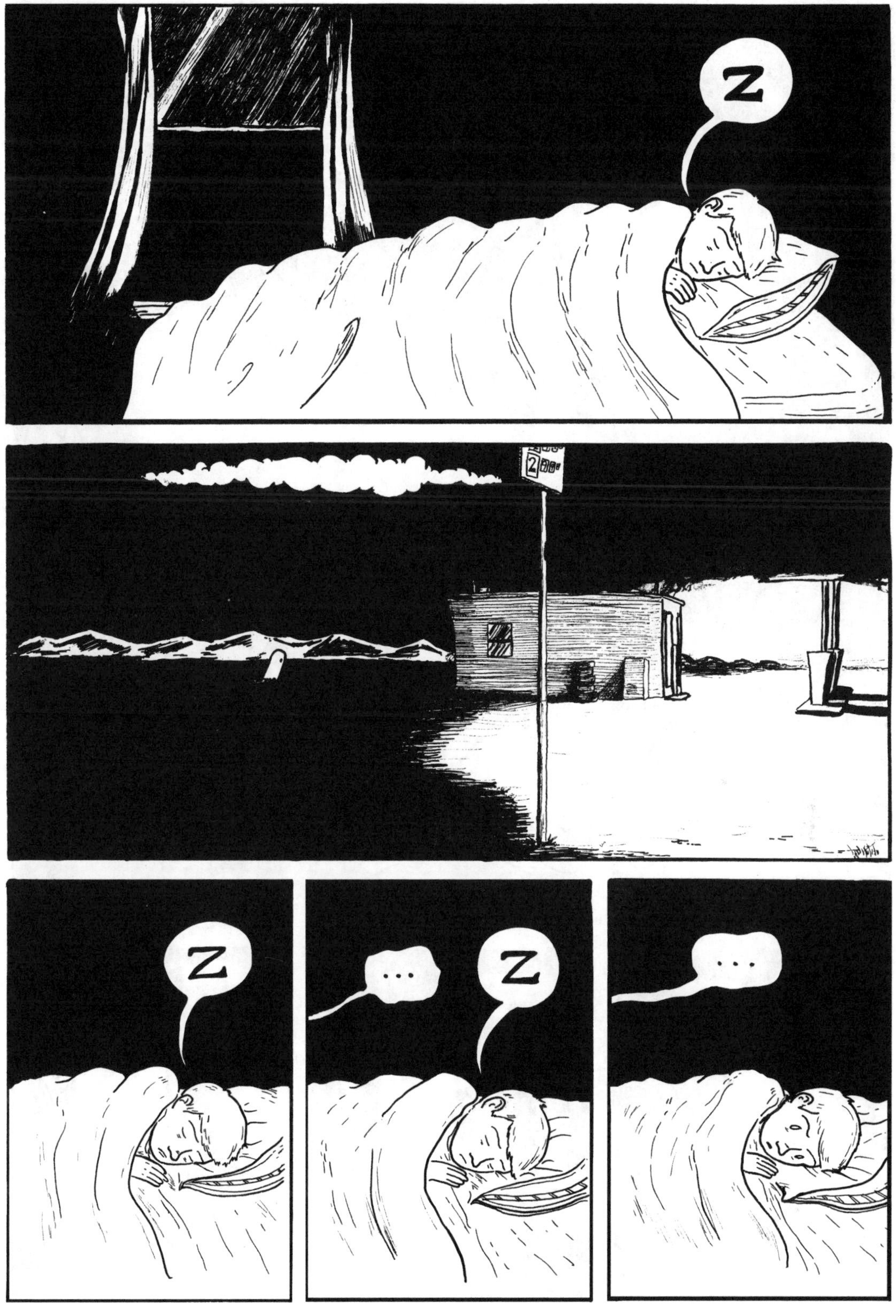
Z
Z
...
Z
...

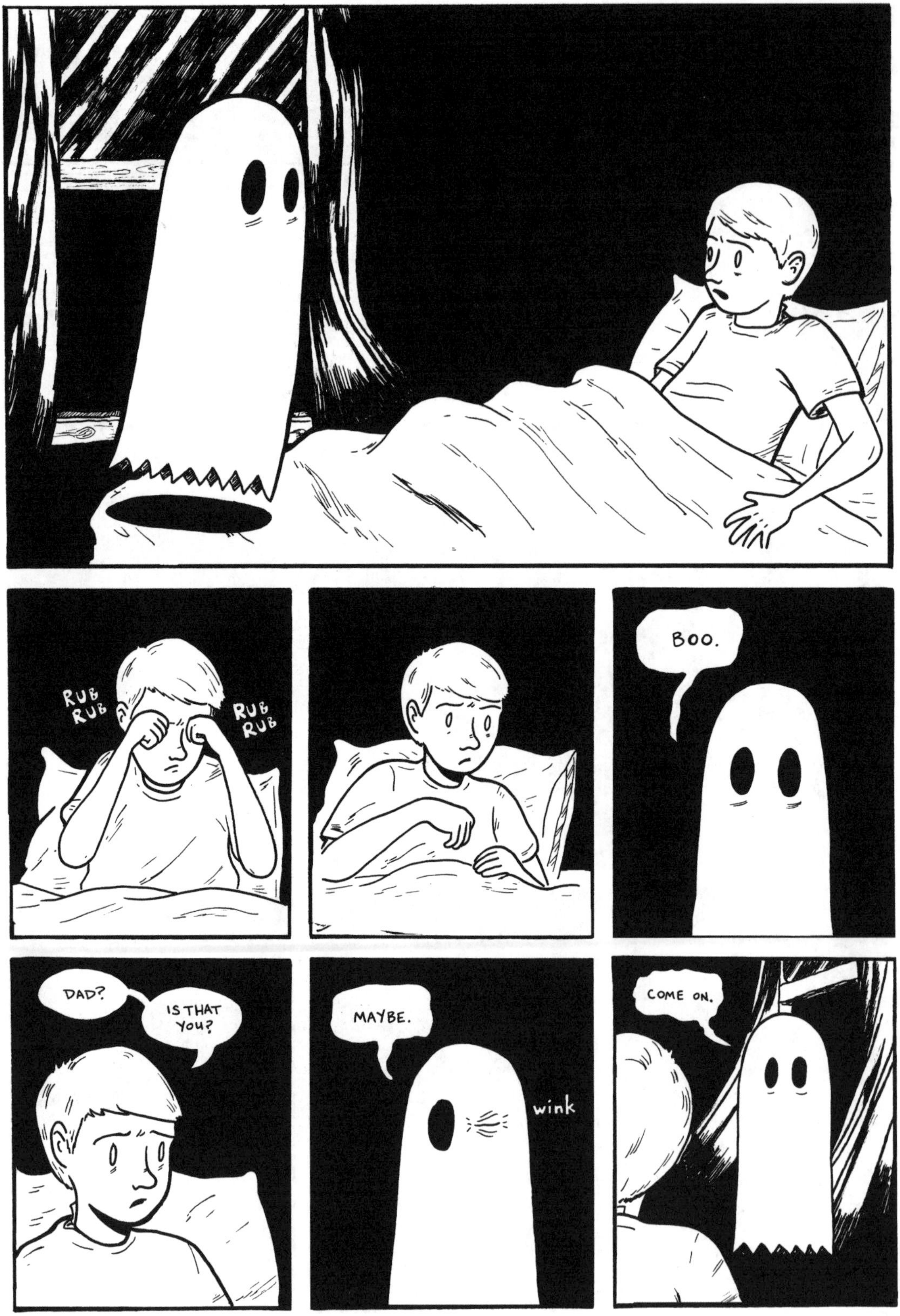
RUB RUB
RUB RUB
BOO.
DAD?
IS THAT YOU?
MAYBE.
wink
COME ON.

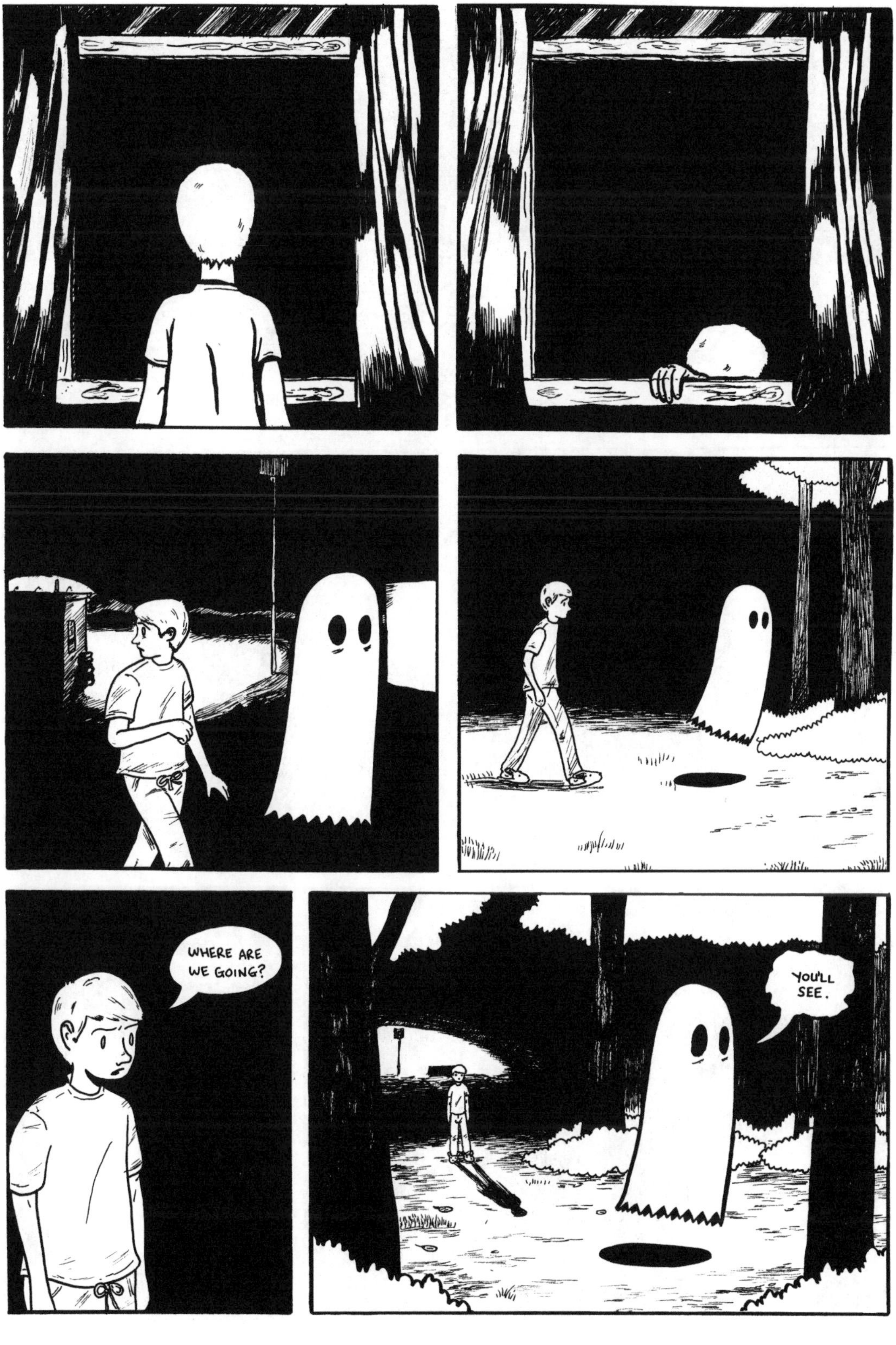
WHERE ARE WE GOING?
YOU'LL SEE.

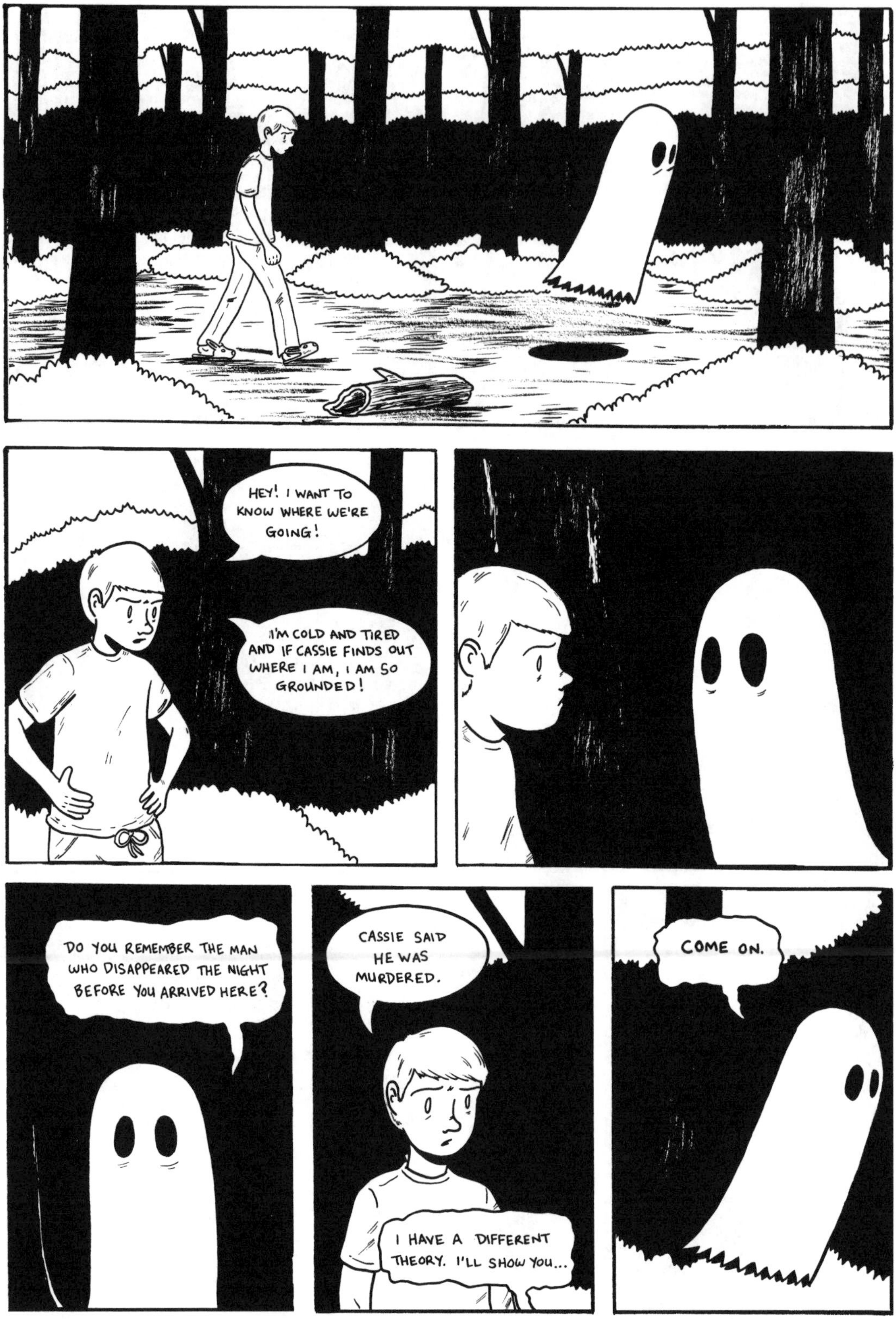
HEY! I WANT TO KNOW WHERE WE'RE GOING!
I'M COLD AND TIRED AND IF CASSIE FINDS OUT WHERE I AM, I AM SO GROUNDED!
DO YOU REMEMBER THE MAN WHO DISAPPEARED THE NIGHT BEFORE YOU ARRIVED HERE?
CASSIE SAID HE WAS MURDERED.
I HAVE A DIFFERENT THEORY. I'LL SHOW YOU...
COME ON.

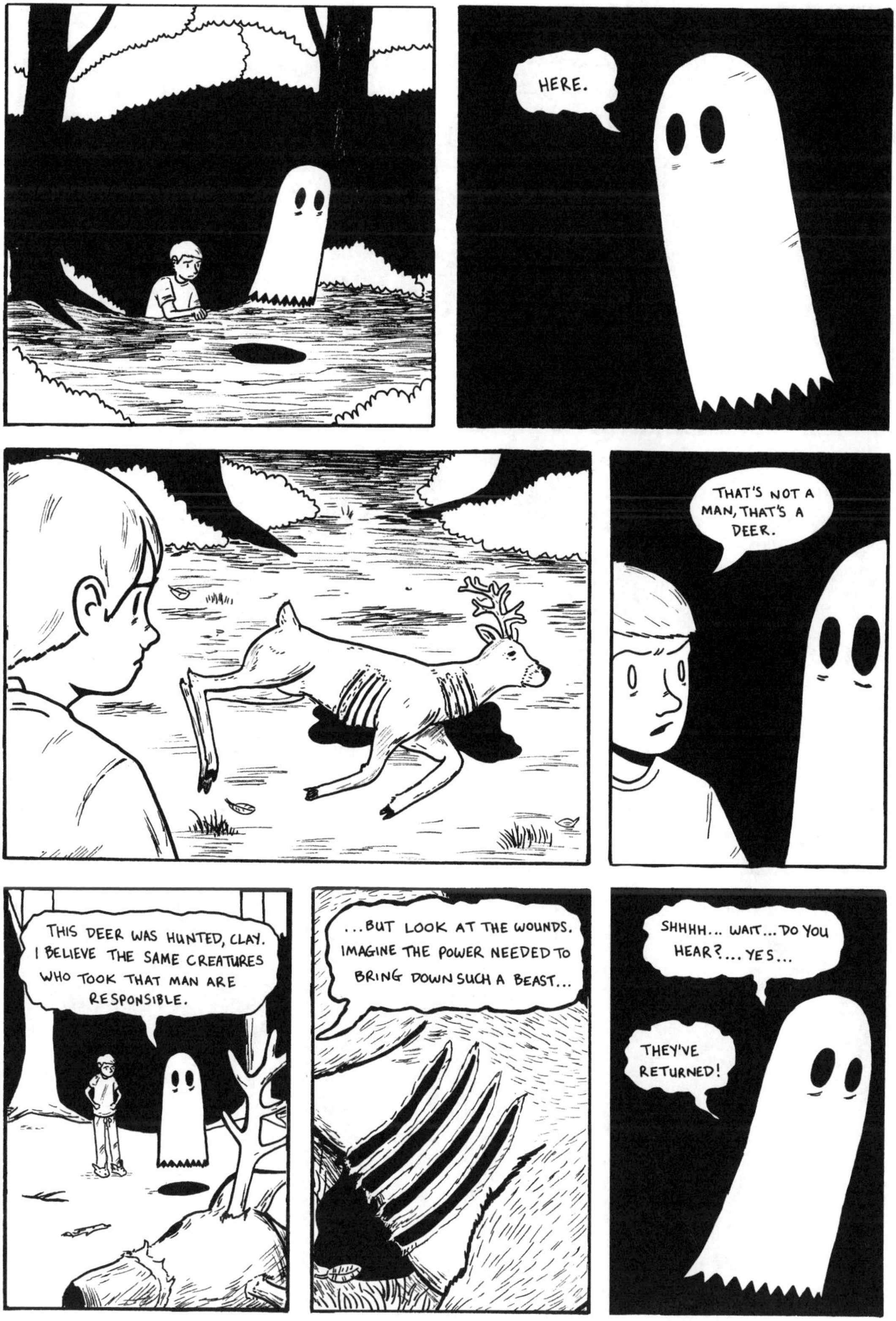
HERE.
THAT'S NOT A MAN, THAT'S A DEER.
THIS DEER WAS HUNTED, CLAY. I BELIEVE THE SAME CREATURES WHO TOOK THAT MAN ARE RESPONSIBLE.
...BUT LOOK AT THE WOUNDS. IMAGINE THE POWER NEEDED TO BRING DOWN SUCH A BEAST...
SHHHH... WAIT... DO YOU HEAR?... YES...
THEY'VE RETURNED!

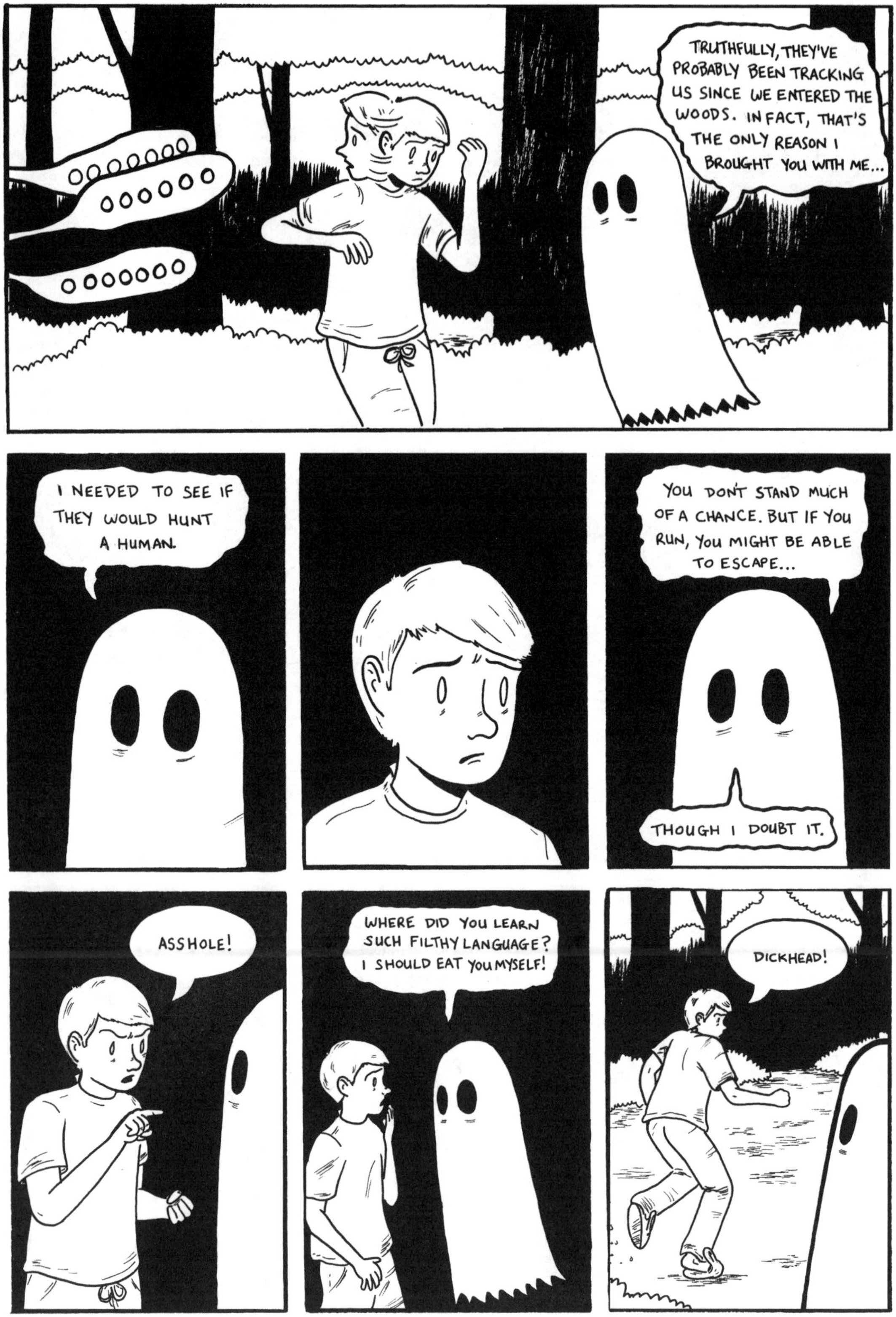
OOOOOOO
OOOOOO
OOOOOOO
TRUTHFULLY, THEY'VE PROBABLY BEEN TRACKING US SINCE WE ENTERED THE WOODS. IN FACT, THAT'S THE ONLY REASON I BROUGHT YOU WITH ME...
I NEEDED TO SEE IF THEY WOULD HUNT A HUMAN.
YOU DON'T STAND MUCH OF A CHANCE. BUT IF YOU RUN, YOU MIGHT BE ABLE TO ESCAPE...
THOUGH I DOUBT IT.
ASSHOLE!
WHERE DID YOU LEARN SUCH FILTHY LANGUAGE? I SHOULD EAT YOU MYSELF!
DICKHEAD!

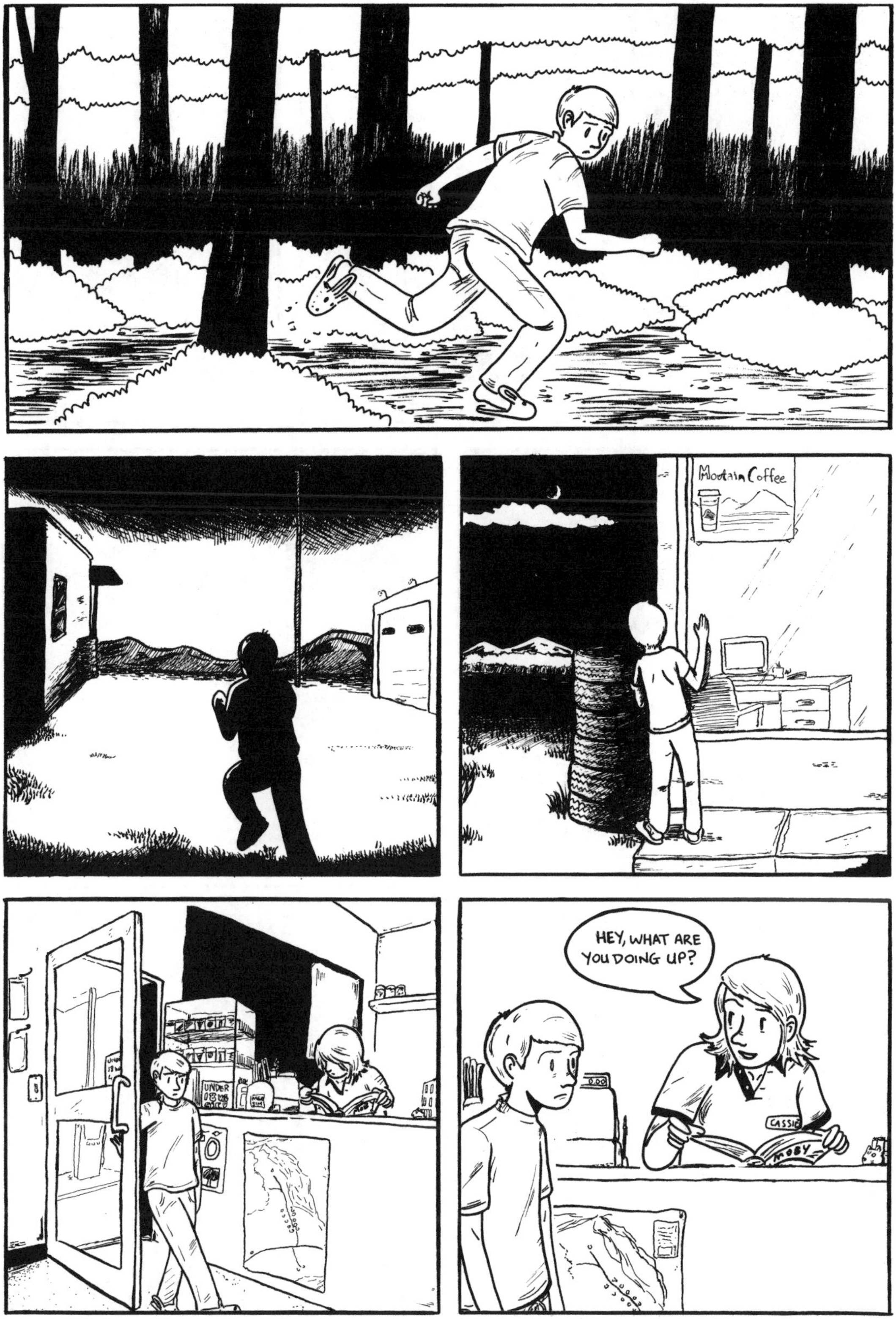
Moutain Coffee
UNDER
HEY, WHAT ARE YOU DOING UP?
CASSIE
MOBY

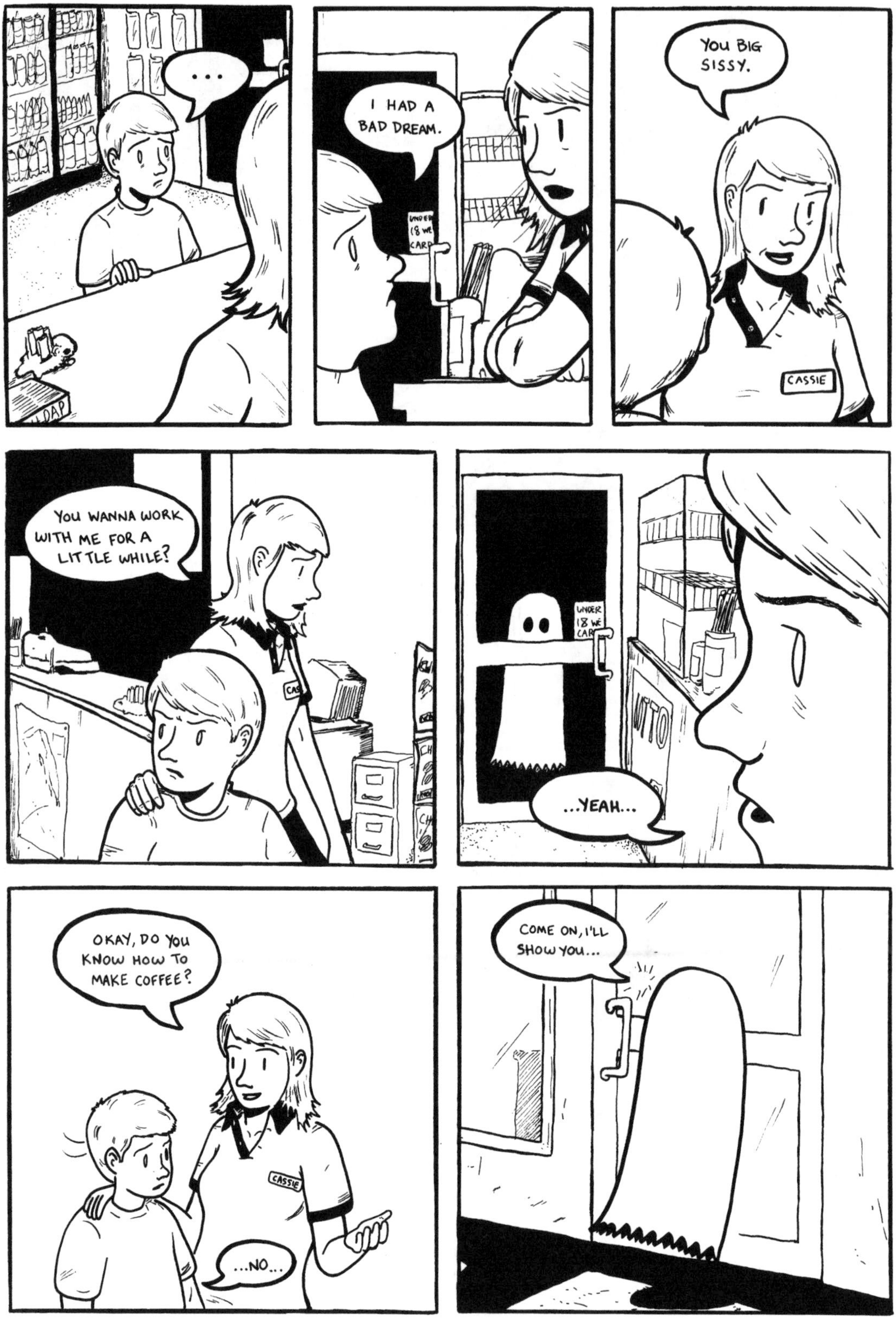
...
I HAD A BAD DREAM.
YOU BIG SISSY.
CASSIE
YOU WANNA WORK WITH ME FOR A LITTLE WHILE?
...YEAH...
OKAY, DO YOU KNOW HOW TO MAKE COFFEE?
...NO...
COME ON, I'LL SHOW YOU...

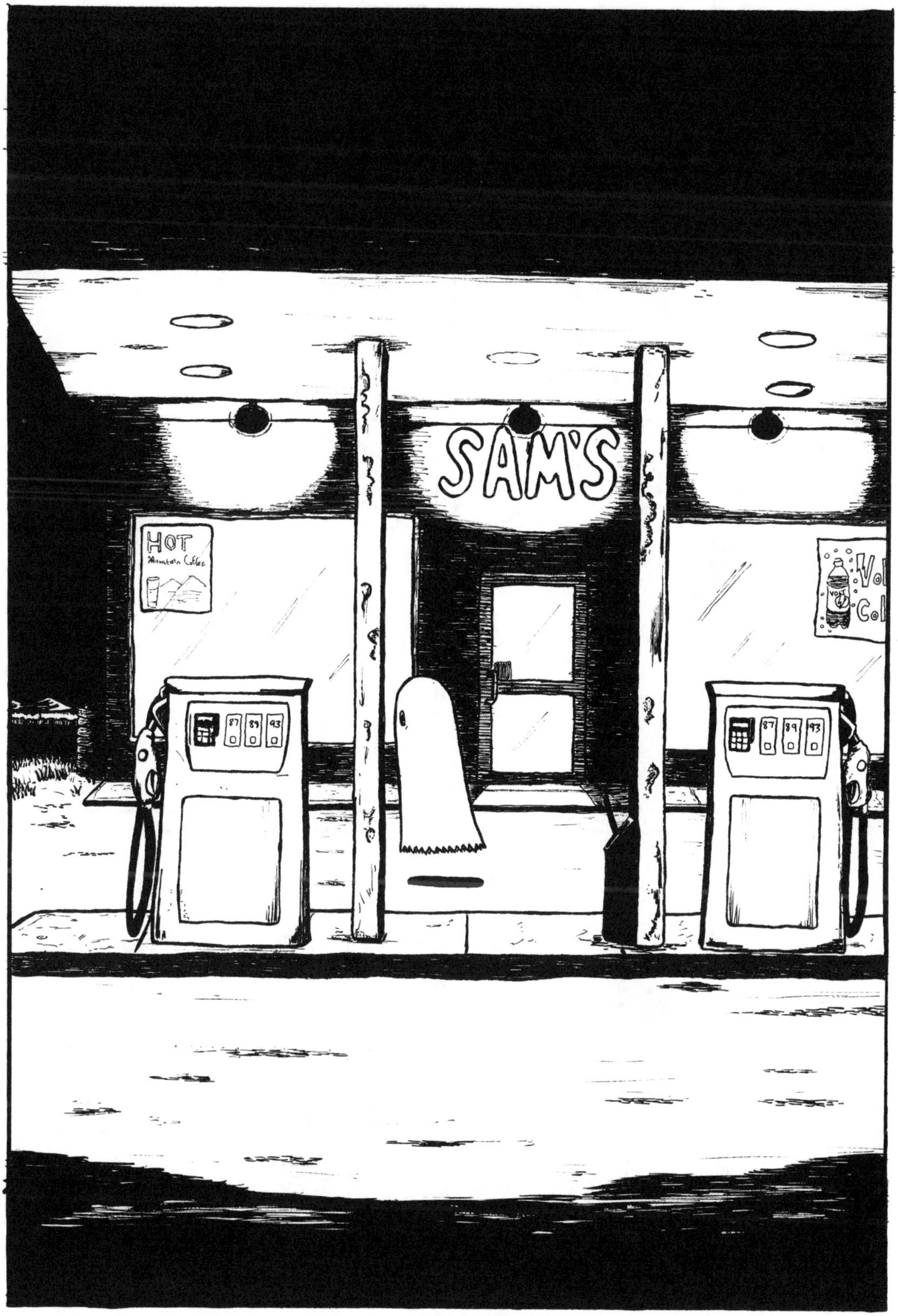
SAM'S
HOT
Mountain Coffee
87 89 93
87 89 93

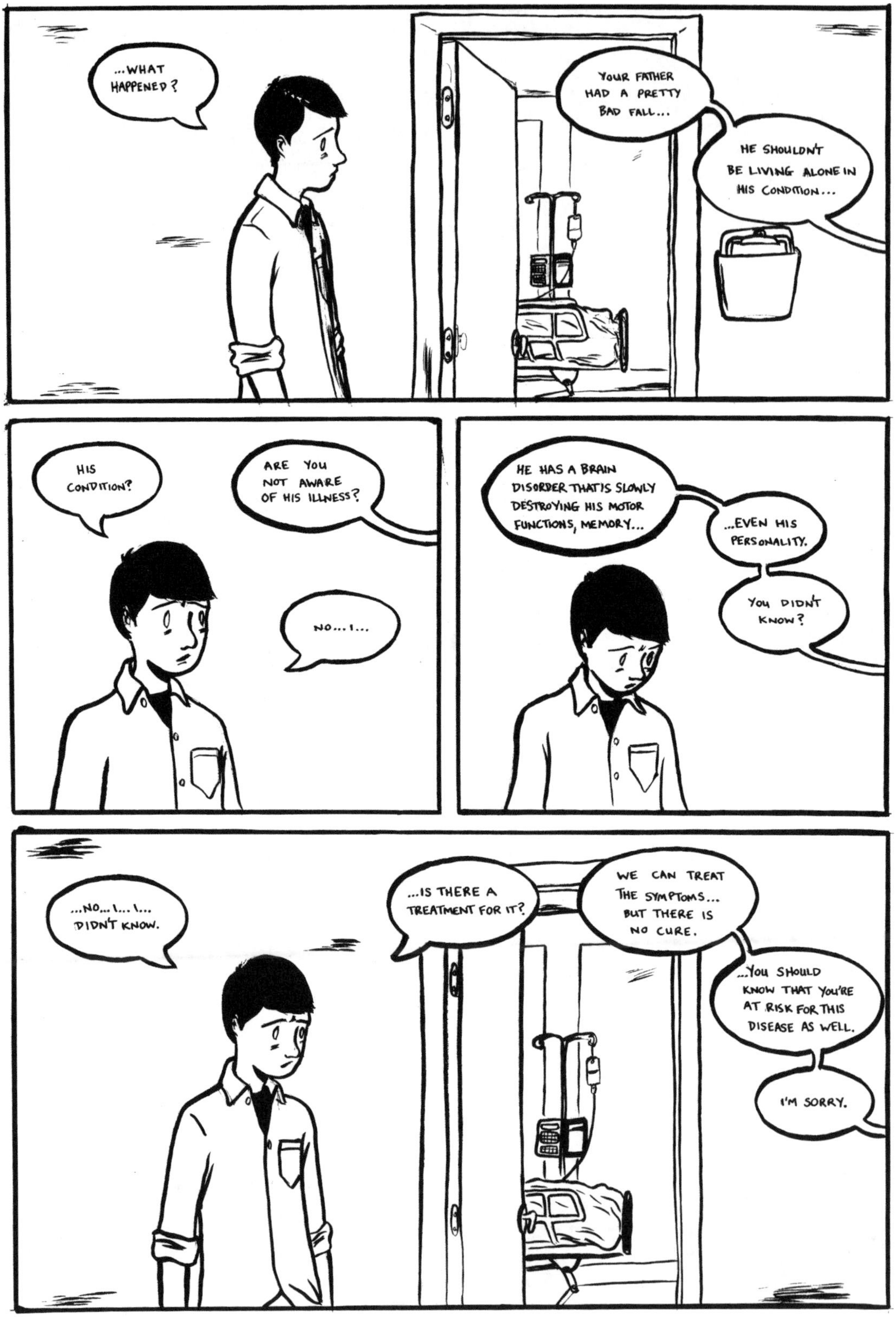
...WHAT HAPPENED?
YOUR FATHER HAD A PRETTY BAD FALL...
HE SHOULDN'T BE LIVING ALONE IN HIS CONDITION...
HIS CONDITION?
ARE YOU NOT AWARE OF HIS ILLNESS?
NO... I...
HE HAS A BRAIN DISORDER THAT IS SLOWLY DESTROYING HIS MOTOR FUNCTIONS, MEMORY...
...EVEN HIS PERSONALITY.
YOU DIDN'T KNOW?
...NO... I... I... DIDN'T KNOW.
...IS THERE A TREATMENT FOR IT?
WE CAN TREAT THE SYMPTOMS... BUT THERE IS NO CURE.
...YOU SHOULD KNOW THAT YOU'RE AT RISK FOR THIS DISEASE AS WELL.
I'M SORRY.

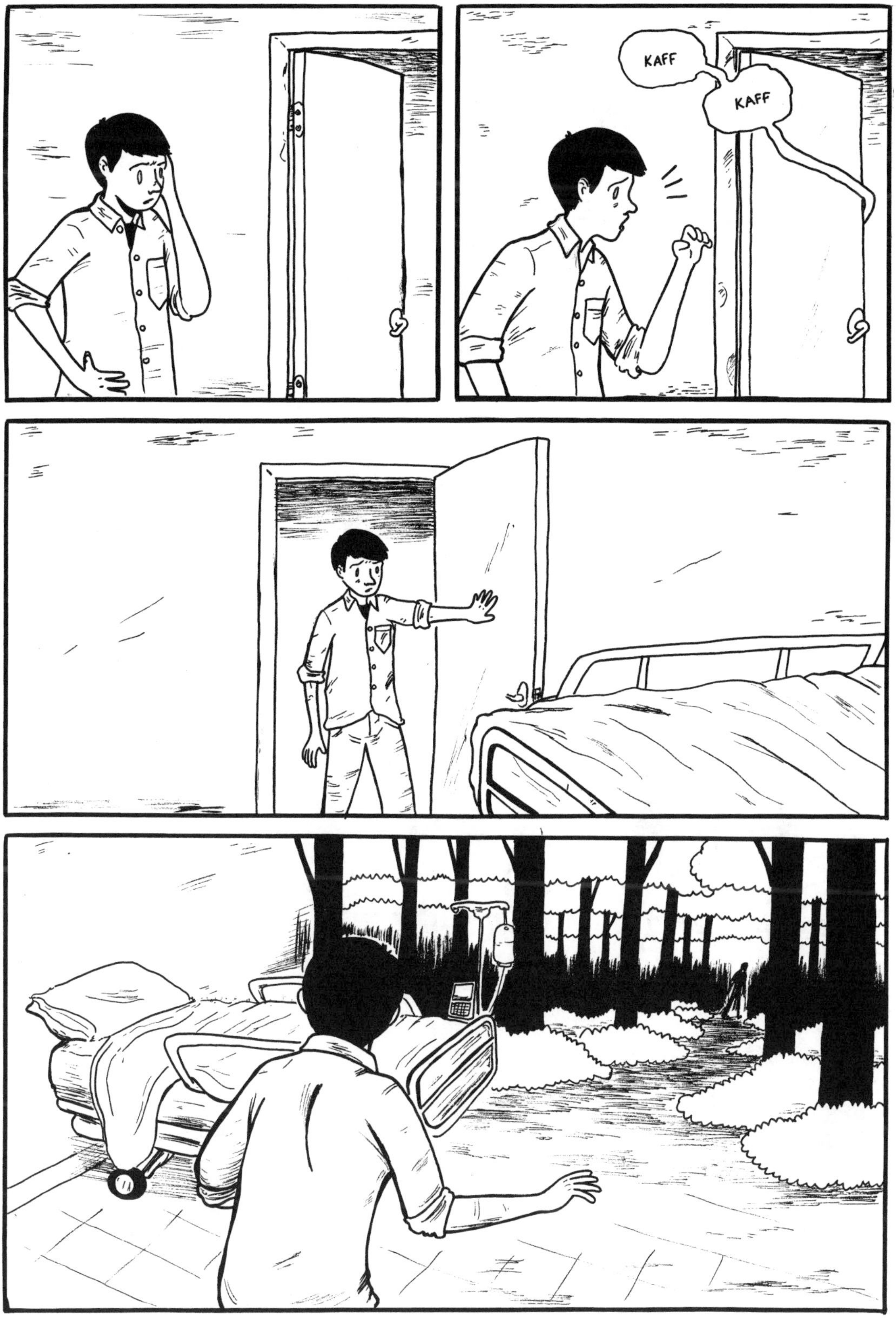
KAFF
KAFF

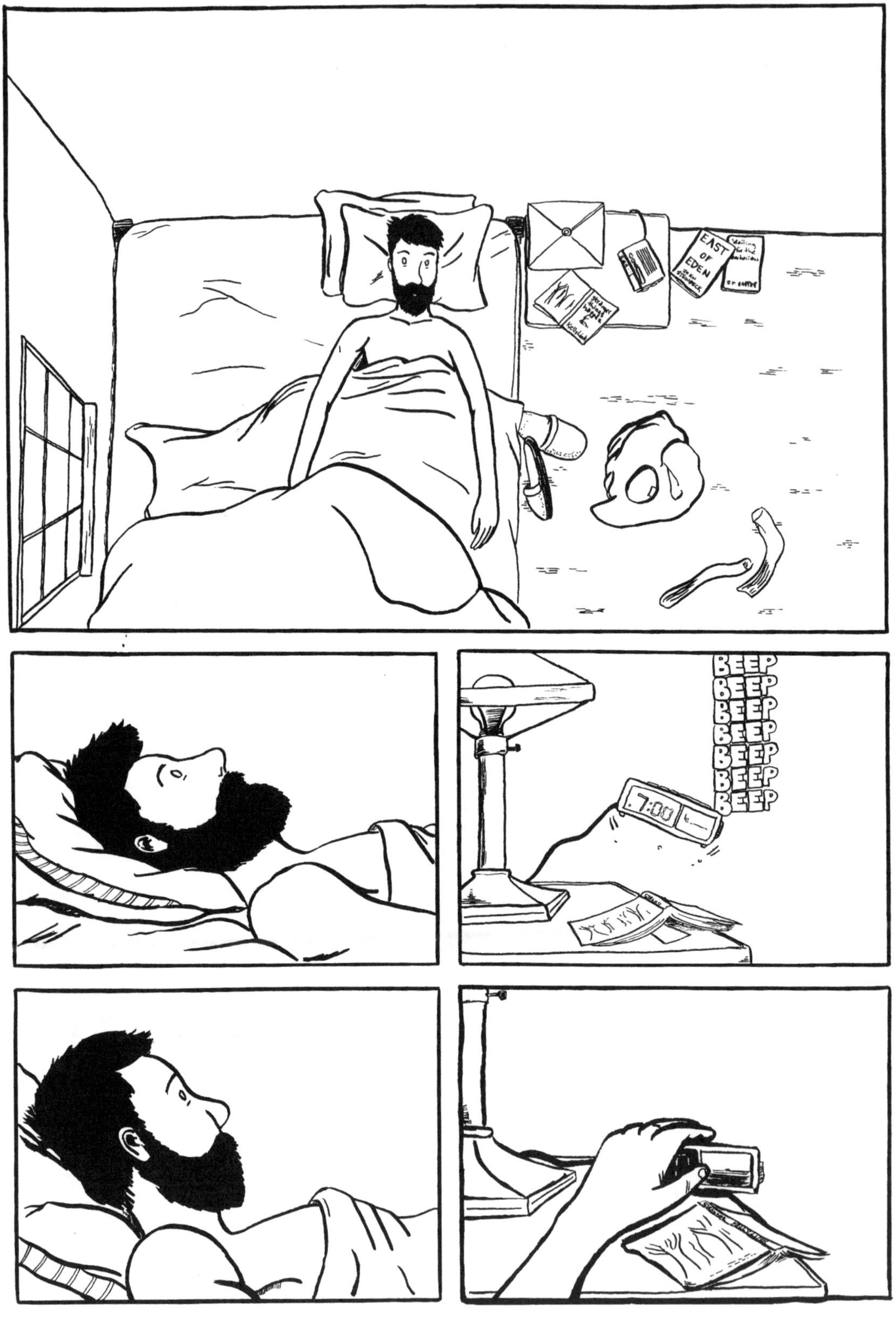
stranger things happen
Kelly Link
EAST OF EDEN
JOHN STEINBECK
Waiting for the
BEEP
BEEP
BEEP
BEEP
BEEP
BEEP
BEEP
7:00

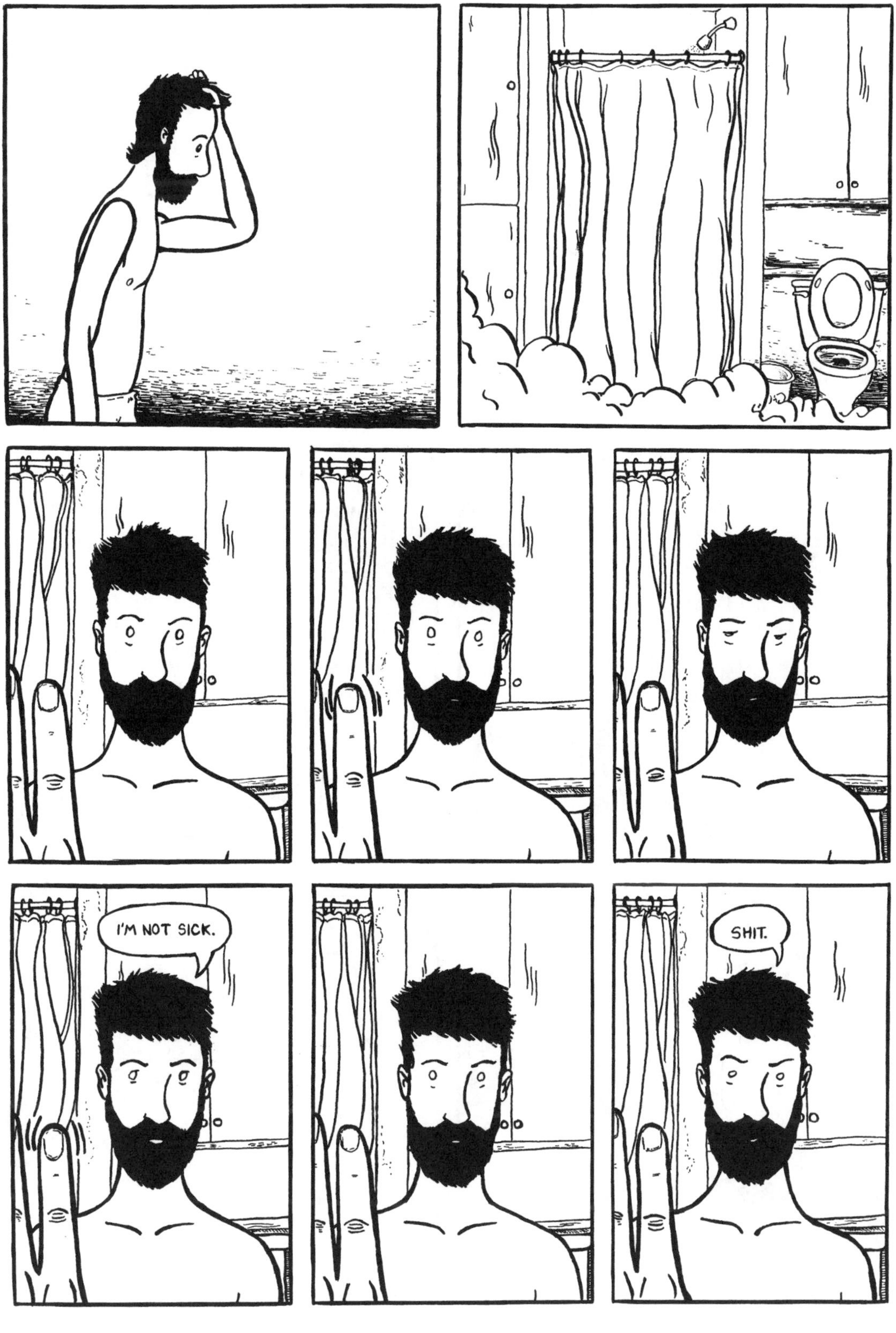
I'M NOT SICK.
SHIT.

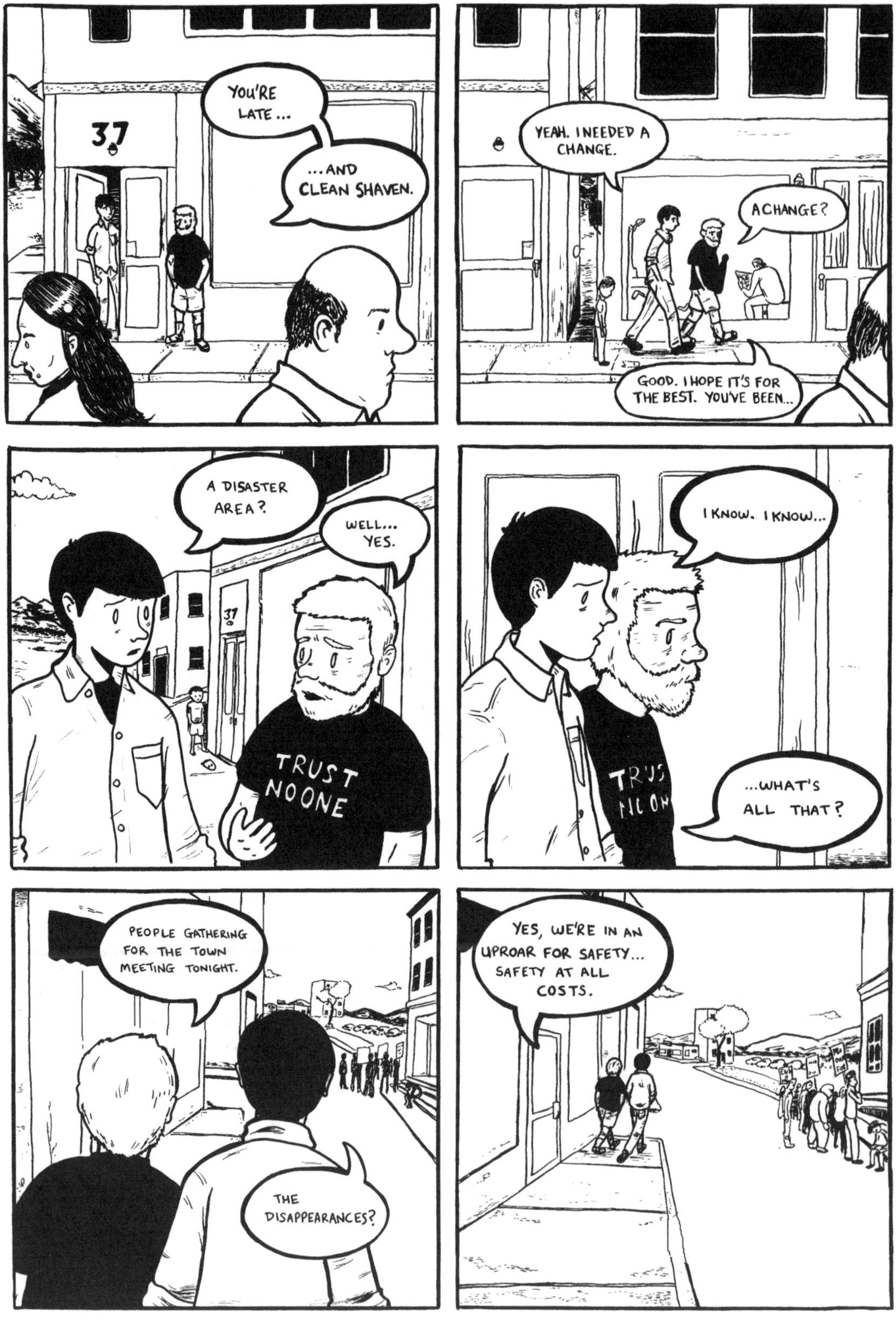
YOU'RE LATE...
...AND CLEAN SHAVEN.
37
YEAH. I NEEDED A CHANGE.
A CHANGE?
GOOD. I HOPE IT'S FOR THE BEST. YOU'VE BEEN...
A DISASTER AREA?
WELL... YES.
37
TRUST NO ONE
I KNOW. I KNOW...
...WHAT'S ALL THAT?
PEOPLE GATHERING FOR THE TOWN MEETING TONIGHT.
THE DISAPPEARANCES?
YES, WE'RE IN AN UPROAR FOR SAFETY... SAFETY AT ALL COSTS.

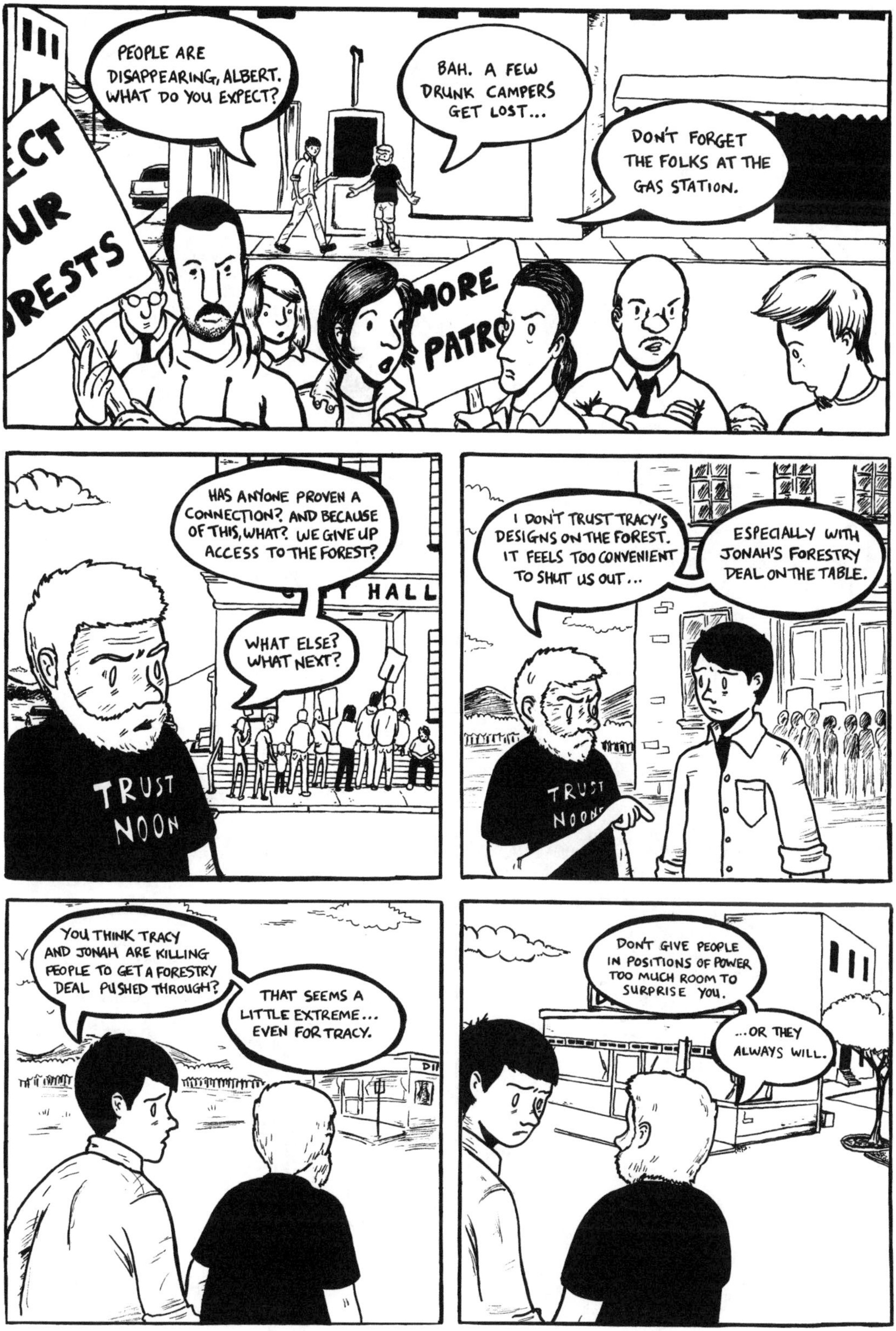
ECT
UR
RESTS
PEOPLE ARE DISAPPEARING, ALBERT. WHAT DO YOU EXPECT?
BAH. A FEW DRUNK CAMPERS GET LOST...
DON'T FORGET THE FOLKS AT THE GAS STATION.
MORE PATR
HALL
HAS ANYONE PROVEN A CONNECTION? AND BECAUSE OF THIS, WHAT? WE GIVE UP ACCESS TO THE FOREST?
WHAT ELSE? WHAT NEXT?
TRUST NOON
I DON'T TRUST TRACY'S DESIGNS ON THE FOREST. IT FEELS TOO CONVENIENT TO SHUT US OUT...
ESPECIALLY WITH JONAH'S FORESTRY DEAL ON THE TABLE.
TRUST NOONE
YOU THINK TRACY AND JONAH ARE KILLING PEOPLE TO GET A FORESTRY DEAL PUSHED THROUGH?
THAT SEEMS A LITTLE EXTREME... EVEN FOR TRACY.
DON'T GIVE PEOPLE IN POSITIONS OF POWER TOO MUCH ROOM TO SURPRISE YOU.
...OR THEY ALWAYS WILL.

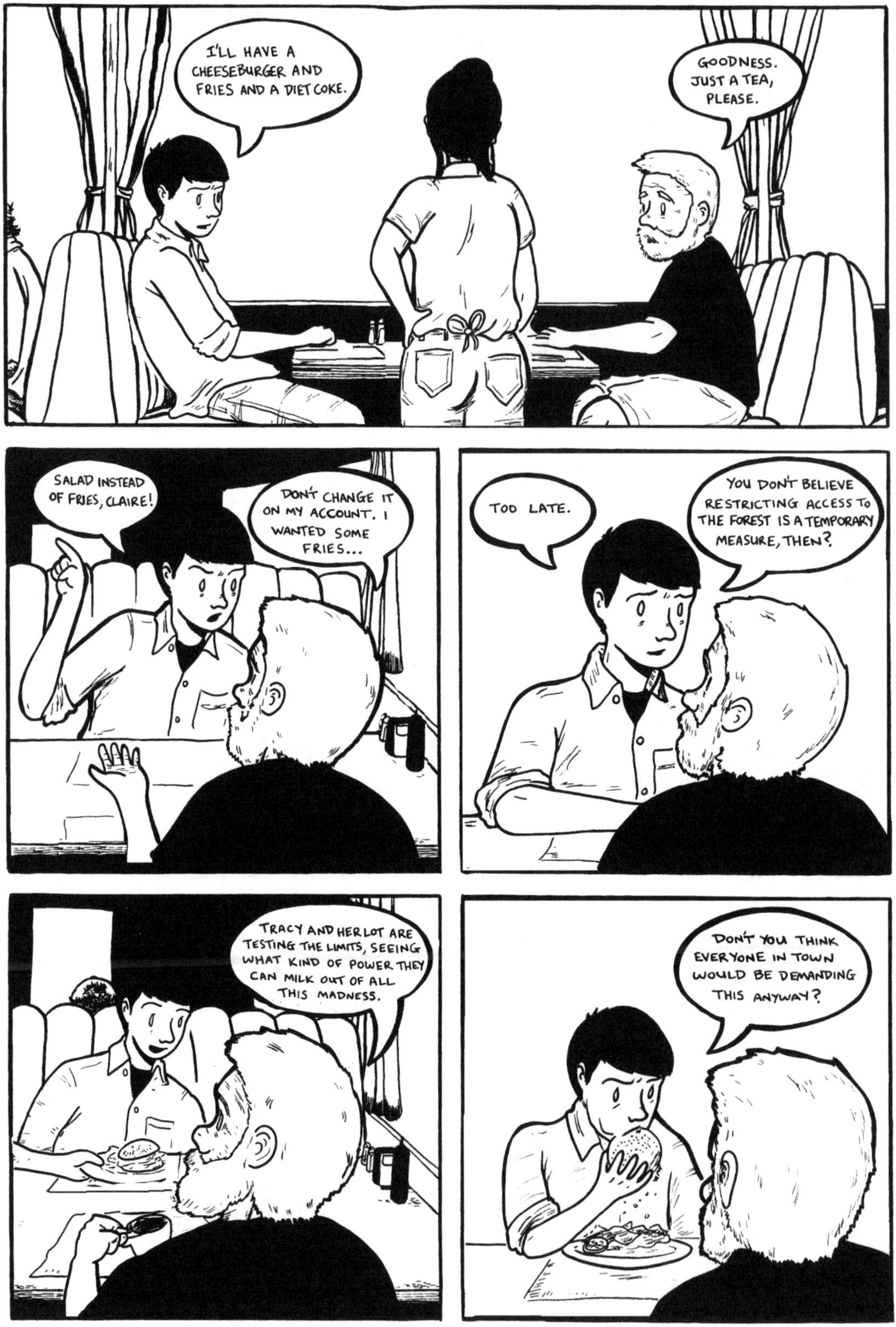
I'LL HAVE A CHEESEBURGER AND FRIES AND A DIET COKE.
GOODNESS. JUST A TEA, PLEASE.
SALAD INSTEAD OF FRIES, CLAIRE!
DON'T CHANGE IT ON MY ACCOUNT. I WANTED SOME FRIES...
TOO LATE.
YOU DON'T BELIEVE RESTRICTING ACCESS TO THE FOREST IS A TEMPORARY MEASURE, THEN?
TRACY AND HER LOT ARE TESTING THE LIMITS, SEEING WHAT KIND OF POWER THEY CAN MILK OUT OF ALL THIS MADNESS.
DON'T YOU THINK EVERYONE IN TOWN WOULD BE DEMANDING THIS ANYWAY?

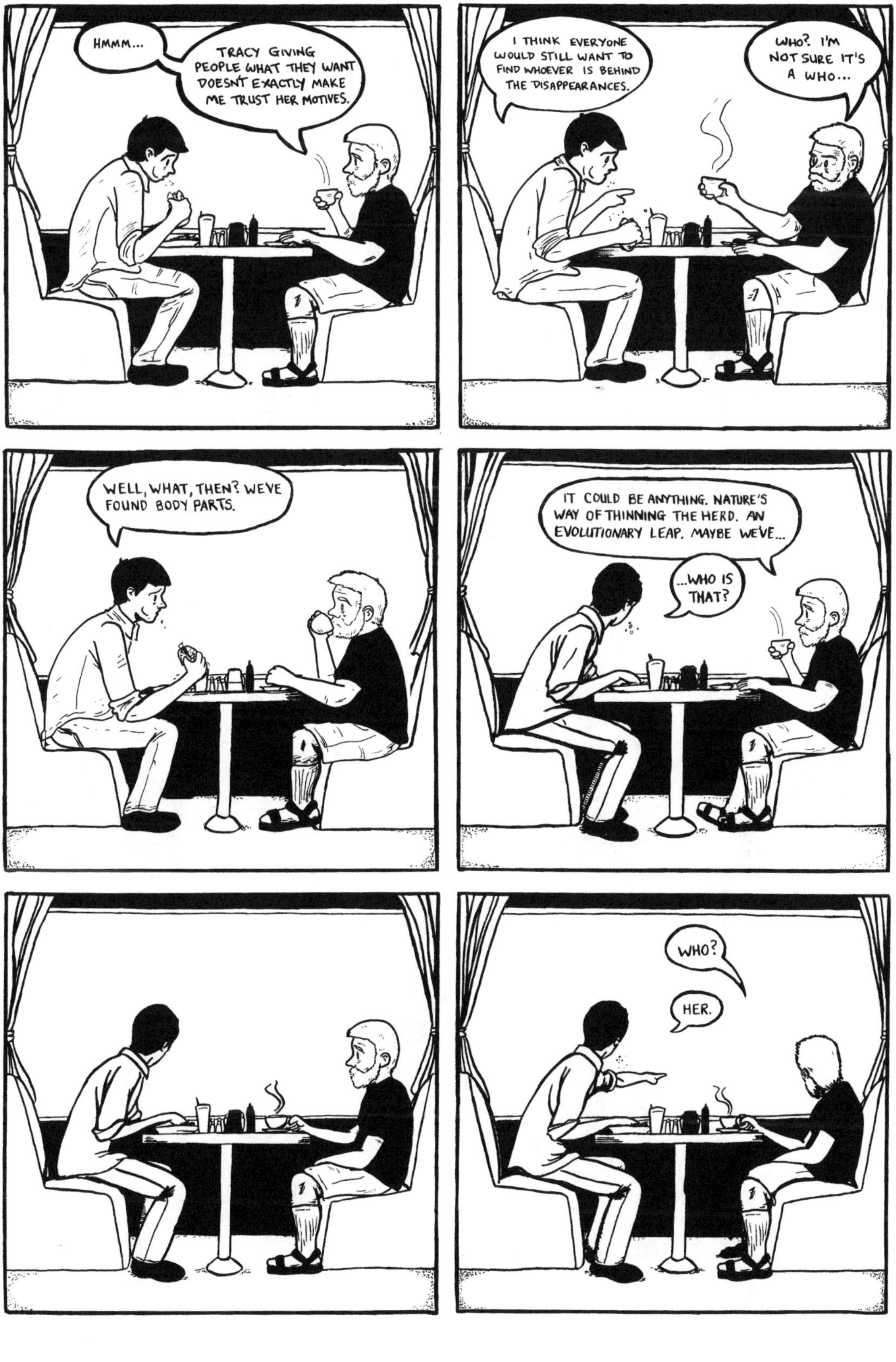
HMMM...
TRACY GIVING PEOPLE WHAT THEY WANT DOESN'T EXACTLY MAKE ME TRUST HER MOTIVES.
I THINK EVERYONE WOULD STILL WANT TO FIND WHOEVER IS BEHIND THE DISAPPEARANCES.
WHO? I'M NOT SURE IT'S A WHO...
WELL, WHAT, THEN? WE'VE FOUND BODY PARTS.
IT COULD BE ANYTHING. NATURE'S WAY OF THINNING THE HERD. AN EVOLUTIONARY LEAP. MAYBE WE'VE...
...WHO IS THAT?
WHO?
HER.

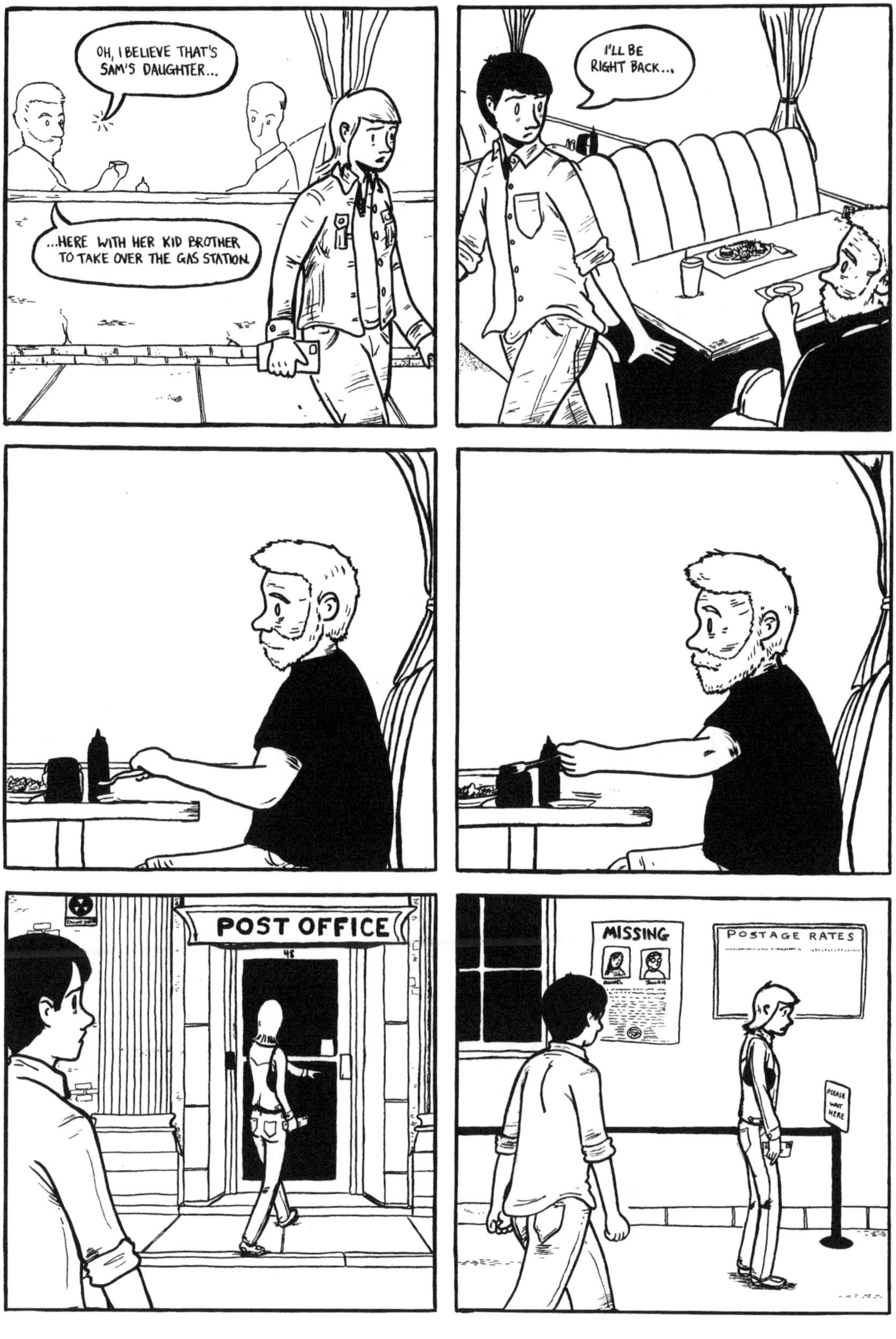
OH, I BELIEVE THAT'S SAM'S DAUGHTER...
...HERE WITH HER KID BROTHER TO TAKE OVER THE GAS STATION.
I'LL BE RIGHT BACK...
POST OFFICE
MISSING
POSTAGE RATES
PLEASE WAIT HERE

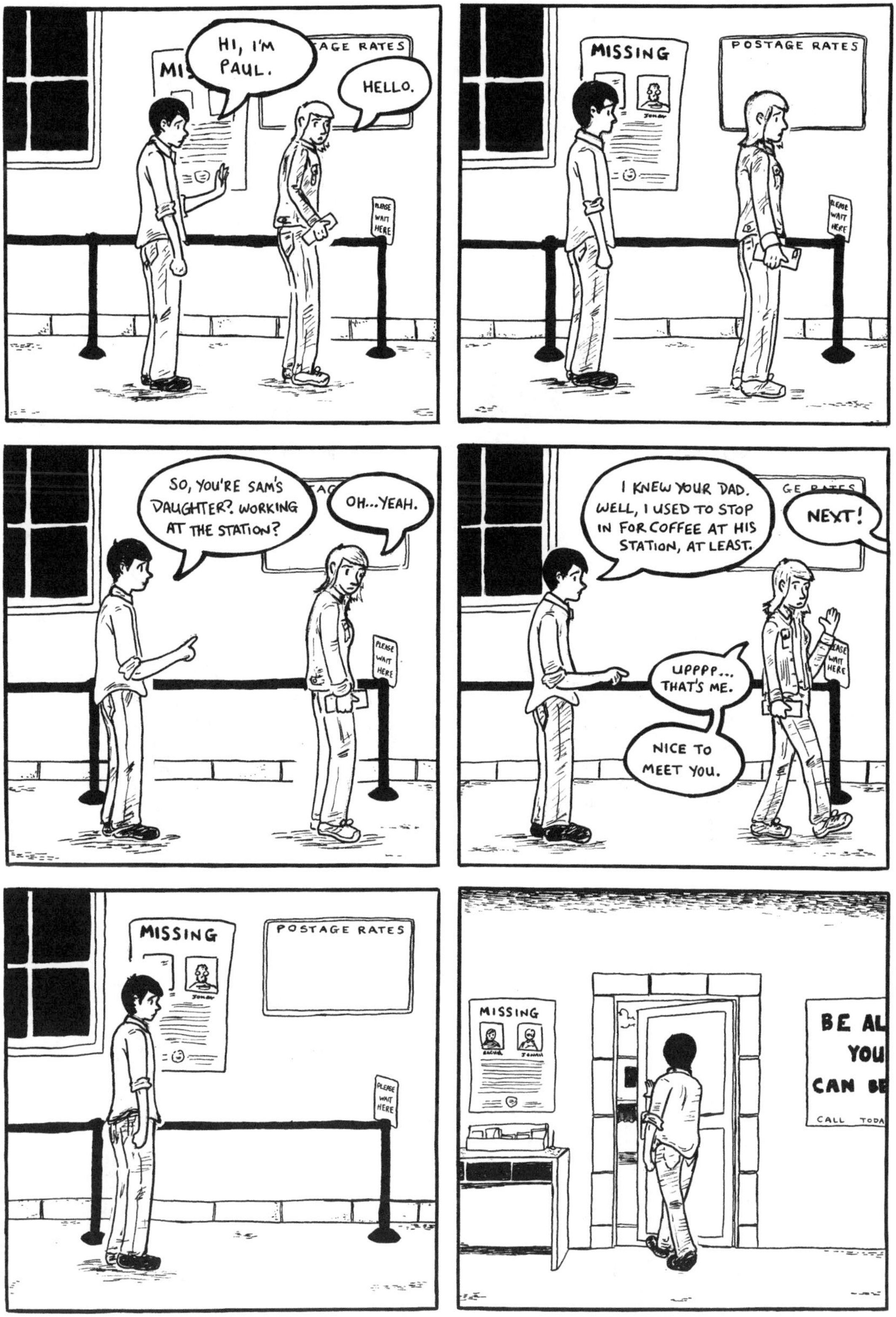
HI, I'M PAUL.
HELLO.
MISSING
POSTAGE RATES
PLEASE WAIT HERE
SO, YOU'RE SAM'S DAUGHTER? WORKING AT THE STATION?
OH...YEAH.
I KNEW YOUR DAD. WELL, I USED TO STOP IN FOR COFFEE AT HIS STATION, AT LEAST.
NEXT!
UPPPP... THAT'S ME.
NICE TO MEET YOU.
MISSING
POSTAGE RATES
PLEASE WAIT HERE
MISSING
RACHEL JONAH
BE AL
YOU
CAN BE
CALL TODA

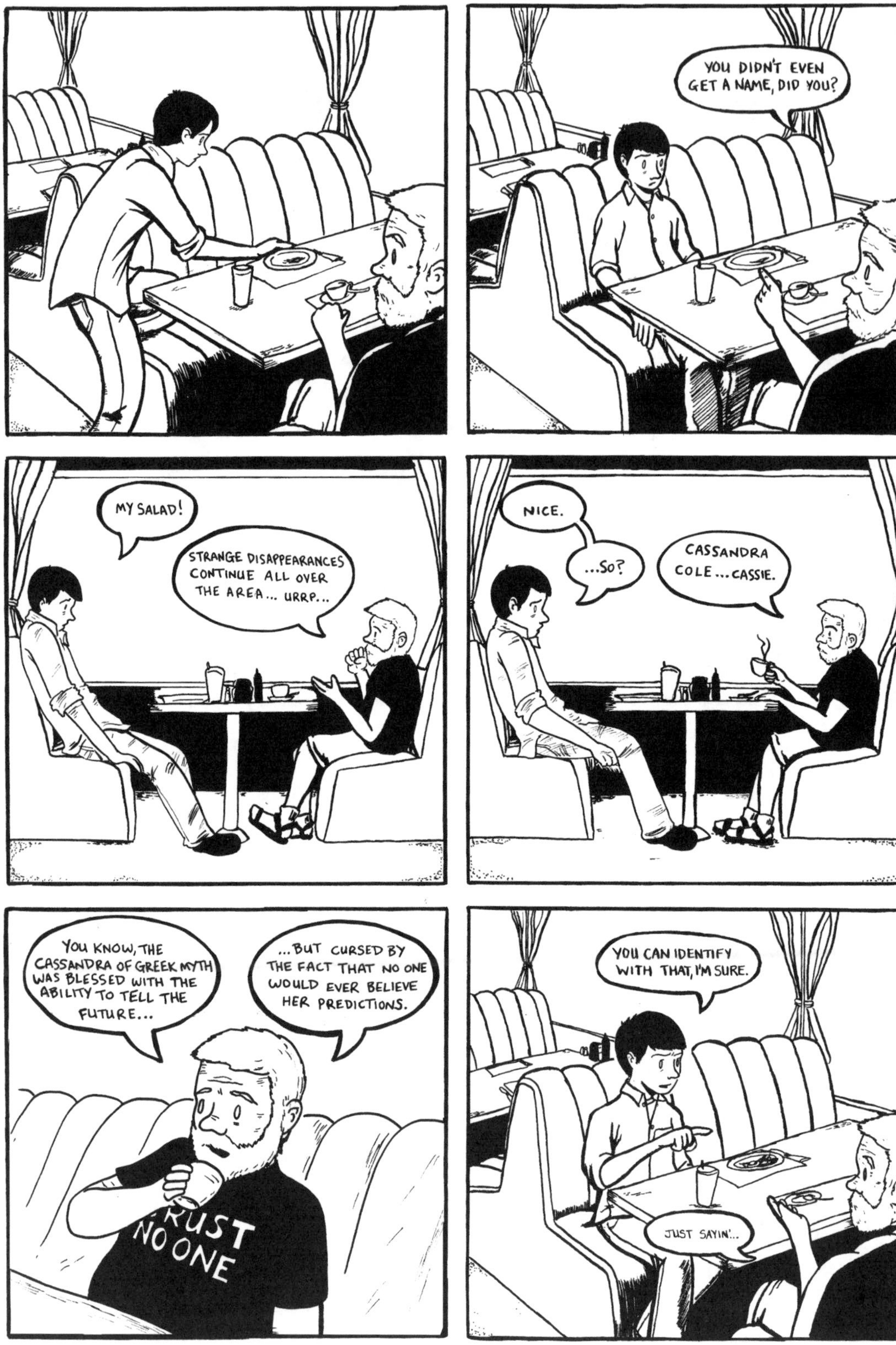
YOU DIDN'T EVEN GET A NAME, DID YOU?
MY SALAD!
STRANGE DISAPPEARANCES CONTINUE ALL OVER THE AREA... URRP...
NICE.
...SO?
CASSANDRA COLE... CASSIE.
YOU KNOW, THE CASSANDRA OF GREEK MYTH WAS BLESSED WITH THE ABILITY TO TELL THE FUTURE...
...BUT CURSED BY THE FACT THAT NO ONE WOULD EVER BELIEVE HER PREDICTIONS.
TRUST NO ONE
YOU CAN IDENTIFY WITH THAT, I'M SURE.
JUST SAYIN'...

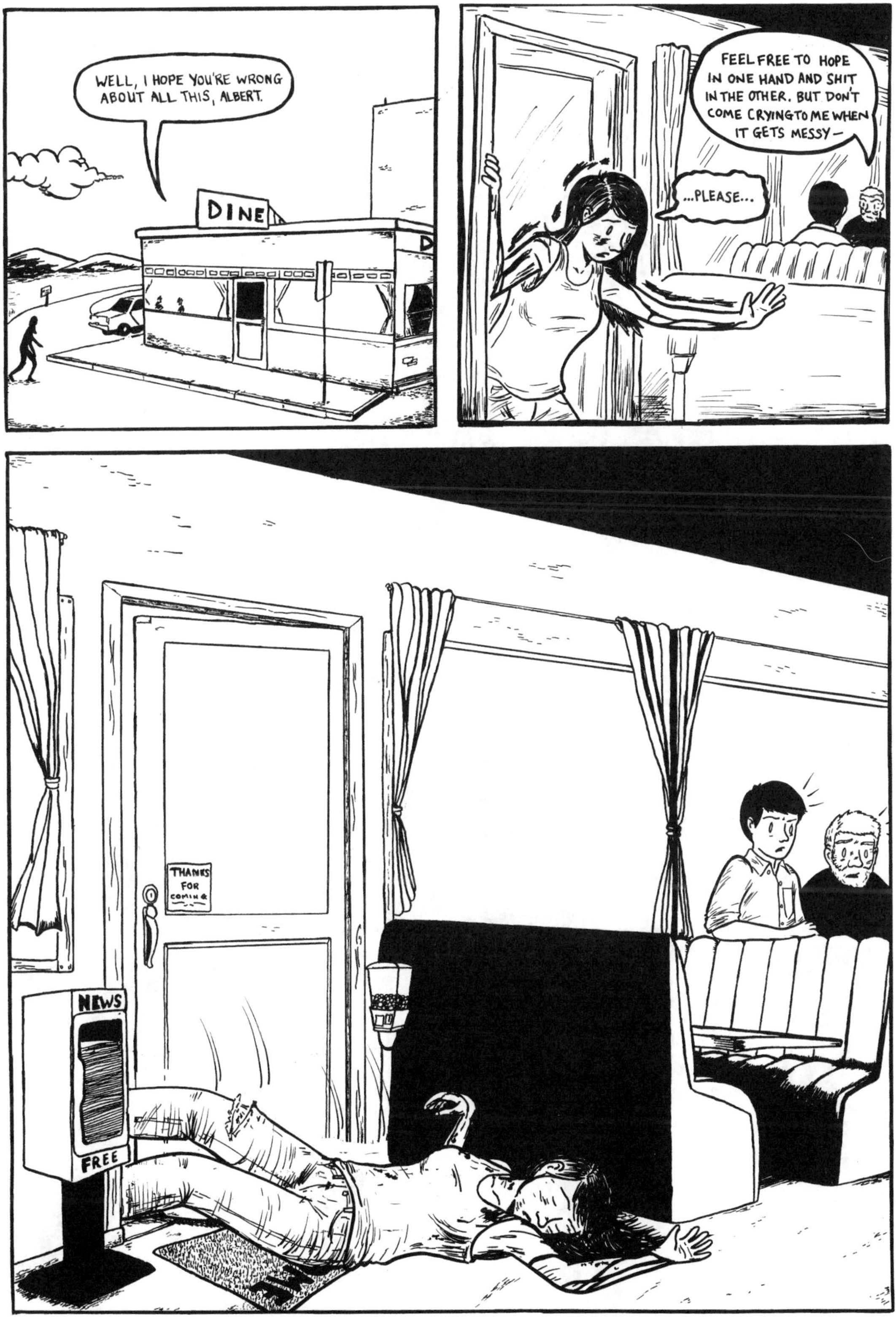
WELL, I HOPE YOU'RE WRONG ABOUT ALL THIS, ALBERT.
DINE
FEEL FREE TO HOPE IN ONE HAND AND SHIT IN THE OTHER. BUT DON'T COME CRYING TO ME WHEN IT GETS MESSY—
...PLEASE...
THANKS FOR COMING
NEWS
FREE

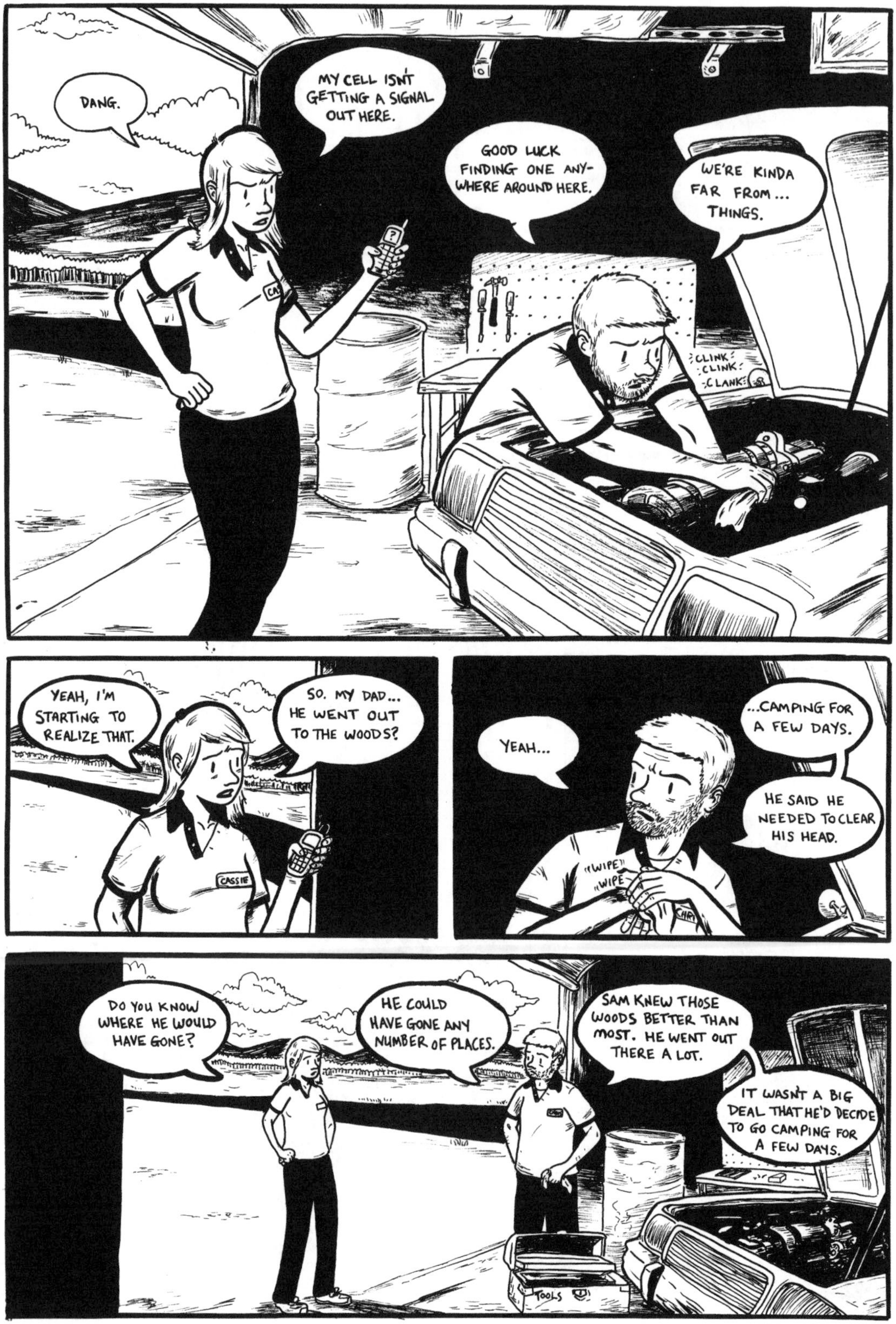
DANG.
MY CELL ISN'T GETTING A SIGNAL OUT HERE.
GOOD LUCK FINDING ONE ANY-WHERE AROUND HERE.
WE'RE KINDA FAR FROM... THINGS.
CLINK CLINK CLANK
YEAH, I'M STARTING TO REALIZE THAT.
SO. MY DAD... HE WENT OUT TO THE WOODS?
CASSIE
YEAH...
...CAMPING FOR A FEW DAYS.
HE SAID HE NEEDED TO CLEAR HIS HEAD.
"WIPE" "WIPE"
DO YOU KNOW WHERE HE WOULD HAVE GONE?
HE COULD HAVE GONE ANY NUMBER OF PLACES.
SAM KNEW THOSE WOODS BETTER THAN MOST. HE WENT OUT THERE A LOT.
IT WASN'T A BIG DEAL THAT HE'D DECIDE TO GO CAMPING FOR A FEW DAYS.
TOOLS

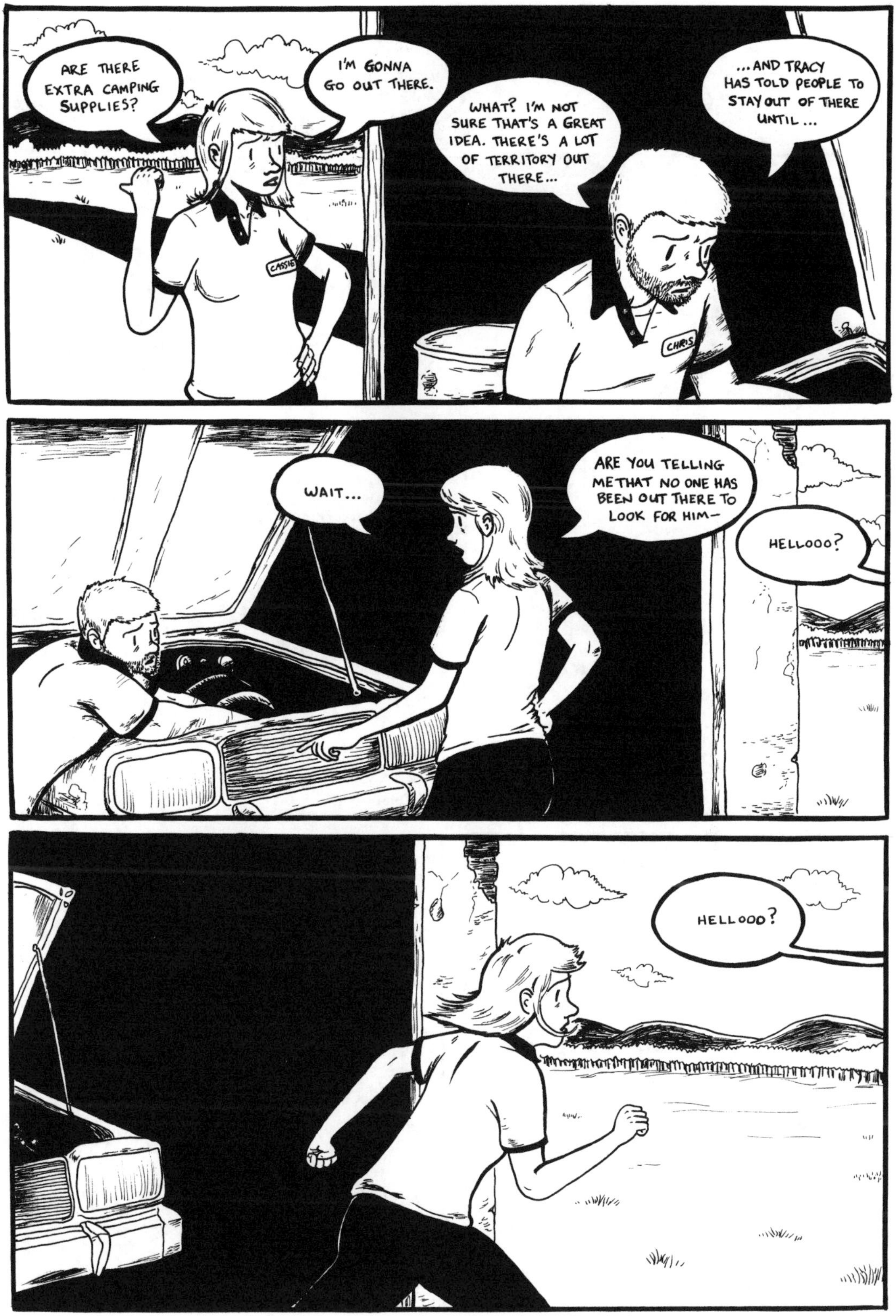
ARE THERE EXTRA CAMPING SUPPLIES?
I'M GONNA GO OUT THERE.
WHAT? I'M NOT SURE THAT'S A GREAT IDEA. THERE'S A LOT OF TERRITORY OUT THERE...
...AND TRACY HAS TOLD PEOPLE TO STAY OUT OF THERE UNTIL...
CASSIE
CHRIS
WAIT...
ARE YOU TELLING ME THAT NO ONE HAS BEEN OUT THERE TO LOOK FOR HIM—
HELLOOO?
HELLOOO?

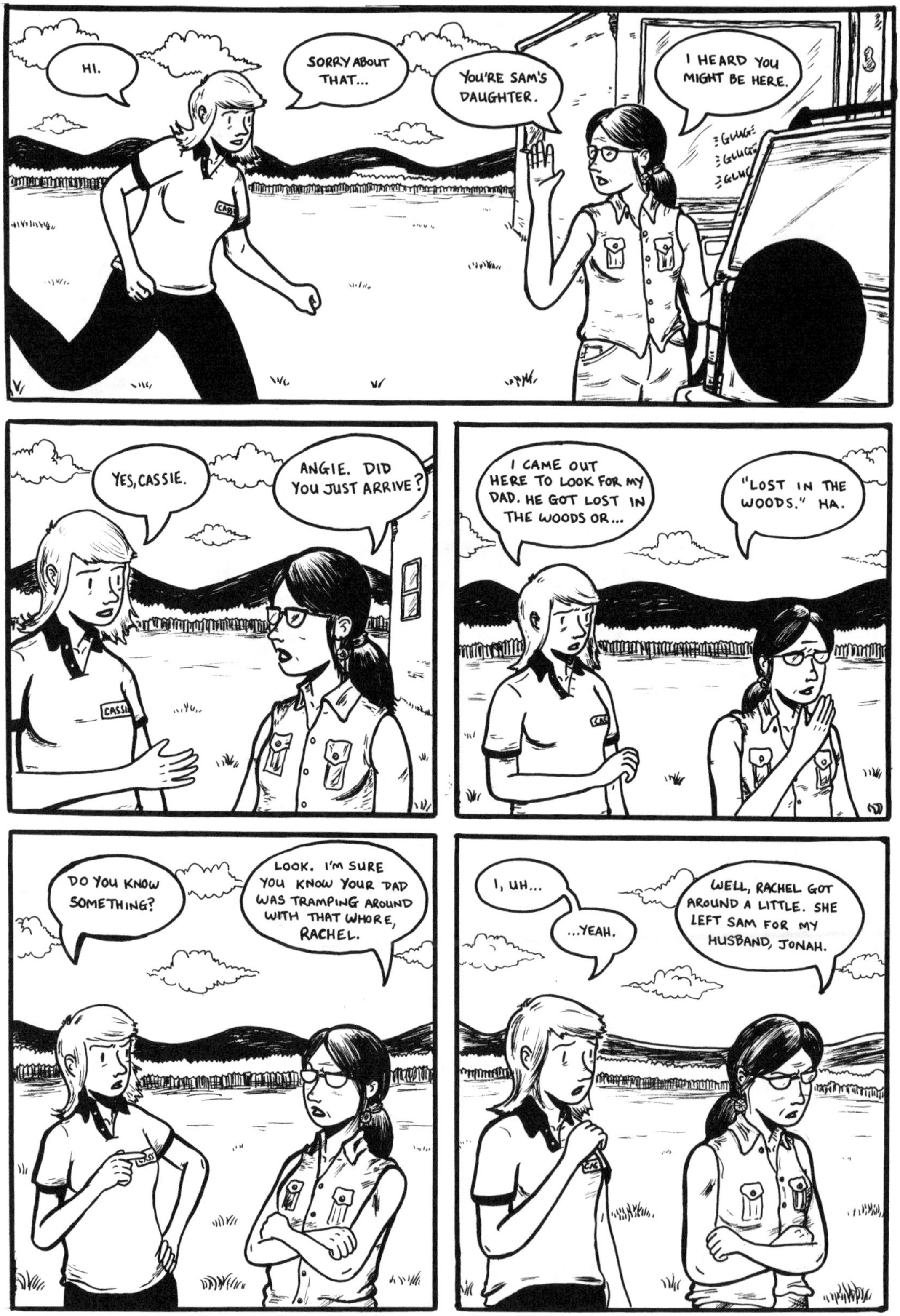
HI.
SORRY ABOUT THAT...
YOU'RE SAM'S DAUGHTER.
I HEARD YOU MIGHT BE HERE.
GLUG GLUG GLUG
YES, CASSIE.
ANGIE. DID YOU JUST ARRIVE?
I CAME OUT HERE TO LOOK FOR MY DAD. HE GOT LOST IN THE WOODS OR...
"LOST IN THE WOODS." HA.
DO YOU KNOW SOMETHING?
LOOK. I'M SURE YOU KNOW YOUR DAD WAS TRAMPING AROUND WITH THAT WHORE, RACHEL.
I, UH...
...YEAH.
WELL, RACHEL GOT AROUND A LITTLE. SHE LEFT SAM FOR MY HUSBAND, JONAH.

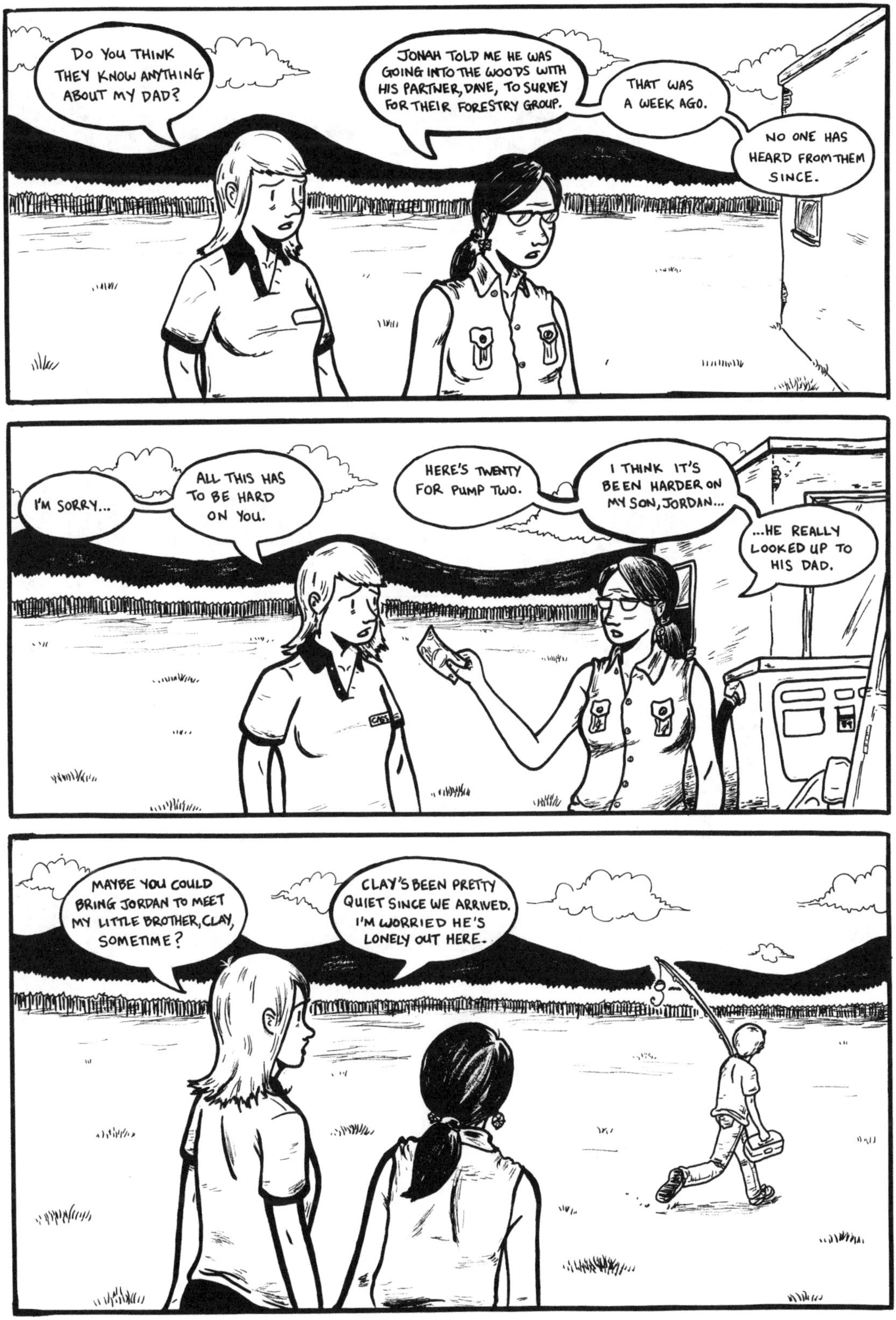
DO YOU THINK THEY KNOW ANYTHING ABOUT MY DAD?
JONAH TOLD ME HE WAS GOING INTO THE WOODS WITH HIS PARTNER, DAVE, TO SURVEY FOR THEIR FORESTRY GROUP.
THAT WAS A WEEK AGO.
NO ONE HAS HEARD FROM THEM SINCE.
I'M SORRY...
ALL THIS HAS TO BE HARD ON YOU.
HERE'S TWENTY FOR PUMP TWO.
I THINK IT'S BEEN HARDER ON MY SON, JORDAN...
...HE REALLY LOOKED UP TO HIS DAD.
MAYBE YOU COULD BRING JORDAN TO MEET MY LITTLE BROTHER, CLAY, SOMETIME?
CLAY'S BEEN PRETTY QUIET SINCE WE ARRIVED. I'M WORRIED HE'S LONELY OUT HERE.

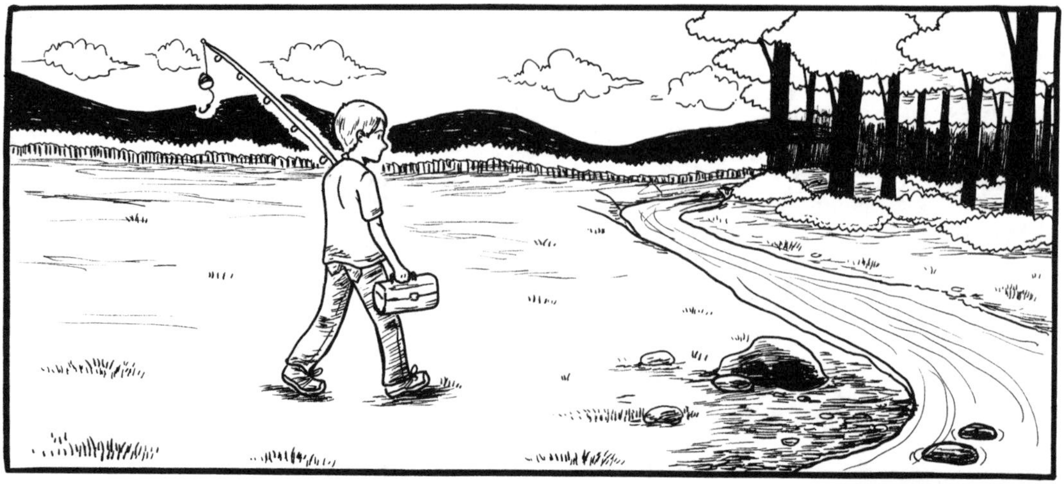
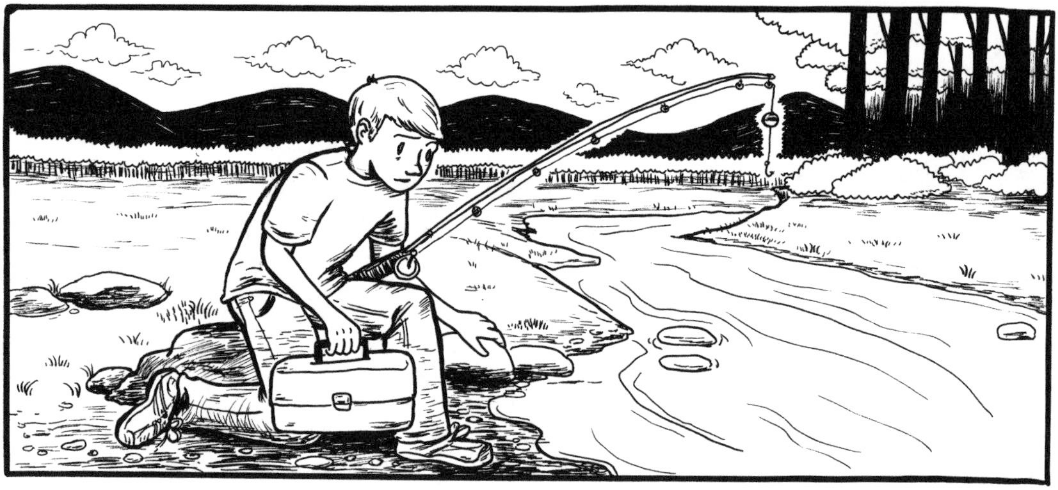
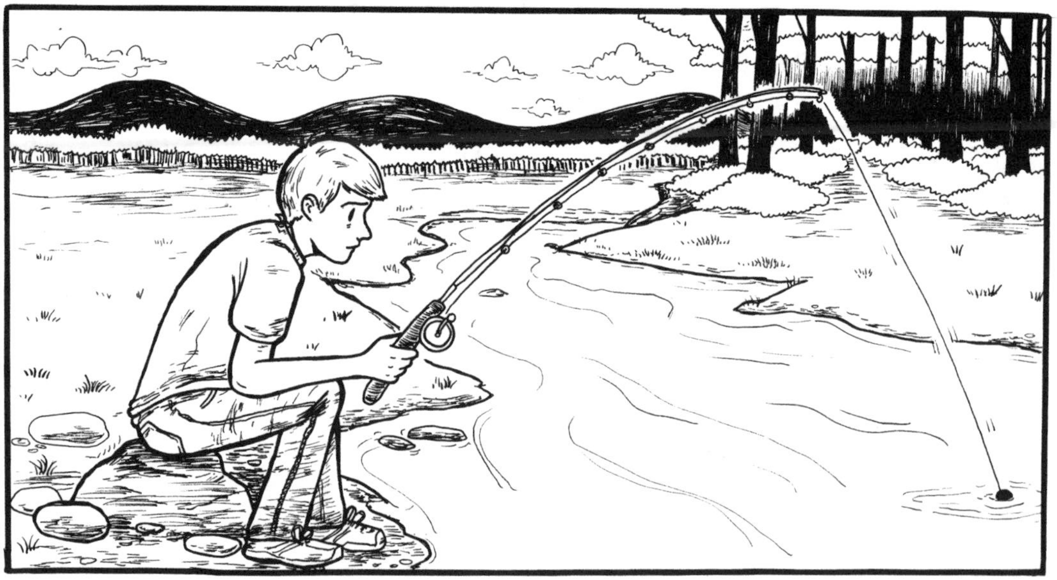

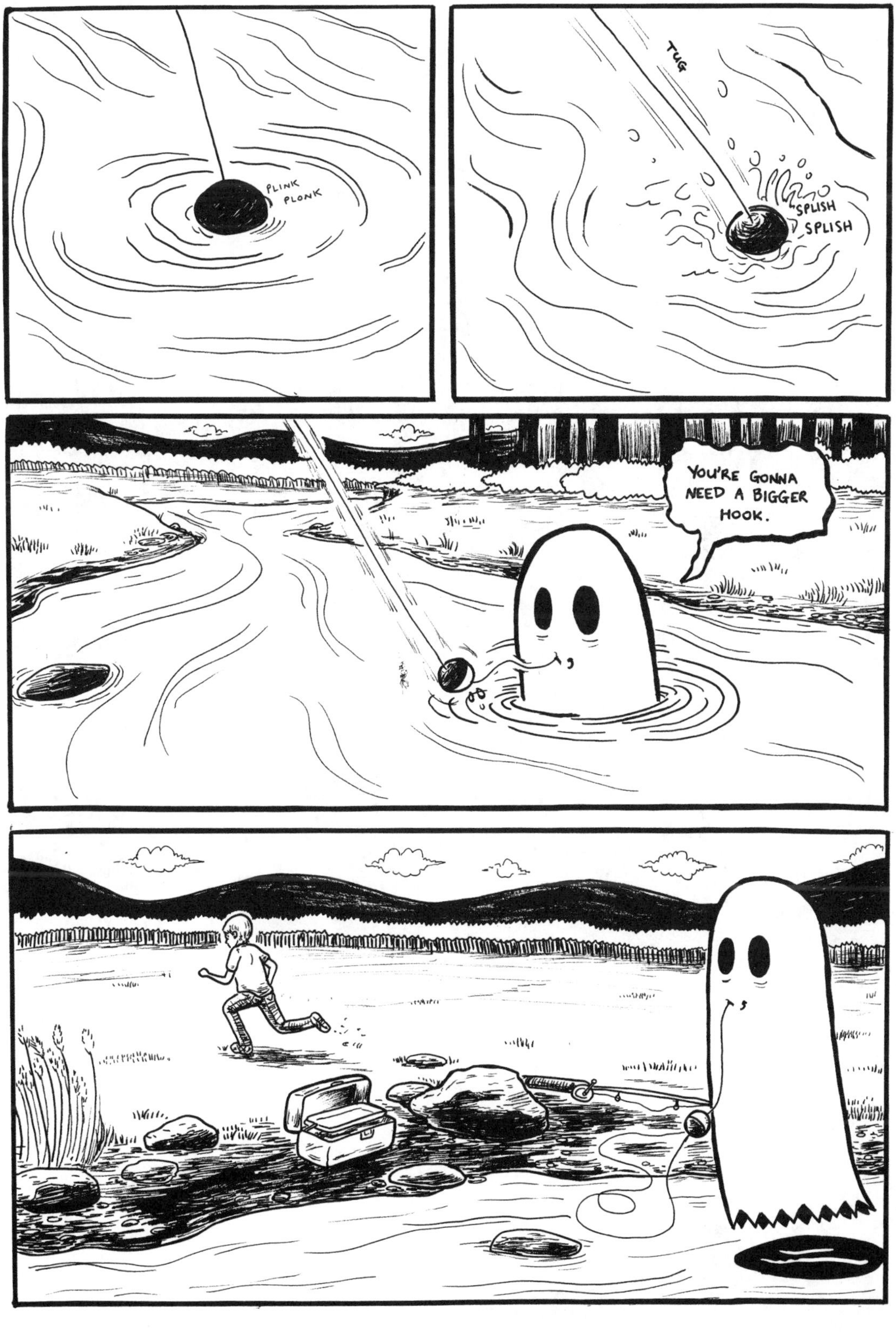
PLINK
PLONK
TUG
SPLISH
SPLISH
YOU'RE GONNA NEED A BIGGER HOOK.

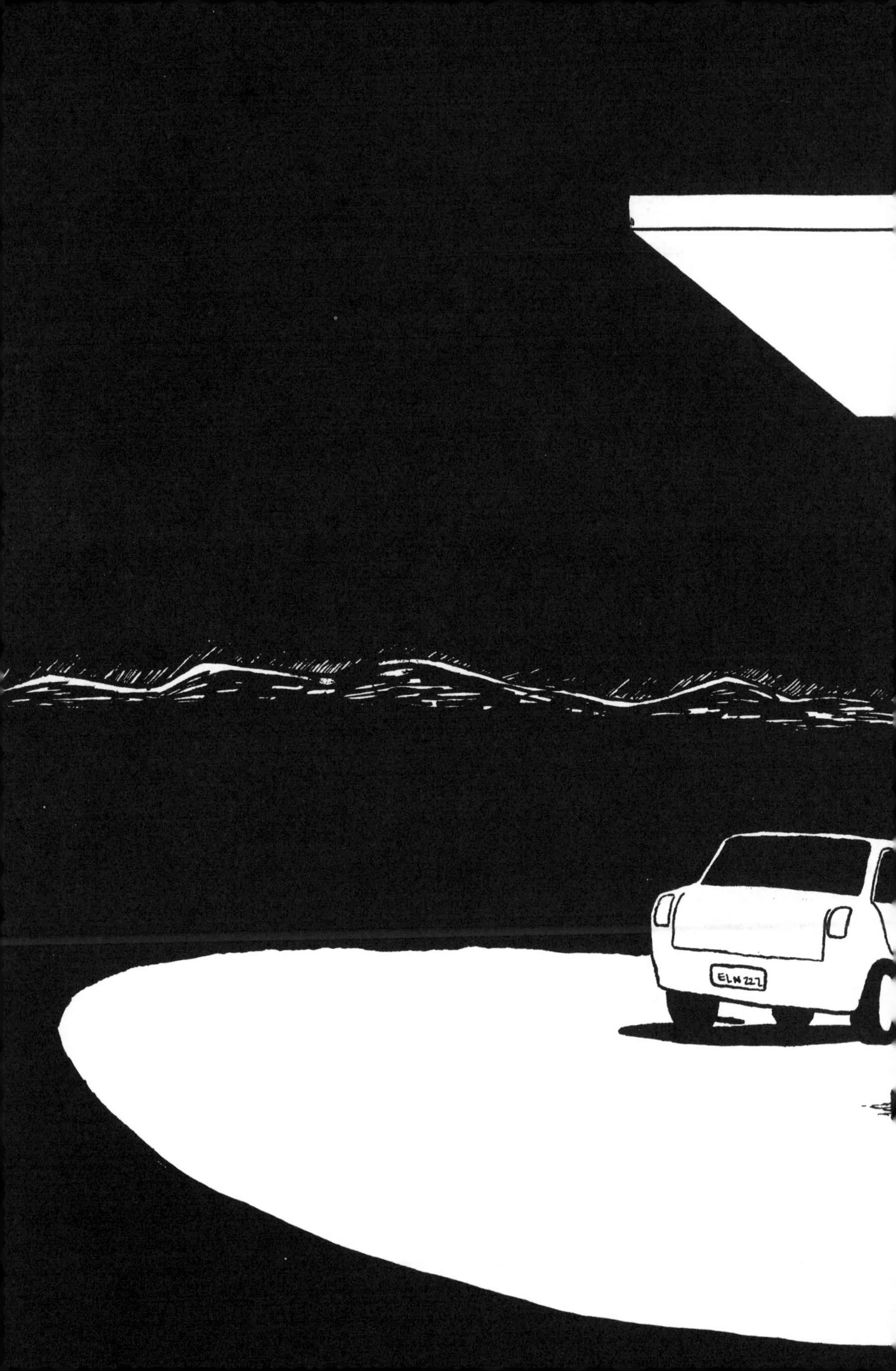

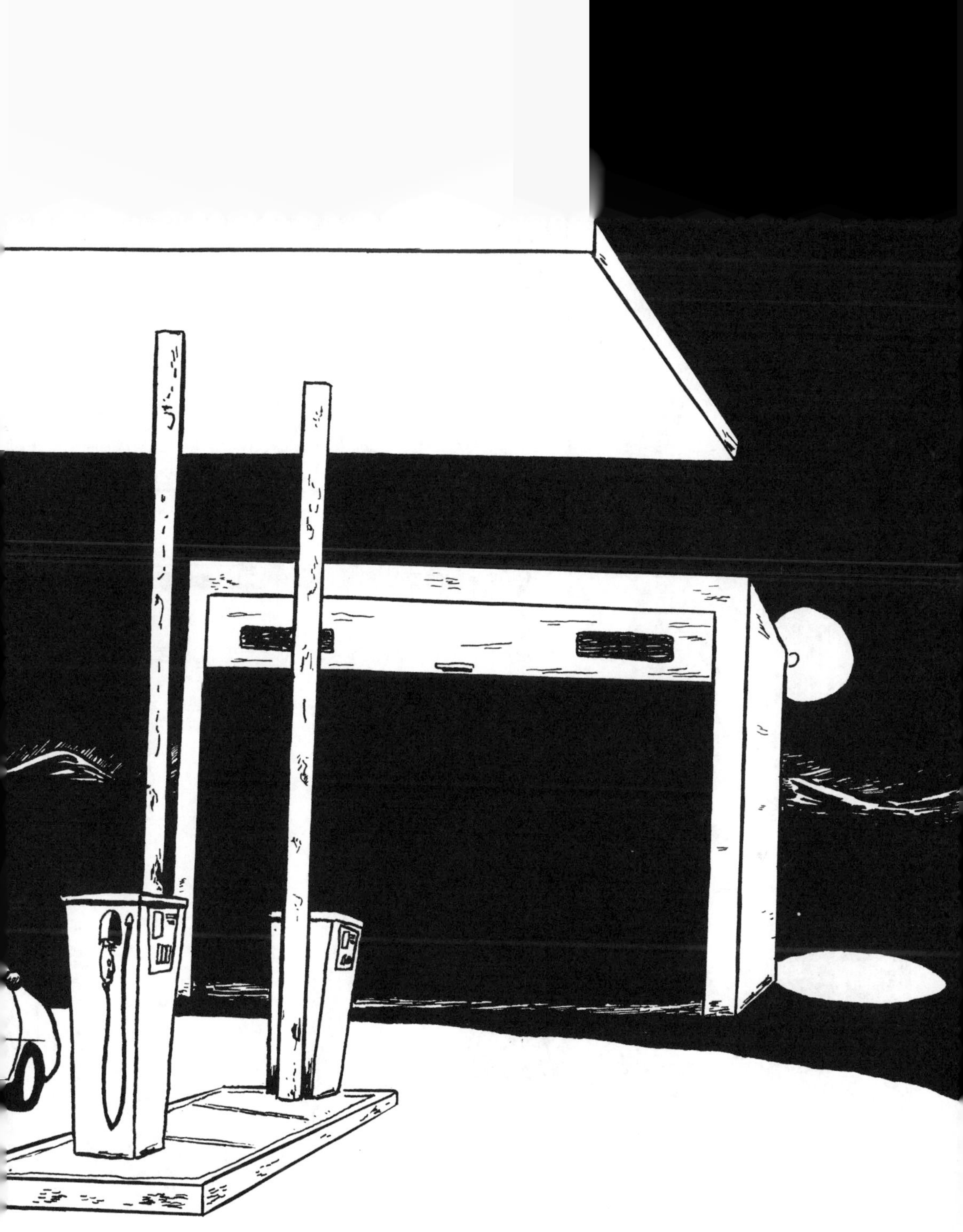

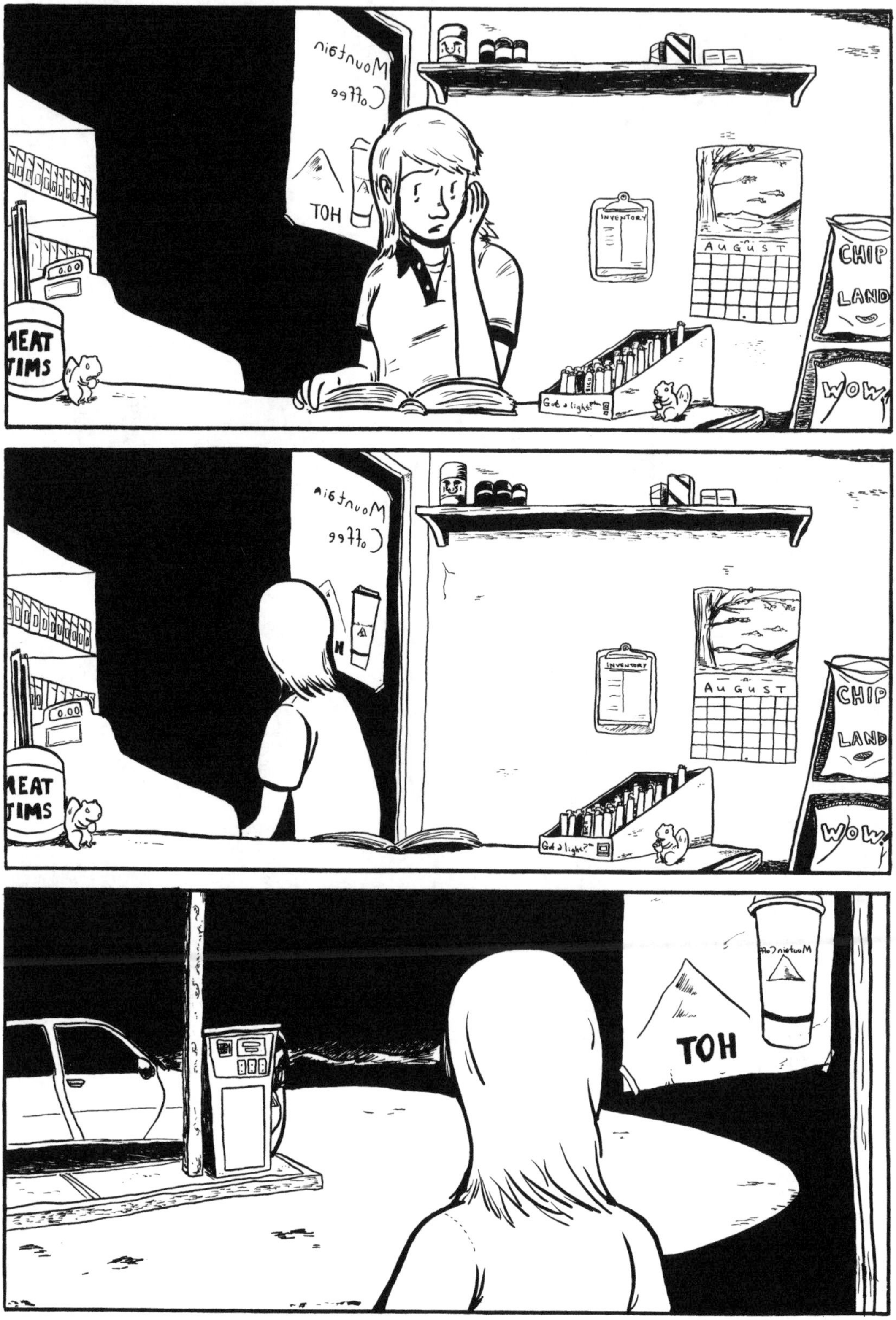
INVENTORY
AUGUST
CHIP LAND
WOW
MEAT TIMS
Got a light?
0.00
INVENTORY
AUGUST
CHIP LAND
WOW
MEAT TIMS
Got a light?
0.00
TOH

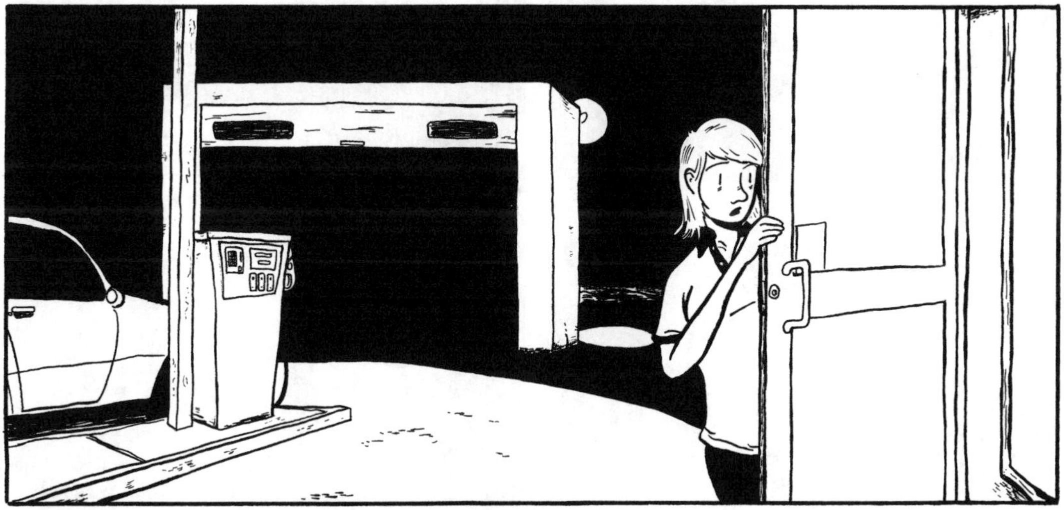

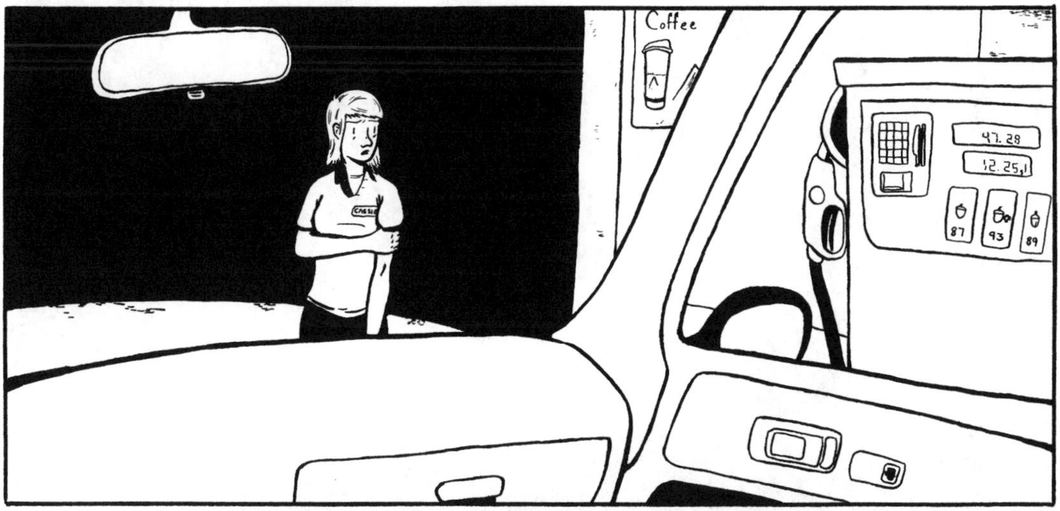
Coffee
CASSIE
47.28
12.25,1
87
93
89

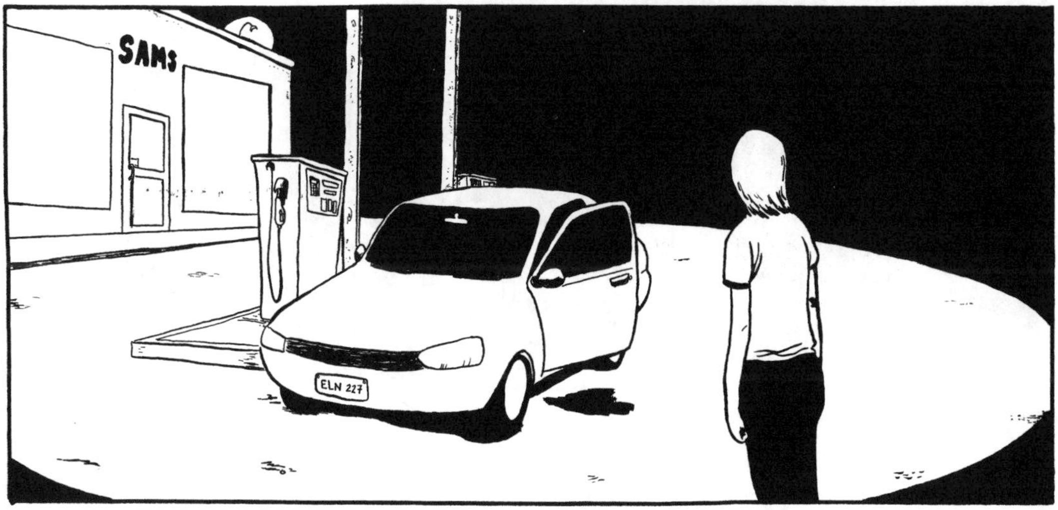
SAMS
ELN 227

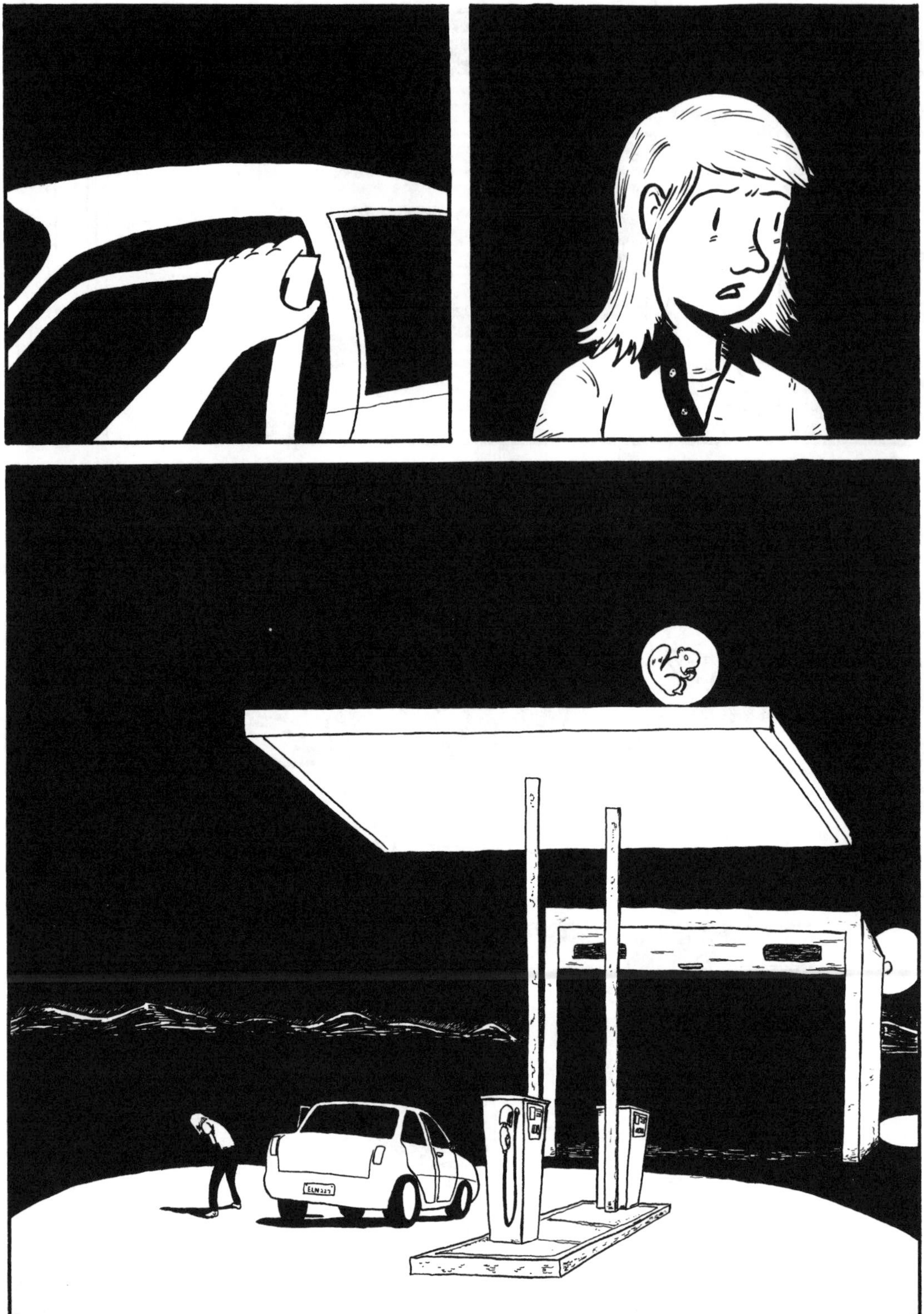
ELN 227

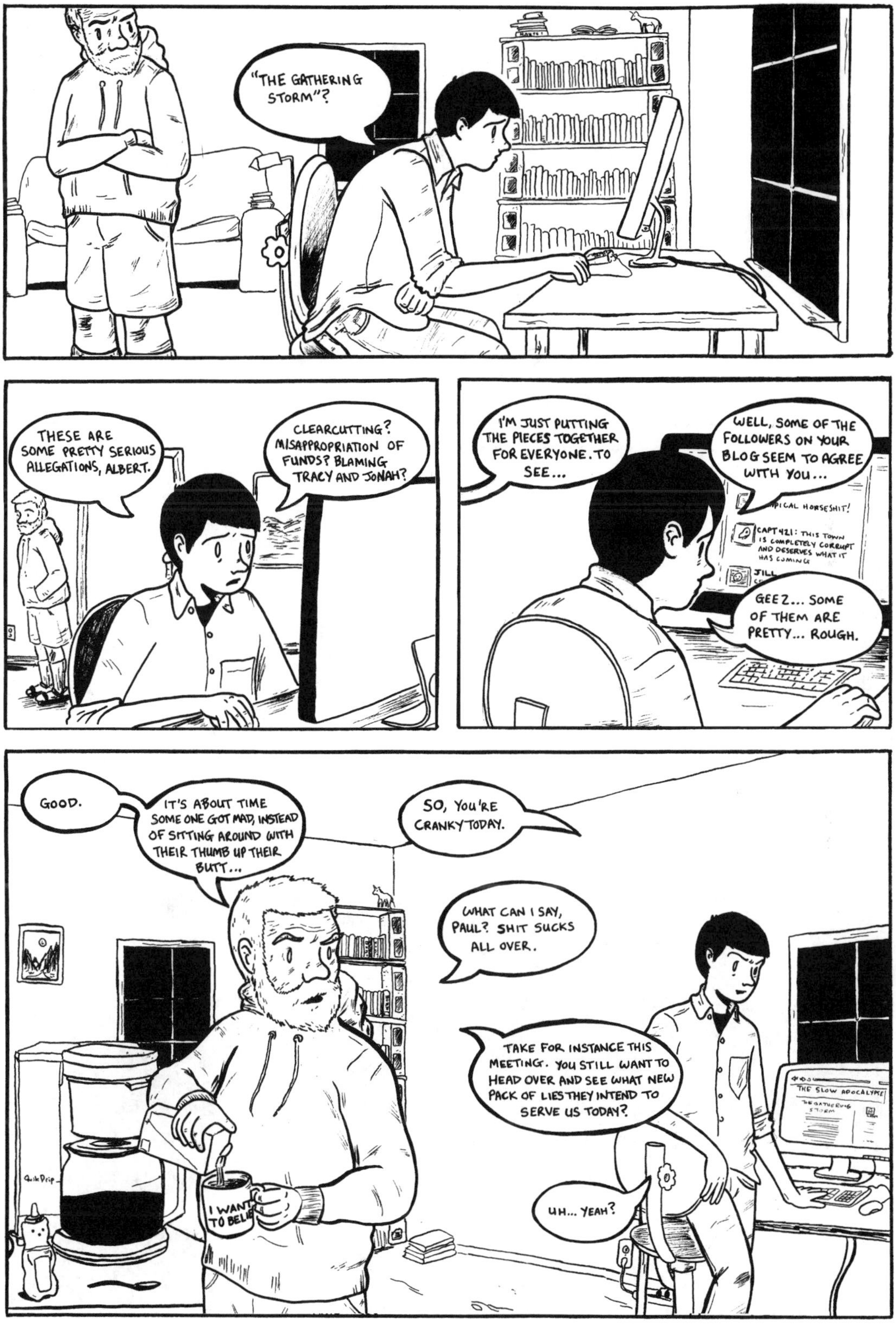
"THE GATHERING STORM"?
THESE ARE SOME PRETTY SERIOUS ALLEGATIONS, ALBERT.
CLEARCUTTING? MISAPPROPRIATION OF FUNDS? BLAMING TRACY AND JONAH?
I'M JUST PUTTING THE PIECES TOGETHER FOR EVERYONE. TO SEE...
WELL, SOME OF THE FOLLOWERS ON YOUR BLOG SEEM TO AGREE WITH YOU...
PICAL HORSESHIT!
CAPT421: THIS TOWN IS COMPLETELY CORRUPT AND DESERVES WHAT IT HAS COMING
GEEZ... SOME OF THEM ARE PRETTY... ROUGH.
GOOD.
IT'S ABOUT TIME SOME ONE GOT MAD, INSTEAD OF SITTING AROUND WITH THEIR THUMB UP THEIR BUTT...
SO, YOU'RE CRANKY TODAY.
WHAT CAN I SAY, PAUL? SHIT SUCKS ALL OVER.
TAKE FOR INSTANCE THIS MEETING. YOU STILL WANT TO HEAD OVER AND SEE WHAT NEW PACK OF LIES THEY INTEND TO SERVE US TODAY?
UH... YEAH?
THE SLOW APOCALYPSE
THE GATHERING STORM
I WANT TO BELI

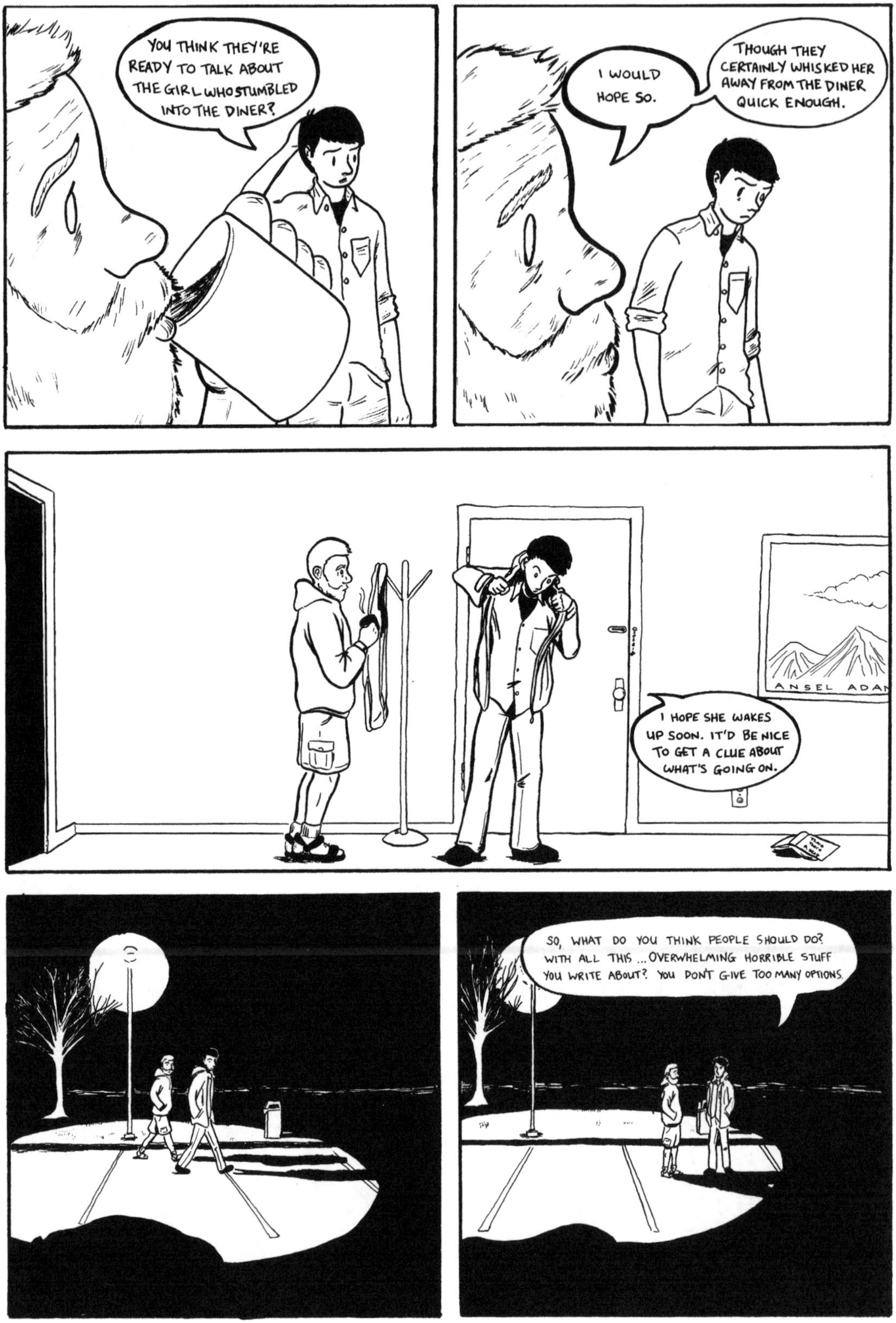
YOU THINK THEY'RE READY TO TALK ABOUT THE GIRL WHO STUMBLED INTO THE DINER?
I WOULD HOPE SO.
THOUGH THEY CERTAINLY WHISKED HER AWAY FROM THE DINER QUICK ENOUGH.
I HOPE SHE WAKES UP SOON. IT'D BE NICE TO GET A CLUE ABOUT WHAT'S GOING ON.
SO, WHAT DO YOU THINK PEOPLE SHOULD DO? WITH ALL THIS ... OVERWHELMING HORRIBLE STUFF YOU WRITE ABOUT? YOU DON'T GIVE TOO MANY OPTIONS.

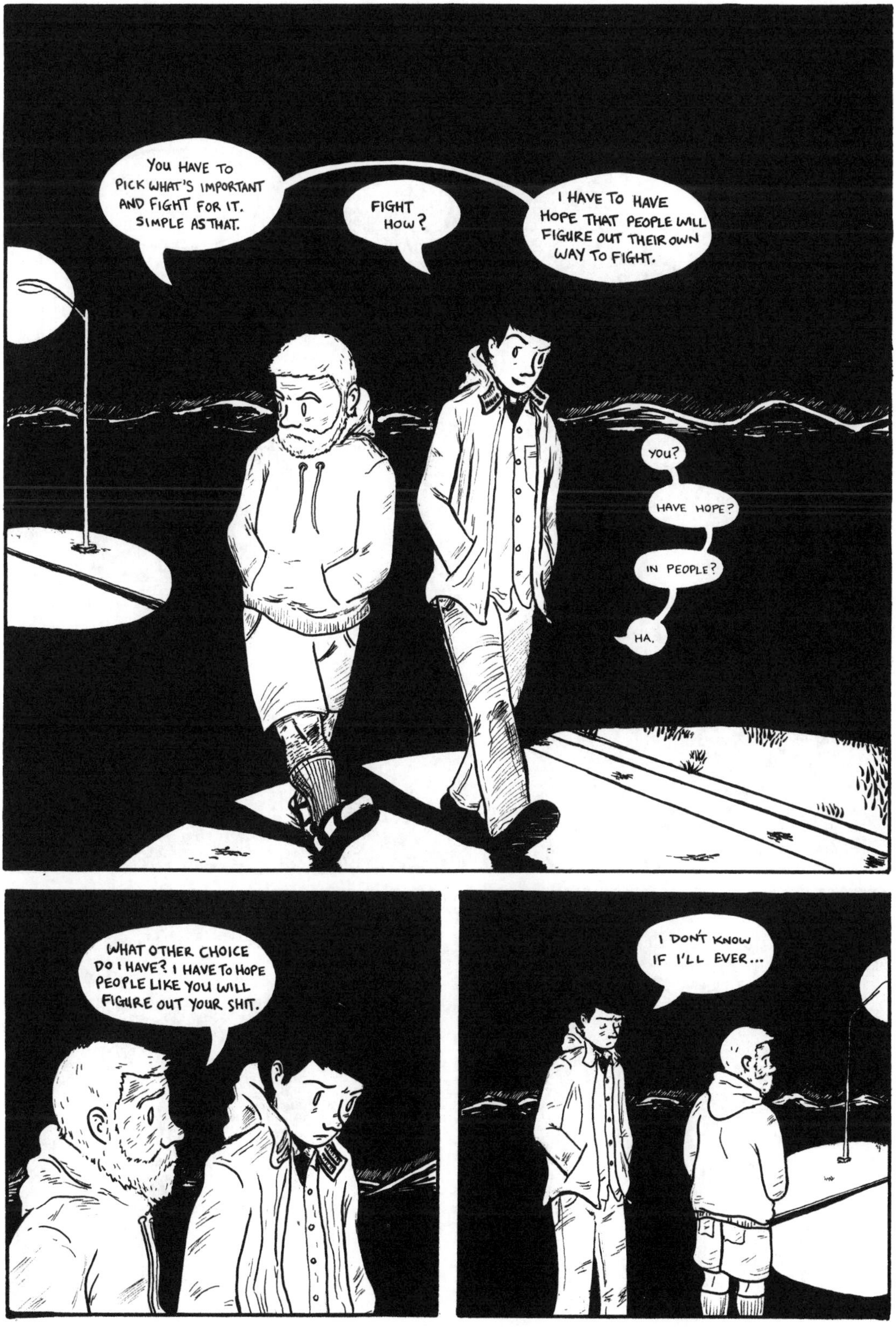
YOU HAVE TO PICK WHAT'S IMPORTANT AND FIGHT FOR IT. SIMPLE AS THAT.
FIGHT HOW?
I HAVE TO HAVE HOPE THAT PEOPLE WILL FIGURE OUT THEIR OWN WAY TO FIGHT.
YOU?
HAVE HOPE?
IN PEOPLE?
HA.
WHAT OTHER CHOICE DO I HAVE? I HAVE TO HOPE PEOPLE LIKE YOU WILL FIGURE OUT YOUR SHIT.
I DON'T KNOW IF I'LL EVER...

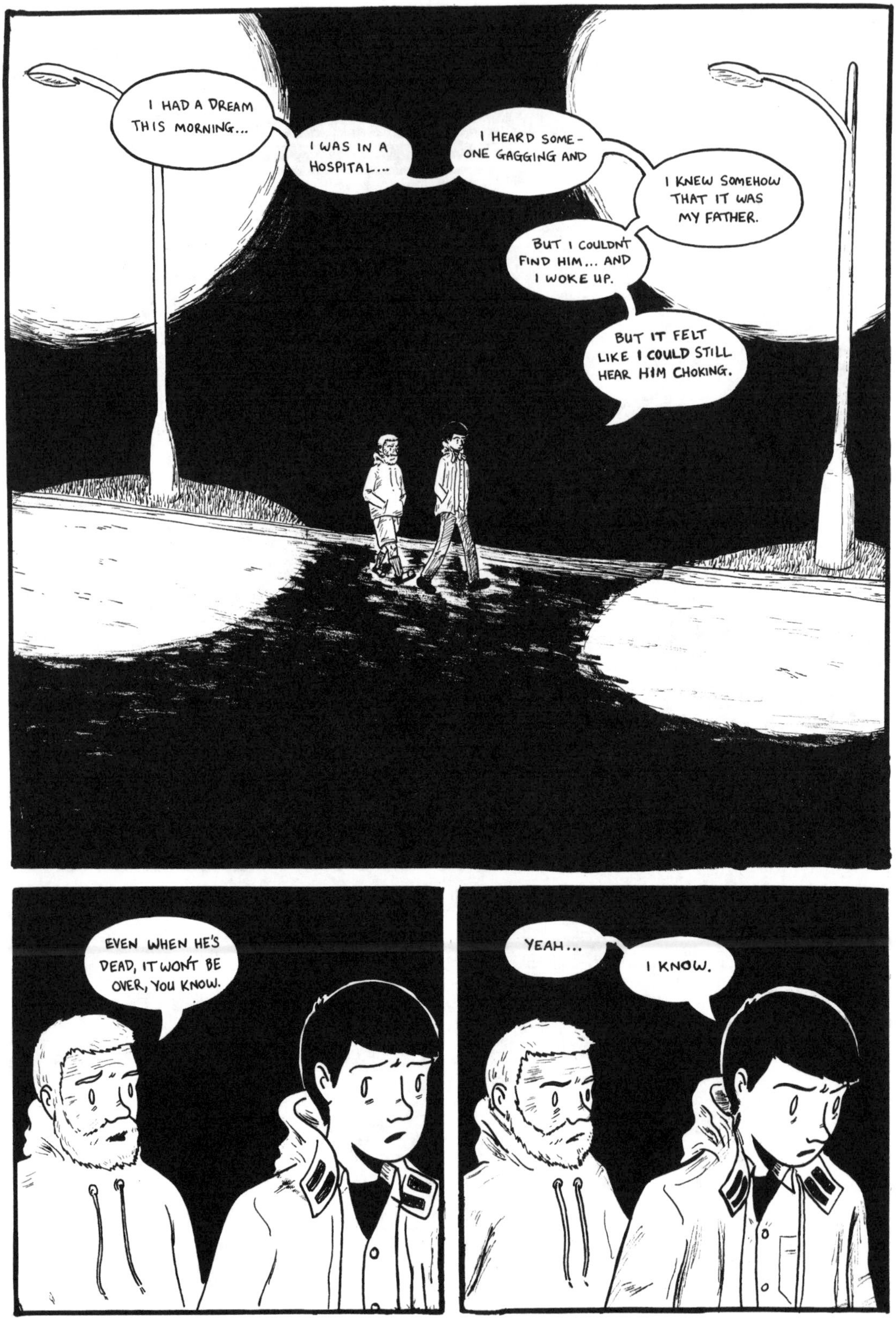
I HAD A DREAM THIS MORNING...
I WAS IN A HOSPITAL...
I HEARD SOME-ONE GAGGING AND
I KNEW SOMEHOW THAT IT WAS MY FATHER.
BUT I COULDN'T FIND HIM... AND I WOKE UP.
BUT IT FELT LIKE I COULD STILL HEAR HIM CHOKING.
EVEN WHEN HE'S DEAD, IT WON'T BE OVER, YOU KNOW.
YEAH...
I KNOW.

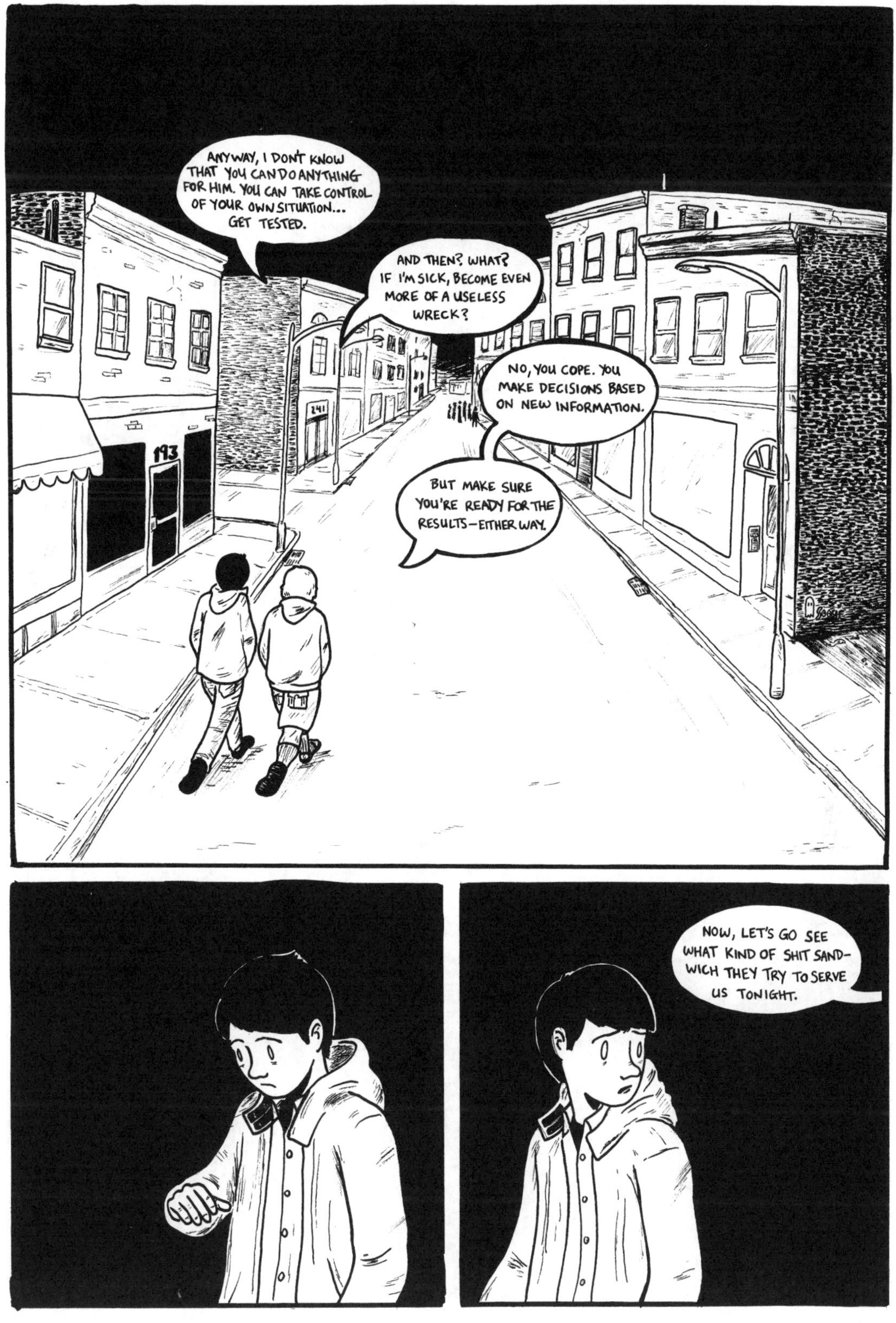
ANYWAY, I DON'T KNOW THAT YOU CAN DO ANYTHING FOR HIM. YOU CAN TAKE CONTROL OF YOUR OWN SITUATION... GET TESTED.
AND THEN? WHAT? IF I'M SICK, BECOME EVEN MORE OF A USELESS WRECK?
NO, YOU COPE. YOU MAKE DECISIONS BASED ON NEW INFORMATION.
BUT MAKE SURE YOU'RE READY FOR THE RESULTS—EITHER WAY.
NOW, LET'S GO SEE WHAT KIND OF SHIT SAND-WICH THEY TRY TO SERVE US TONIGHT.

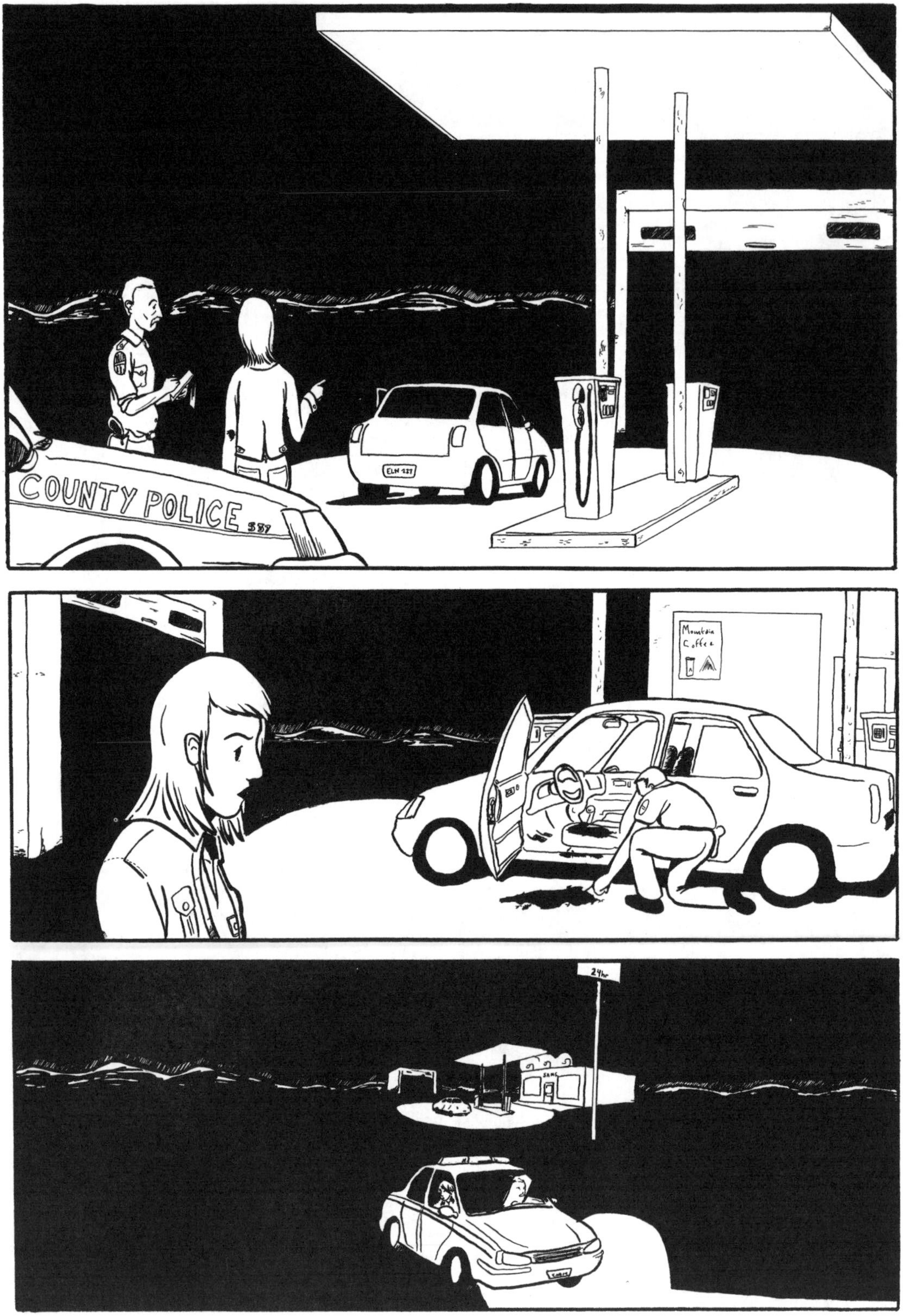
COUNTY POLICE 537
ELN 227
Mountain Coffee
24hr

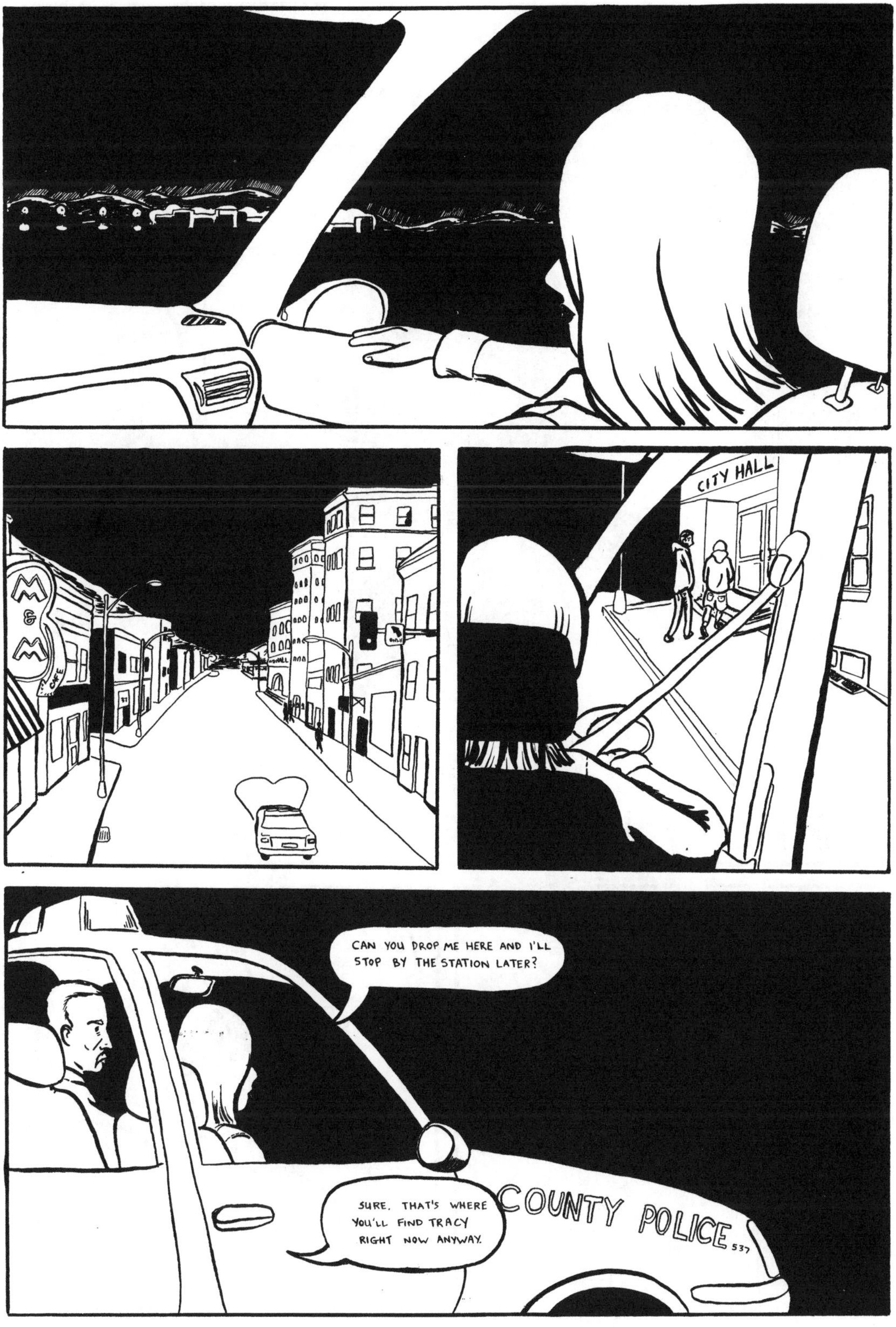
M & M
CAFE
CITY HALL
CAN YOU DROP ME HERE AND I'LL STOP BY THE STATION LATER?
SURE. THAT'S WHERE YOU'LL FIND TRACY RIGHT NOW ANYWAY.
COUNTY POLICE
537

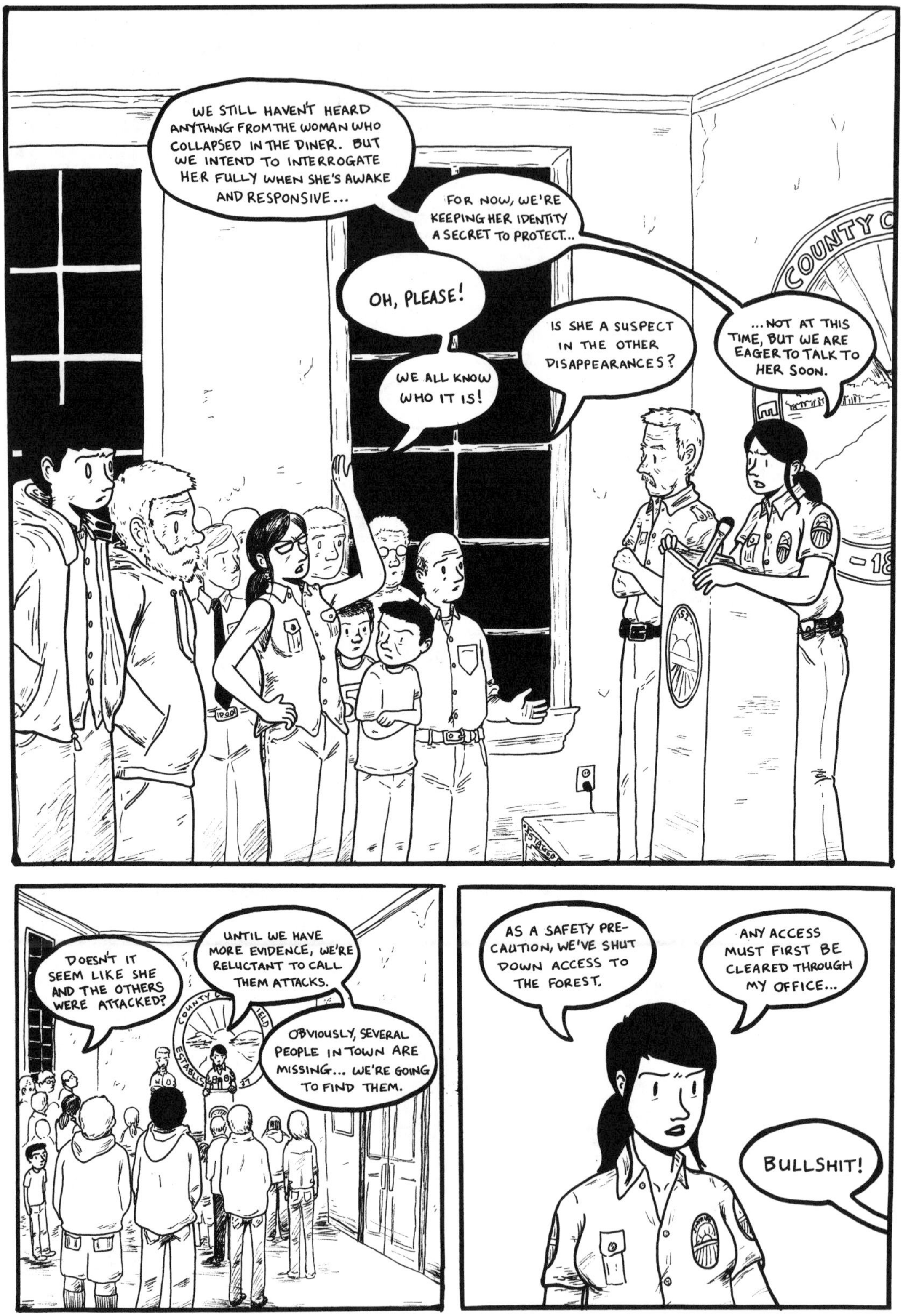
WE STILL HAVEN'T HEARD ANYTHING FROM THE WOMAN WHO COLLAPSED IN THE DINER. BUT WE INTEND TO INTERROGATE HER FULLY WHEN SHE'S AWAKE AND RESPONSIVE...
FOR NOW, WE'RE KEEPING HER IDENTITY A SECRET TO PROTECT...
OH, PLEASE!
WE ALL KNOW WHO IT IS!
IS SHE A SUSPECT IN THE OTHER DISAPPEARANCES?
...NOT AT THIS TIME, BUT WE ARE EAGER TO TALK TO HER SOON.
DOESN'T IT SEEM LIKE SHE AND THE OTHERS WERE ATTACKED?
UNTIL WE HAVE MORE EVIDENCE, WE'RE RELUCTANT TO CALL THEM ATTACKS.
OBVIOUSLY, SEVERAL PEOPLE IN TOWN ARE MISSING... WE'RE GOING TO FIND THEM.
AS A SAFETY PRE-CAUTION, WE'VE SHUT DOWN ACCESS TO THE FOREST.
ANY ACCESS MUST FIRST BE CLEARED THROUGH MY OFFICE...
BULLSHIT!

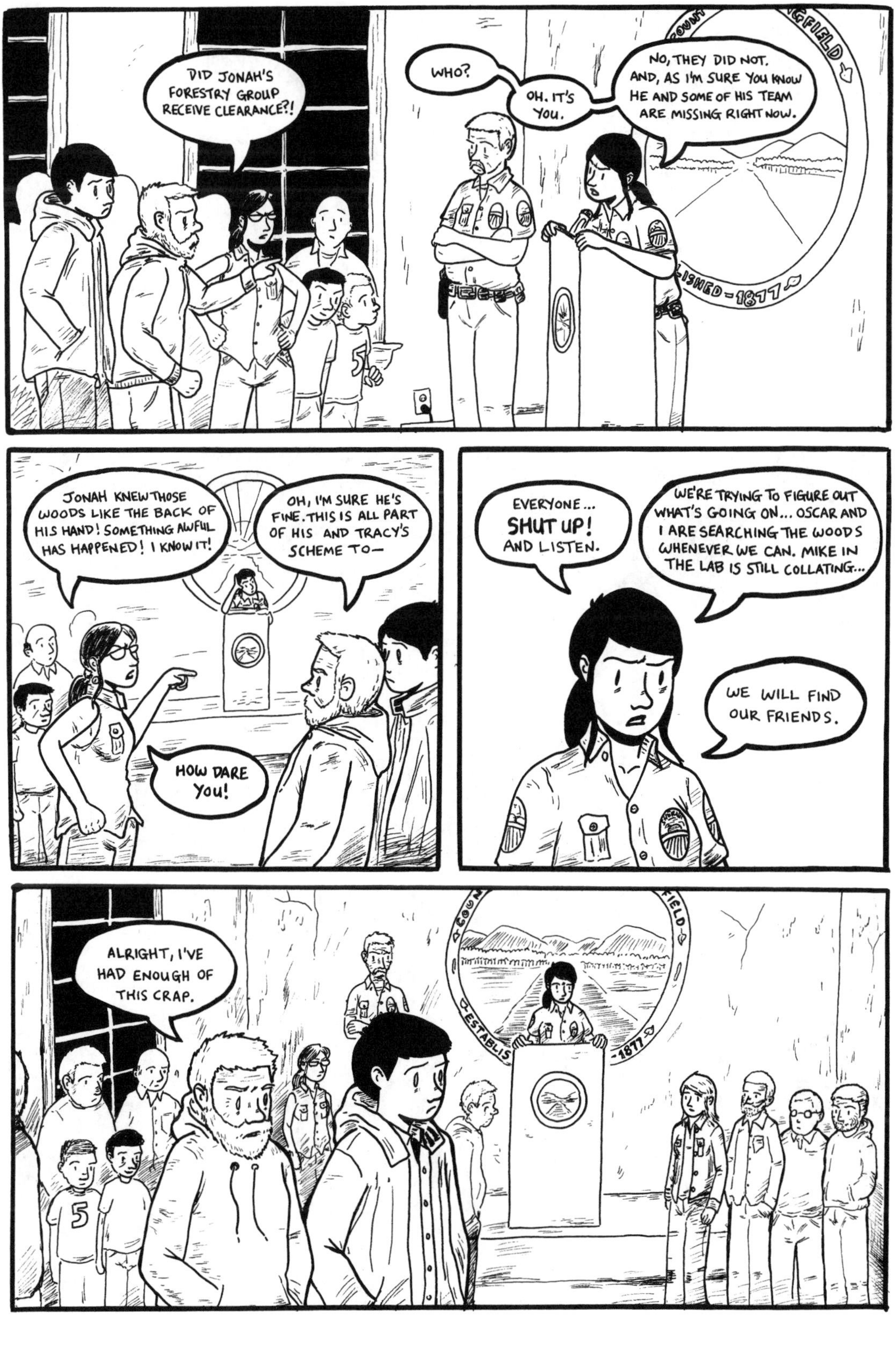

DID JONAH'S FORESTRY GROUP RECEIVE CLEARANCE?!
WHO?
OH. IT'S YOU.
NO, THEY DID NOT. AND, AS I'M SURE YOU KNOW HE AND SOME OF HIS TEAM ARE MISSING RIGHT NOW.
JONAH KNEW THOSE WOODS LIKE THE BACK OF HIS HAND! SOMETHING AWFUL HAS HAPPENED! I KNOW IT!
OH, I'M SURE HE'S FINE. THIS IS ALL PART OF HIS AND TRACY'S SCHEME TO—
HOW DARE YOU!
EVERYONE... SHUT UP! AND LISTEN.
WE'RE TRYING TO FIGURE OUT WHAT'S GOING ON... OSCAR AND I ARE SEARCHING THE WOODS WHENEVER WE CAN. MIKE IN THE LAB IS STILL COLLATING...
WE WILL FIND OUR FRIENDS.
ALRIGHT, I'VE HAD ENOUGH OF THIS CRAP.

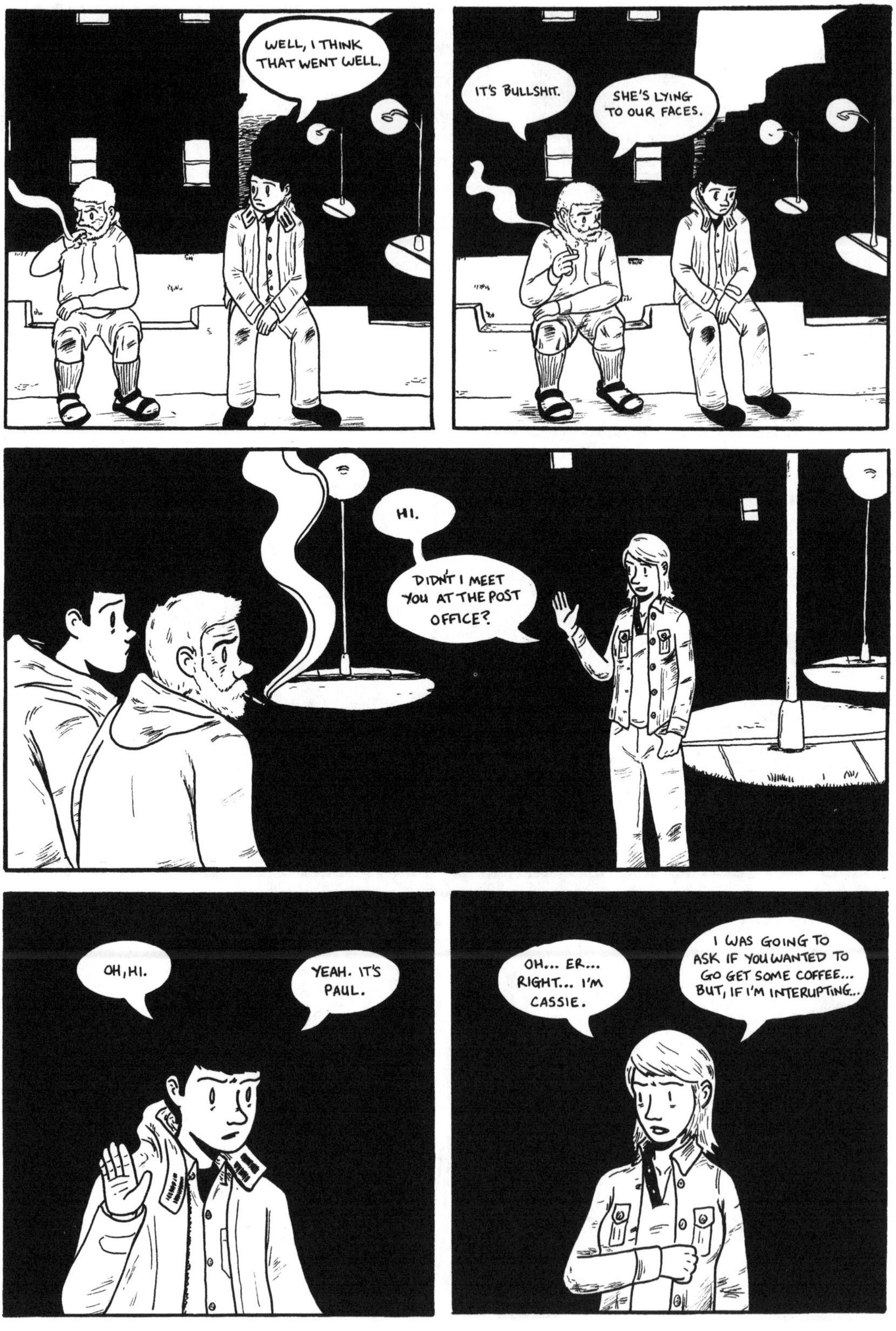
WELL, I THINK THAT WENT WELL.
IT'S BULLSHIT.
SHE'S LYING TO OUR FACES.
HI.
DIDN'T I MEET YOU AT THE POST OFFICE?
OH, HI.
YEAH. IT'S PAUL.
OH... ER... RIGHT... I'M CASSIE.
I WAS GOING TO ASK IF YOU WANTED TO GO GET SOME COFFEE... BUT, IF I'M INTERUPTING...

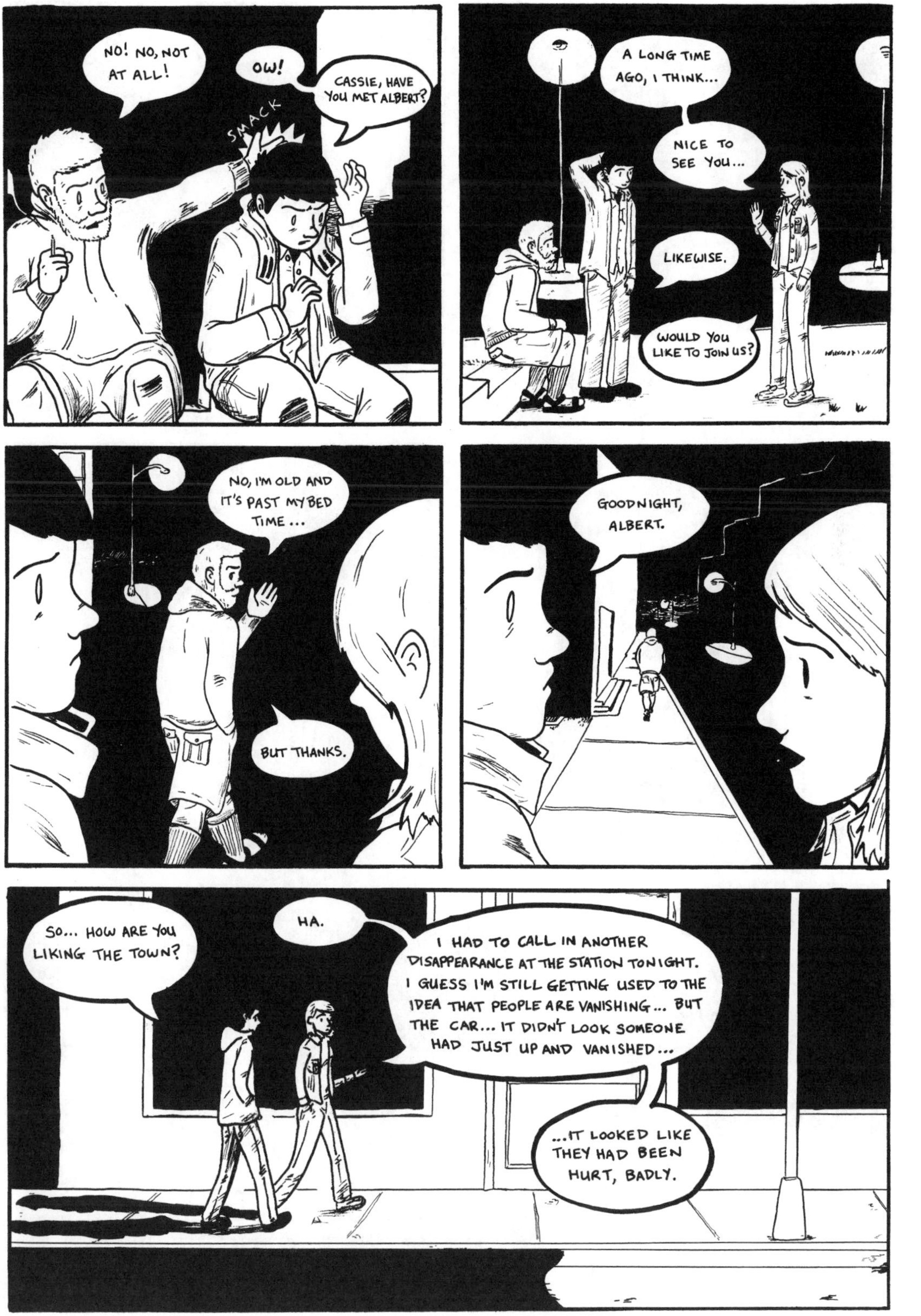
NO! NO, NOT AT ALL!
OW!
SMACK
CASSIE, HAVE YOU MET ALBERT?
A LONG TIME AGO, I THINK...
NICE TO SEE YOU...
LIKEWISE.
WOULD YOU LIKE TO JOIN US?
NO, I'M OLD AND IT'S PAST MY BED TIME...
BUT THANKS.
GOODNIGHT, ALBERT.
SO... HOW ARE YOU LIKING THE TOWN?
HA.
I HAD TO CALL IN ANOTHER DISAPPEARANCE AT THE STATION TONIGHT. I GUESS I'M STILL GETTING USED TO THE IDEA THAT PEOPLE ARE VANISHING... BUT THE CAR... IT DIDN'T LOOK SOMEONE HAD JUST UP AND VANISHED...
...IT LOOKED LIKE THEY HAD BEEN HURT, BADLY.

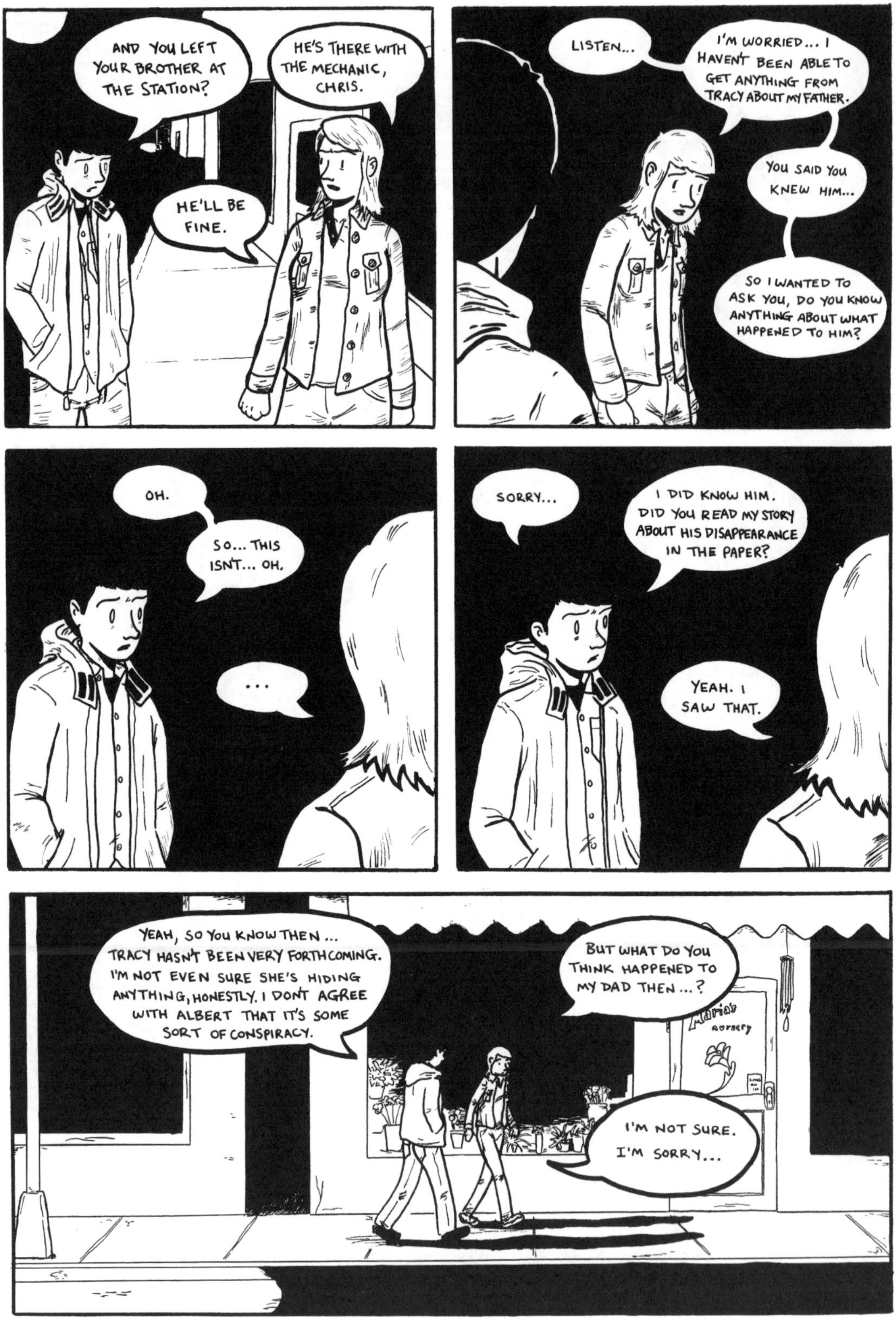
AND YOU LEFT YOUR BROTHER AT THE STATION?
HE'S THERE WITH THE MECHANIC, CHRIS.
HE'LL BE FINE.
LISTEN...
I'M WORRIED... I HAVEN'T BEEN ABLE TO GET ANYTHING FROM TRACY ABOUT MY FATHER.
YOU SAID YOU KNEW HIM...
SO I WANTED TO ASK YOU, DO YOU KNOW ANYTHING ABOUT WHAT HAPPENED TO HIM?
OH.
SO... THIS ISN'T... OH.
...
SORRY...
I DID KNOW HIM. DID YOU READ MY STORY ABOUT HIS DISAPPEARANCE IN THE PAPER?
YEAH. I SAW THAT.
YEAH, SO YOU KNOW THEN... TRACY HASN'T BEEN VERY FORTHCOMING. I'M NOT EVEN SURE SHE'S HIDING ANYTHING, HONESTLY. I DON'T AGREE WITH ALBERT THAT IT'S SOME SORT OF CONSPIRACY.
BUT WHAT DO YOU THINK HAPPENED TO MY DAD THEN...?
Maria's nursery
I'M NOT SURE. I'M SORRY...

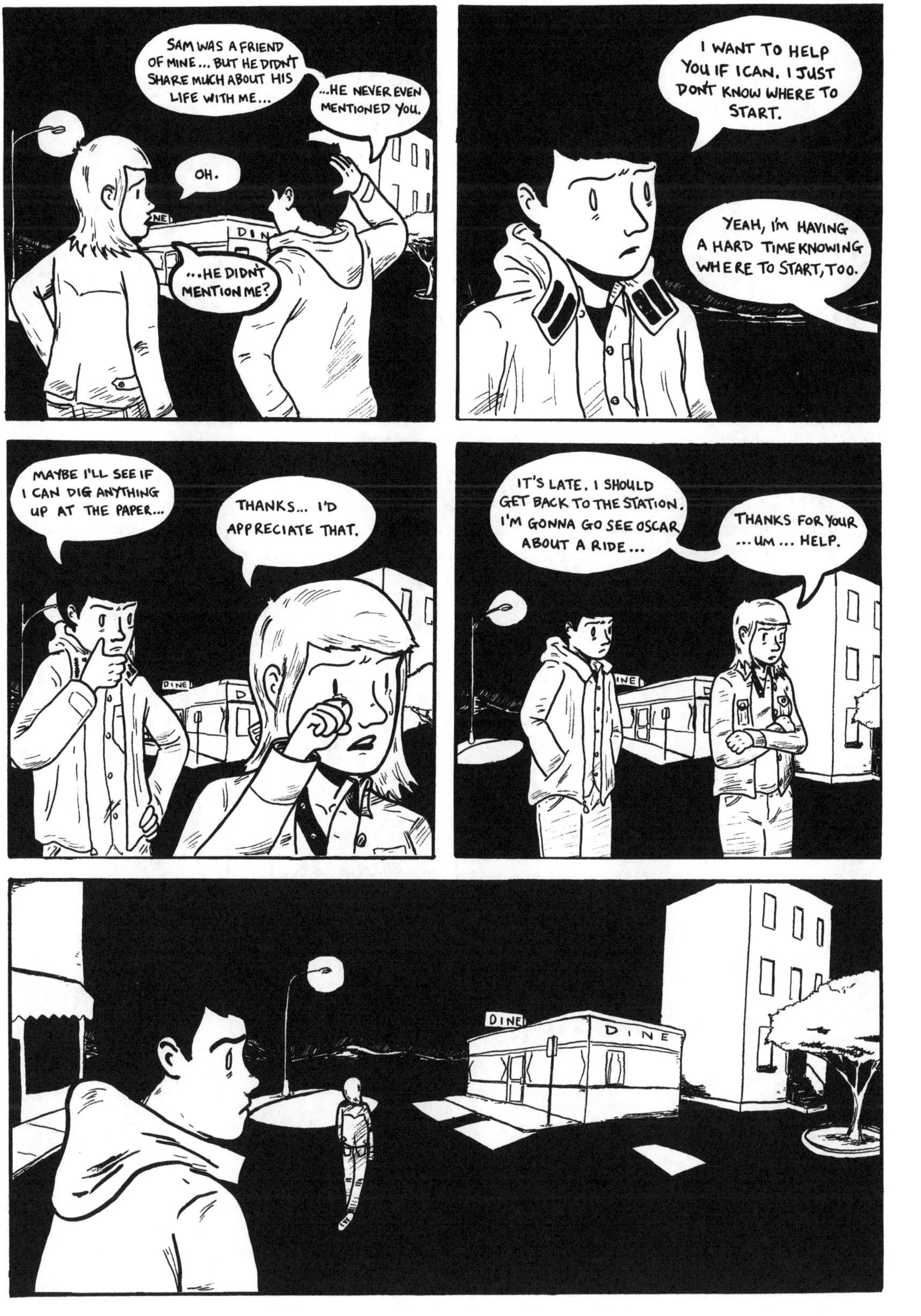
SAM WAS A FRIEND OF MINE... BUT HE DIDN'T SHARE MUCH ABOUT HIS LIFE WITH ME...
...HE NEVER EVEN MENTIONED YOU.
OH.
...HE DIDN'T MENTION ME?
DINE
I WANT TO HELP YOU IF I CAN. I JUST DON'T KNOW WHERE TO START.
YEAH, I'M HAVING A HARD TIME KNOWING WHERE TO START, TOO.
MAYBE I'LL SEE IF I CAN DIG ANYTHING UP AT THE PAPER...
THANKS... I'D APPRECIATE THAT.
DINE
IT'S LATE. I SHOULD GET BACK TO THE STATION. I'M GONNA GO SEE OSCAR ABOUT A RIDE...
THANKS FOR YOUR ...UM... HELP.
DINE
DINE

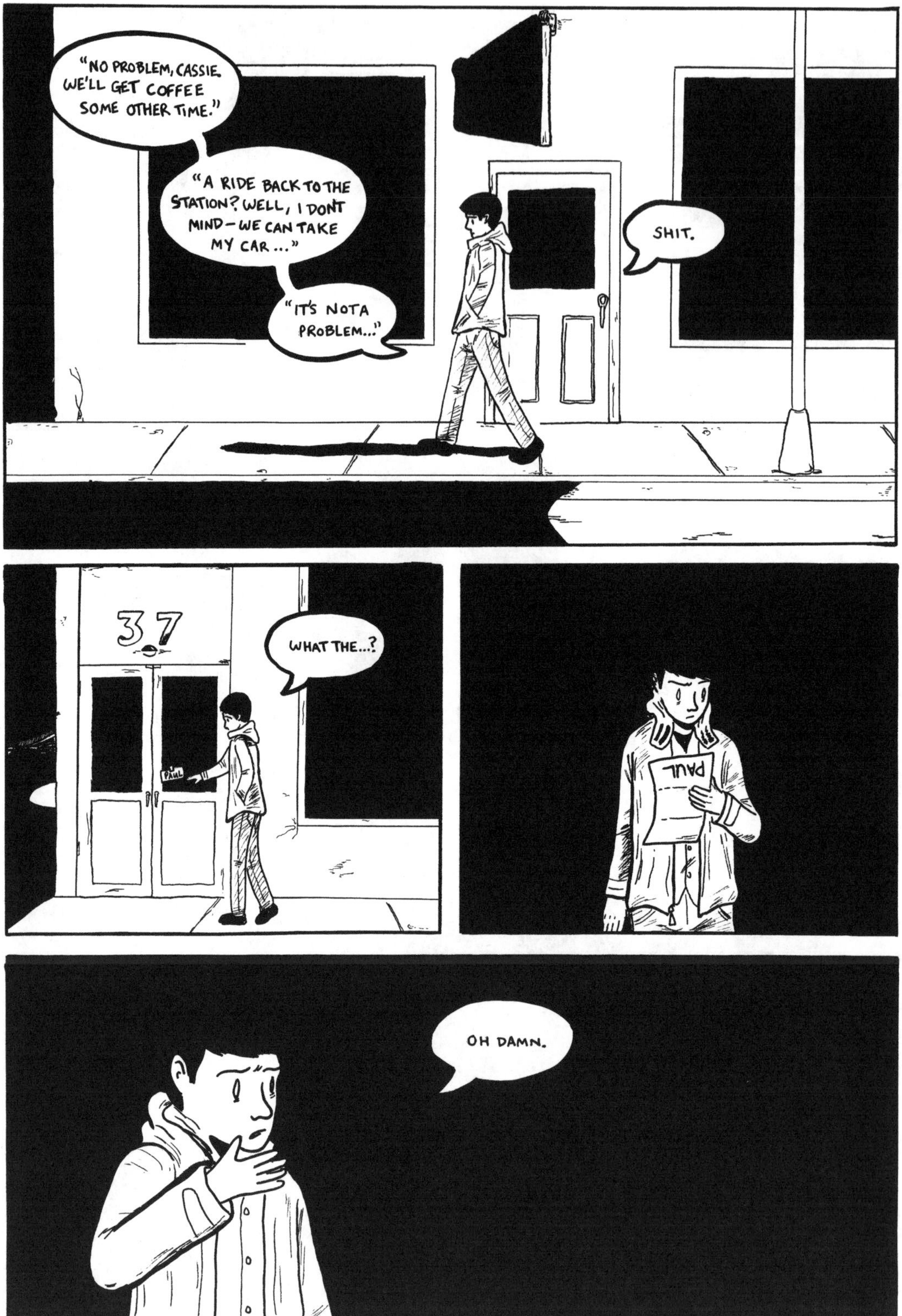
"NO PROBLEM, CASSIE. WE'LL GET COFFEE SOME OTHER TIME."
"A RIDE BACK TO THE STATION? WELL, I DONT MIND—WE CAN TAKE MY CAR..."
"IT'S NOT A PROBLEM..."
SHIT.
37
PAUL
WHAT THE...?
PAUL
OH DAMN.

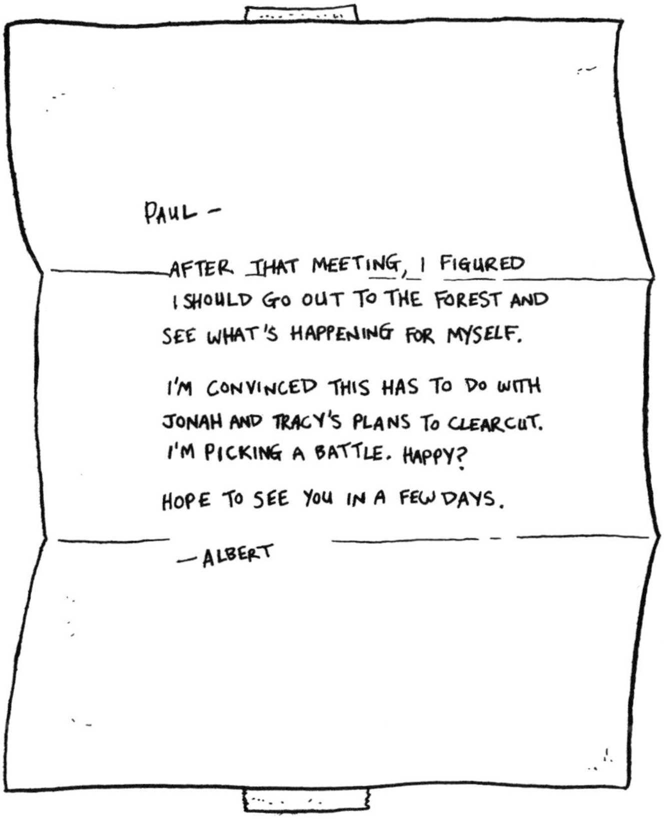
PAUL -

AFTER THAT MEETING, I FIGURED I SHOULD GO OUT TO THE FOREST AND SEE WHAT'S HAPPENING FOR MYSELF.

I'M CONVINCED THIS HAS TO DO WITH JONAH AND TRACY'S PLANS TO CLEARCUT. I'M PICKING A BATTLE. HAPPY?

HOPE TO SEE YOU IN A FEW DAYS.

— ALBERT

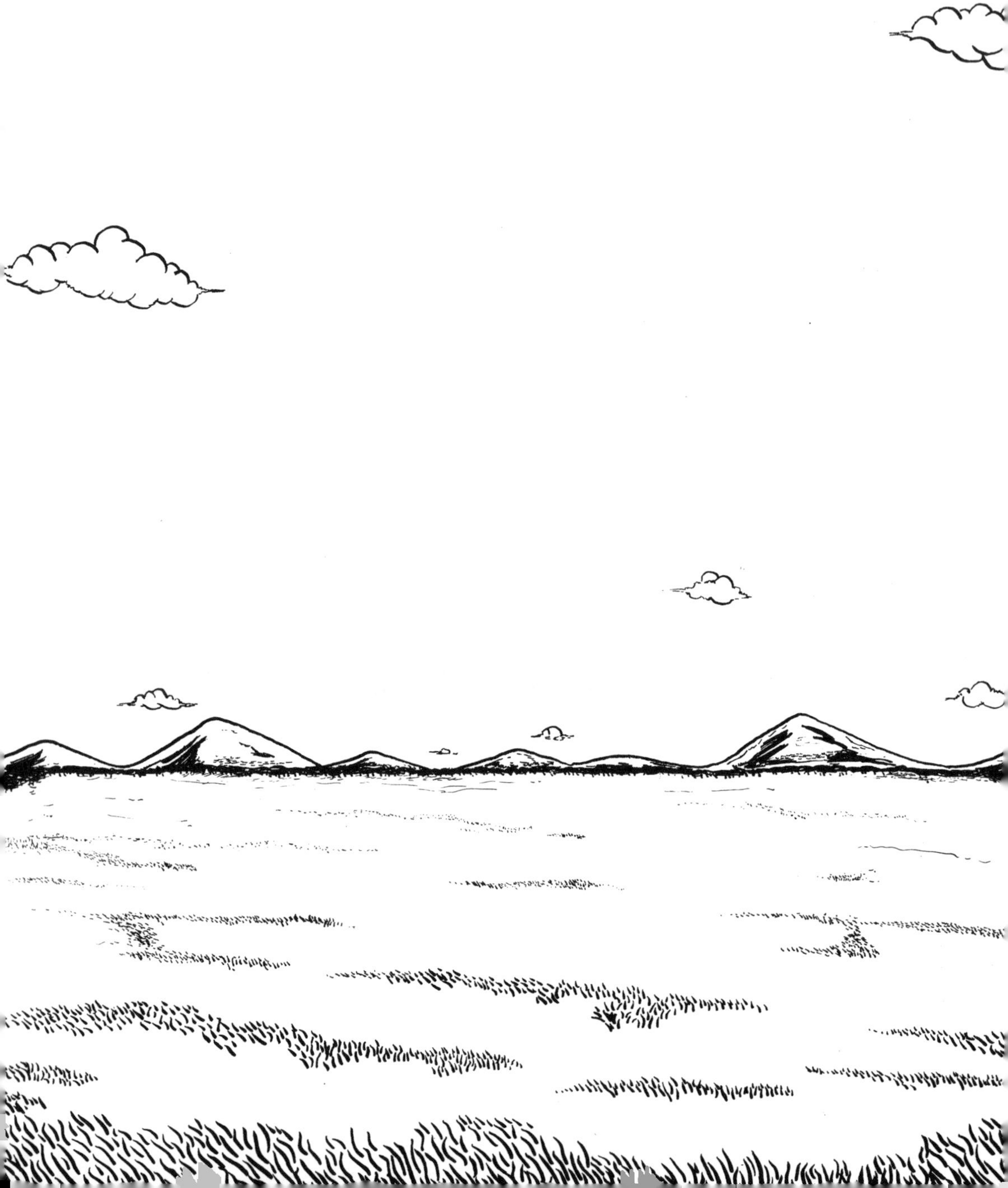

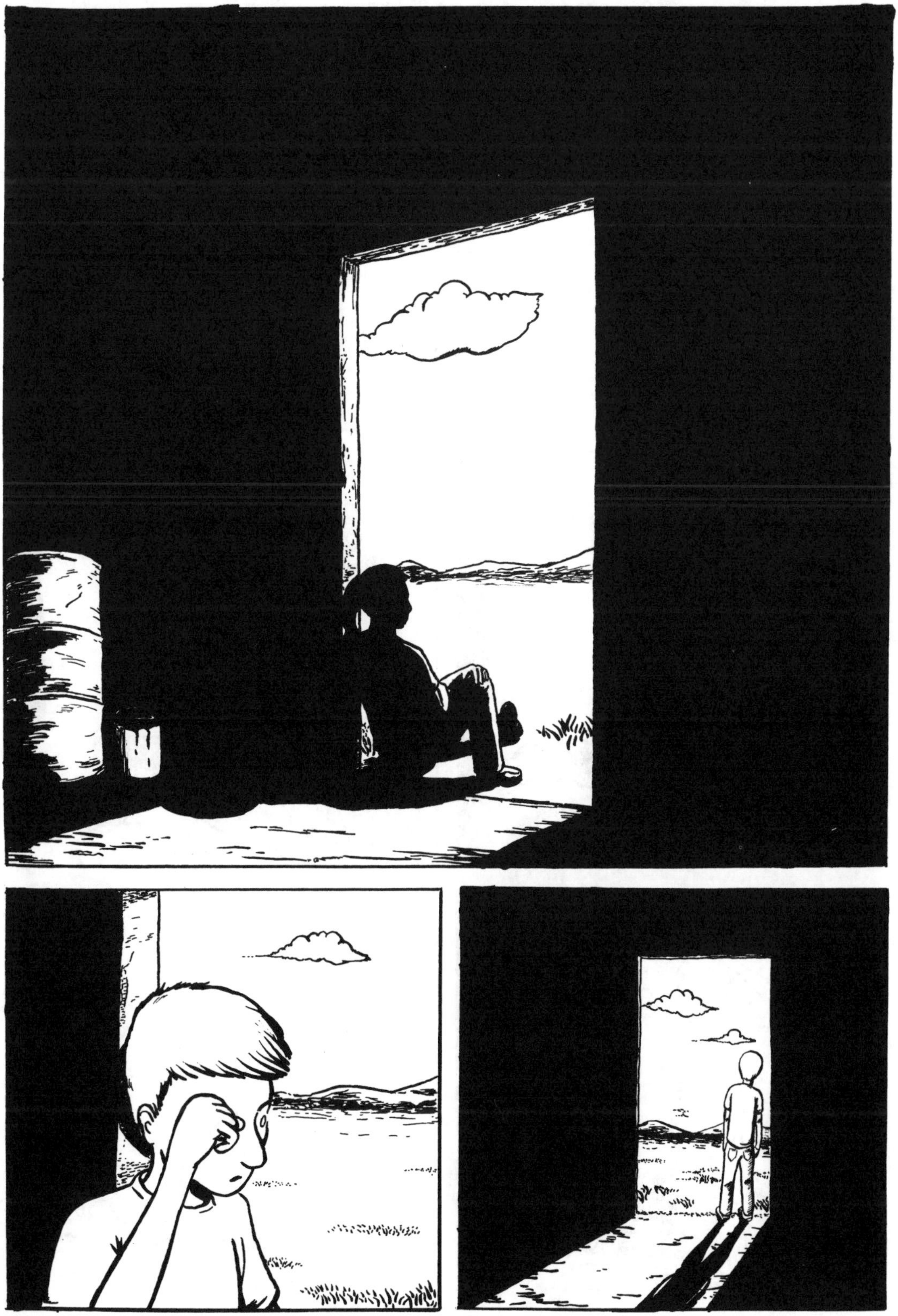

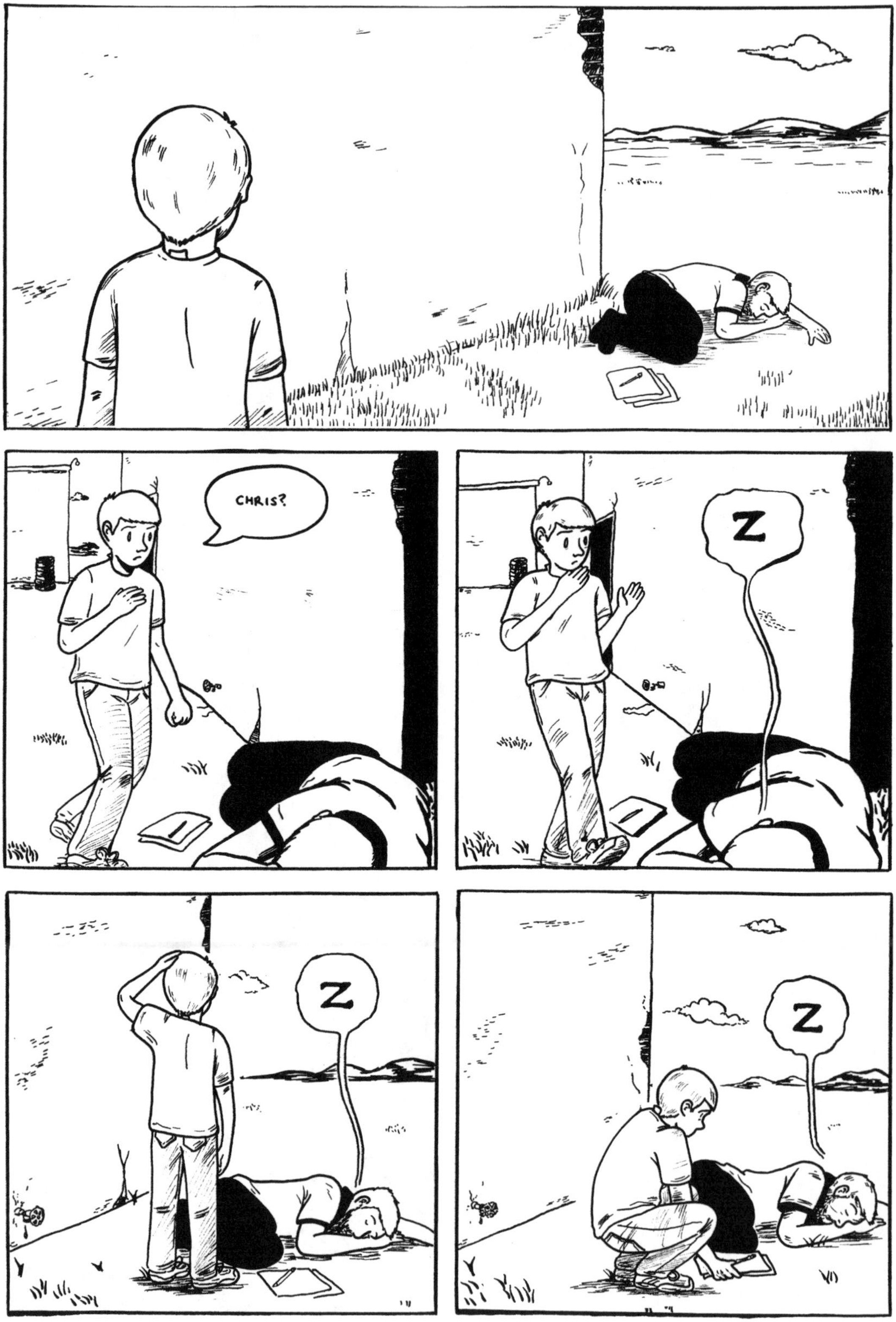
CHRIS?
Z
Z
Z

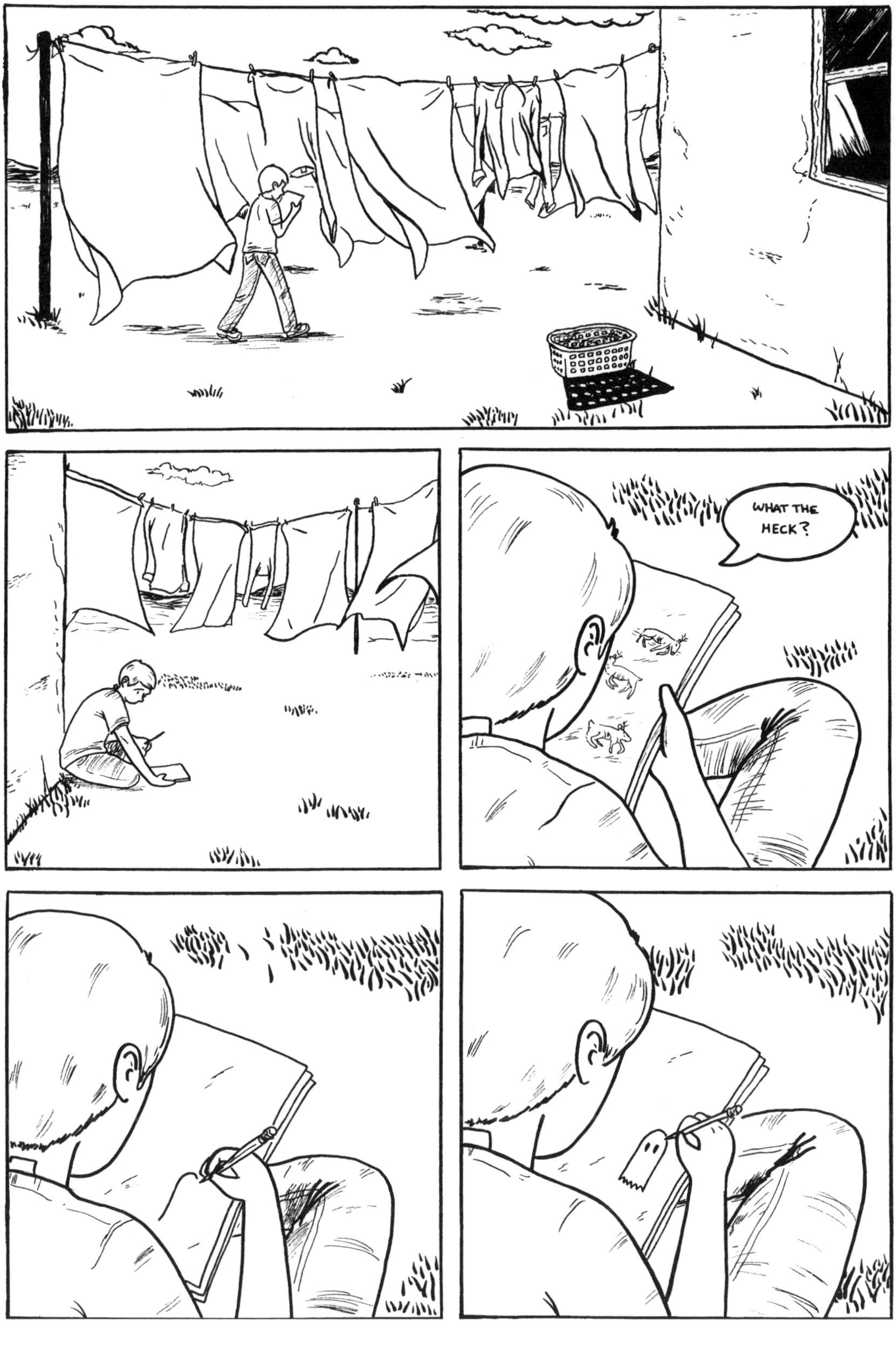
WHAT THE HECK?

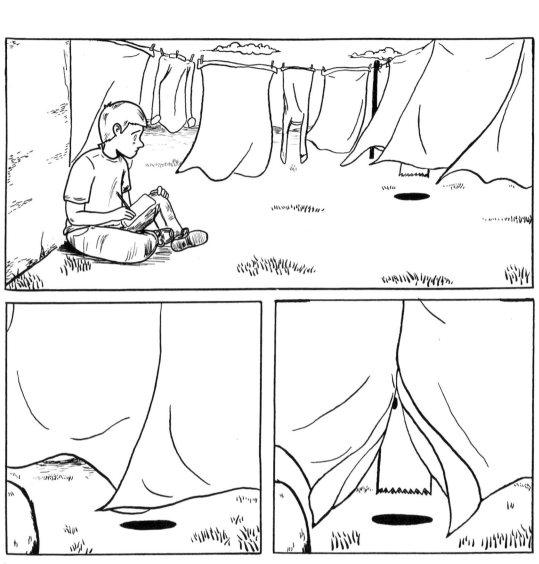

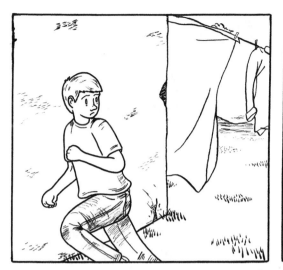

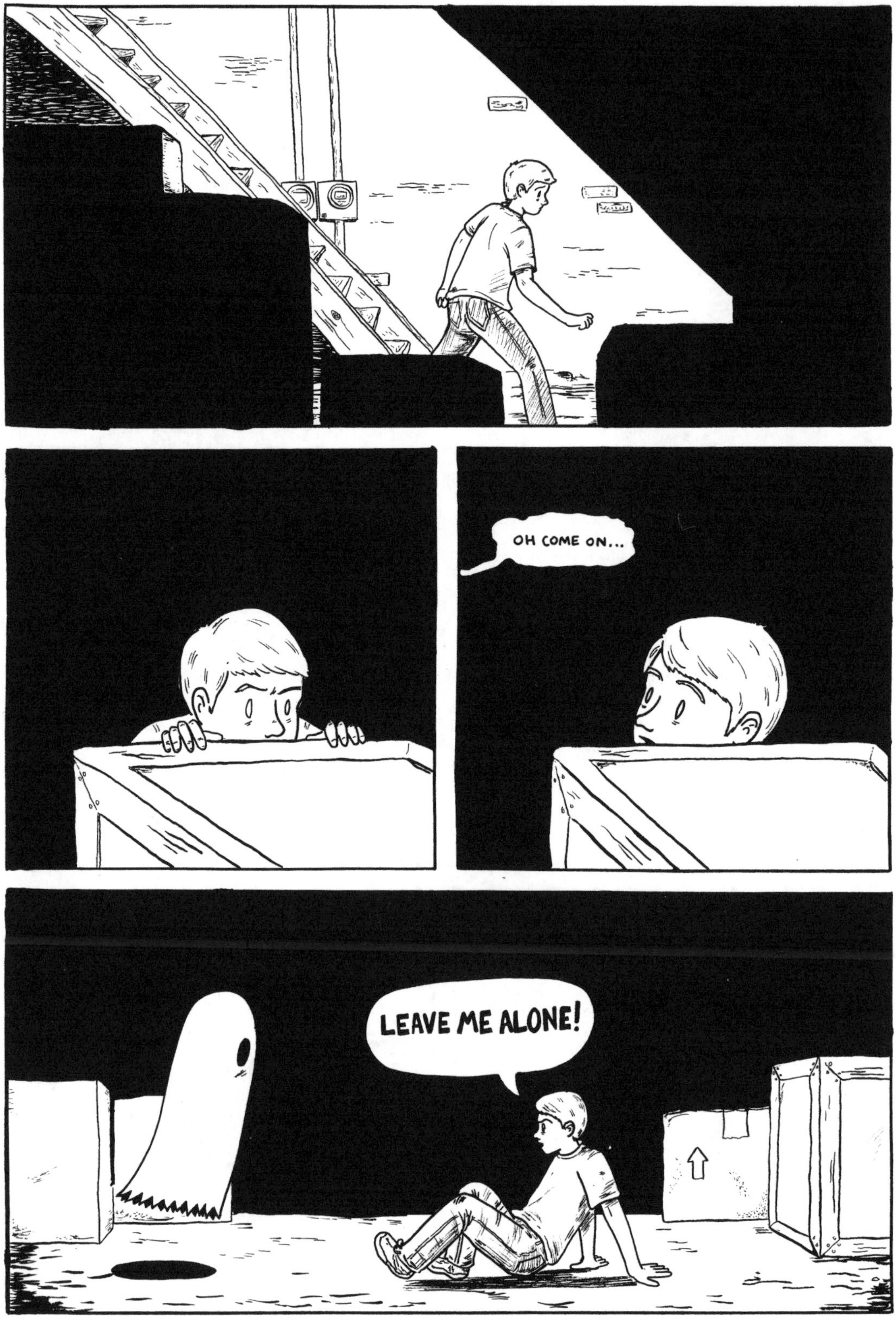
OH COME ON...
LEAVE ME ALONE!

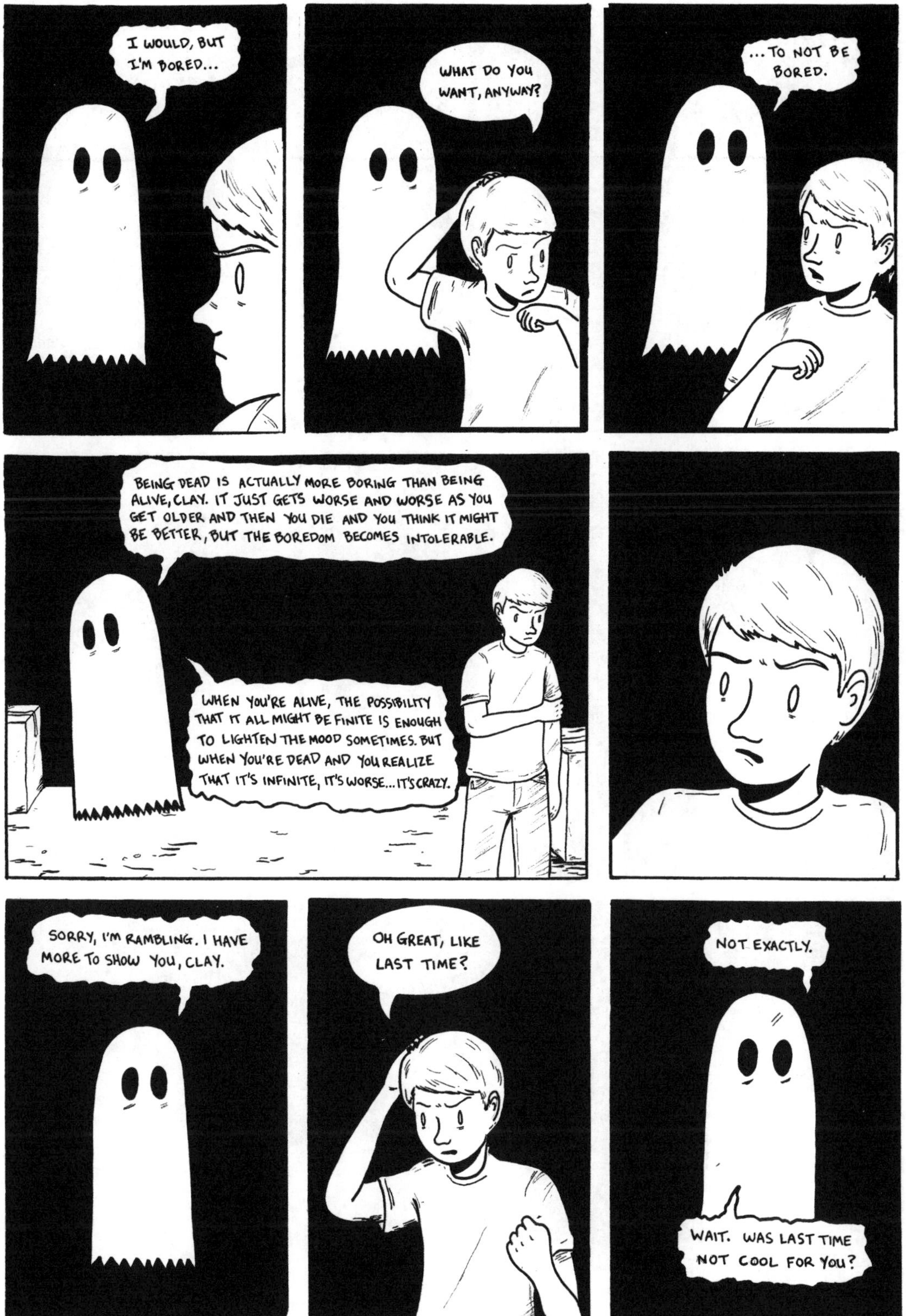
I WOULD, BUT I'M BORED...
WHAT DO YOU WANT, ANYWAY?
...TO NOT BE BORED.
BEING DEAD IS ACTUALLY MORE BORING THAN BEING ALIVE, CLAY. IT JUST GETS WORSE AND WORSE AS YOU GET OLDER AND THEN YOU DIE AND YOU THINK IT MIGHT BE BETTER, BUT THE BOREDOM BECOMES INTOLERABLE.
WHEN YOU'RE ALIVE, THE POSSIBILITY THAT IT ALL MIGHT BE FINITE IS ENOUGH TO LIGHTEN THE MOOD SOMETIMES. BUT WHEN YOU'RE DEAD AND YOU REALIZE THAT IT'S INFINITE, IT'S WORSE... IT'S CRAZY.
SORRY, I'M RAMBLING. I HAVE MORE TO SHOW YOU, CLAY.
OH GREAT, LIKE LAST TIME?
NOT EXACTLY.
WAIT. WAS LAST TIME NOT COOL FOR YOU?

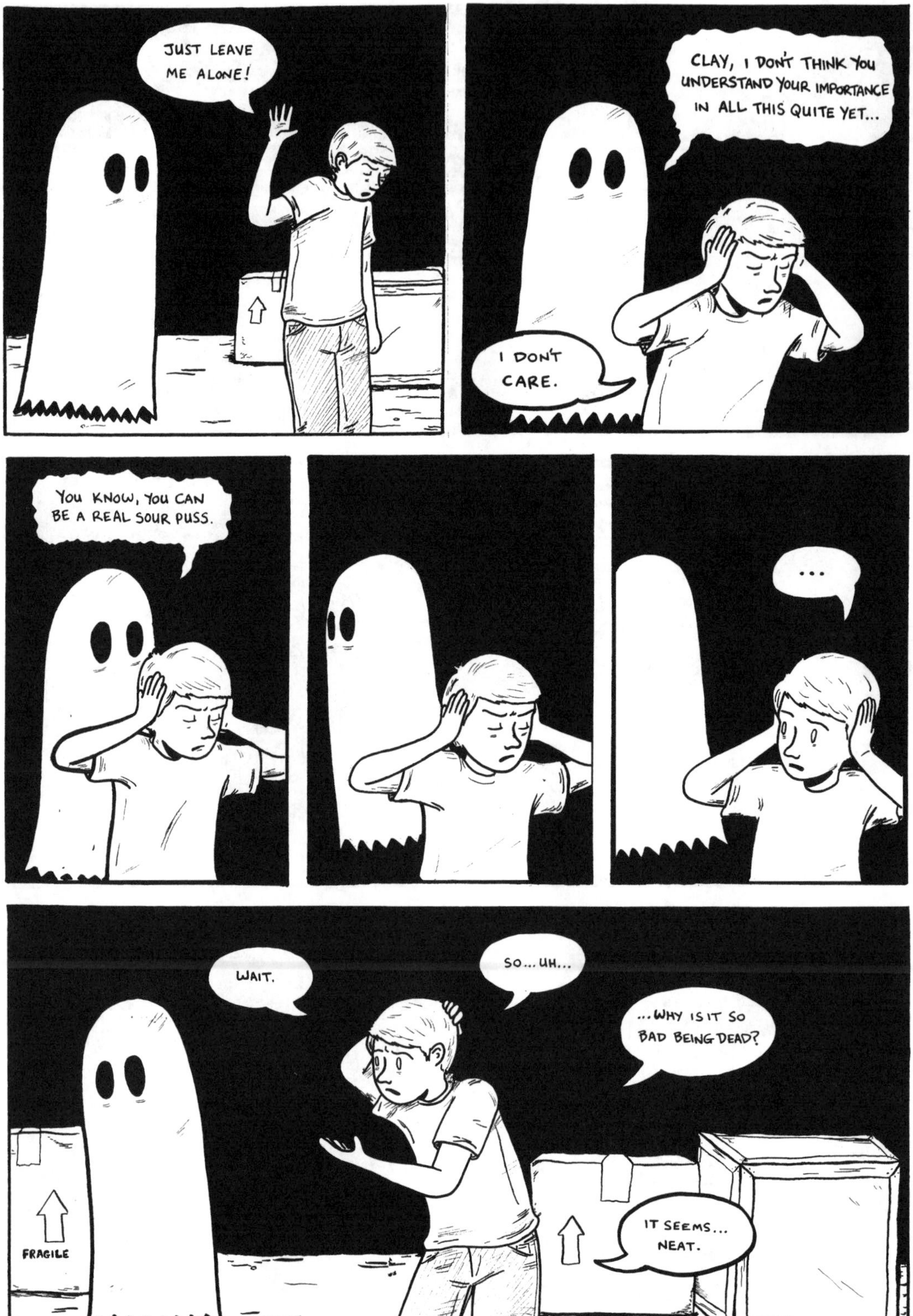
JUST LEAVE ME ALONE!
CLAY, I DON'T THINK YOU UNDERSTAND YOUR IMPORTANCE IN ALL THIS QUITE YET...
I DON'T CARE.
YOU KNOW, YOU CAN BE A REAL SOUR PUSS.
...
WAIT.
SO... UH...
...WHY IS IT SO BAD BEING DEAD?
FRAGILE
IT SEEMS... NEAT.

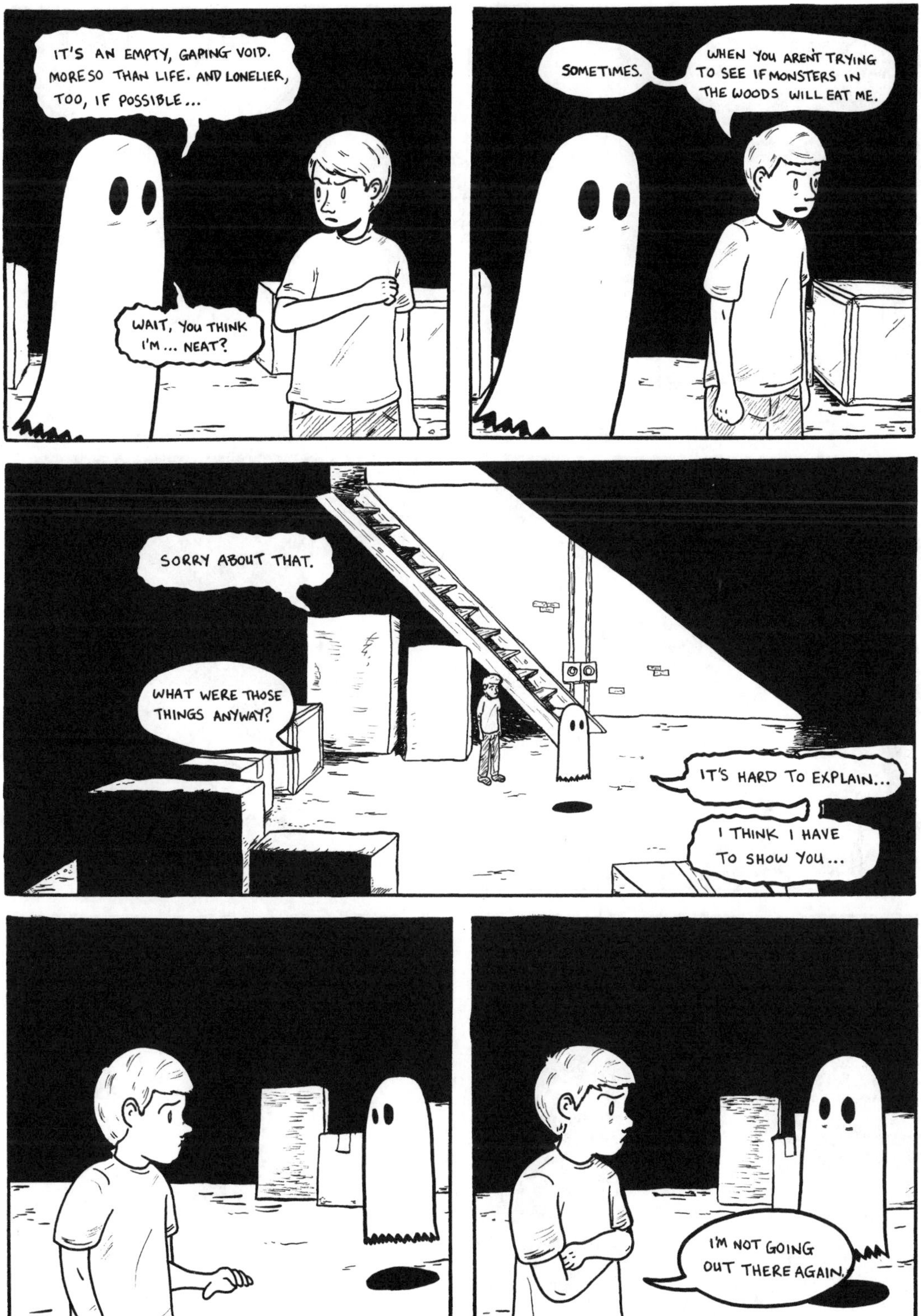
IT'S AN EMPTY, GAPING VOID. MORESO THAN LIFE. AND LONELIER, TOO, IF POSSIBLE...
WAIT, YOU THINK I'M... NEAT?
SOMETIMES.
WHEN YOU AREN'T TRYING TO SEE IF MONSTERS IN THE WOODS WILL EAT ME.
SORRY ABOUT THAT.
WHAT WERE THOSE THINGS ANYWAY?
IT'S HARD TO EXPLAIN...
I THINK I HAVE TO SHOW YOU...
I'M NOT GOING OUT THERE AGAIN.

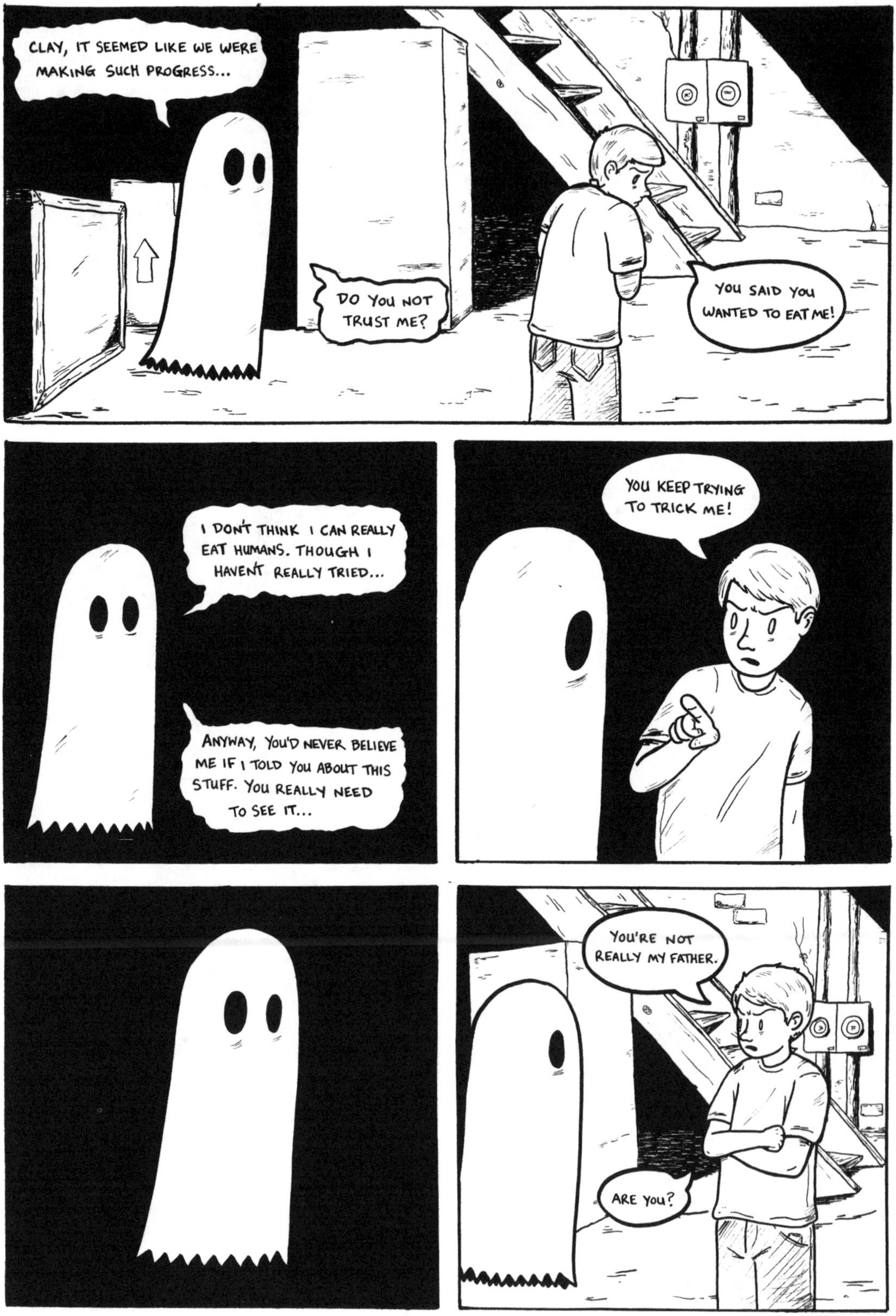
CLAY, IT SEEMED LIKE WE WERE MAKING SUCH PROGRESS...
DO YOU NOT TRUST ME?
YOU SAID YOU WANTED TO EAT ME!
I DON'T THINK I CAN REALLY EAT HUMANS. THOUGH I HAVEN'T REALLY TRIED...
ANYWAY, YOU'D NEVER BELIEVE ME IF I TOLD YOU ABOUT THIS STUFF. YOU REALLY NEED TO SEE IT...
YOU KEEP TRYING TO TRICK ME!
YOU'RE NOT REALLY MY FATHER.
ARE YOU?

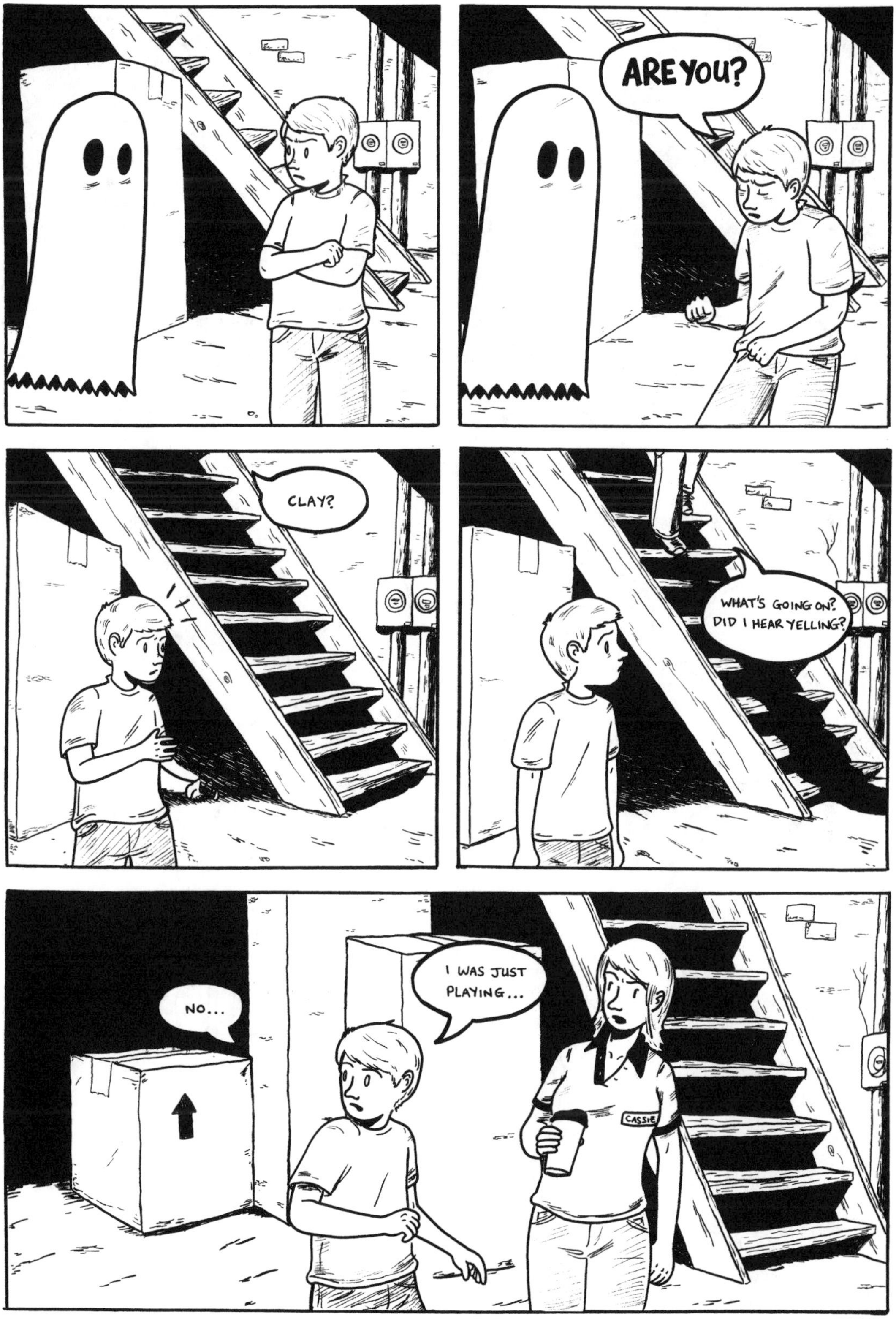

ARE YOU?
CLAY?
WHAT'S GOING ON? DID I HEAR YELLING?
NO...
I WAS JUST PLAYING...
CASSIE

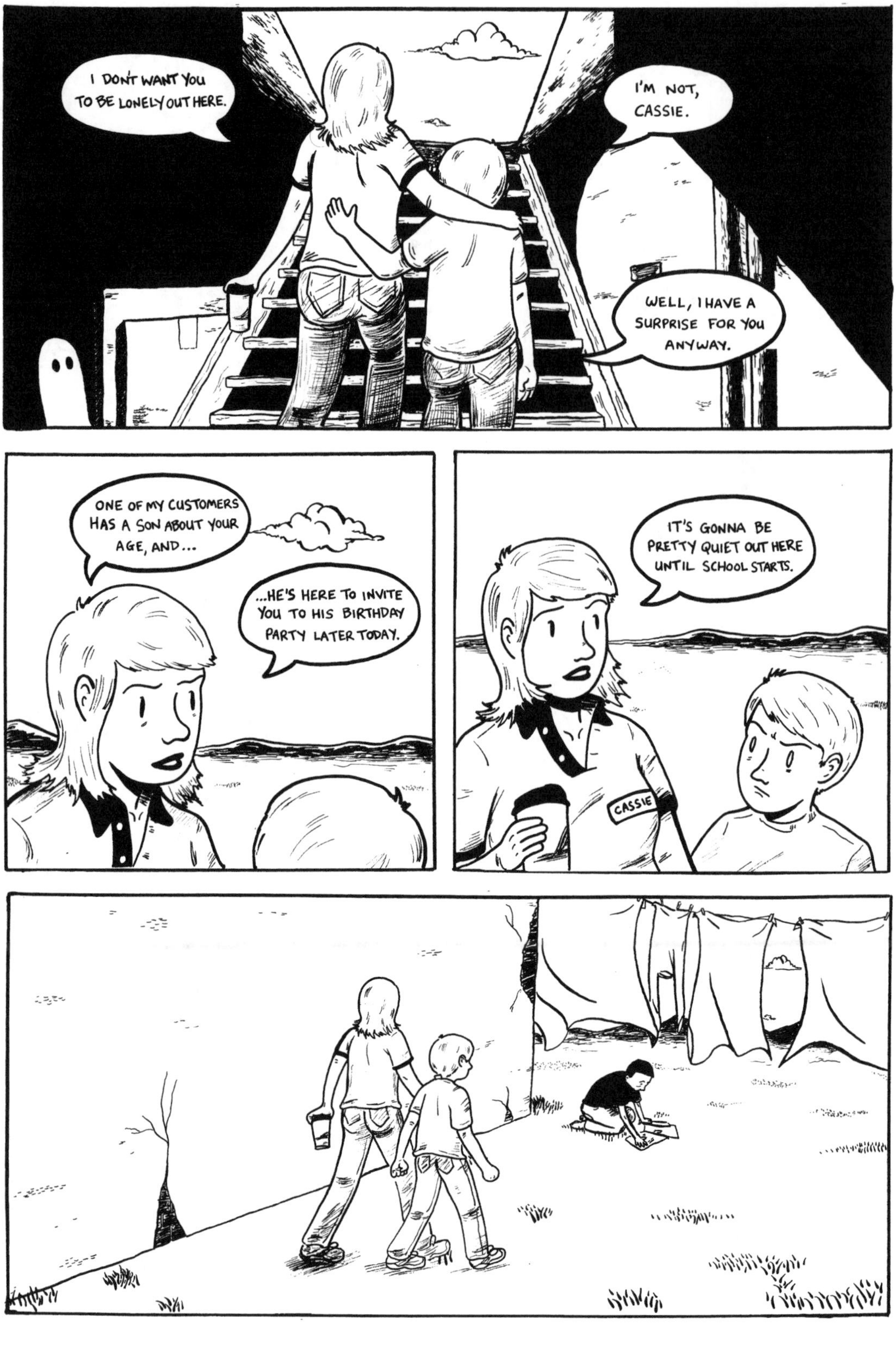
I DON'T WANT YOU TO BE LONELY OUT HERE.
I'M NOT, CASSIE.
WELL, I HAVE A SURPRISE FOR YOU ANYWAY.
ONE OF MY CUSTOMERS HAS A SON ABOUT YOUR AGE, AND...
...HE'S HERE TO INVITE YOU TO HIS BIRTHDAY PARTY LATER TODAY.
IT'S GONNA BE PRETTY QUIET OUT HERE UNTIL SCHOOL STARTS.
CASSIE

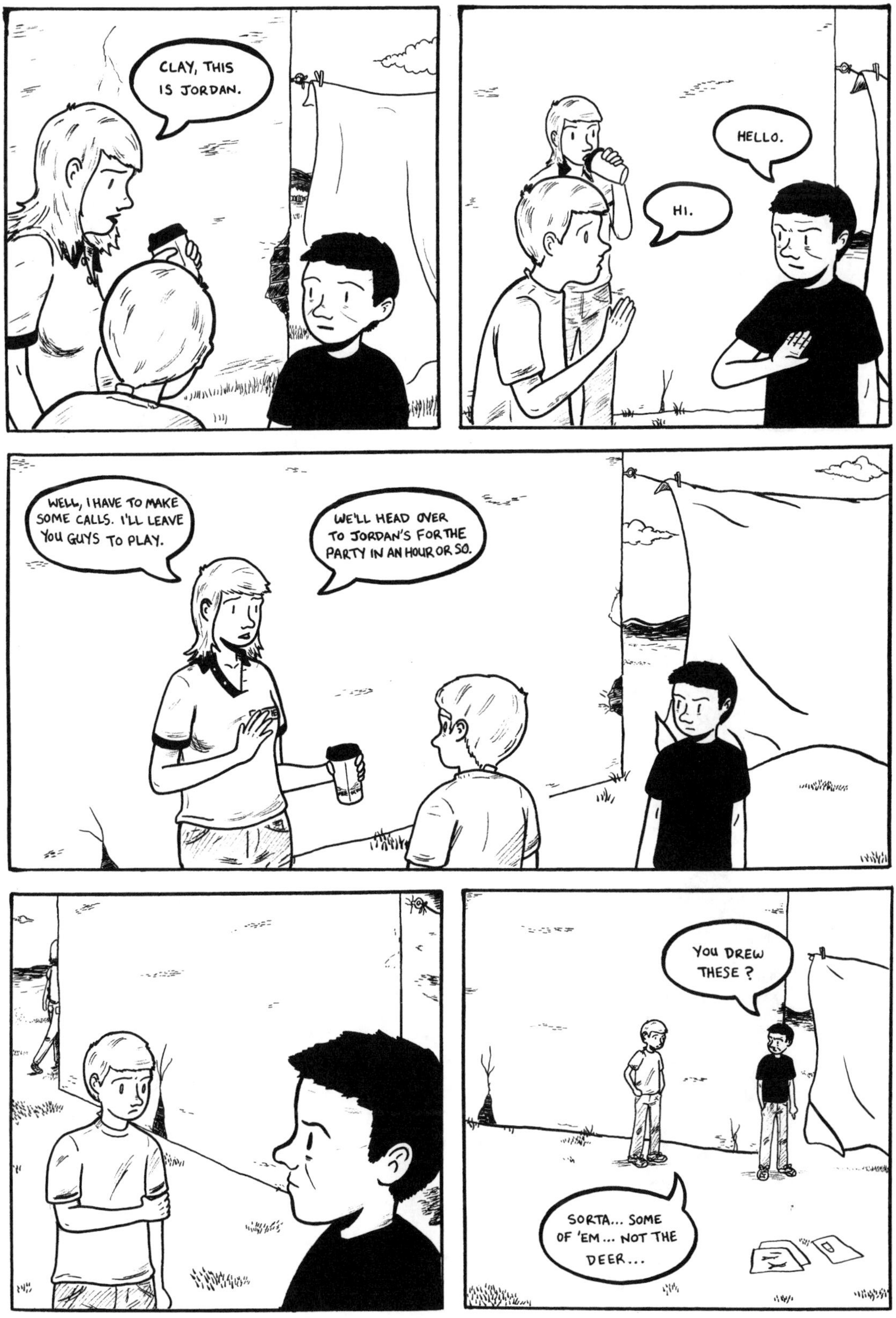
CLAY, THIS IS JORDAN.
HELLO.
HI.
WELL, I HAVE TO MAKE SOME CALLS. I'LL LEAVE YOU GUYS TO PLAY.
WE'LL HEAD OVER TO JORDAN'S FOR THE PARTY IN AN HOUR OR SO.
YOU DREW THESE?
SORTA... SOME OF 'EM... NOT THE DEER...

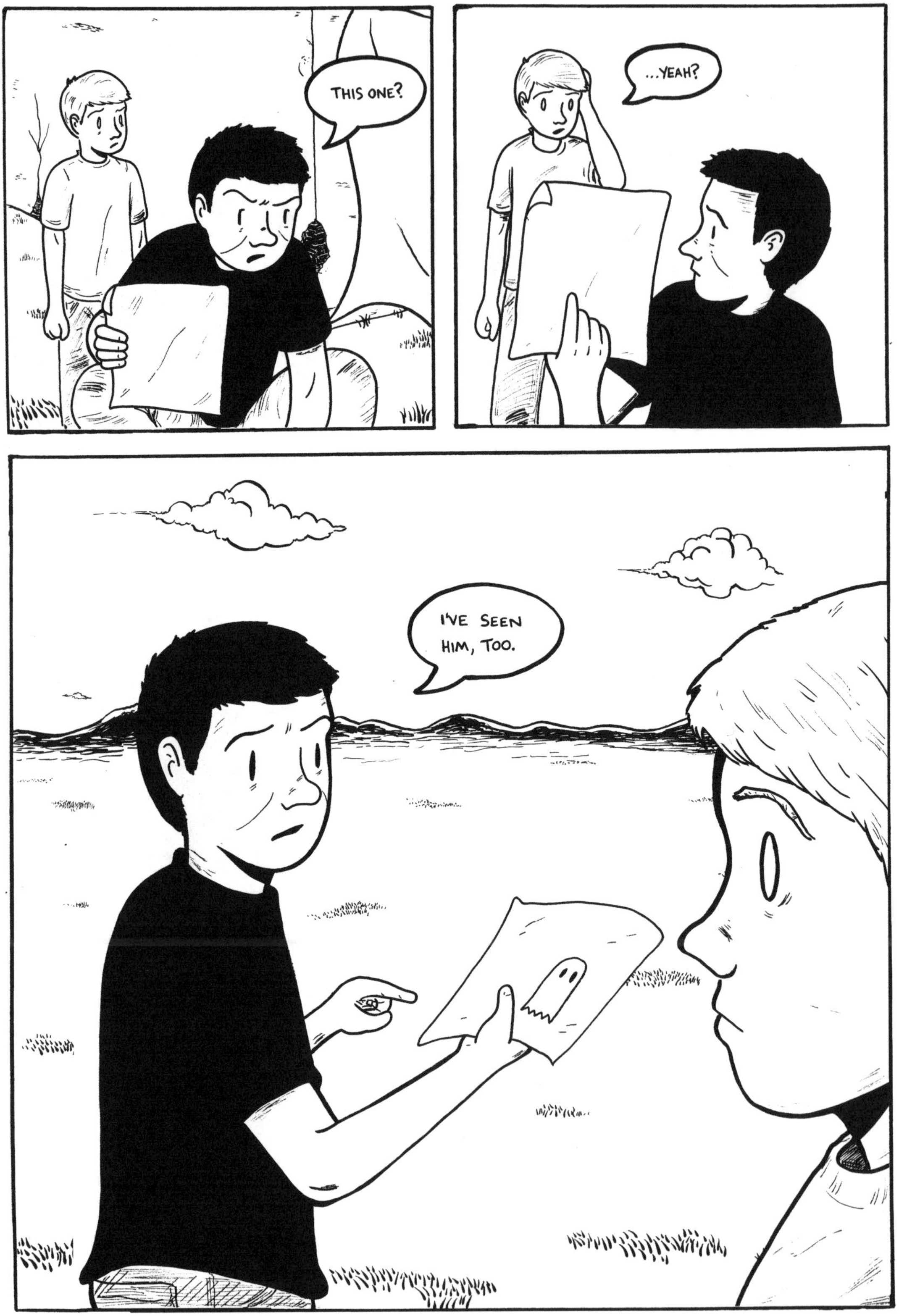
THIS ONE?
...YEAH?
I'VE SEEN HIM, TOO.

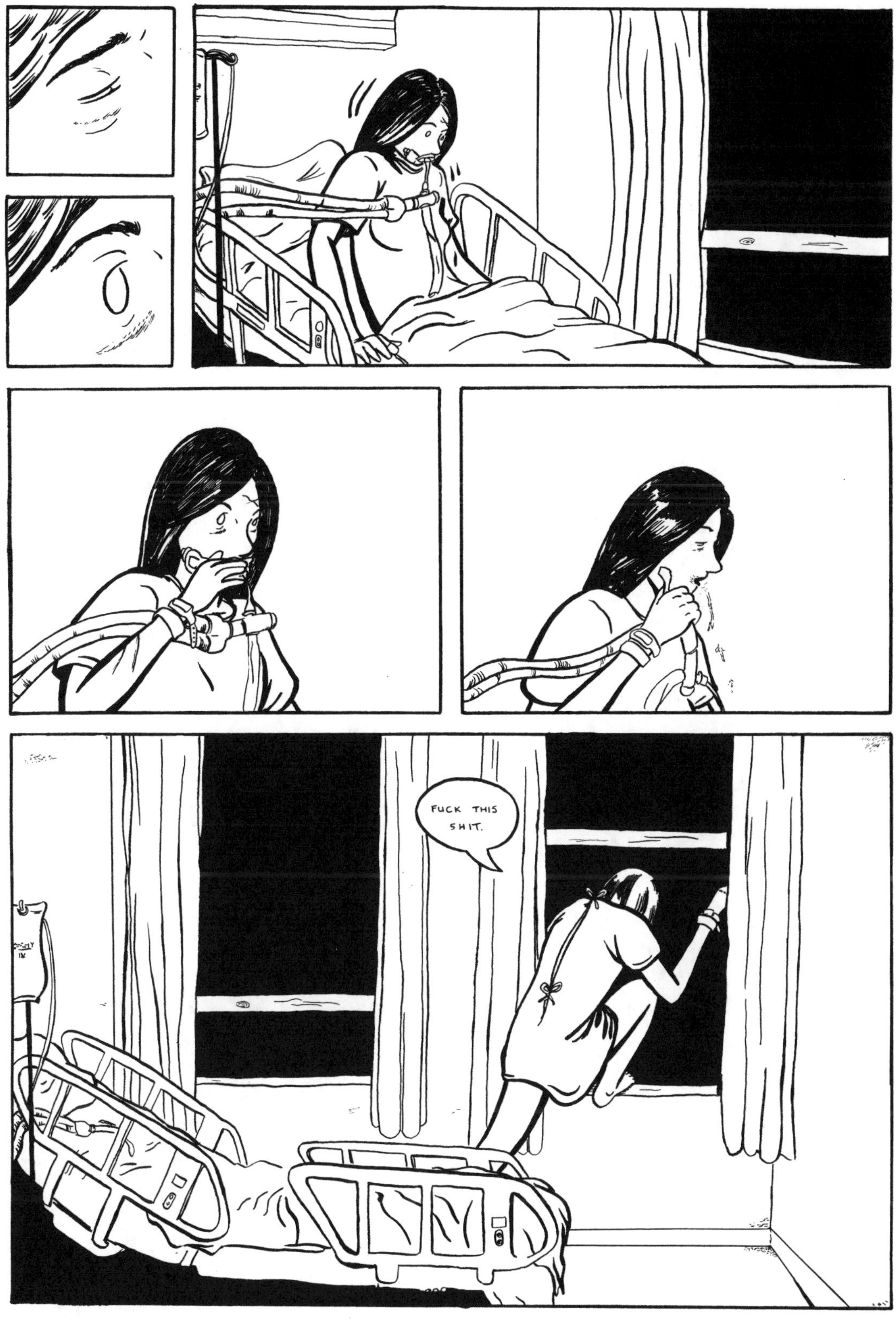
FUCK THIS SHIT.

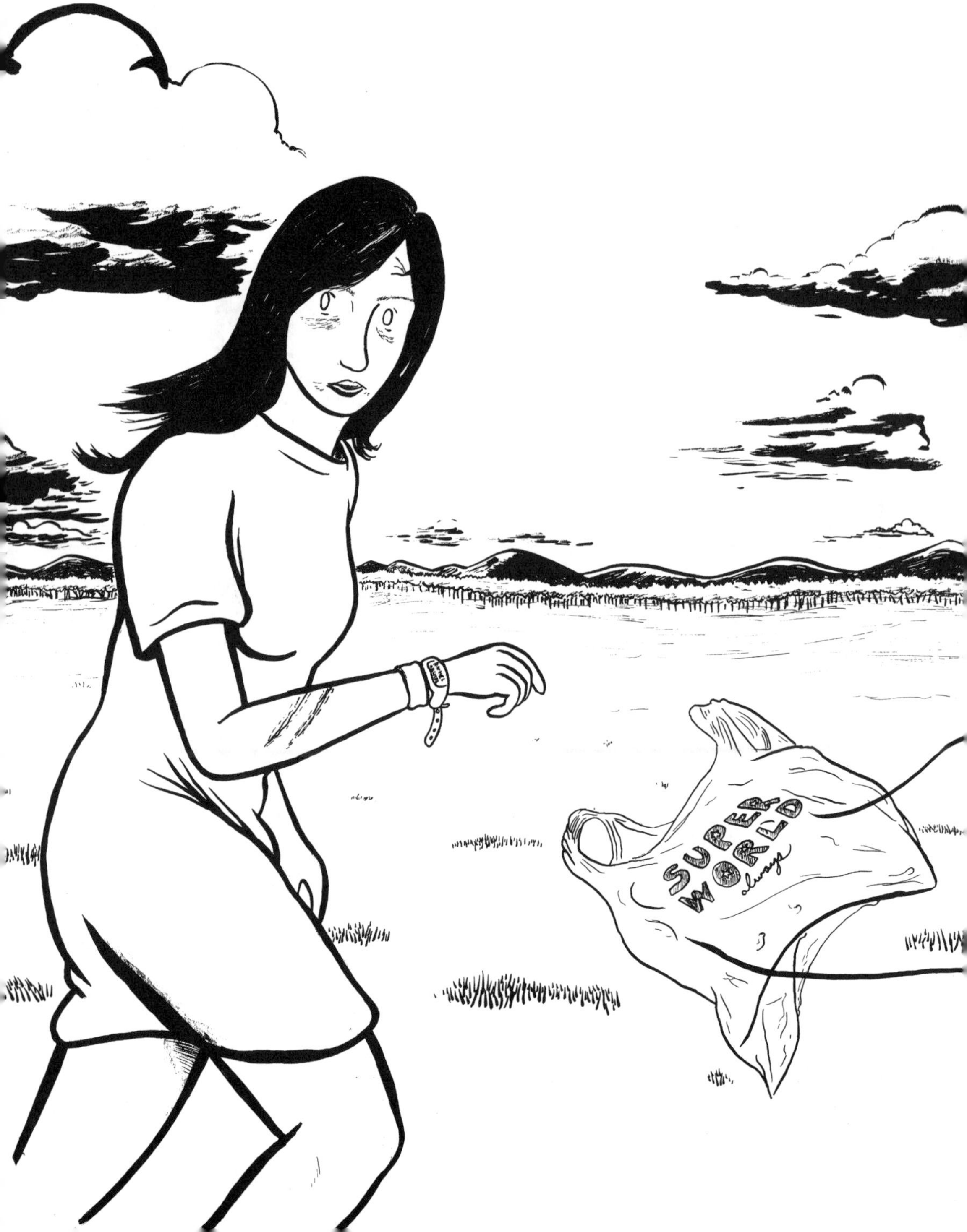
SUPER WORLD
always

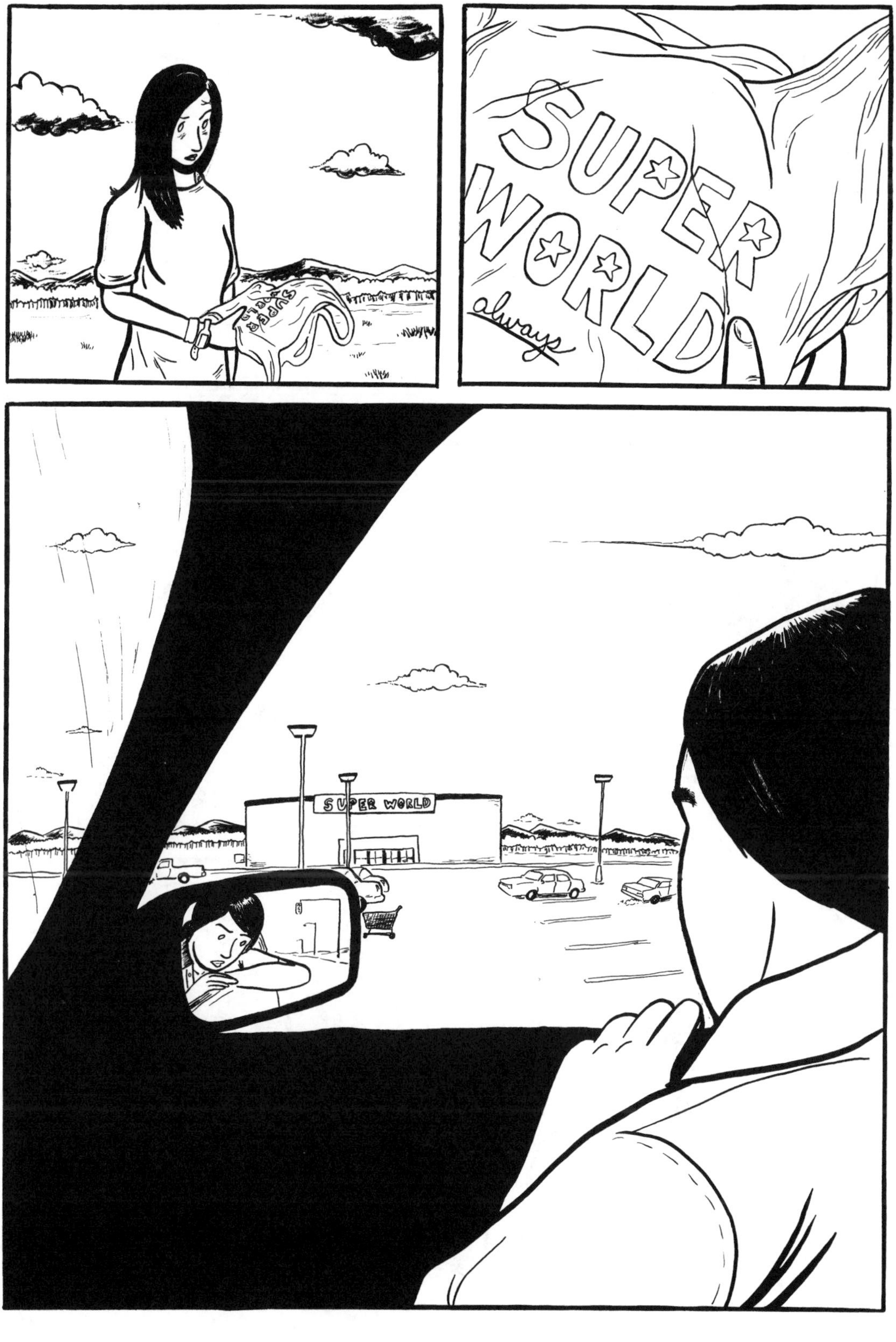
SUPER WORLD
always
SUPER WORLD

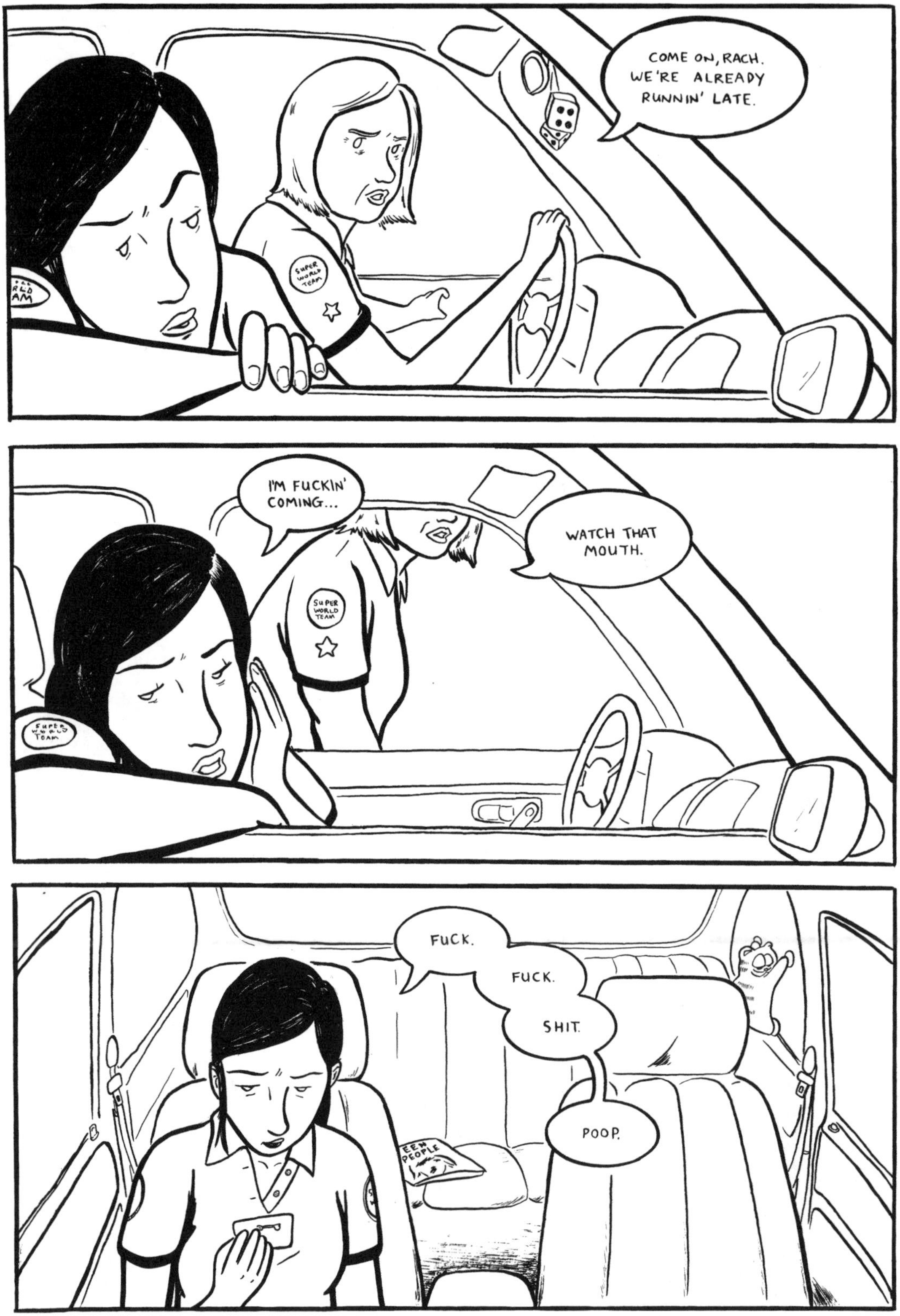
COME ON, RACH. WE'RE ALREADY RUNNIN' LATE.
SUPER WORLD TEAM
I'M FUCKIN' COMING...
WATCH THAT MOUTH.
SUPER WORLD TEAM
FUCK.
FUCK.
SHIT.
POOP.

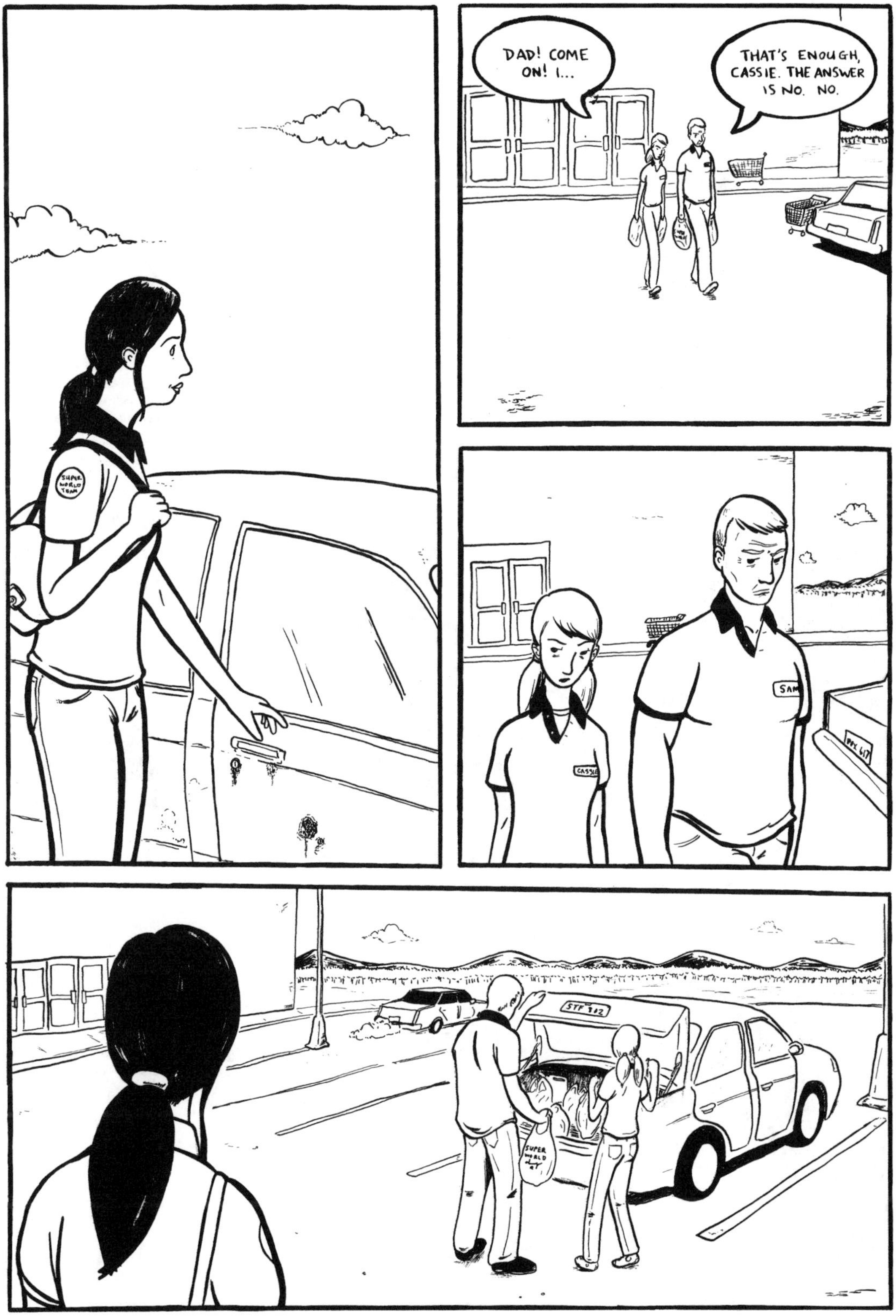

DAD! COME ON! I...
THAT'S ENOUGH, CASSIE. THE ANSWER IS NO. NO.

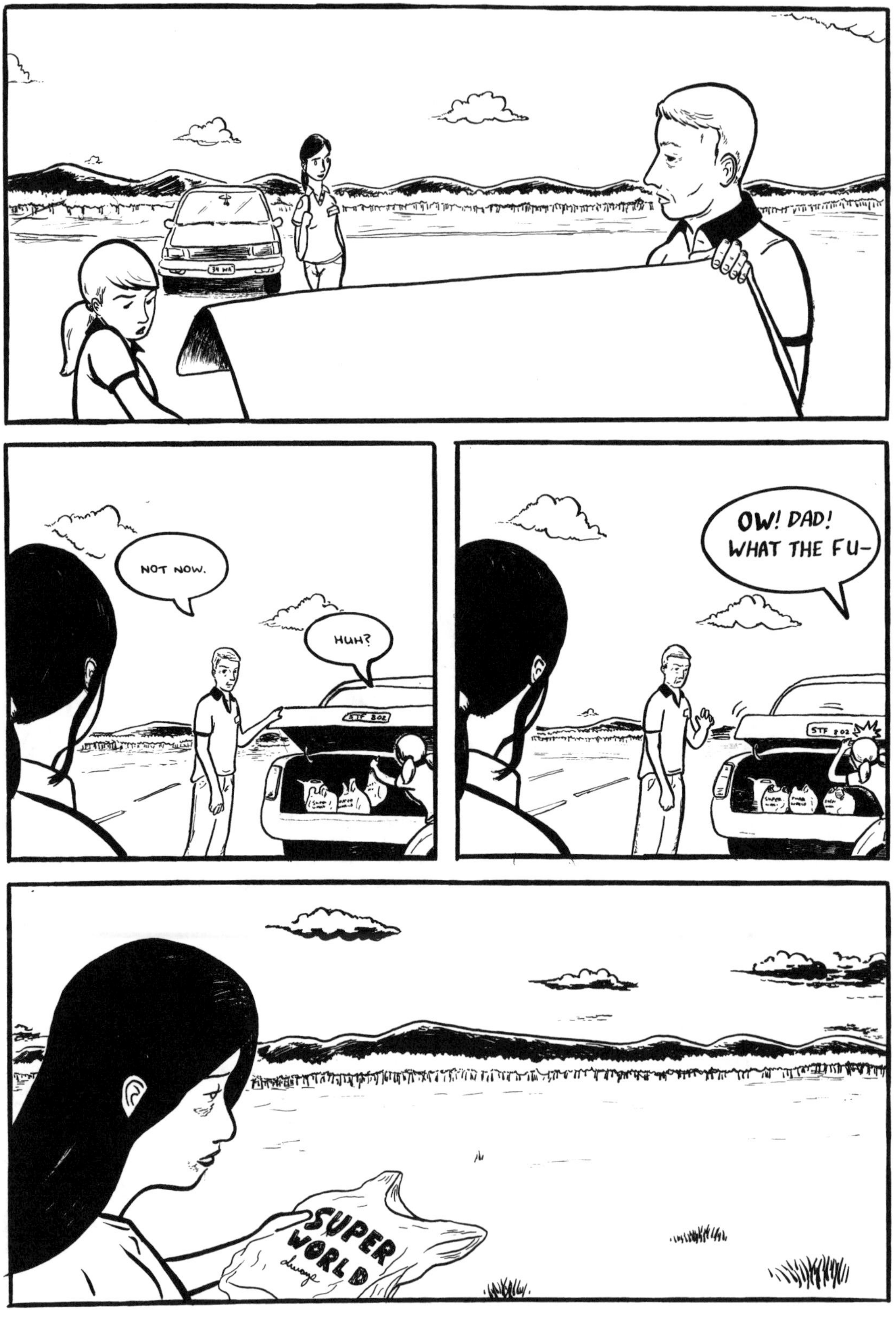
NOT NOW.
HUH?
OW! DAD! WHAT THE FU-
SUPER WORLD

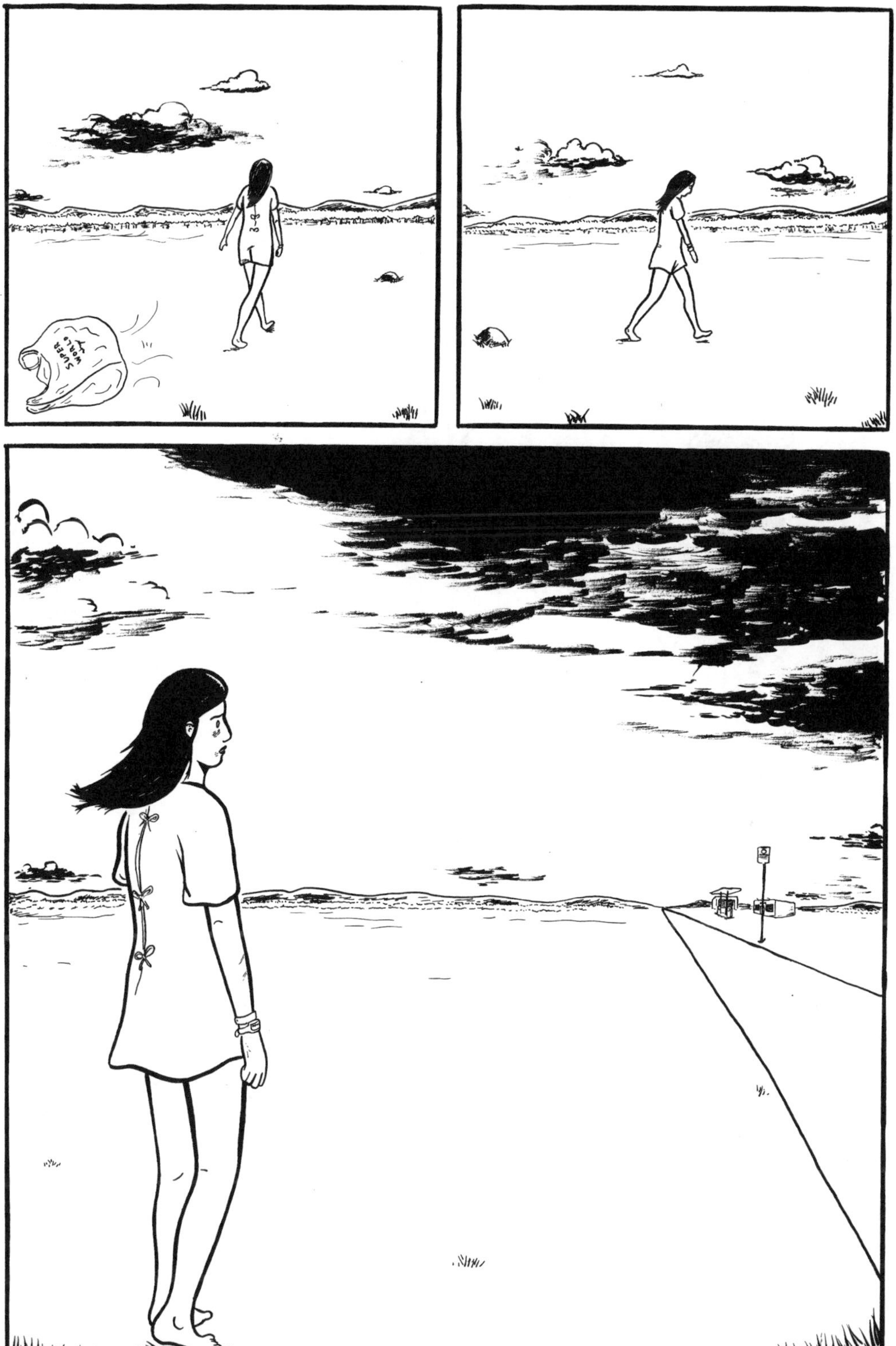
SUPER WORLD

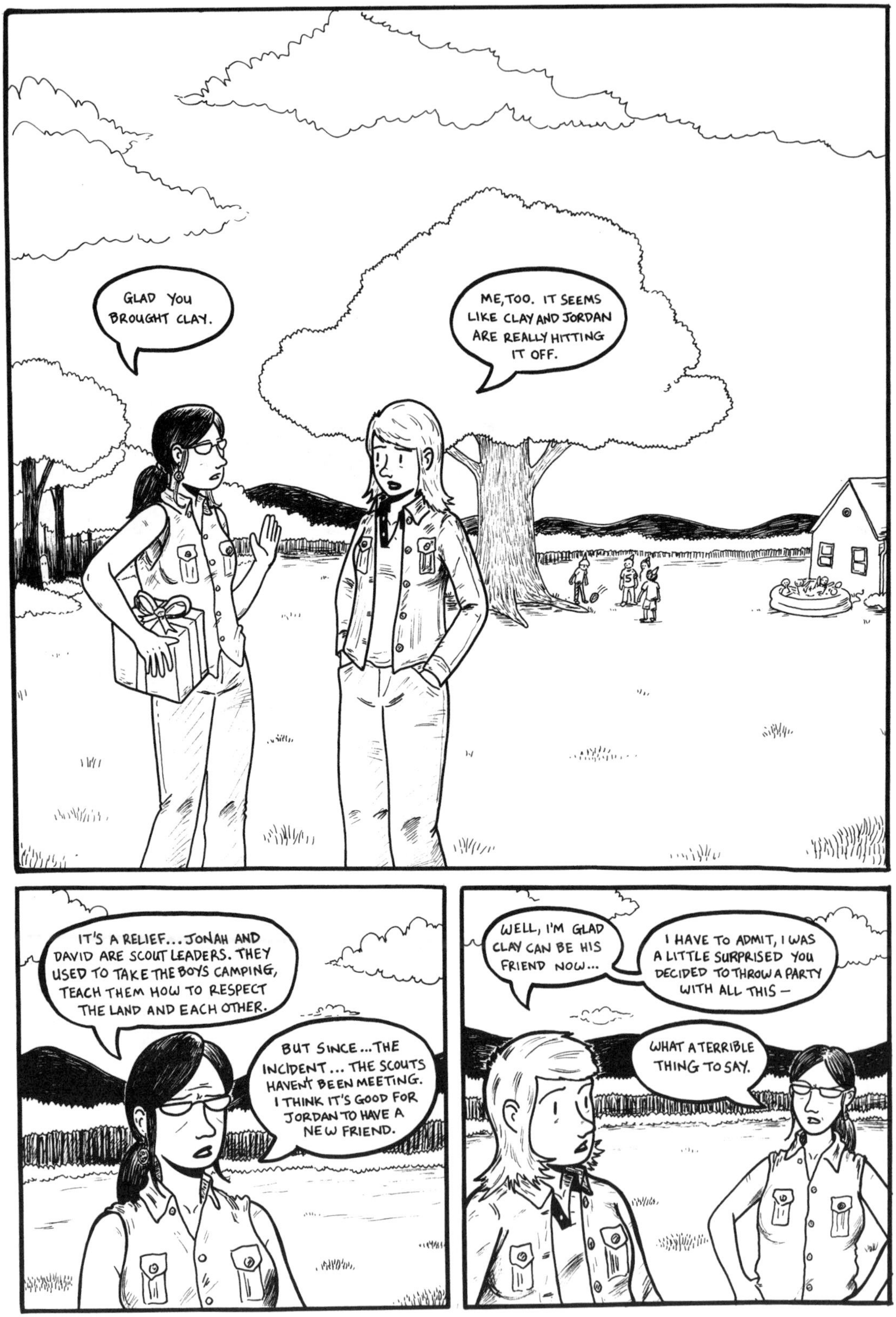
GLAD YOU BROUGHT CLAY.
ME, TOO. IT SEEMS LIKE CLAY AND JORDAN ARE REALLY HITTING IT OFF.
IT'S A RELIEF... JONAH AND DAVID ARE SCOUT LEADERS. THEY USED TO TAKE THE BOYS CAMPING, TEACH THEM HOW TO RESPECT THE LAND AND EACH OTHER.
BUT SINCE... THE INCIDENT... THE SCOUTS HAVEN'T BEEN MEETING. I THINK IT'S GOOD FOR JORDAN TO HAVE A NEW FRIEND.
WELL, I'M GLAD CLAY CAN BE HIS FRIEND NOW...
I HAVE TO ADMIT, I WAS A LITTLE SURPRISED YOU DECIDED TO THROW A PARTY WITH ALL THIS —
WHAT A TERRIBLE THING TO SAY.

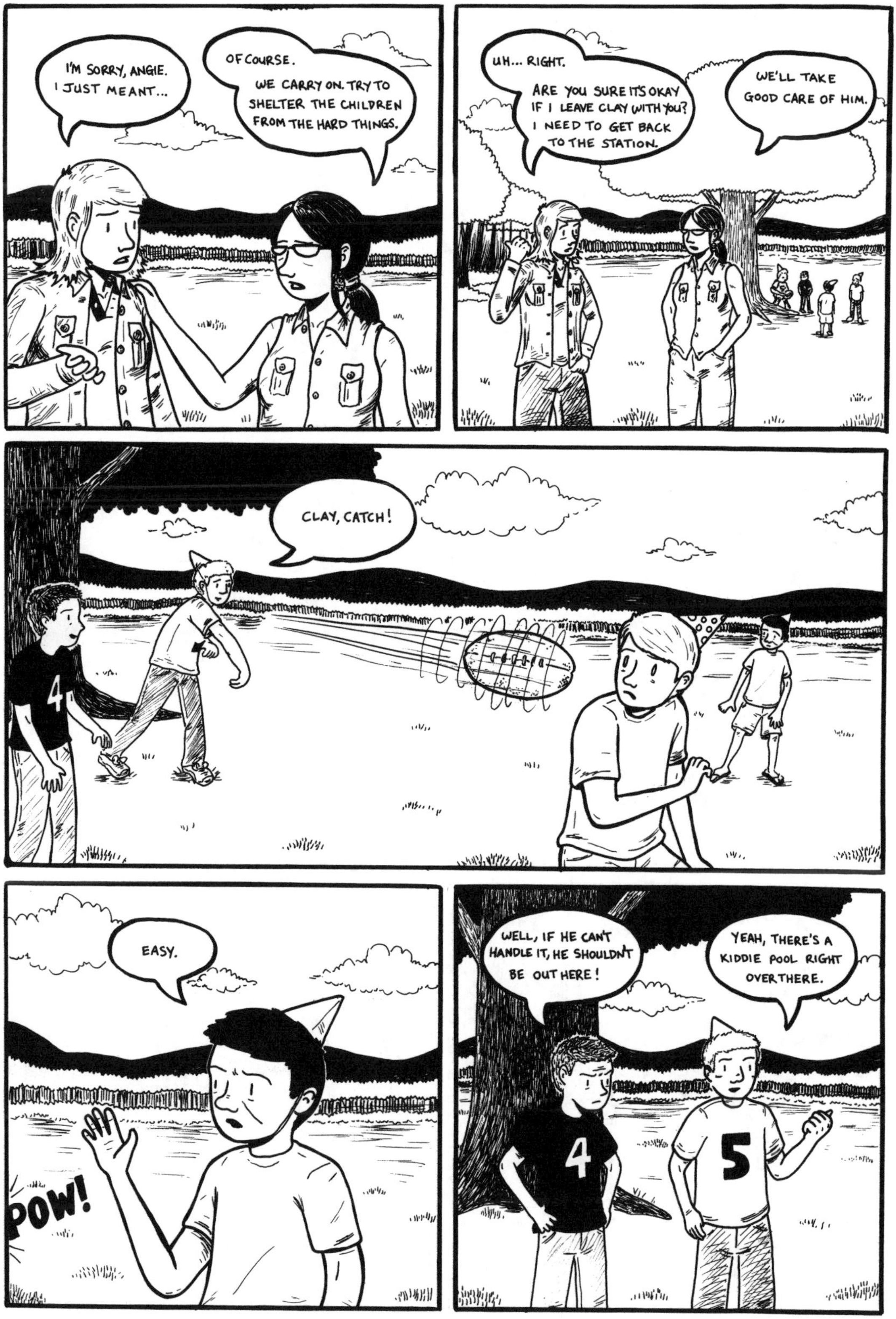
I'M SORRY, ANGIE. I JUST MEANT...
OF COURSE.
WE CARRY ON. TRY TO SHELTER THE CHILDREN FROM THE HARD THINGS.
UH... RIGHT.
ARE YOU SURE IT'S OKAY IF I LEAVE CLAY WITH YOU? I NEED TO GET BACK TO THE STATION.
WE'LL TAKE GOOD CARE OF HIM.
CLAY, CATCH!
EASY.
POW!
WELL, IF HE CAN'T HANDLE IT, HE SHOULDN'T BE OUT HERE!
YEAH, THERE'S A KIDDIE POOL RIGHT OVER THERE.

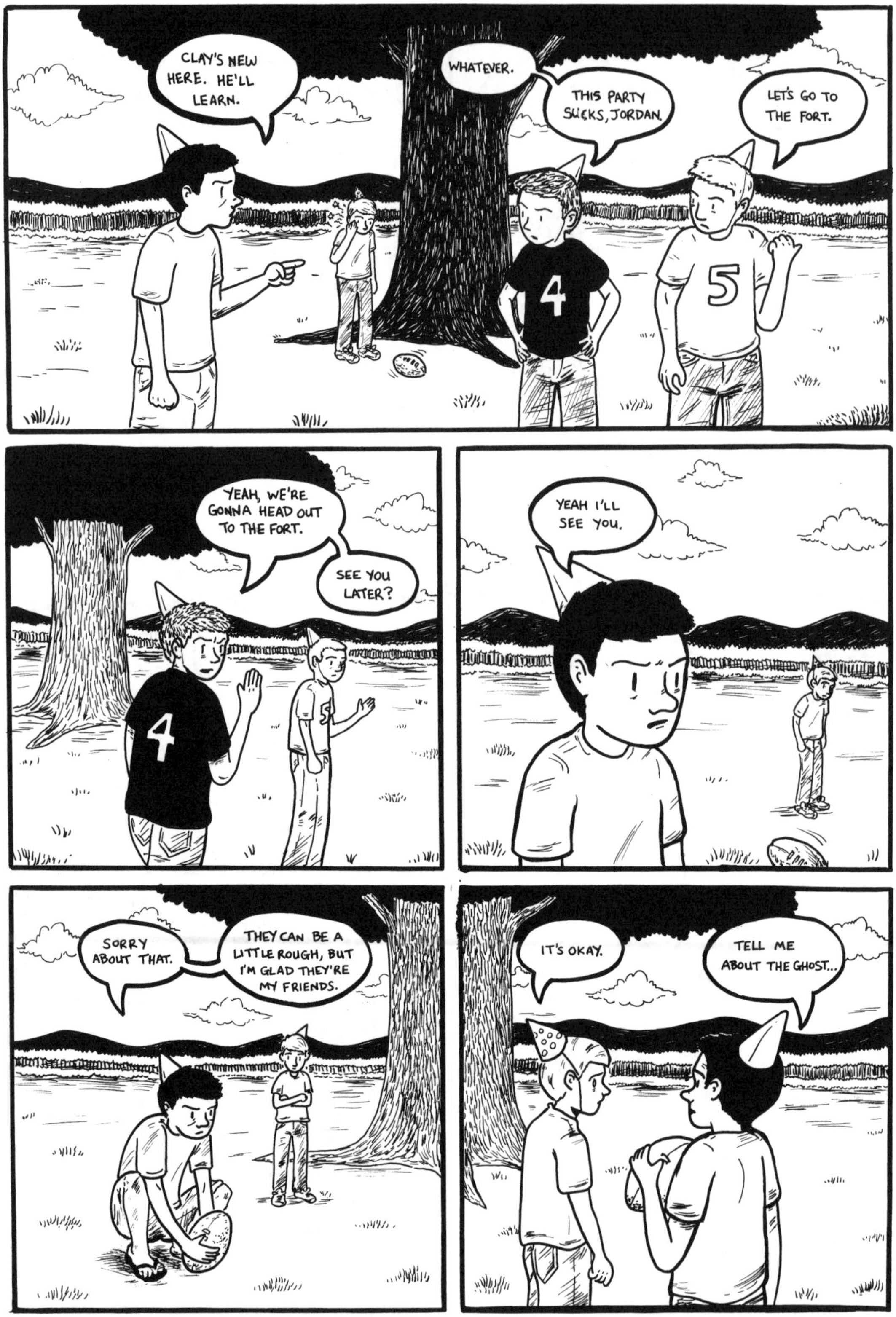
CLAY'S NEW HERE. HE'LL LEARN.
WHATEVER.
THIS PARTY SUCKS, JORDAN.
LET'S GO TO THE FORT.
YEAH, WE'RE GONNA HEAD OUT TO THE FORT.
SEE YOU LATER?
YEAH I'LL SEE YOU.
SORRY ABOUT THAT.
THEY CAN BE A LITTLE ROUGH, BUT I'M GLAD THEY'RE MY FRIENDS.
IT'S OKAY.
TELL ME ABOUT THE GHOST...

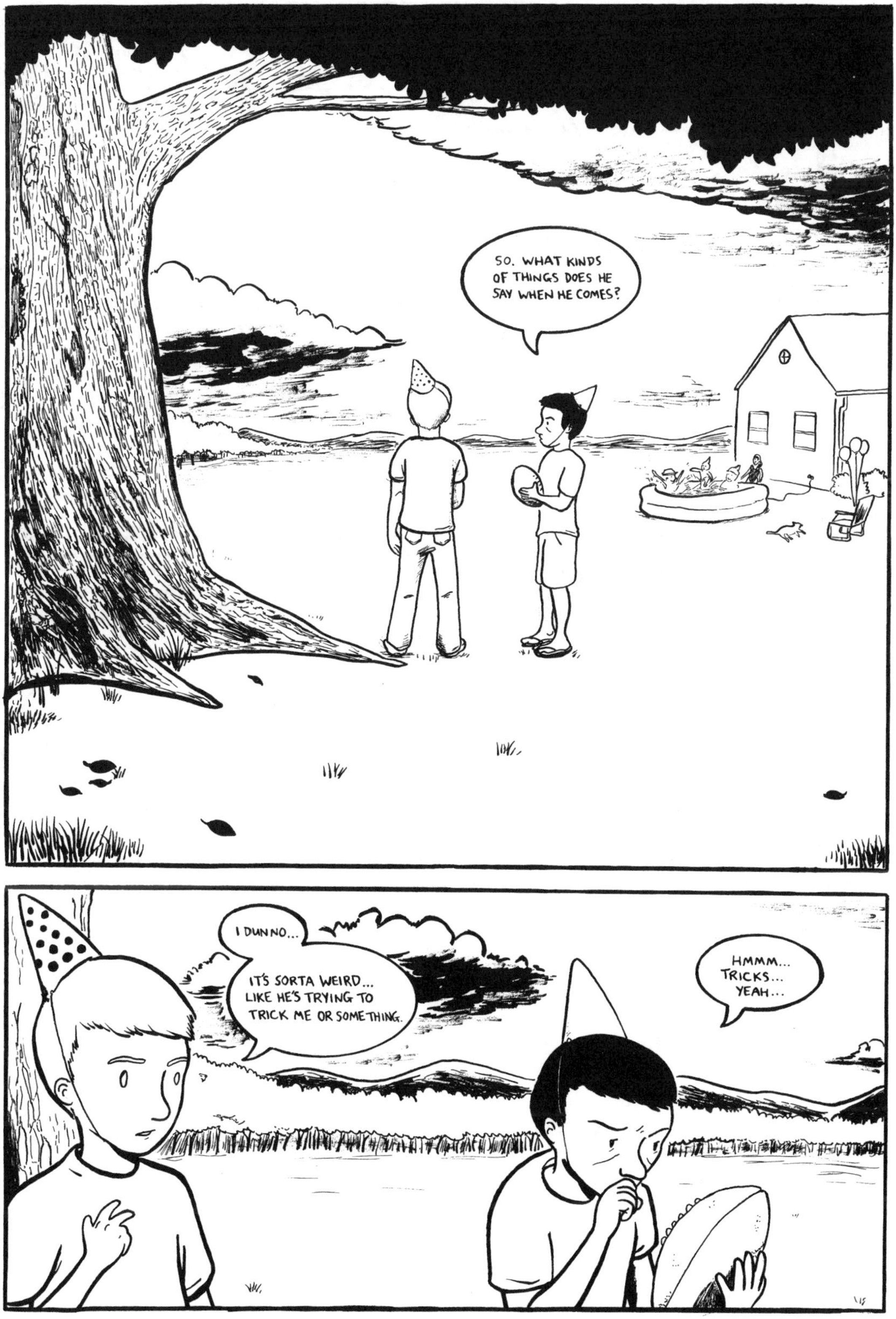
SO. WHAT KINDS OF THINGS DOES HE SAY WHEN HE COMES?
I DUNNO...
IT'S SORTA WEIRD... LIKE HE'S TRYING TO TRICK ME OR SOMETHING.
HMMM... TRICKS... YEAH...

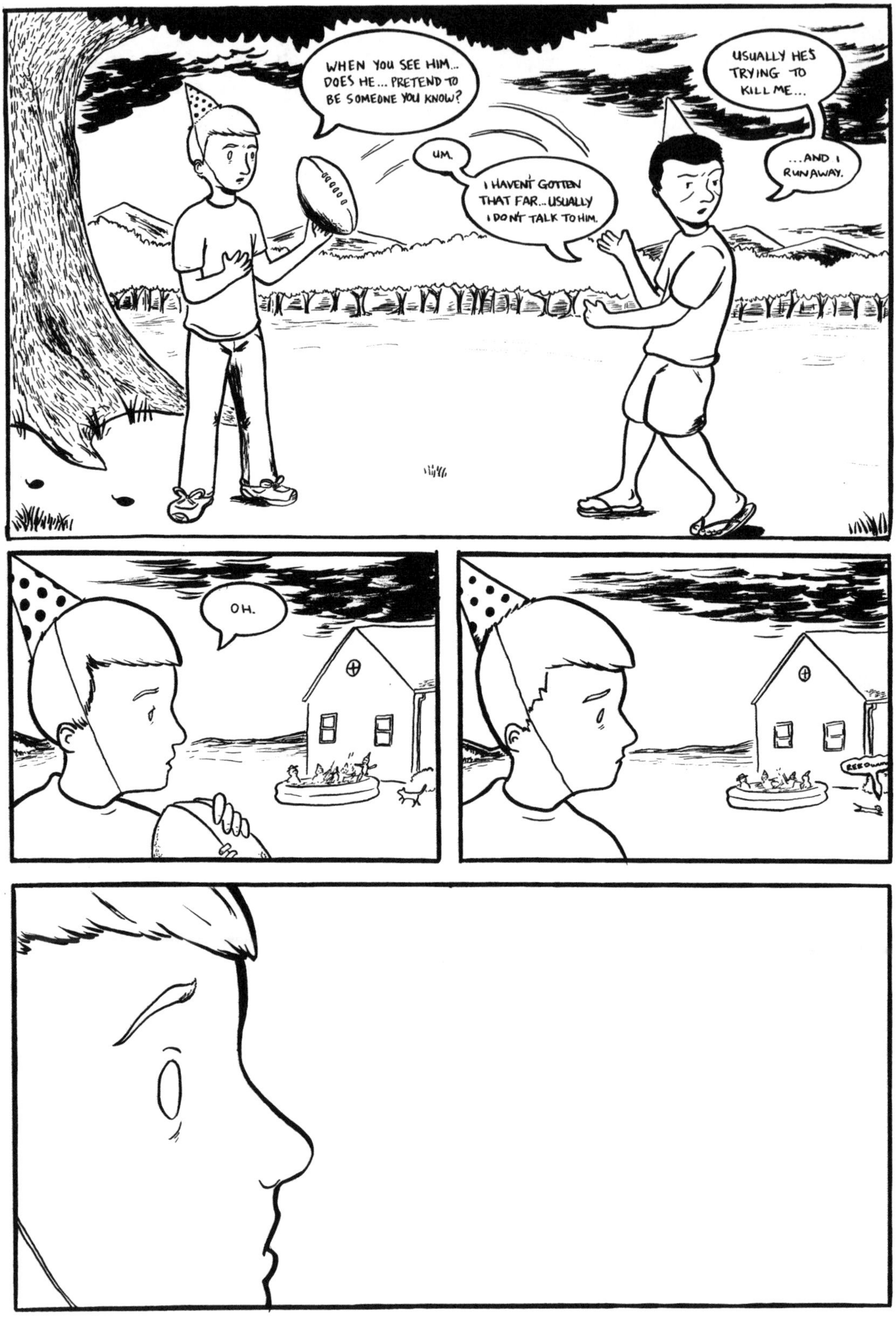
WHEN YOU SEE HIM... DOES HE... PRETEND TO BE SOMEONE YOU KNOW?
UM.
I HAVEN'T GOTTEN THAT FAR... USUALLY I DON'T TALK TO HIM.
USUALLY HE'S TRYING TO KILL ME...
...AND I RUNAWAY.
OH.

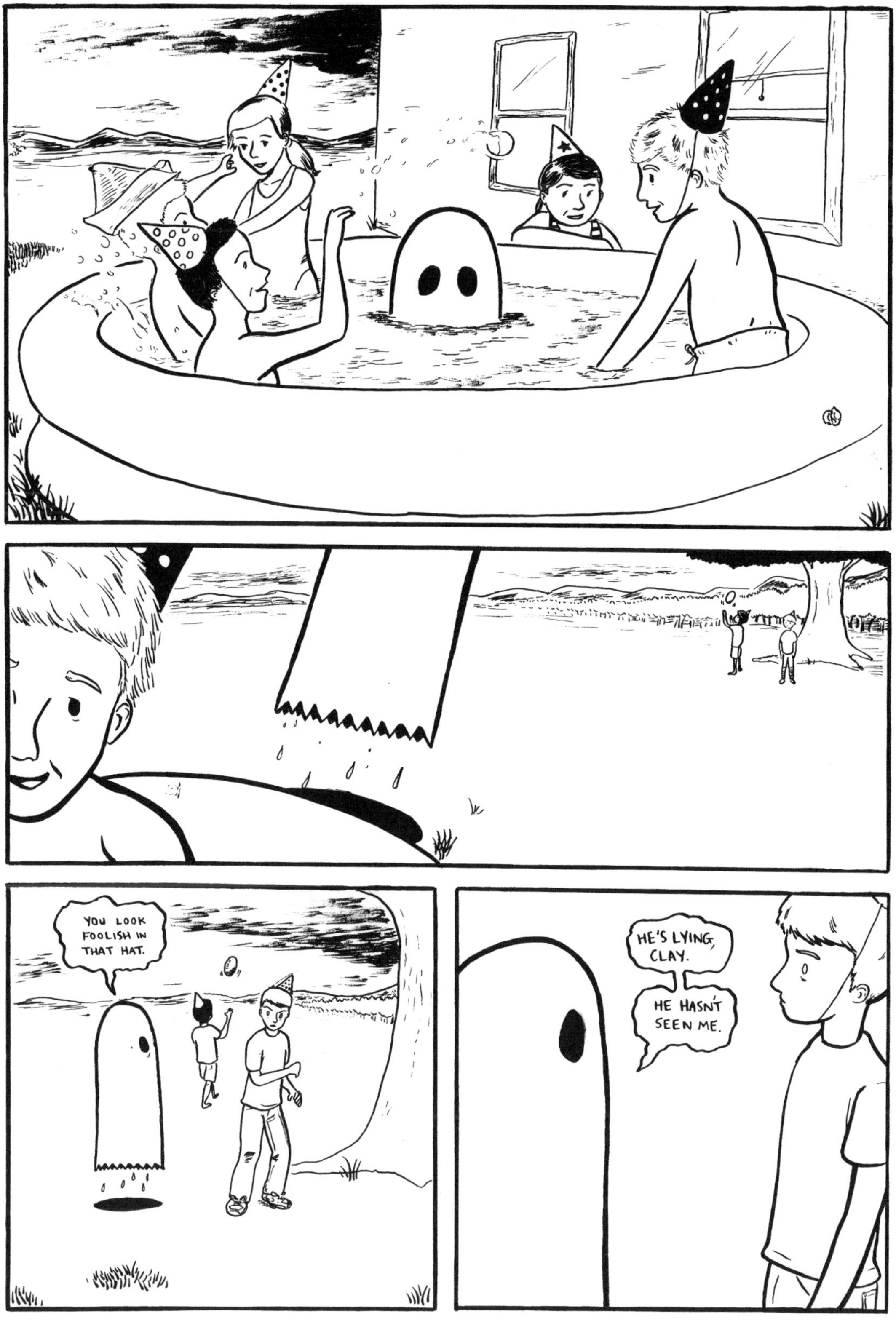
YOU LOOK FOOLISH IN THAT HAT.
HE'S LYING, CLAY.
HE HASN'T SEEN ME.

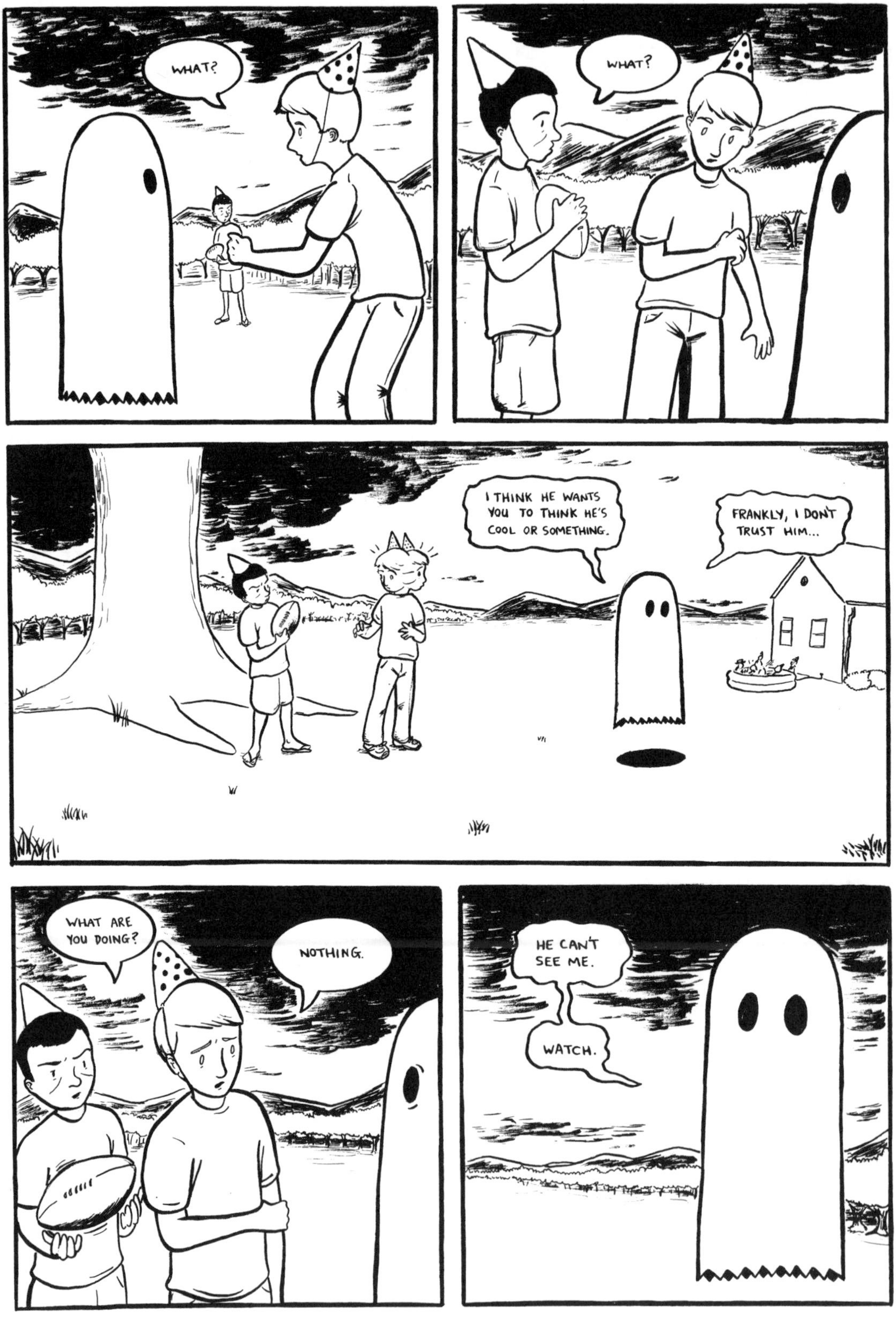
WHAT?
WHAT?
I THINK HE WANTS YOU TO THINK HE'S COOL OR SOMETHING.
FRANKLY, I DON'T TRUST HIM...
WHAT ARE YOU DOING?
NOTHING.
HE CAN'T SEE ME.
WATCH.

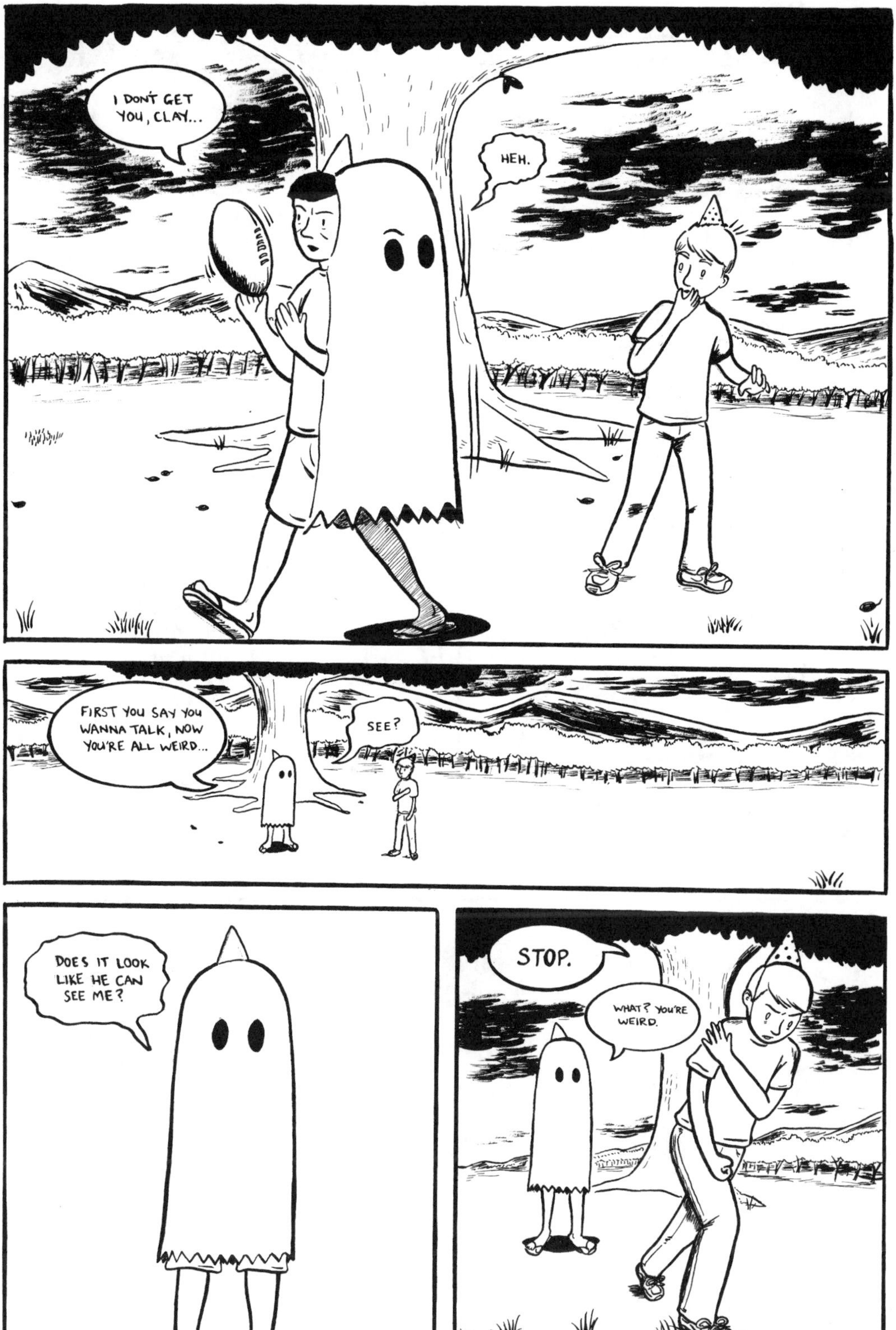
I DON'T GET YOU, CLAY...
HEH.
FIRST YOU SAY YOU WANNA TALK, NOW YOU'RE ALL WEIRD...
SEE?
DOES IT LOOK LIKE HE CAN SEE ME?
STOP.
WHAT? YOU'RE WEIRD.

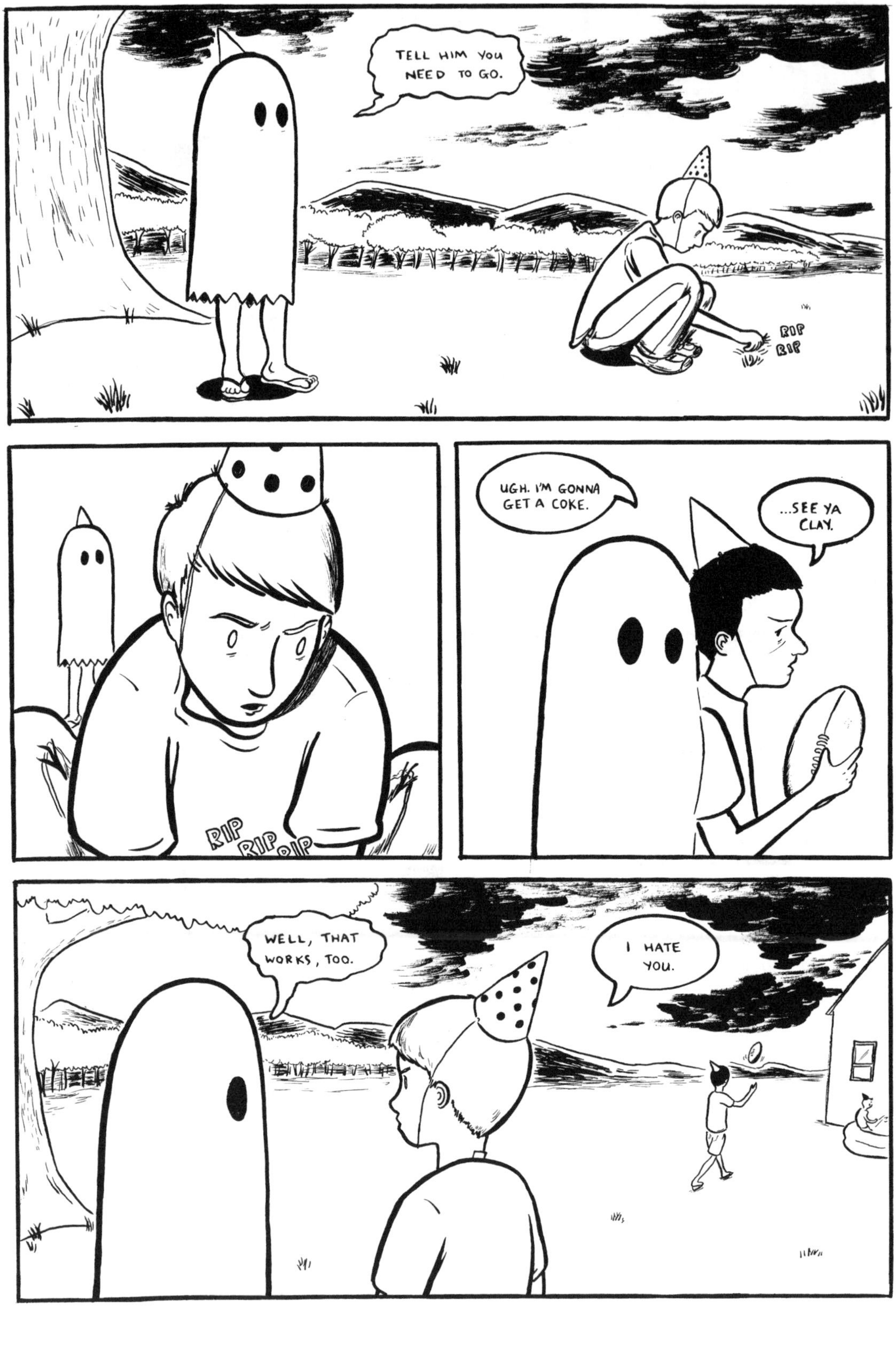
TELL HIM YOU NEED TO GO.
RIP RIP
RIP RIP RIP
UGH. I'M GONNA GET A COKE.
...SEE YA CLAY.
WELL, THAT WORKS, TOO.
I HATE YOU.

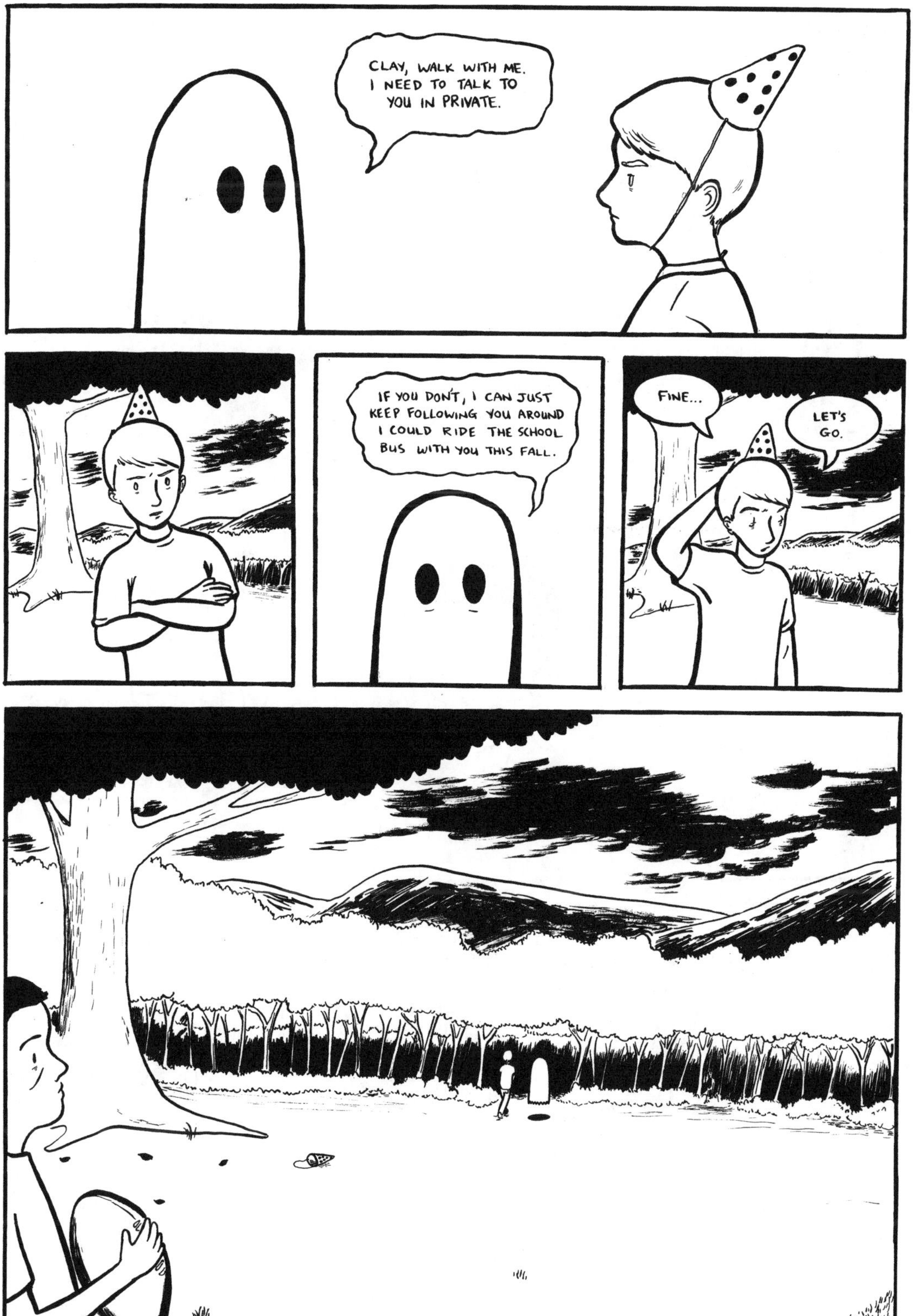
CLAY, WALK WITH ME. I NEED TO TALK TO YOU IN PRIVATE.
IF YOU DON'T, I CAN JUST KEEP FOLLOWING YOU AROUND I COULD RIDE THE SCHOOL BUS WITH YOU THIS FALL.
FINE...
LET'S GO.

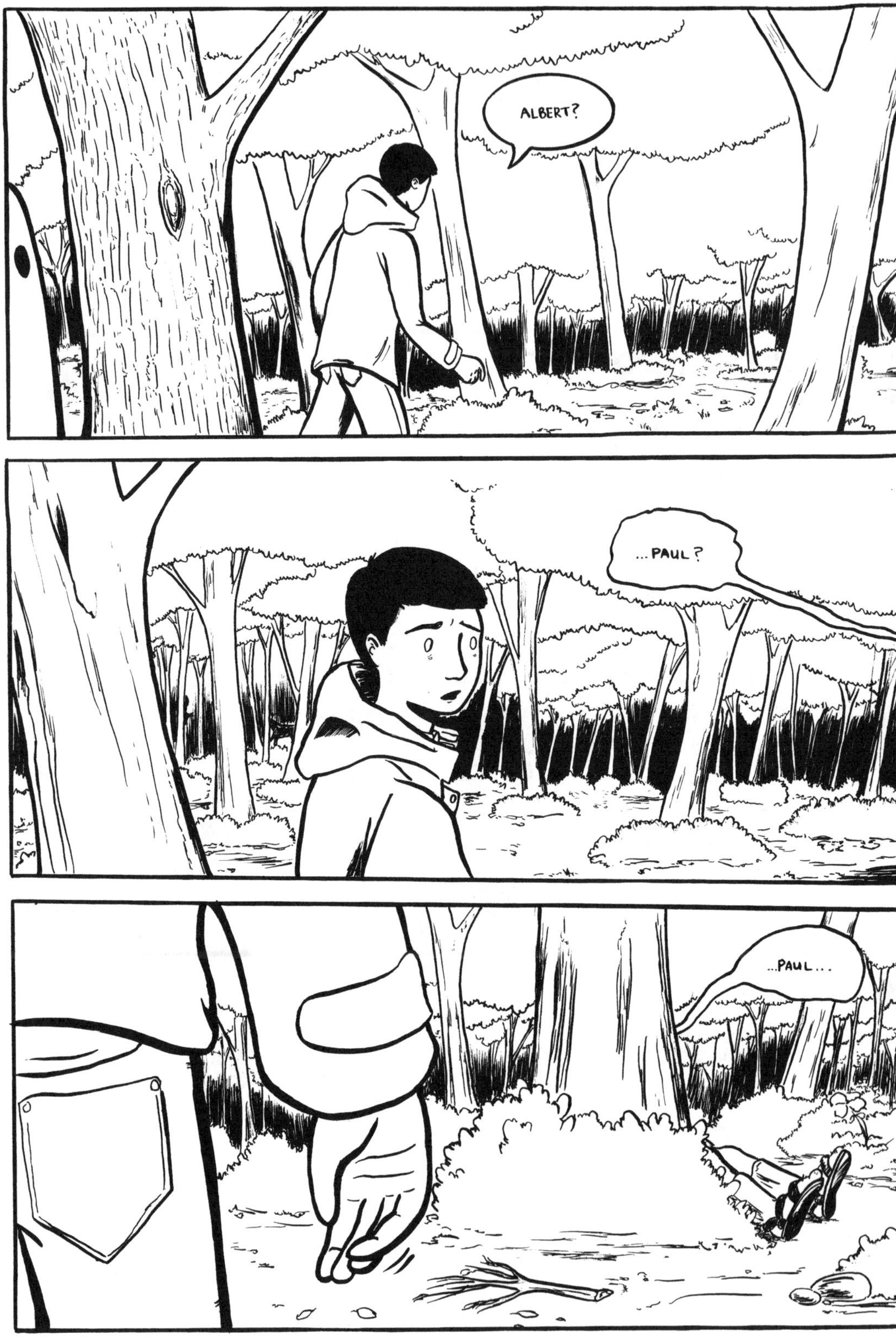
ALBERT?
...PAUL?
...PAUL...

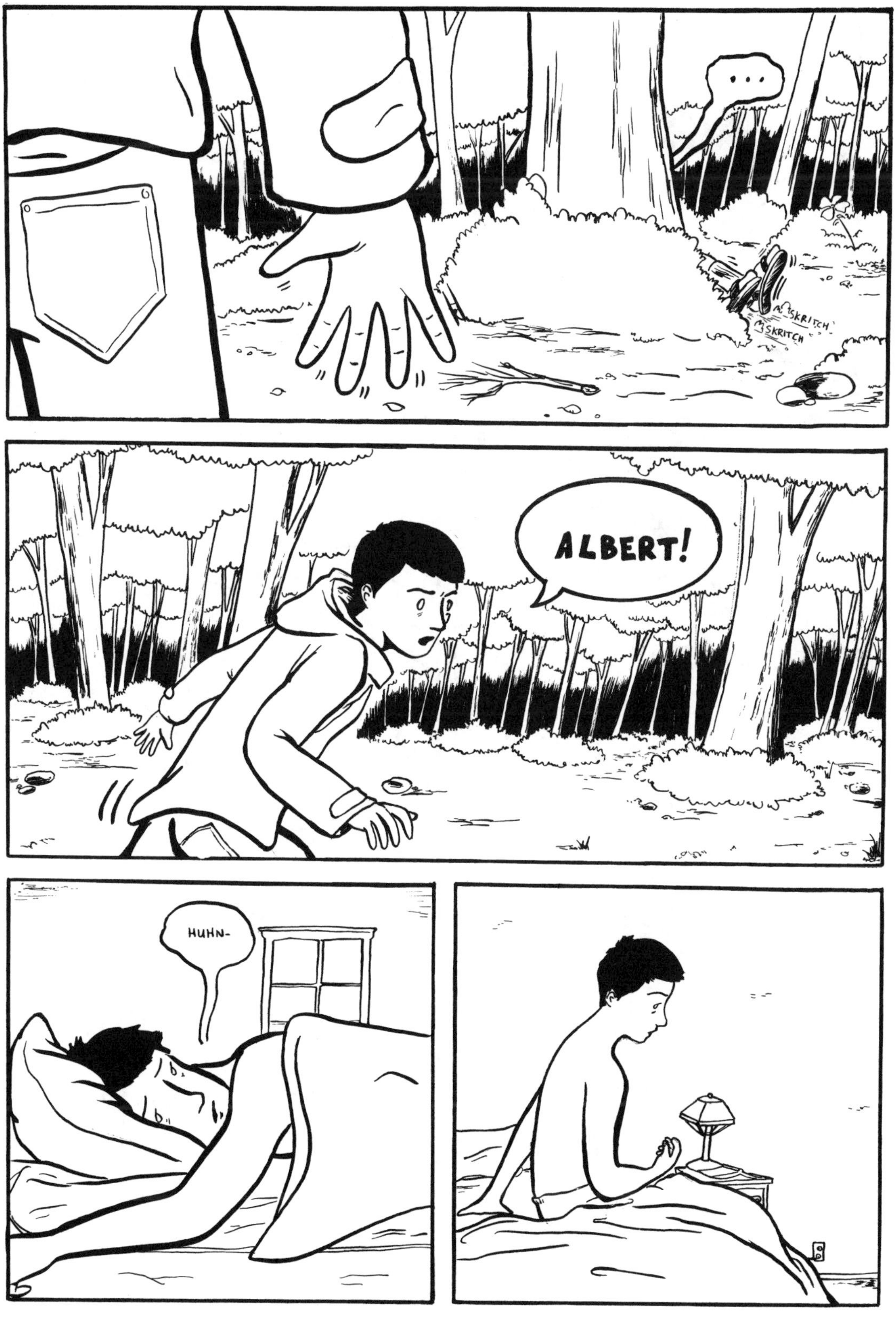
...
SKRITCH
SKRITCH
ALBERT!
HUHN-

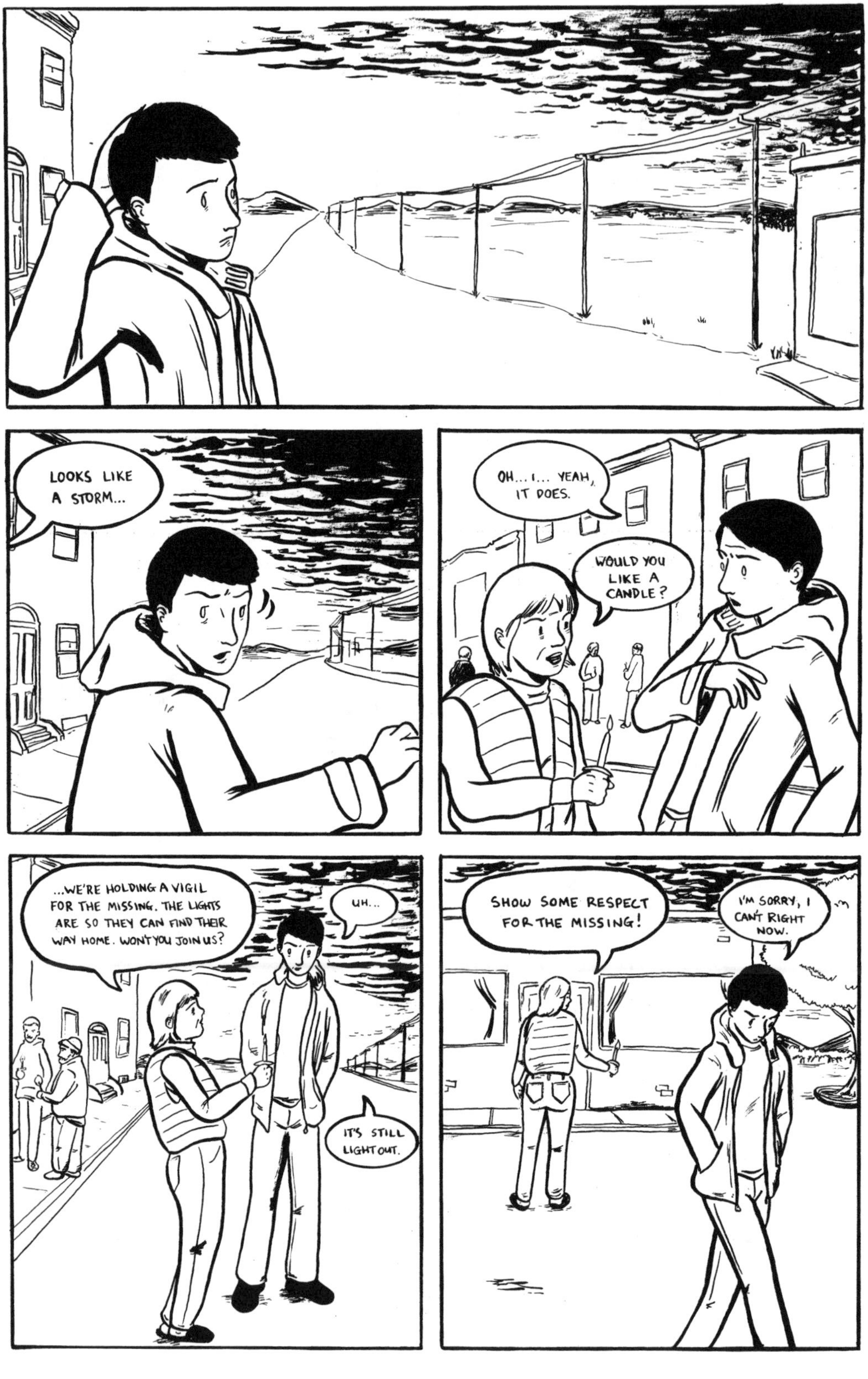
LOOKS LIKE A STORM...
OH... I... YEAH, IT DOES.
WOULD YOU LIKE A CANDLE?
...WE'RE HOLDING A VIGIL FOR THE MISSING. THE LIGHTS ARE SO THEY CAN FIND THEIR WAY HOME. WON'T YOU JOIN US?
UH...
IT'S STILL LIGHT OUT.
SHOW SOME RESPECT FOR THE MISSING!
I'M SORRY, I CAN'T RIGHT NOW.

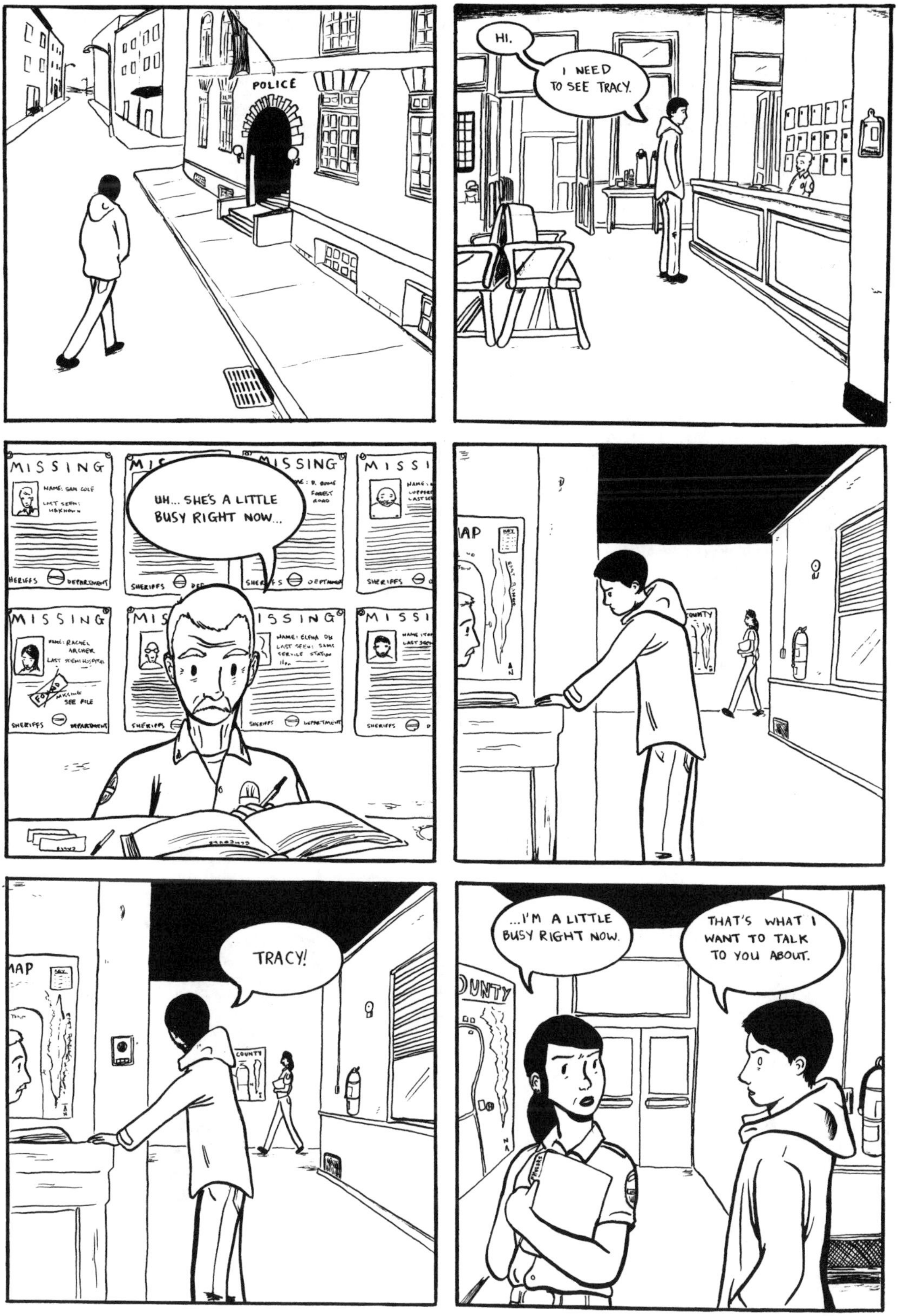
POLICE
HI.
I NEED TO SEE TRACY.
UH... SHE'S A LITTLE BUSY RIGHT NOW...
TRACY!
...I'M A LITTLE BUSY RIGHT NOW.
THAT'S WHAT I WANT TO TALK TO YOU ABOUT.

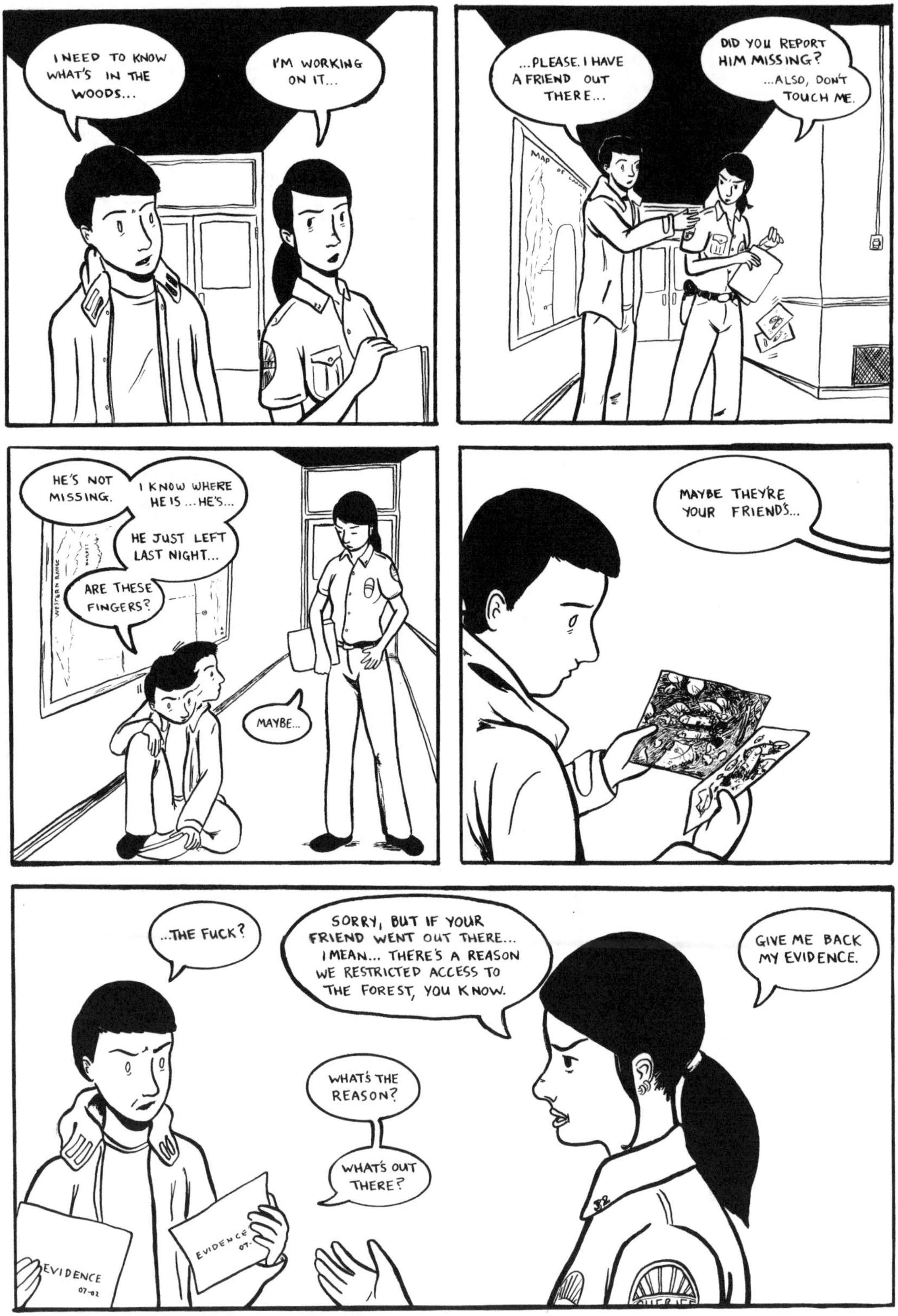
I NEED TO KNOW WHAT'S IN THE WOODS...
I'M WORKING ON IT...
...PLEASE. I HAVE A FRIEND OUT THERE...
DID YOU REPORT HIM MISSING?
...ALSO, DON'T TOUCH ME.
HE'S NOT MISSING.
I KNOW WHERE HE IS... HE'S...
HE JUST LEFT LAST NIGHT...
ARE THESE FINGERS?
MAYBE...
MAYBE THEY'RE YOUR FRIEND'S...
...THE FUCK?
SORRY, BUT IF YOUR FRIEND WENT OUT THERE... I MEAN... THERE'S A REASON WE RESTRICTED ACCESS TO THE FOREST, YOU KNOW.
GIVE ME BACK MY EVIDENCE.
WHAT'S THE REASON?
WHAT'S OUT THERE?
EVIDENCE 07-02
EVIDENCE 07-

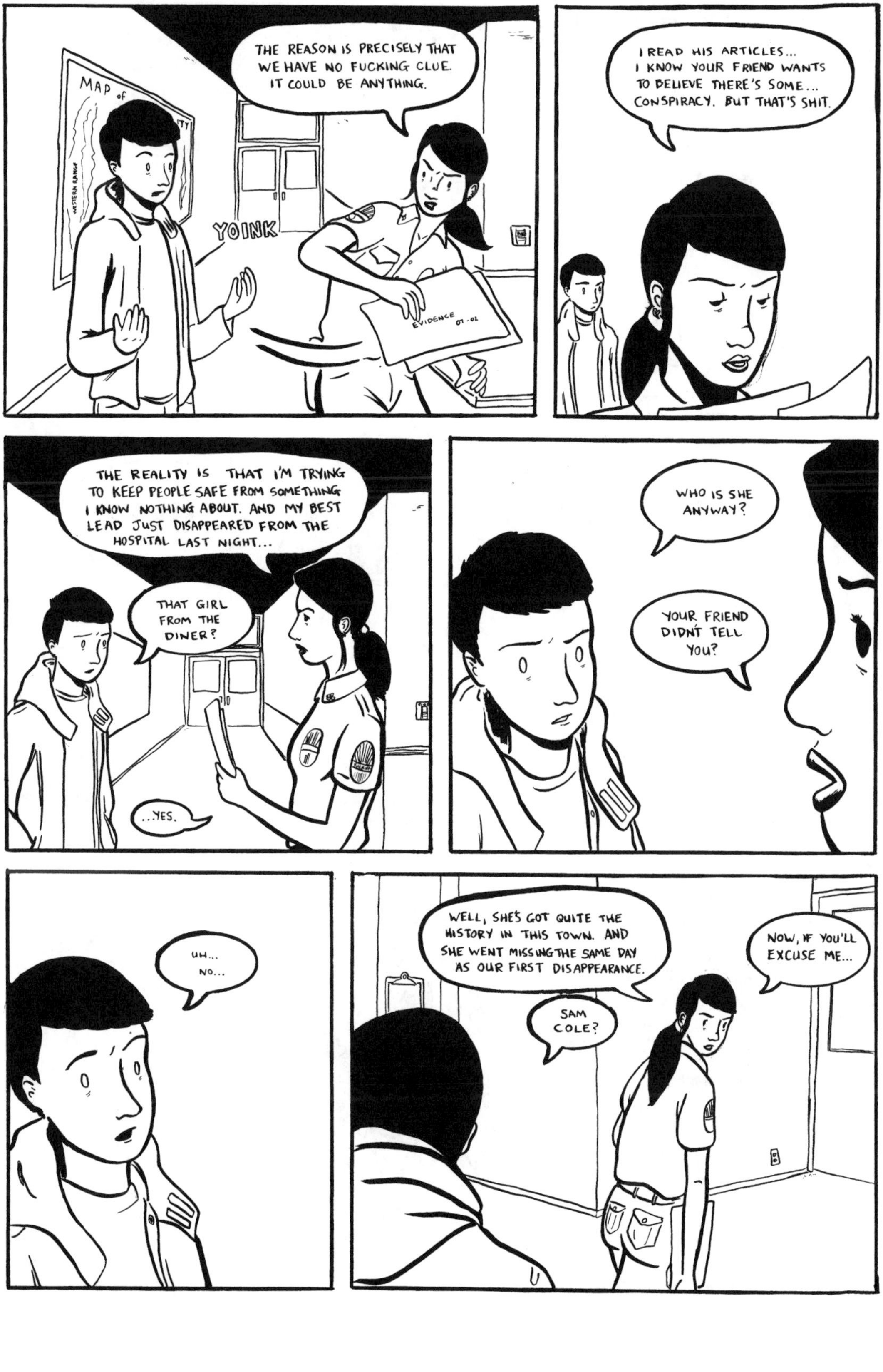
THE REASON IS PRECISELY THAT WE HAVE NO FUCKING CLUE. IT COULD BE ANYTHING.
MAP of
YOINK
EVIDENCE 07-02
I READ HIS ARTICLES... I KNOW YOUR FRIEND WANTS TO BELIEVE THERE'S SOME... CONSPIRACY. BUT THAT'S SHIT.
THE REALITY IS THAT I'M TRYING TO KEEP PEOPLE SAFE FROM SOMETHING I KNOW NOTHING ABOUT. AND MY BEST LEAD JUST DISAPPEARED FROM THE HOSPITAL LAST NIGHT...
THAT GIRL FROM THE DINER?
...YES.
WHO IS SHE ANYWAY?
YOUR FRIEND DIDN'T TELL YOU?
UH... NO...
WELL, SHE'S GOT QUITE THE HISTORY IN THIS TOWN. AND SHE WENT MISSING THE SAME DAY AS OUR FIRST DISAPPEARANCE.
SAM COLE?
NOW, IF YOU'LL EXCUSE ME...

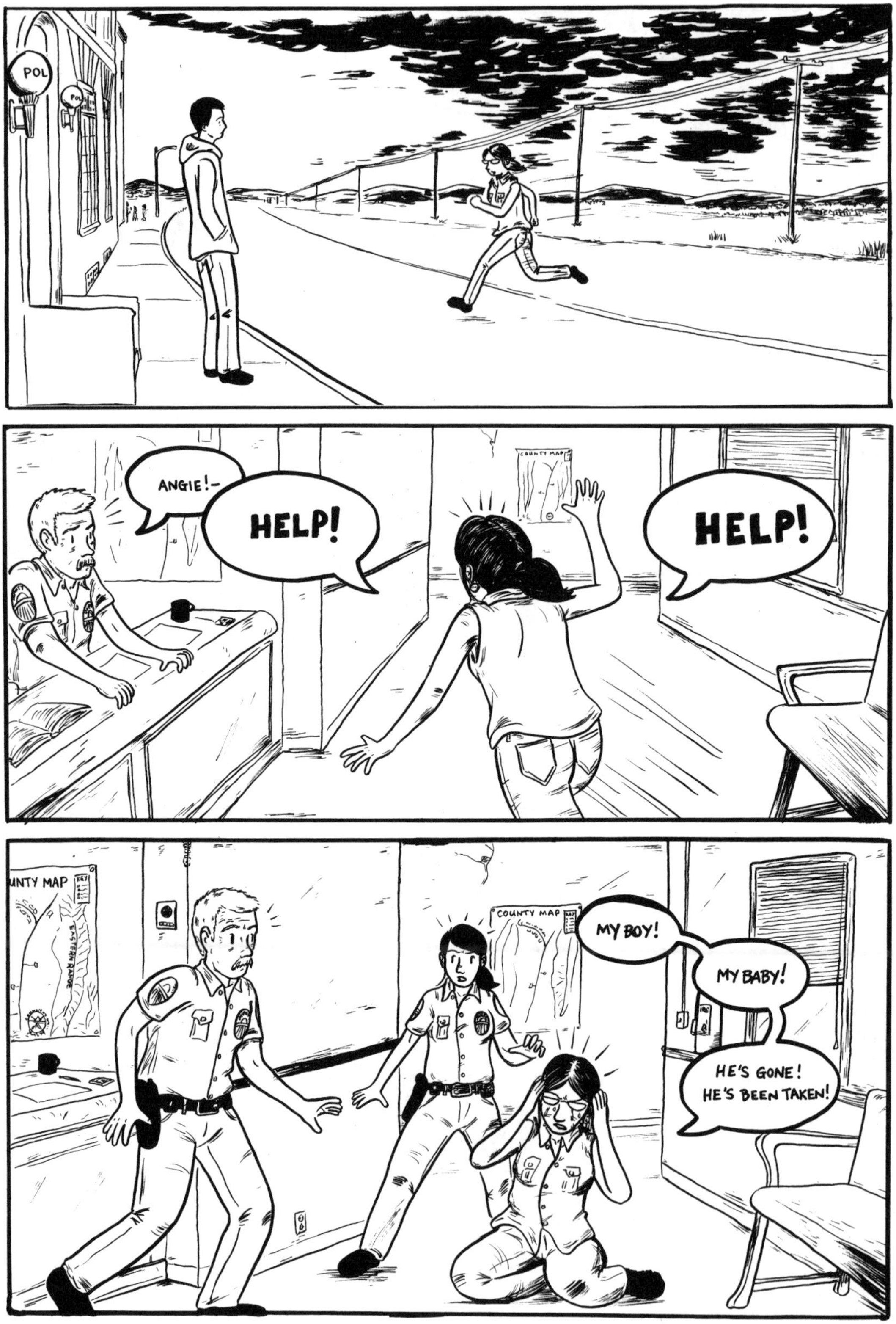
POL
POL
ANGIE! –
HELP!
HELP!
COUNTY MAP
UNTY MAP
KEY
EASTERN RANGE
COUNTY MAP
MY BOY!
MY BABY!
HE'S GONE! HE'S BEEN TAKEN!

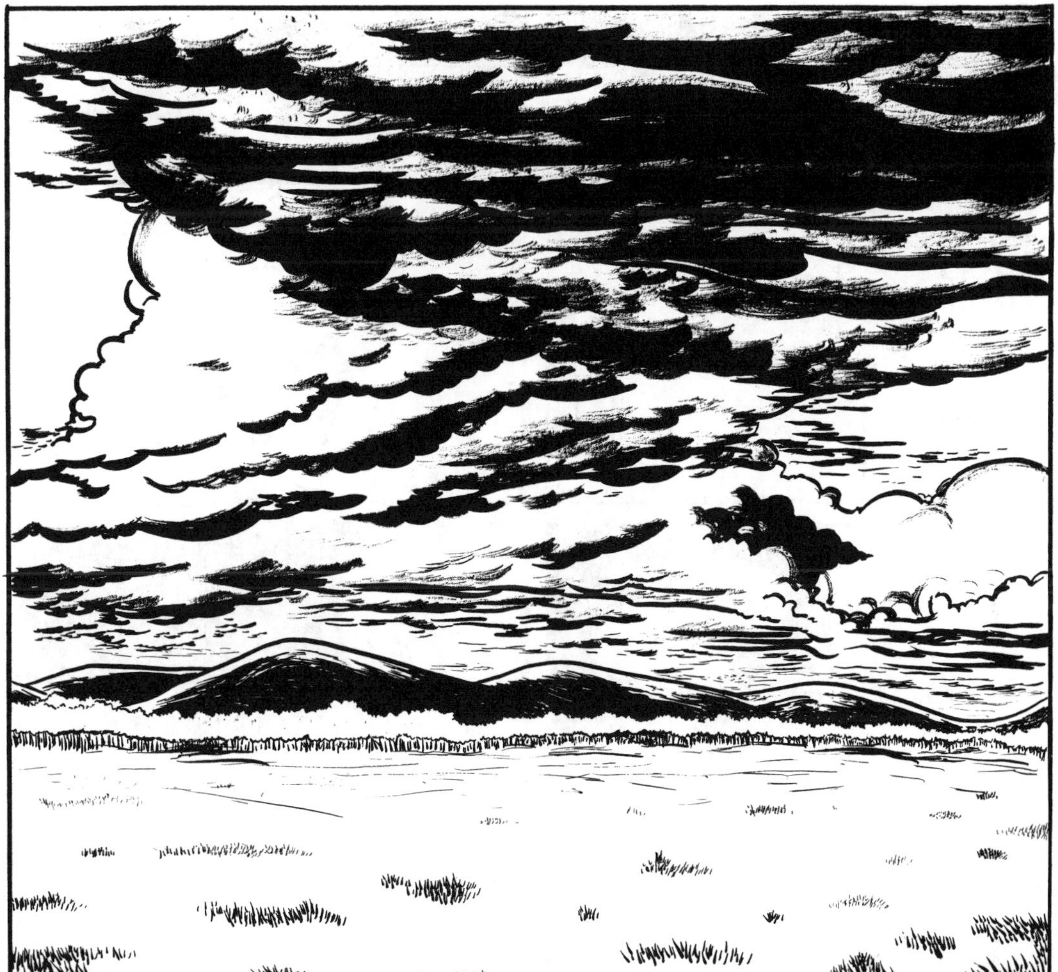
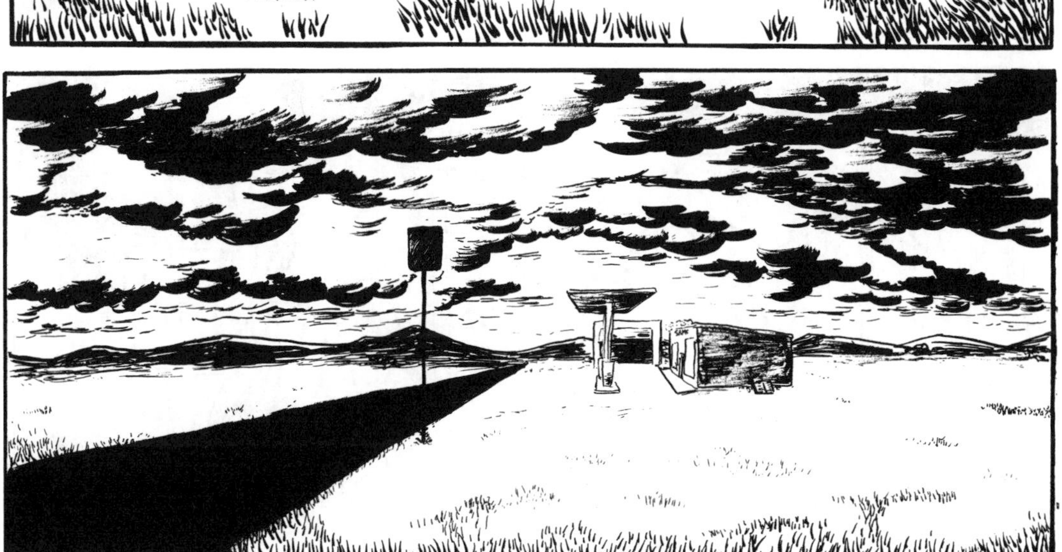

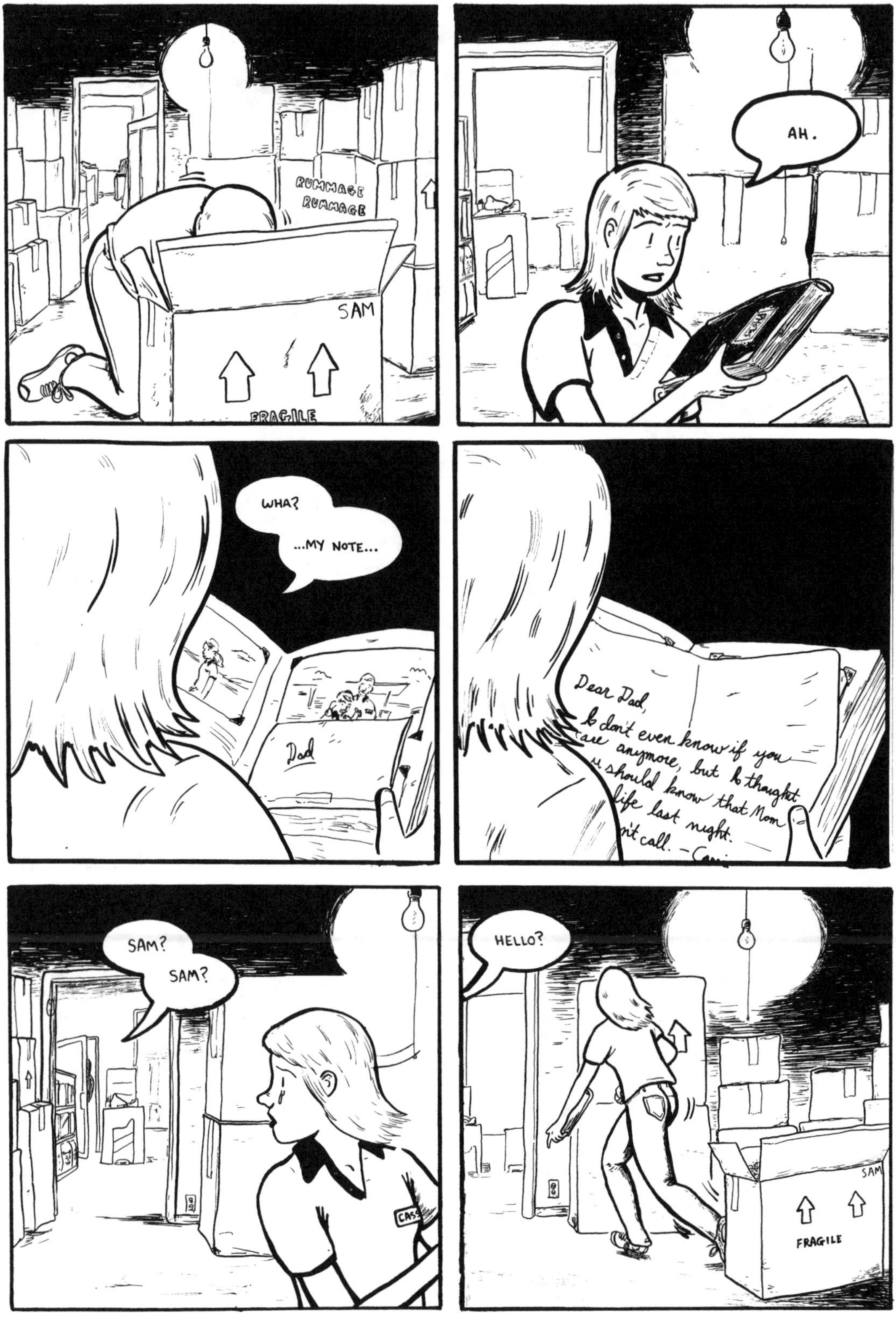
RUMMAGE
RUMMAGE
SAM
FRAGILE
AH.
WHA?
...MY NOTE...
Dad
Dear Dad,
I don't even know if you
are anymore, but I thought
u should know that Mom
life last night.
n't call. —Ca
SAM?
SAM?
CASS
HELLO?
SAM
FRAGILE

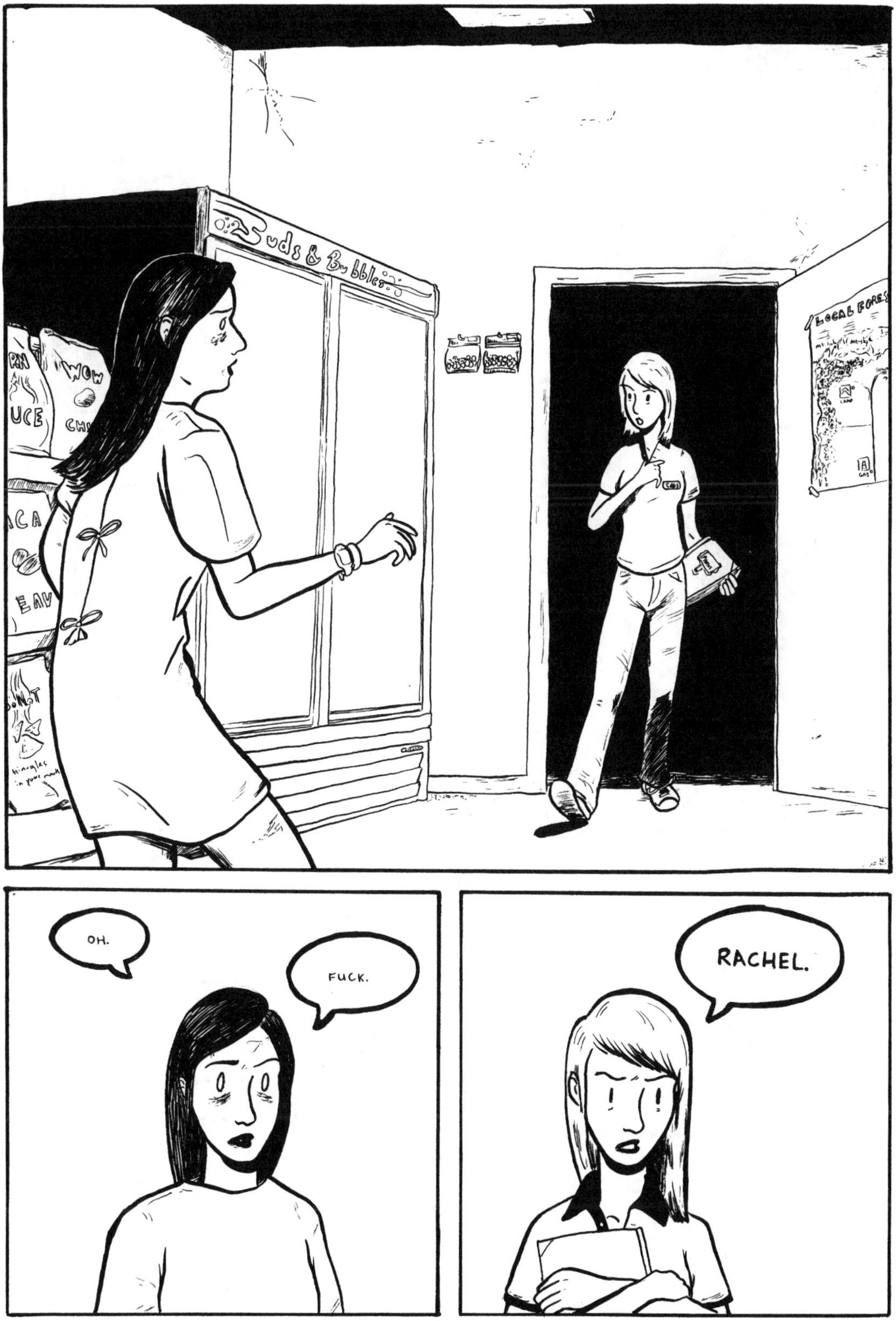
Suds & Bubbles
LOCAL FORES
OH.
FUCK.
RACHEL.

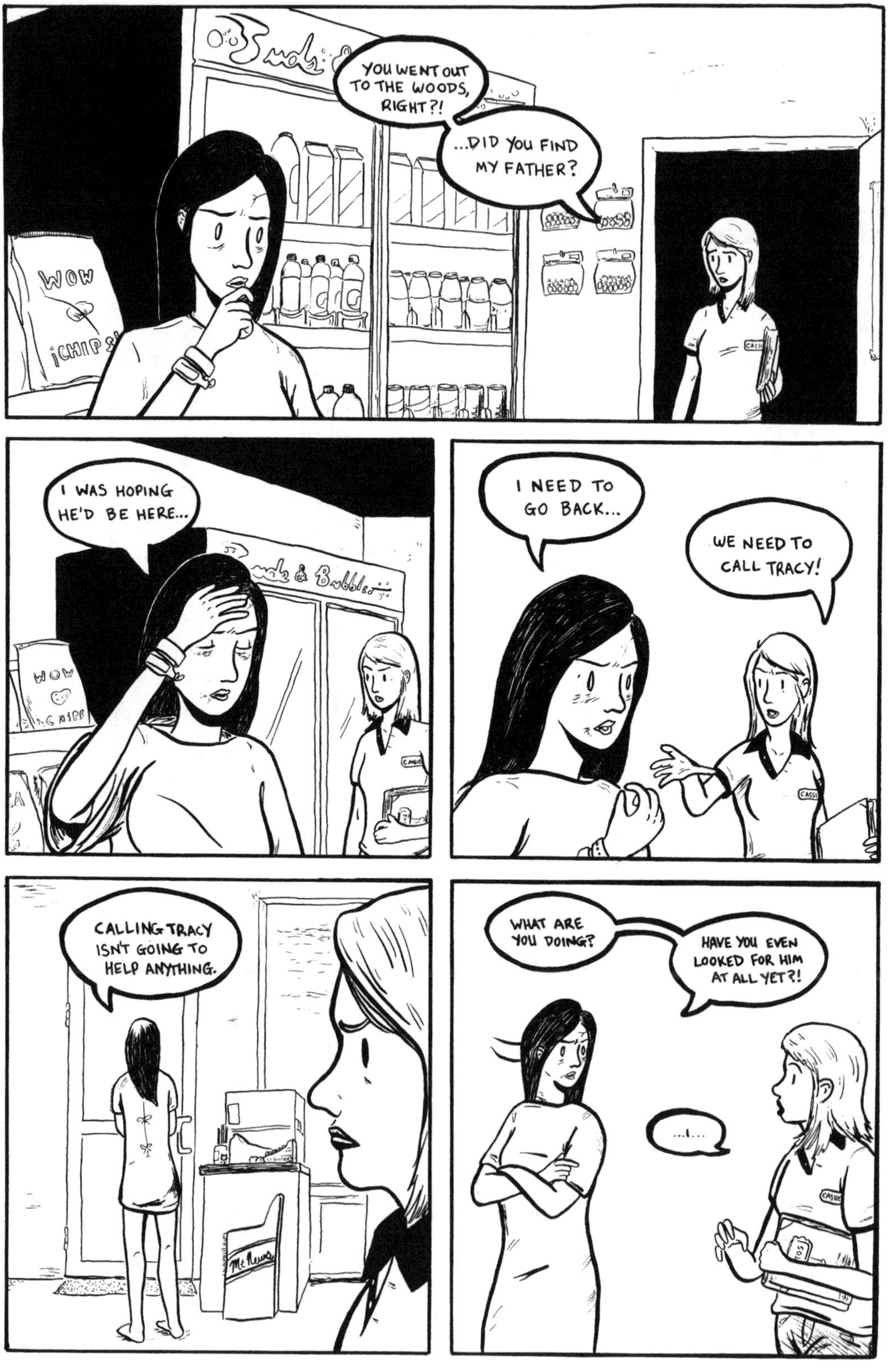
YOU WENT OUT TO THE WOODS, RIGHT?!
...DID YOU FIND MY FATHER?
WOW iCHIPS
I WAS HOPING HE'D BE HERE...
I NEED TO GO BACK...
WE NEED TO CALL TRACY!
CALLING TRACY ISN'T GOING TO HELP ANYTHING.
WHAT ARE YOU DOING?
HAVE YOU EVEN LOOKED FOR HIM AT ALL YET?!
...I...

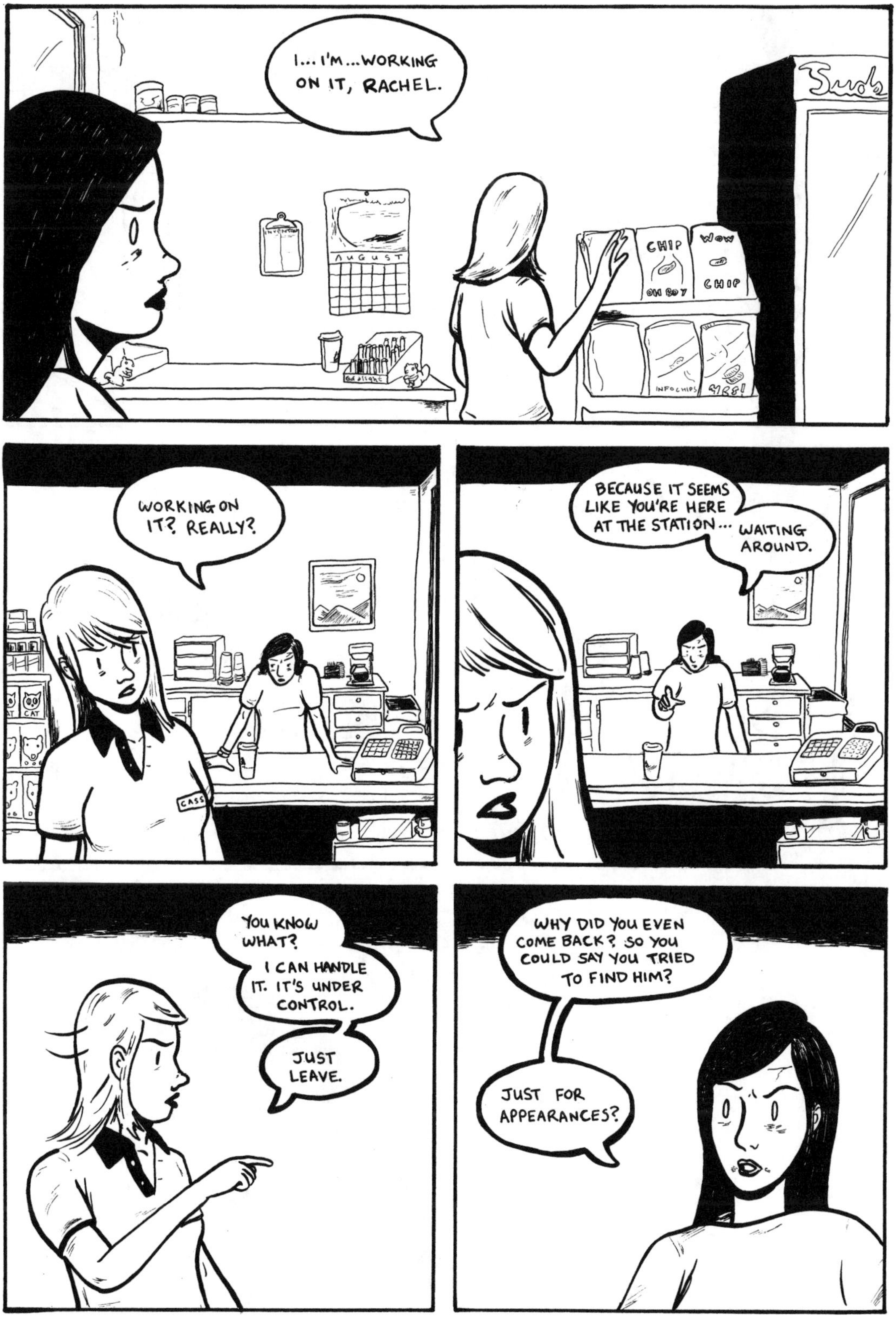
I... I'M... WORKING ON IT, RACHEL.
Suds
AUGUST
CHIP
OH BOY
WOW
CHIP
INFOCHIPS
WORKING ON IT? REALLY?
CASS
BECAUSE IT SEEMS LIKE YOU'RE HERE AT THE STATION...
WAITING AROUND.
YOU KNOW WHAT?
I CAN HANDLE IT. IT'S UNDER CONTROL.
JUST LEAVE.
WHY DID YOU EVEN COME BACK? SO YOU COULD SAY YOU TRIED TO FIND HIM?
JUST FOR APPEARANCES?

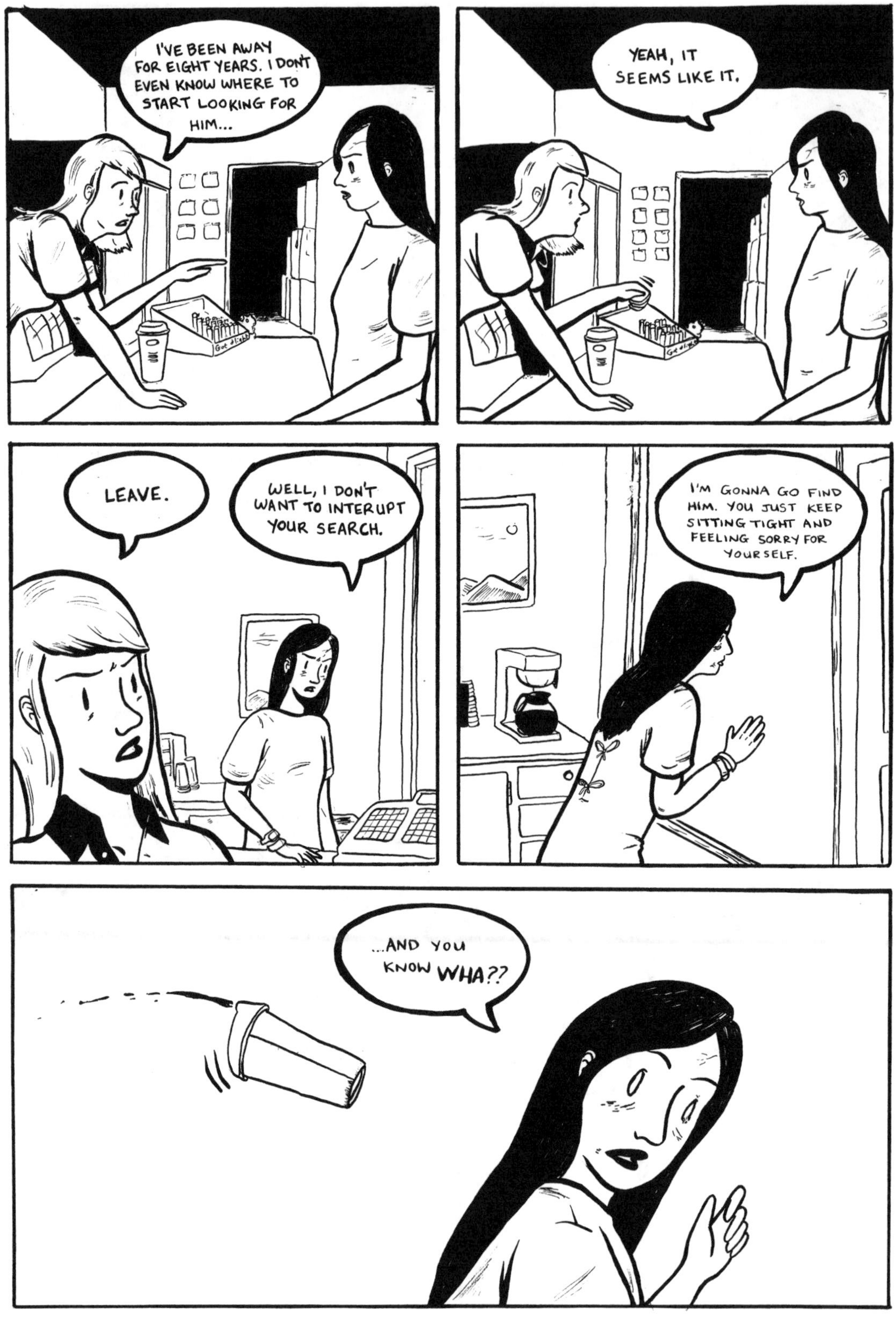
I'VE BEEN AWAY FOR EIGHT YEARS. I DON'T EVEN KNOW WHERE TO START LOOKING FOR HIM...
YEAH, IT SEEMS LIKE IT.
LEAVE.
WELL, I DON'T WANT TO INTERUPT YOUR SEARCH.
I'M GONNA GO FIND HIM. YOU JUST KEEP SITTING TIGHT AND FEELING SORRY FOR YOURSELF.
...AND YOU KNOW WHA??

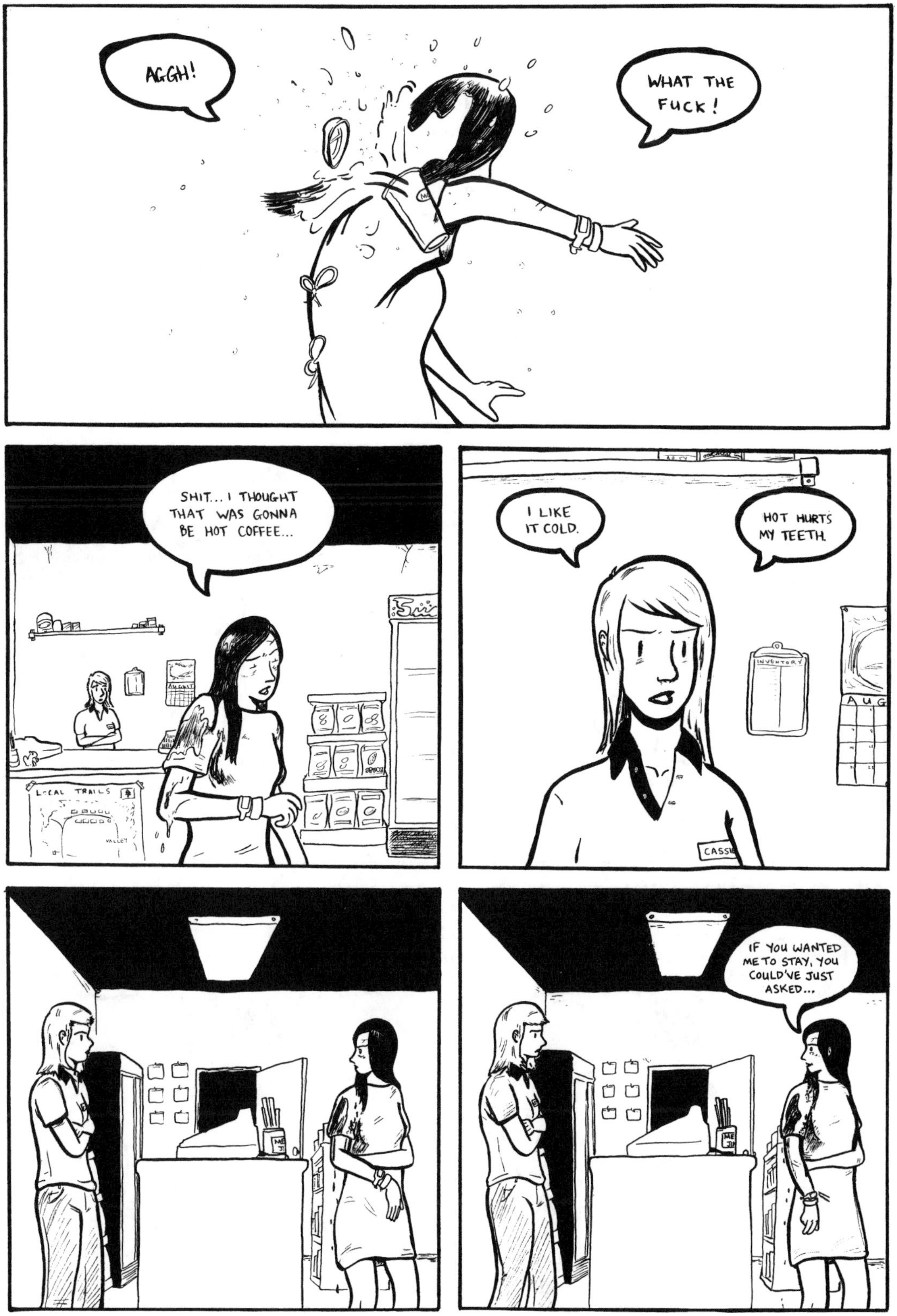
AGGH!
WHAT THE FUCK!
SHIT... I THOUGHT THAT WAS GONNA BE HOT COFFEE...
LOCAL TRAILS
VALLEY
I LIKE IT COLD.
HOT HURTS MY TEETH.
INVENTORY
AUG
CASSIE
IF YOU WANTED ME TO STAY, YOU COULD'VE JUST ASKED...

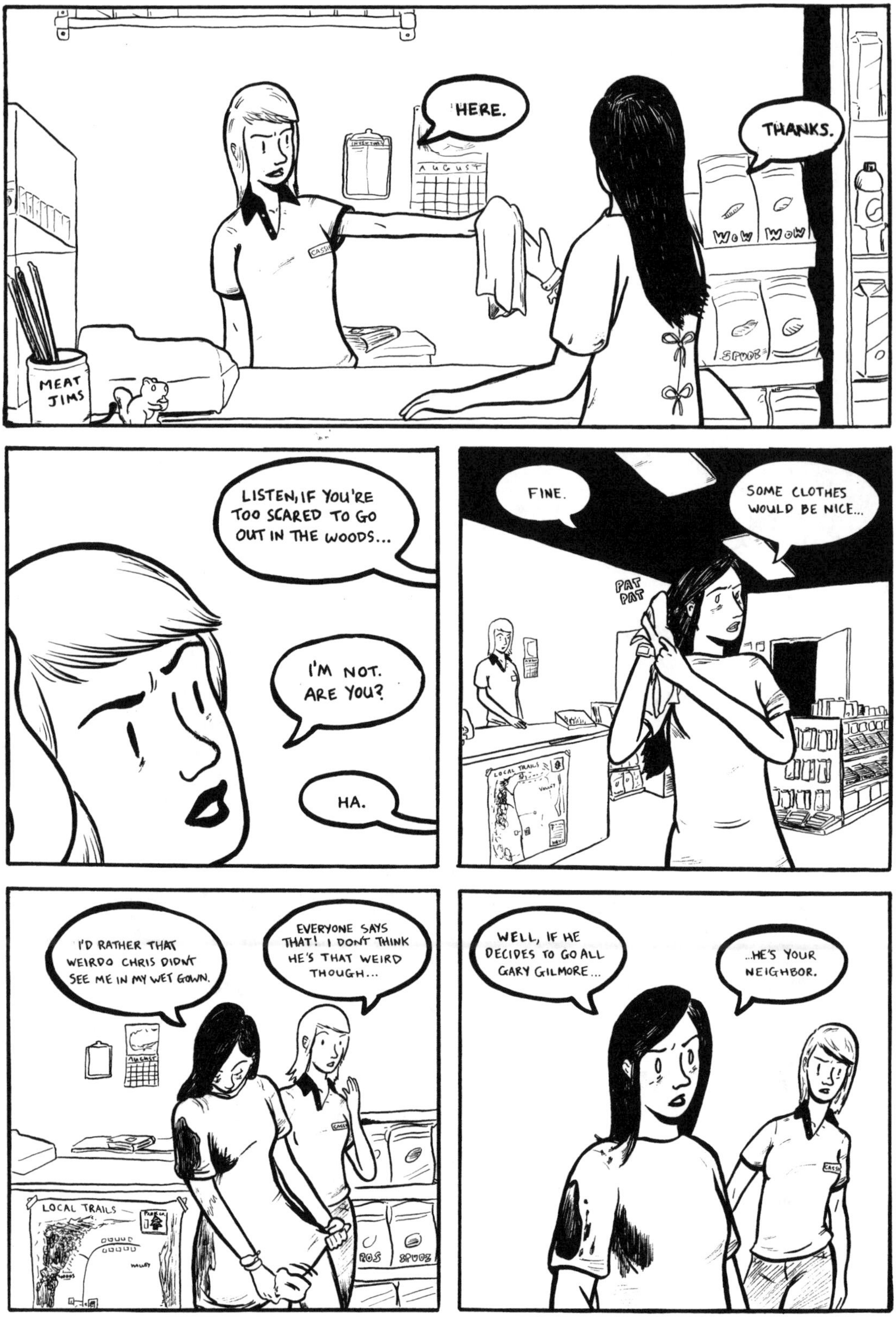
HERE.
THANKS.
MEAT JIMS
AUGUST
CASSIE
WOW WOW
SPUDZ
LISTEN, IF YOU'RE TOO SCARED TO GO OUT IN THE WOODS...
I'M NOT. ARE YOU?
HA.
FINE.
SOME CLOTHES WOULD BE NICE...
PAT PAT
LOCAL TRAILS
I'D RATHER THAT WEIRDO CHRIS DIDN'T SEE ME IN MY WET GOWN.
EVERYONE SAYS THAT! I DON'T THINK HE'S THAT WEIRD THOUGH...
LOCAL TRAILS
AUGUST
ROS SPUDZ
WELL, IF HE DECIDES TO GO ALL GARY GILMORE...
...HE'S YOUR NEIGHBOR.

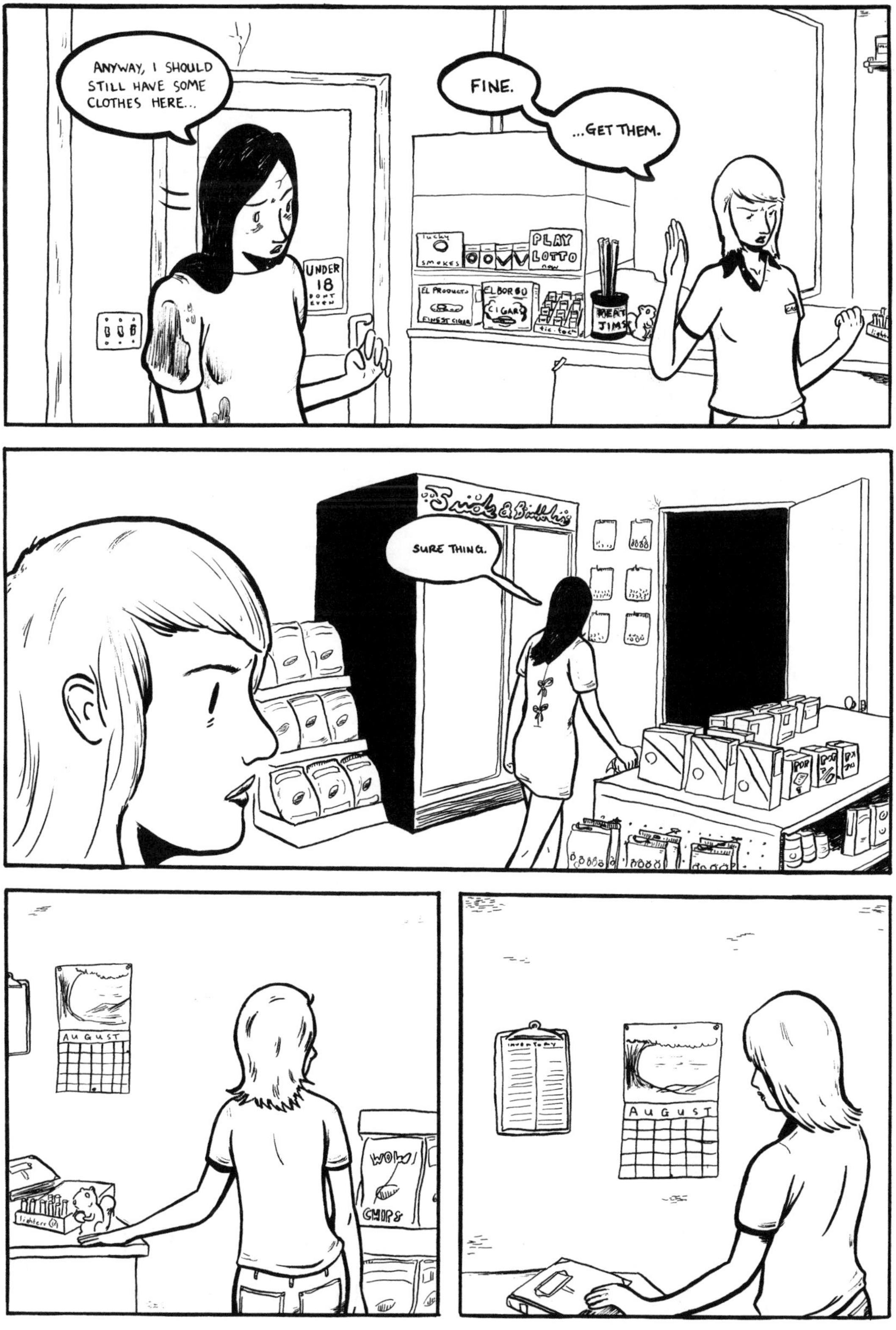
ANYWAY, I SHOULD STILL HAVE SOME CLOTHES HERE...
UNDER 18 DONT EVEN
FINE.
...GET THEM.
PLAY LOTTO now
FINEST CIGAR
MEAT JIMS
SURE THING.
AUGUST
CHIPS
AUGUST

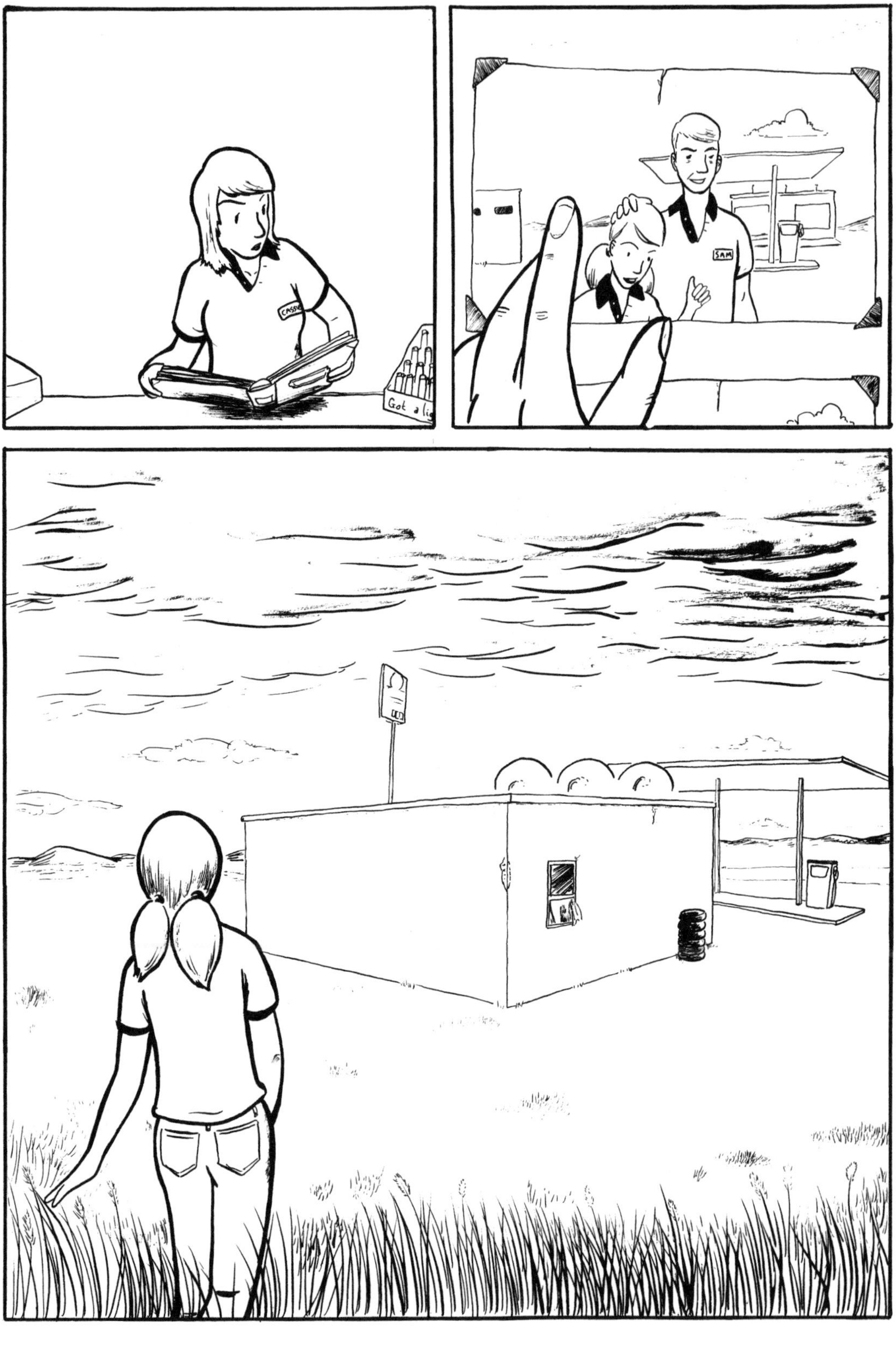
SAM

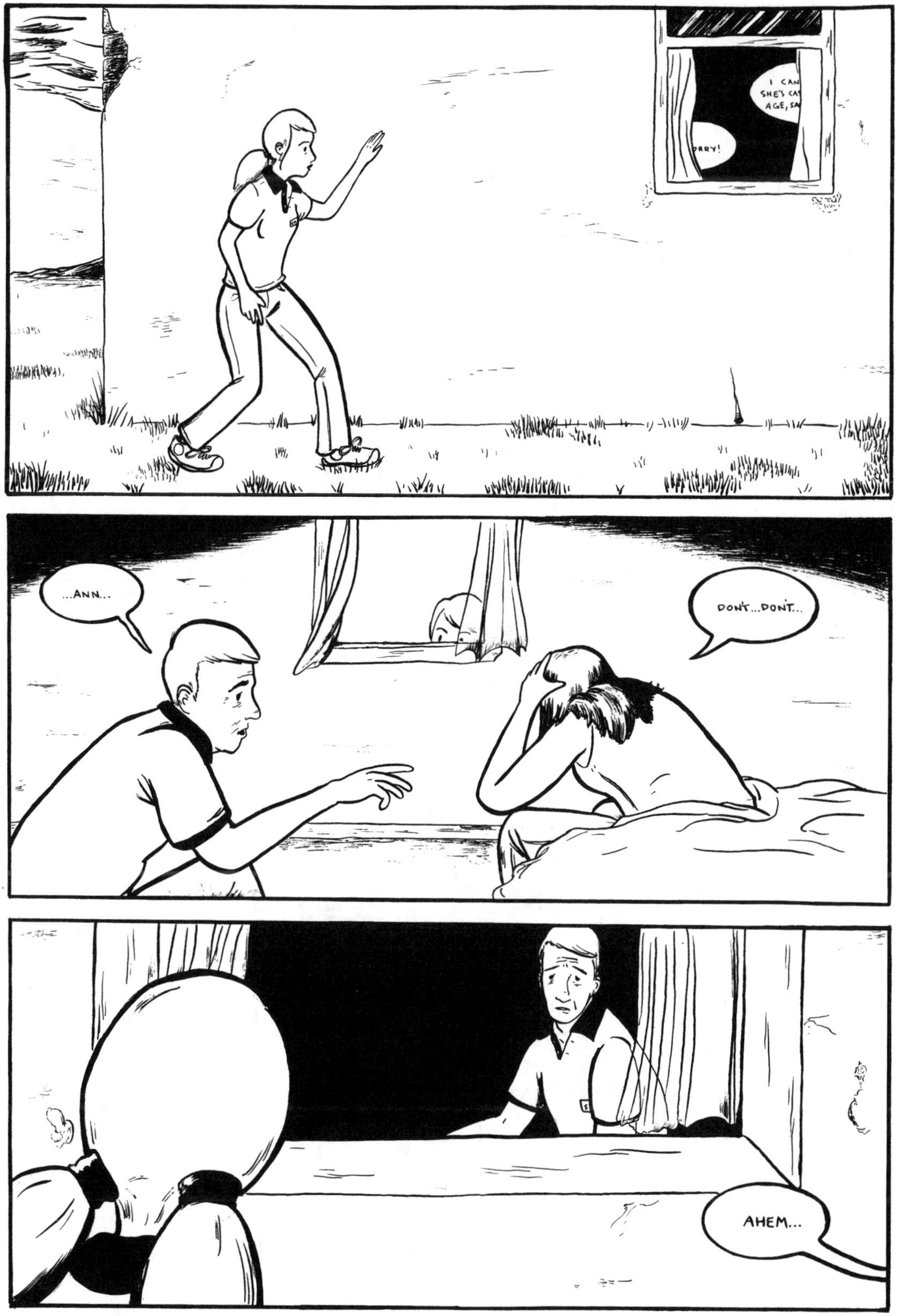
...ANN...
DON'T...DON'T...
AHEM...

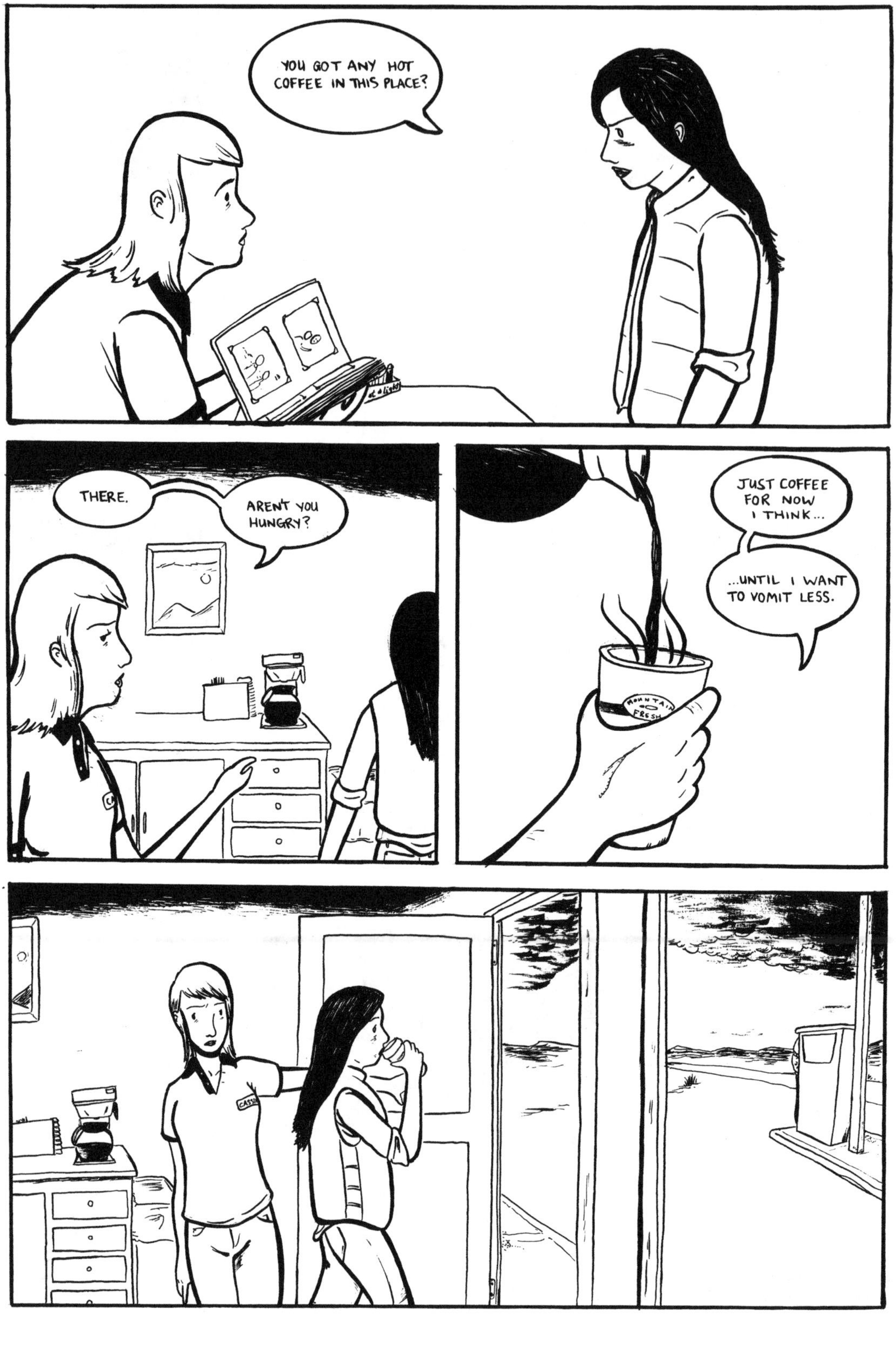
YOU GOT ANY HOT COFFEE IN THIS PLACE?
THERE.
AREN'T YOU HUNGRY?
JUST COFFEE FOR NOW I THINK...
...UNTIL I WANT TO VOMIT LESS.
MOUNTAIN FRESH
CASSI

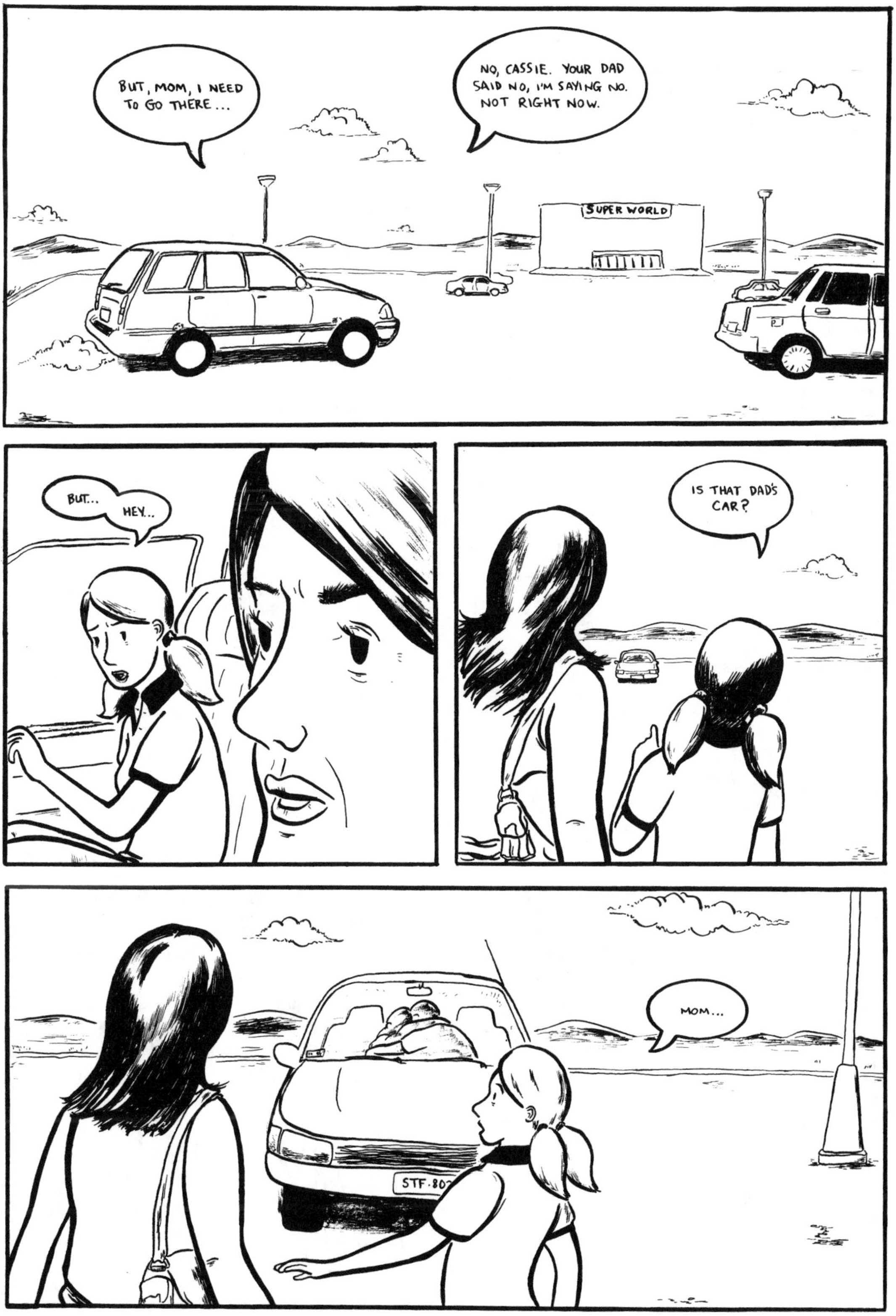
BUT, MOM, I NEED TO GO THERE...
NO, CASSIE. YOUR DAD SAID NO, I'M SAYING NO. NOT RIGHT NOW.
SUPER WORLD
BUT...
HEY...
IS THAT DAD'S CAR?
MOM...

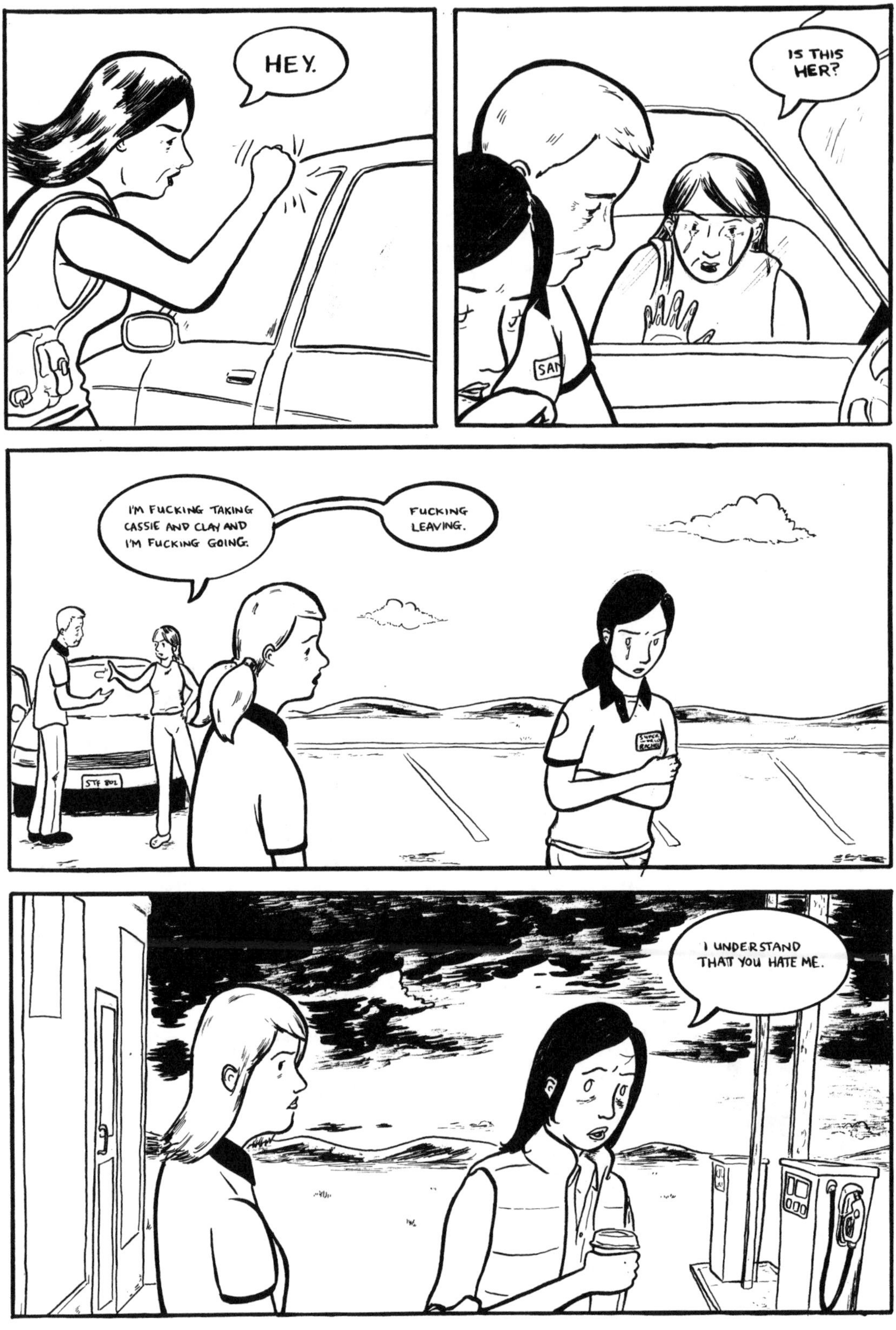
HEY.
IS THIS HER?
I'M FUCKING TAKING CASSIE AND CLAY AND I'M FUCKING GOING.
FUCKING LEAVING.
I UNDERSTAND THAT YOU HATE ME.

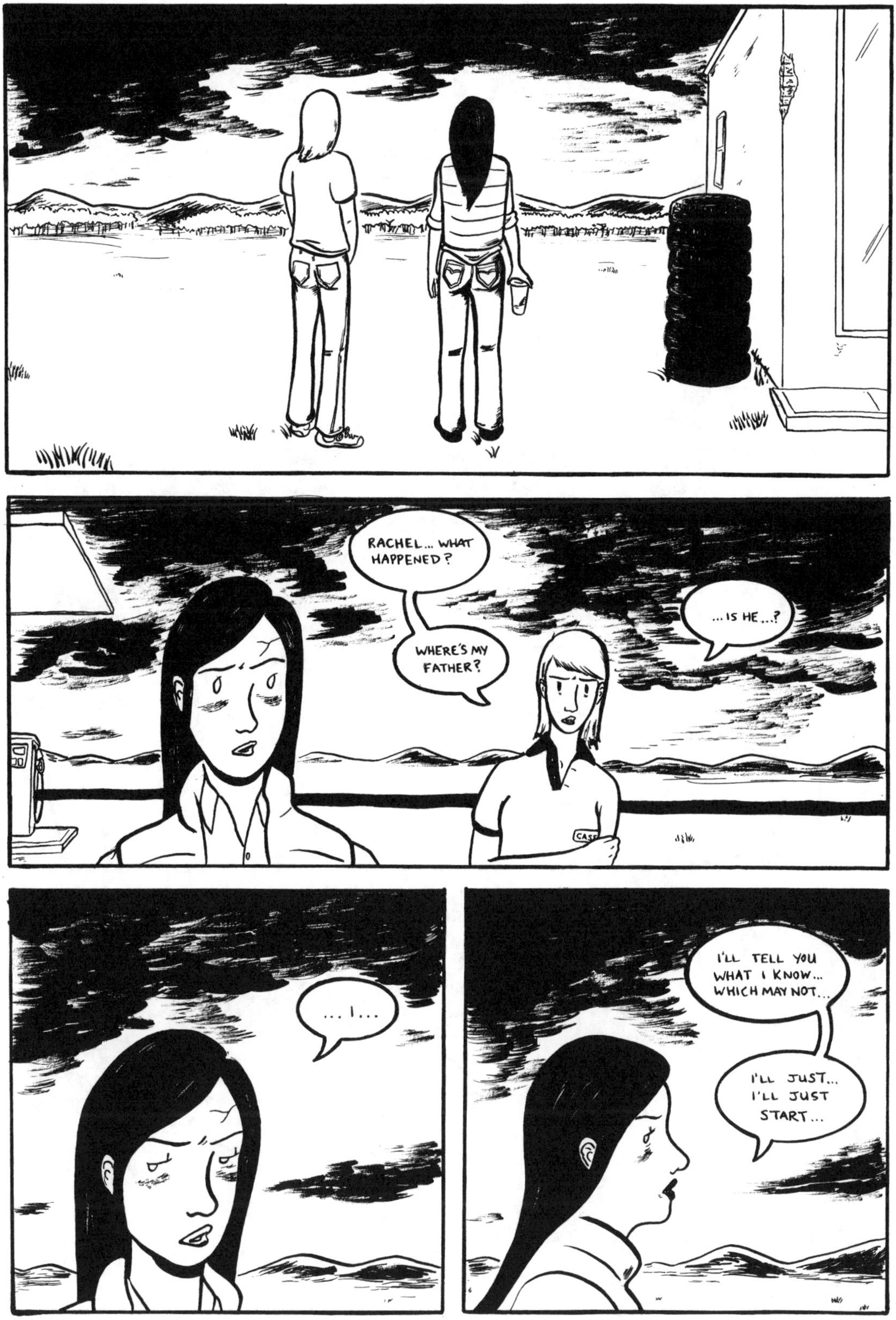
RACHEL... WHAT HAPPENED?
WHERE'S MY FATHER?
...IS HE...?
CASS
...I...
I'LL TELL YOU WHAT I KNOW... WHICH MAY NOT...
I'LL JUST... I'LL JUST START...

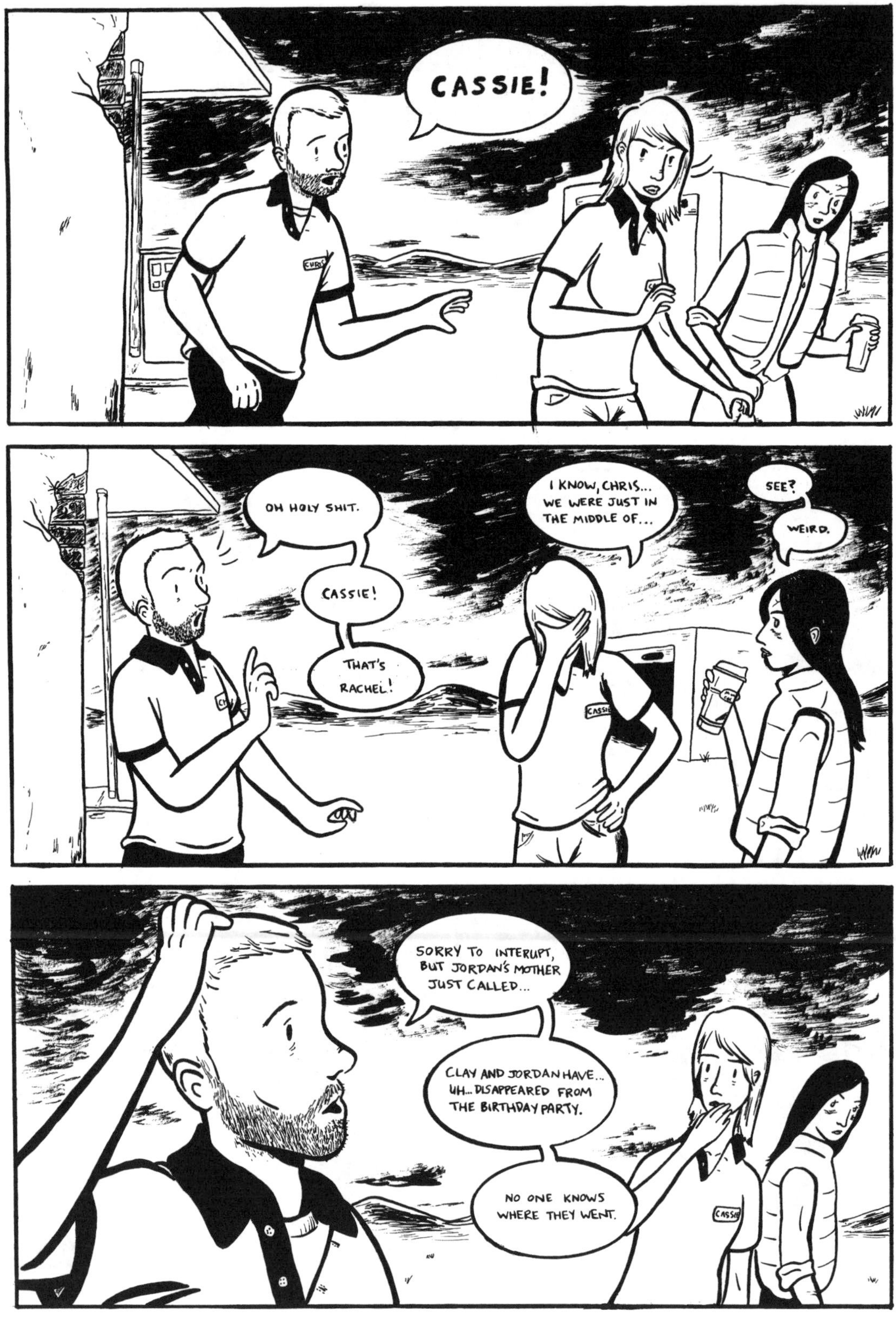
CASSIE!
OH HOLY SHIT.
CASSIE!
THAT'S RACHEL!
I KNOW, CHRIS... WE WERE JUST IN THE MIDDLE OF...
SEE?
WEIRD.
SORRY TO INTERUPT, BUT JORDAN'S MOTHER JUST CALLED...
CLAY AND JORDAN HAVE... UH... DISAPPEARED FROM THE BIRTHDAY PARTY.
NO ONE KNOWS WHERE THEY WENT.

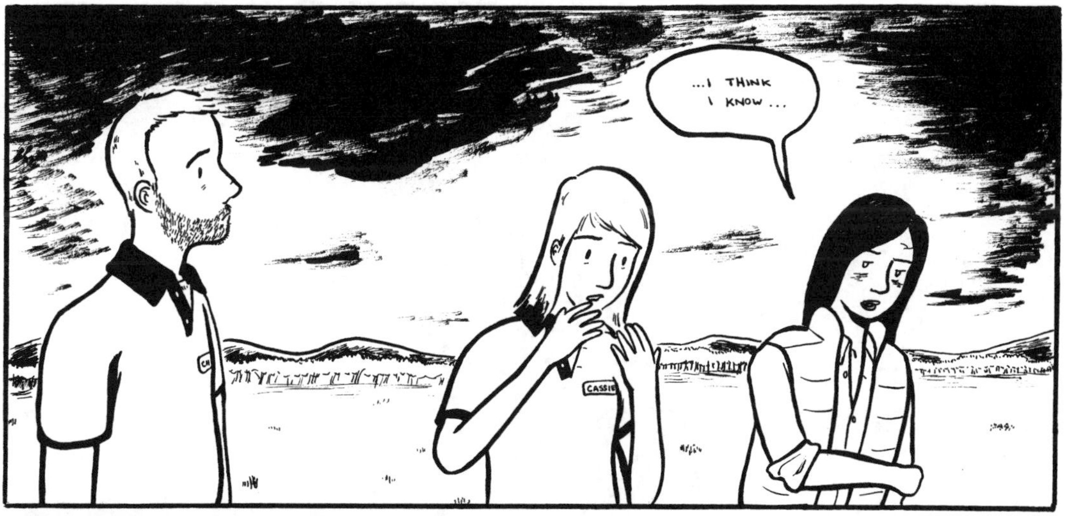
CASSIE
...I THINK I KNOW...

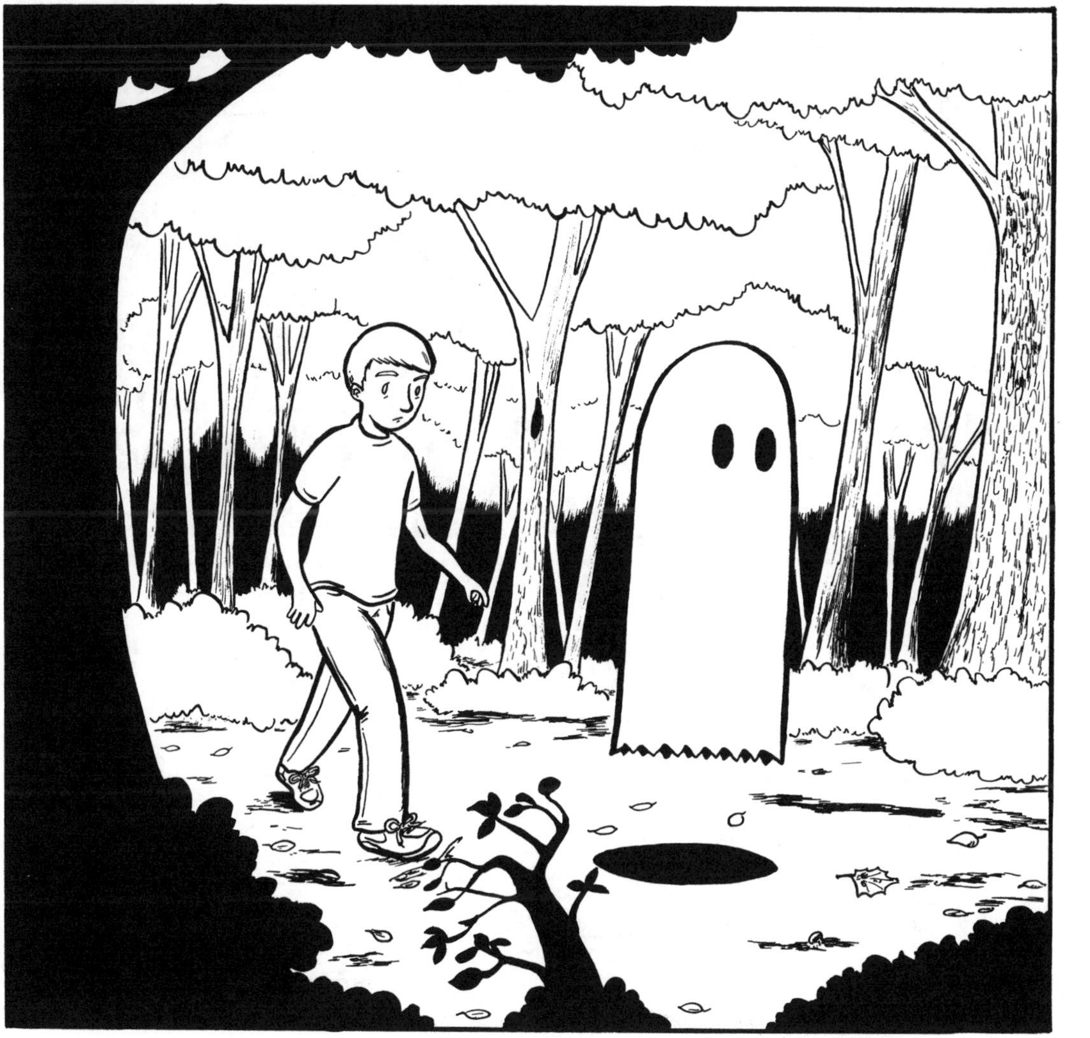

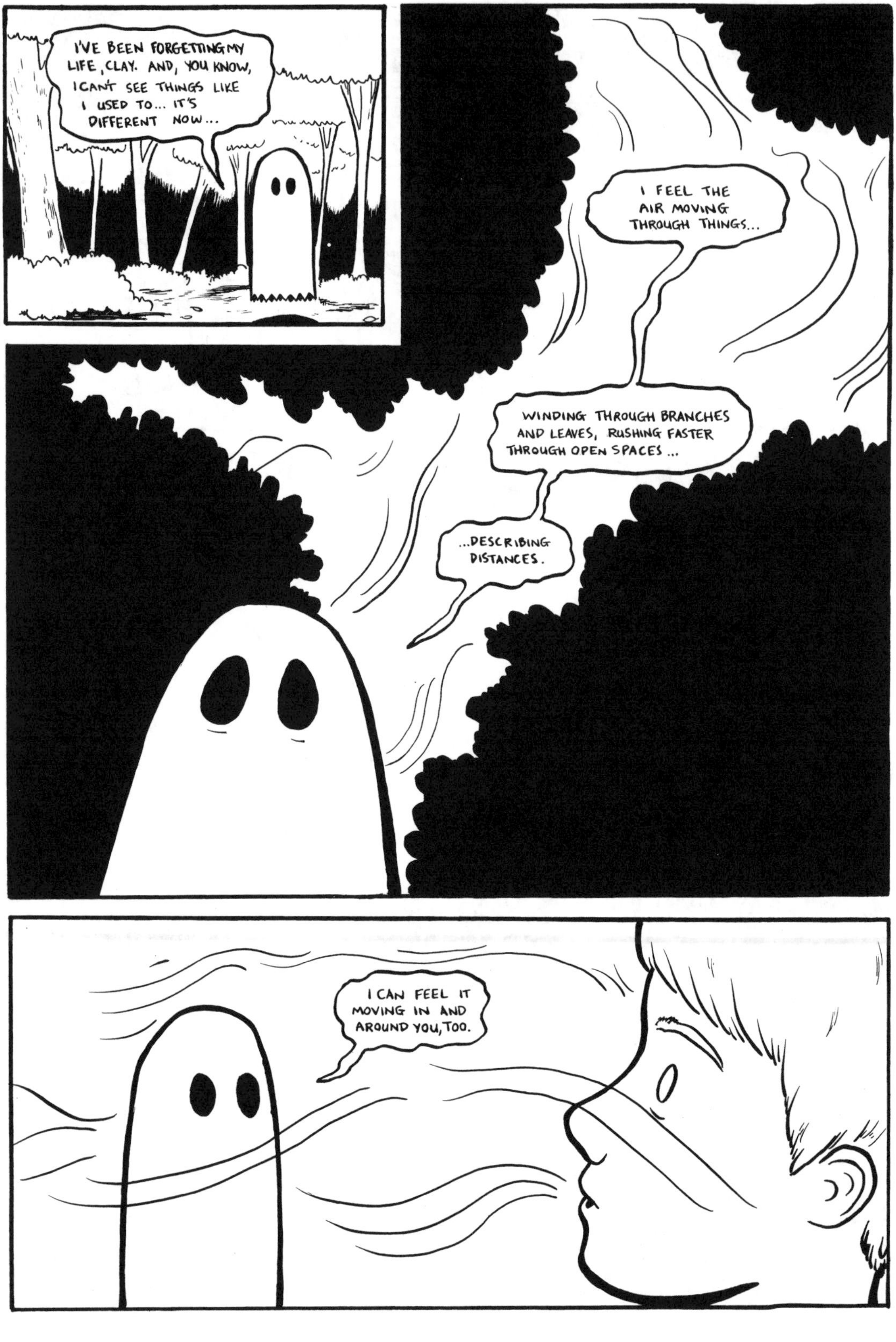
I'VE BEEN FORGETTING MY LIFE, CLAY. AND, YOU KNOW, I CAN'T SEE THINGS LIKE I USED TO... IT'S DIFFERENT NOW...
I FEEL THE AIR MOVING THROUGH THINGS...
WINDING THROUGH BRANCHES AND LEAVES, RUSHING FASTER THROUGH OPEN SPACES...
...DESCRIBING DISTANCES.
I CAN FEEL IT MOVING IN AND AROUND YOU, TOO.

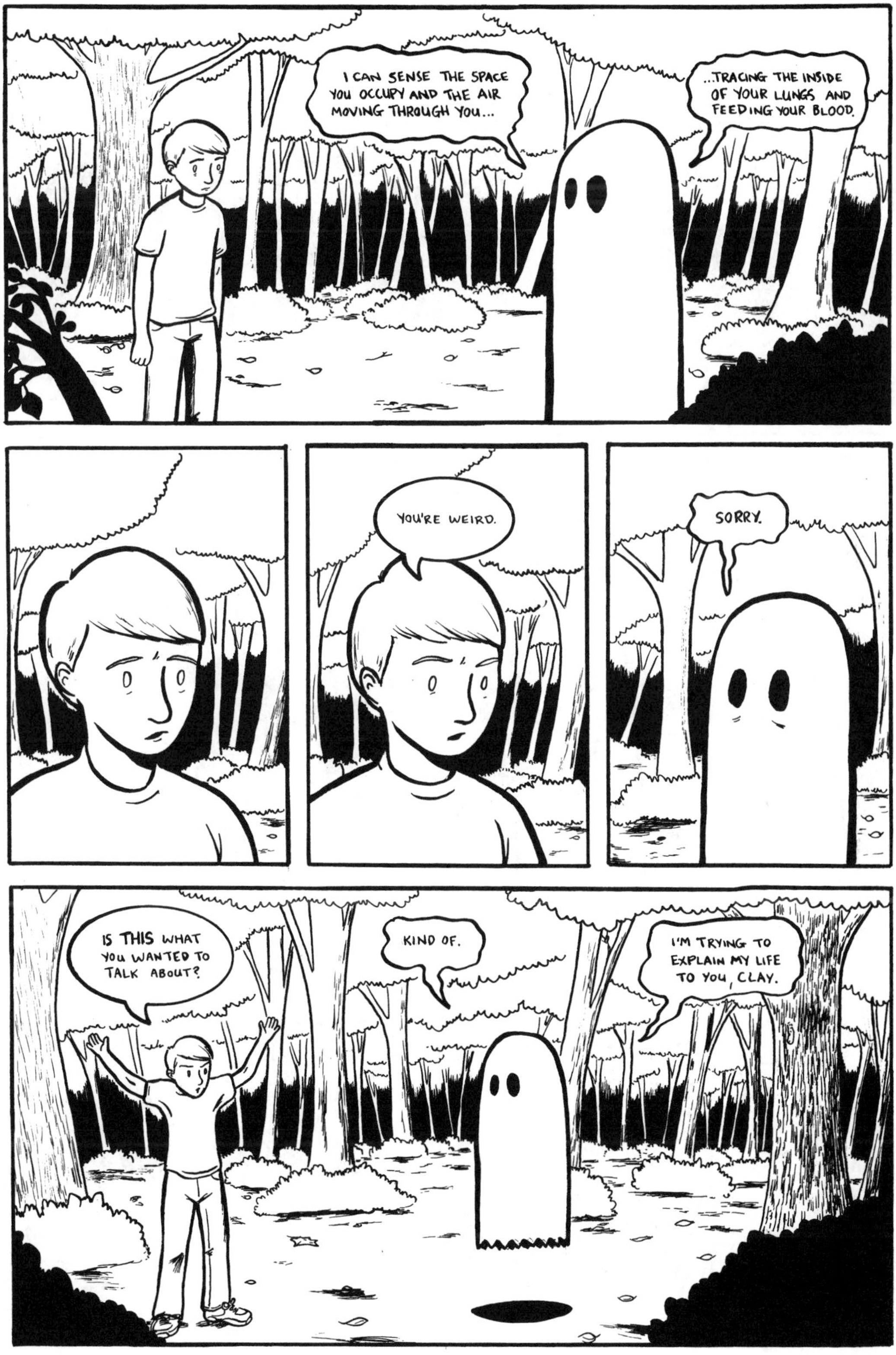

I CAN SENSE THE SPACE YOU OCCUPY AND THE AIR MOVING THROUGH YOU...
...TRACING THE INSIDE OF YOUR LUNGS AND FEEDING YOUR BLOOD.
YOU'RE WEIRD.
SORRY.
IS THIS WHAT YOU WANTED TO TALK ABOUT?
KIND OF.
I'M TRYING TO EXPLAIN MY LIFE TO YOU, CLAY.

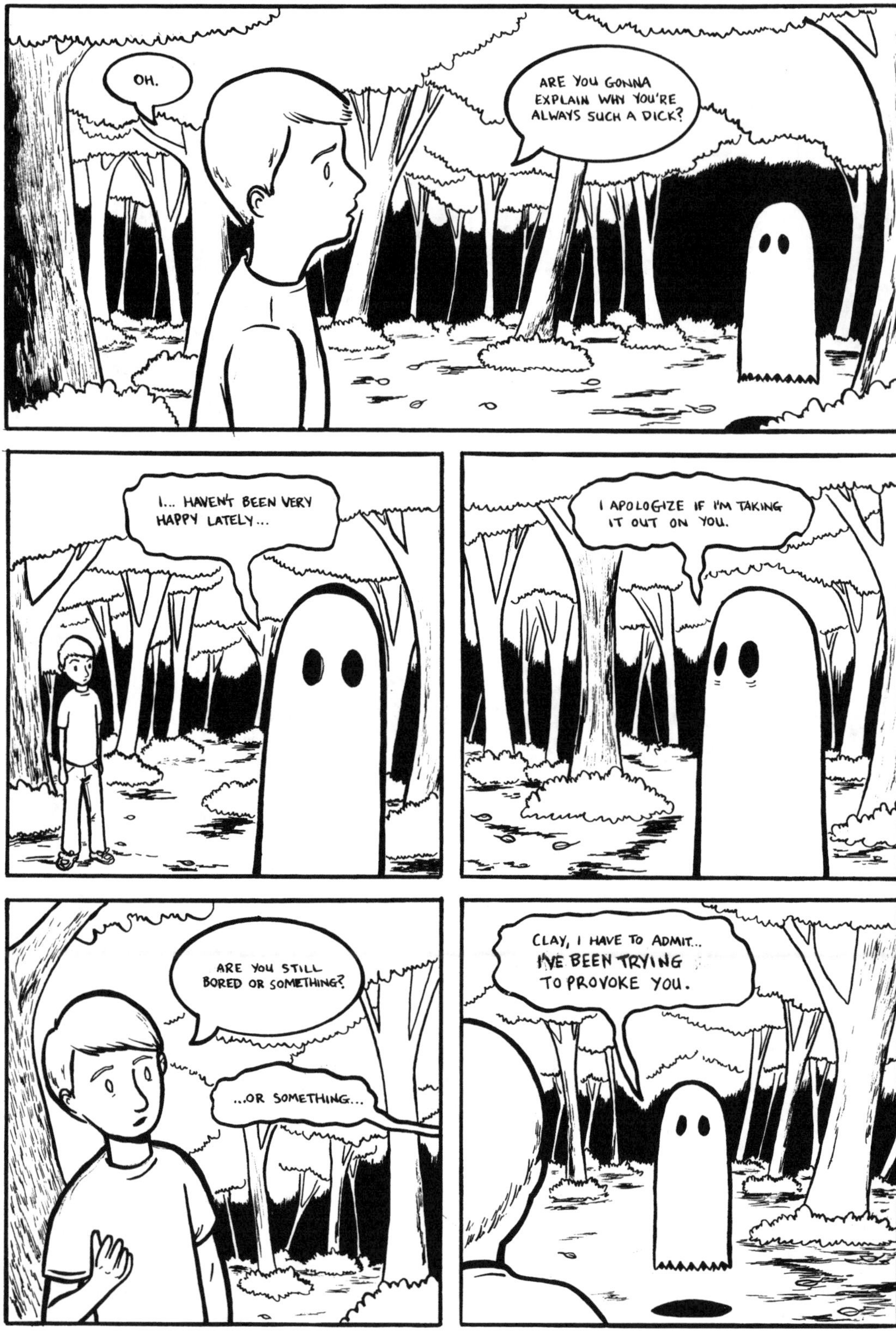
OH.
ARE YOU GONNA EXPLAIN WHY YOU'RE ALWAYS SUCH A DICK?
I... HAVEN'T BEEN VERY HAPPY LATELY...
I APOLOGIZE IF I'M TAKING IT OUT ON YOU.
ARE YOU STILL BORED OR SOMETHING?
...OR SOMETHING...
CLAY, I HAVE TO ADMIT... I'VE BEEN TRYING TO PROVOKE YOU.

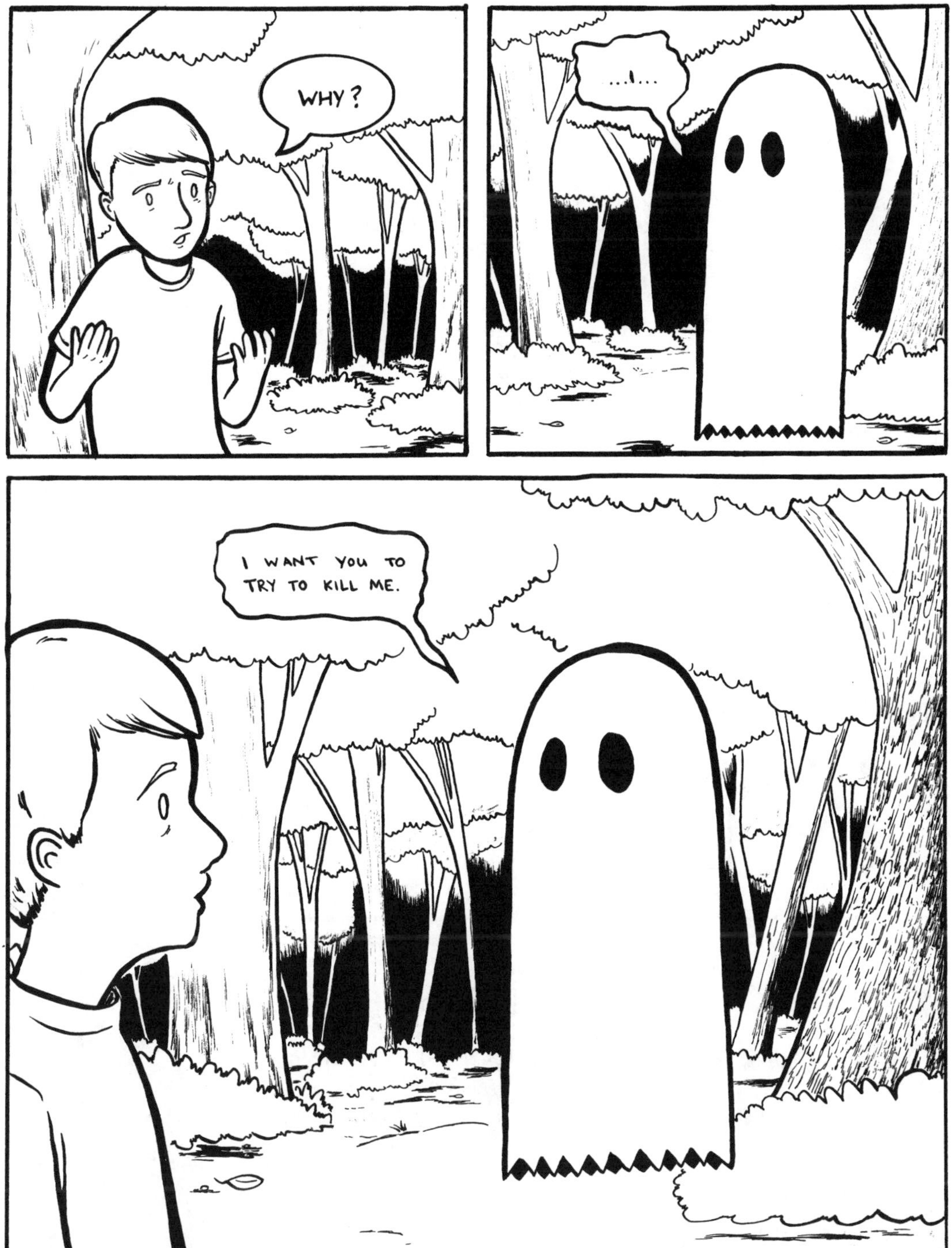
WHY?
...I...
I WANT YOU TO TRY TO KILL ME.

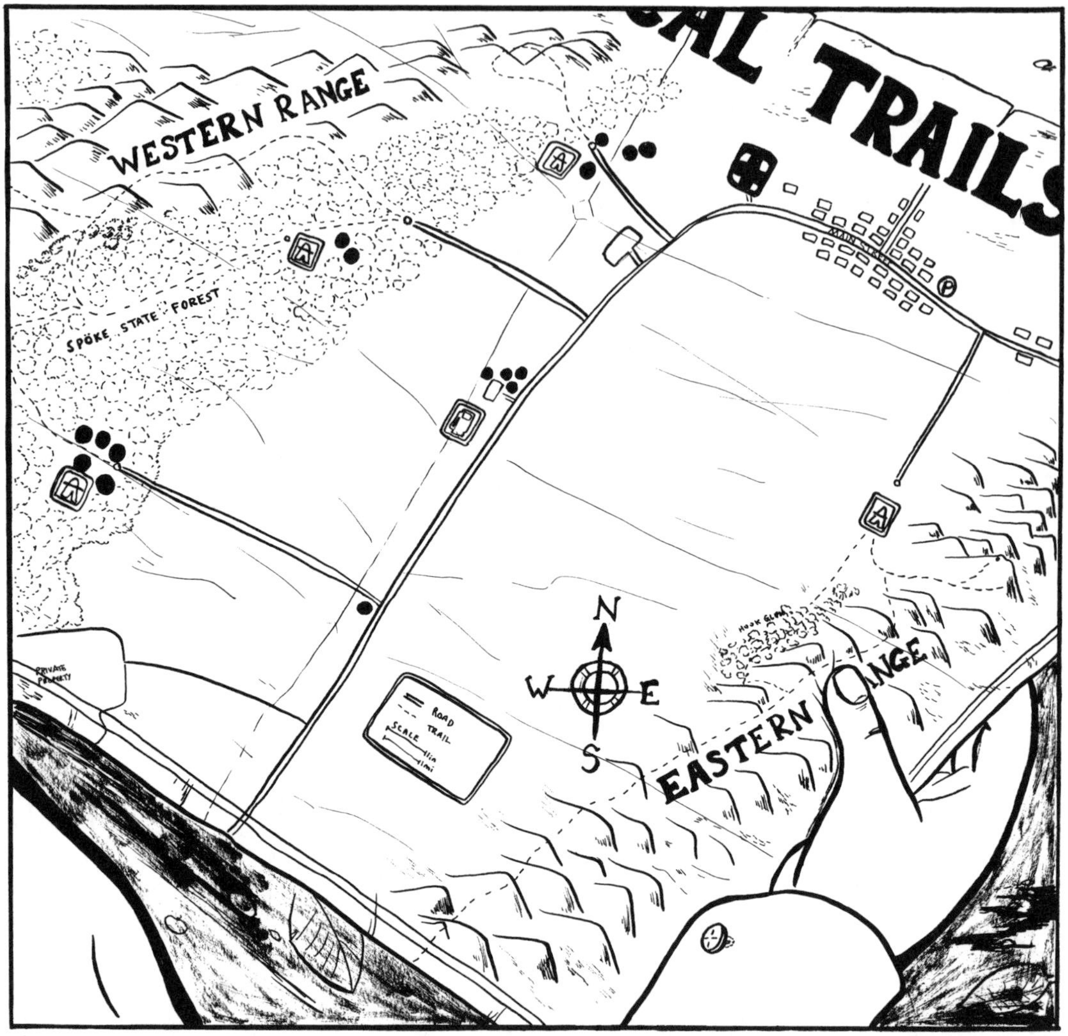
CAL TRAILS
WESTERN RANGE
SPÖKE STATE FOREST
PRIVATE PROPERTY
ROAD
TRAIL
SCALE
N
W
E
S
EASTERN
NGE

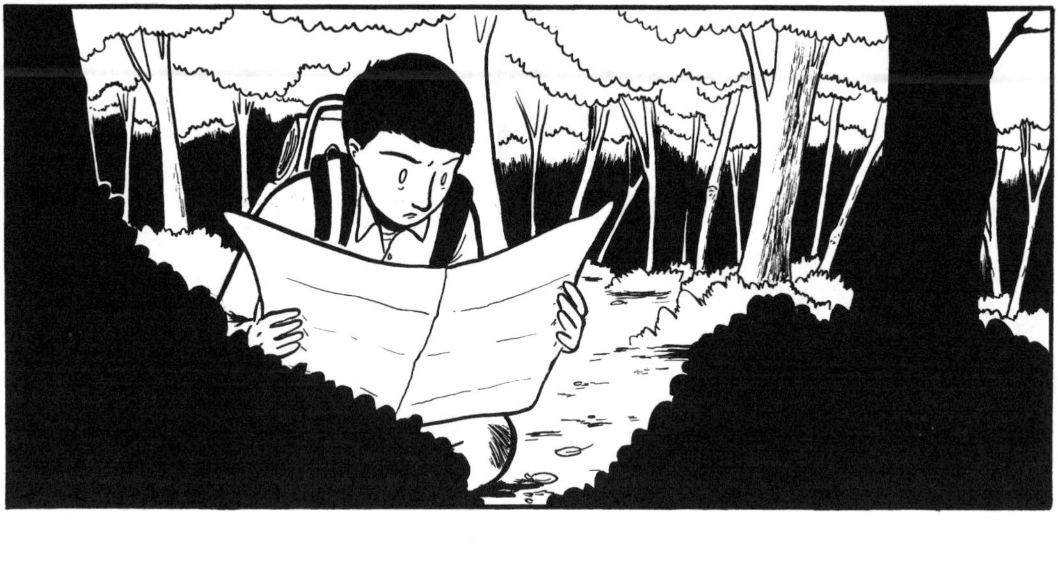

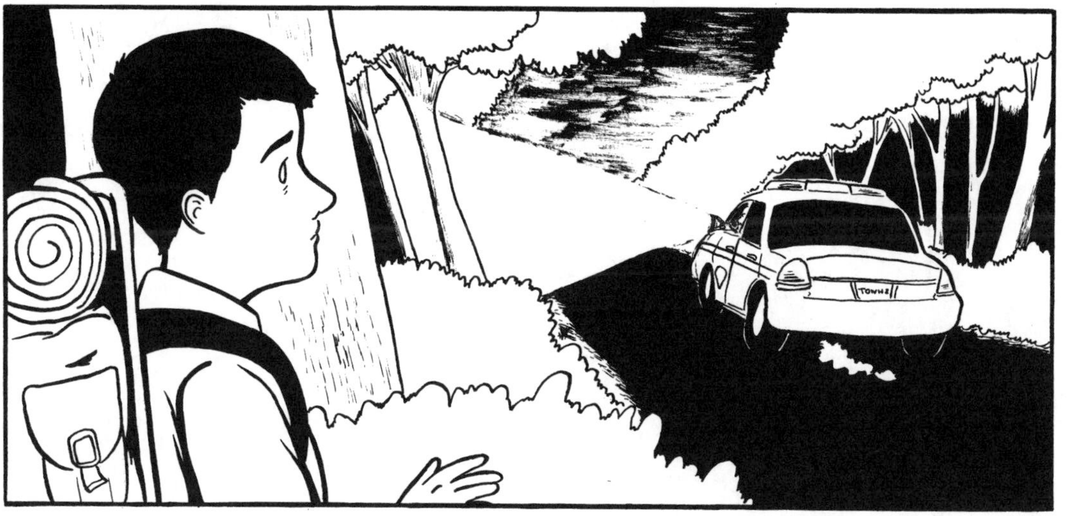
TOWNE

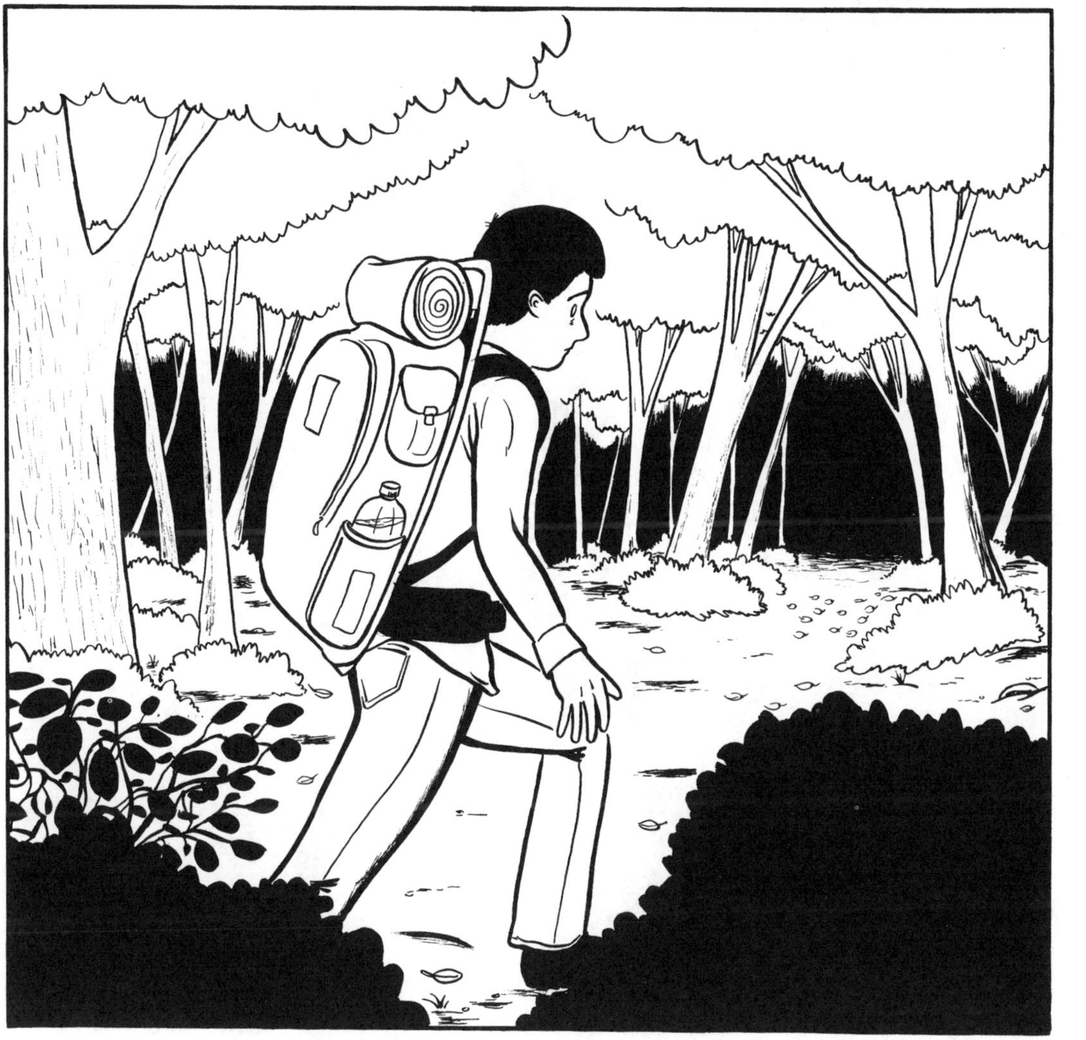

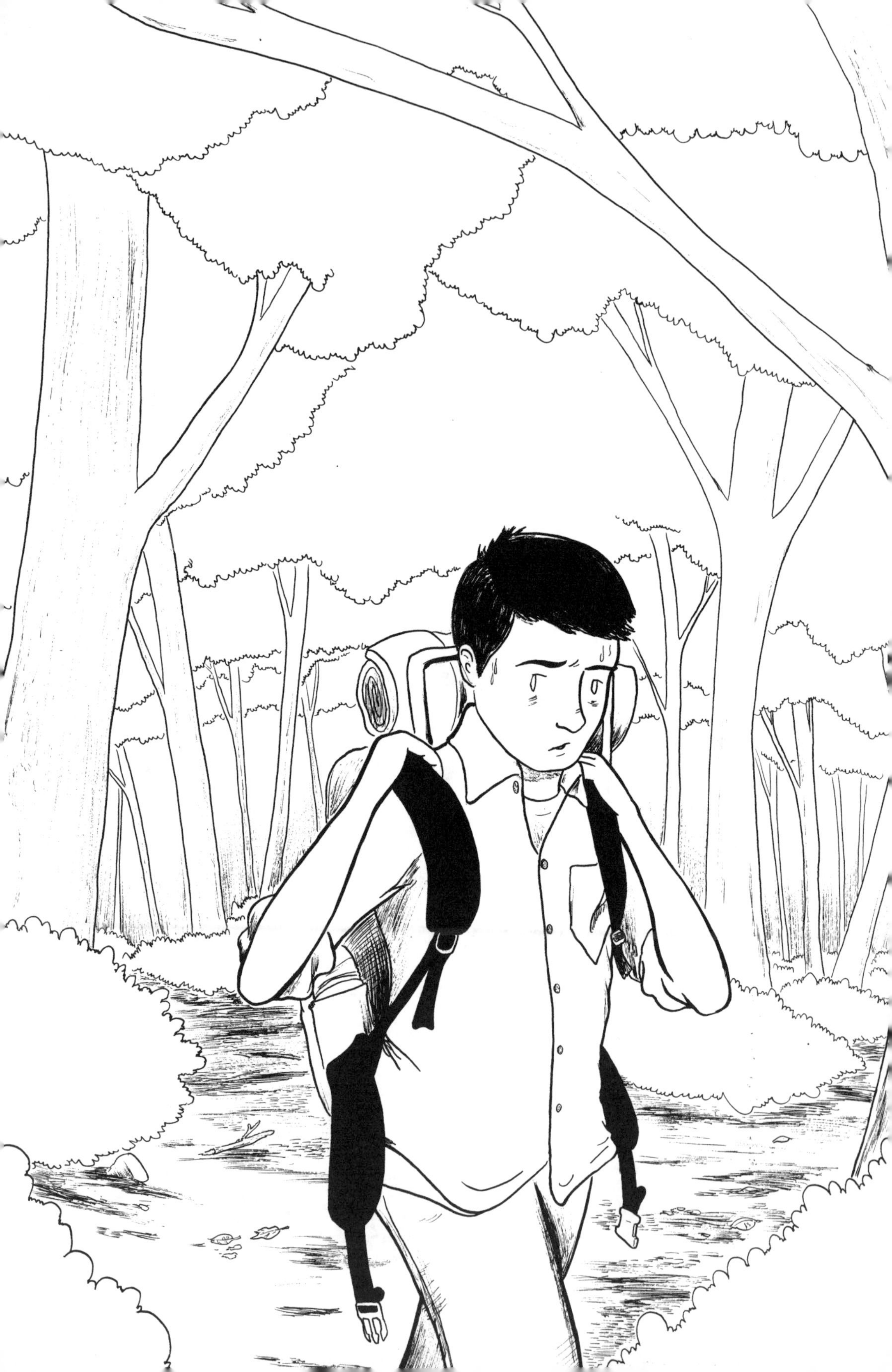

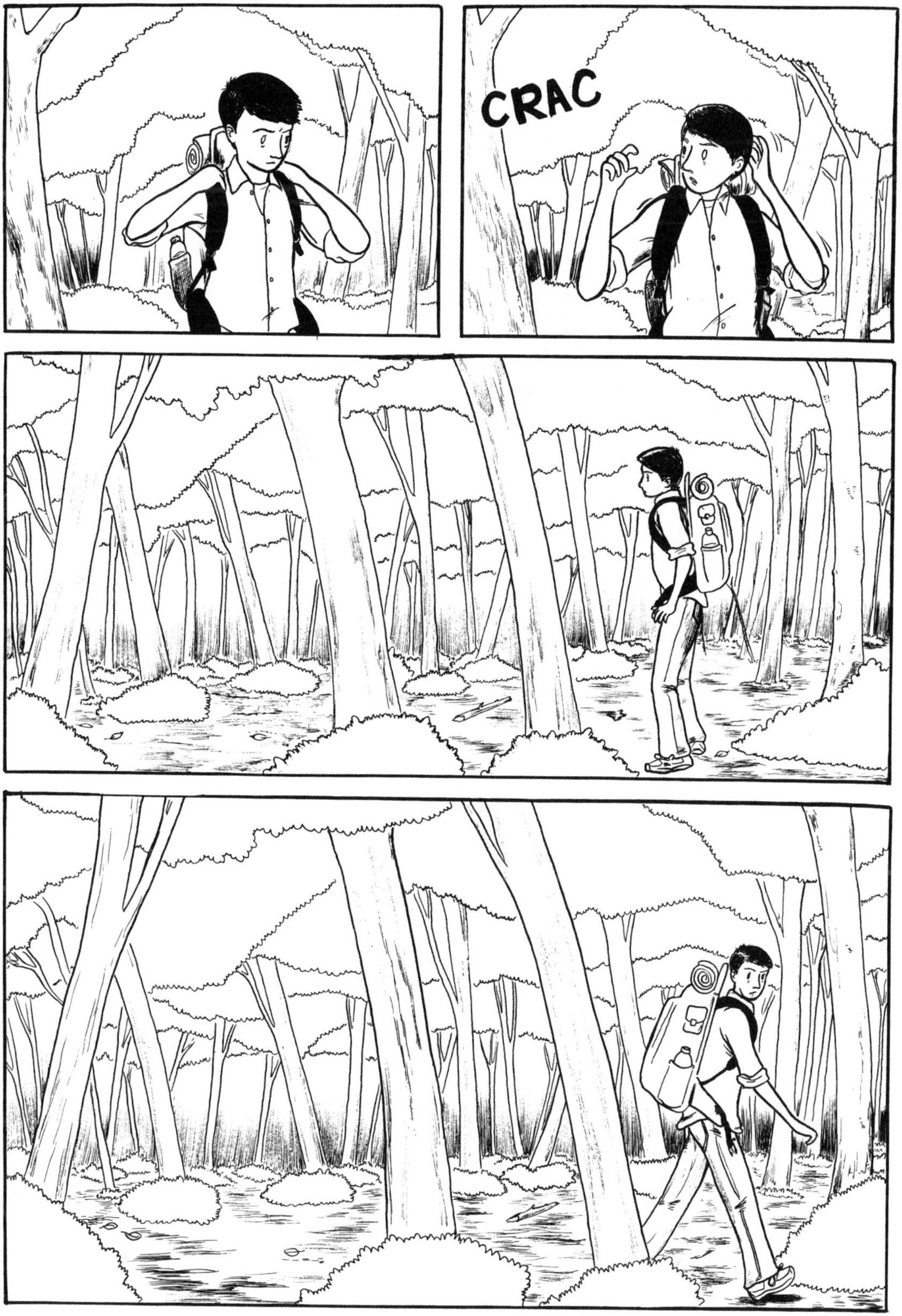
CRAC

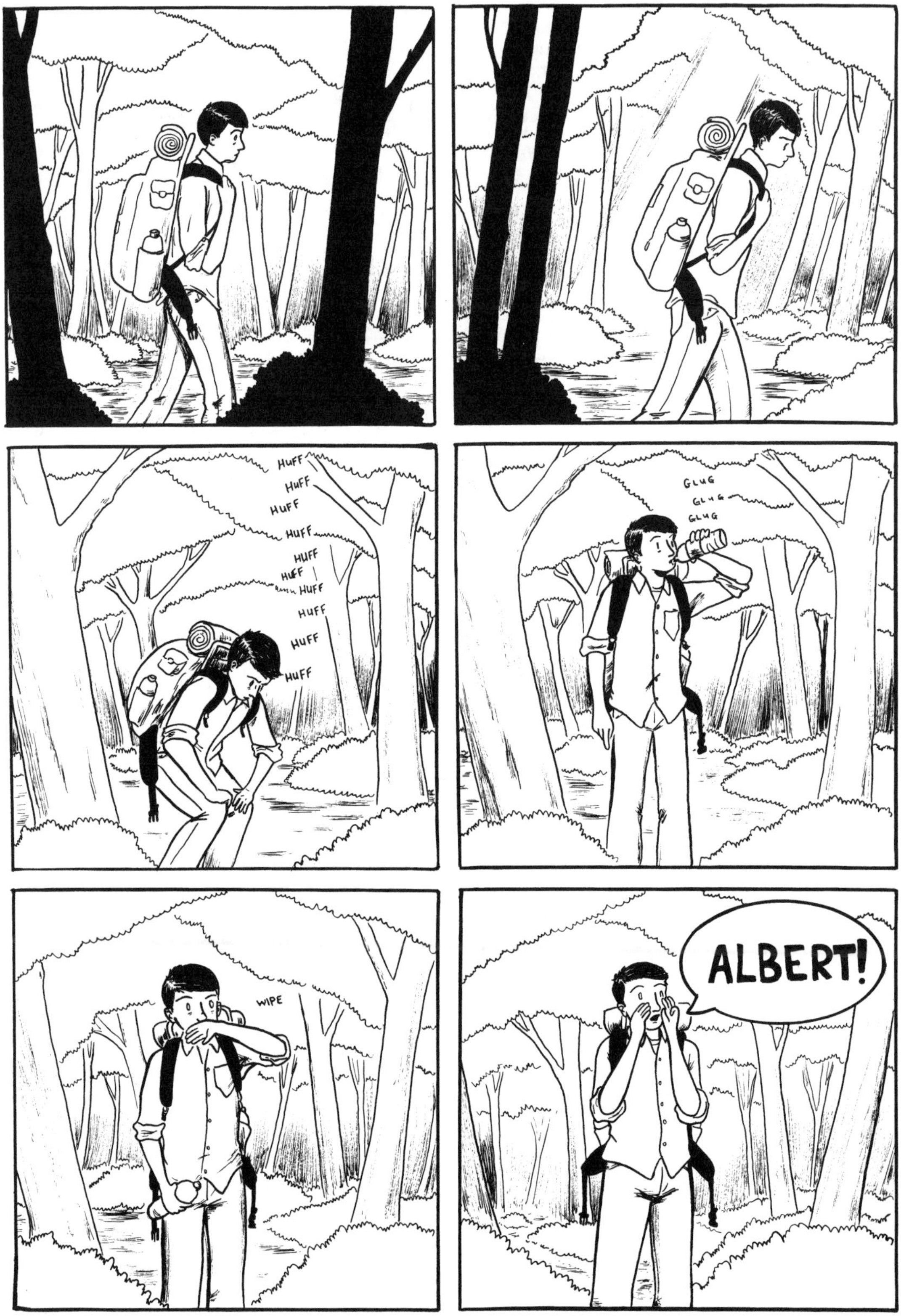
HUFF
HUFF
HUFF
HUFF
HUFF
HUFF
HUFF
HUFF
HUFF
HUFF
GLUG
GLUG
GLUG
WIPE
ALBERT!

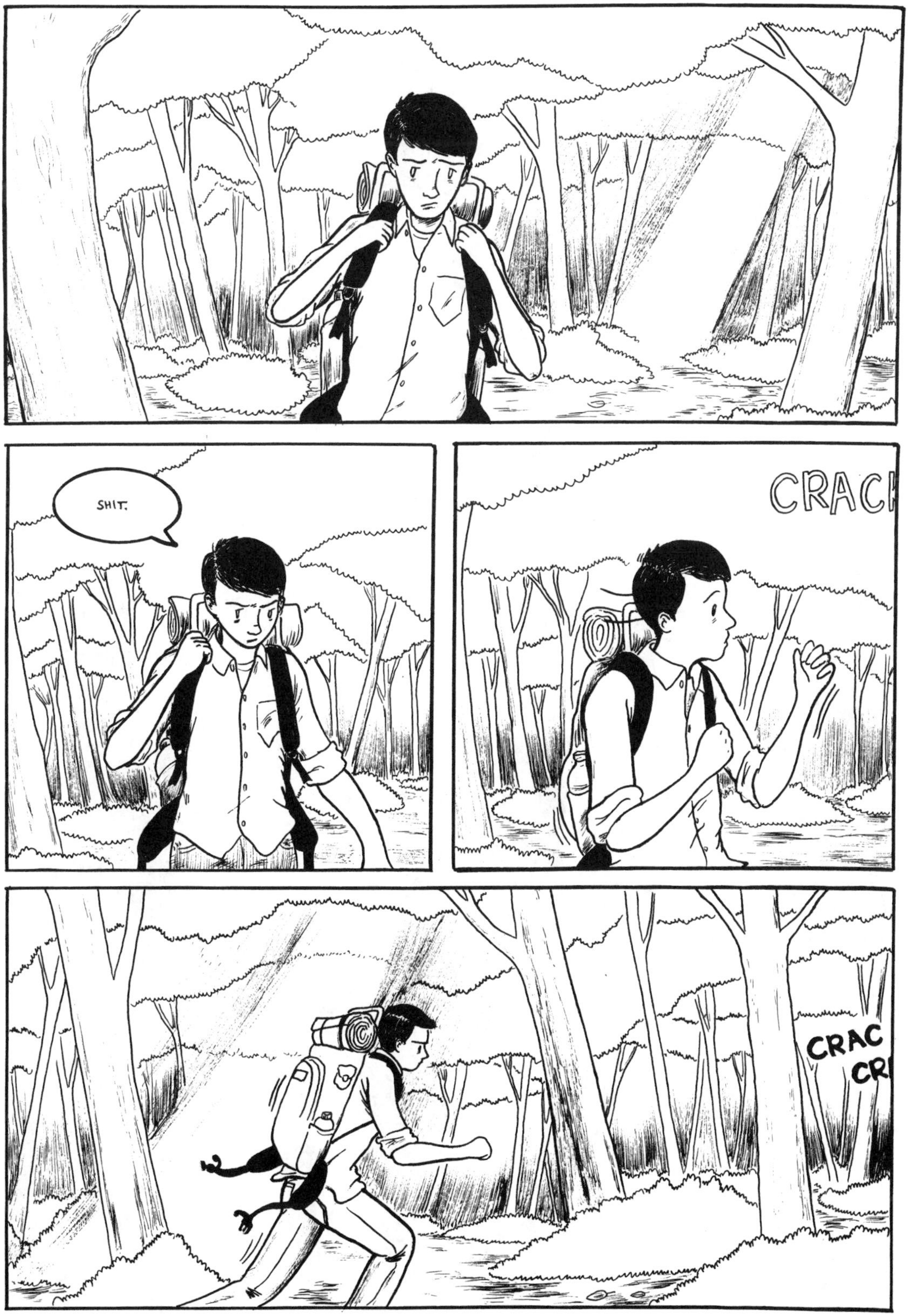
SHIT.
CRACK
CRAC
CR

HUFF
HUFF
HUFF
CRA
CR

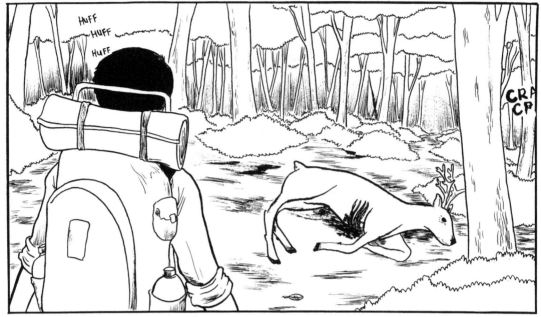

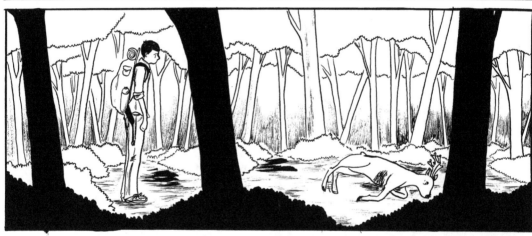

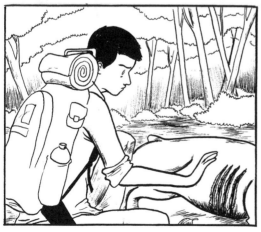

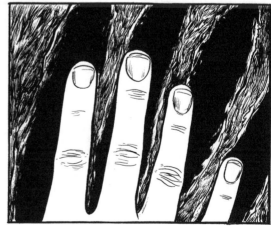

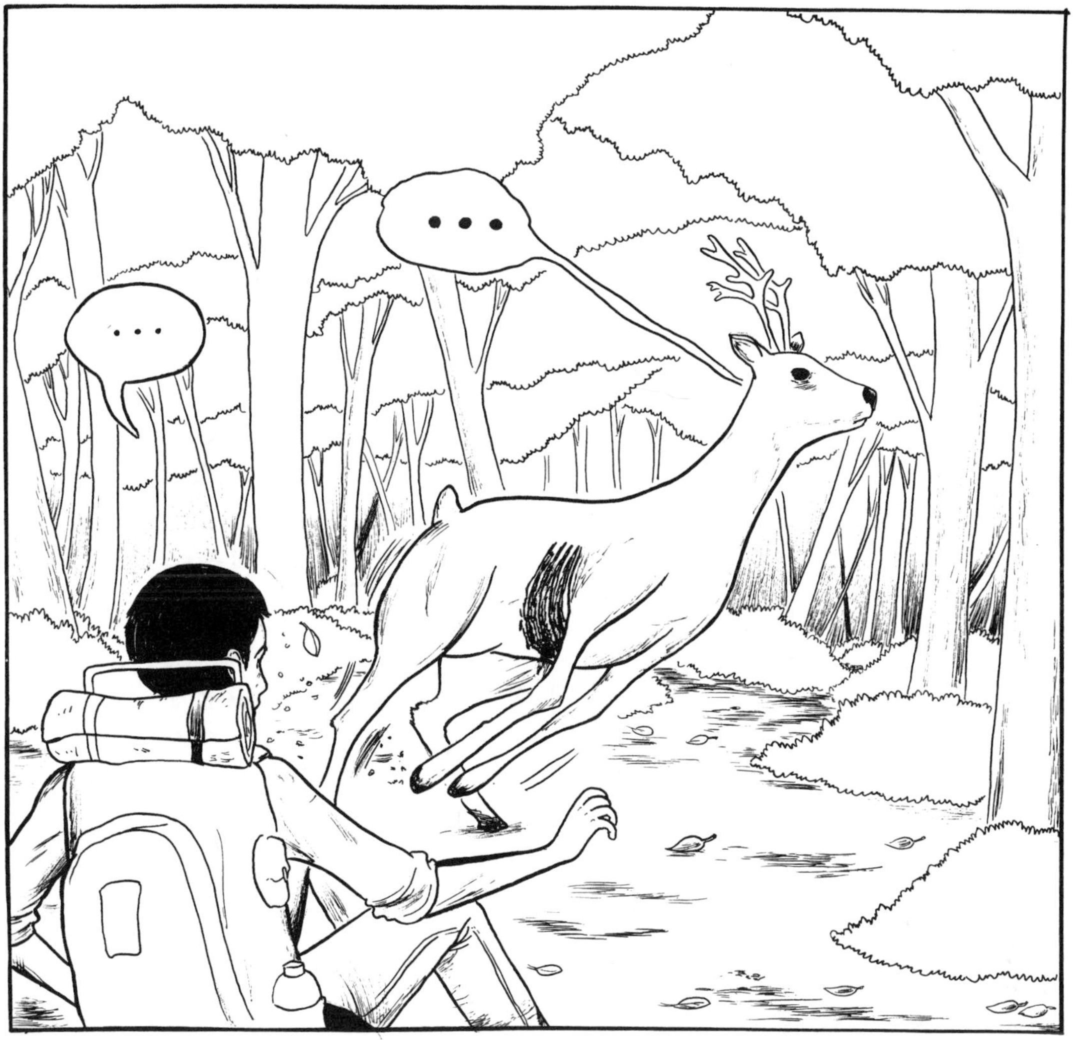
...
...

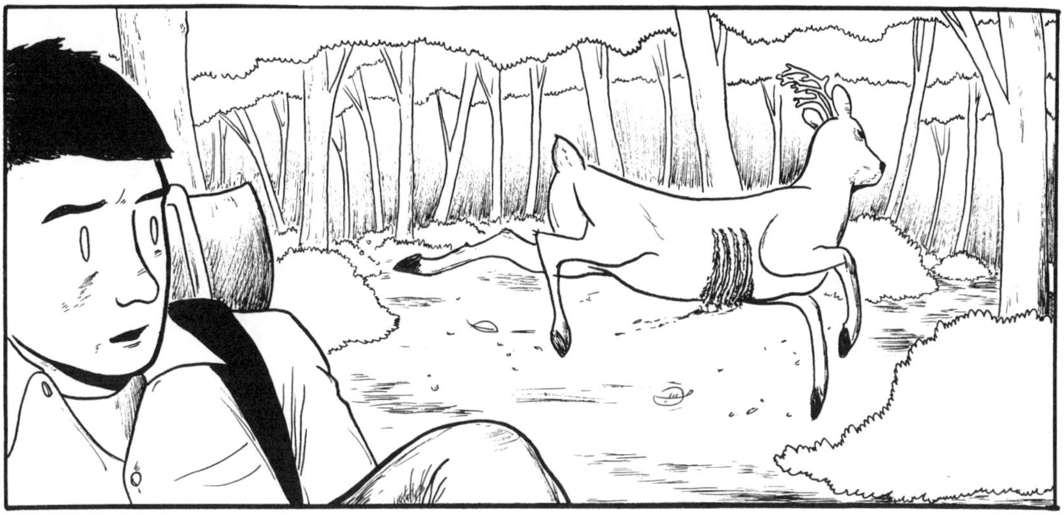

RING
RING
...HELLO?
SAM COLE?
...YES...
...MISSING?
PULL

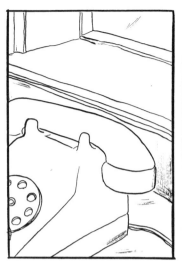

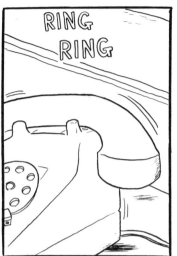

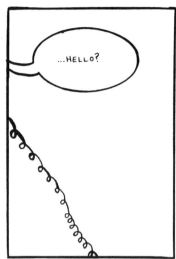

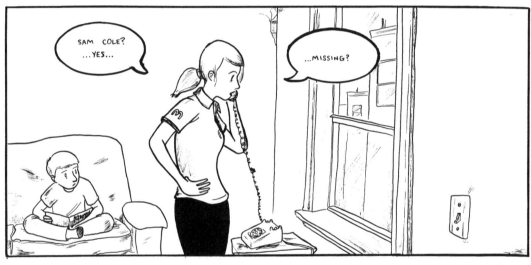

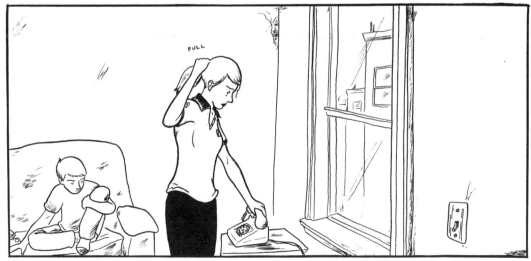

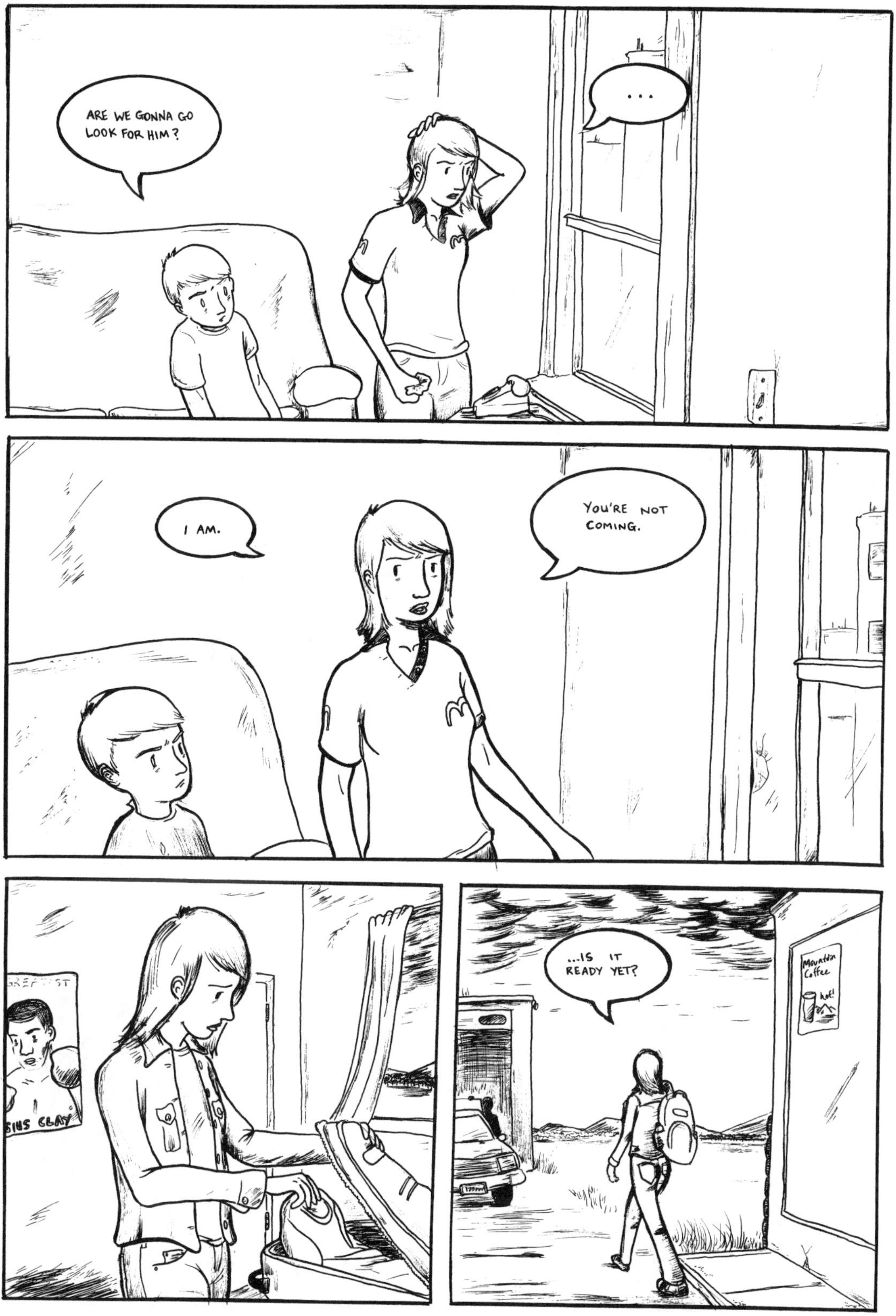

ARE WE GONNA GO LOOK FOR HIM?
...
I AM.
YOU'RE NOT COMING.
GREATEST
SIUS CLAY
...IS IT READY YET?
Mountain Coffee
hot!

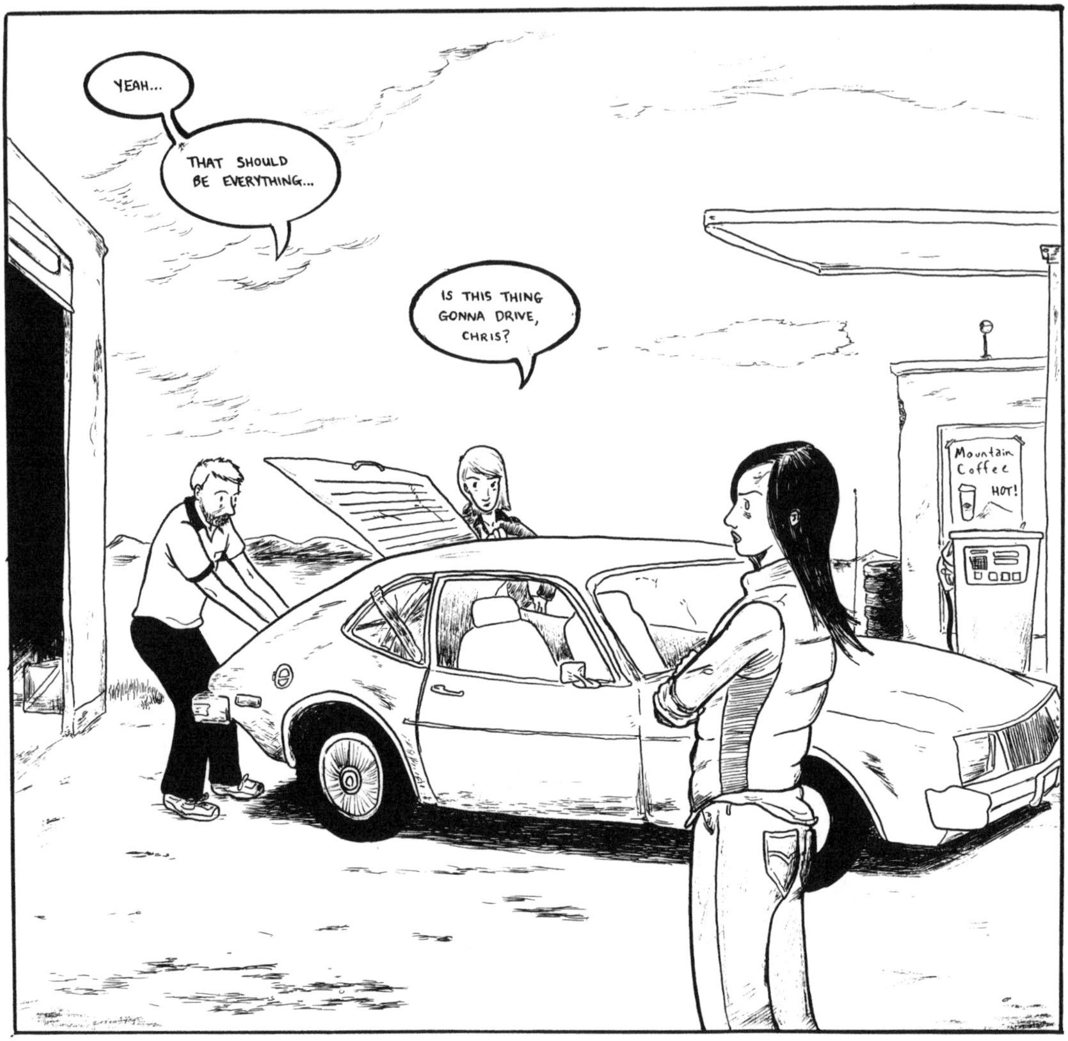
YEAH...
THAT SHOULD BE EVERYTHING...
IS THIS THING GONNA DRIVE, CHRIS?
Mountain Coffee HOT!

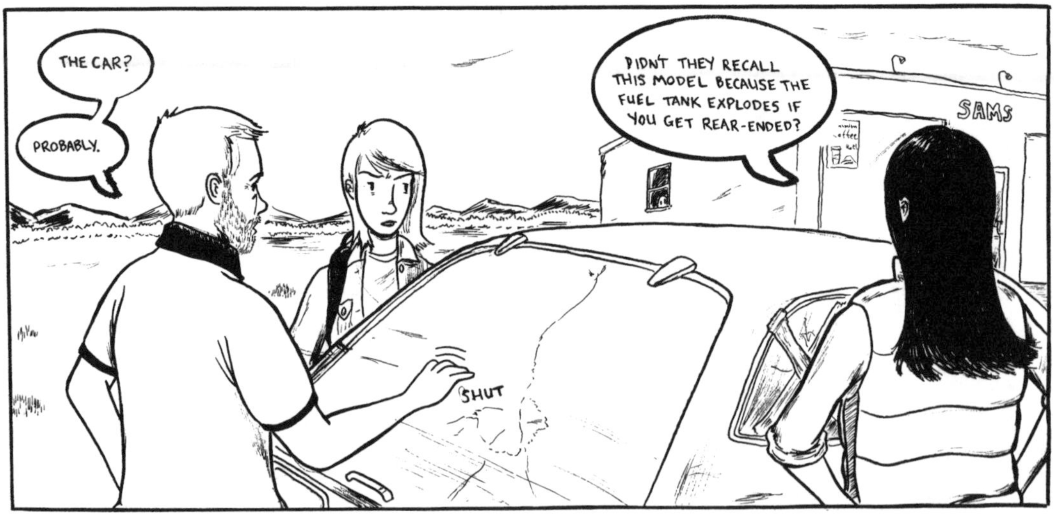
THE CAR?
PROBABLY.
DIDN'T THEY RECALL THIS MODEL BECAUSE THE FUEL TANK EXPLODES IF YOU GET REAR-ENDED?
SAMS
SHUT

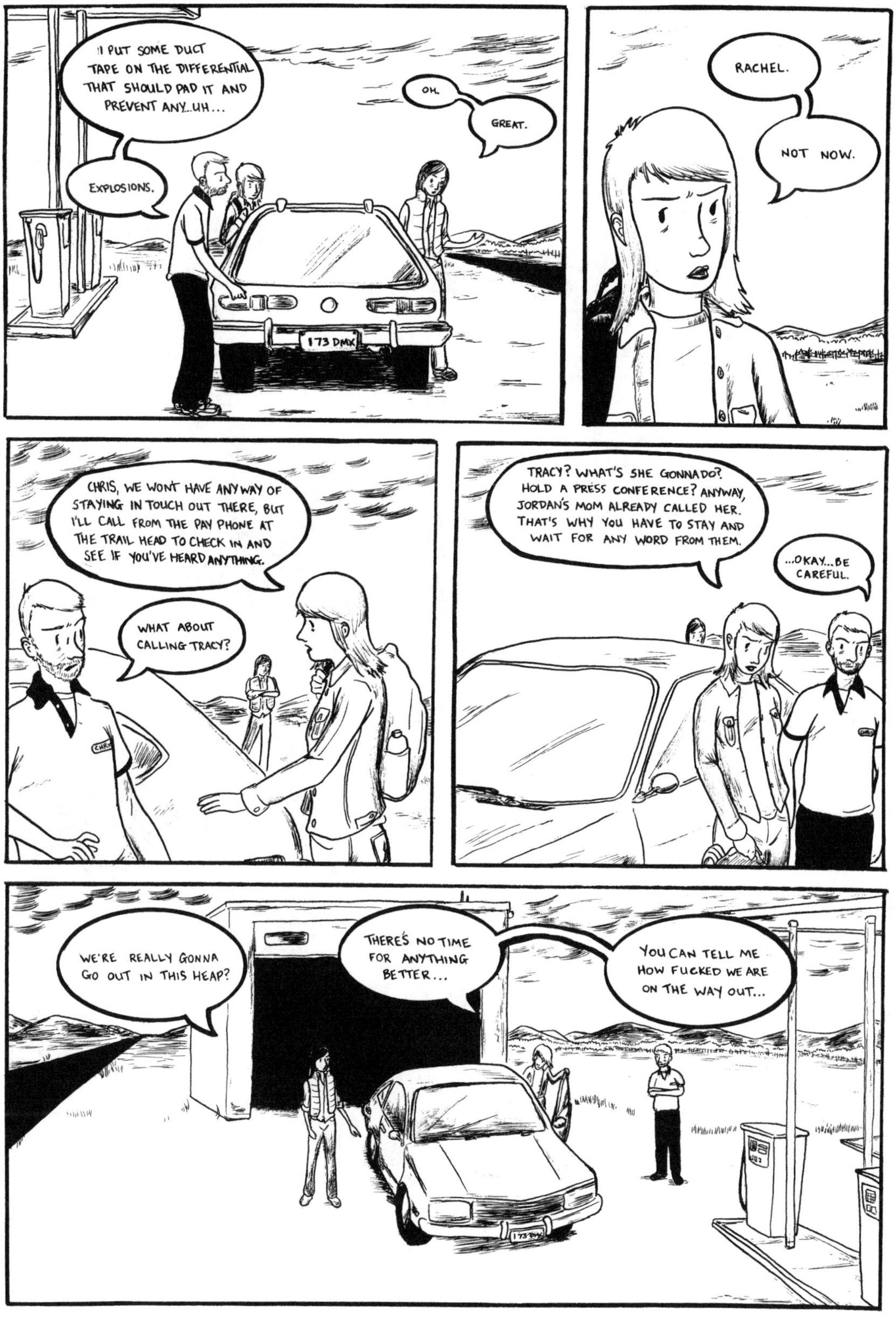

I PUT SOME DUCT TAPE ON THE DIFFERENTIAL THAT SHOULD PAD IT AND PREVENT ANY...UH...
EXPLOSIONS.
OH.
GREAT.
RACHEL.
NOT NOW.
CHRIS, WE WON'T HAVE ANY WAY OF STAYING IN TOUCH OUT THERE, BUT I'LL CALL FROM THE PAY PHONE AT THE TRAIL HEAD TO CHECK IN AND SEE IF YOU'VE HEARD ANYTHING.
WHAT ABOUT CALLING TRACY?
TRACY? WHAT'S SHE GONNA DO? HOLD A PRESS CONFERENCE? ANYWAY, JORDAN'S MOM ALREADY CALLED HER. THAT'S WHY YOU HAVE TO STAY AND WAIT FOR ANY WORD FROM THEM.
...OKAY...BE CAREFUL.
WE'RE REALLY GONNA GO OUT IN THIS HEAP?
THERE'S NO TIME FOR ANYTHING BETTER...
YOU CAN TELL ME HOW FUCKED WE ARE ON THE WAY OUT...

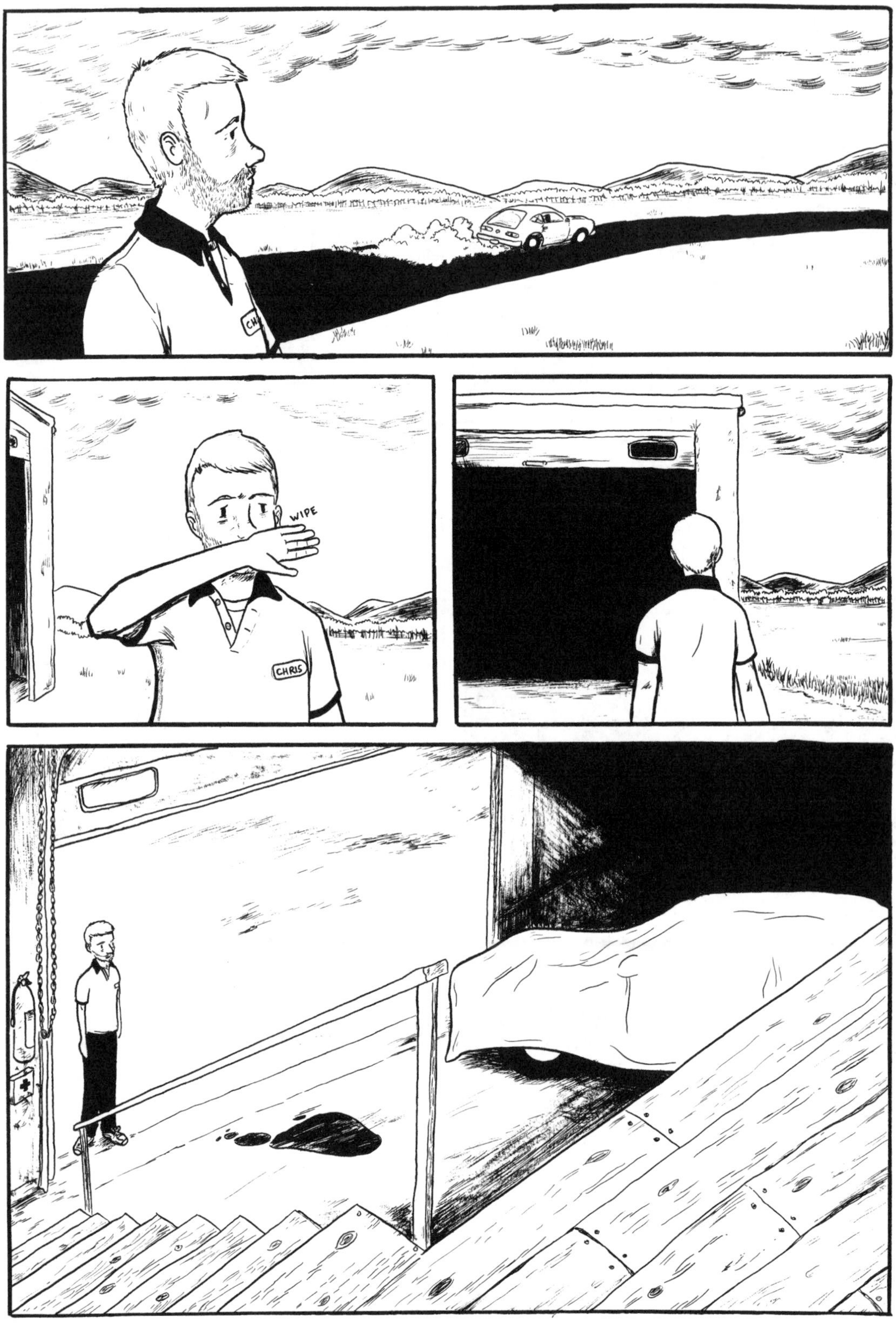
CH
WIPE
CHRIS

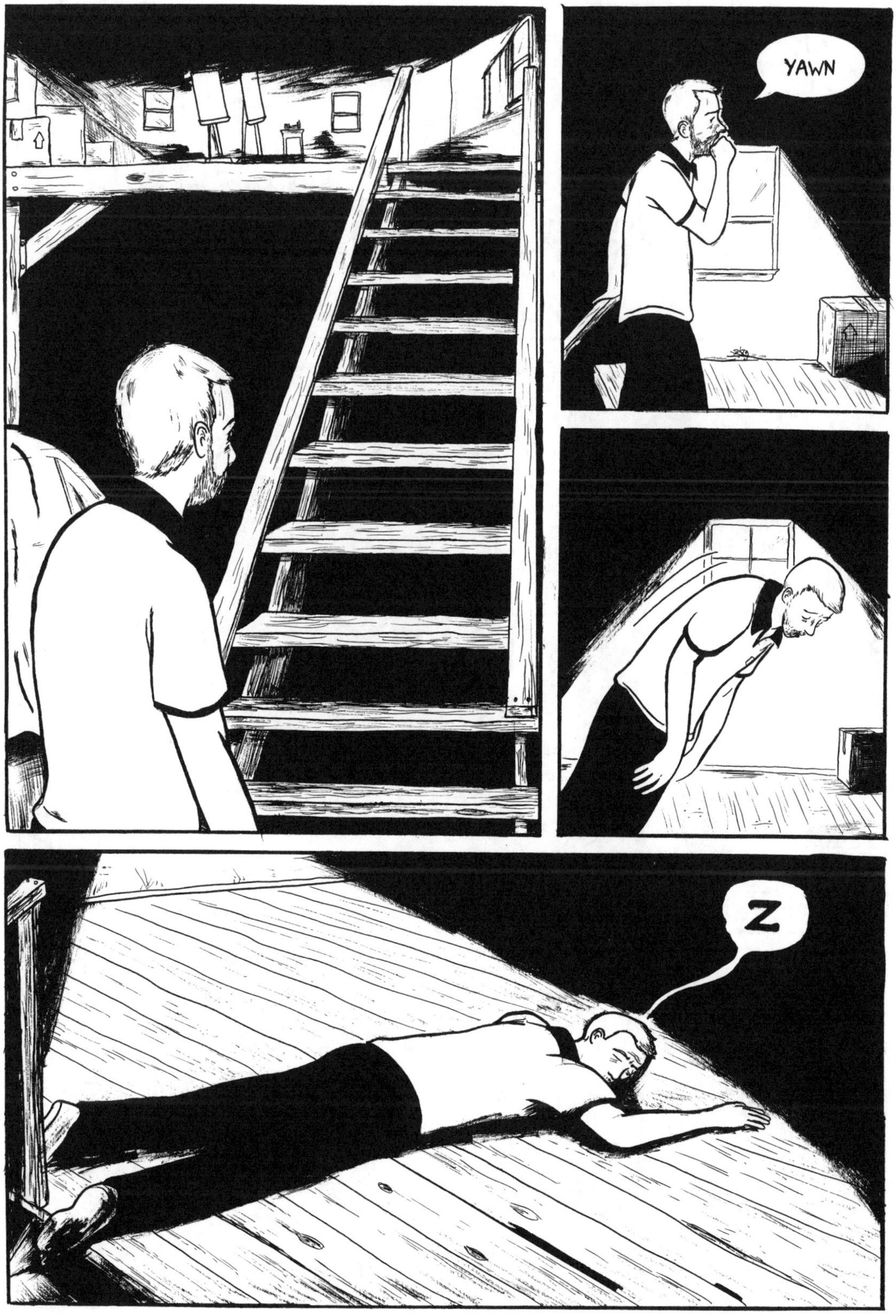
YAWN
Z

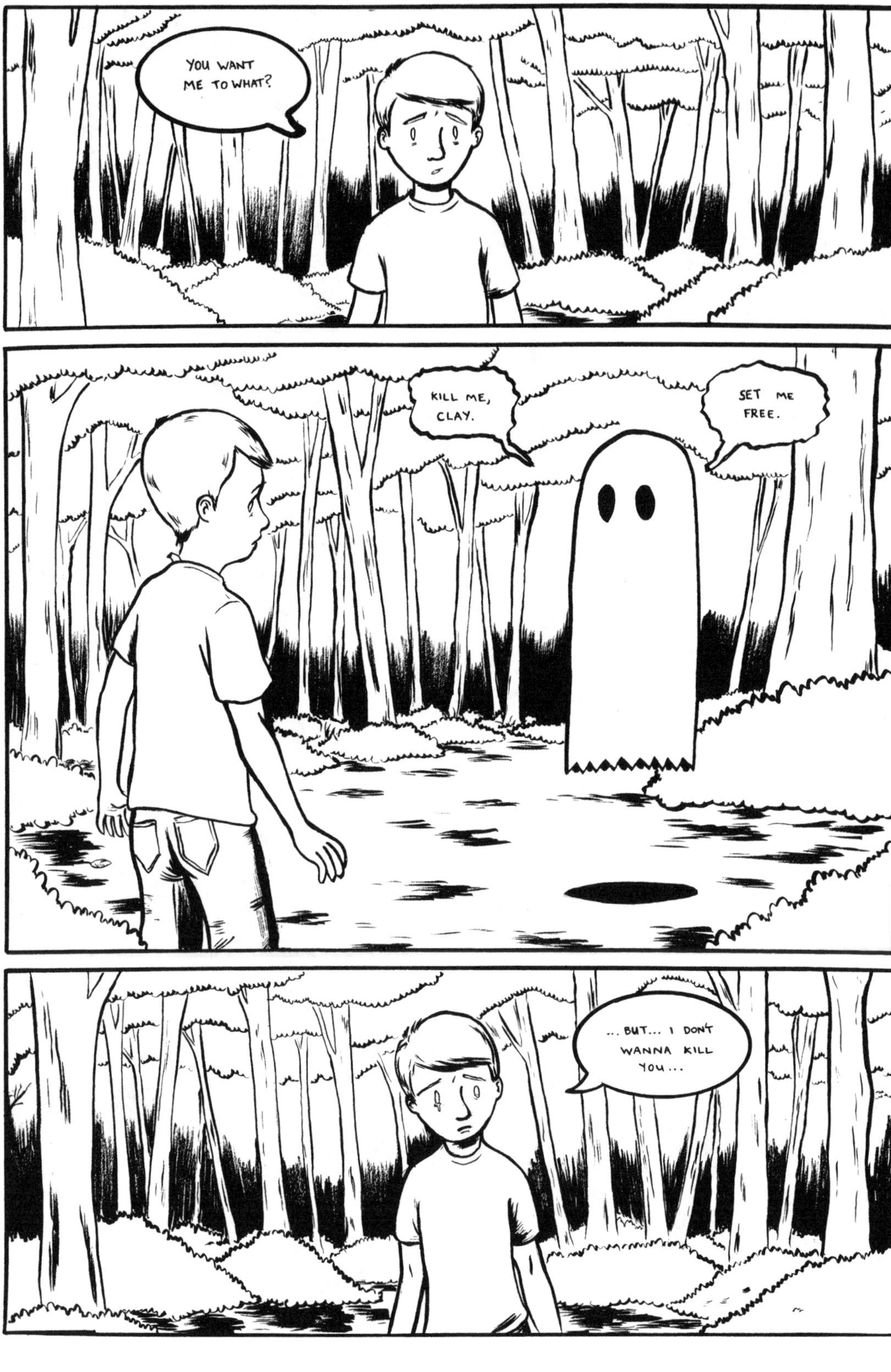
YOU WANT ME TO WHAT?
KILL ME, CLAY.
SET ME FREE.
...BUT... I DON'T WANNA KILL YOU...

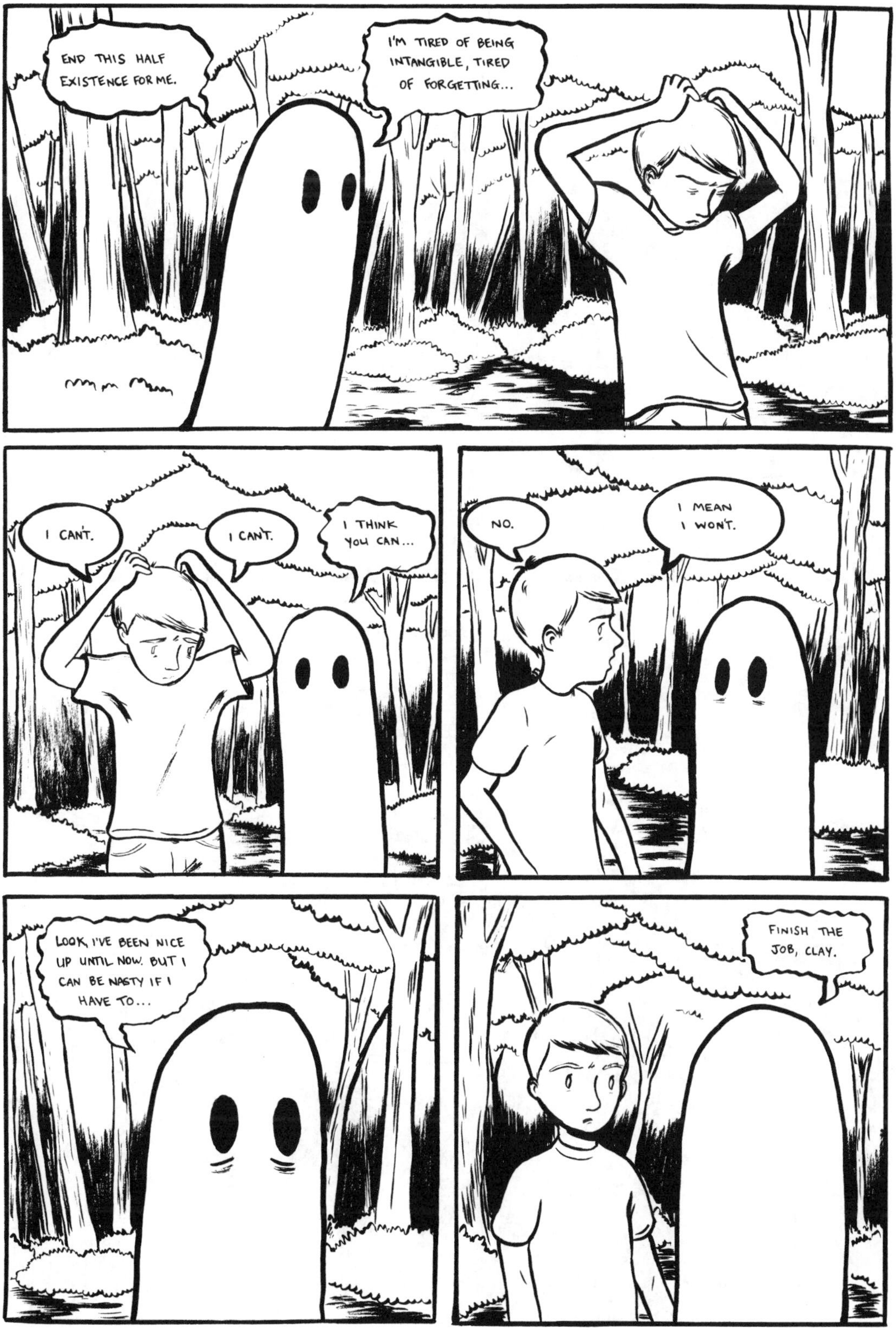
END THIS HALF EXISTENCE FOR ME.
I'M TIRED OF BEING INTANGIBLE, TIRED OF FORGETTING...
I CAN'T.
I CAN'T.
I THINK YOU CAN...
NO.
I MEAN I WON'T.
LOOK, I'VE BEEN NICE UP UNTIL NOW. BUT I CAN BE NASTY IF I HAVE TO...
FINISH THE JOB, CLAY.

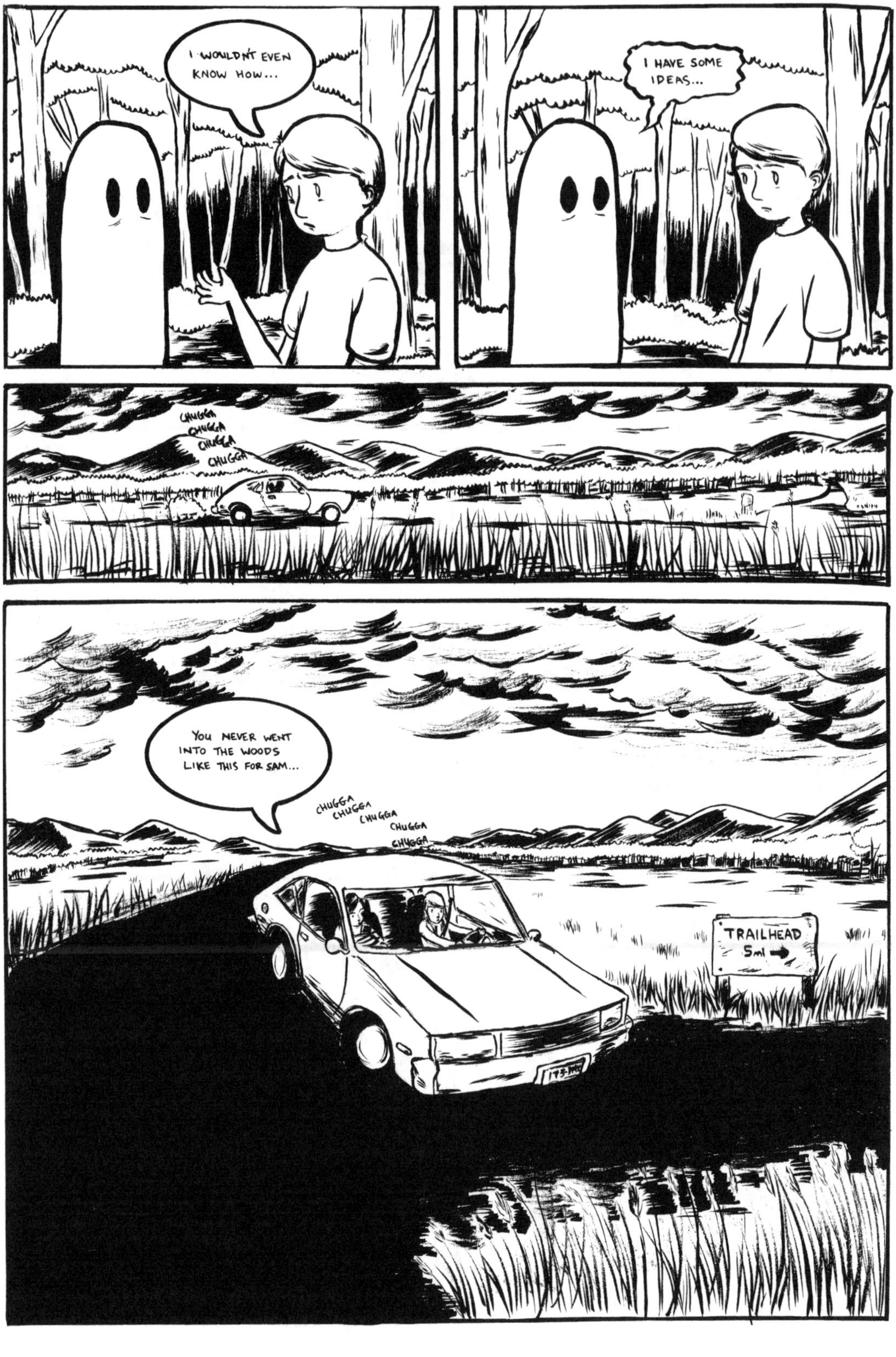
I WOULDN'T EVEN KNOW HOW...
I HAVE SOME IDEAS...
CHUGGA CHUGGA CHUGGA CHUGGA
YOU NEVER WENT INTO THE WOODS LIKE THIS FOR SAM...
CHUGGA CHUGGA CHUGGA CHUGGA CHUGGA
TRAILHEAD
5 mi →

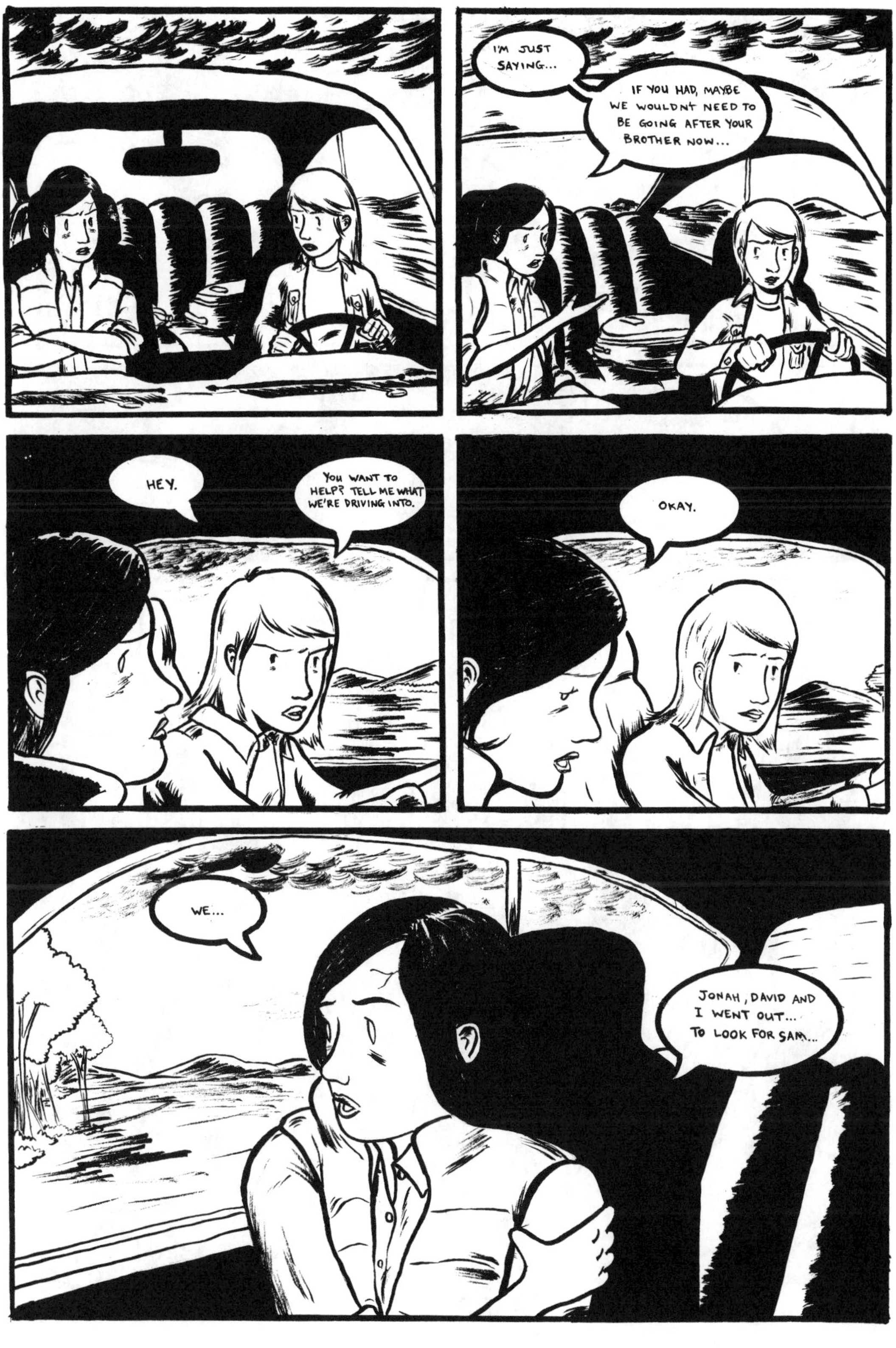
I'M JUST SAYING...
IF YOU HAD, MAYBE WE WOULDN'T NEED TO BE GOING AFTER YOUR BROTHER NOW...
HEY.
YOU WANT TO HELP? TELL ME WHAT WE'RE DRIVING INTO.
OKAY.
WE...
JONAH, DAVID AND I WENT OUT... TO LOOK FOR SAM...

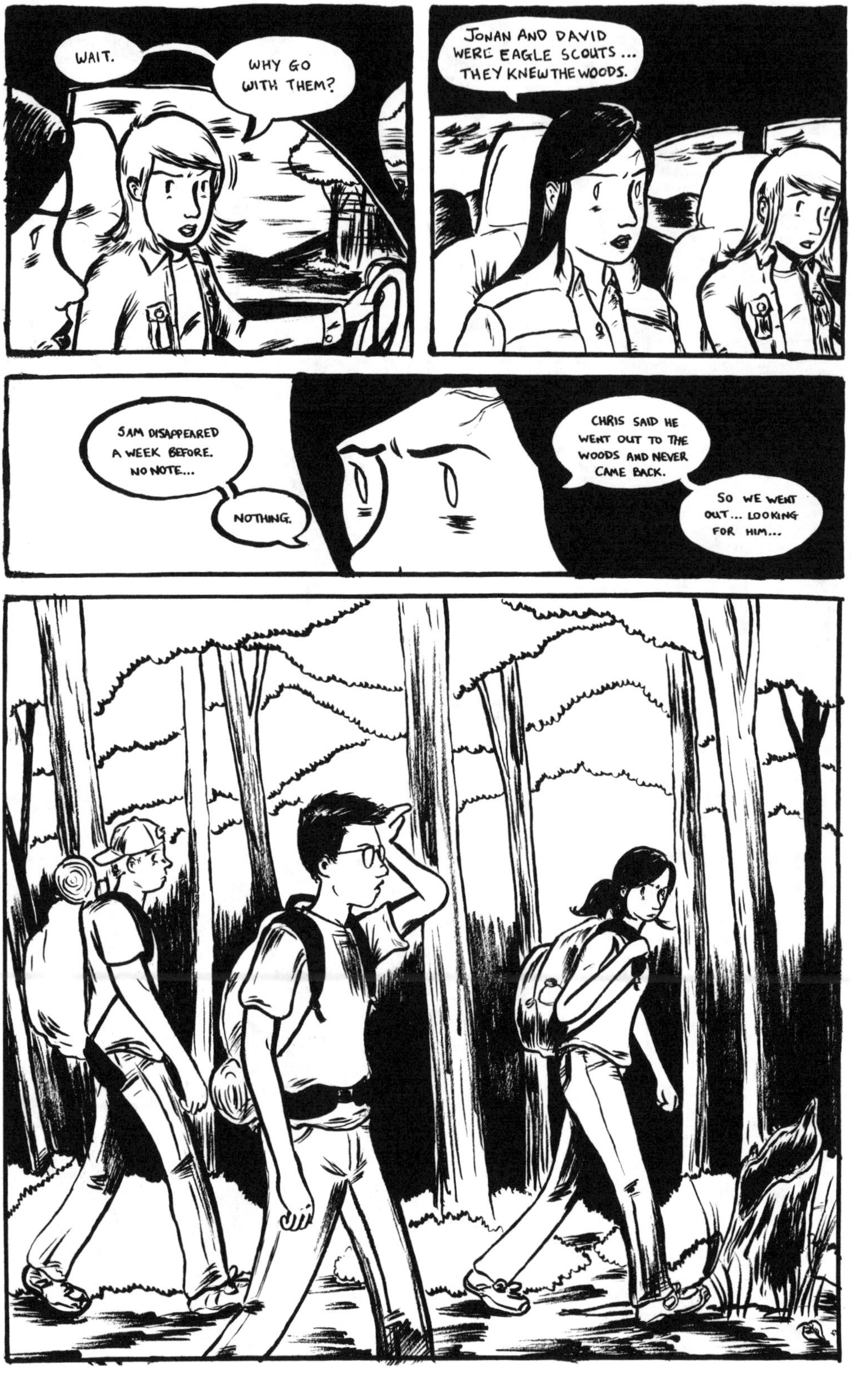
WAIT.
WHY GO WITH THEM?
JONAN AND DAVID WERE EAGLE SCOUTS ... THEY KNEW THE WOODS.
SAM DISAPPEARED A WEEK BEFORE. NO NOTE...
NOTHING.
CHRIS SAID HE WENT OUT TO THE WOODS AND NEVER CAME BACK.
SO WE WENT OUT... LOOKING FOR HIM...

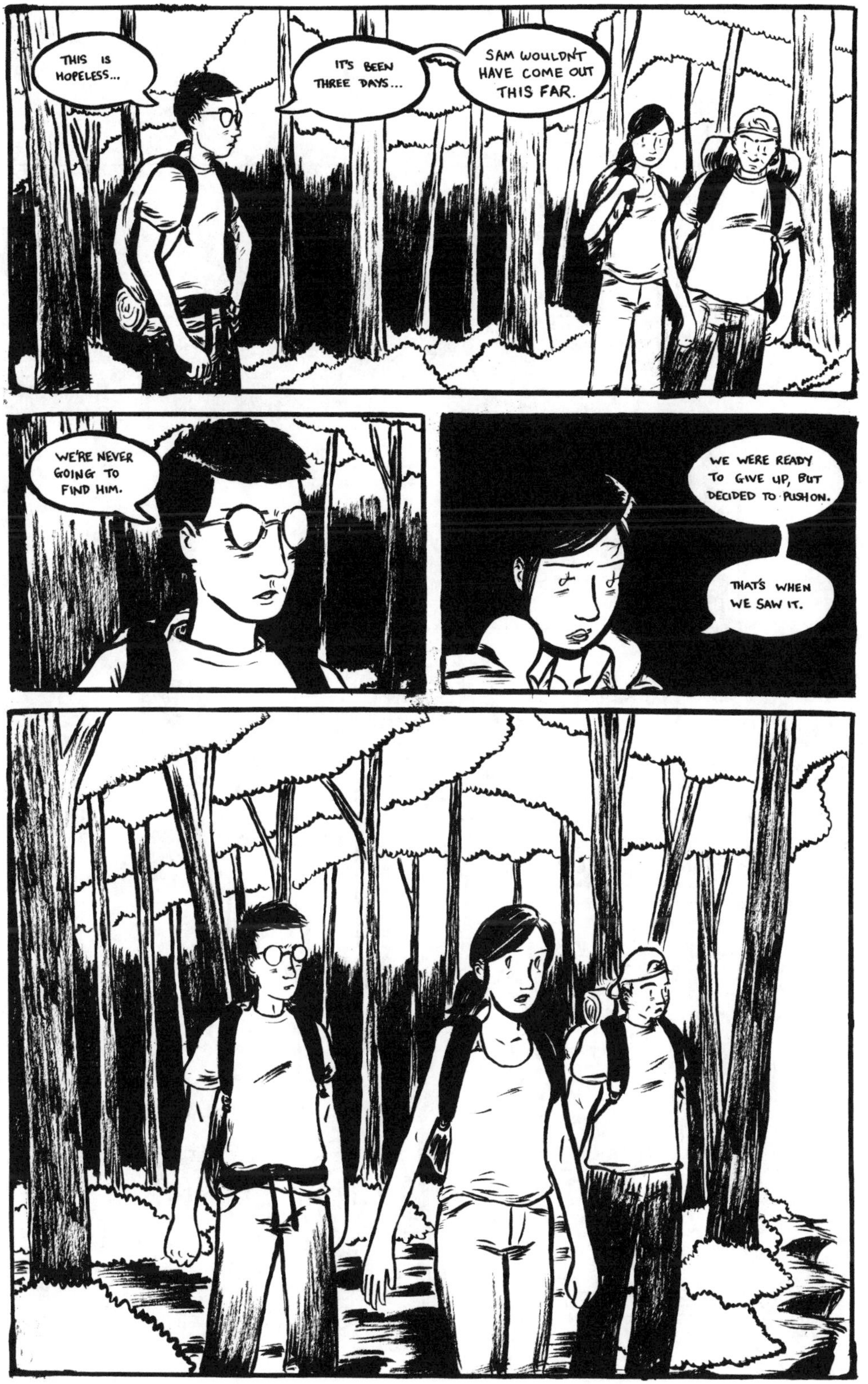
THIS IS HOPELESS...
IT'S BEEN THREE DAYS...
SAM WOULDN'T HAVE COME OUT THIS FAR.
WE'RE NEVER GOING TO FIND HIM.
WE WERE READY TO GIVE UP, BUT DECIDED TO PUSH ON.
THAT'S WHEN WE SAW IT.

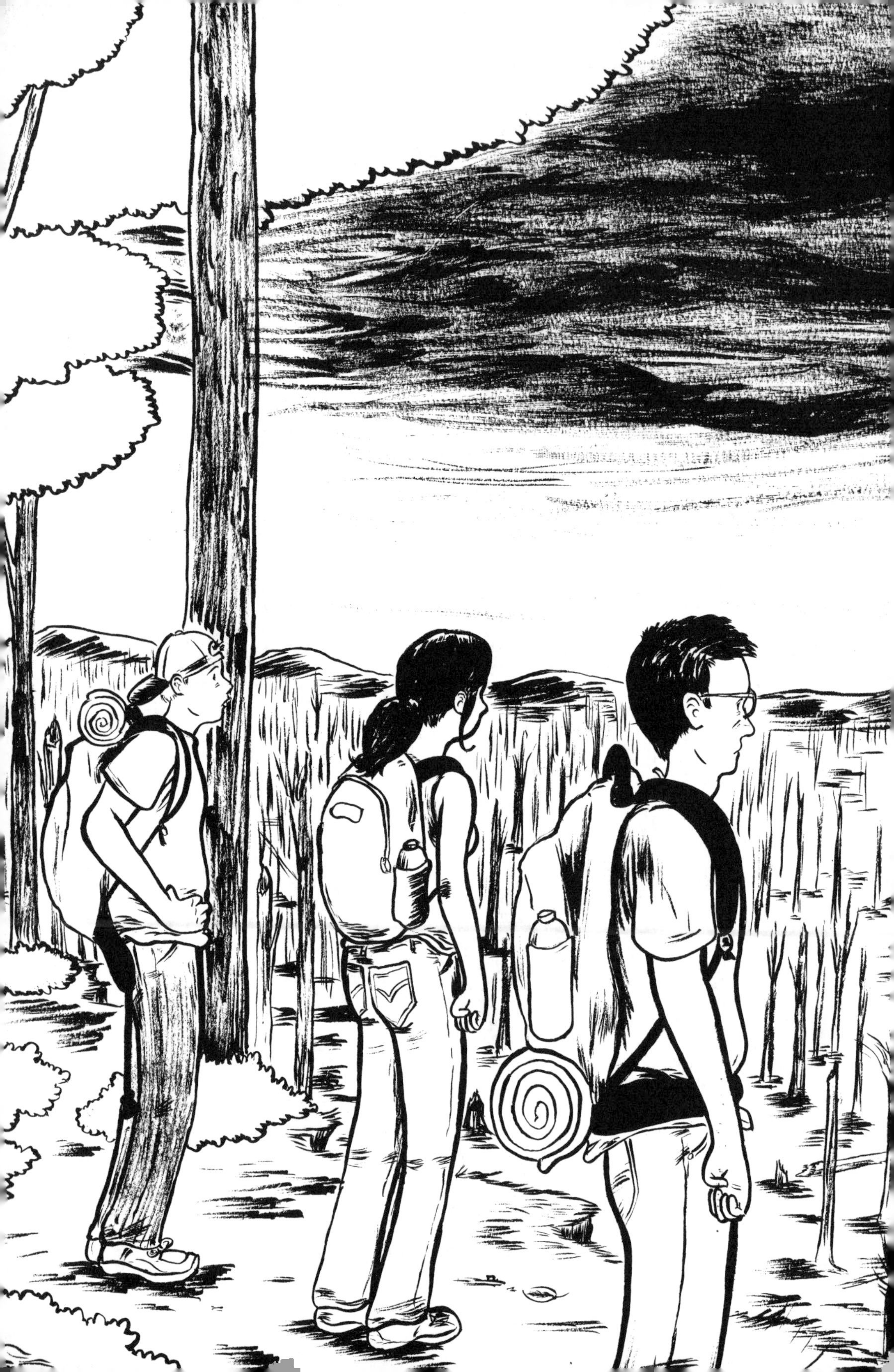

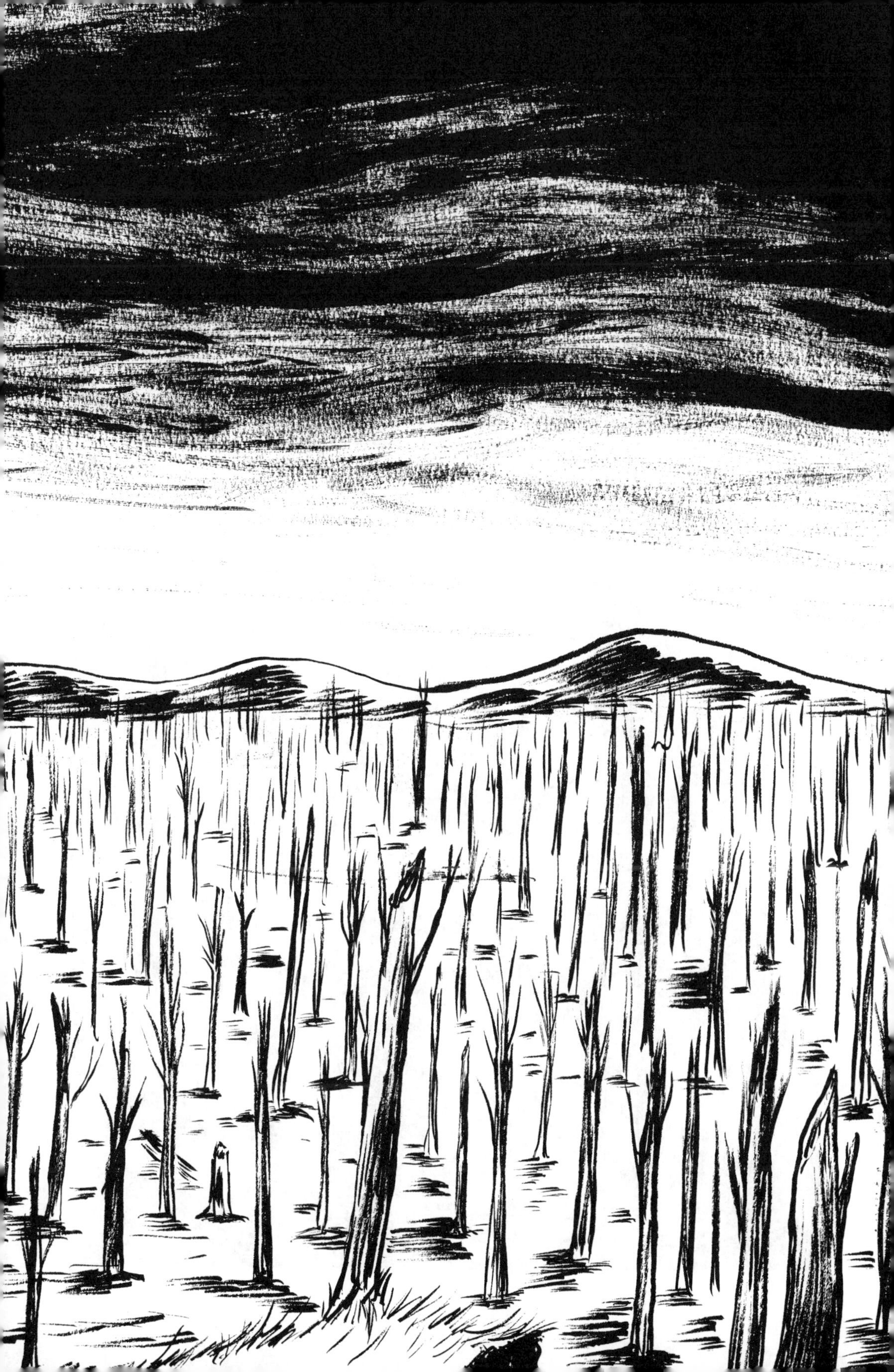

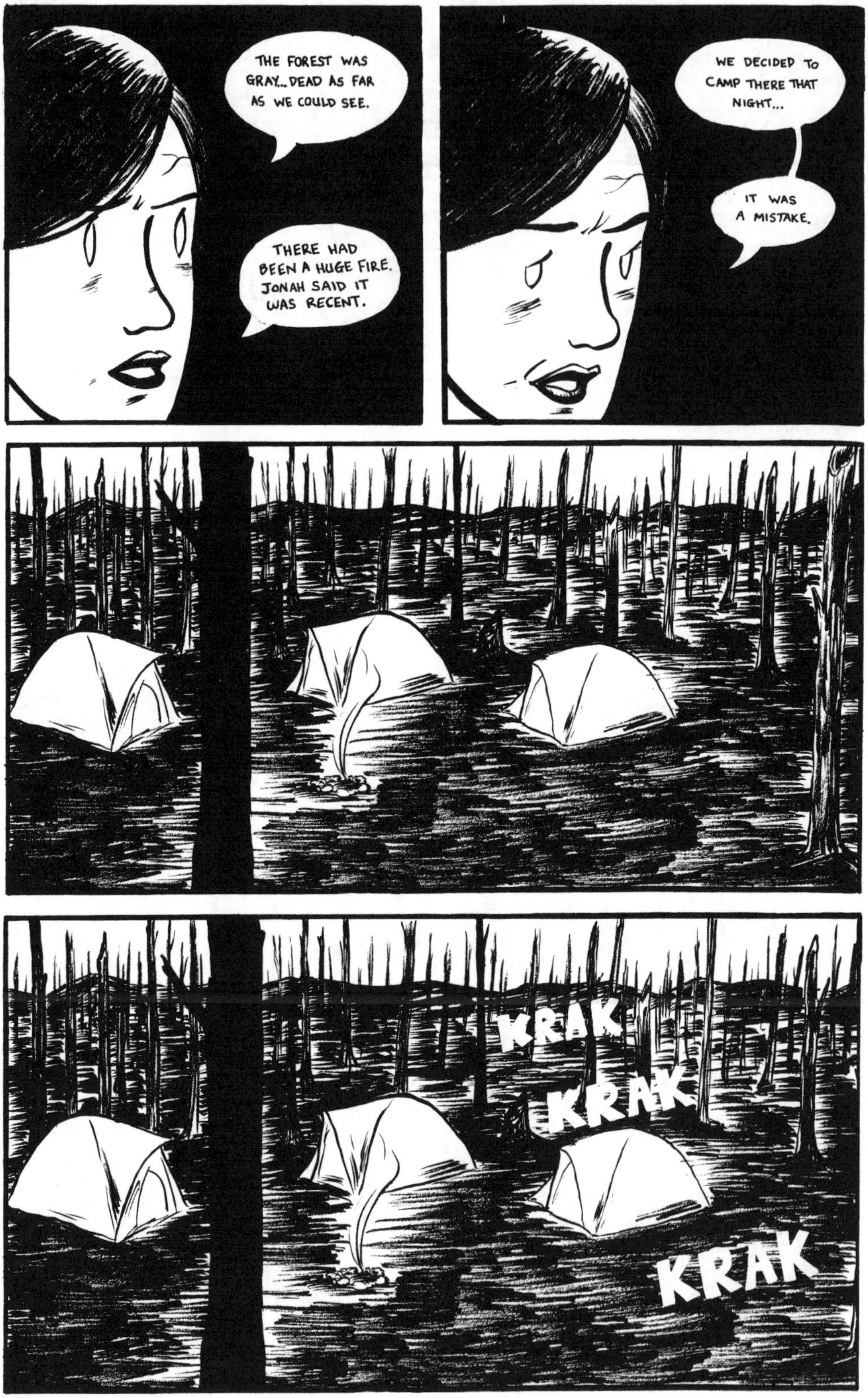
THE FOREST WAS GRAY... DEAD AS FAR AS WE COULD SEE.
THERE HAD BEEN A HUGE FIRE. JONAH SAID IT WAS RECENT.
WE DECIDED TO CAMP THERE THAT NIGHT...
IT WAS A MISTAKE.
KRAK
KRAK
KRAK

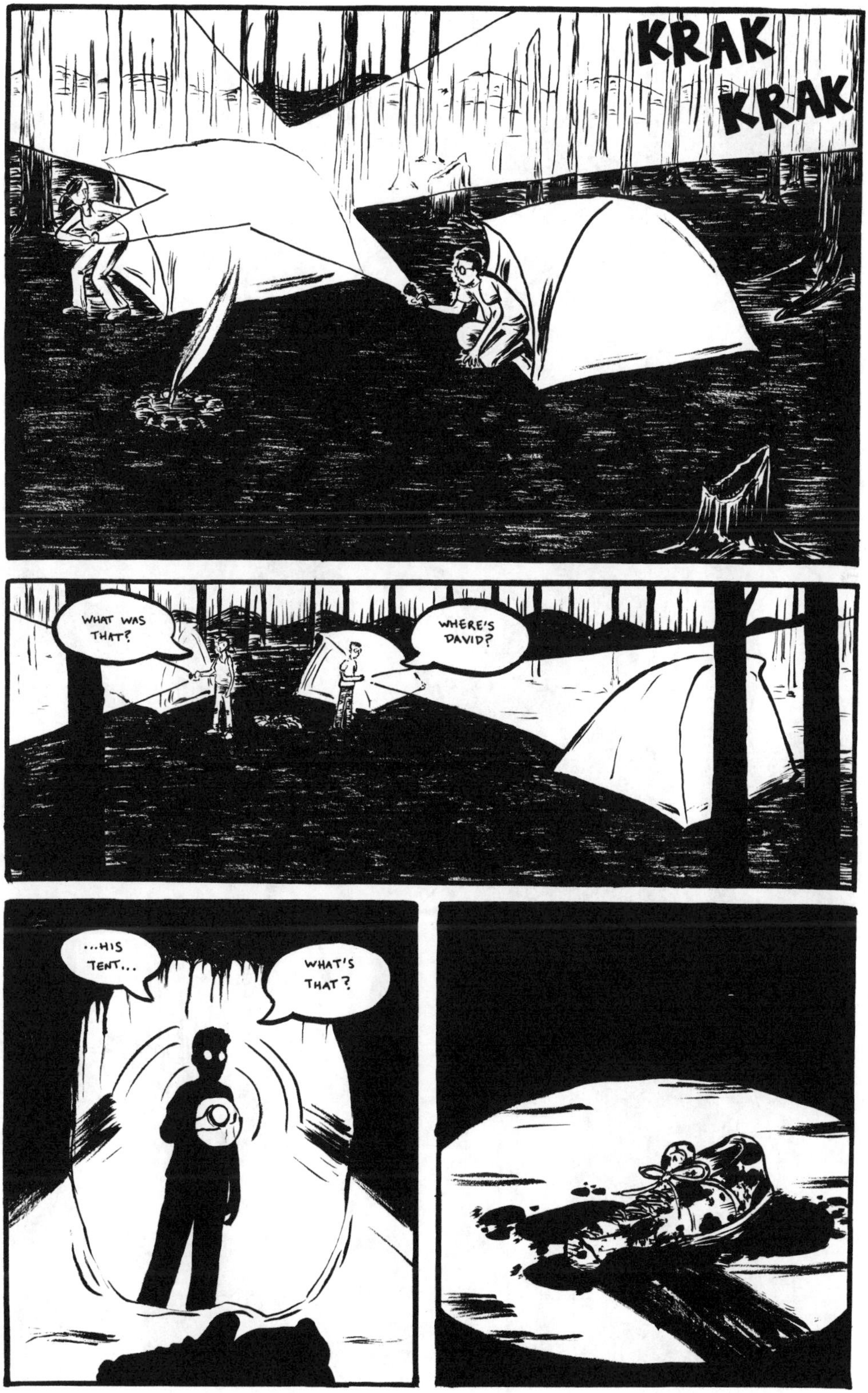
KRAK
KRAK
WHAT WAS THAT?
WHERE'S DAVID?
...HIS TENT...
WHAT'S THAT?

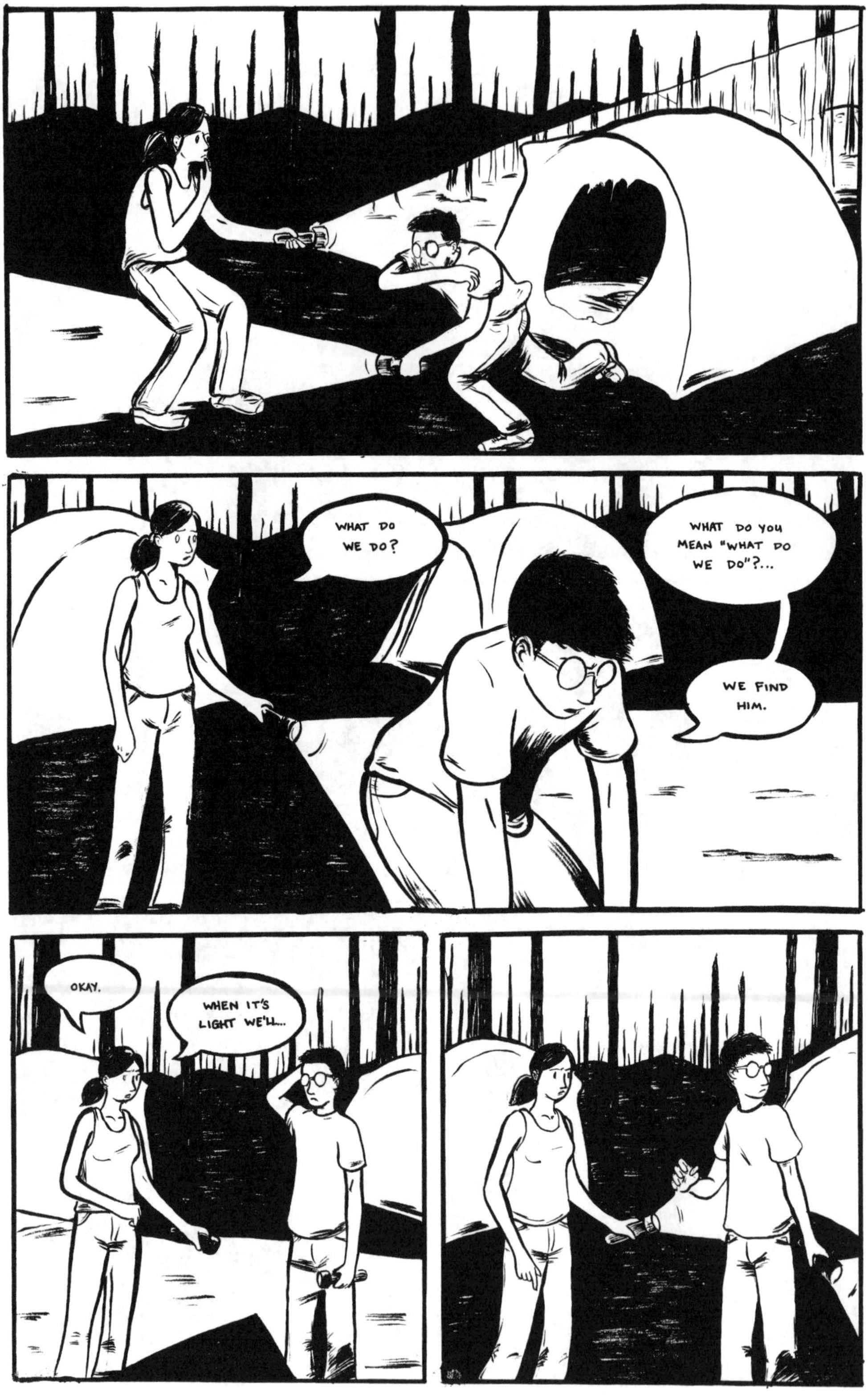
WHAT DO WE DO?
WHAT DO YOU MEAN "WHAT DO WE DO"?...
WE FIND HIM.
OKAY.
WHEN IT'S LIGHT WE'LL...

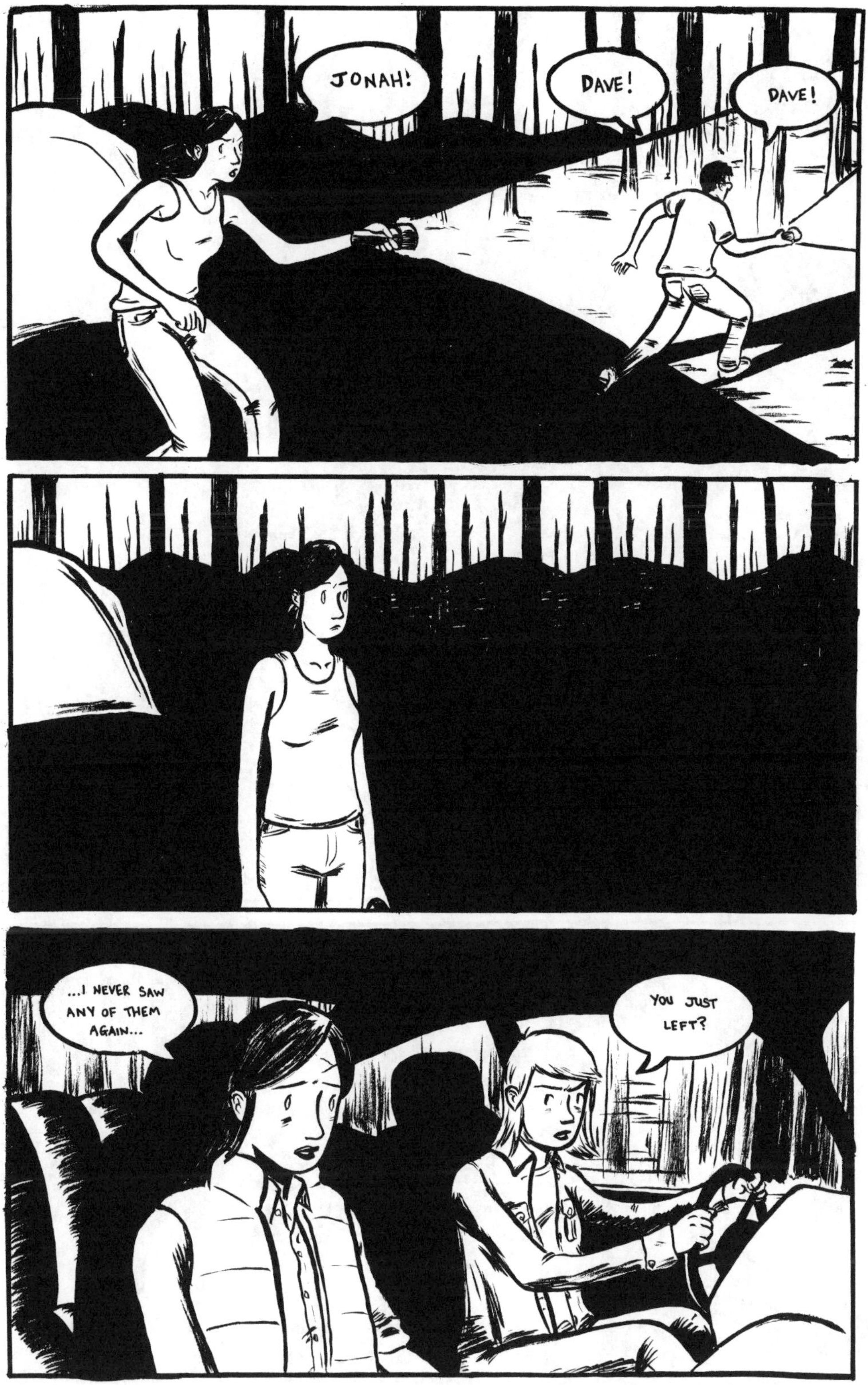
JONAH!
DAVE!
DAVE!
...I NEVER SAW ANY OF THEM AGAIN...
YOU JUST LEFT?

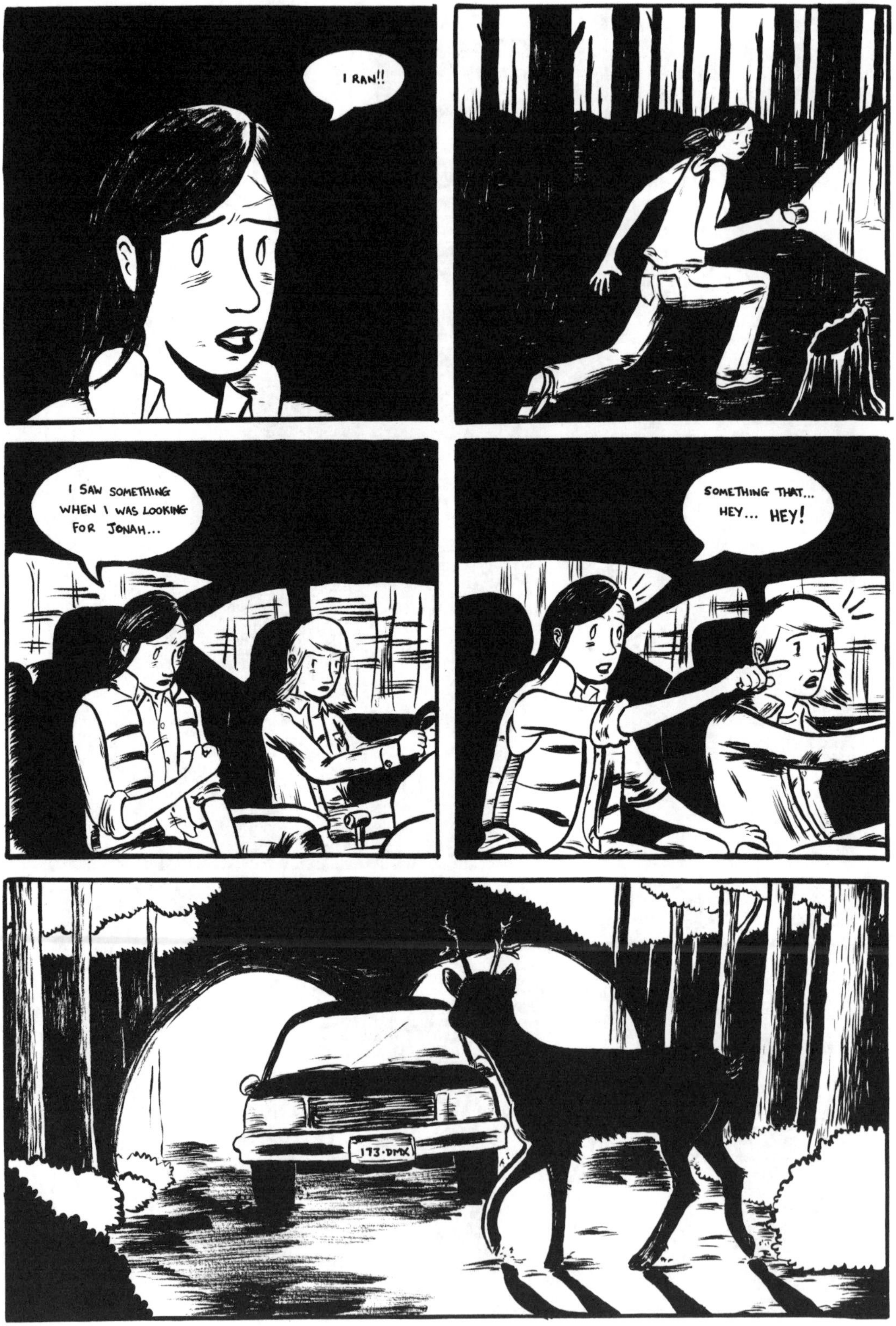
I RAN!!
I SAW SOMETHING WHEN I WAS LOOKING FOR JONAH...
SOMETHING THAT... HEY... HEY!
173·DMX

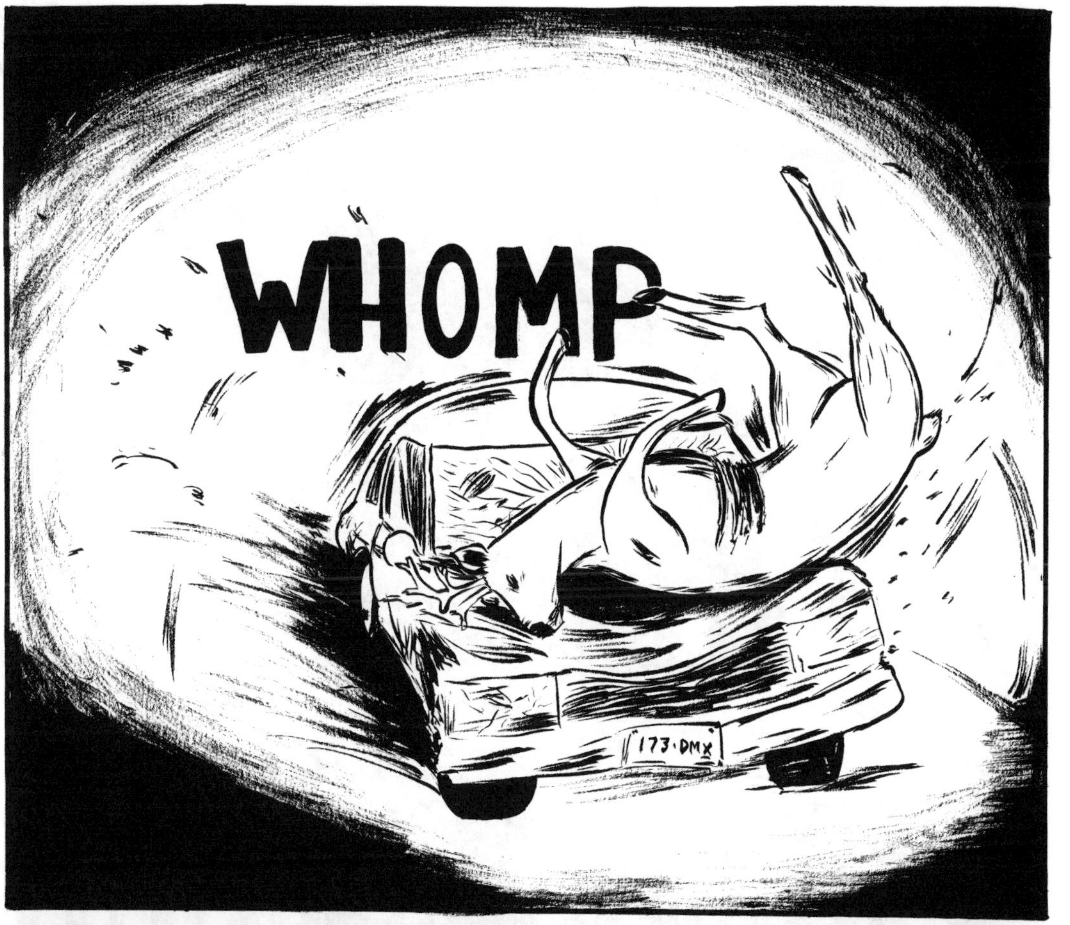
WHOMP
173·DMX

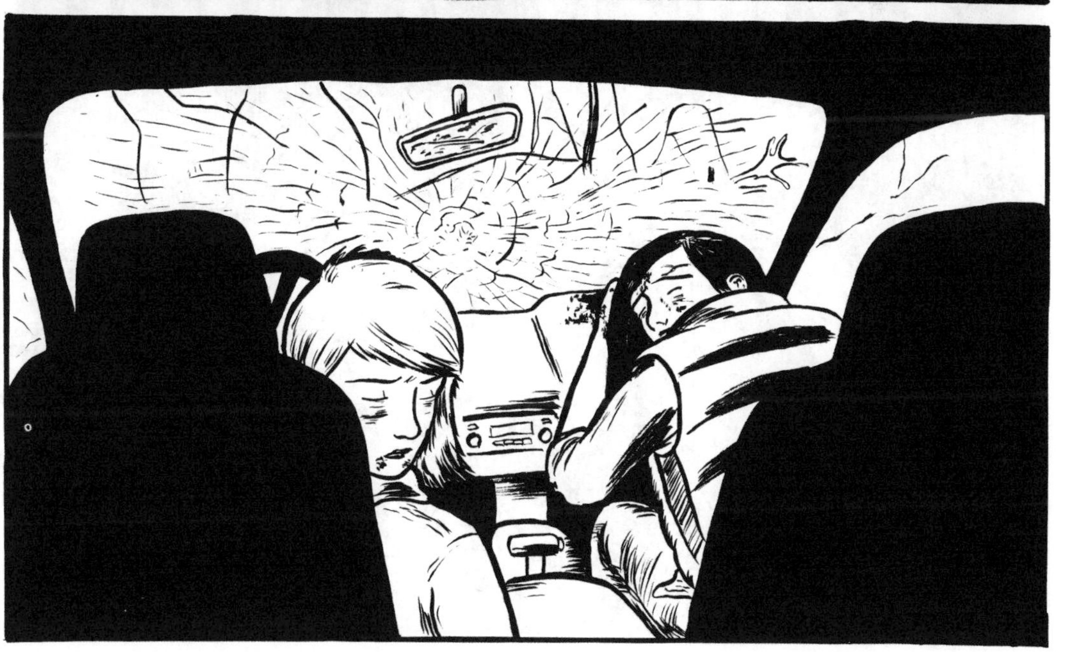

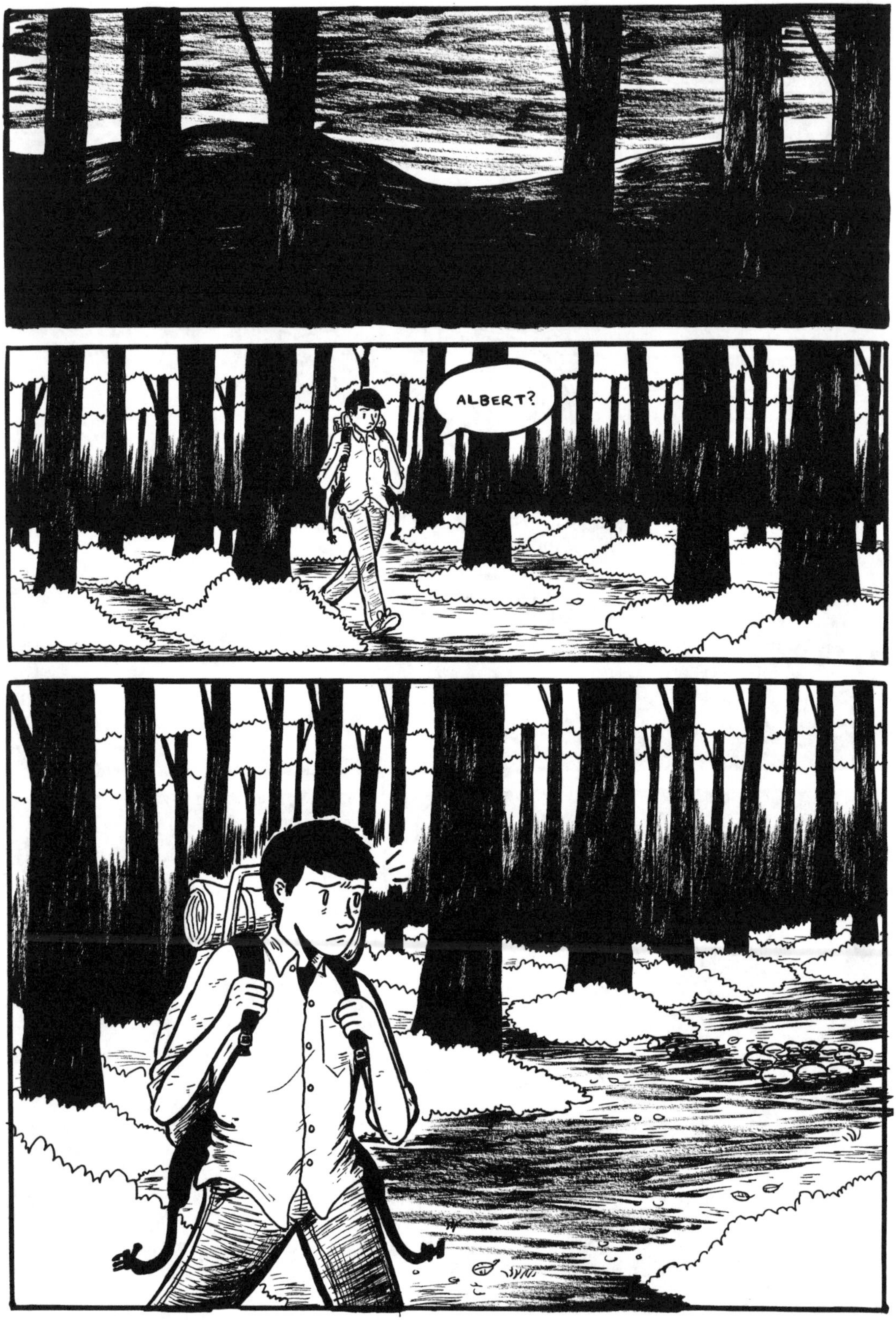
ALBERT?

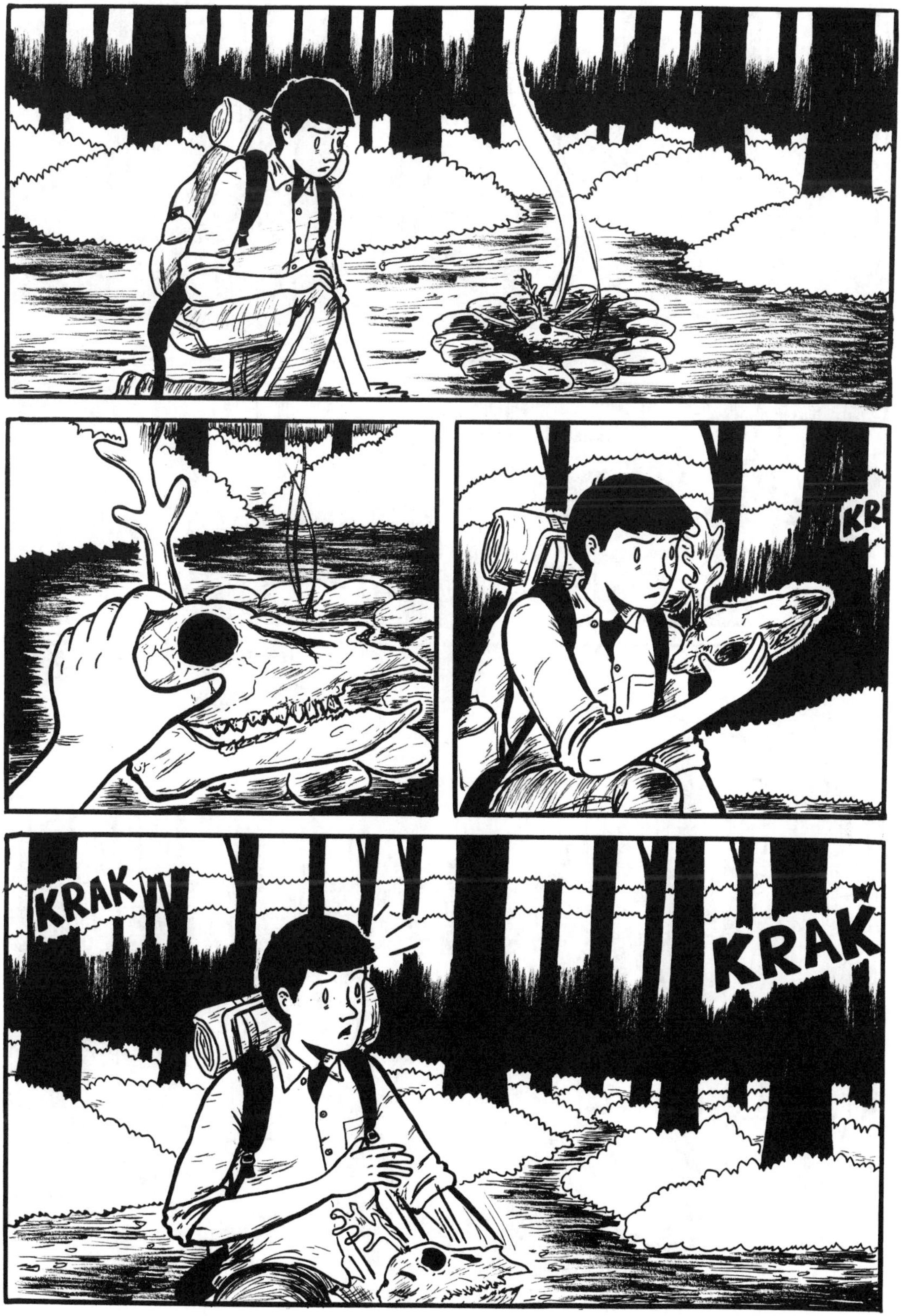
KR
KRAK
KRAK

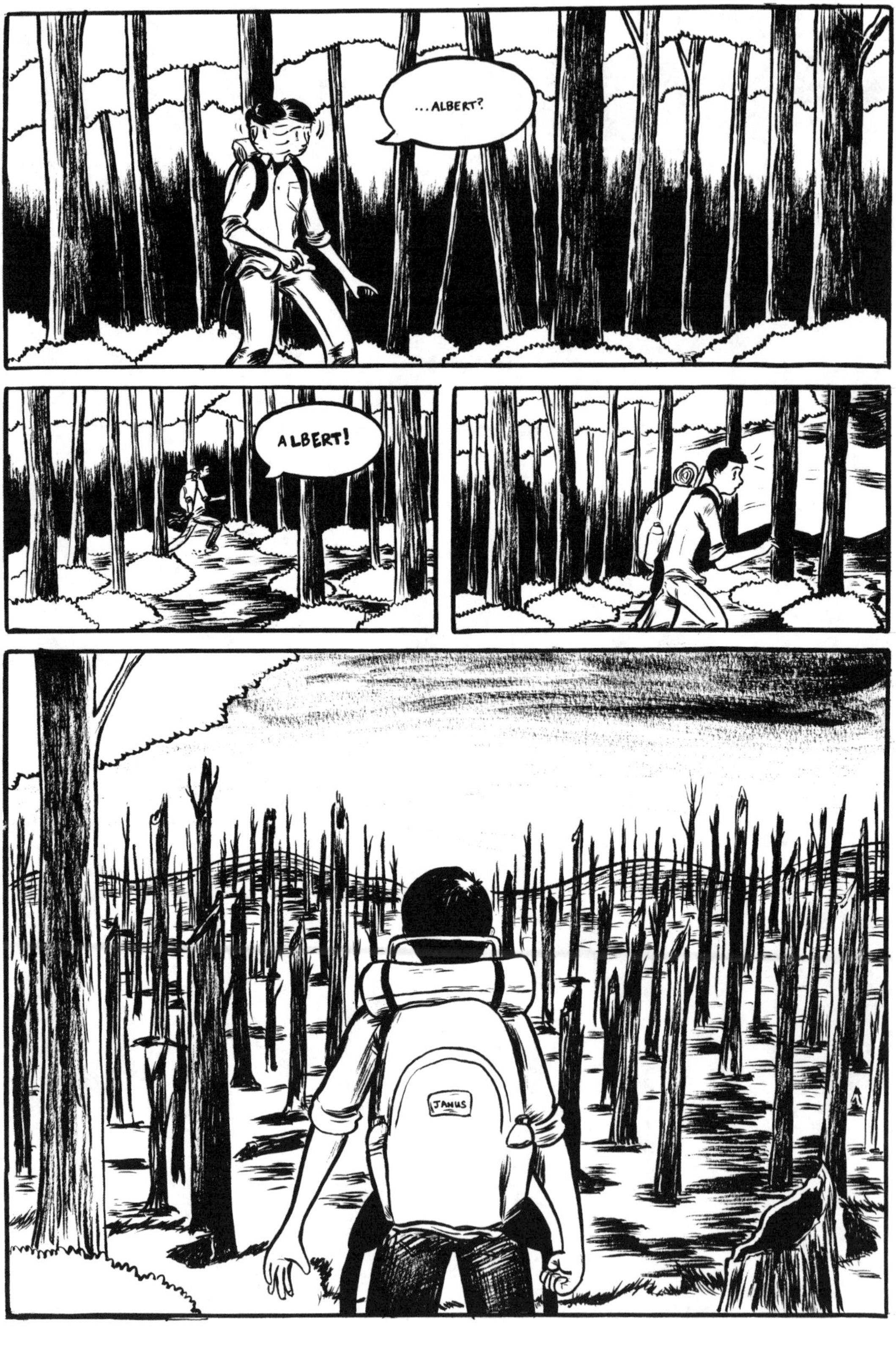
...ALBERT?
ALBERT!
JANUS

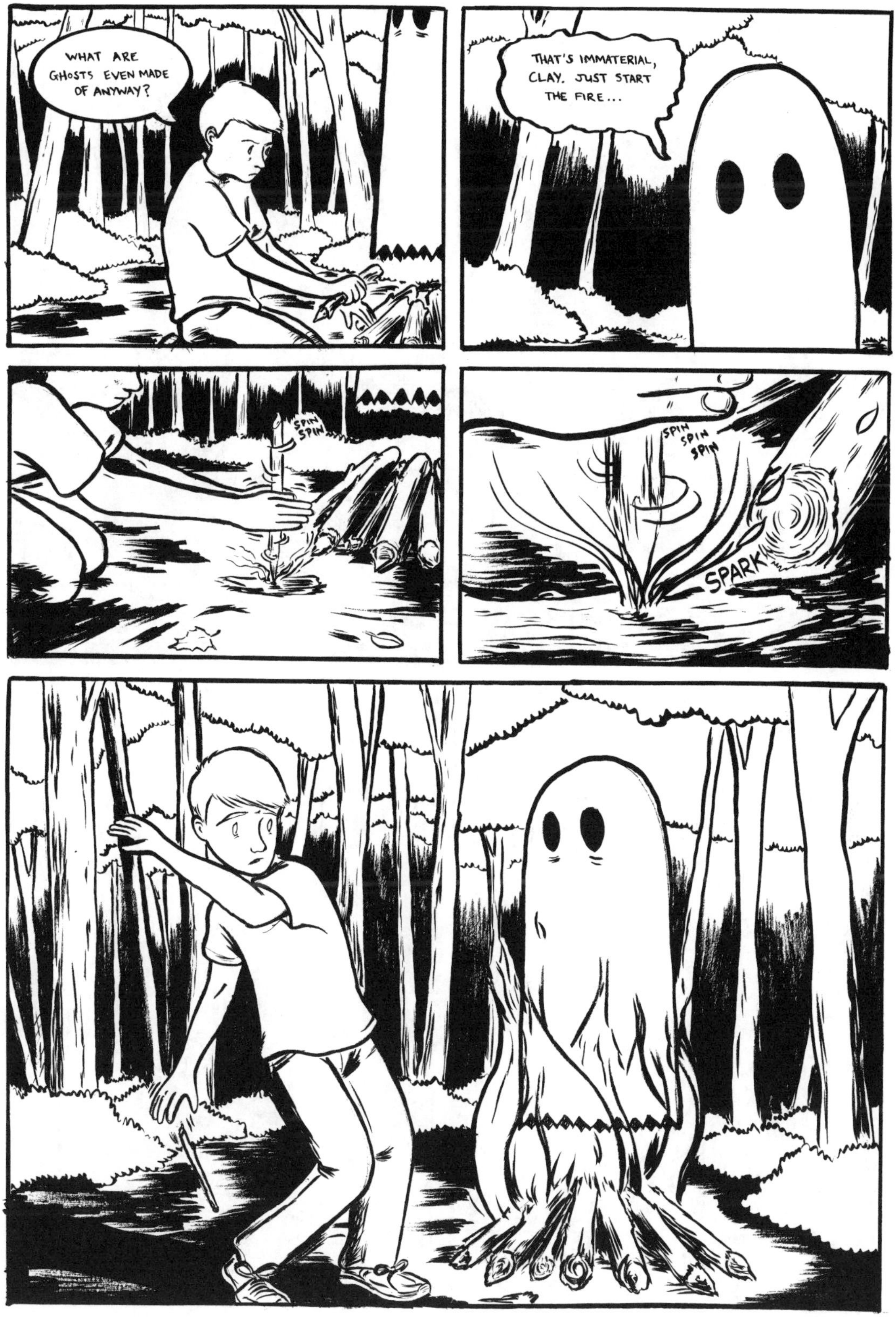
WHAT ARE GHOSTS EVEN MADE OF ANYWAY?
THAT'S IMMATERIAL, CLAY. JUST START THE FIRE...
SPIN SPIN
SPIN SPIN SPIN
SPARK

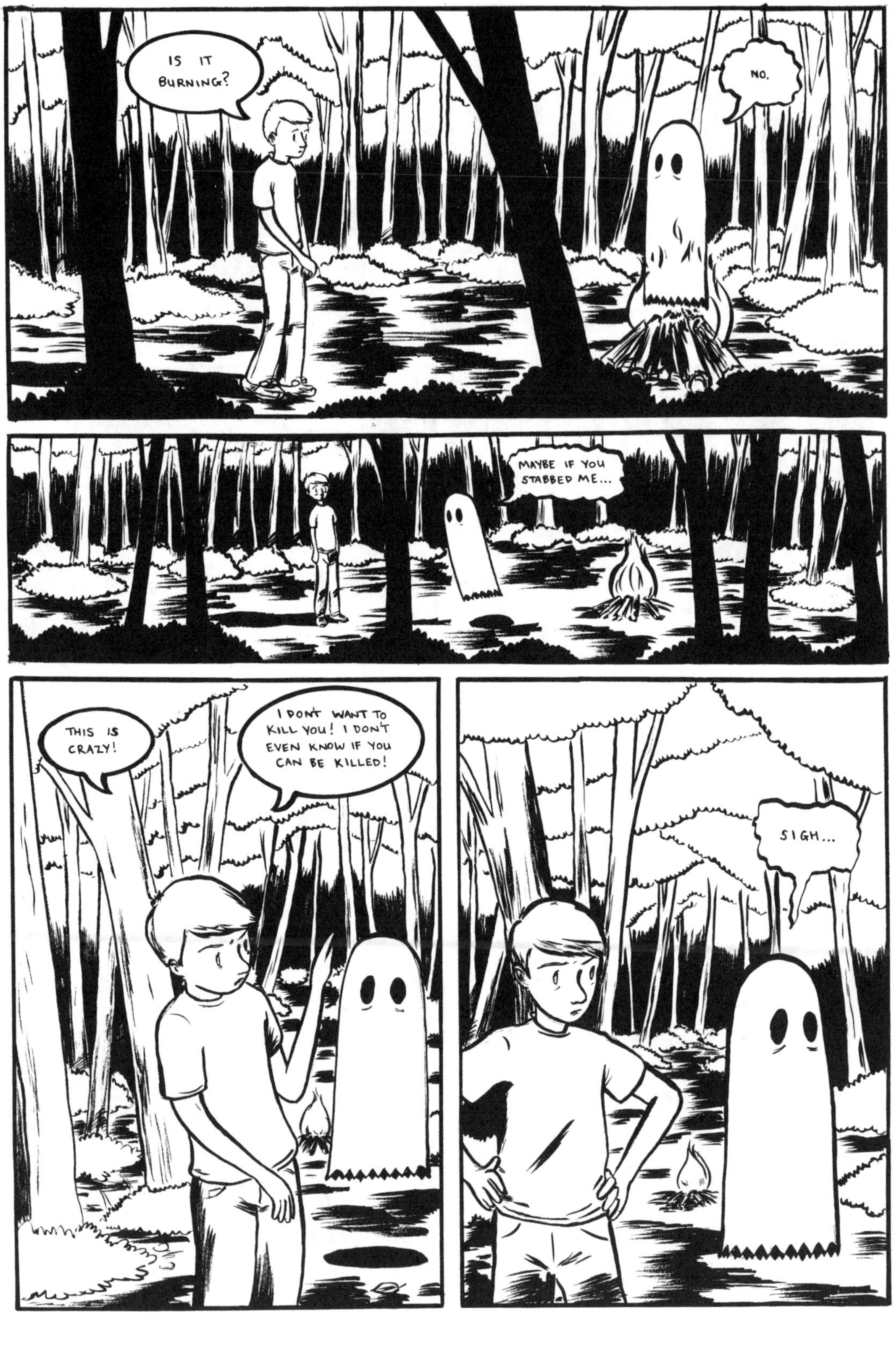
IS IT BURNING?
NO.
MAYBE IF YOU STABBED ME...
THIS IS CRAZY!
I DON'T WANT TO KILL YOU! I DON'T EVEN KNOW IF YOU CAN BE KILLED!
SIGH...

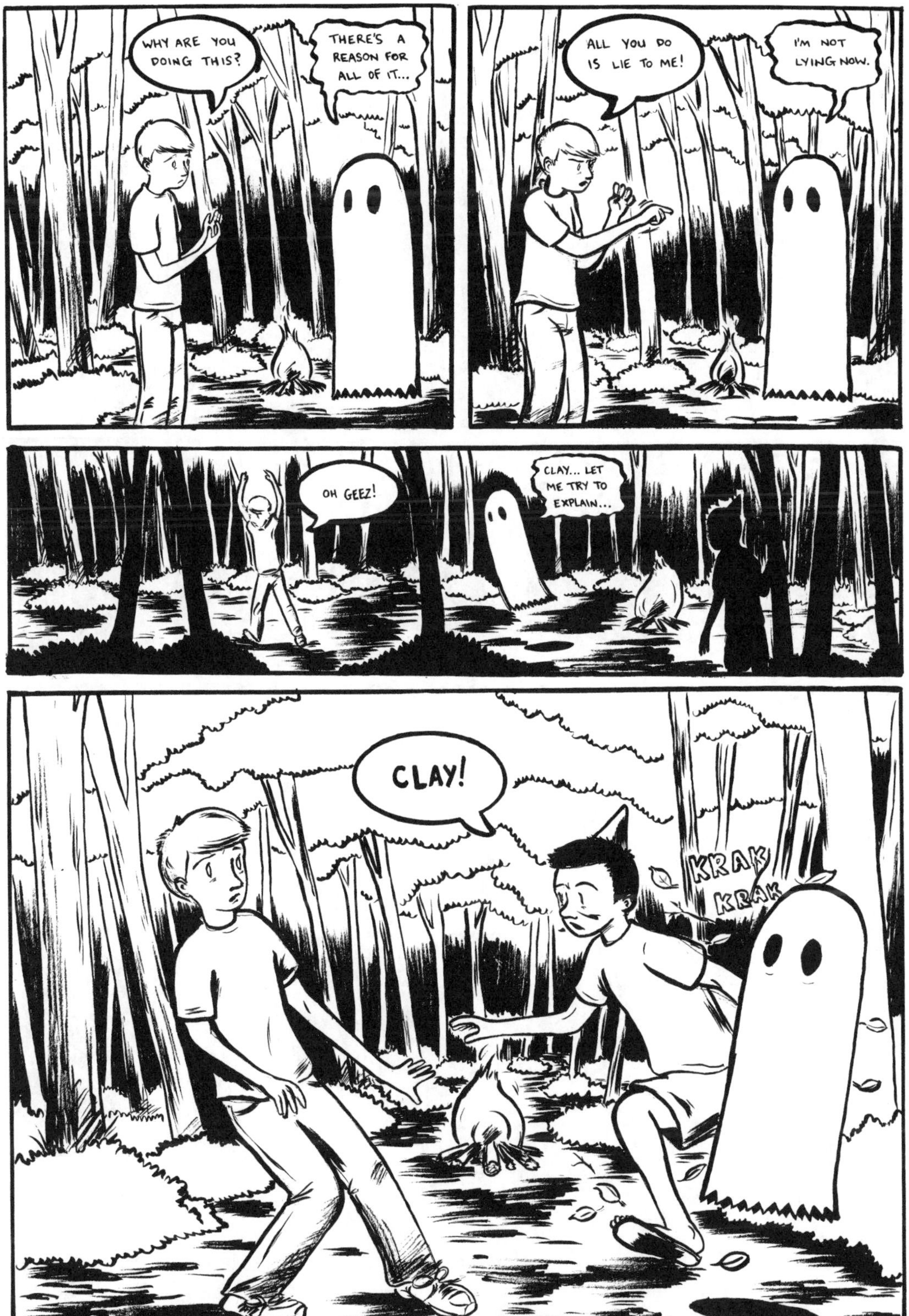
WHY ARE YOU DOING THIS?
THERE'S A REASON FOR ALL OF IT...
ALL YOU DO IS LIE TO ME!
I'M NOT LYING NOW.
OH GEEZ!
CLAY... LET ME TRY TO EXPLAIN...
CLAY!
KRAK
KRAK

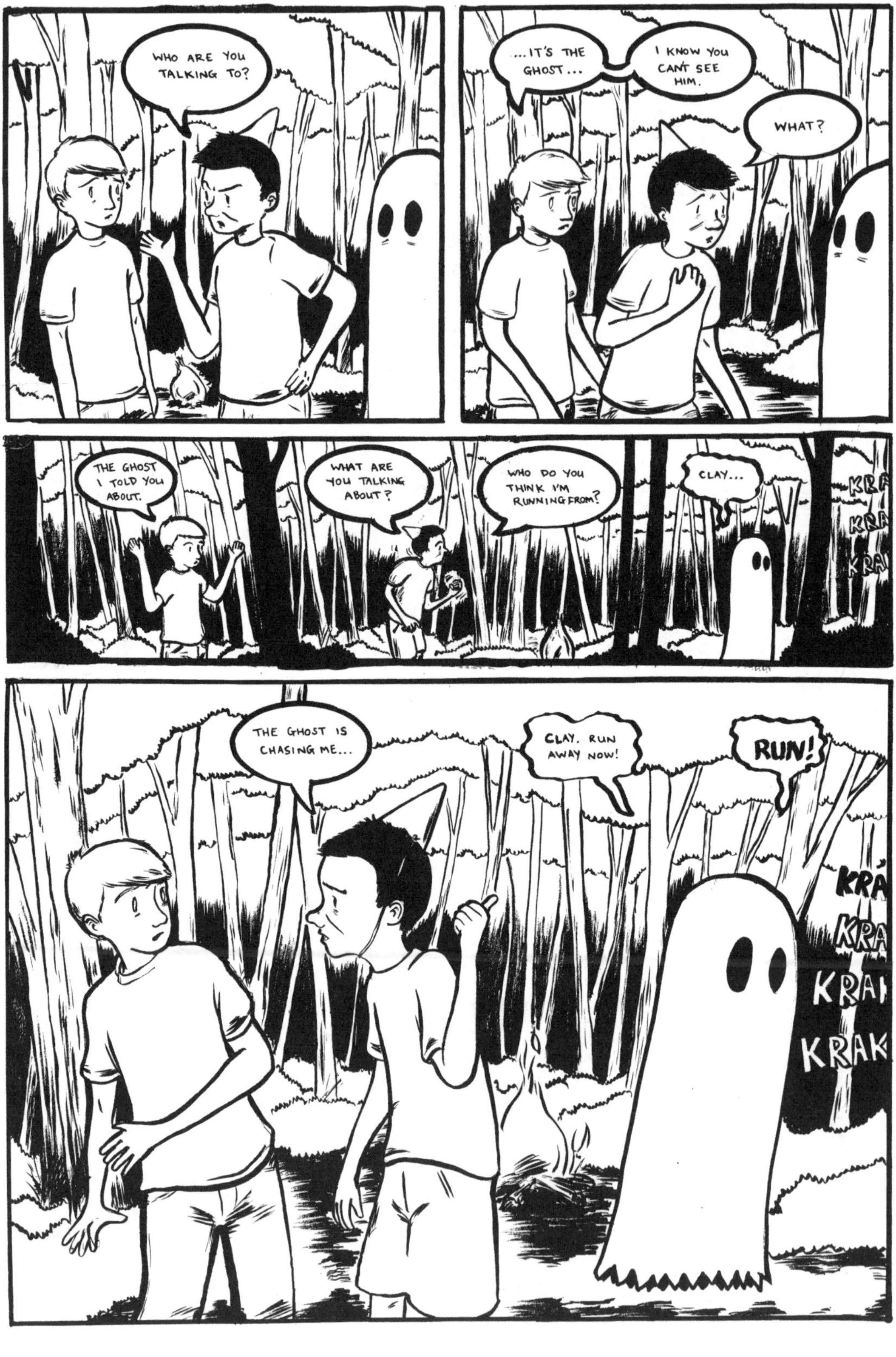
WHO ARE YOU TALKING TO?
...IT'S THE GHOST...
I KNOW YOU CAN'T SEE HIM.
WHAT?
THE GHOST I TOLD YOU ABOUT.
WHAT ARE YOU TALKING ABOUT?
WHO DO YOU THINK I'M RUNNING FROM?
CLAY...
THE GHOST IS CHASING ME...
CLAY. RUN AWAY NOW!
RUN!
KRAK

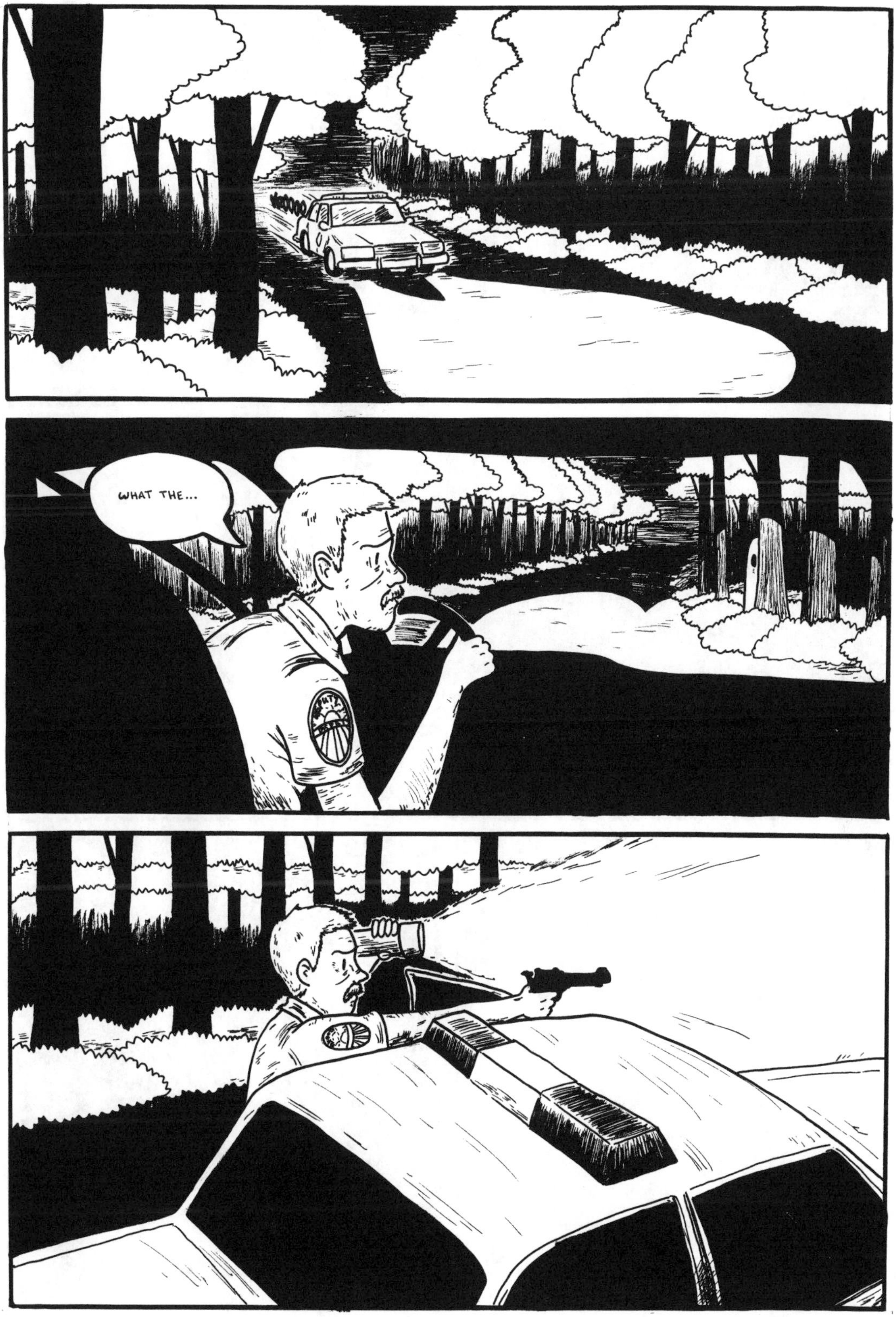
WHAT THE...

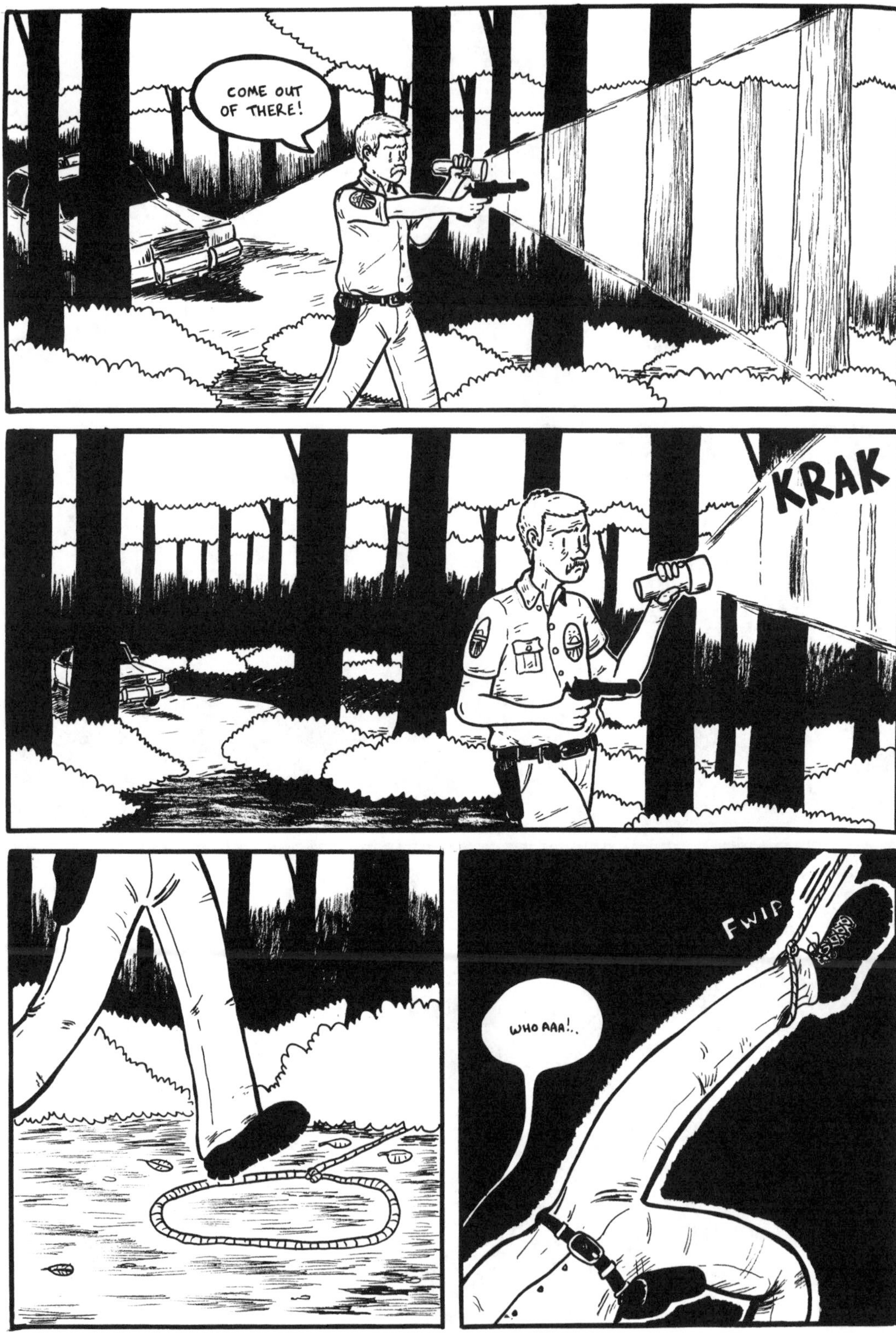
COME OUT OF THERE!
KRAK
FWIP
WHOAAA!..

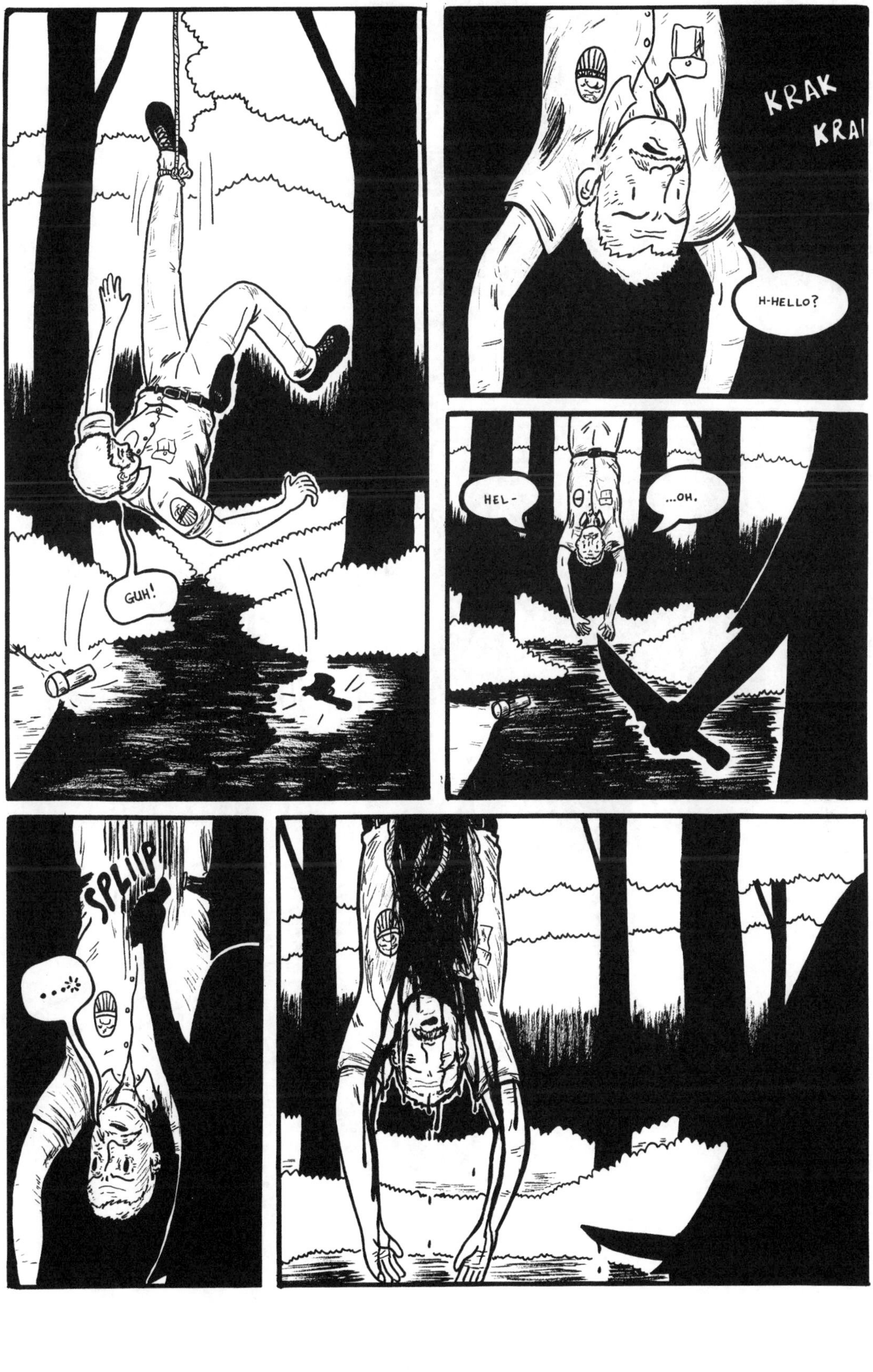
GUH!
KRAK
KRA
H-HELLO?
HEL-
...OH.
SPLIIP
...

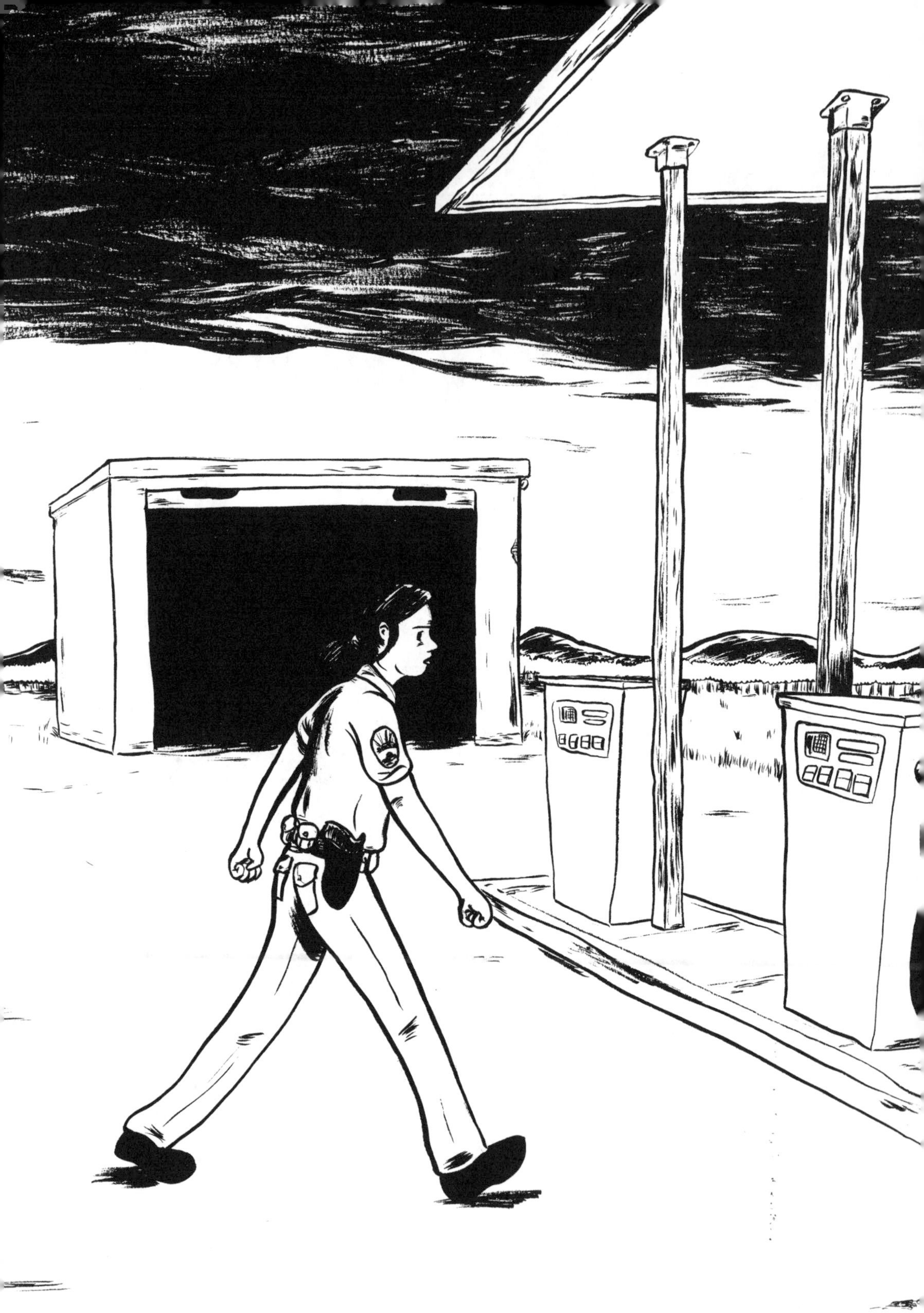

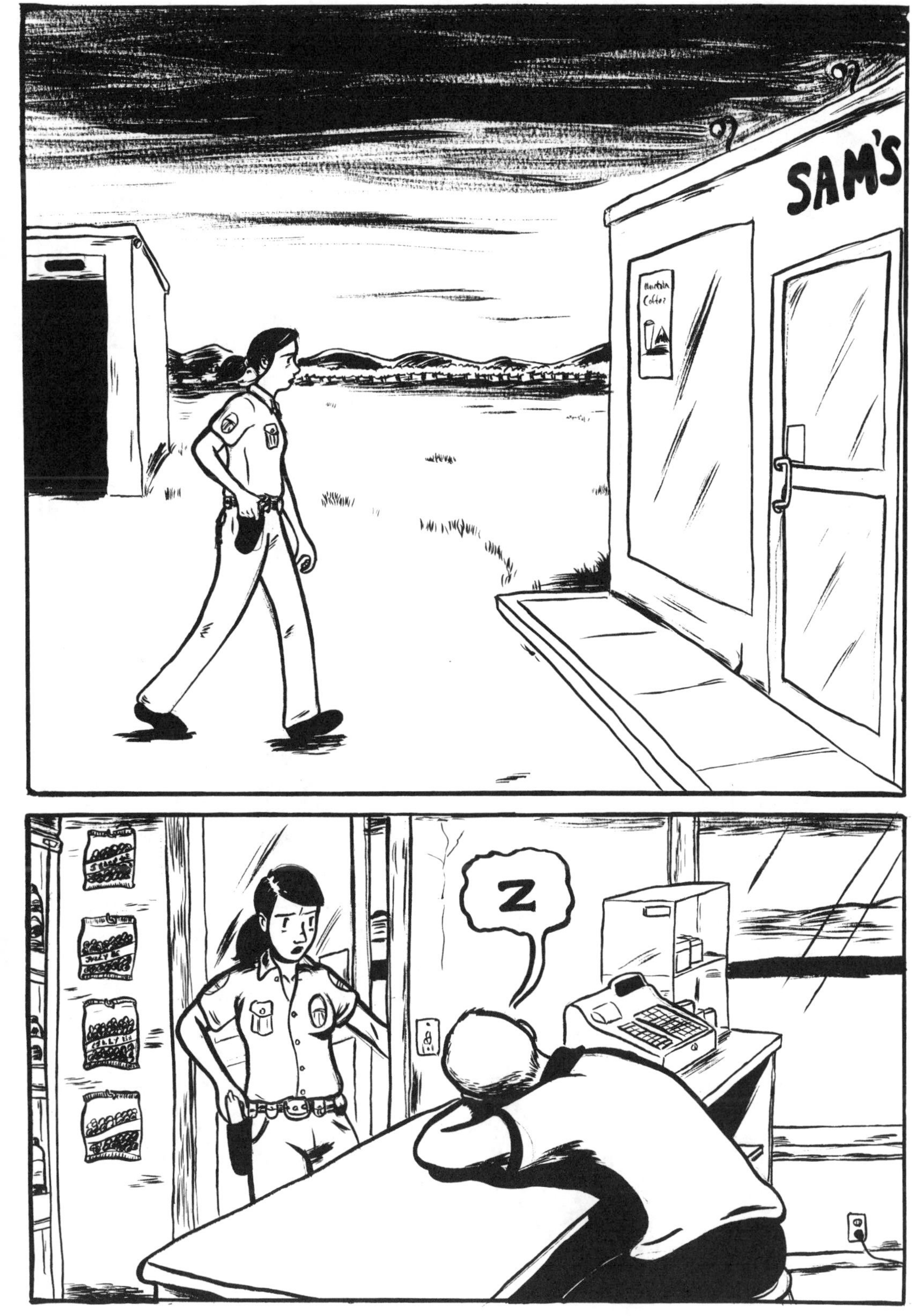
SAM'S
Z

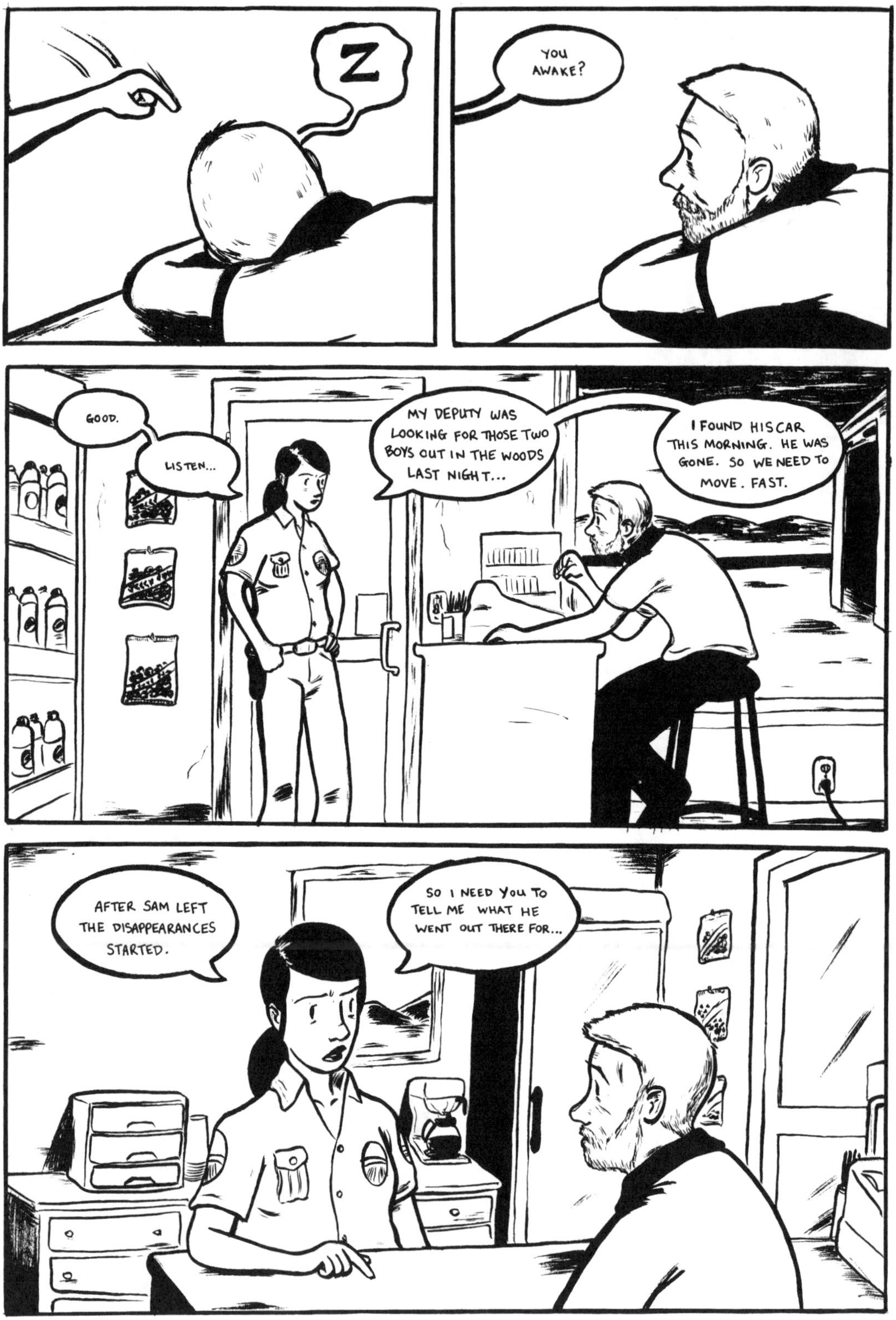
Z
YOU AWAKE?
GOOD.
LISTEN...
MY DEPUTY WAS LOOKING FOR THOSE TWO BOYS OUT IN THE WOODS LAST NIGHT...
I FOUND HIS CAR THIS MORNING. HE WAS GONE. SO WE NEED TO MOVE. FAST.
AFTER SAM LEFT THE DISAPPEARANCES STARTED.
SO I NEED YOU TO TELL ME WHAT HE WENT OUT THERE FOR...

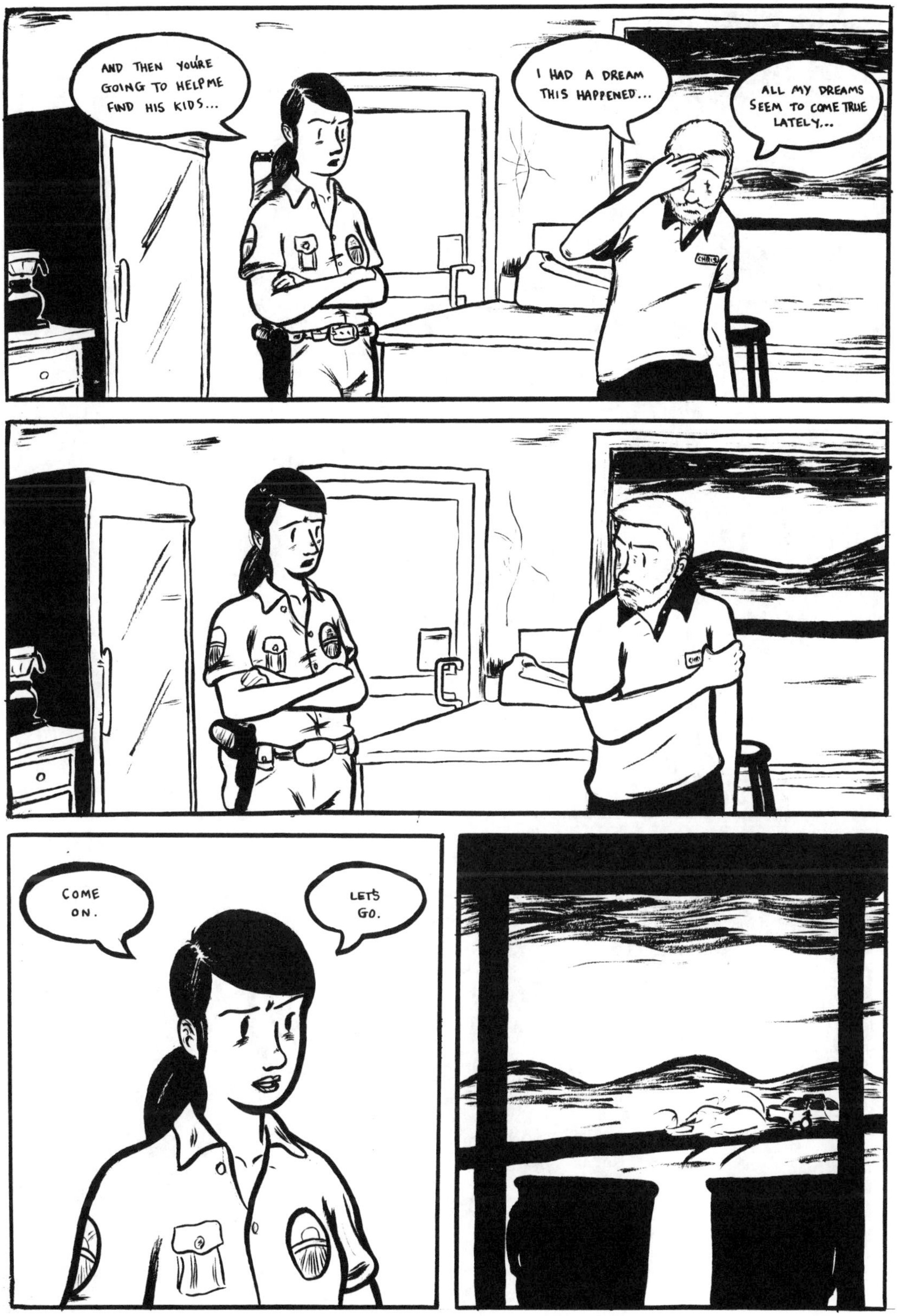
AND THEN YOU'RE GOING TO HELP ME FIND HIS KIDS...
I HAD A DREAM THIS HAPPENED...
ALL MY DREAMS SEEM TO COME TRUE LATELY...
CHRIS
CHRIS
COME ON.
LET'S GO.

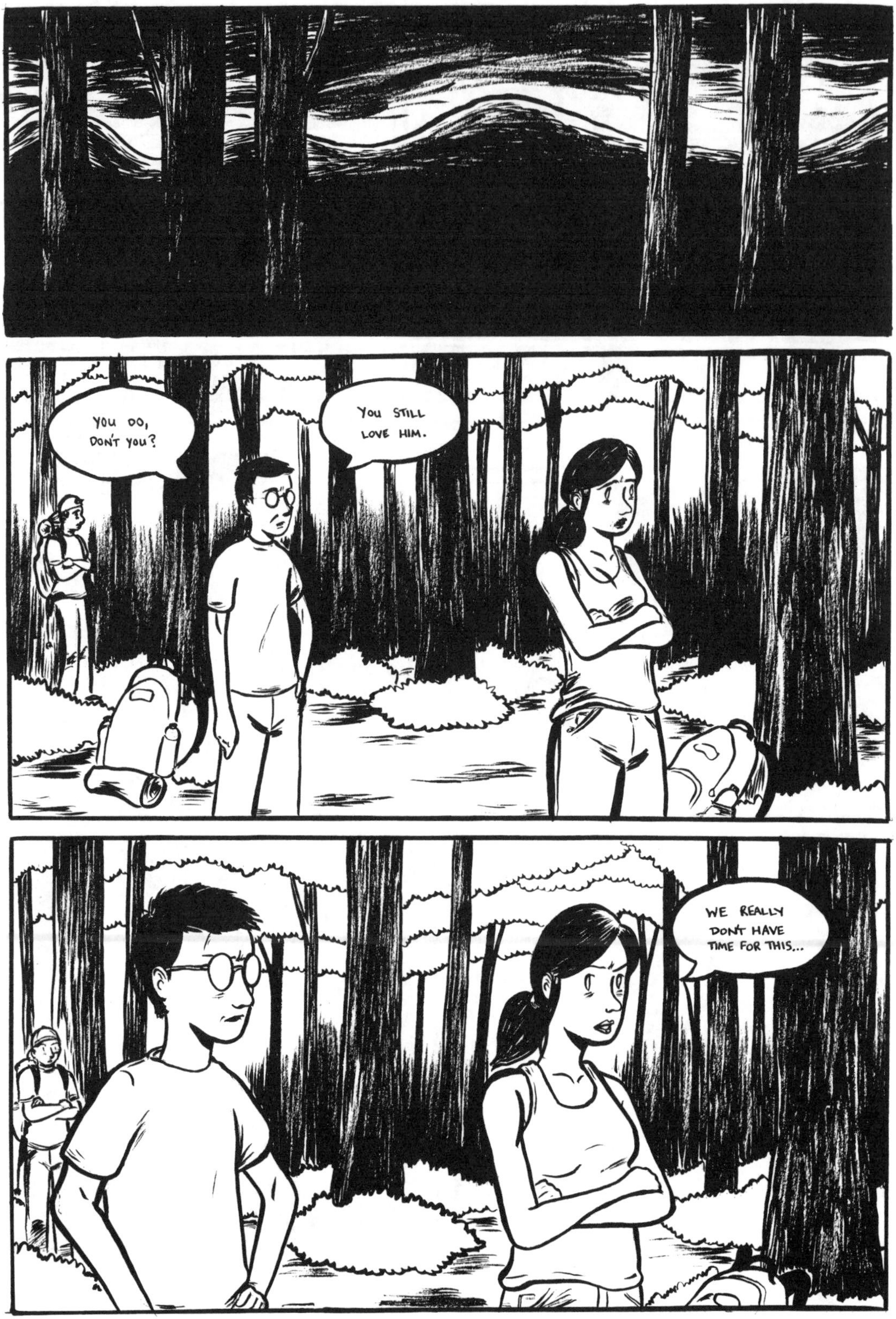
YOU DO,
DON'T YOU?
YOU STILL
LOVE HIM.
WE REALLY
DON'T HAVE
TIME FOR THIS...

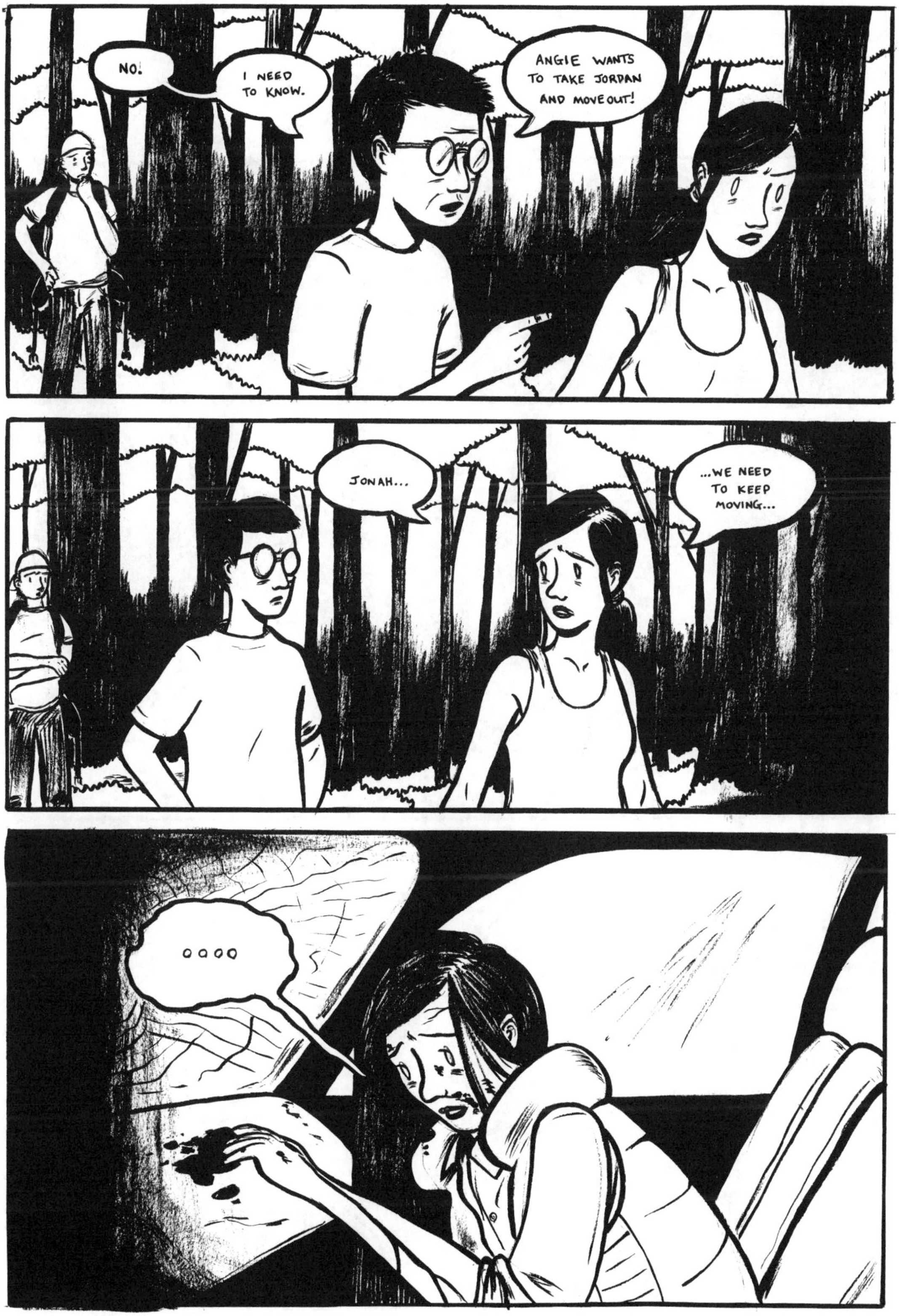
NO!
I NEED TO KNOW.
ANGIE WANTS TO TAKE JORDAN AND MOVE OUT!
JONAH...
...WE NEED TO KEEP MOVING...

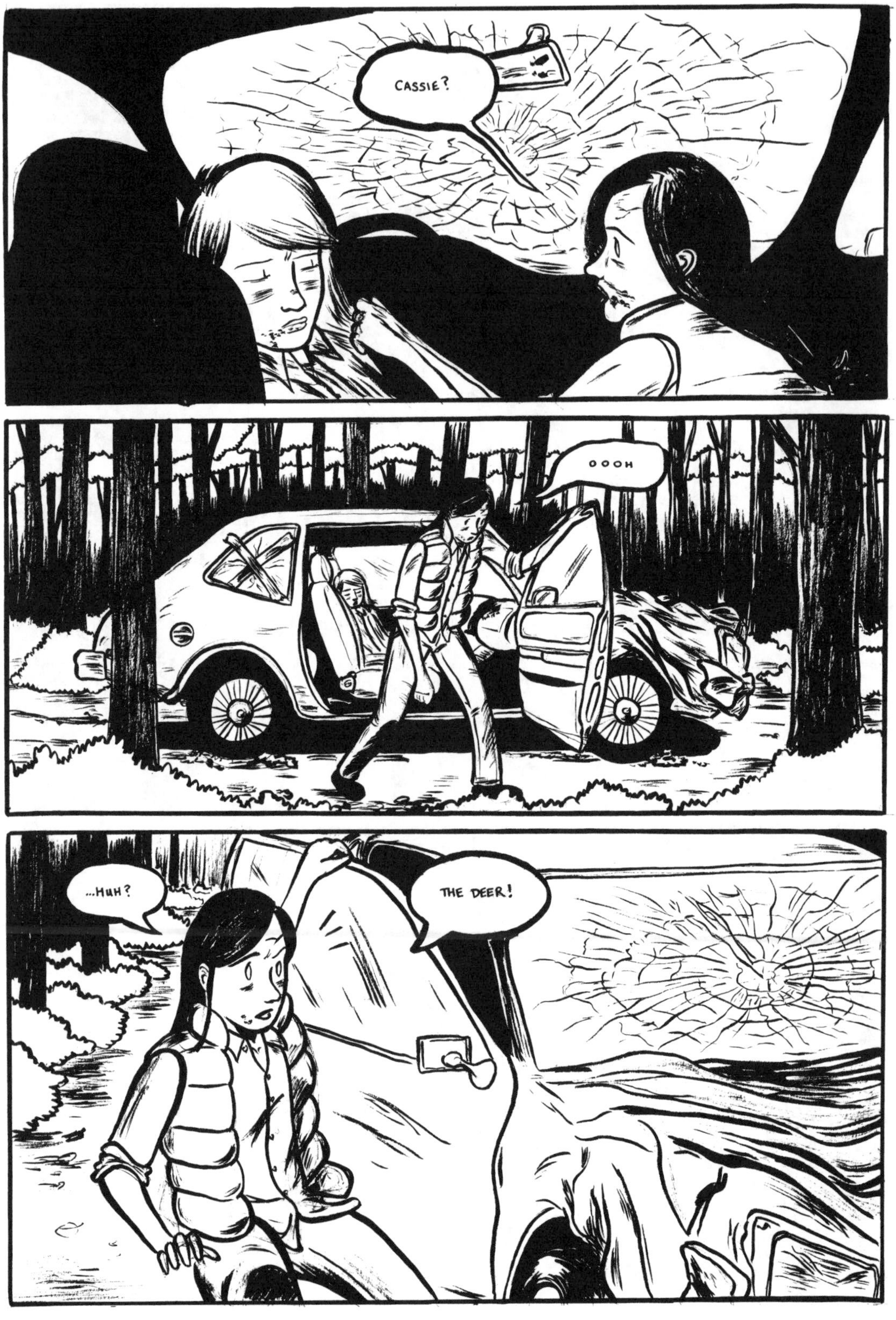
CASSIE?
OOOH
...HUH?
THE DEER!

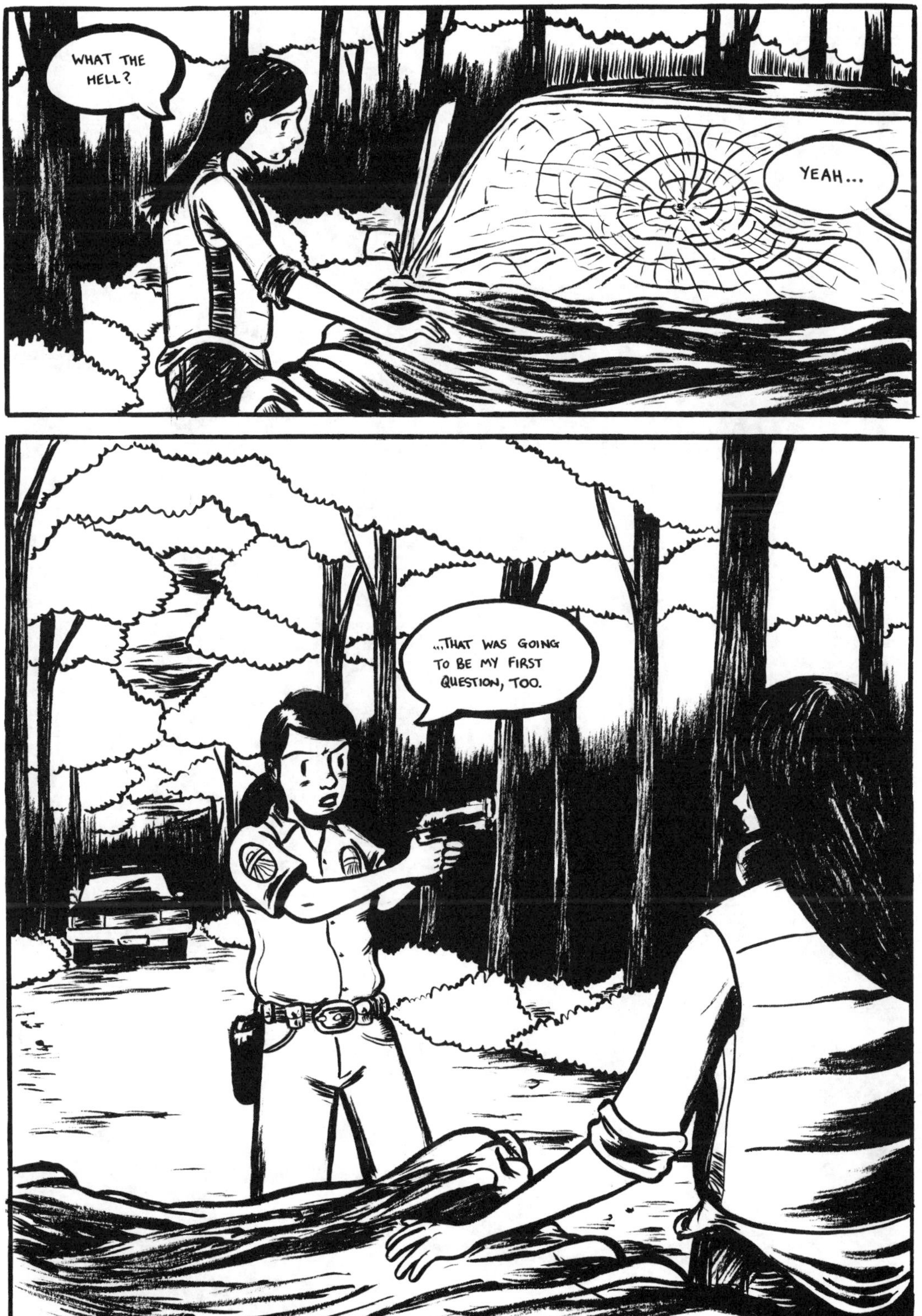
WHAT THE HELL?
YEAH...
...THAT WAS GOING TO BE MY FIRST QUESTION, TOO.

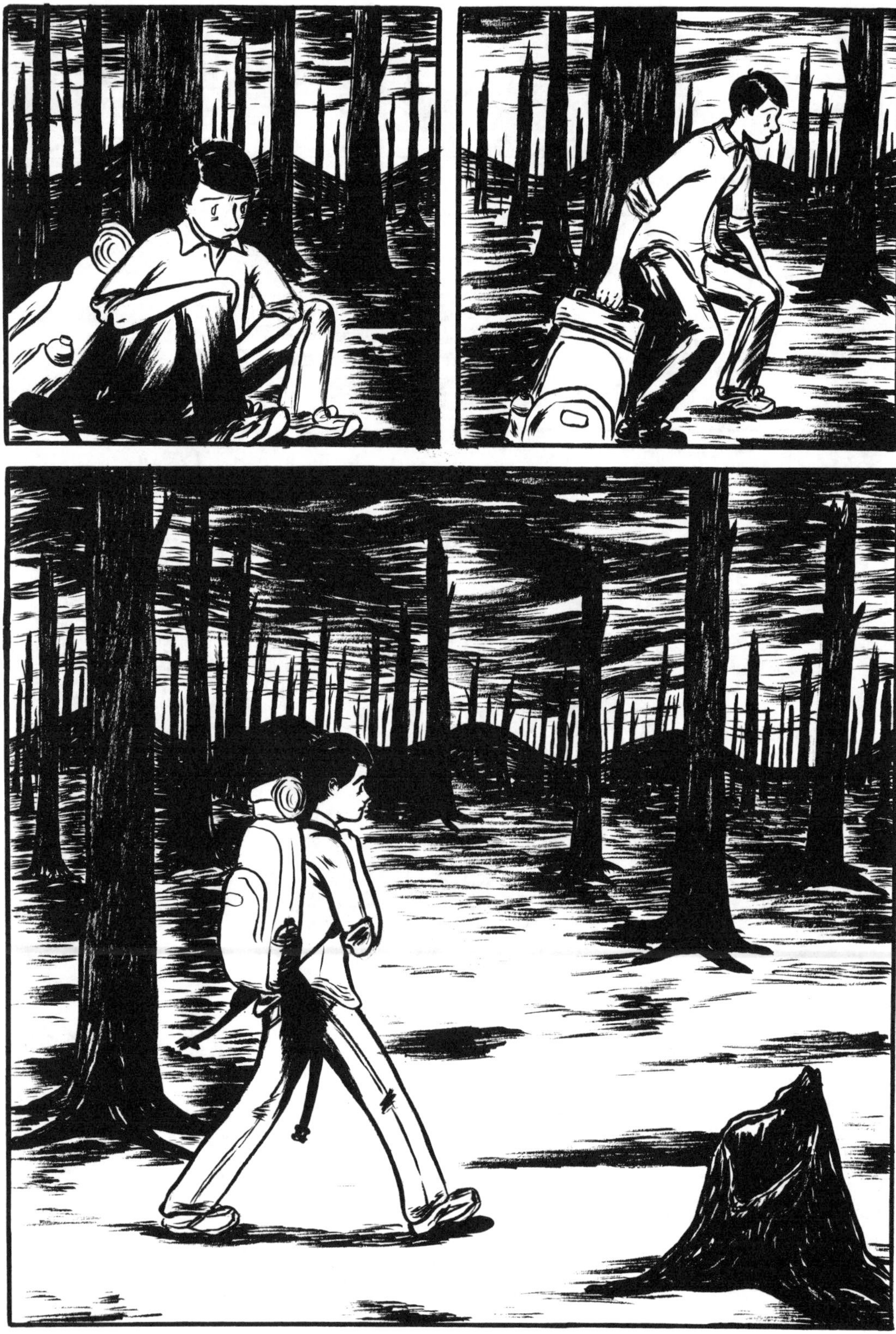

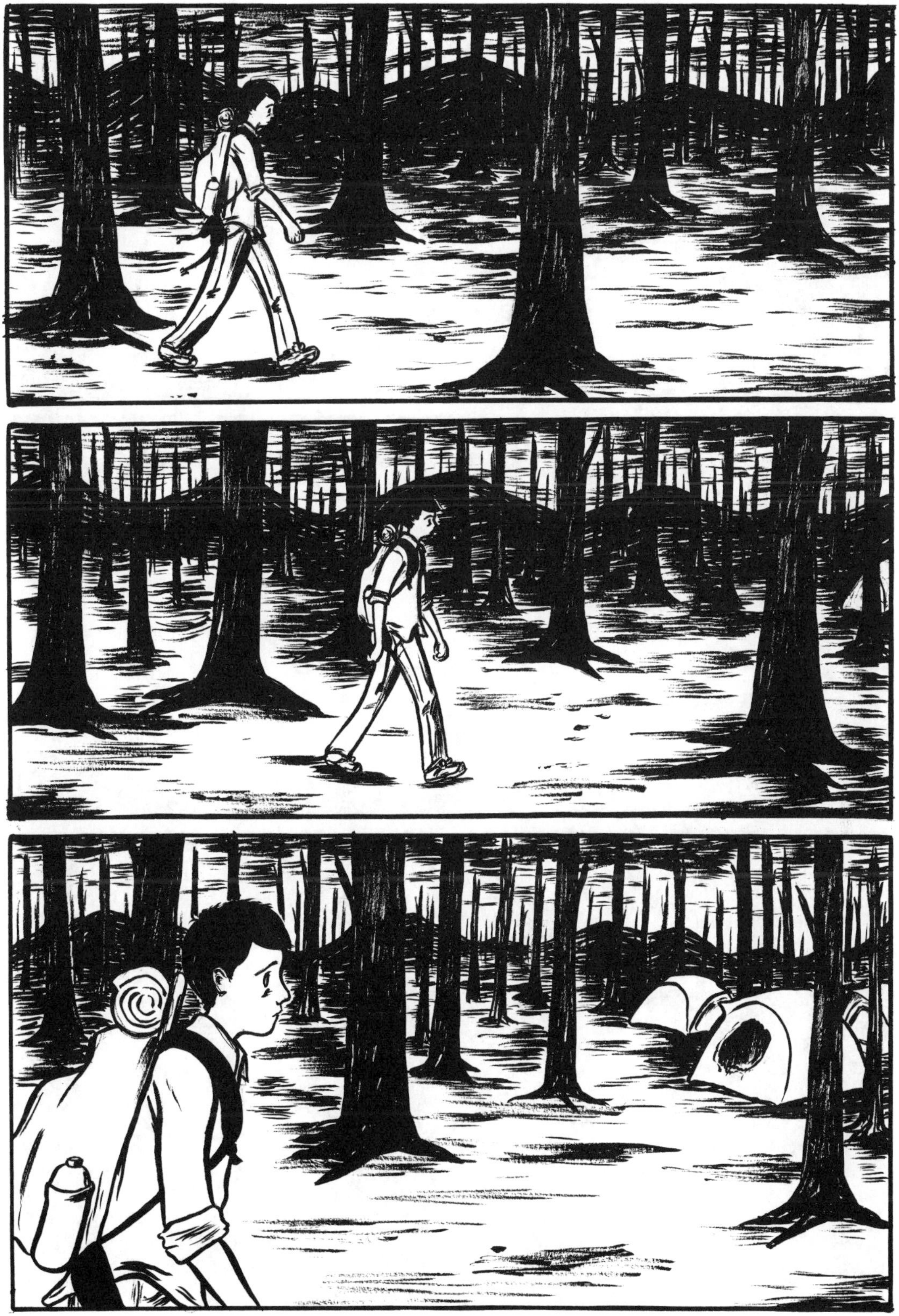

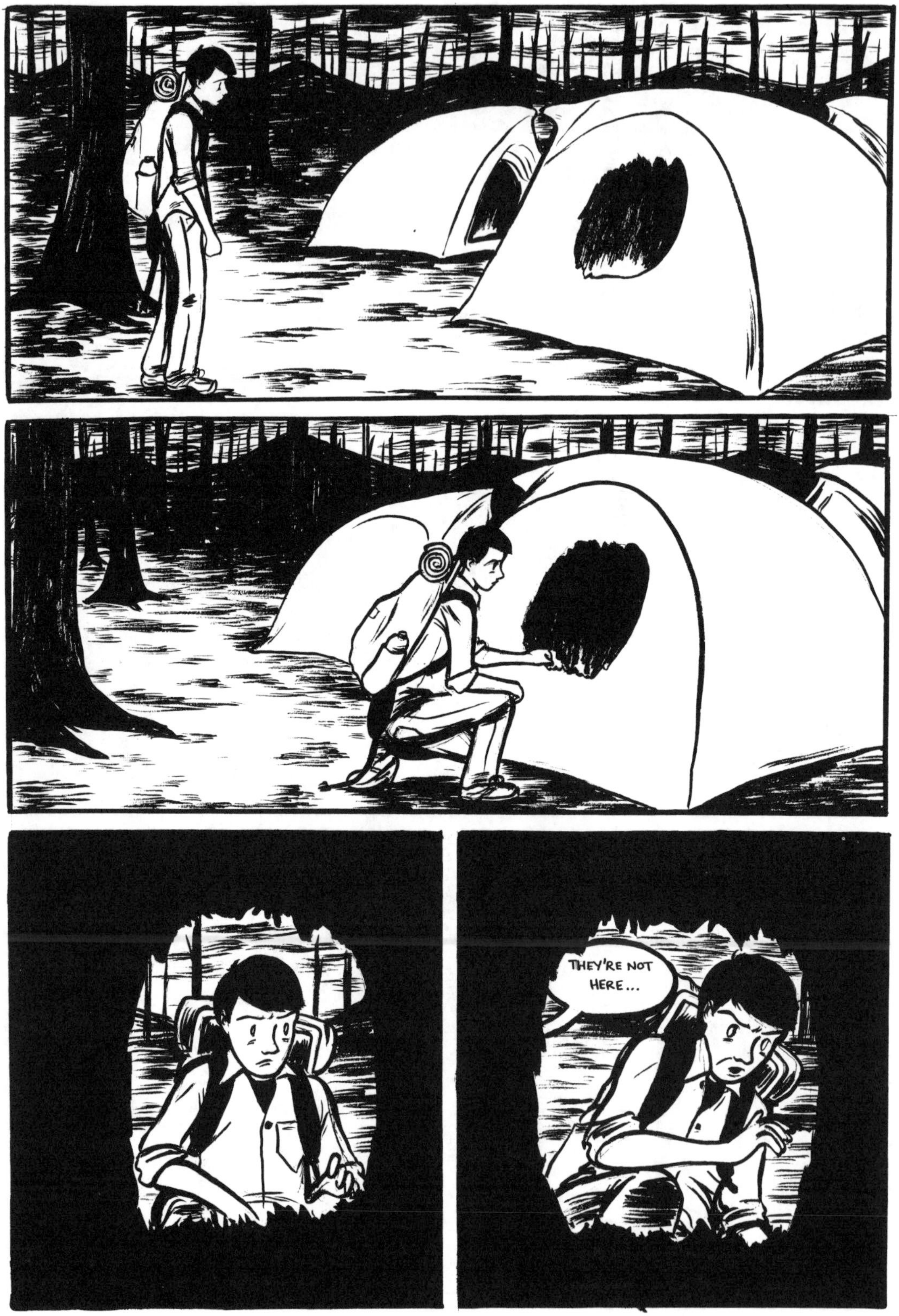
THEY'RE NOT HERE...

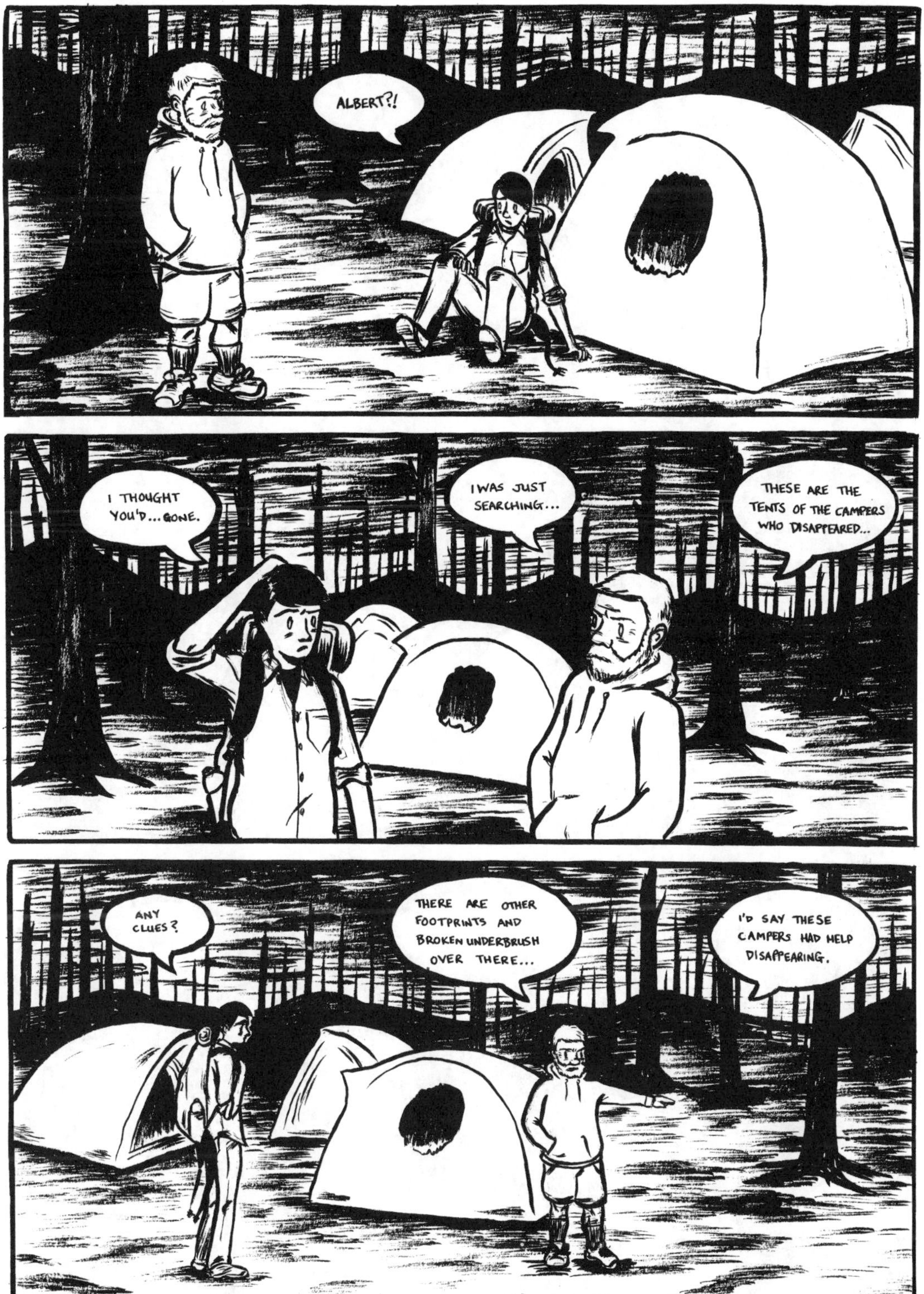
ALBERT?!
I THOUGHT YOU'D... GONE.
I WAS JUST SEARCHING...
THESE ARE THE TENTS OF THE CAMPERS WHO DISAPPEARED...
ANY CLUES?
THERE ARE OTHER FOOTPRINTS AND BROKEN UNDERBRUSH OVER THERE...
I'D SAY THESE CAMPERS HAD HELP DISAPPEARING.

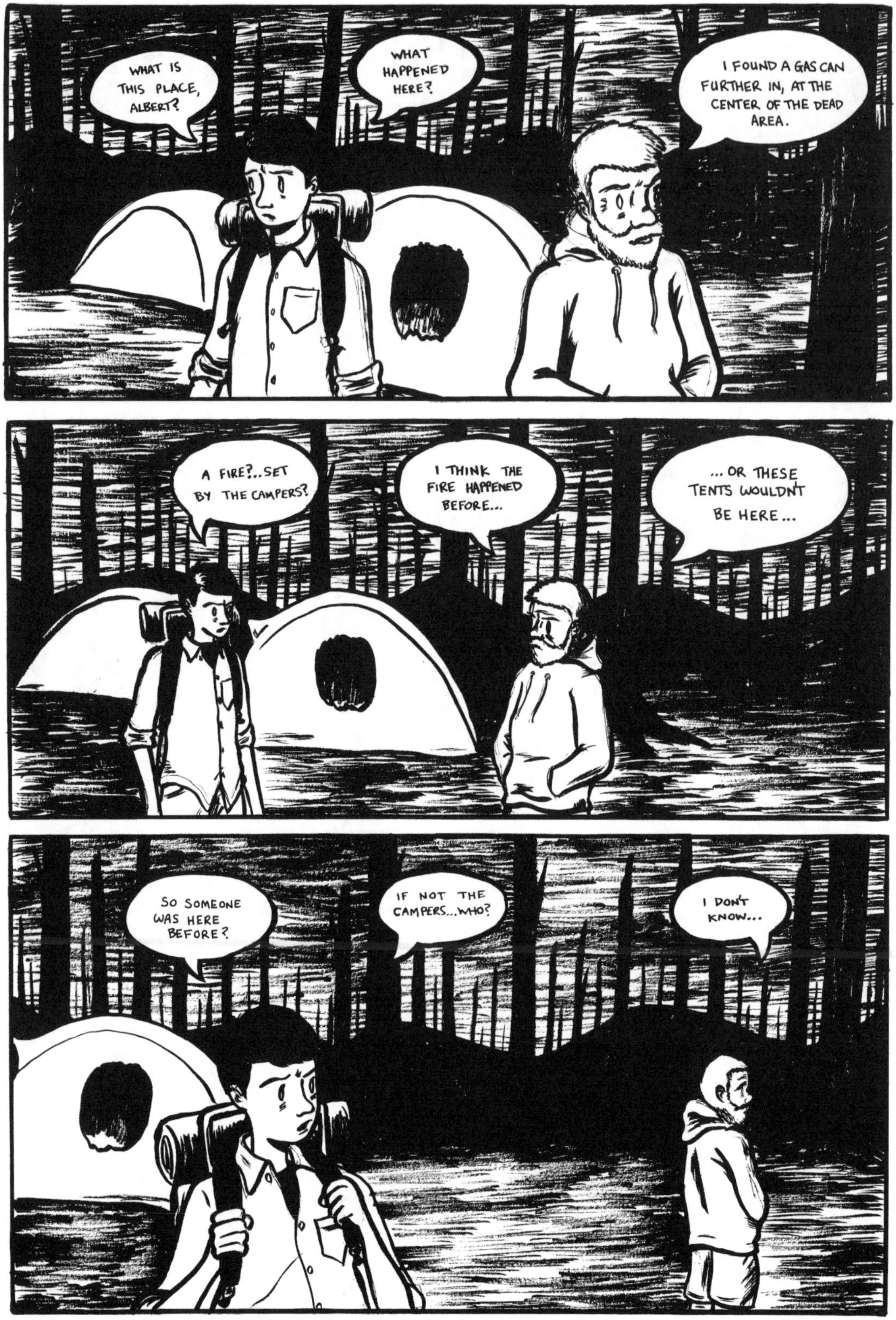
WHAT IS THIS PLACE, ALBERT?
WHAT HAPPENED HERE?
I FOUND A GAS CAN FURTHER IN, AT THE CENTER OF THE DEAD AREA.
A FIRE?.. SET BY THE CAMPERS?
I THINK THE FIRE HAPPENED BEFORE...
... OR THESE TENTS WOULDN'T BE HERE...
SO SOMEONE WAS HERE BEFORE?
IF NOT THE CAMPERS... WHO?
I DON'T KNOW...

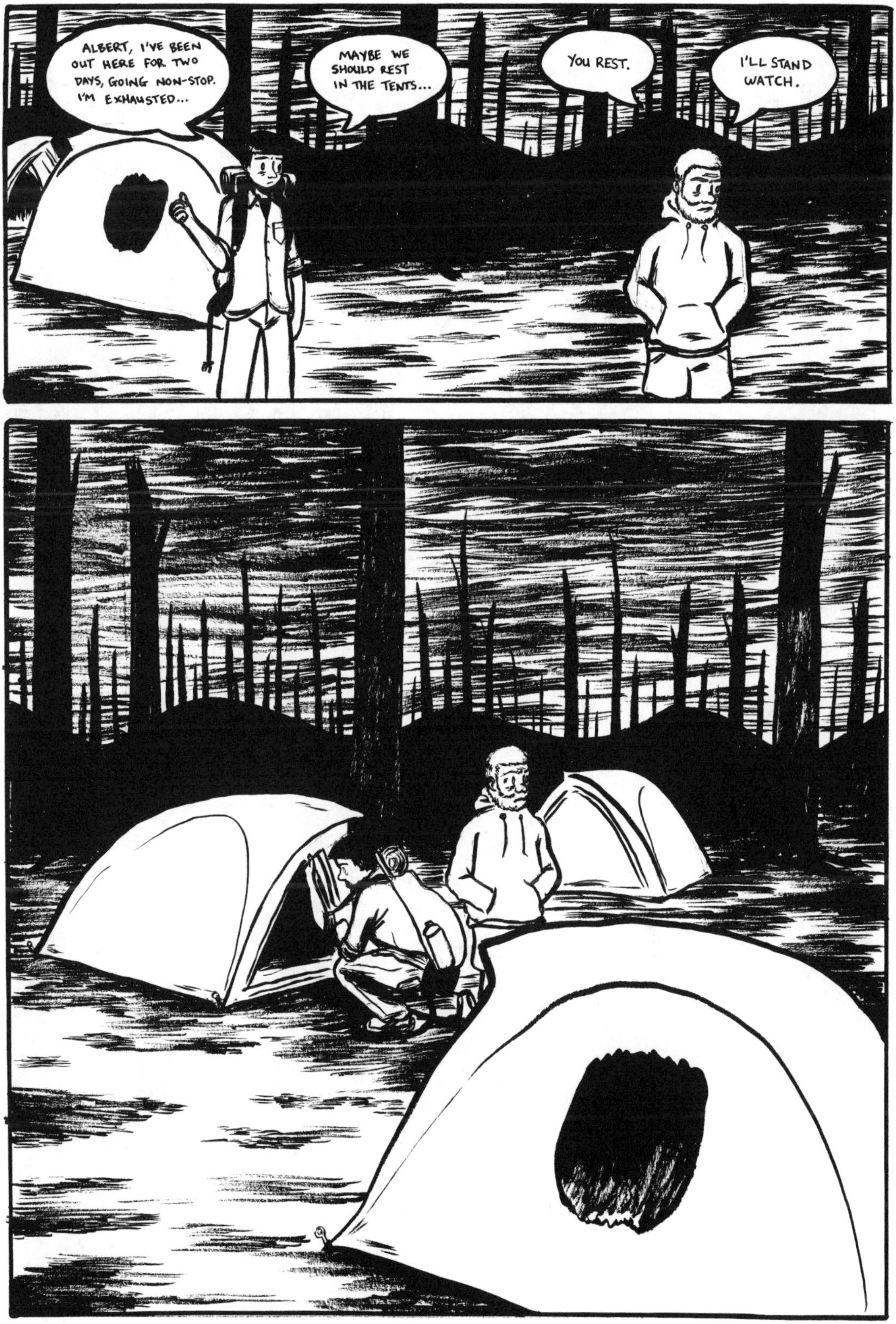
ALBERT, I'VE BEEN OUT HERE FOR TWO DAYS, GOING NON-STOP. I'M EXHAUSTED...
MAYBE WE SHOULD REST IN THE TENTS...
YOU REST.
I'LL STAND WATCH.

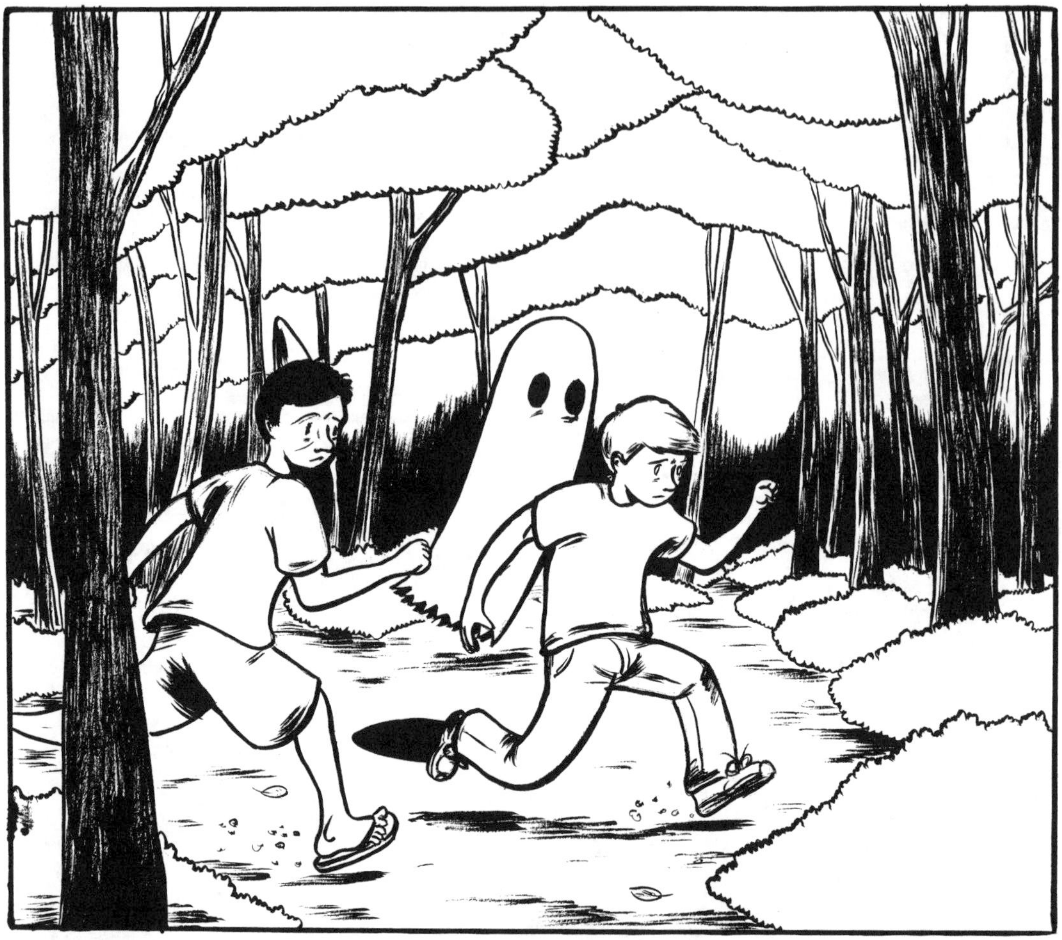

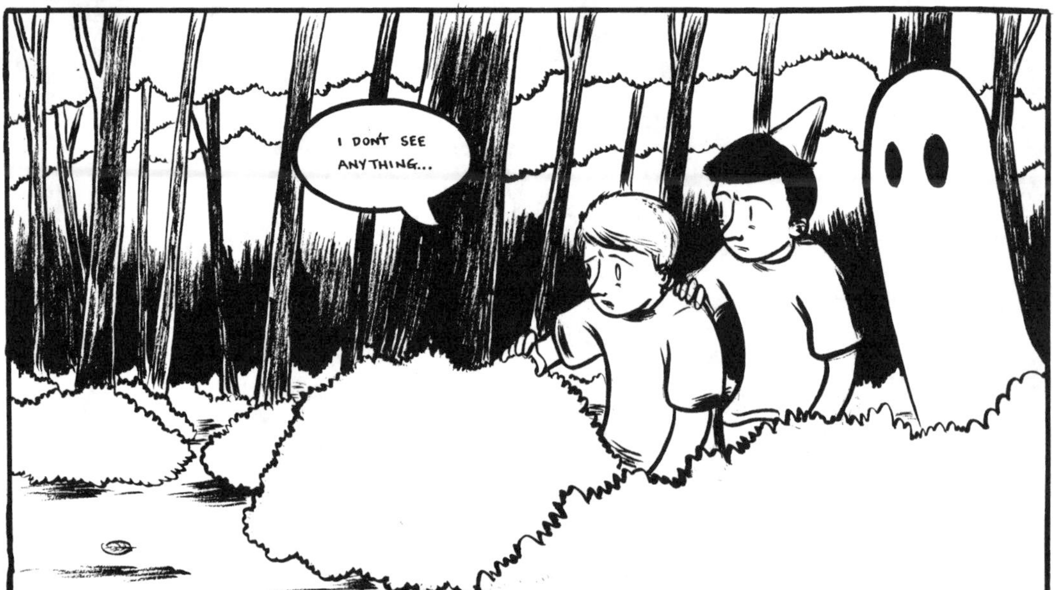
I DON'T SEE ANYTHING...

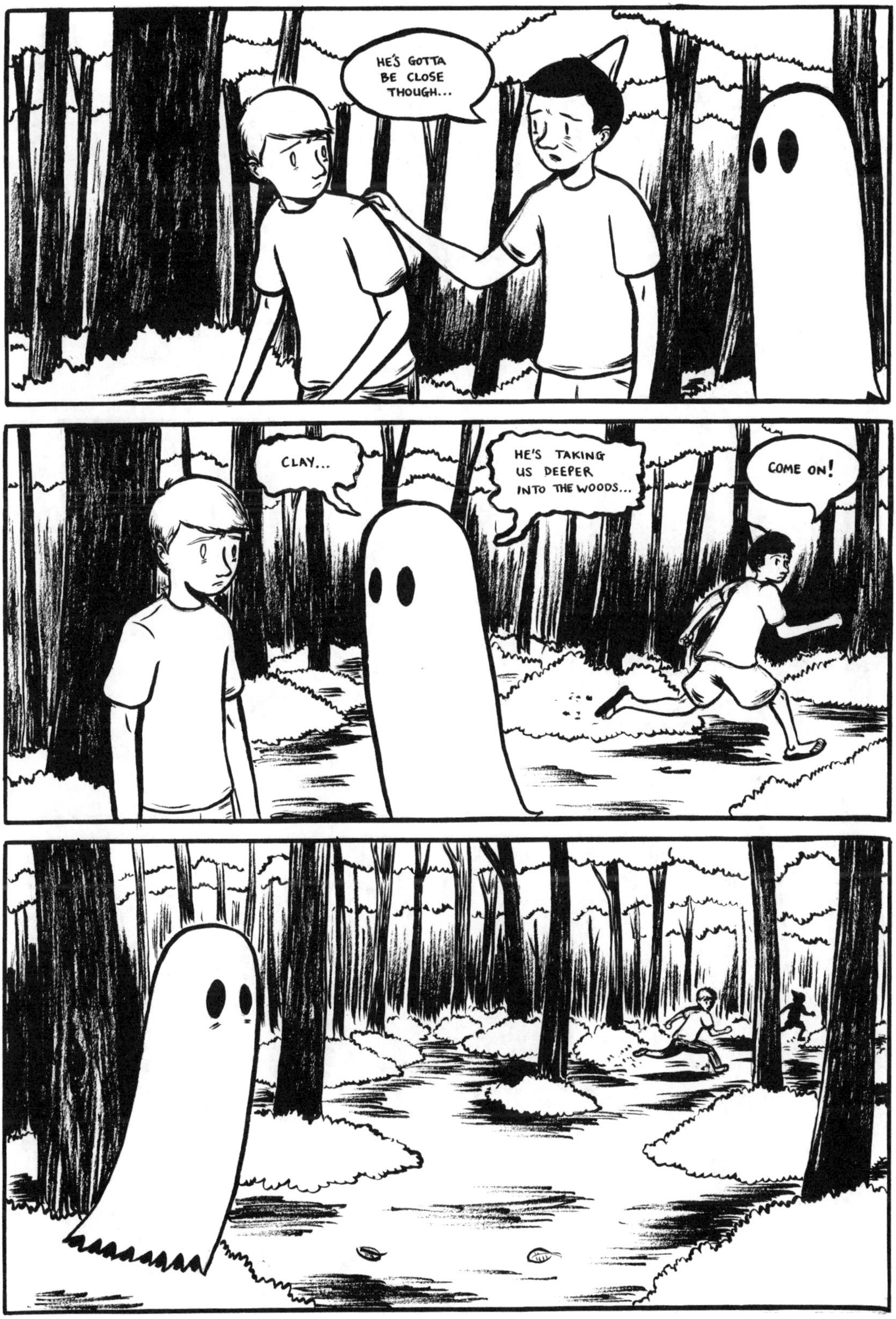
HE'S GOTTA BE CLOSE THOUGH...
CLAY...
HE'S TAKING US DEEPER INTO THE WOODS...
COME ON!

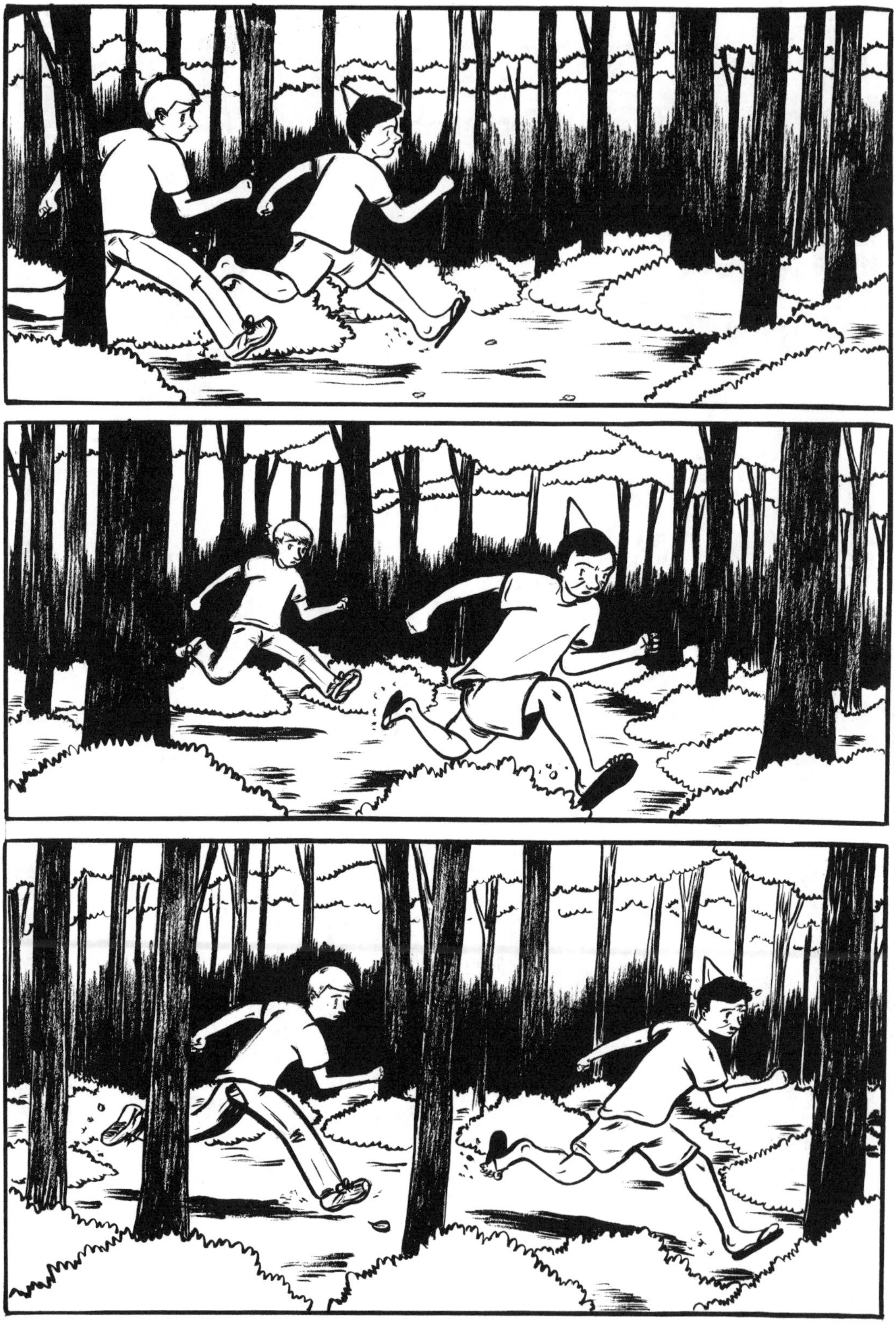

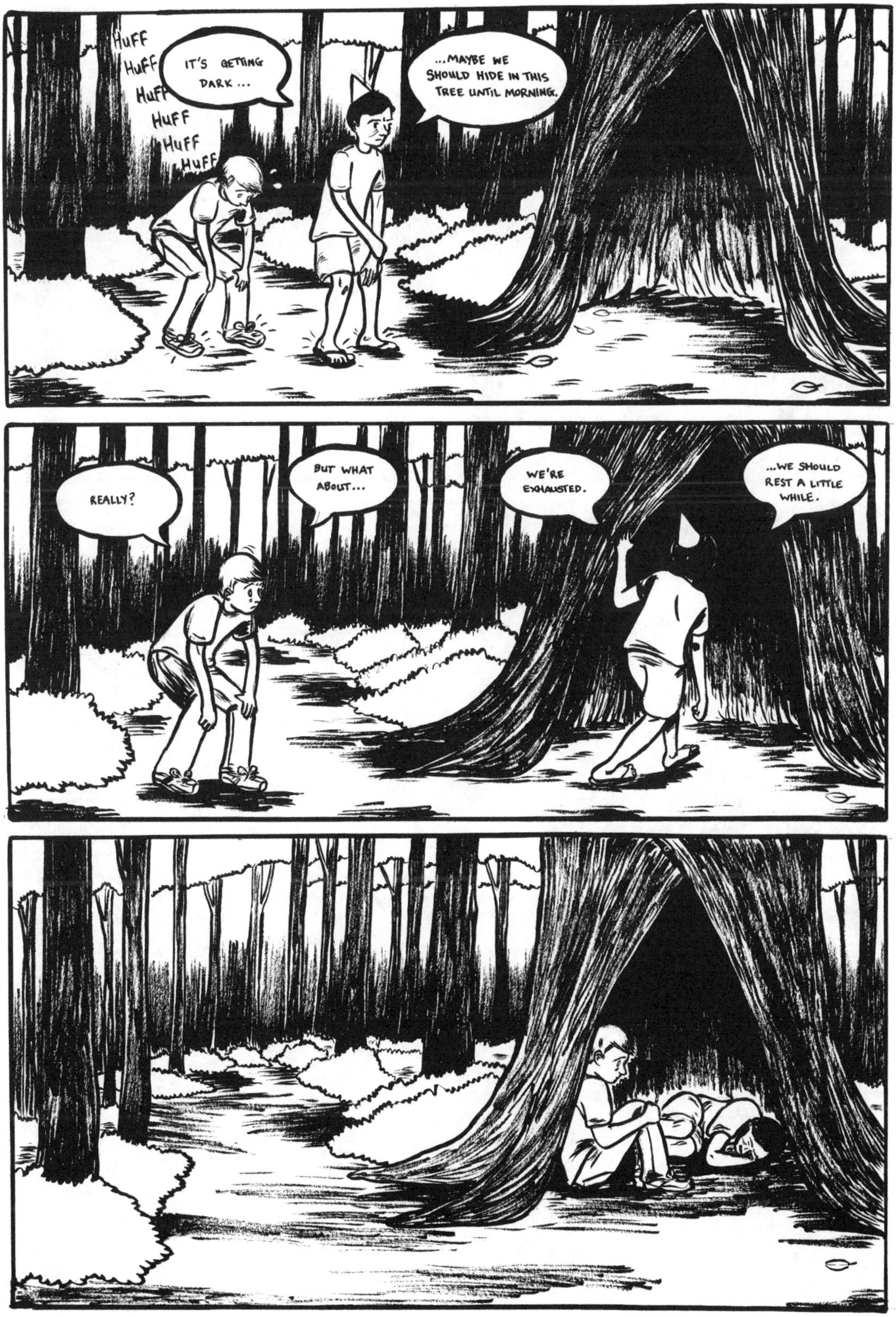
HUFF HUFF HUFF HUFF HUFF HUFF
IT'S GETTING DARK...
...MAYBE WE SHOULD HIDE IN THIS TREE UNTIL MORNING.
REALLY?
BUT WHAT ABOUT...
WE'RE EXHAUSTED.
...WE SHOULD REST A LITTLE WHILE.

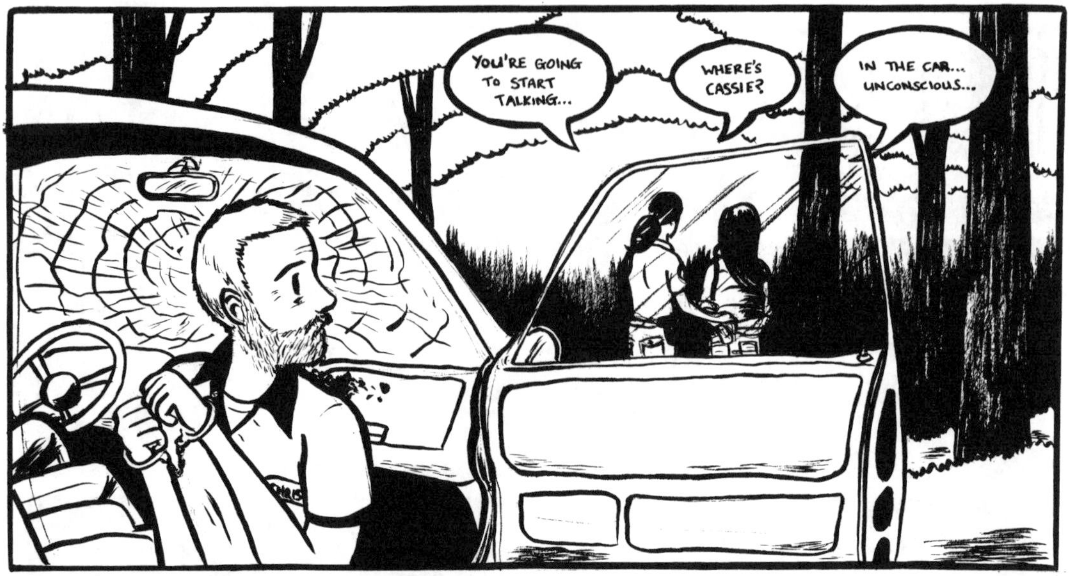
YOU'RE GOING TO START TALKING...
WHERE'S CASSIE?
IN THE CAR... UNCONSCIOUS...

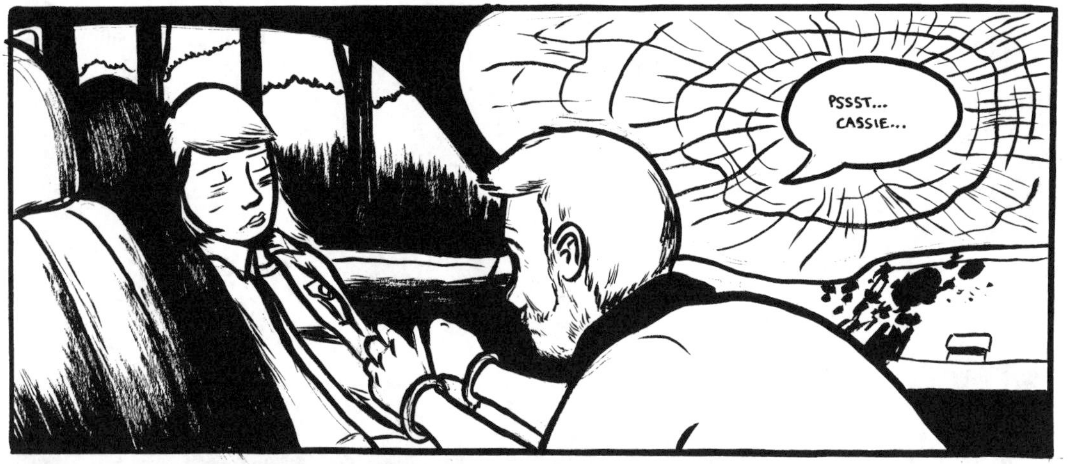
PSSST... CASSIE...

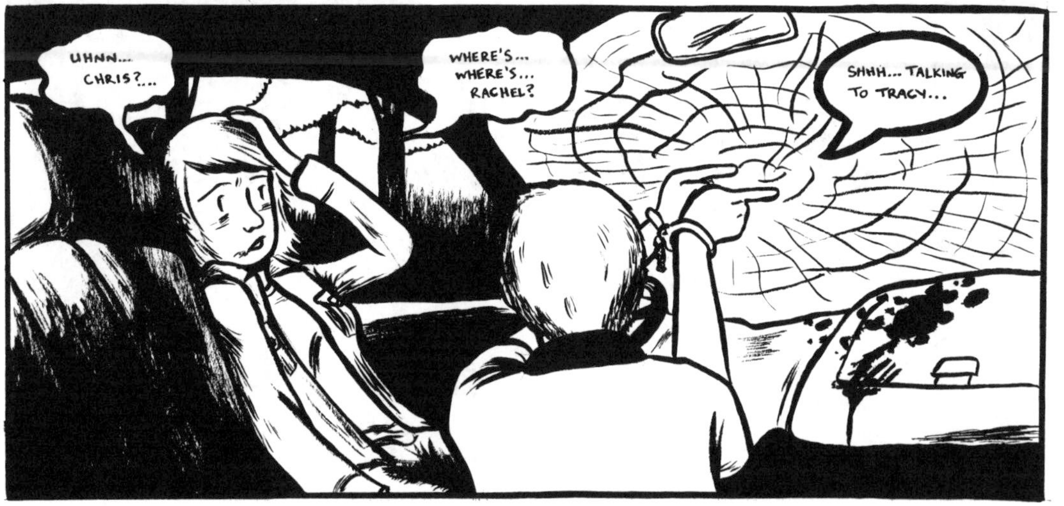
UHNN... CHRIS?...
WHERE'S... WHERE'S... RACHEL?
SHHH... TALKING TO TRACY...

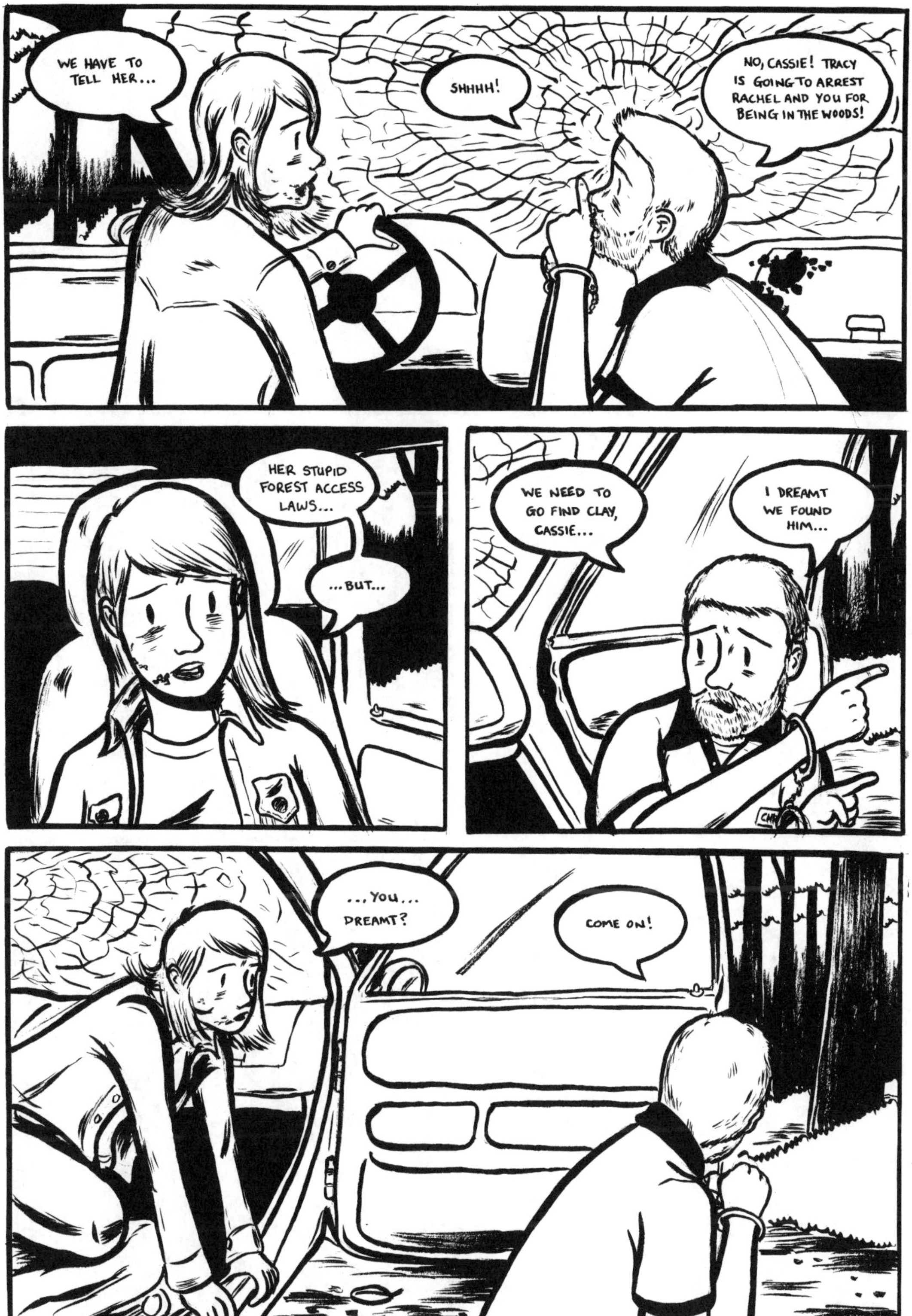
WE HAVE TO TELL HER...
SHHHH!
NO, CASSIE! TRACY IS GOING TO ARREST RACHEL AND YOU FOR BEING IN THE WOODS!
HER STUPID FOREST ACCESS LAWS...
...BUT...
WE NEED TO GO FIND CLAY, CASSIE...
I DREAMT WE FOUND HIM...
...YOU... DREAMT?
COME ON!

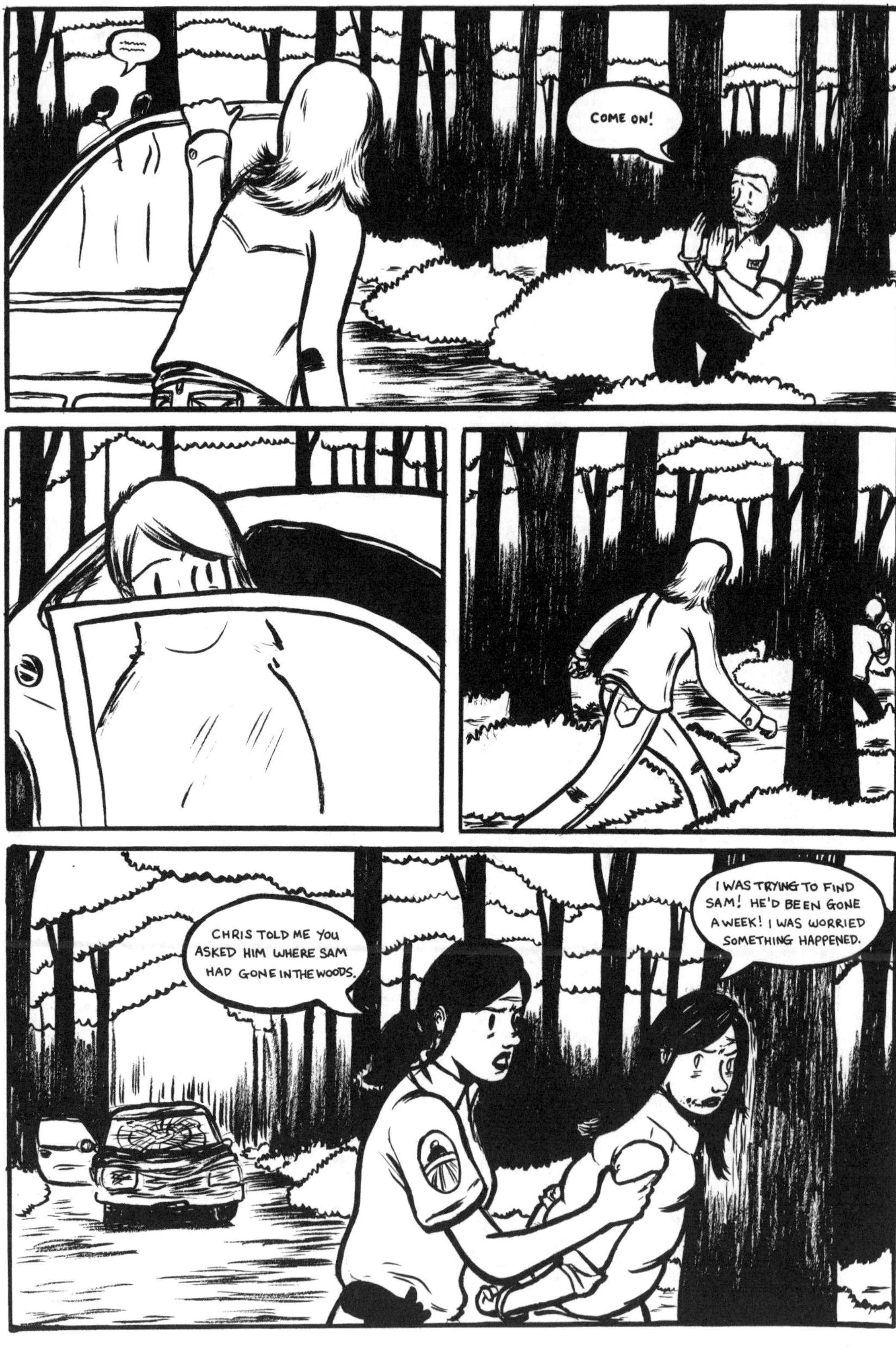
COME ON!
CHRIS TOLD ME YOU ASKED HIM WHERE SAM HAD GONE IN THE WOODS.
I WAS TRYING TO FIND SAM! HE'D BEEN GONE A WEEK! I WAS WORRIED SOMETHING HAPPENED.

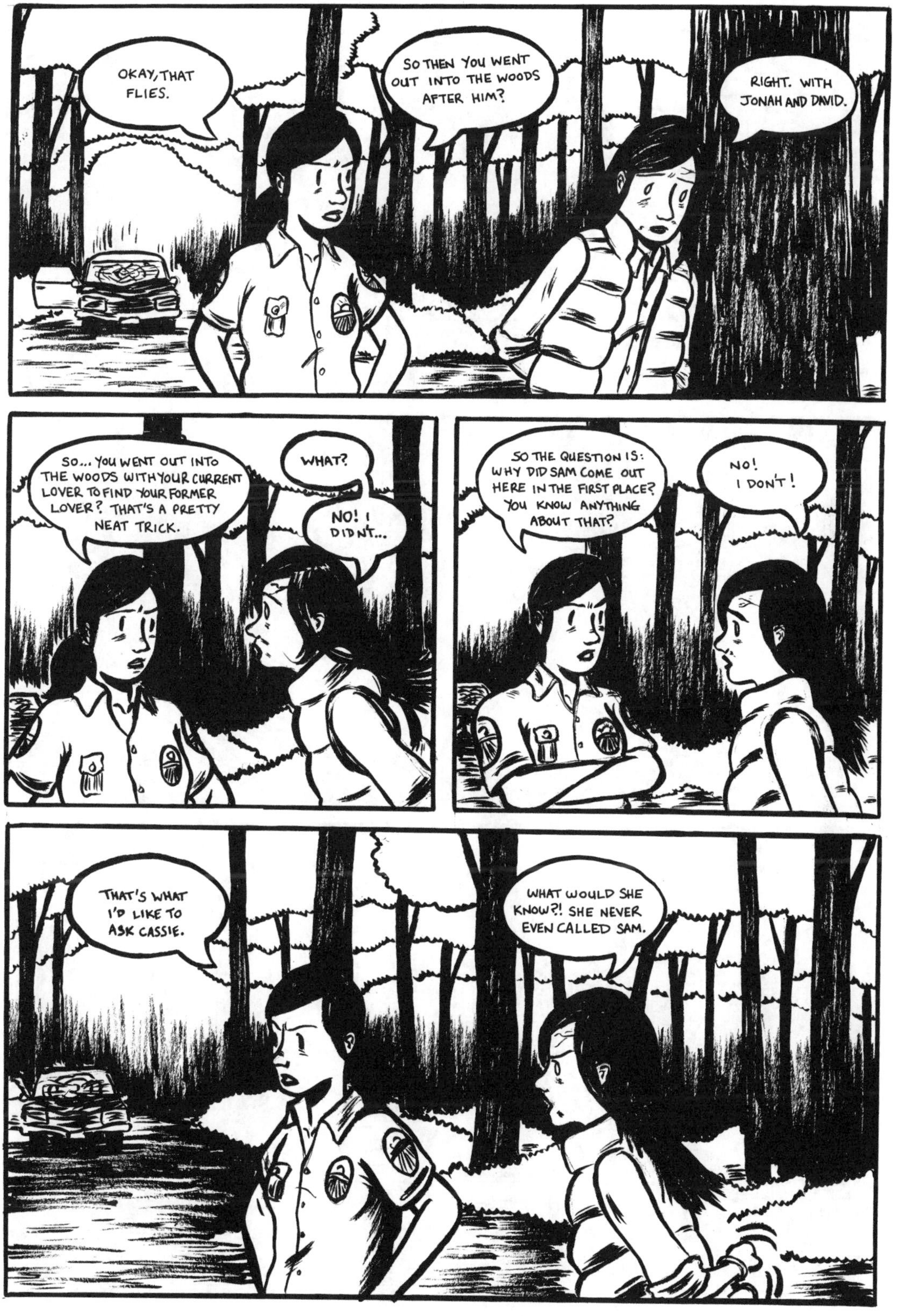
OKAY, THAT FLIES.
SO THEN YOU WENT OUT INTO THE WOODS AFTER HIM?
RIGHT. WITH JONAH AND DAVID.
SO... YOU WENT OUT INTO THE WOODS WITH YOUR CURRENT LOVER TO FIND YOUR FORMER LOVER? THAT'S A PRETTY NEAT TRICK.
WHAT?
NO! I DIDN'T...
SO THE QUESTION IS: WHY DID SAM COME OUT HERE IN THE FIRST PLACE? YOU KNOW ANYTHING ABOUT THAT?
NO! I DON'T!
THAT'S WHAT I'D LIKE TO ASK CASSIE.
WHAT WOULD SHE KNOW?! SHE NEVER EVEN CALLED SAM.

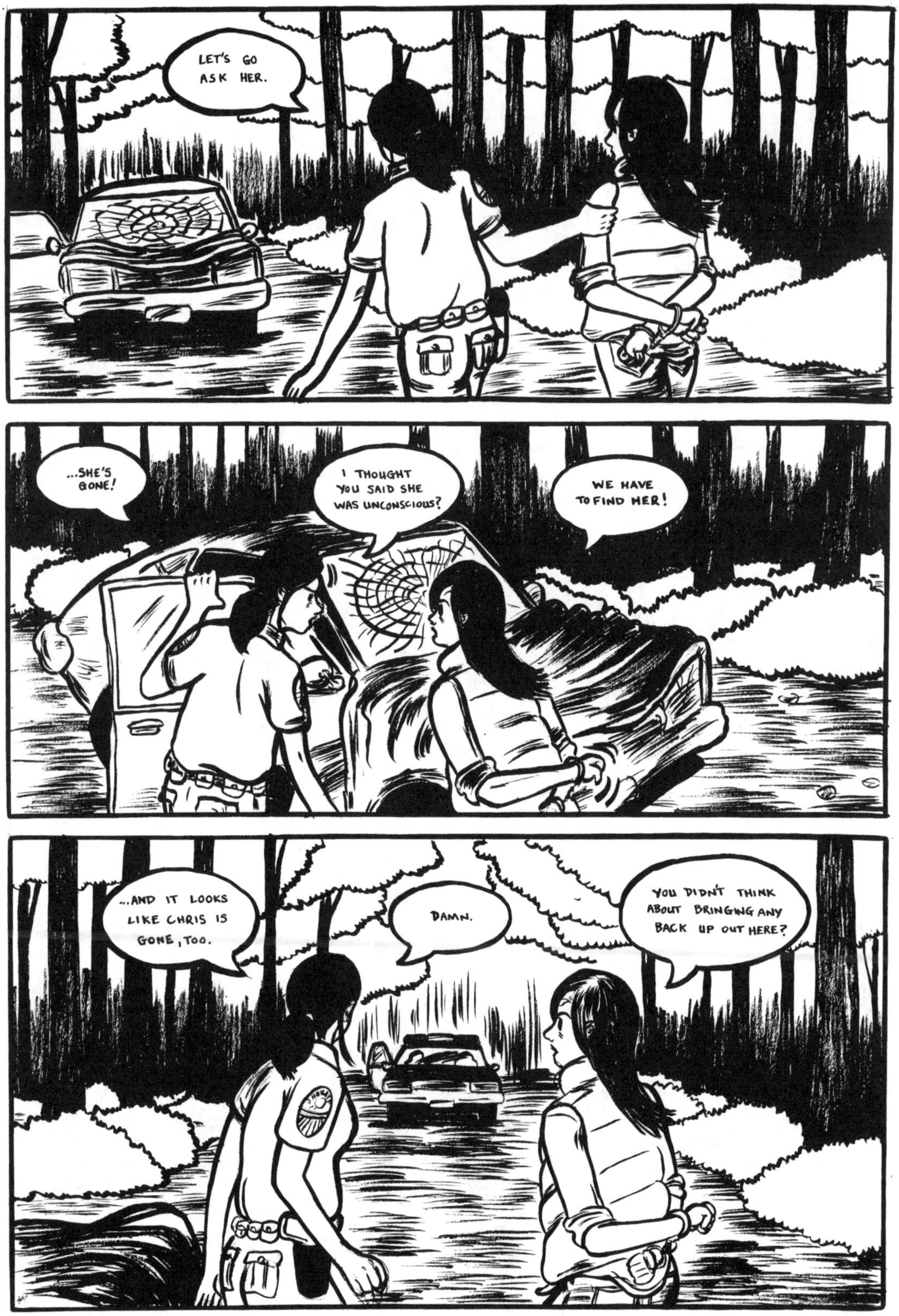
LET'S GO ASK HER.
...SHE'S GONE!
I THOUGHT YOU SAID SHE WAS UNCONSCIOUS?
WE HAVE TO FIND HER!
...AND IT LOOKS LIKE CHRIS IS GONE, TOO.
DAMN.
YOU DIDN'T THINK ABOUT BRINGING ANY BACK UP OUT HERE?

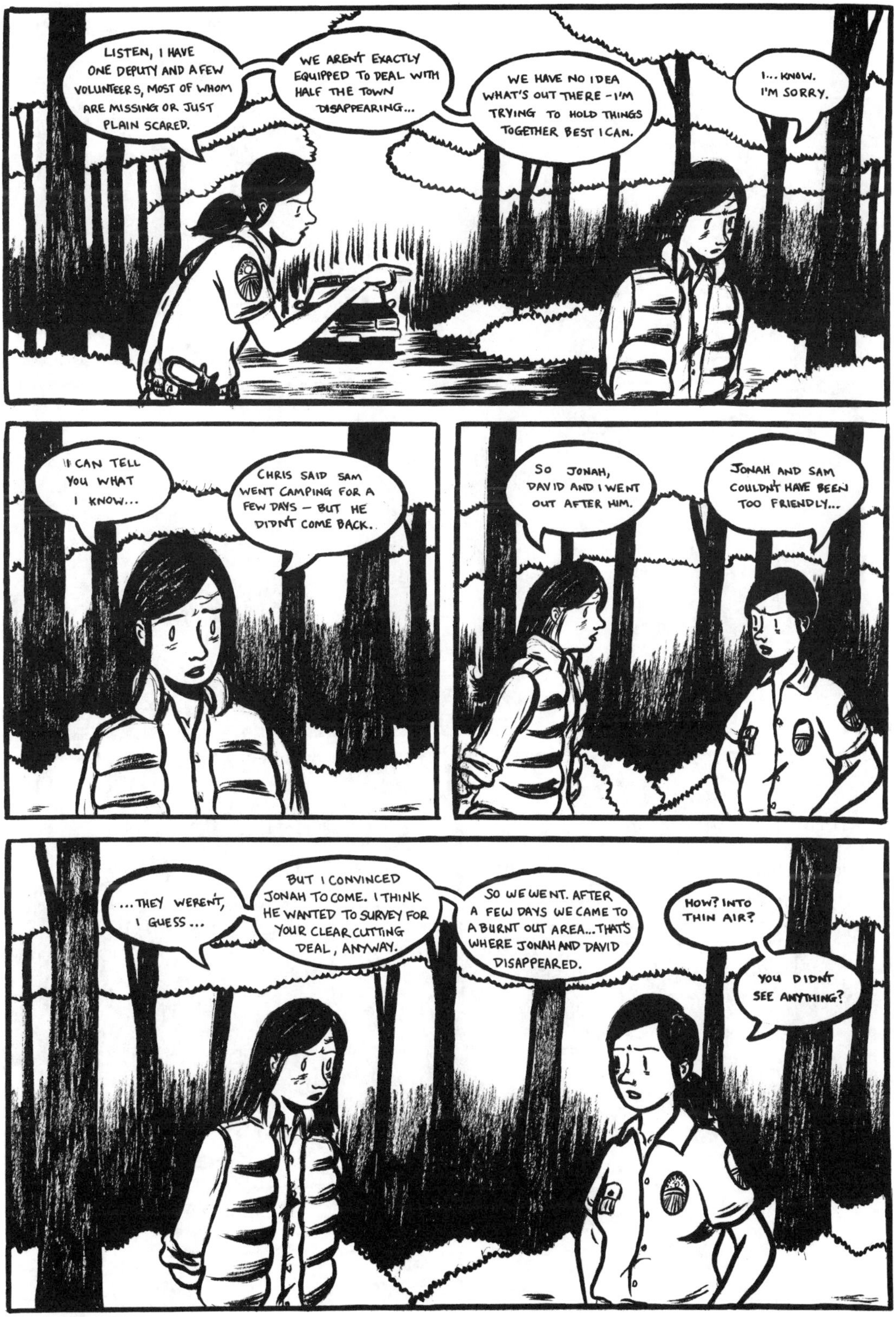
LISTEN, I HAVE ONE DEPUTY AND A FEW VOLUNTEERS, MOST OF WHOM ARE MISSING OR JUST PLAIN SCARED.
WE AREN'T EXACTLY EQUIPPED TO DEAL WITH HALF THE TOWN DISAPPEARING...
WE HAVE NO IDEA WHAT'S OUT THERE - I'M TRYING TO HOLD THINGS TOGETHER BEST I CAN.
I... KNOW. I'M SORRY.
I CAN TELL YOU WHAT I KNOW...
CHRIS SAID SAM WENT CAMPING FOR A FEW DAYS - BUT HE DIDN'T COME BACK.
SO JONAH, DAVID AND I WENT OUT AFTER HIM.
JONAH AND SAM COULDN'T HAVE BEEN TOO FRIENDLY...
...THEY WEREN'T, I GUESS...
BUT I CONVINCED JONAH TO COME. I THINK HE WANTED TO SURVEY FOR YOUR CLEAR CUTTING DEAL, ANYWAY.
SO WE WENT. AFTER A FEW DAYS WE CAME TO A BURNT OUT AREA... THAT'S WHERE JONAH AND DAVID DISAPPEARED.
HOW? INTO THIN AIR?
YOU DIDN'T SEE ANYTHING?

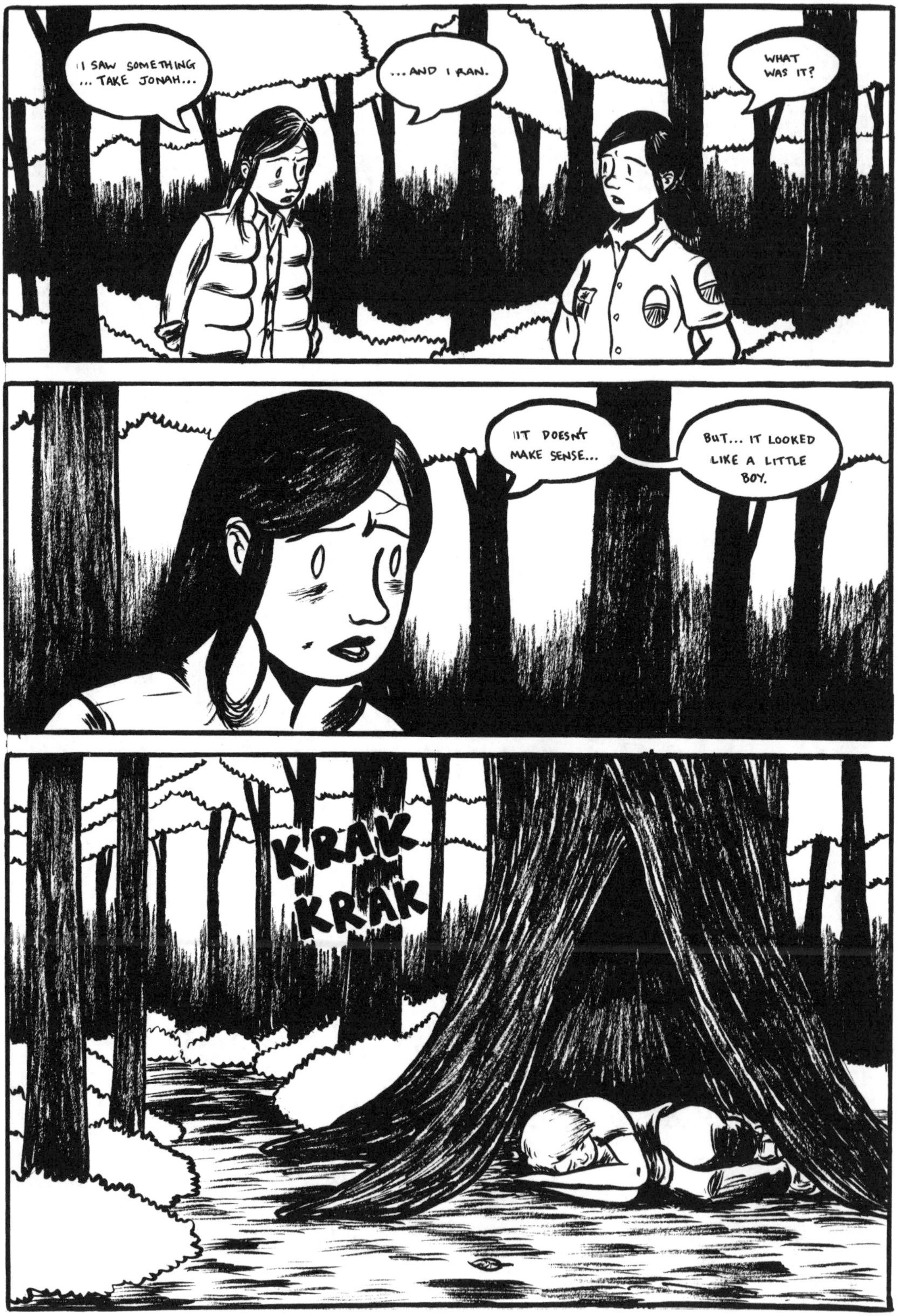

I SAW SOMETHING ... TAKE JONAH...
...AND I RAN.
WHAT WAS IT?
IT DOESN'T MAKE SENSE...
BUT... IT LOOKED LIKE A LITTLE BOY.
KRAK KRAK

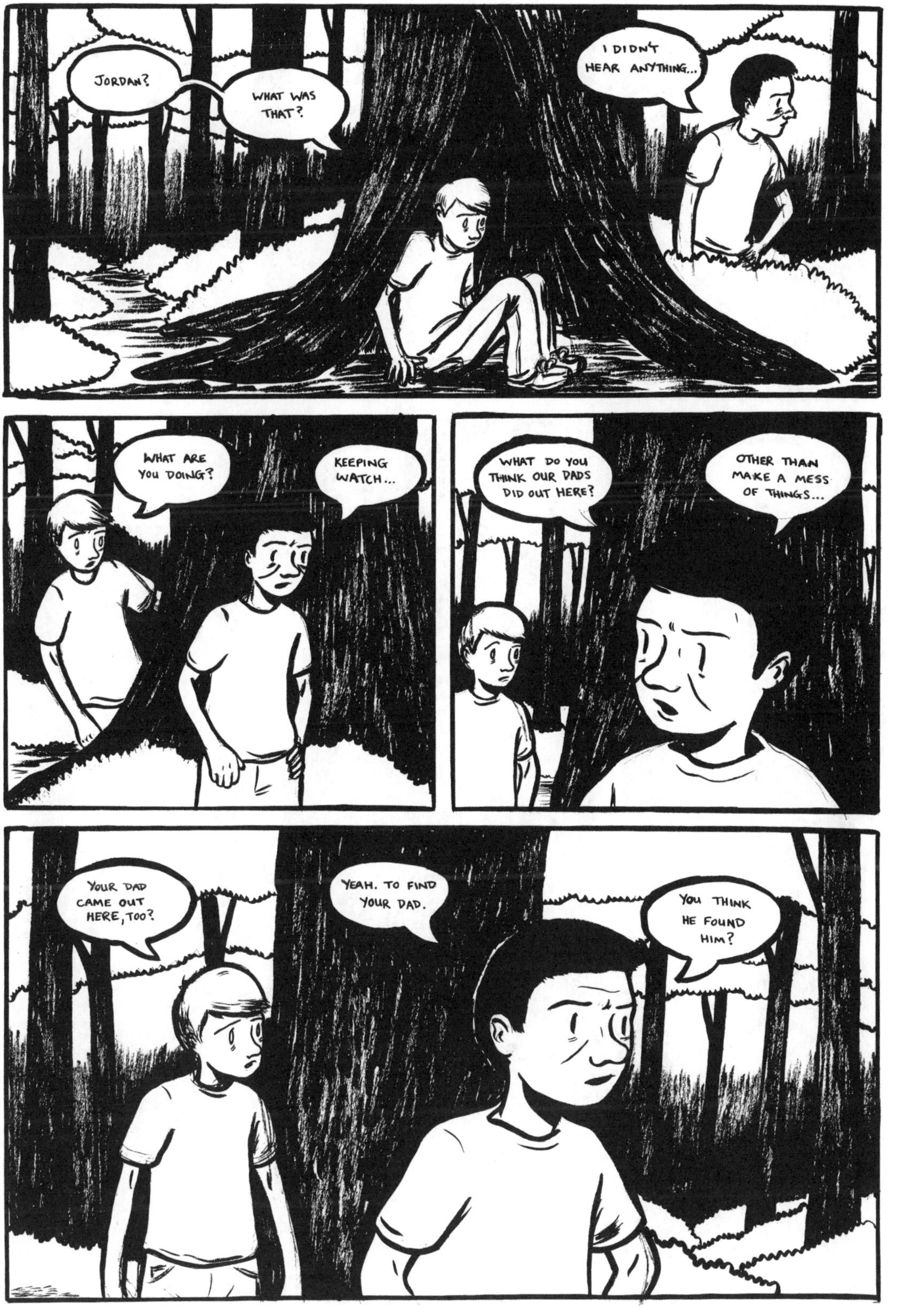
JORDAN?
WHAT WAS THAT?
I DIDN'T HEAR ANYTHING...
WHAT ARE YOU DOING?
KEEPING WATCH...
WHAT DO YOU THINK OUR DADS DID OUT HERE?
OTHER THAN MAKE A MESS OF THINGS...
YOUR DAD CAME OUT HERE, TOO?
YEAH. TO FIND YOUR DAD.
YOU THINK HE FOUND HIM?

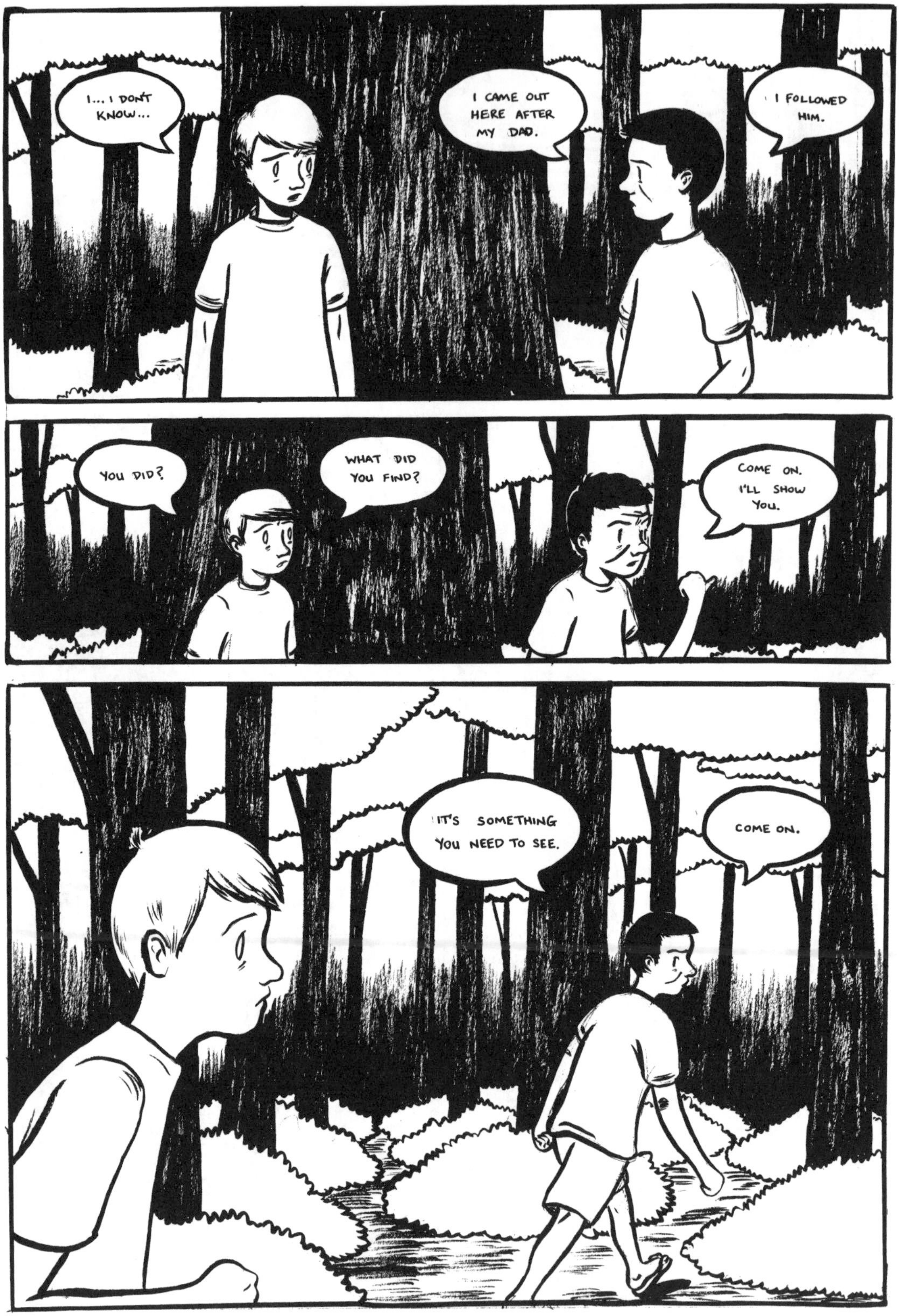
I... I DON'T KNOW...
I CAME OUT HERE AFTER MY DAD.
I FOLLOWED HIM.
YOU DID?
WHAT DID YOU FIND?
COME ON. I'LL SHOW YOU.
IT'S SOMETHING YOU NEED TO SEE.
COME ON.

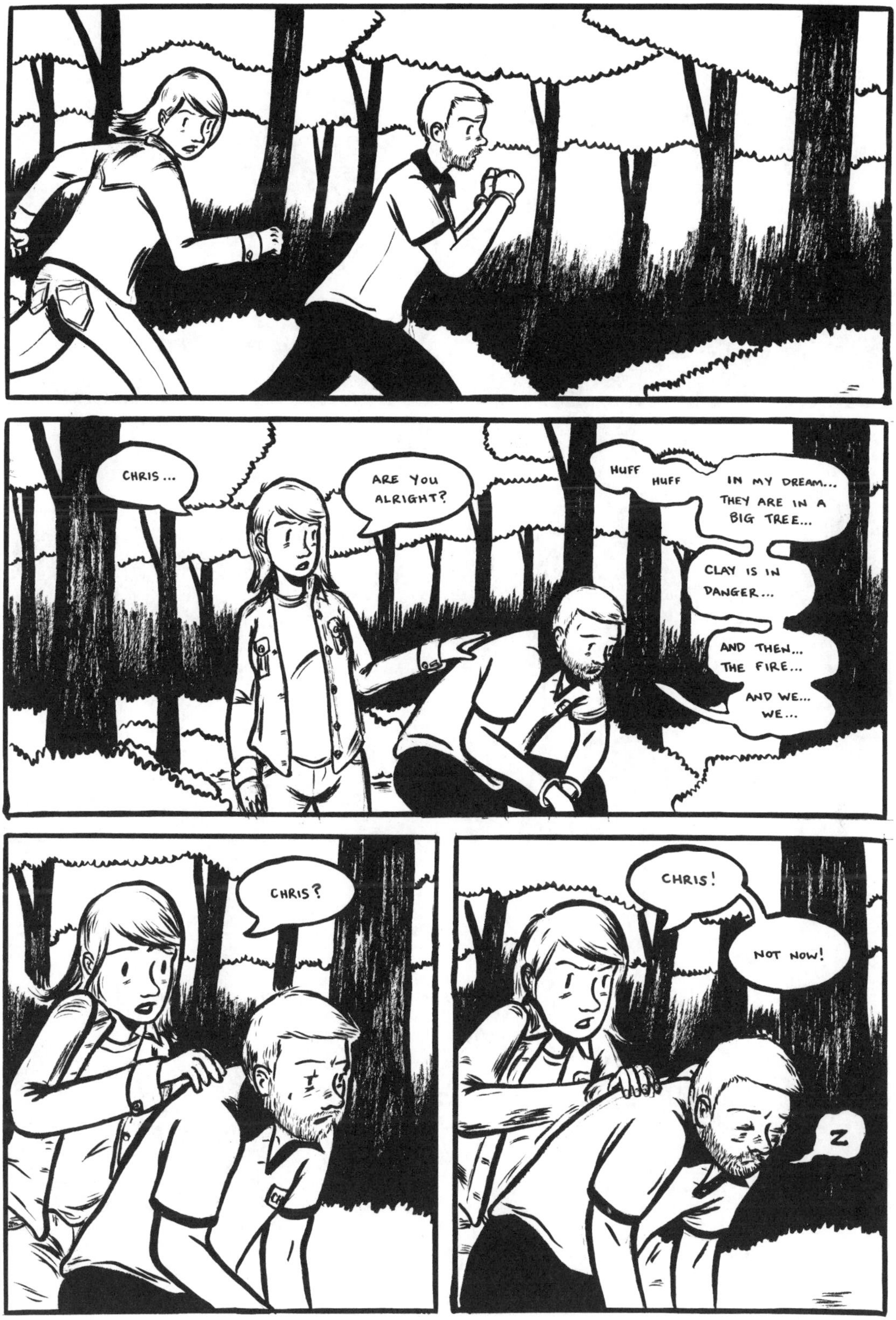
CHRIS...
ARE YOU ALRIGHT?
HUFF HUFF
IN MY DREAM... THEY ARE IN A BIG TREE...
CLAY IS IN DANGER...
AND THEN... THE FIRE...
AND WE... WE...
CHRIS?
CHRIS!
NOT NOW!
Z

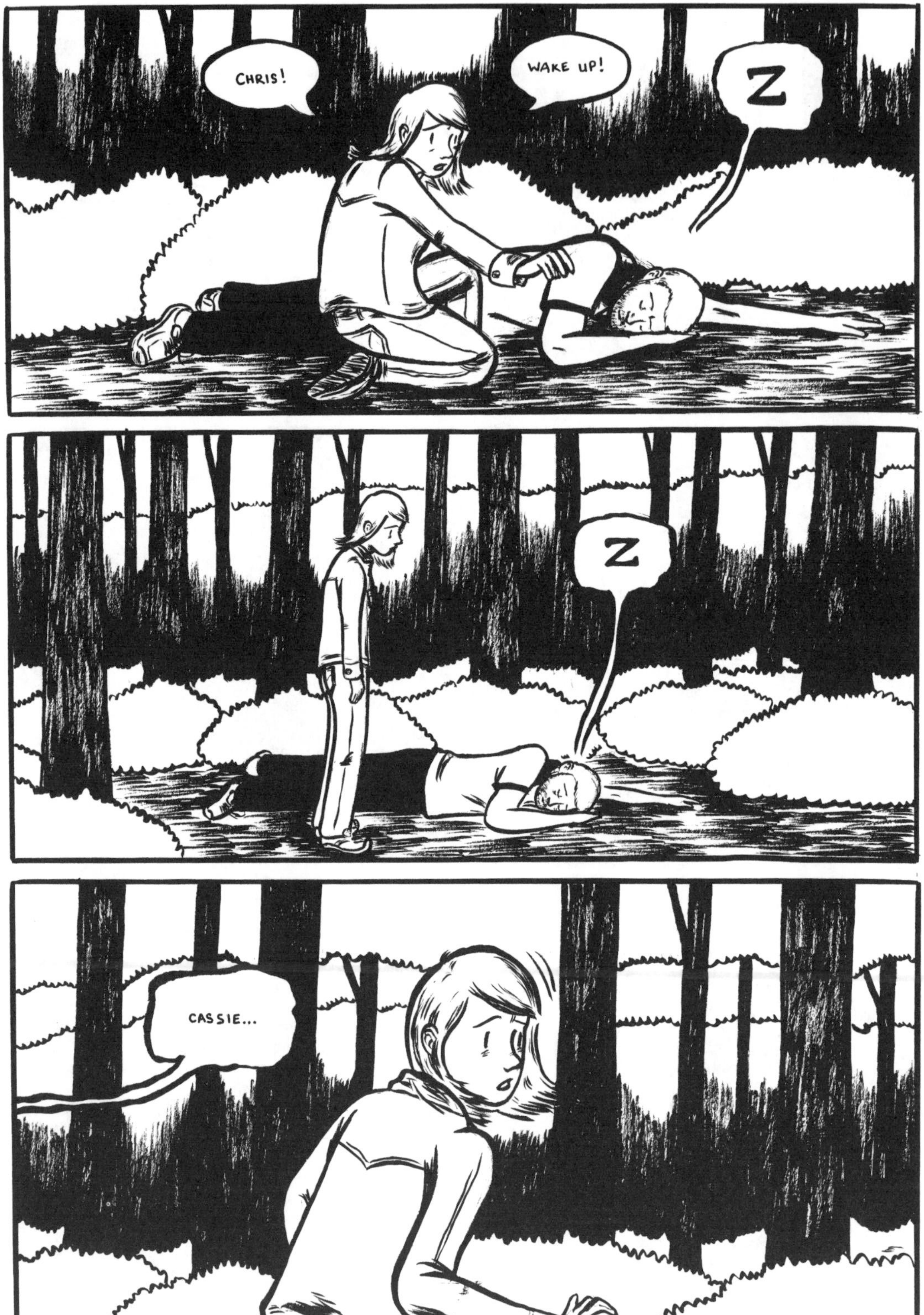
CHRIS!
WAKE UP!
Z
Z
CASSIE...

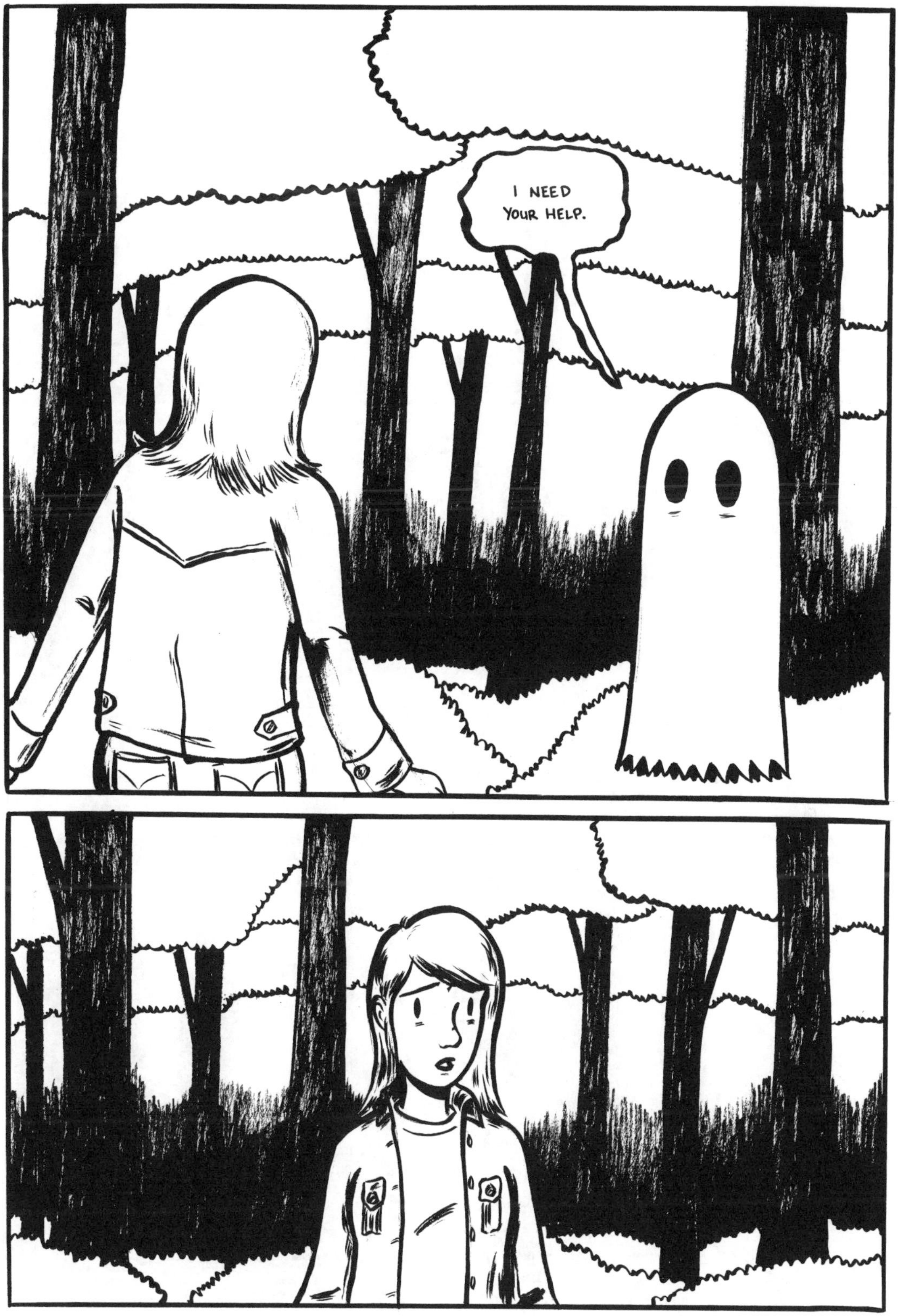
I NEED YOUR HELP.

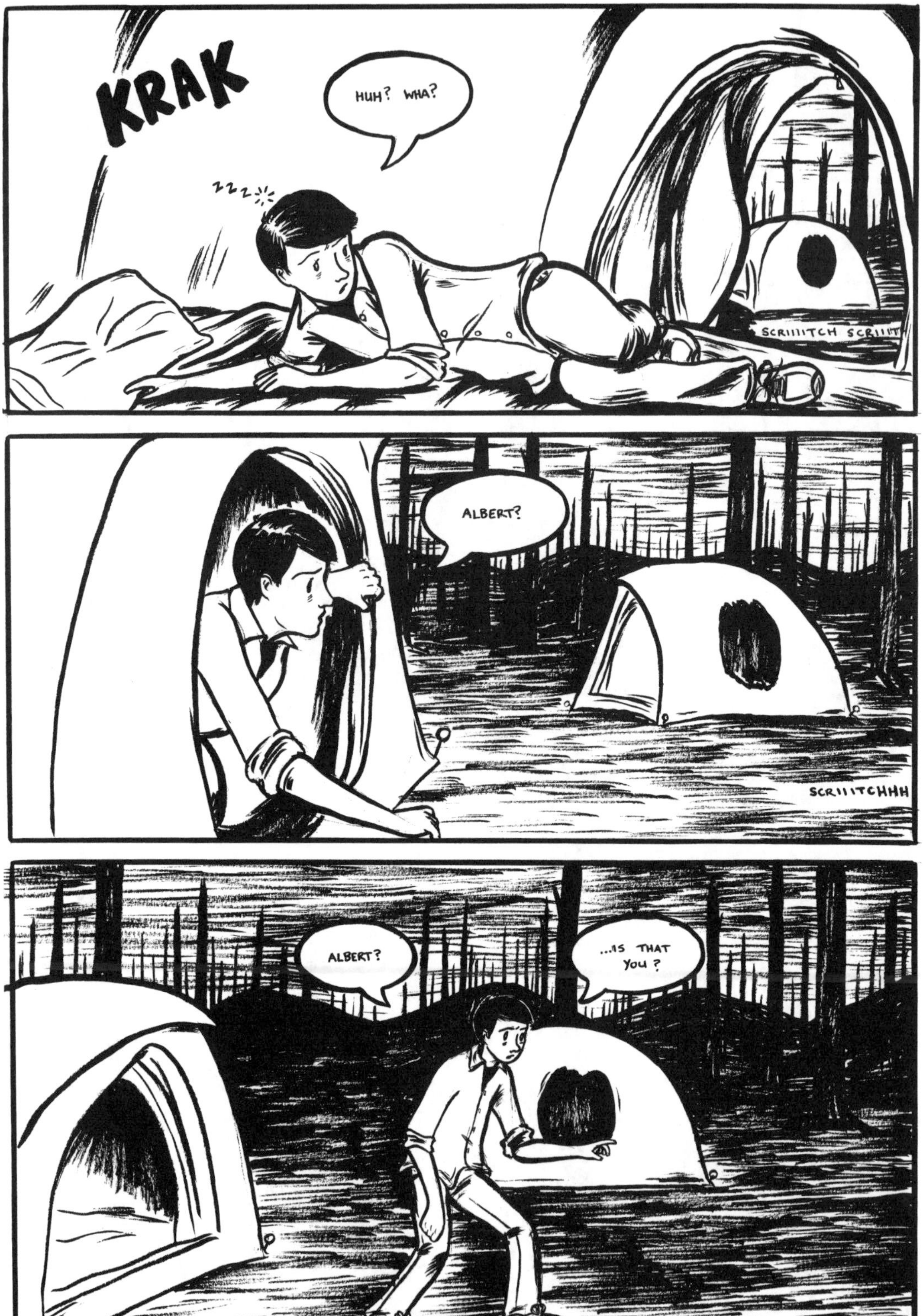
KRAK
HUH? WHA?
ZZZ
SCRIIIIITCH SCRIIIT
ALBERT?
SCRIIITCHHH
ALBERT?
...IS THAT YOU?

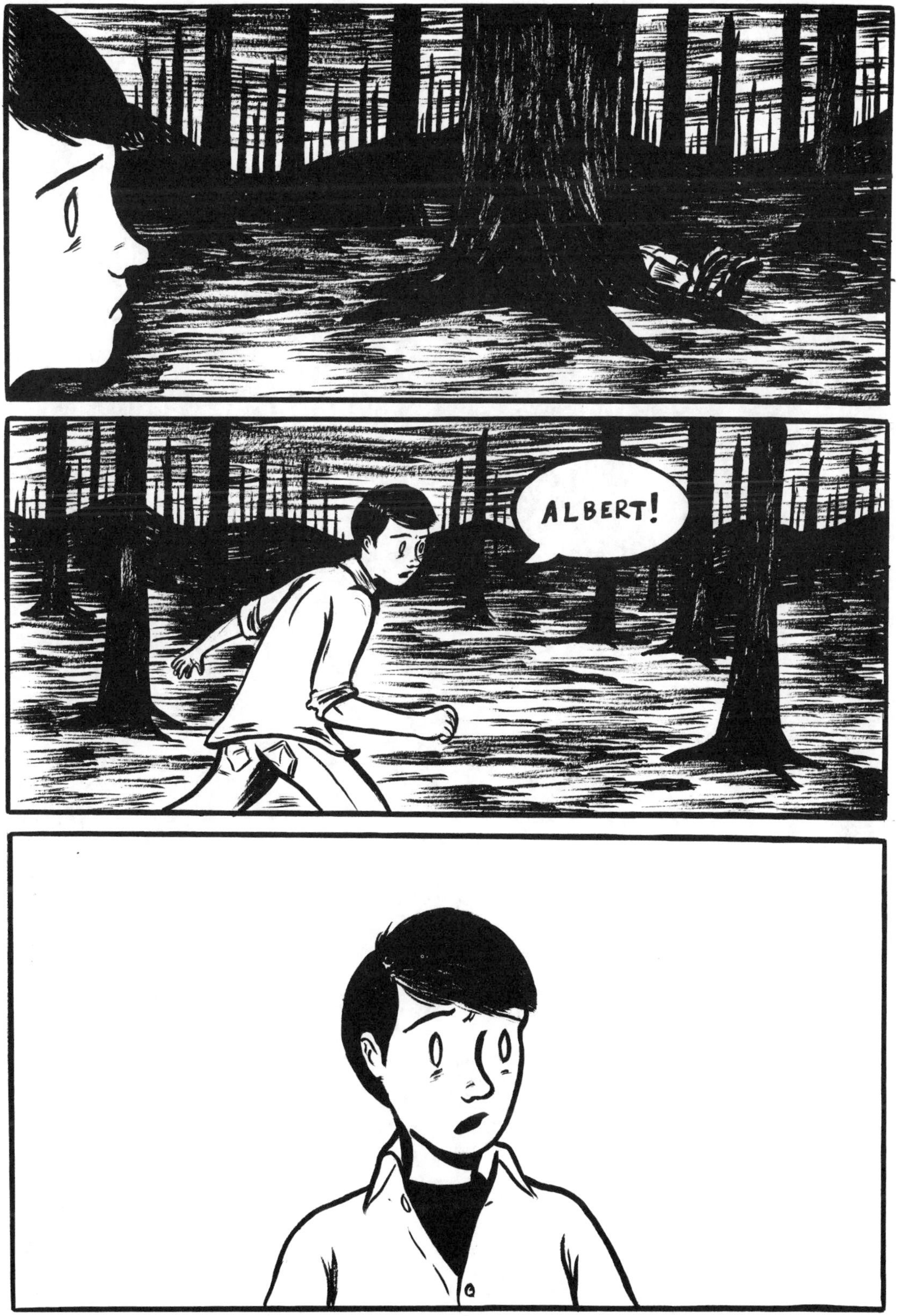
ALBERT!

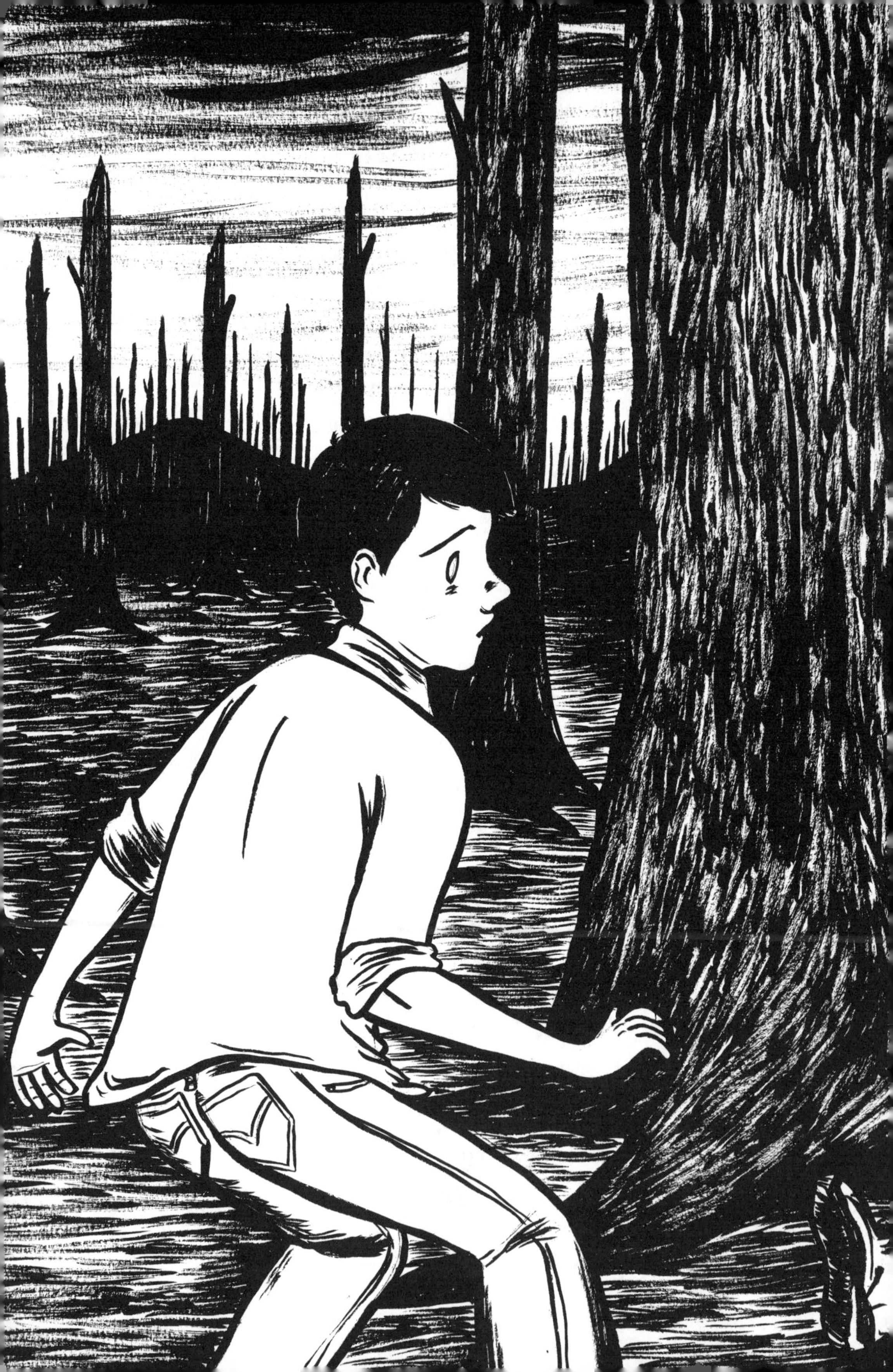

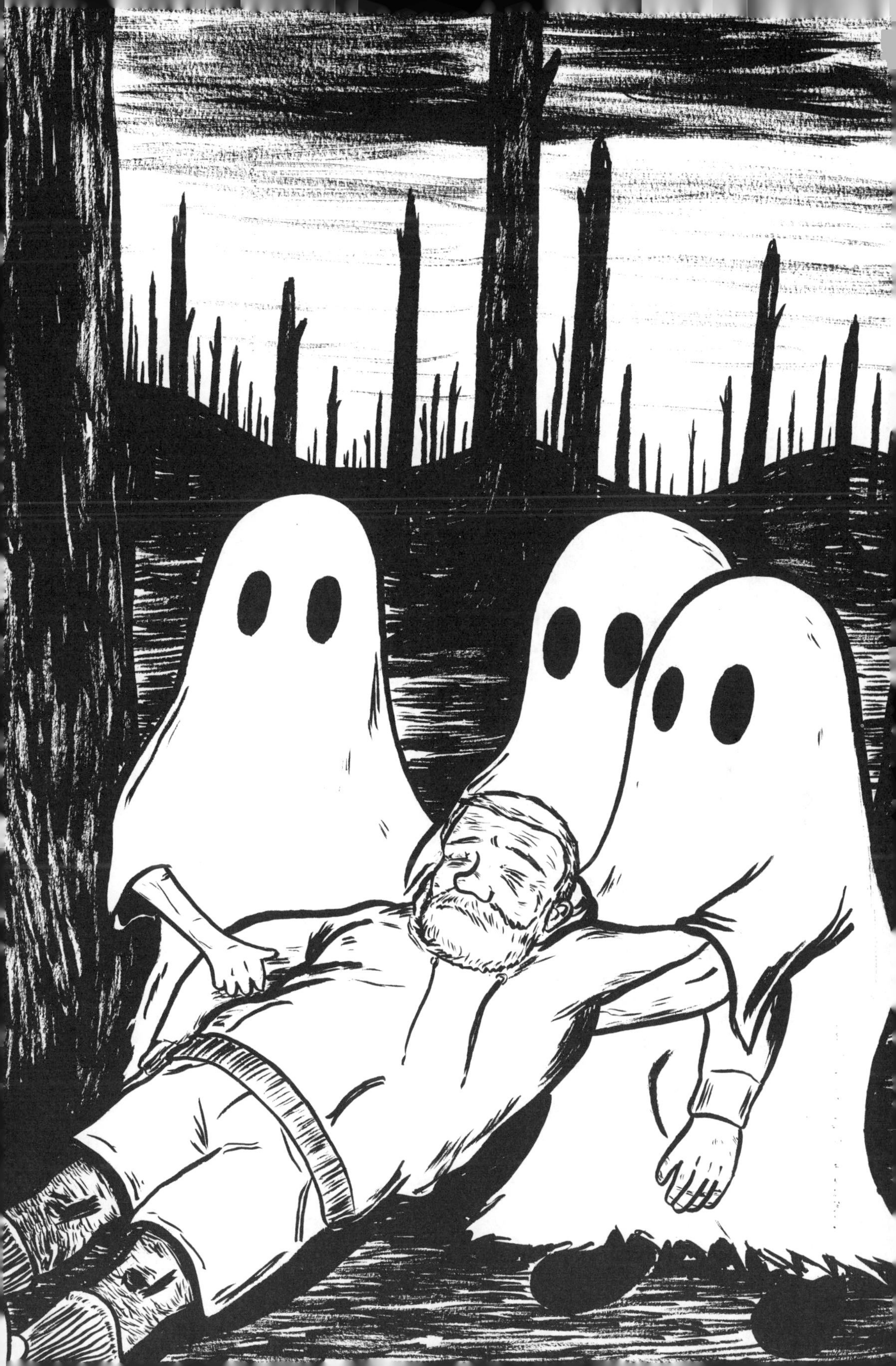

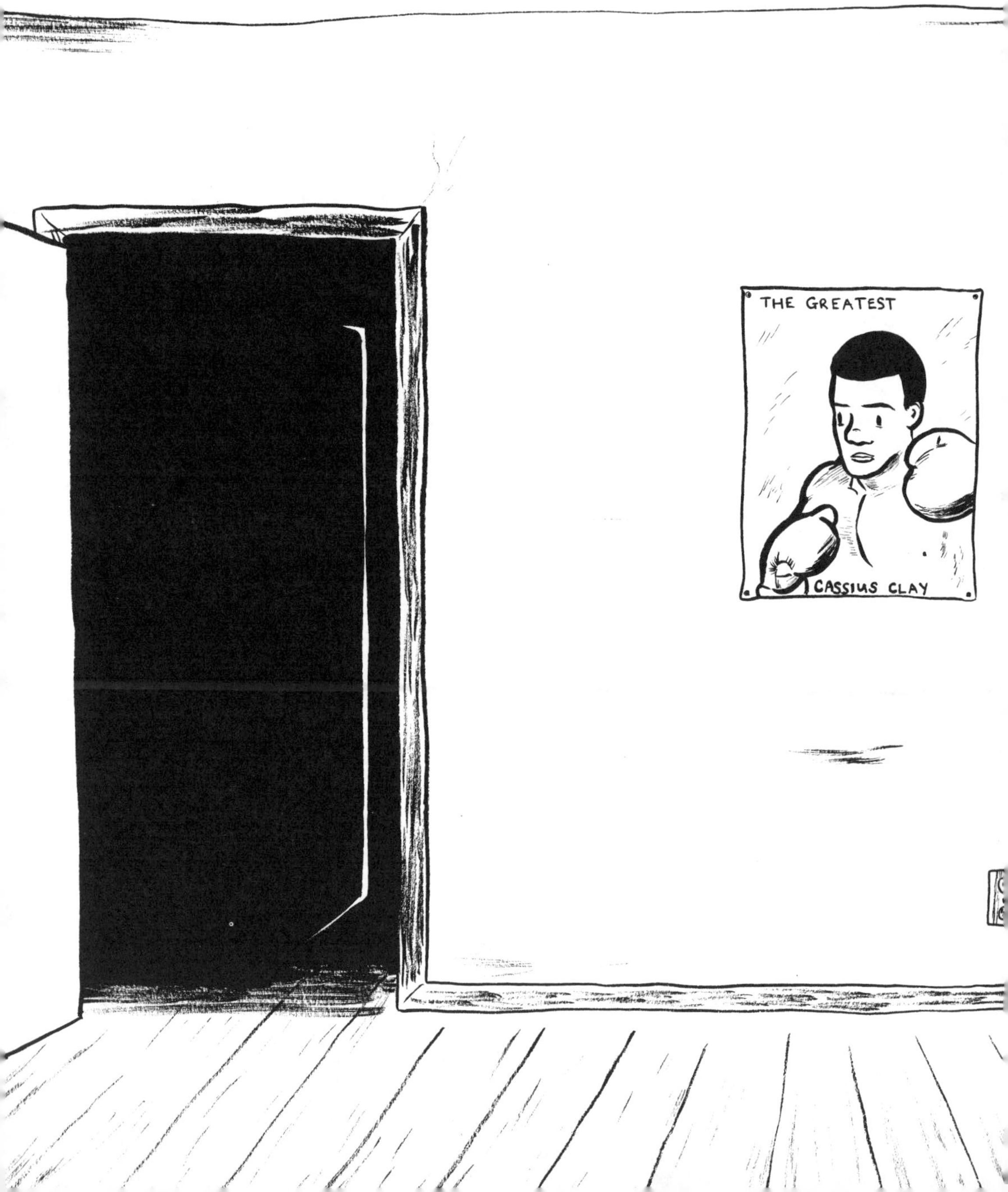
THE GREATEST
CASSIUS CLAY

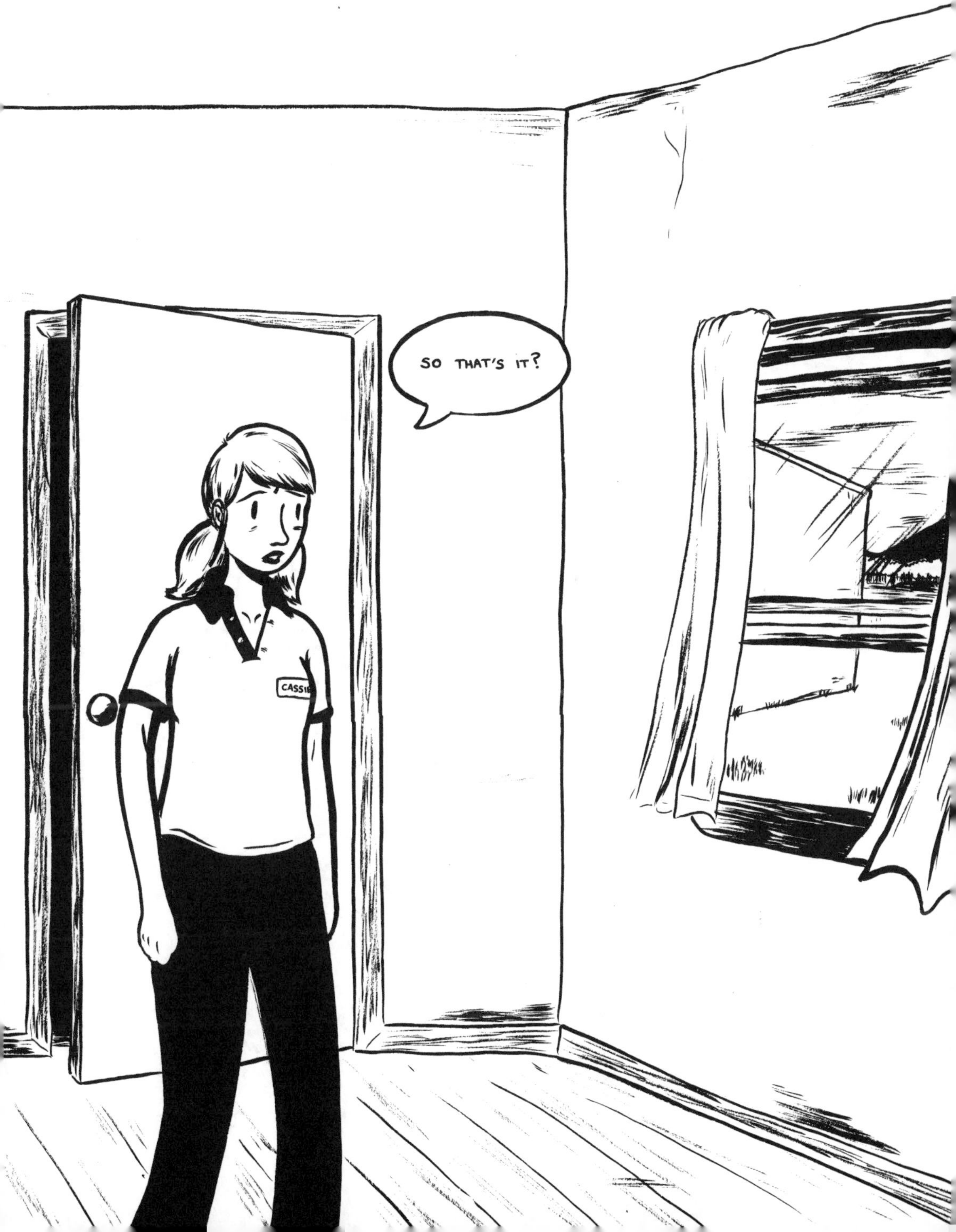
SO THAT'S IT?
CASSIE

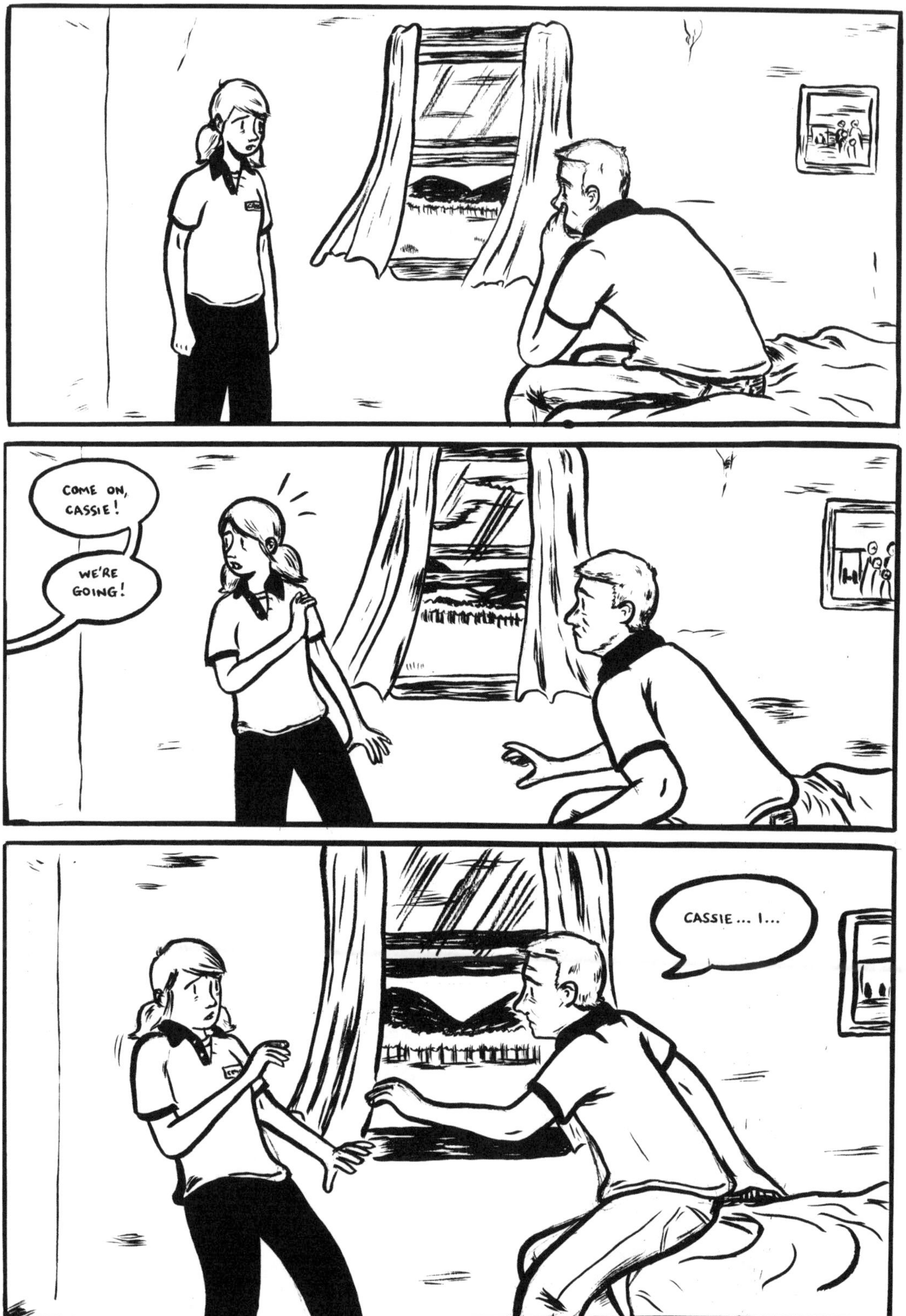
COME ON, CASSIE!
WE'RE GOING!
CASSIE... I...

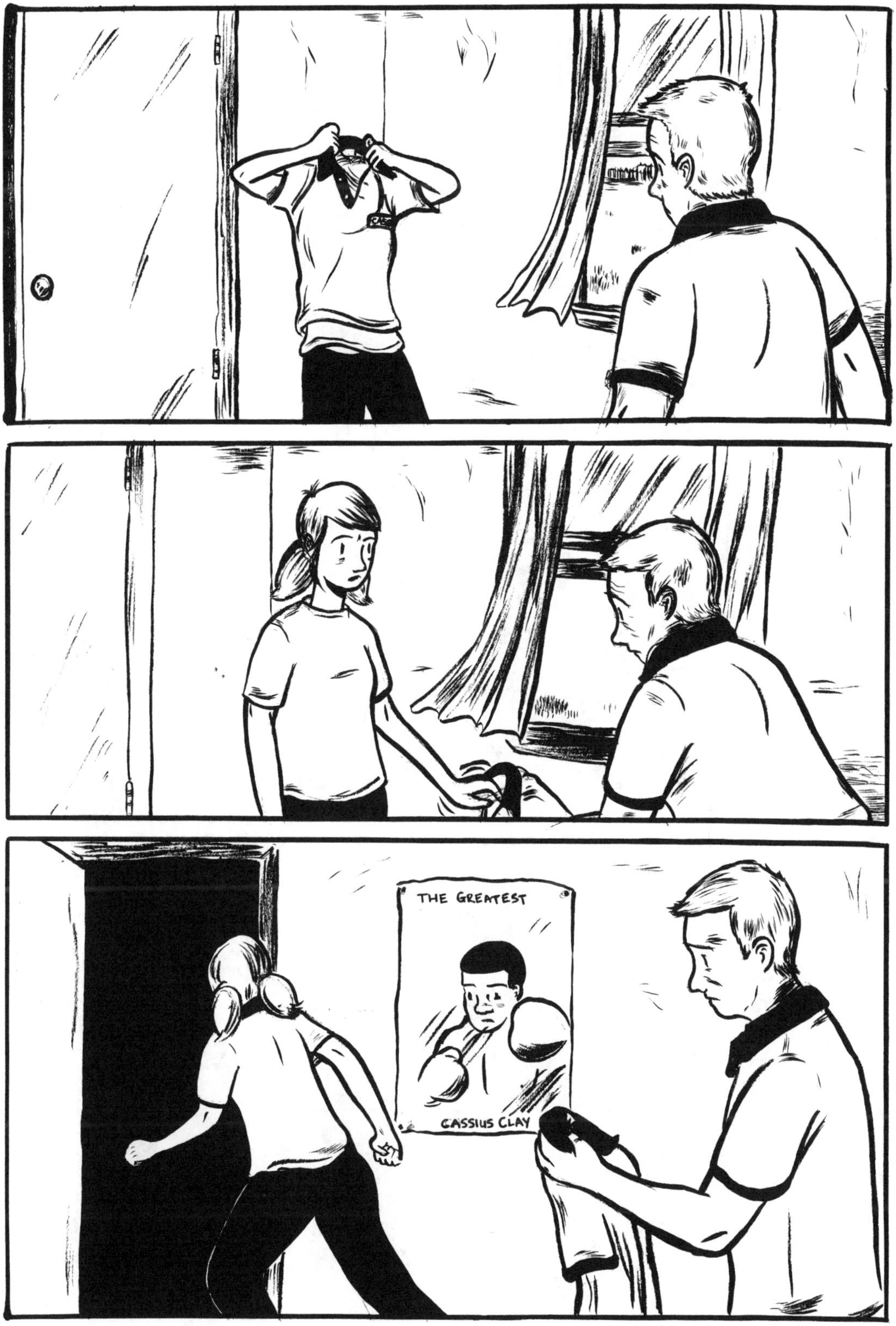
THE GREATEST
CASSIUS CLAY

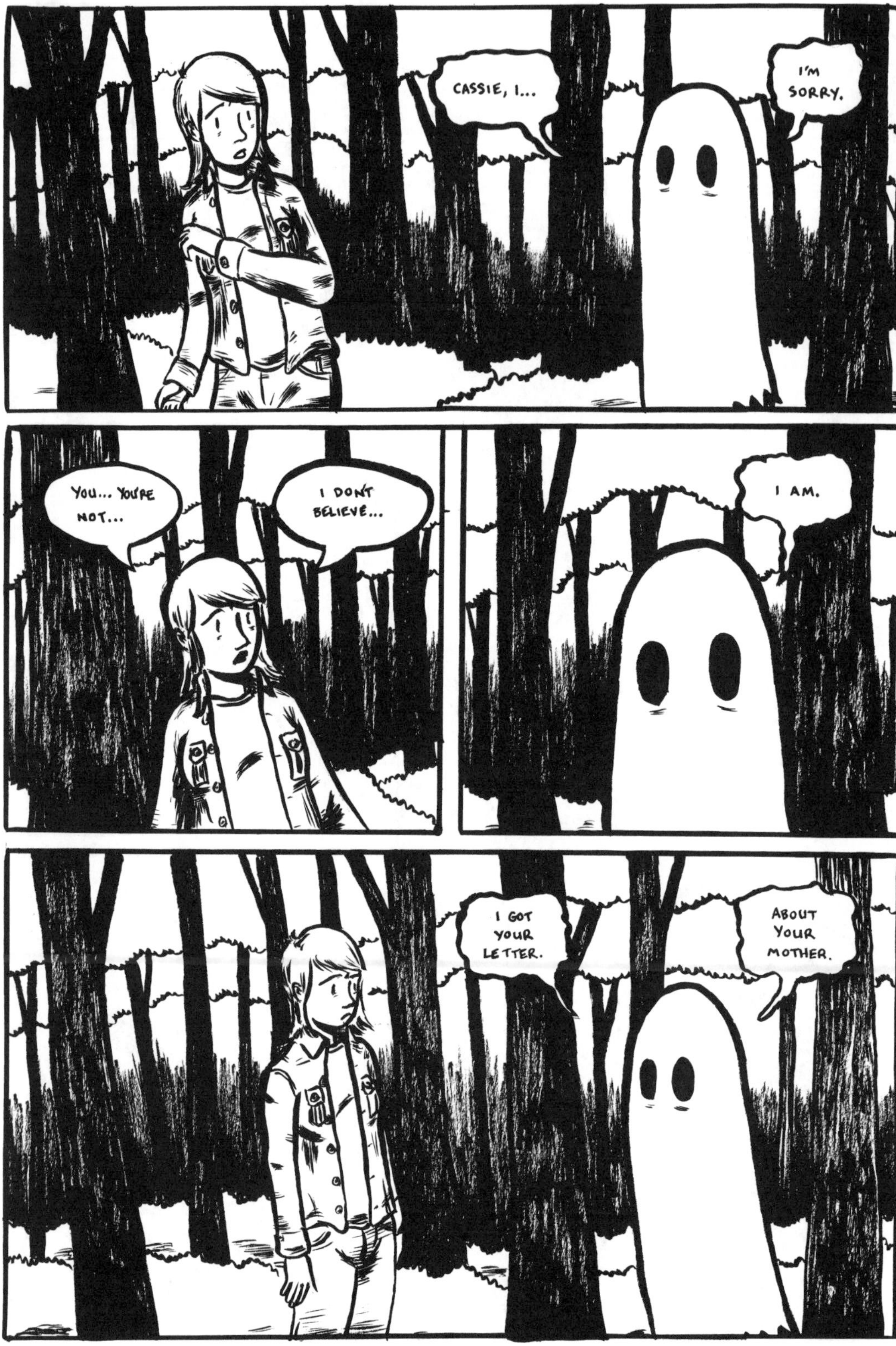
CASSIE, I...
I'M SORRY.
YOU... YOU'RE NOT...
I DON'T BELIEVE...
I AM.
I GOT YOUR LETTER.
ABOUT YOUR MOTHER.

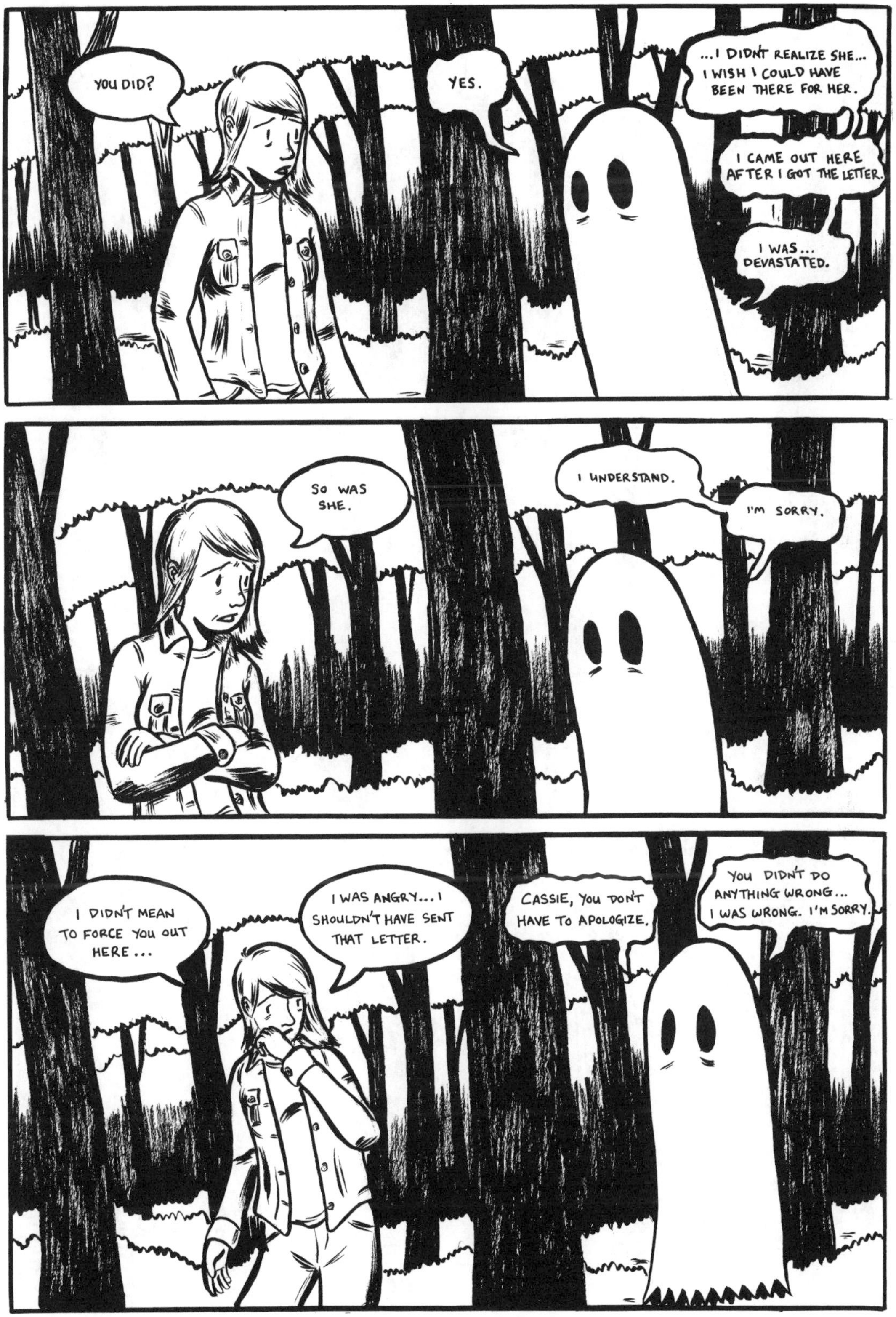
YOU DID?
YES.
...I DIDN'T REALIZE SHE... I WISH I COULD HAVE BEEN THERE FOR HER.
I CAME OUT HERE AFTER I GOT THE LETTER.
I WAS... DEVASTATED.
SO WAS SHE.
I UNDERSTAND.
I'M SORRY.
I DIDN'T MEAN TO FORCE YOU OUT HERE...
I WAS ANGRY... I SHOULDN'T HAVE SENT THAT LETTER.
CASSIE, YOU DON'T HAVE TO APOLOGIZE.
YOU DIDN'T DO ANYTHING WRONG... I WAS WRONG. I'M SORRY.

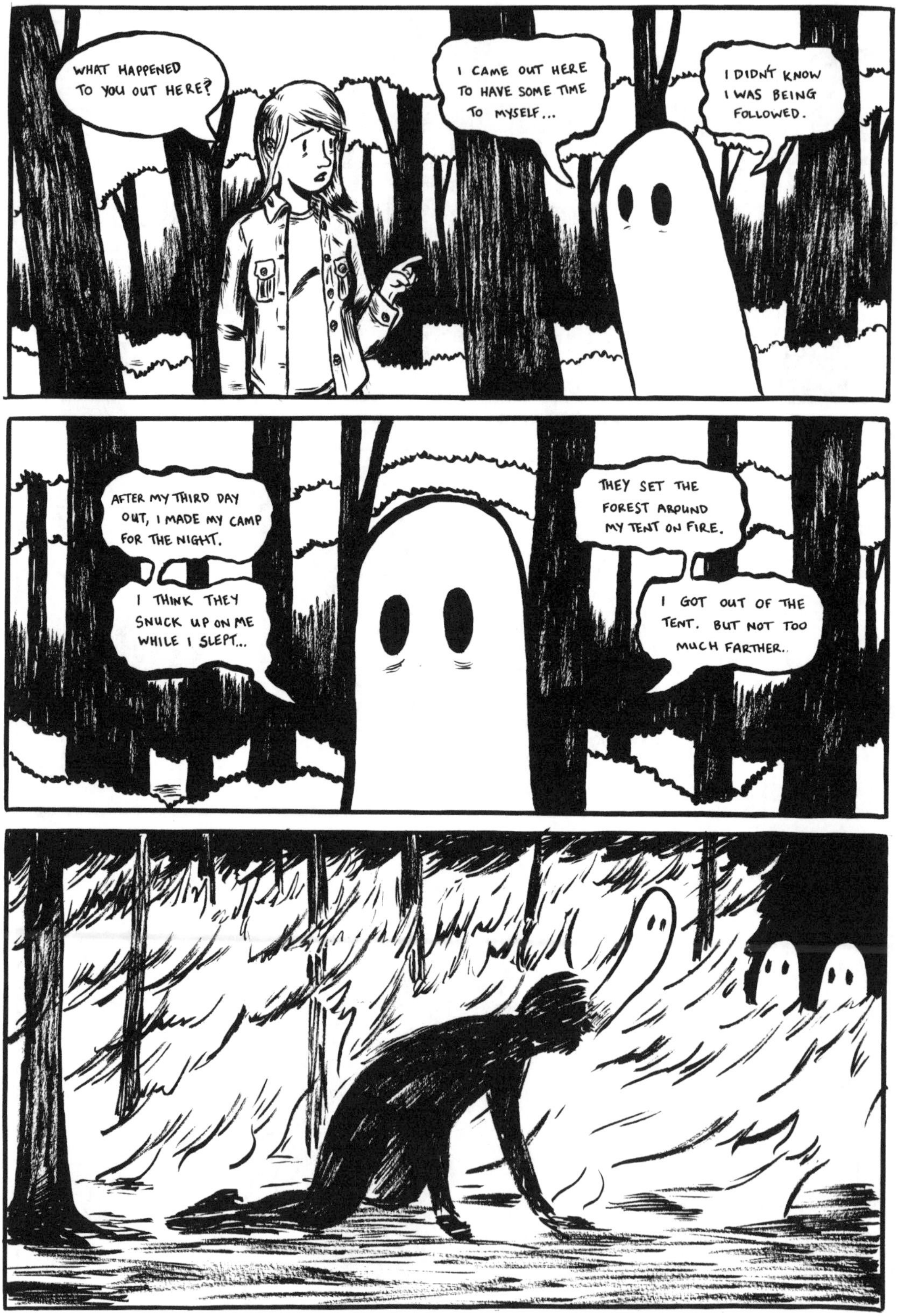
WHAT HAPPENED TO YOU OUT HERE?
I CAME OUT HERE TO HAVE SOME TIME TO MYSELF...
I DIDN'T KNOW I WAS BEING FOLLOWED.
AFTER MY THIRD DAY OUT, I MADE MY CAMP FOR THE NIGHT.
I THINK THEY SNUCK UP ON ME WHILE I SLEPT...
THEY SET THE FOREST AROUND MY TENT ON FIRE.
I GOT OUT OF THE TENT. BUT NOT TOO MUCH FARTHER..

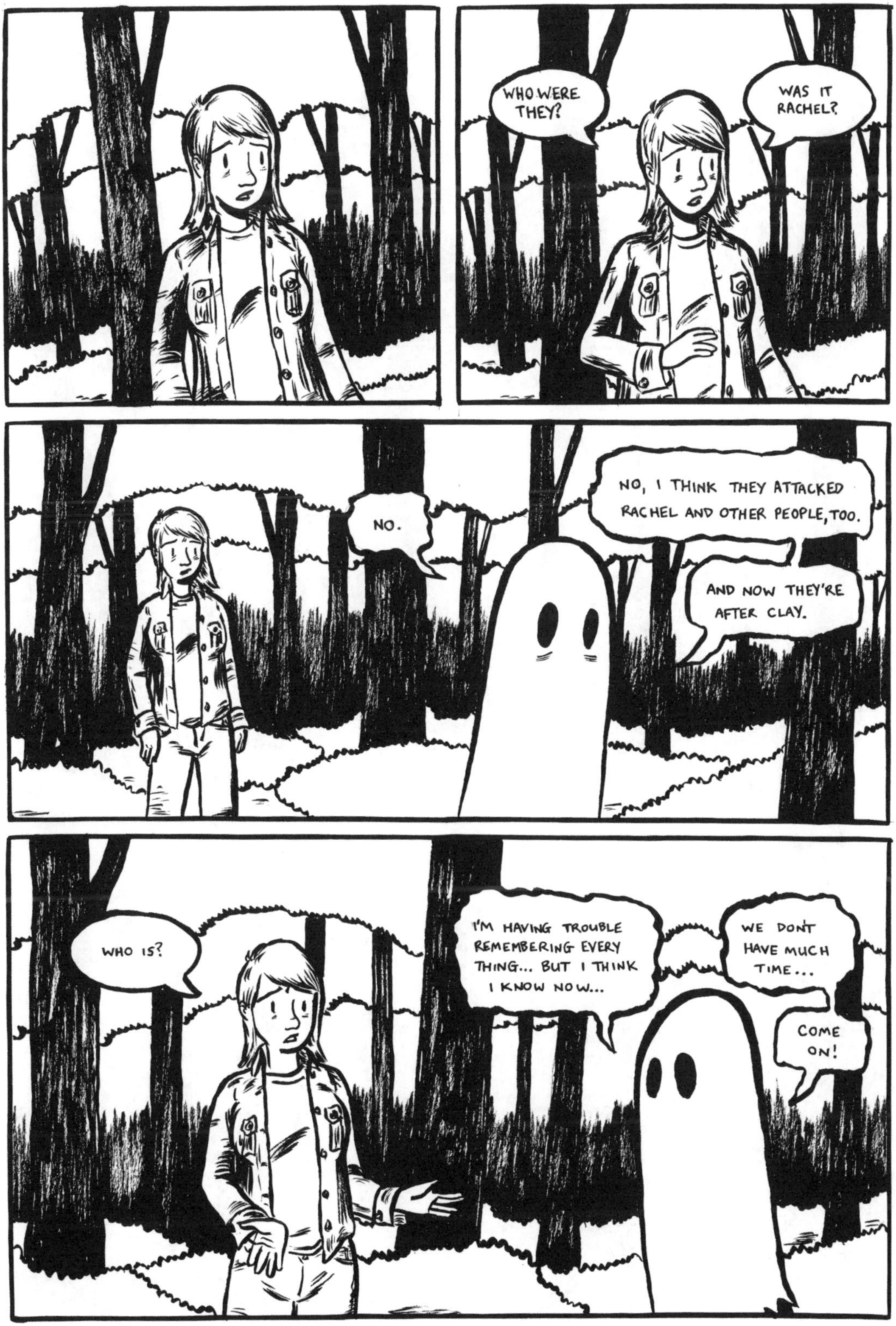
WHO WERE THEY?
WAS IT RACHEL?
NO.
NO, I THINK THEY ATTACKED RACHEL AND OTHER PEOPLE, TOO.
AND NOW THEY'RE AFTER CLAY.
WHO IS?
I'M HAVING TROUBLE REMEMBERING EVERY THING... BUT I THINK I KNOW NOW...
WE DON'T HAVE MUCH TIME...
COME ON!

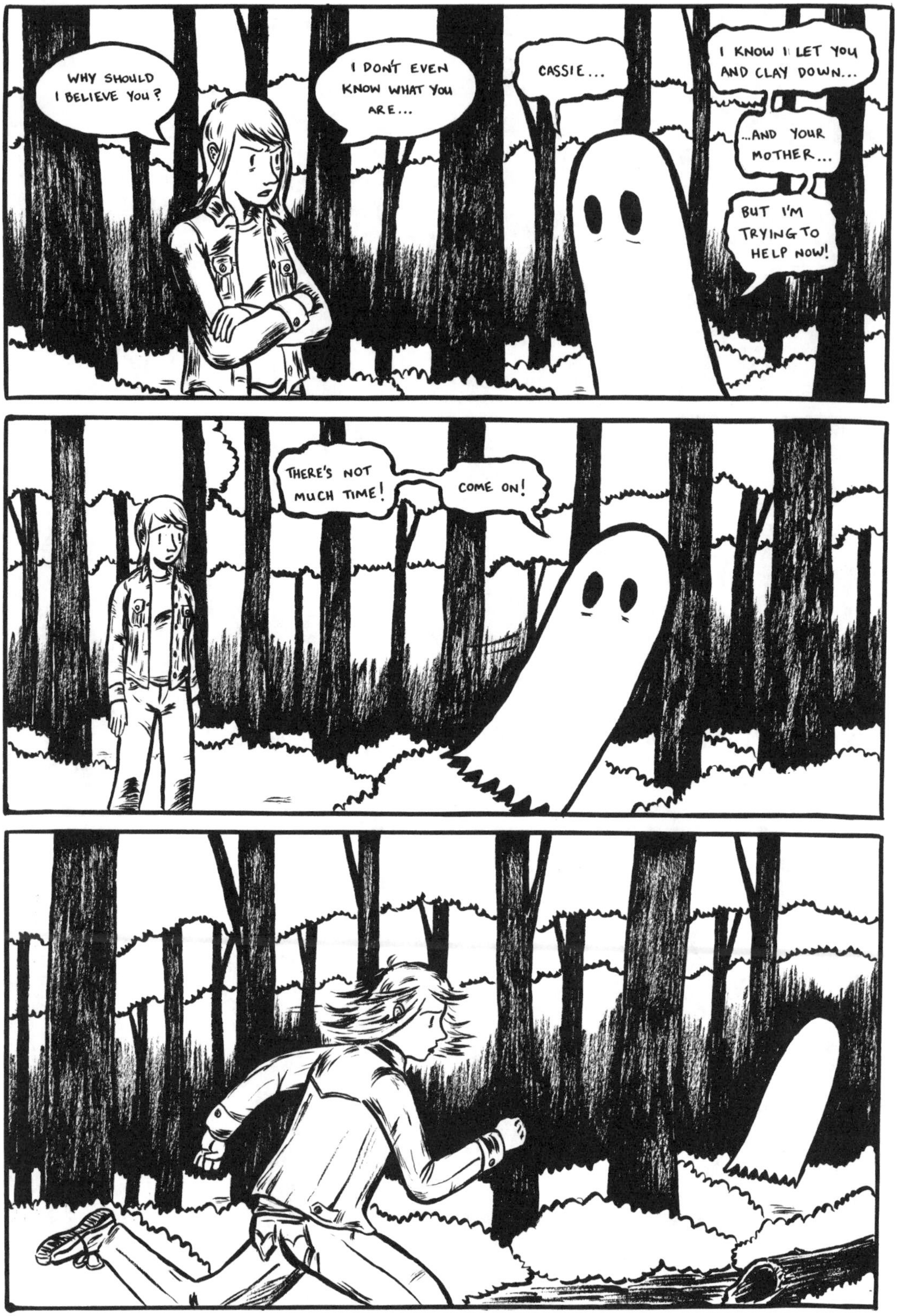
WHY SHOULD I BELIEVE YOU?
I DON'T EVEN KNOW WHAT YOU ARE...
CASSIE...
I KNOW I LET YOU AND CLAY DOWN...
...AND YOUR MOTHER...
BUT I'M TRYING TO HELP NOW!
THERE'S NOT MUCH TIME!
COME ON!

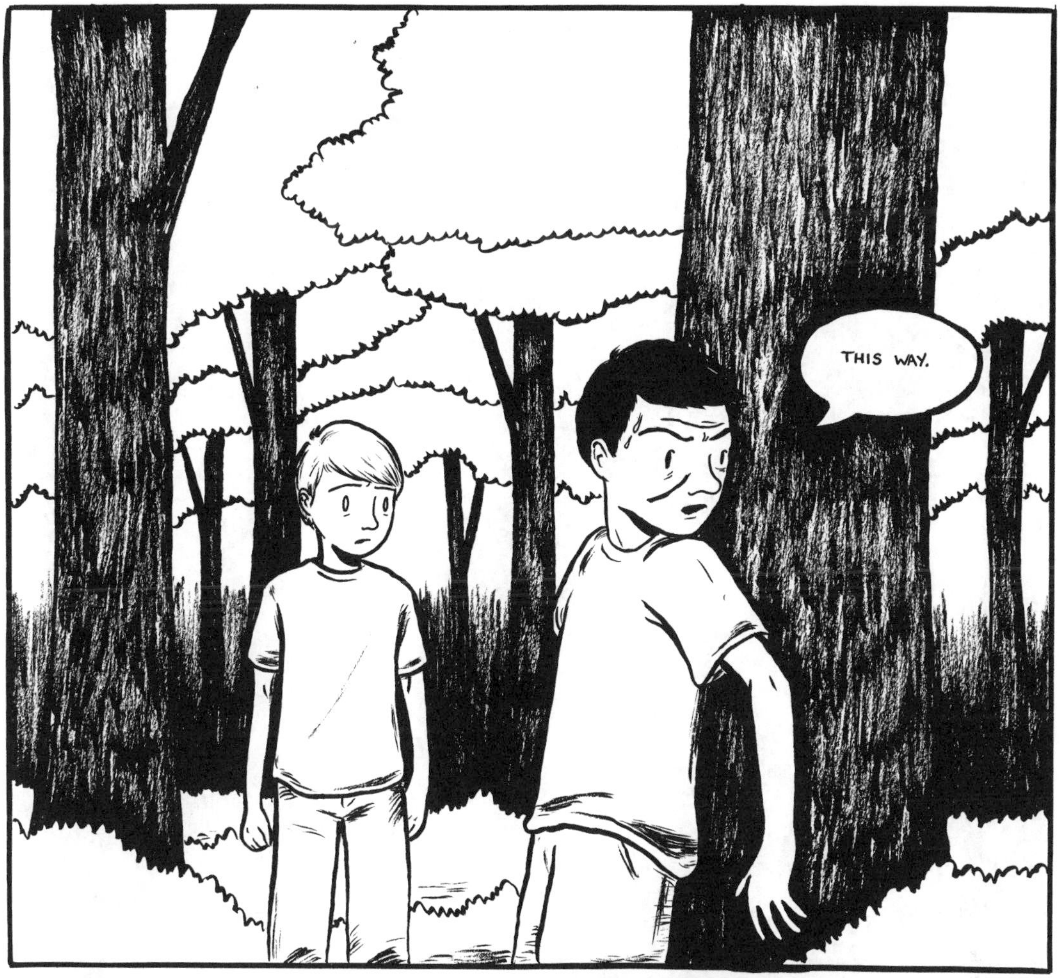
THIS WAY.

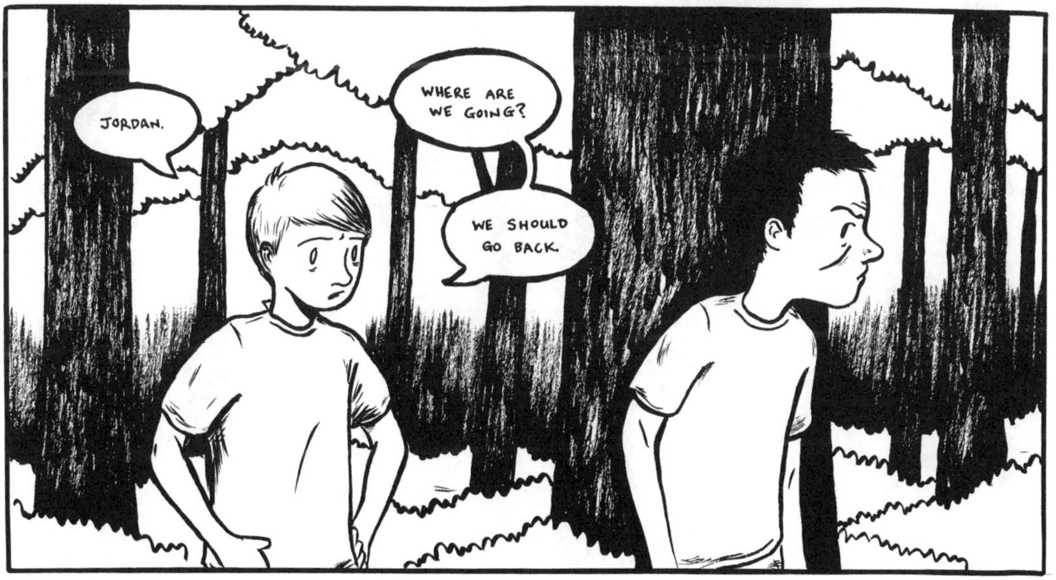
JORDAN.
WHERE ARE WE GOING?
WE SHOULD GO BACK.

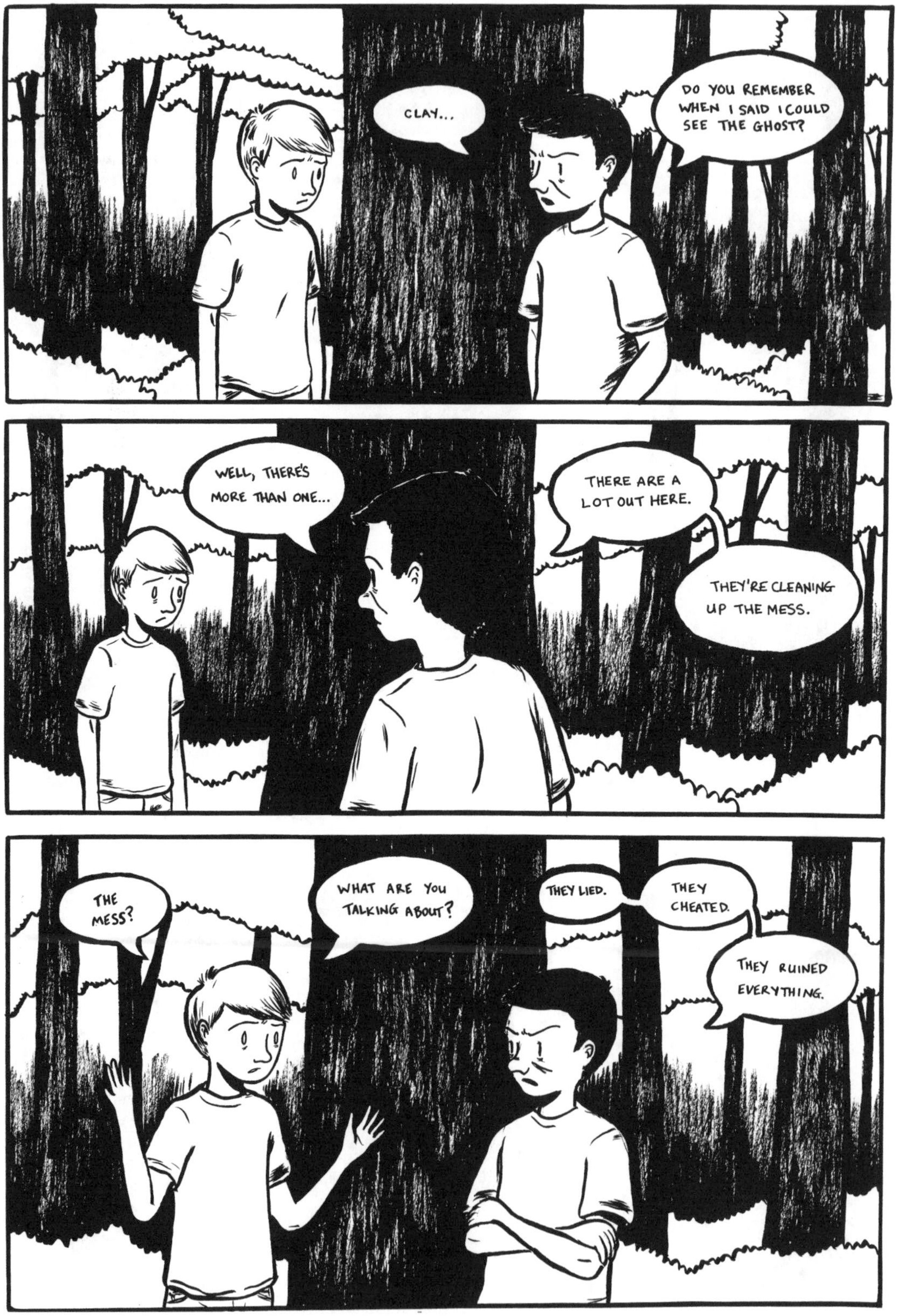
CLAY...
DO YOU REMEMBER WHEN I SAID I COULD SEE THE GHOST?
WELL, THERE'S MORE THAN ONE...
THERE ARE A LOT OUT HERE.
THEY'RE CLEANING UP THE MESS.
THE MESS?
WHAT ARE YOU TALKING ABOUT?
THEY LIED.
THEY CHEATED.
THEY RUINED EVERYTHING.

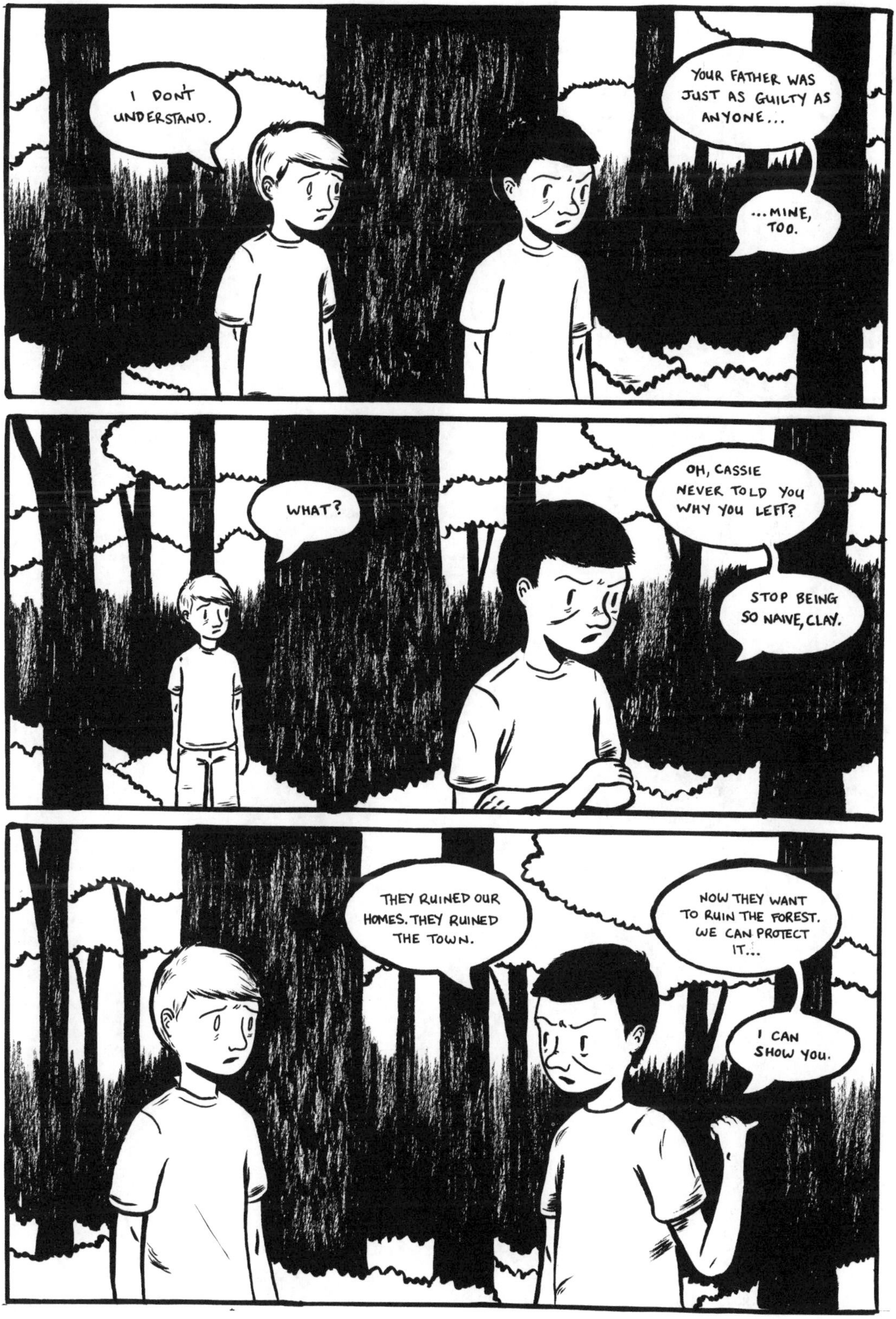
I DON'T UNDERSTAND.
YOUR FATHER WAS JUST AS GUILTY AS ANYONE...
...MINE, TOO.
WHAT?
OH, CASSIE NEVER TOLD YOU WHY YOU LEFT?
STOP BEING SO NAIVE, CLAY.
THEY RUINED OUR HOMES. THEY RUINED THE TOWN.
NOW THEY WANT TO RUIN THE FOREST. WE CAN PROTECT IT...
I CAN SHOW YOU.

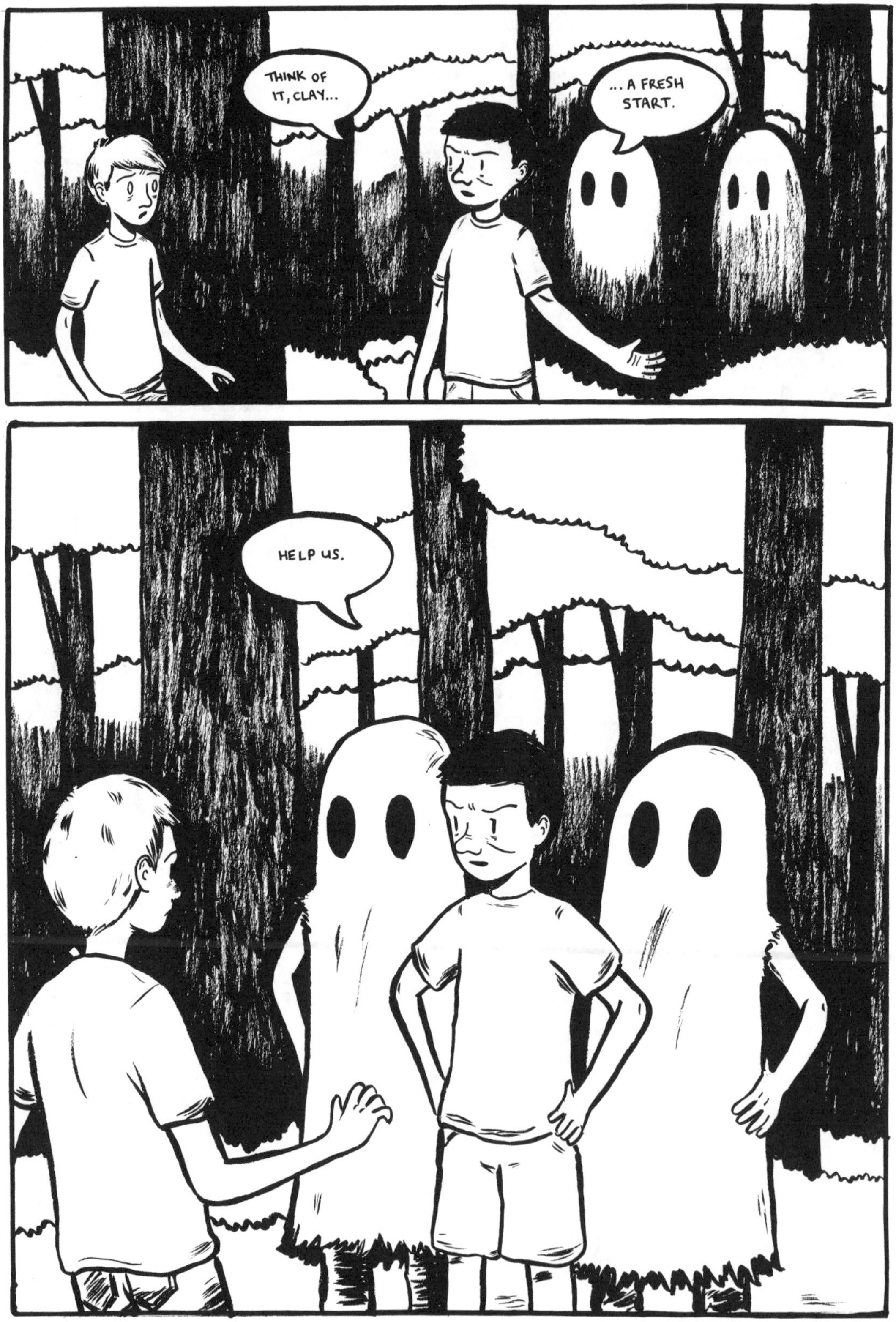
THINK OF IT, CLAY...
... A FRESH START.
HELP US.

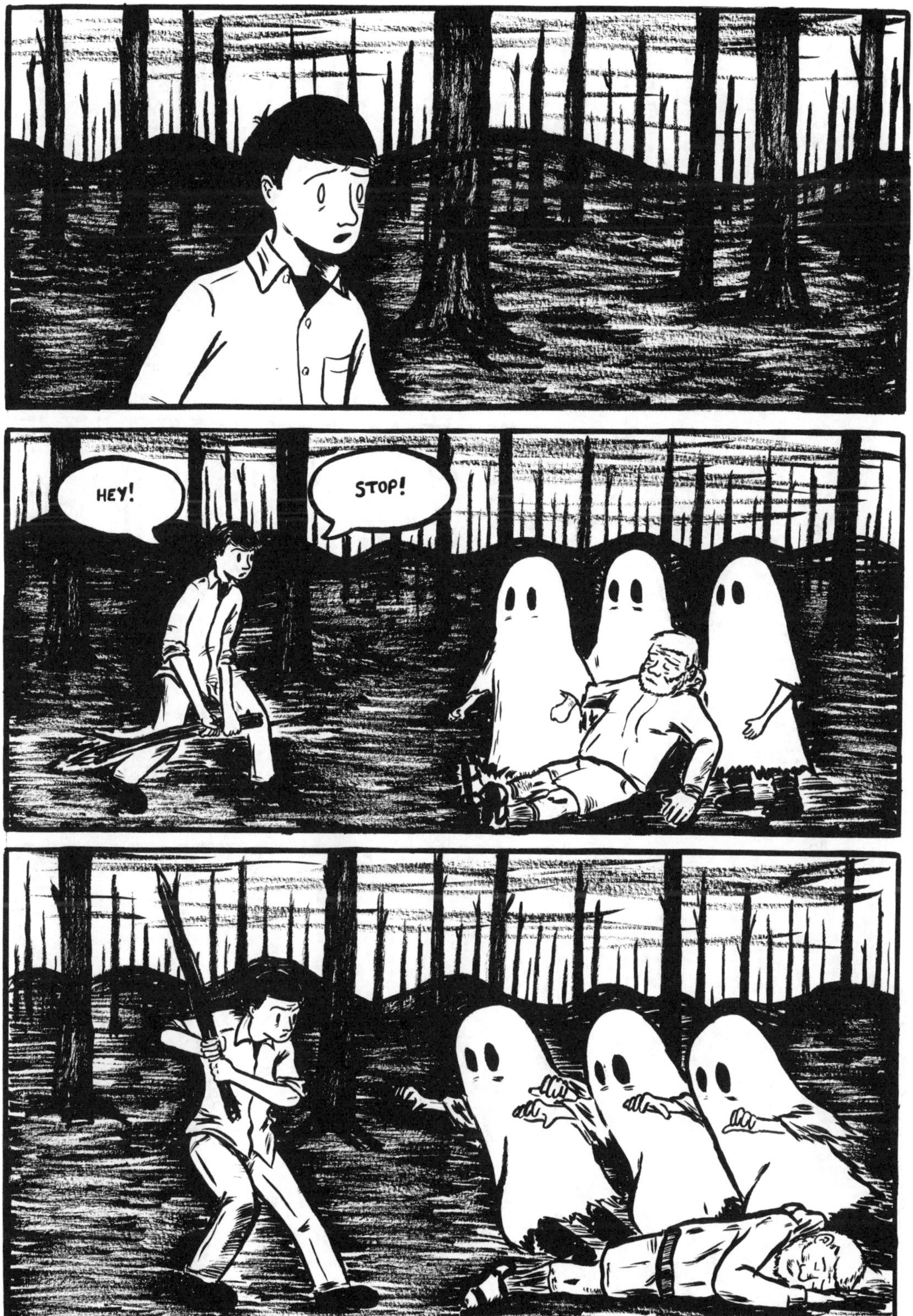
HEY!
STOP!

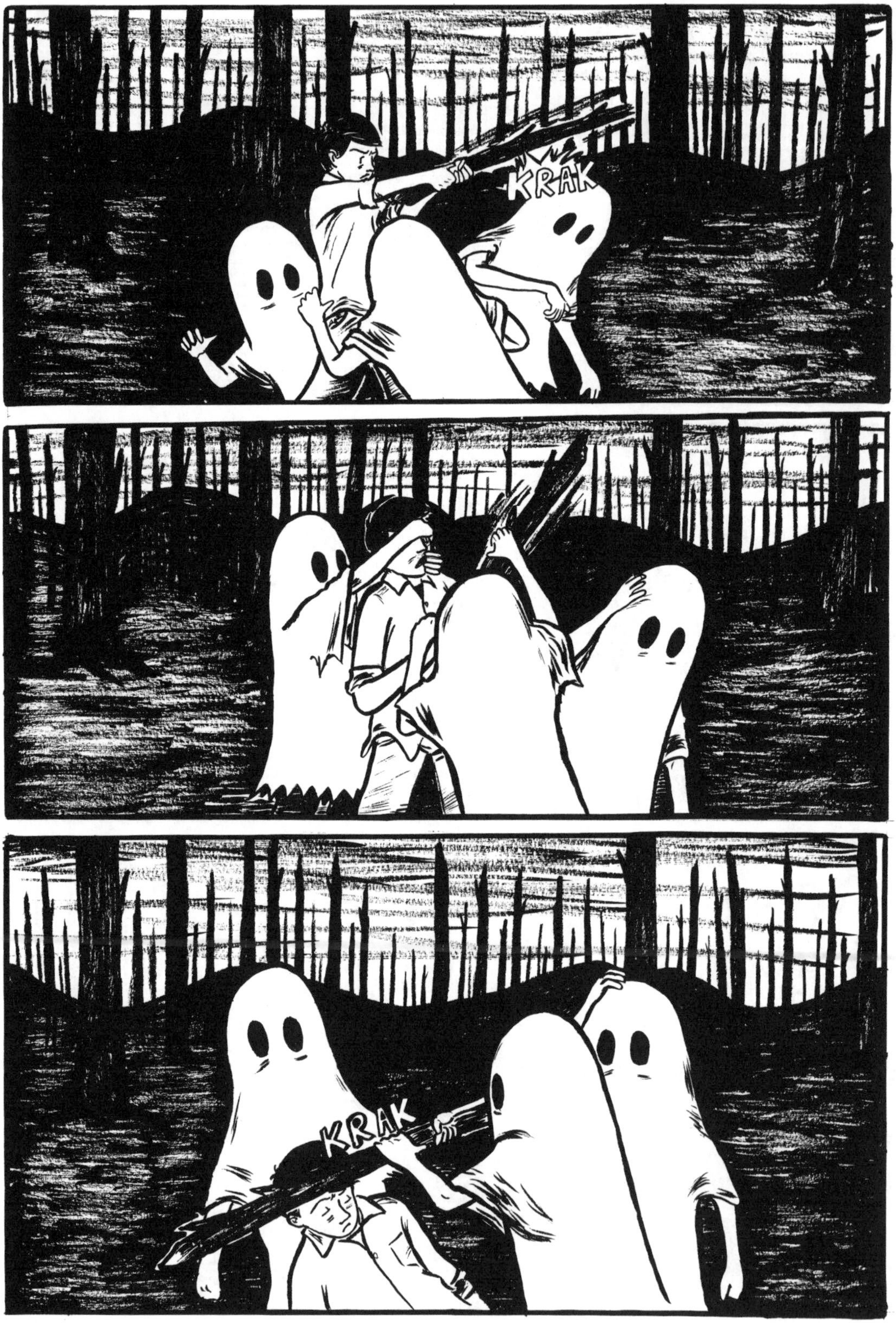
KRAK
KRAK

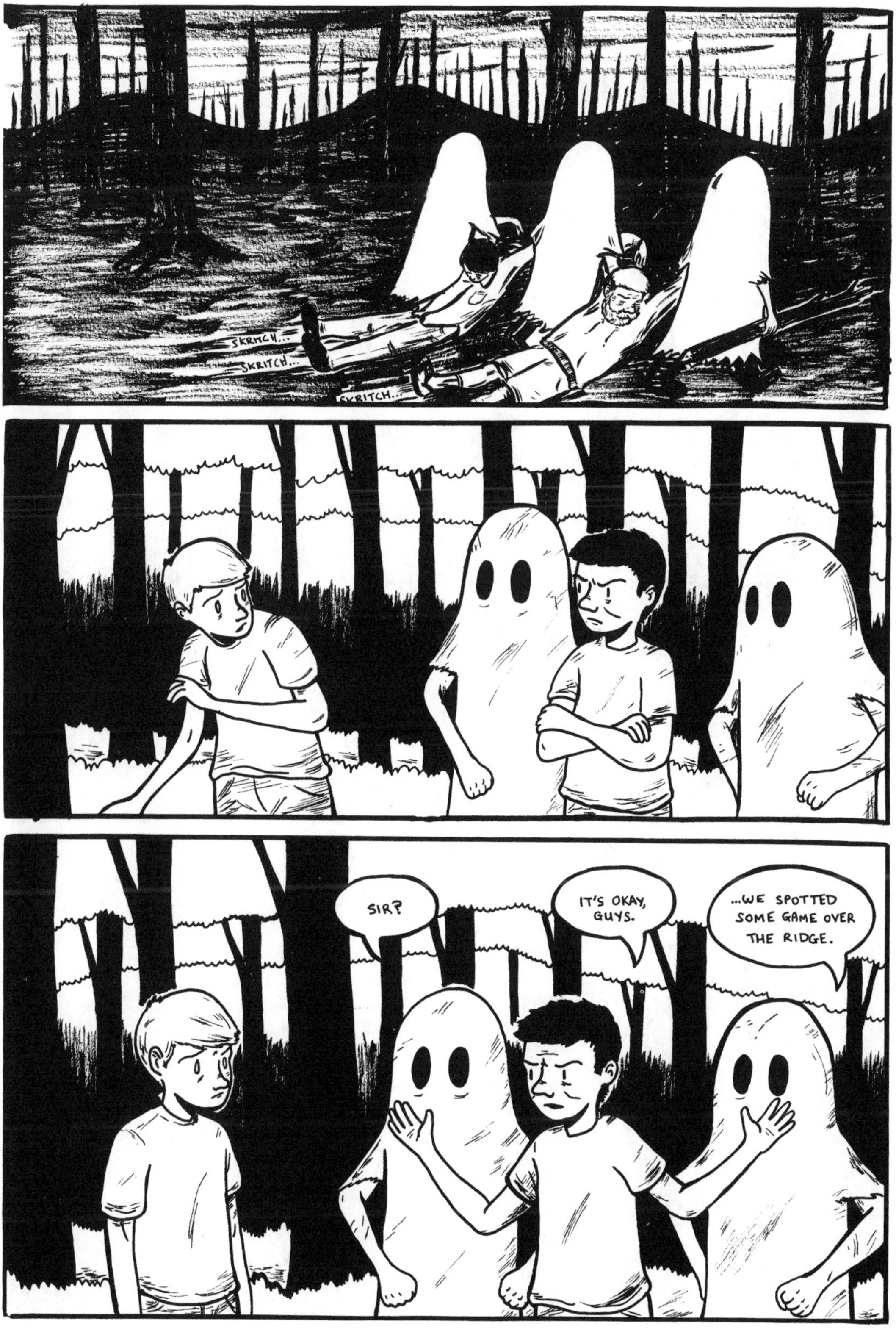
SKRITCH...
SKRITCH...
SKRITCH...
SIR?
IT'S OKAY, GUYS.
...WE SPOTTED SOME GAME OVER THE RIDGE.

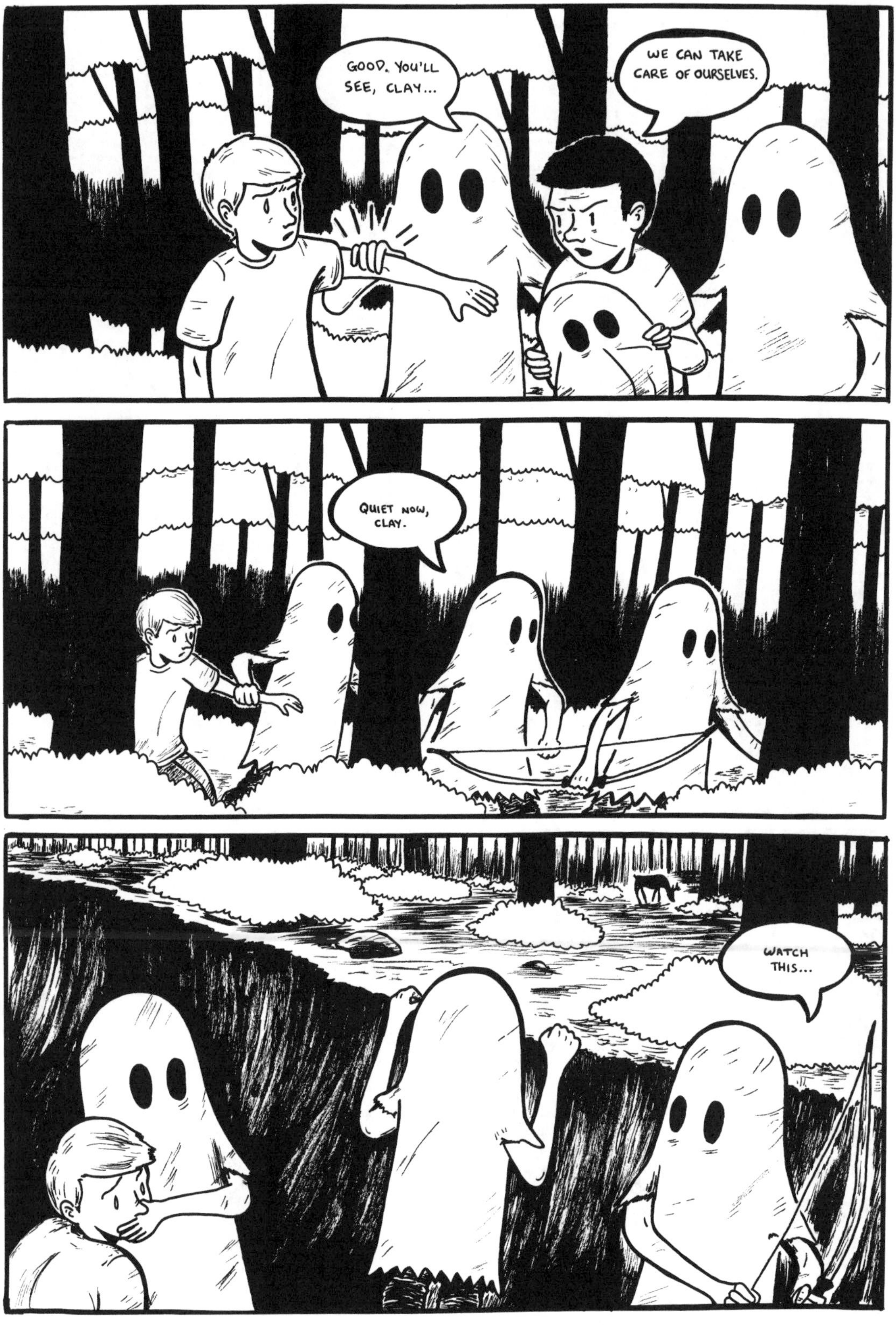
GOOD. YOU'LL SEE, CLAY...
WE CAN TAKE CARE OF OURSELVES.
QUIET NOW, CLAY.
WATCH THIS...

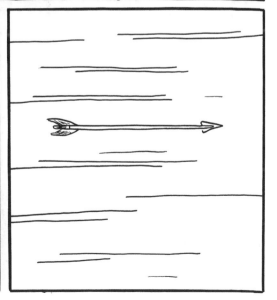

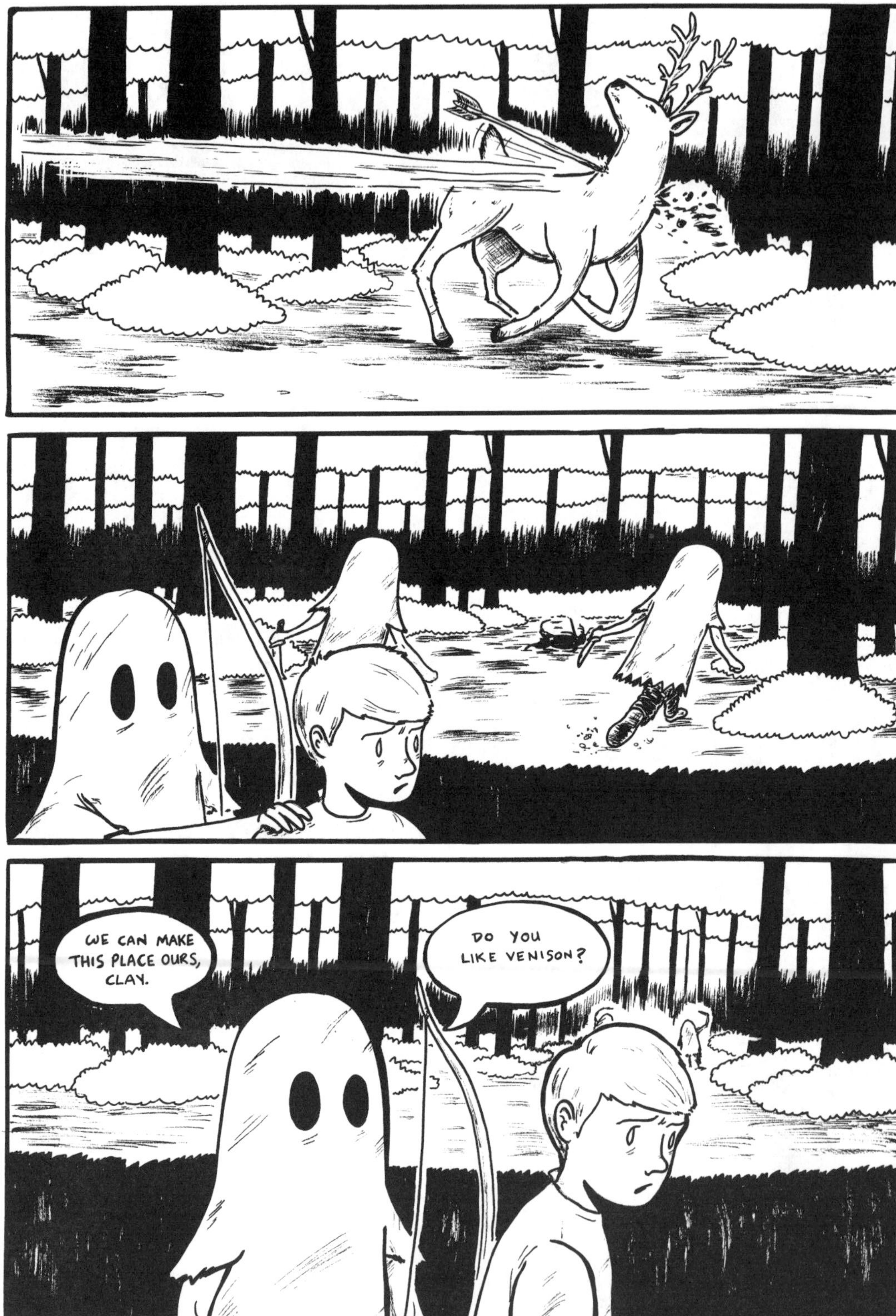
WE CAN MAKE THIS PLACE OURS, CLAY.
DO YOU LIKE VENISON?

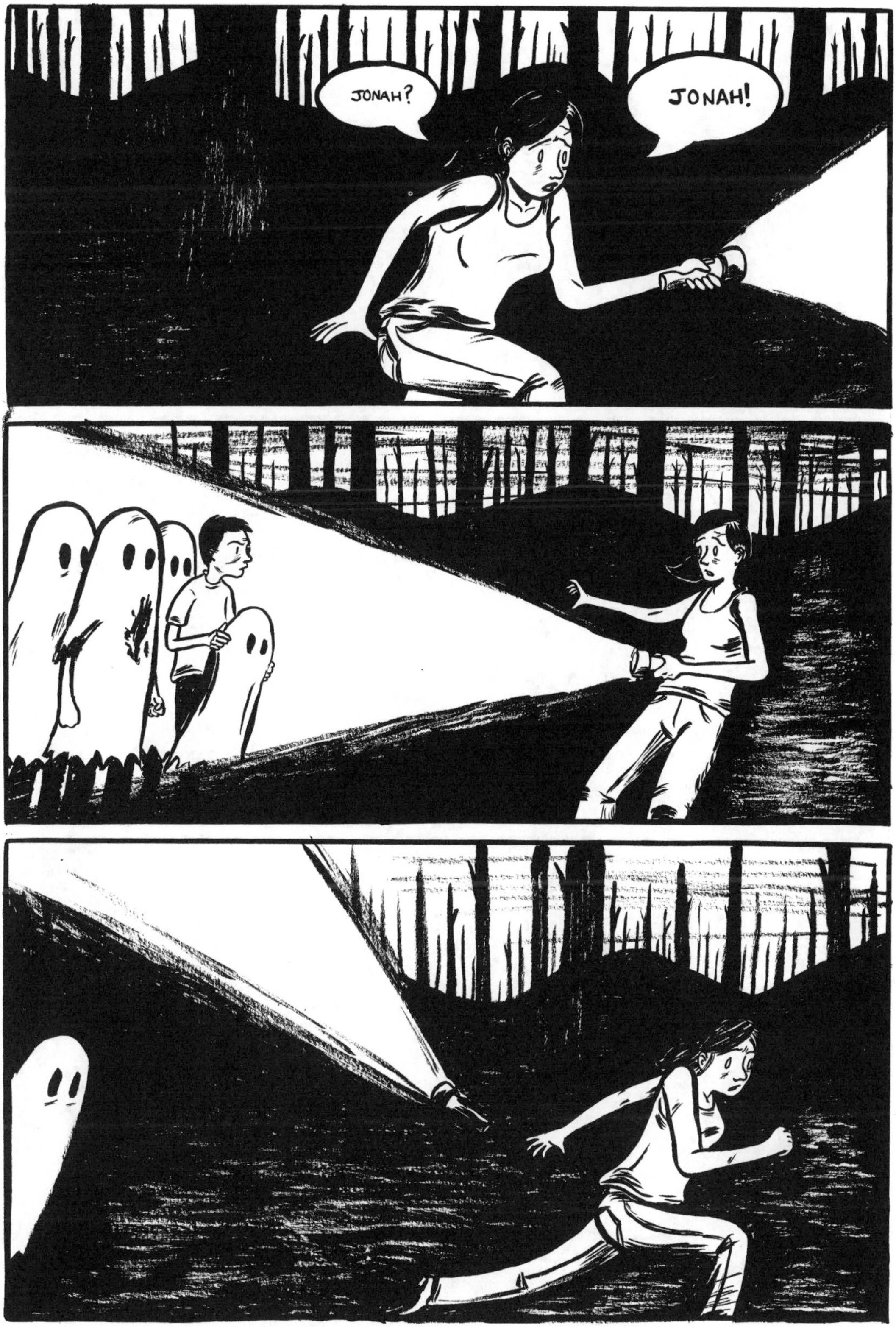
JONAH?
JONAH!

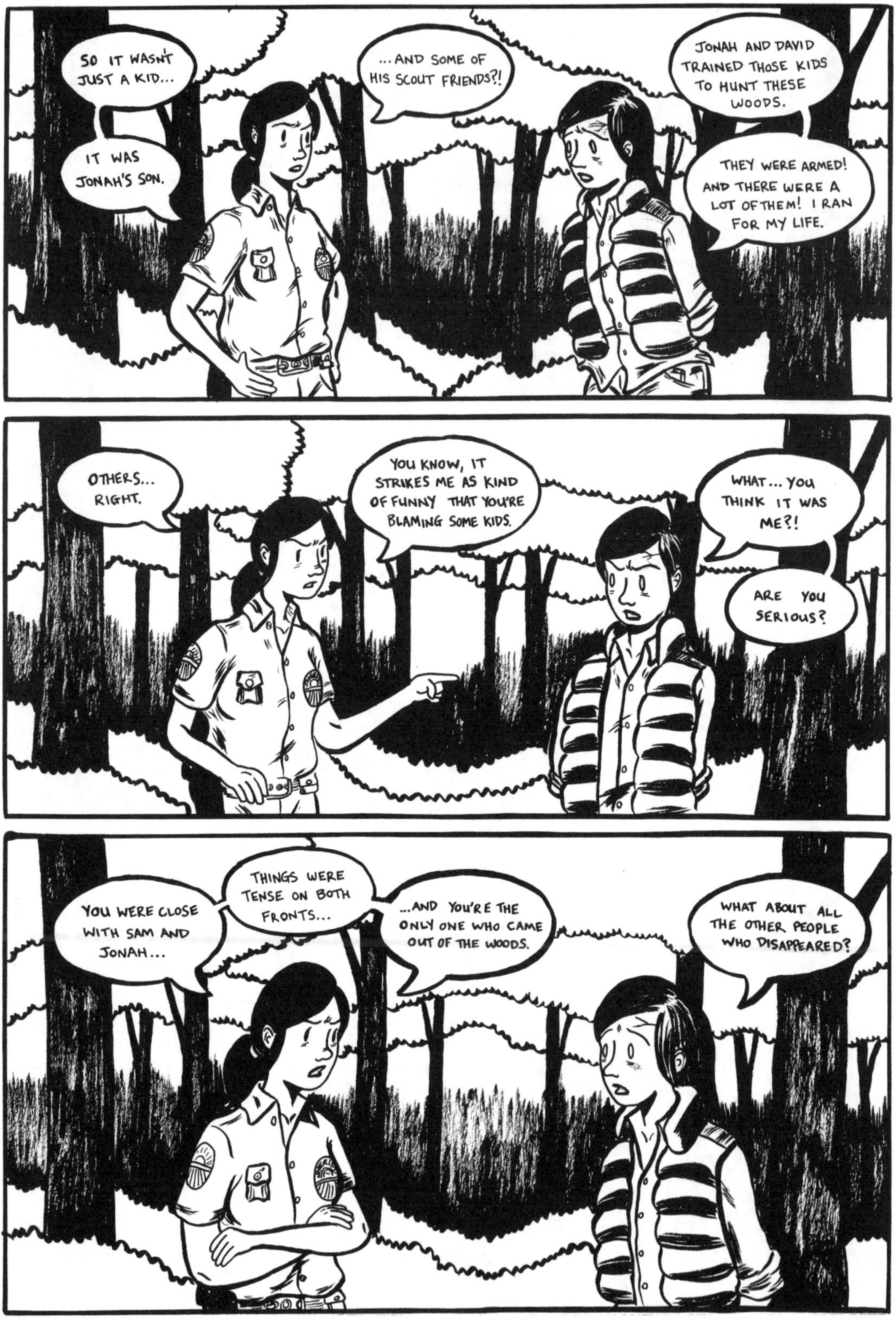
SO IT WASN'T JUST A KID...
IT WAS JONAH'S SON.
...AND SOME OF HIS SCOUT FRIENDS?!
JONAH AND DAVID TRAINED THOSE KIDS TO HUNT THESE WOODS.
THEY WERE ARMED! AND THERE WERE A LOT OF THEM! I RAN FOR MY LIFE.
OTHERS... RIGHT.
YOU KNOW, IT STRIKES ME AS KIND OF FUNNY THAT YOU'RE BLAMING SOME KIDS.
WHAT... YOU THINK IT WAS ME?!
ARE YOU SERIOUS?
YOU WERE CLOSE WITH SAM AND JONAH...
THINGS WERE TENSE ON BOTH FRONTS...
...AND YOU'RE THE ONLY ONE WHO CAME OUT OF THE WOODS.
WHAT ABOUT ALL THE OTHER PEOPLE WHO DISAPPEARED?

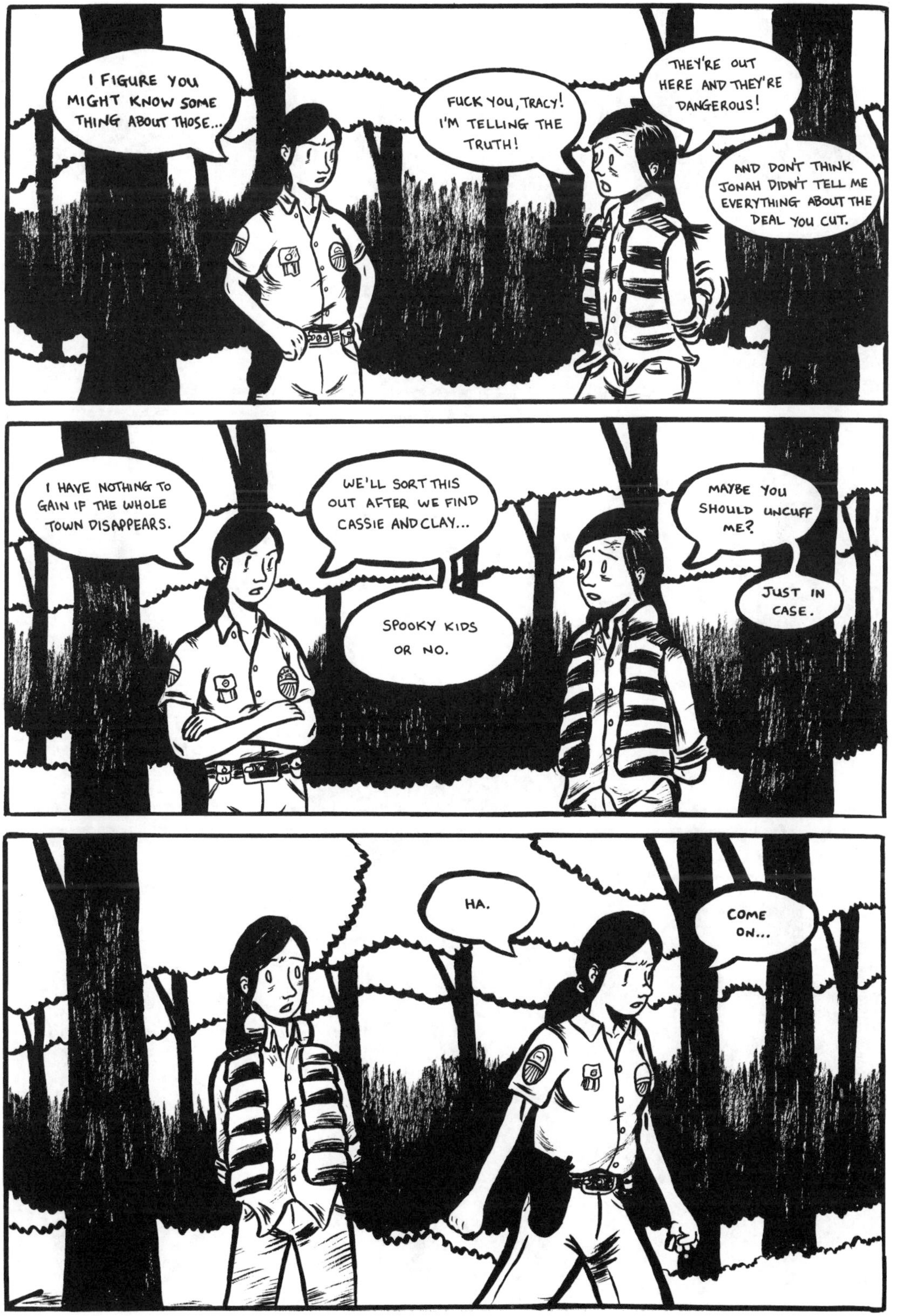
I FIGURE YOU MIGHT KNOW SOME THING ABOUT THOSE...
FUCK YOU, TRACY! I'M TELLING THE TRUTH!
THEY'RE OUT HERE AND THEY'RE DANGEROUS!
AND DON'T THINK JONAH DIDN'T TELL ME EVERYTHING ABOUT THE DEAL YOU CUT.
I HAVE NOTHING TO GAIN IF THE WHOLE TOWN DISAPPEARS.
WE'LL SORT THIS OUT AFTER WE FIND CASSIE AND CLAY...
SPOOKY KIDS OR NO.
MAYBE YOU SHOULD UNCUFF ME?
JUST IN CASE.
HA.
COME ON...

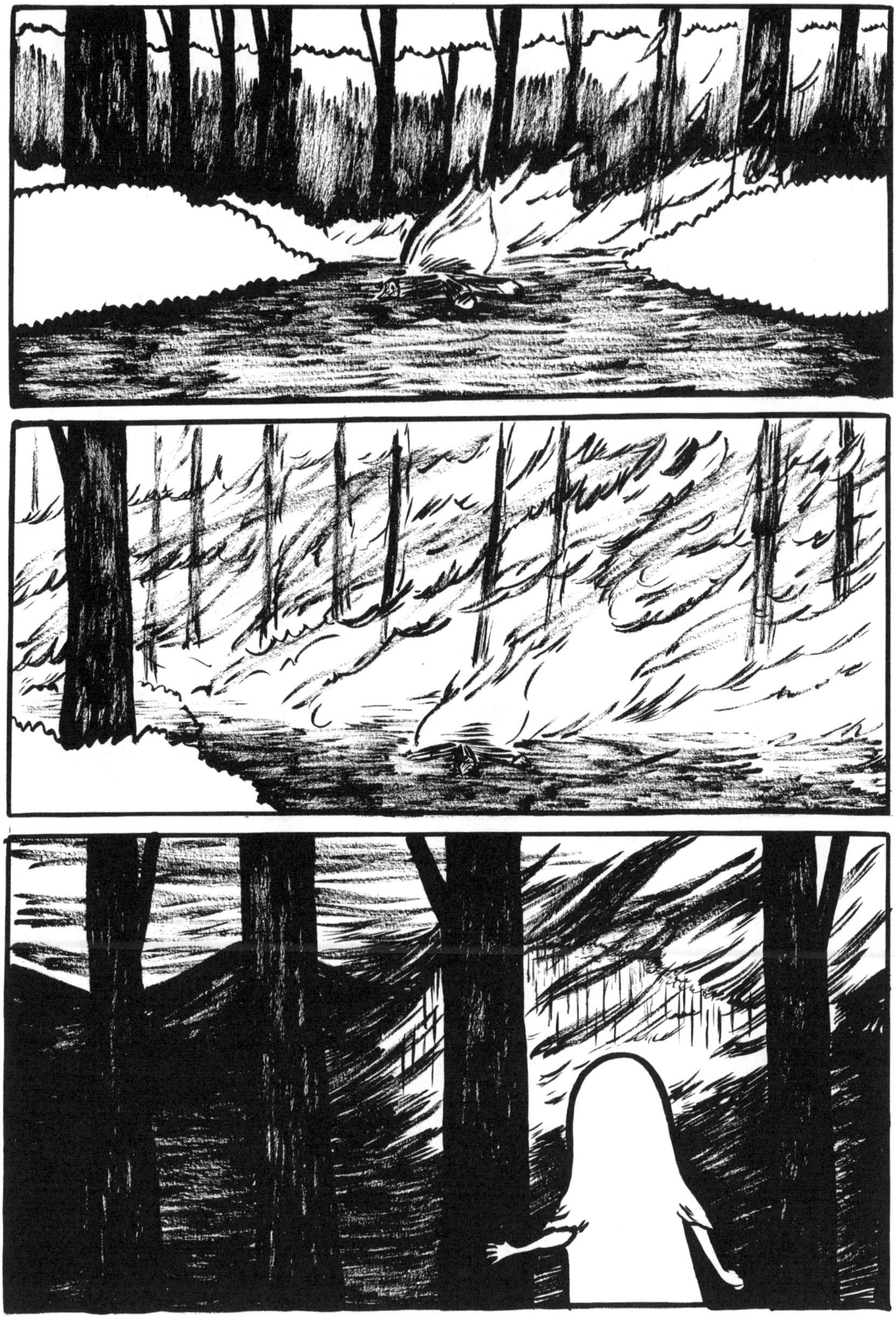

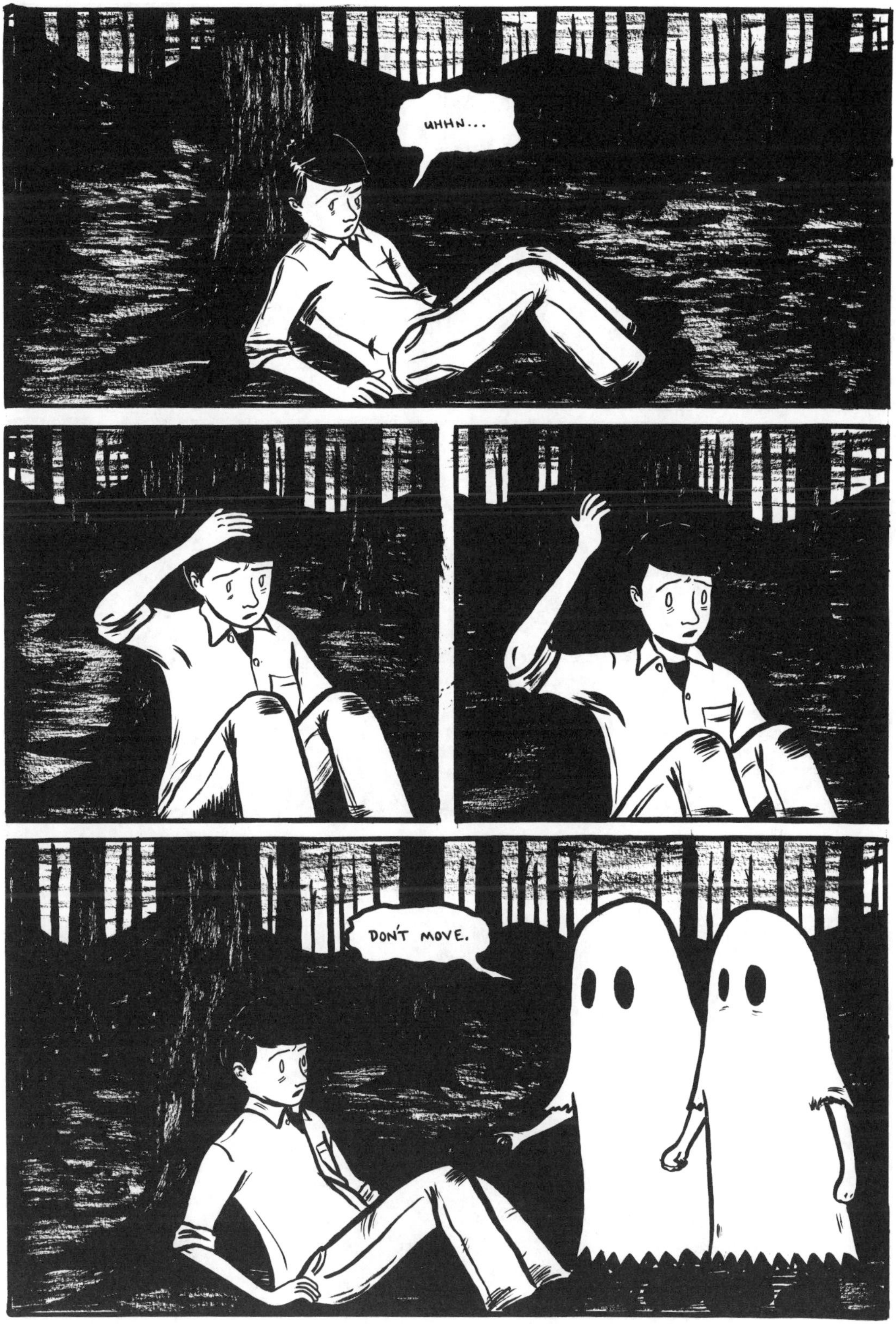
UHHN...
DON'T MOVE.

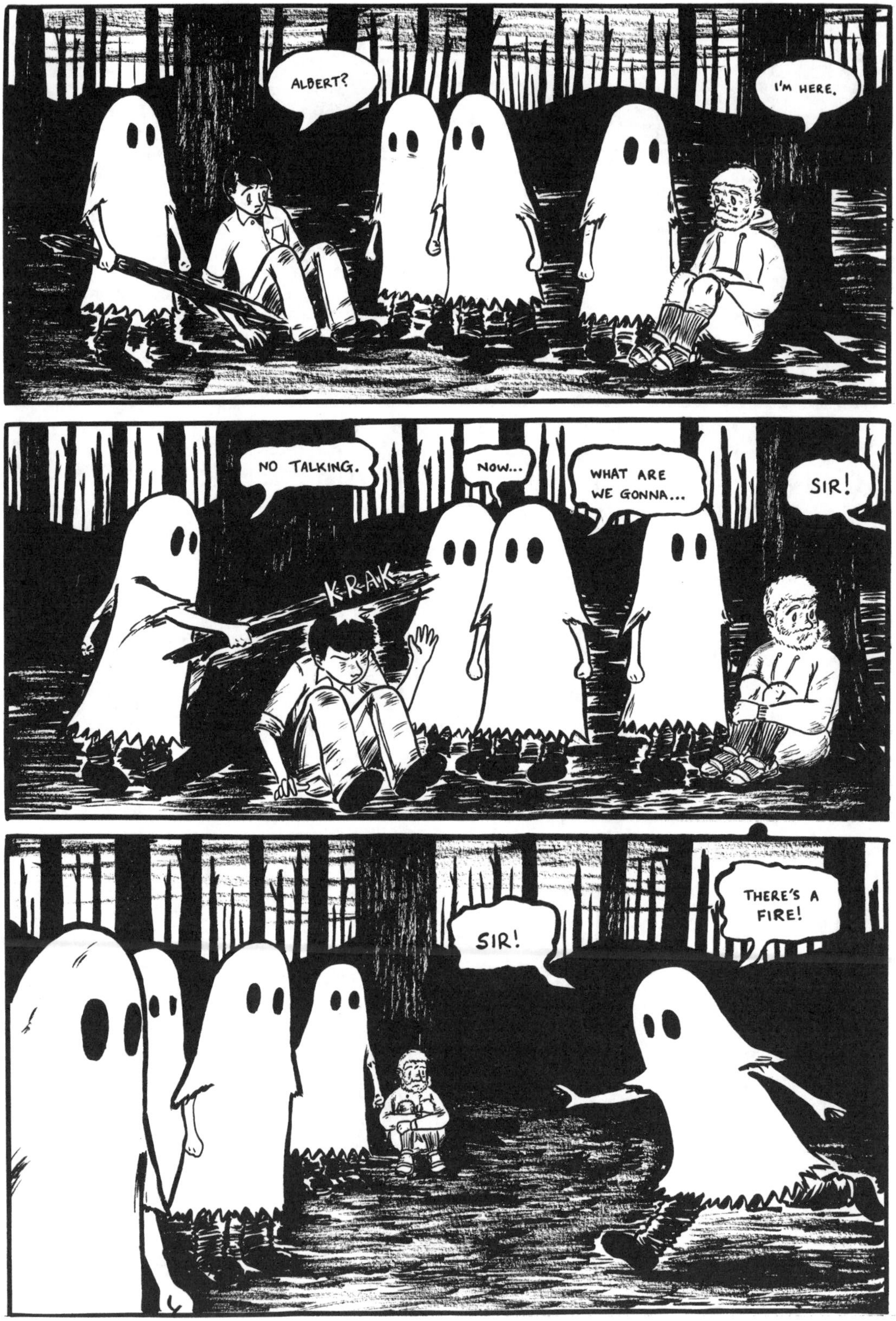
ALBERT?
I'M HERE.
NO TALKING.
KRAK
NOW...
WHAT ARE WE GONNA...
SIR!
SIR!
THERE'S A FIRE!

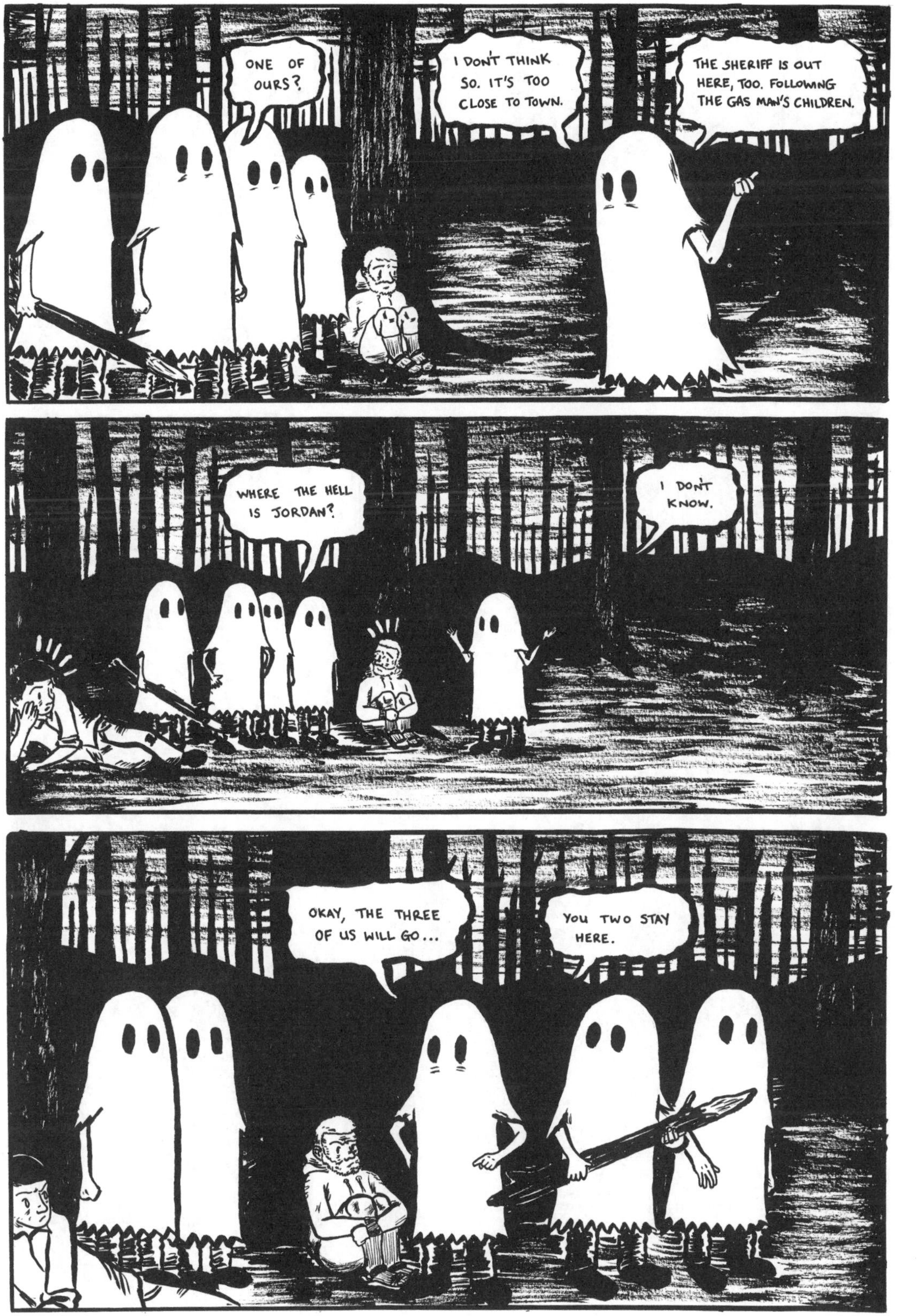

ONE OF OURS?
I DON'T THINK SO. IT'S TOO CLOSE TO TOWN.
THE SHERIFF IS OUT HERE, TOO. FOLLOWING THE GAS MAN'S CHILDREN.
WHERE THE HELL IS JORDAN?
I DON'T KNOW.
OKAY, THE THREE OF US WILL GO...
YOU TWO STAY HERE.

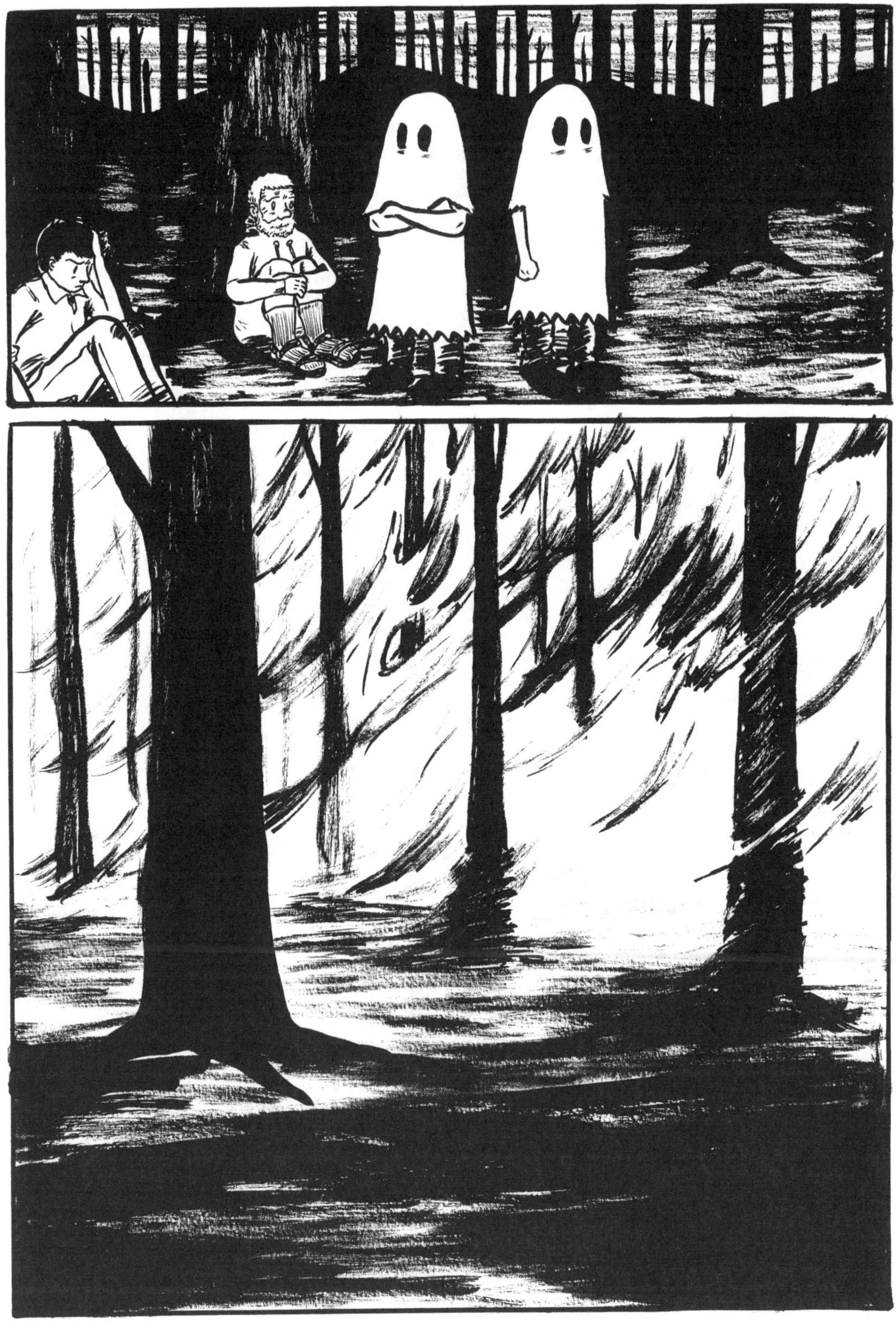

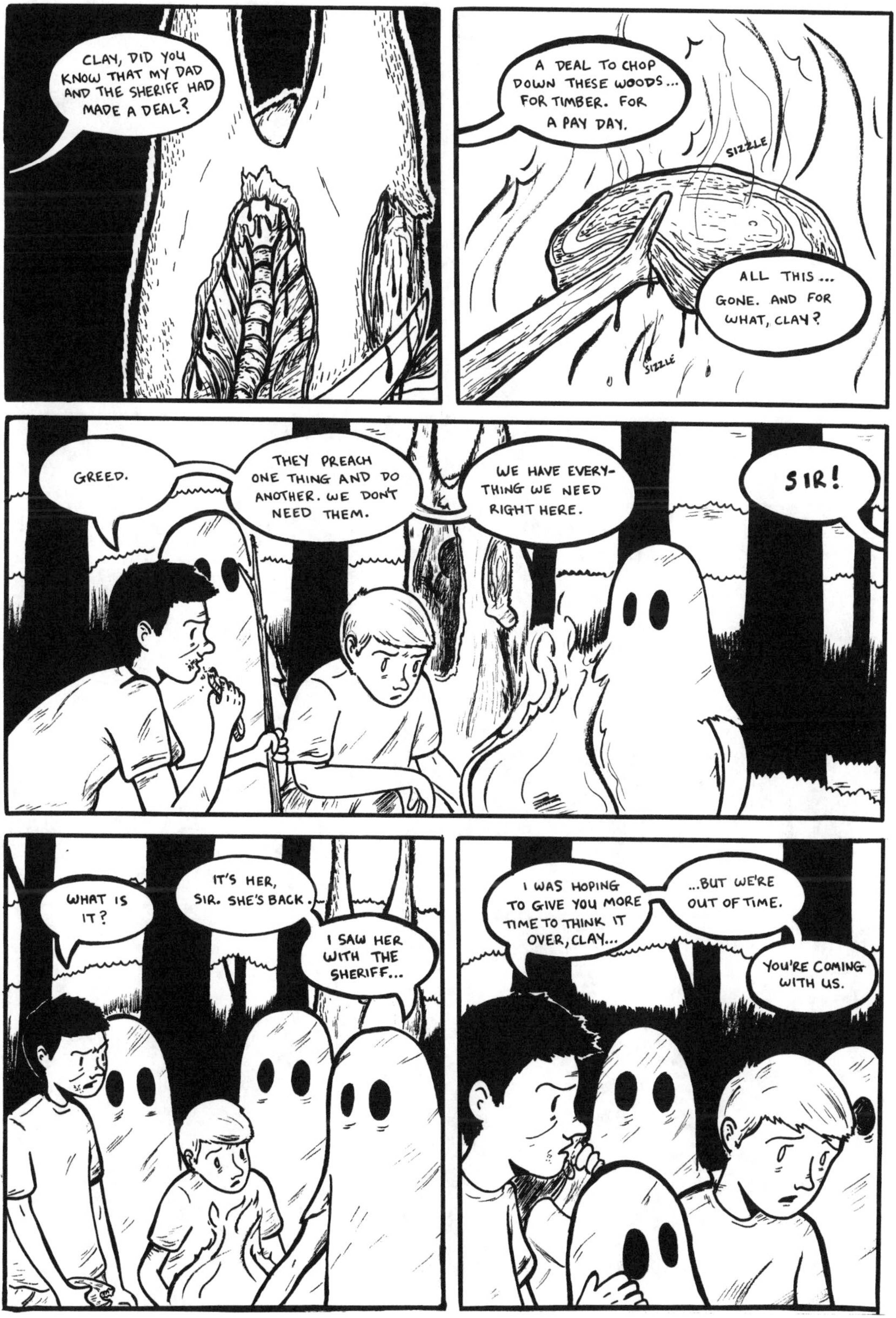
CLAY, DID YOU KNOW THAT MY DAD AND THE SHERIFF HAD MADE A DEAL?
A DEAL TO CHOP DOWN THESE WOODS... FOR TIMBER. FOR A PAY DAY.
SIZZLE
ALL THIS... GONE. AND FOR WHAT, CLAY?
SIZZLE
GREED.
THEY PREACH ONE THING AND DO ANOTHER. WE DON'T NEED THEM.
WE HAVE EVERYTHING WE NEED RIGHT HERE.
SIR!
WHAT IS IT?
IT'S HER, SIR. SHE'S BACK.
I SAW HER WITH THE SHERIFF...
I WAS HOPING TO GIVE YOU MORE TIME TO THINK IT OVER, CLAY...
...BUT WE'RE OUT OF TIME.
YOU'RE COMING WITH US.

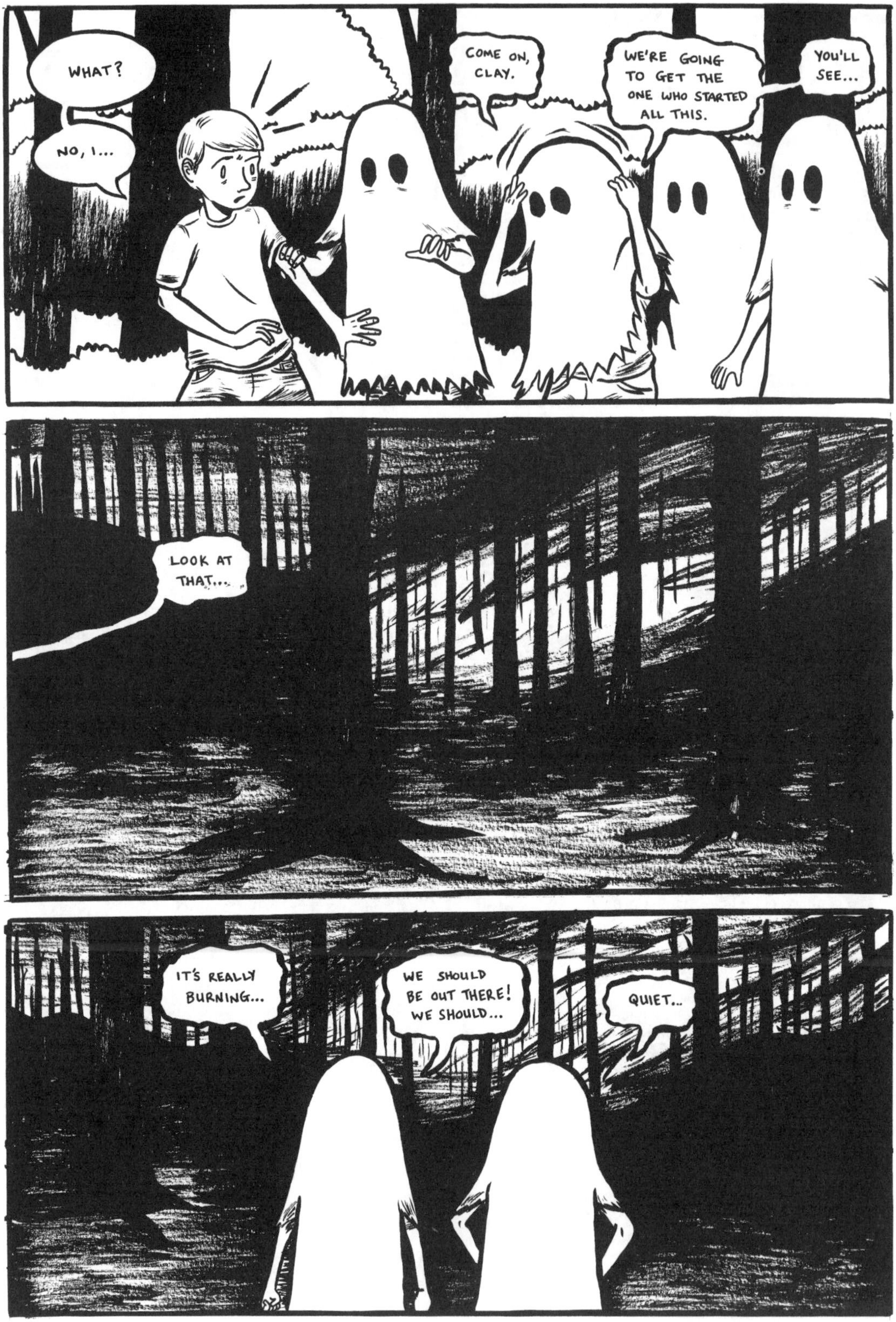
WHAT?
NO, I...
COME ON, CLAY.
WE'RE GOING TO GET THE ONE WHO STARTED ALL THIS.
YOU'LL SEE...
LOOK AT THAT...
IT'S REALLY BURNING...
WE SHOULD BE OUT THERE! WE SHOULD...
QUIET...

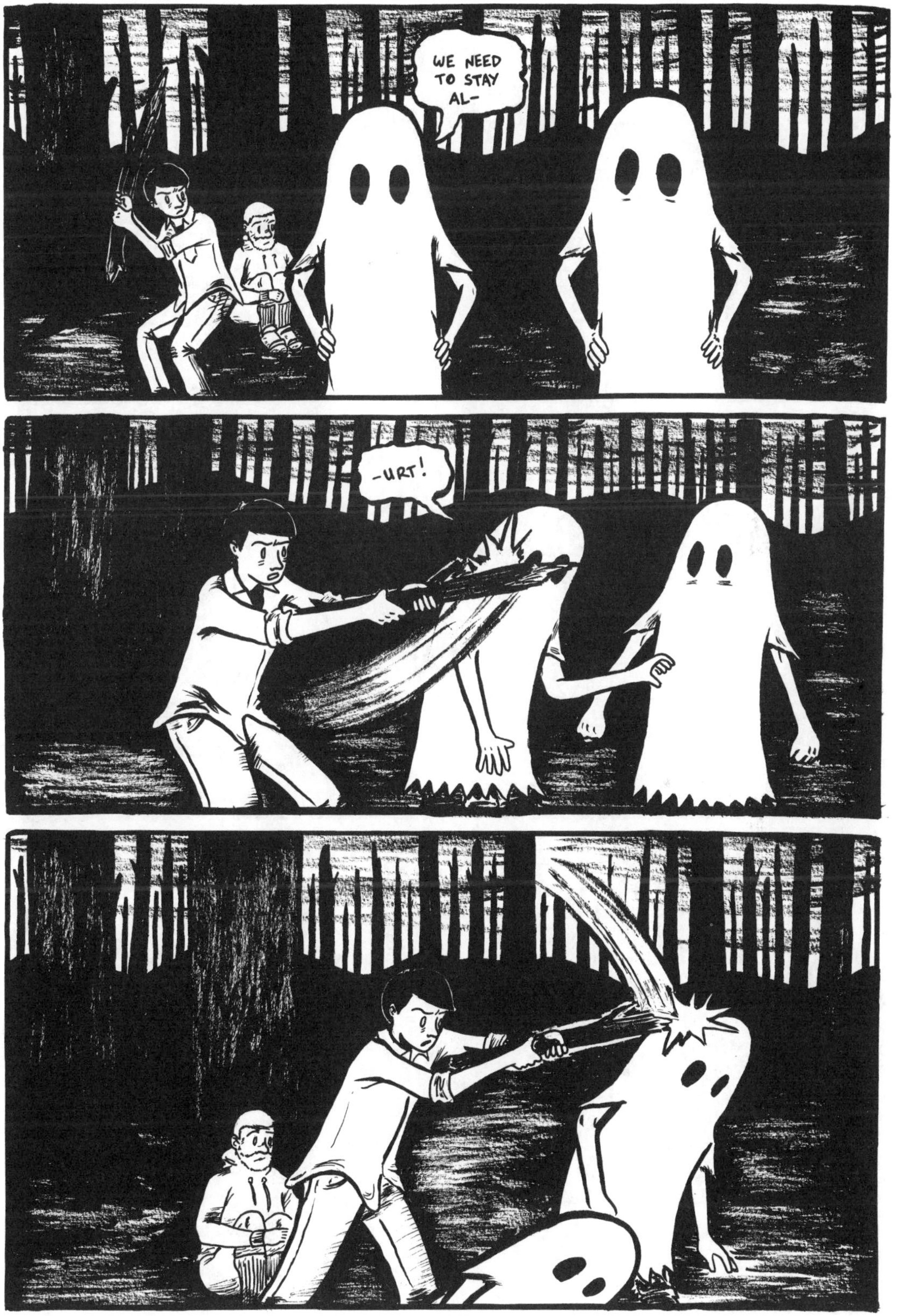
WE NEED TO STAY AL-
-URT!

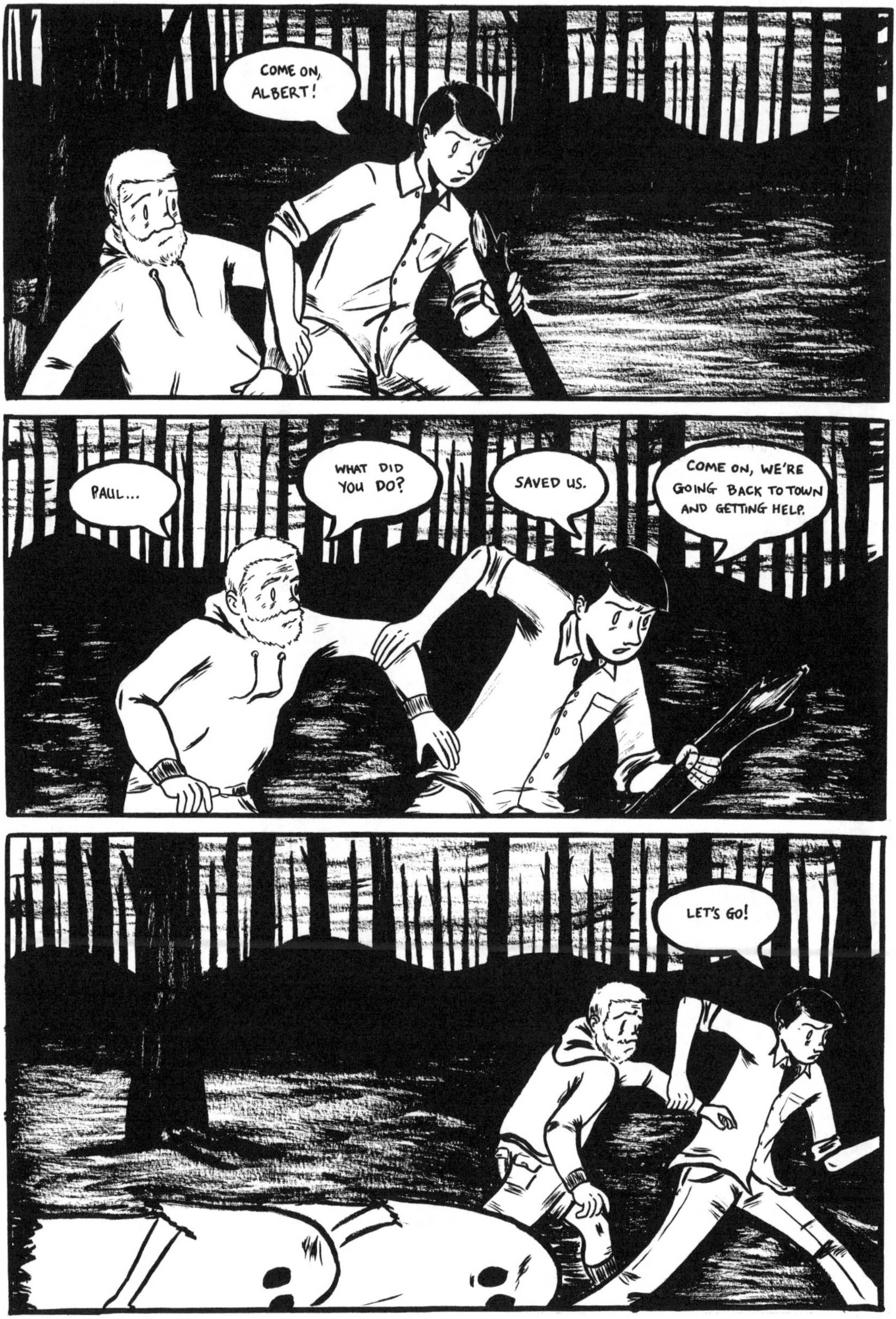
COME ON, ALBERT!
PAUL...
WHAT DID YOU DO?
SAVED US.
COME ON, WE'RE GOING BACK TO TOWN AND GETTING HELP.
LET'S GO!

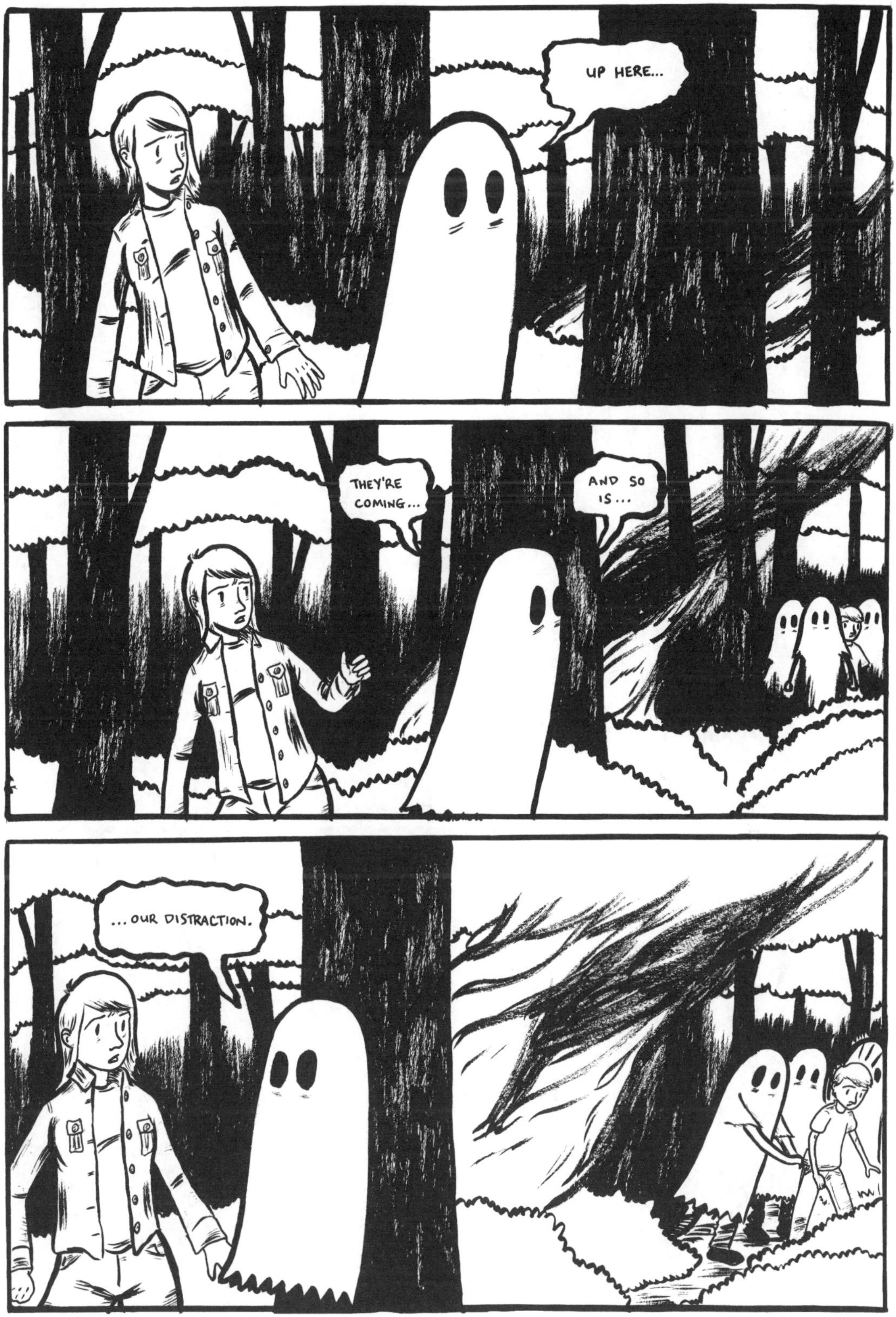

UP HERE...
THEY'RE COMING...
AND SO IS...
...OUR DISTRACTION.

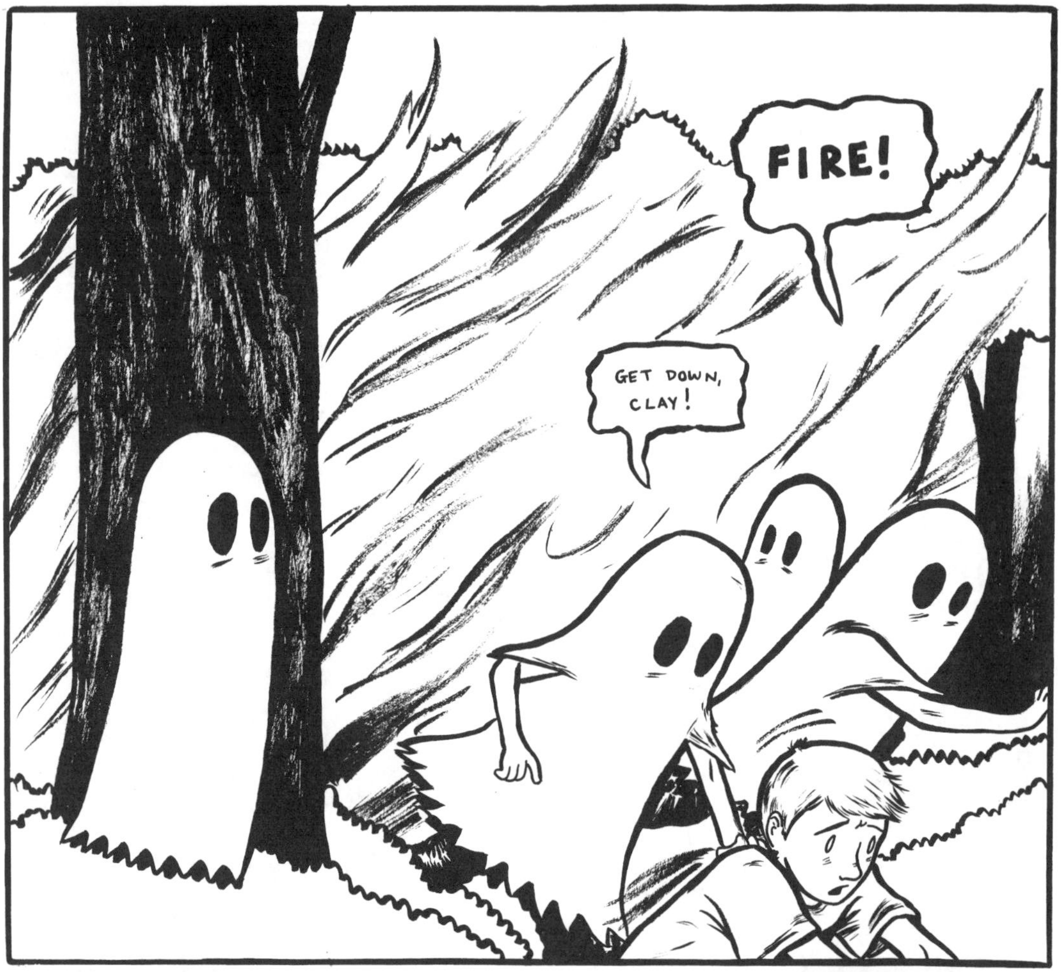
FIRE!
GET DOWN, CLAY!

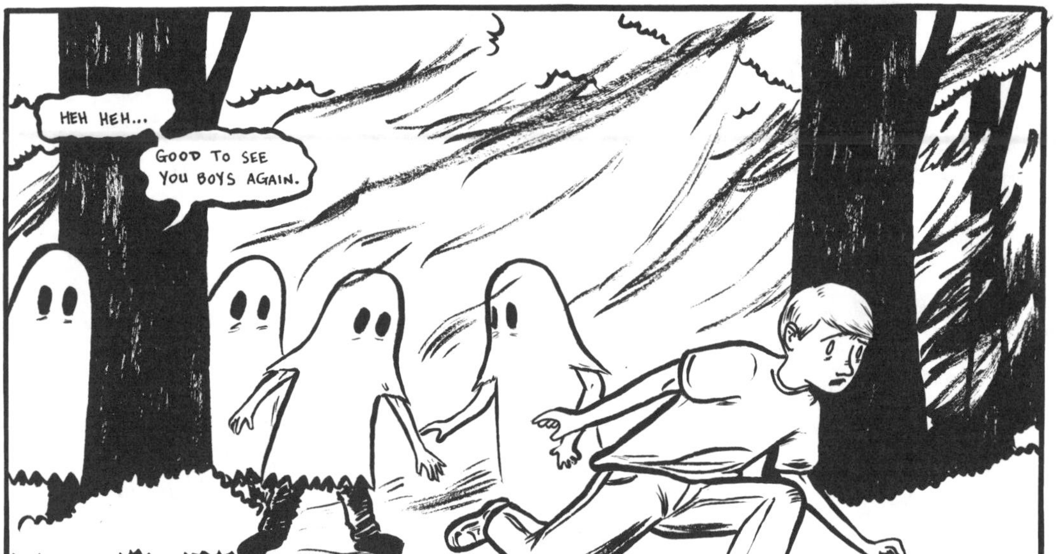
HEH HEH...
GOOD TO SEE YOU BOYS AGAIN.

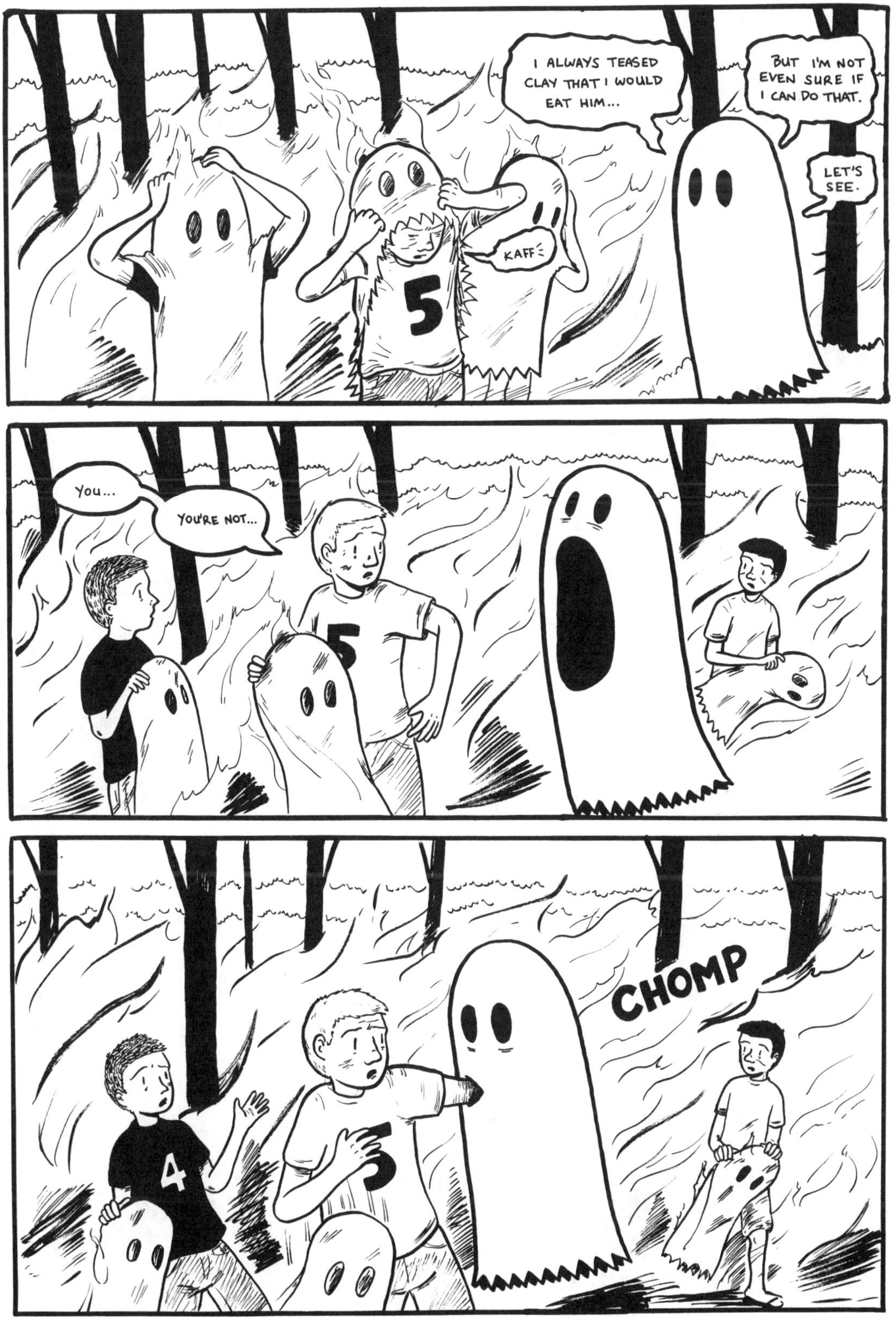

I ALWAYS TEASED CLAY THAT I WOULD EAT HIM...
BUT I'M NOT EVEN SURE IF I CAN DO THAT.
LET'S SEE.
KAFF
YOU...
YOU'RE NOT...
CHOMP
4
5

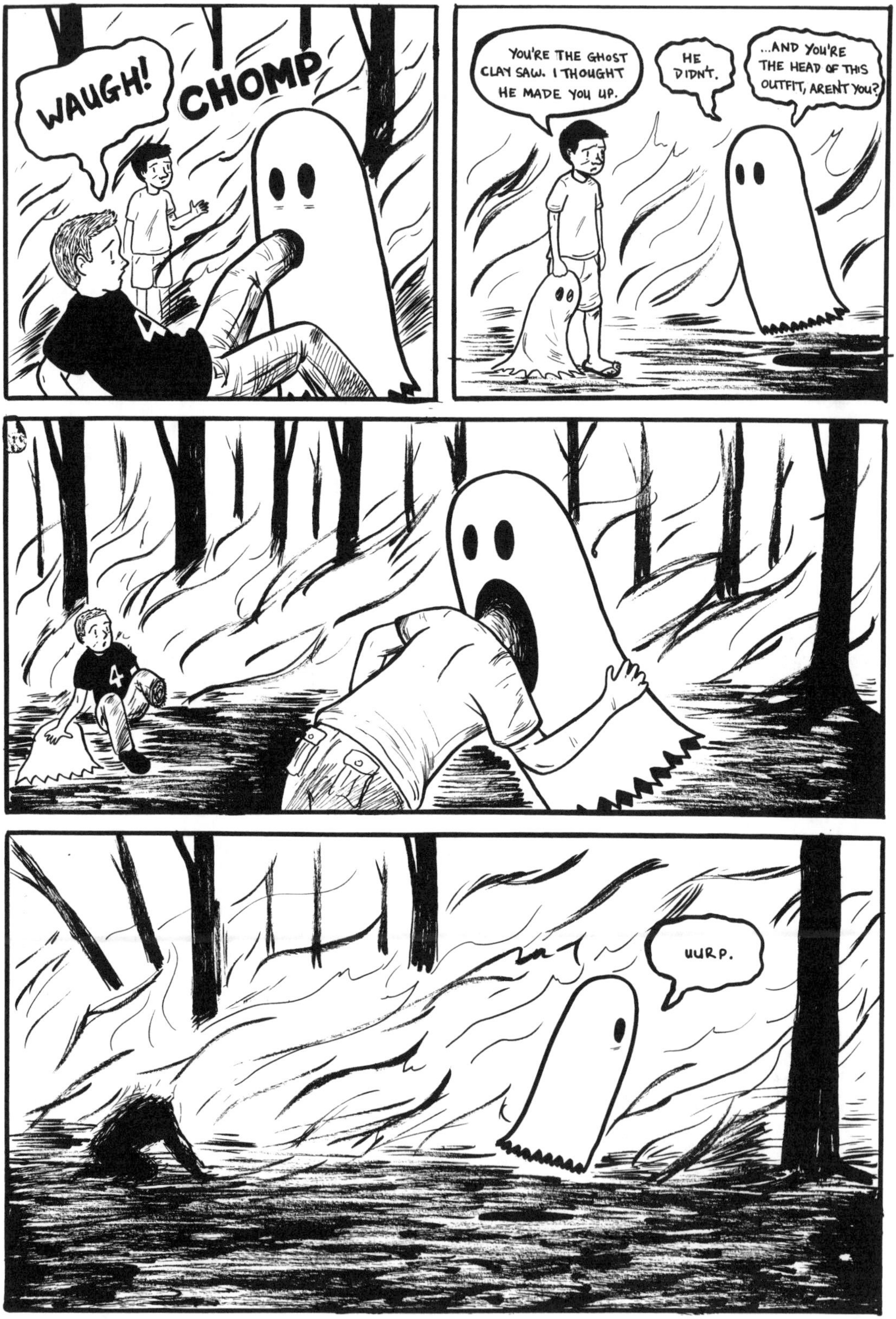
WAUGH!
CHOMP
YOU'RE THE GHOST CLAY SAW. I THOUGHT HE MADE YOU UP.
HE DIDN'T.
...AND YOU'RE THE HEAD OF THIS OUTFIT, AREN'T YOU?
UURP.

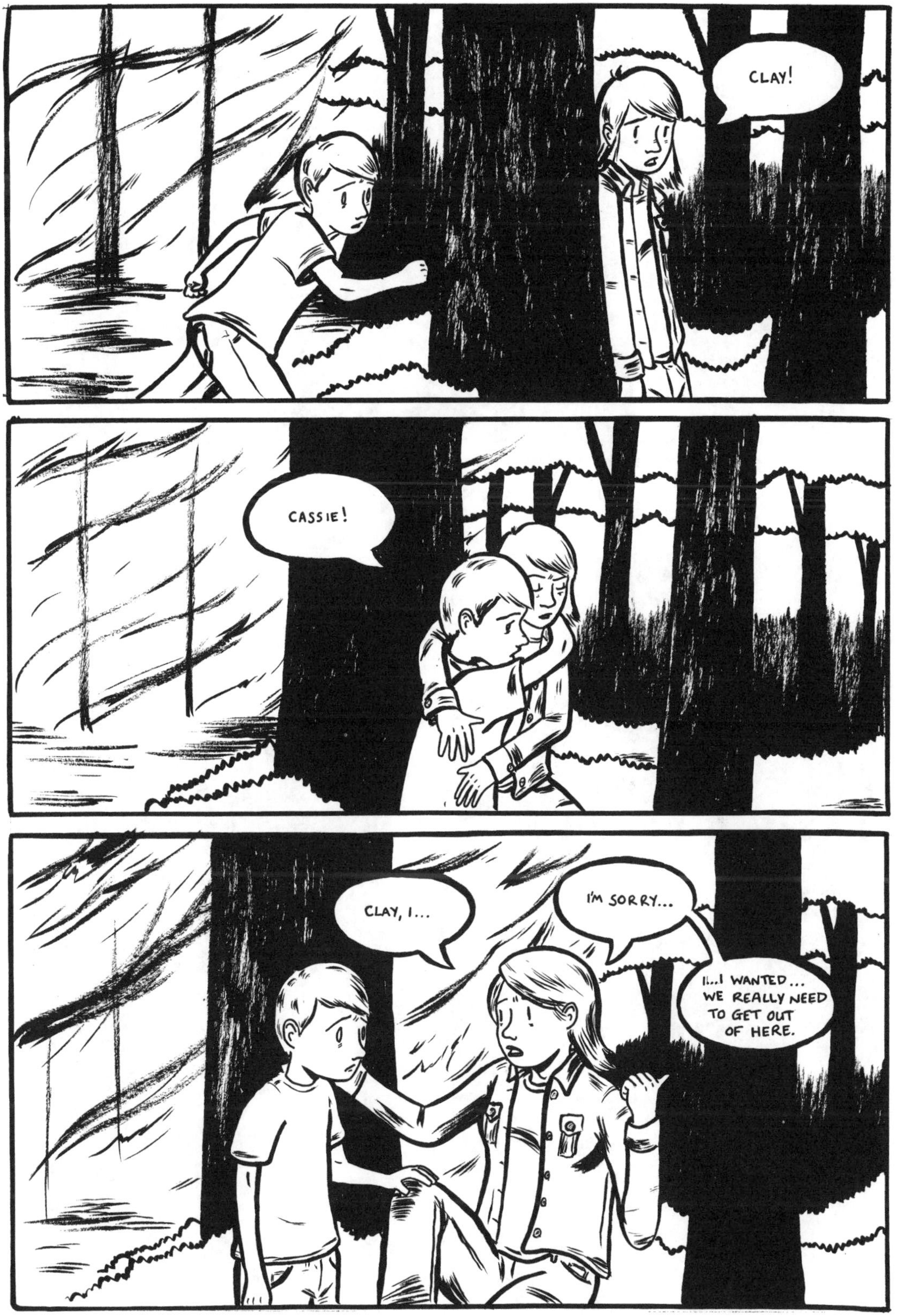
CLAY!
CASSIE!
CLAY, I...
I'M SORRY...
I...I WANTED... WE REALLY NEED TO GET OUT OF HERE.

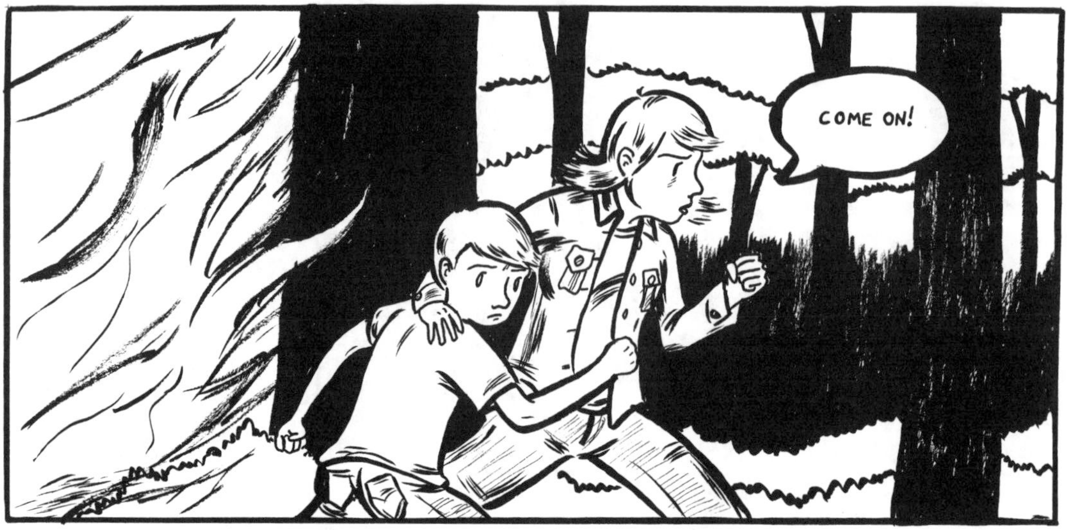
COME ON!

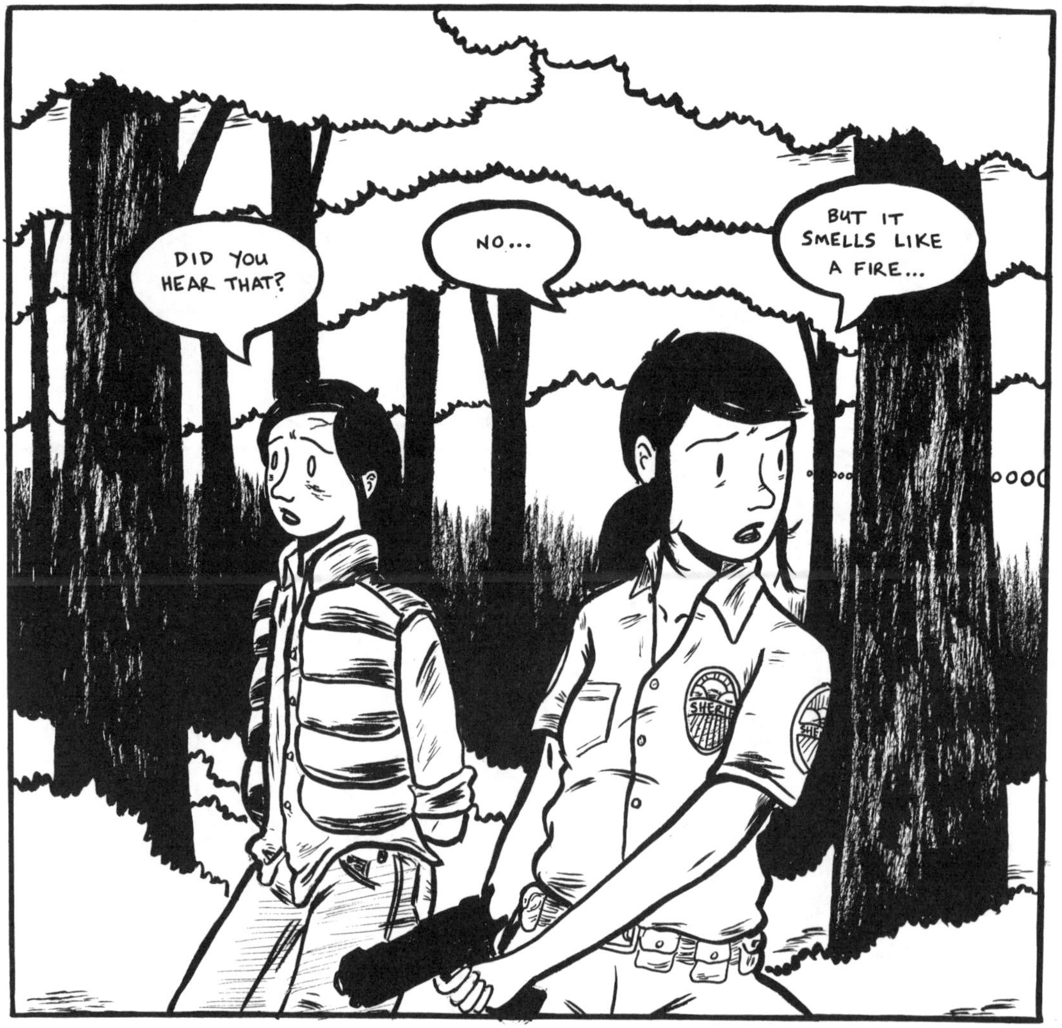
DID YOU HEAR THAT?
NO...
BUT IT SMELLS LIKE A FIRE...

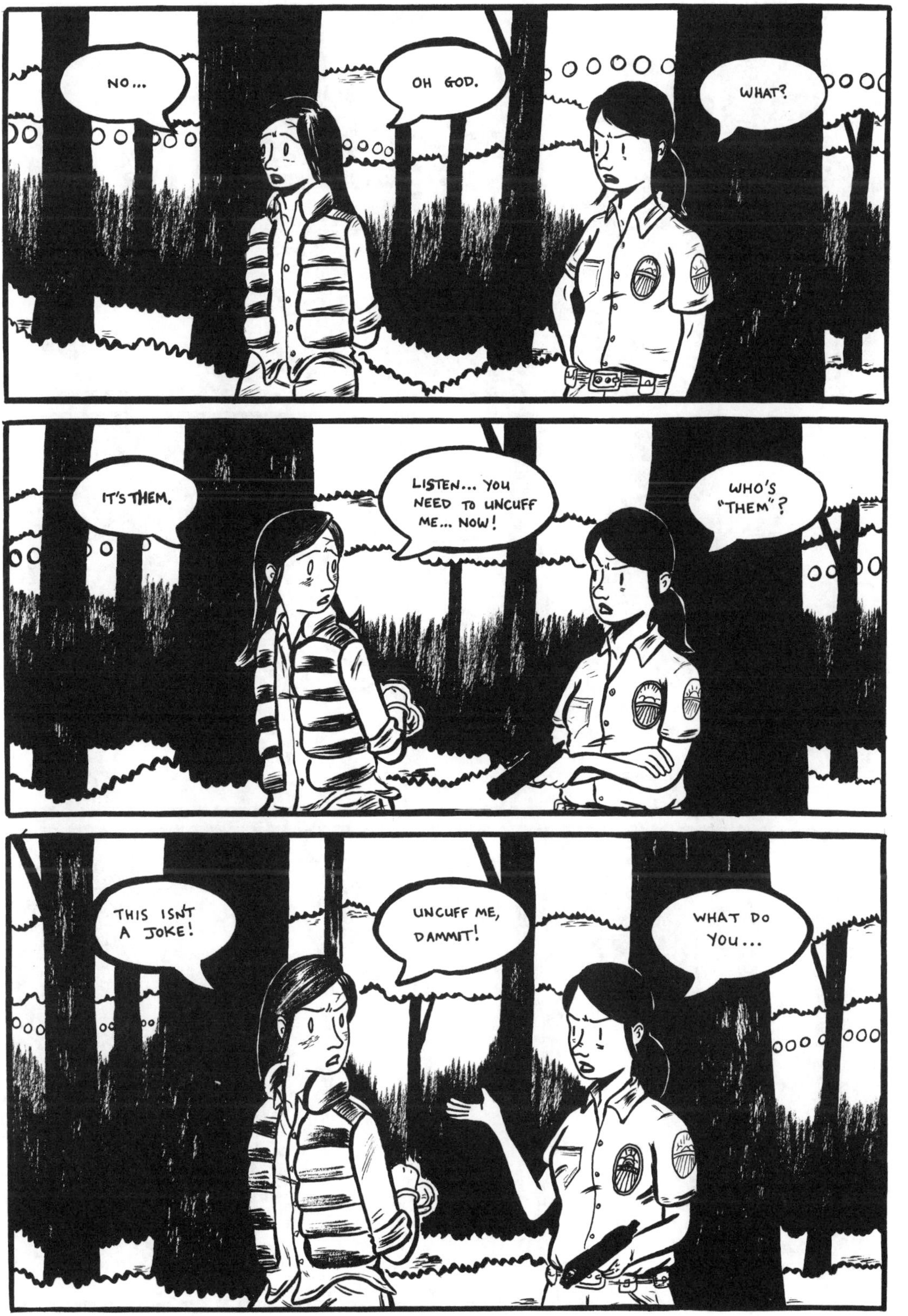

NO...
OH GOD.
WHAT?
IT'S THEM.
LISTEN... YOU NEED TO UNCUFF ME... NOW!
WHO'S "THEM"?
THIS ISN'T A JOKE!
UNCUFF ME, DAMMIT!
WHAT DO YOU...

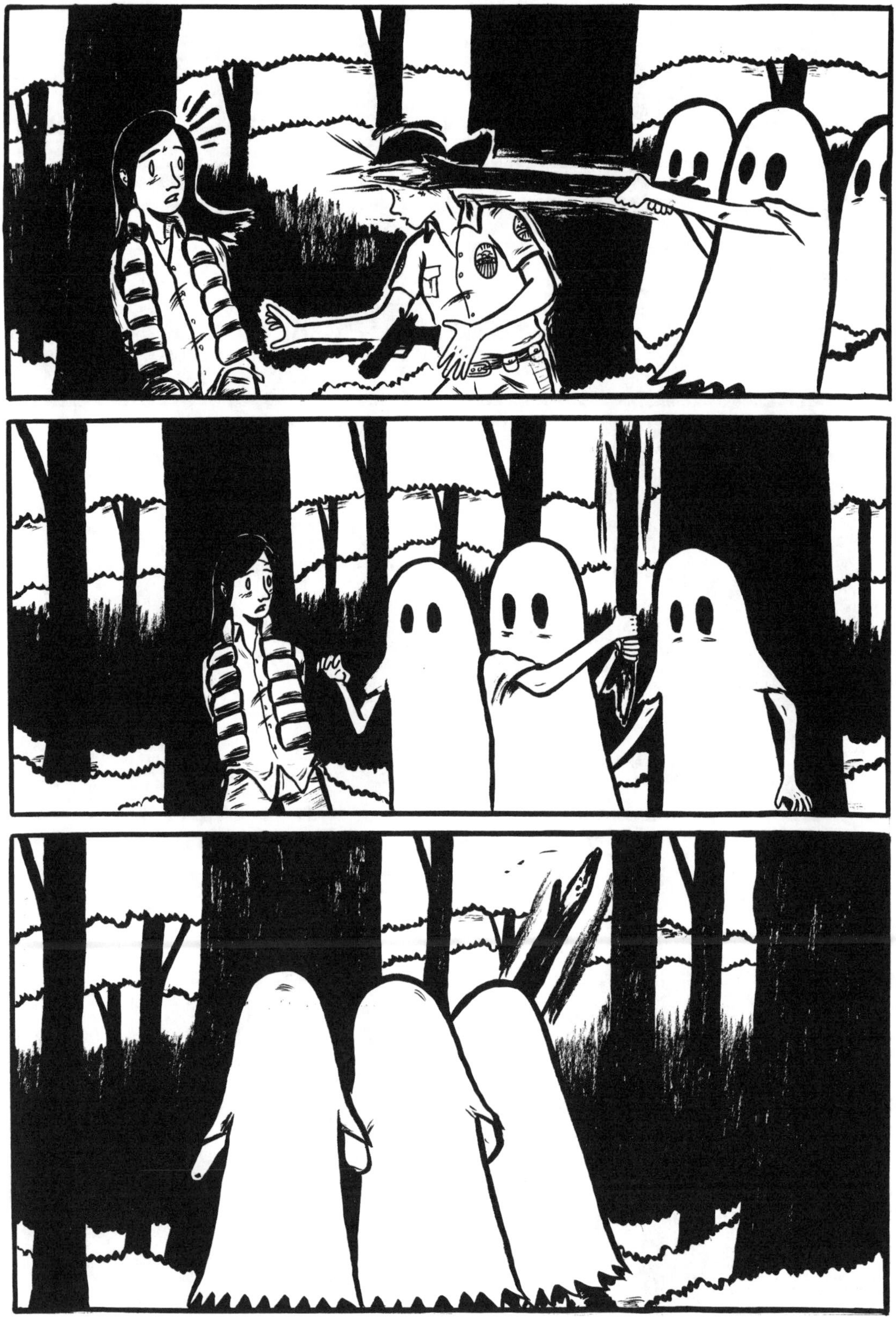

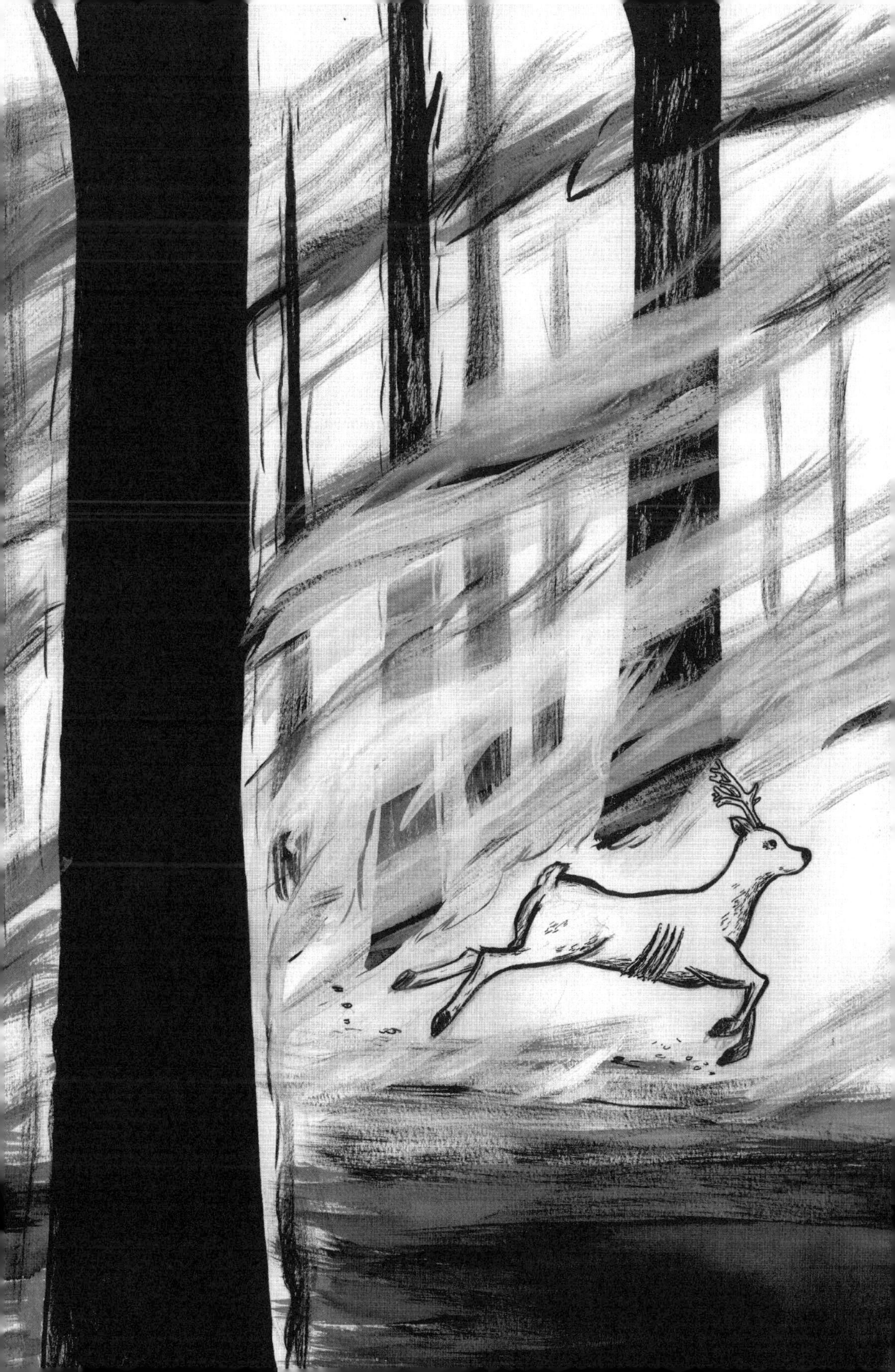

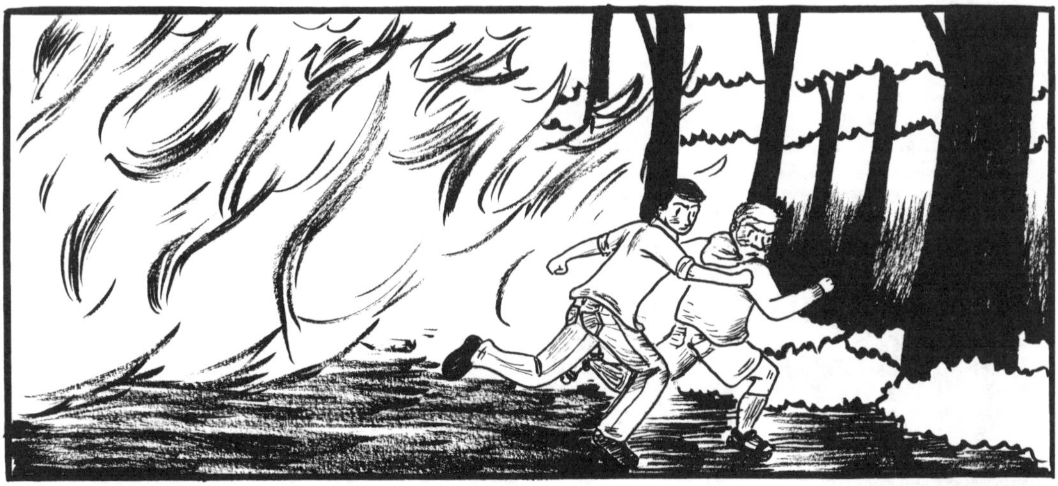

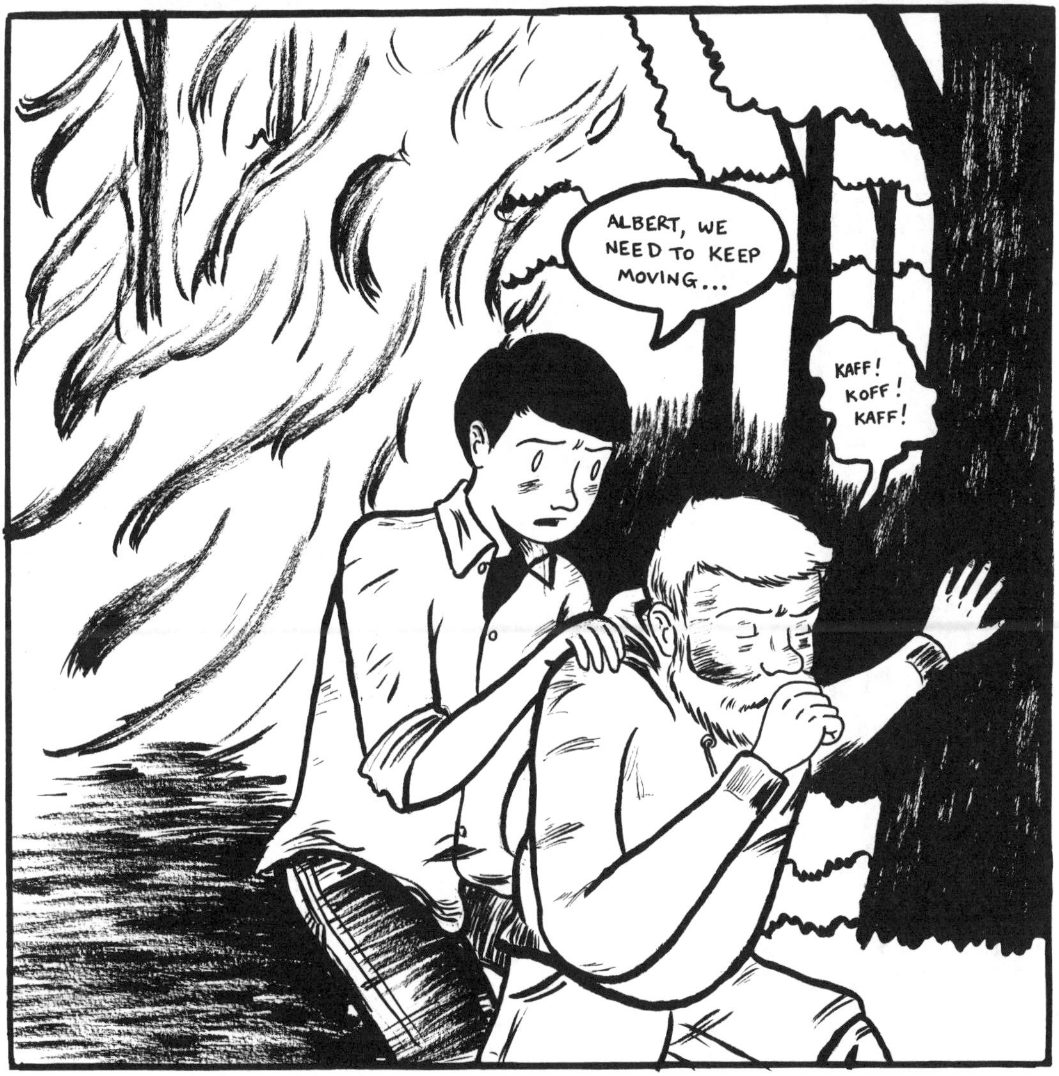
ALBERT, WE NEED TO KEEP MOVING...
KAFF! KOFF! KAFF!

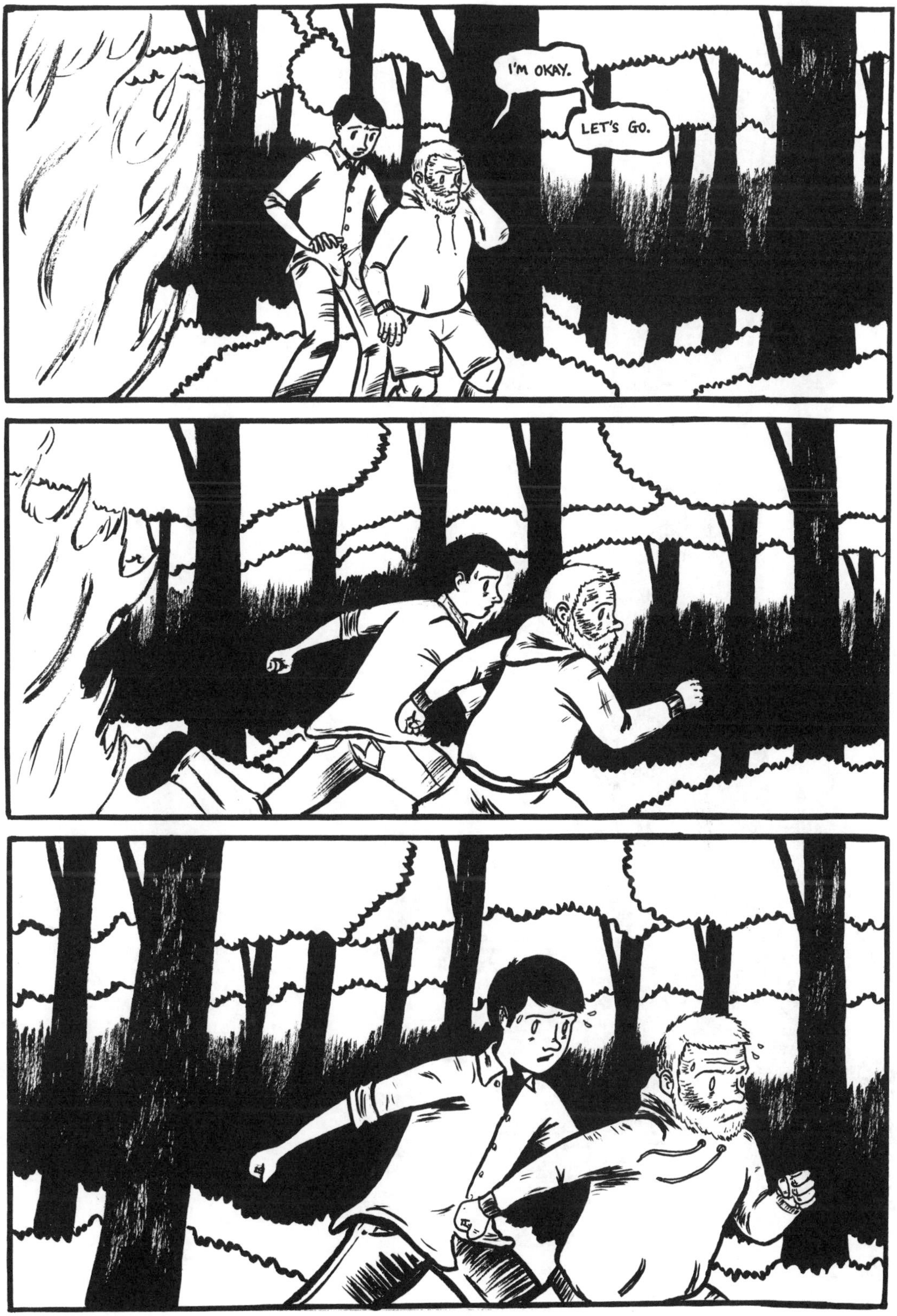
I'M OKAY.
LET'S GO.

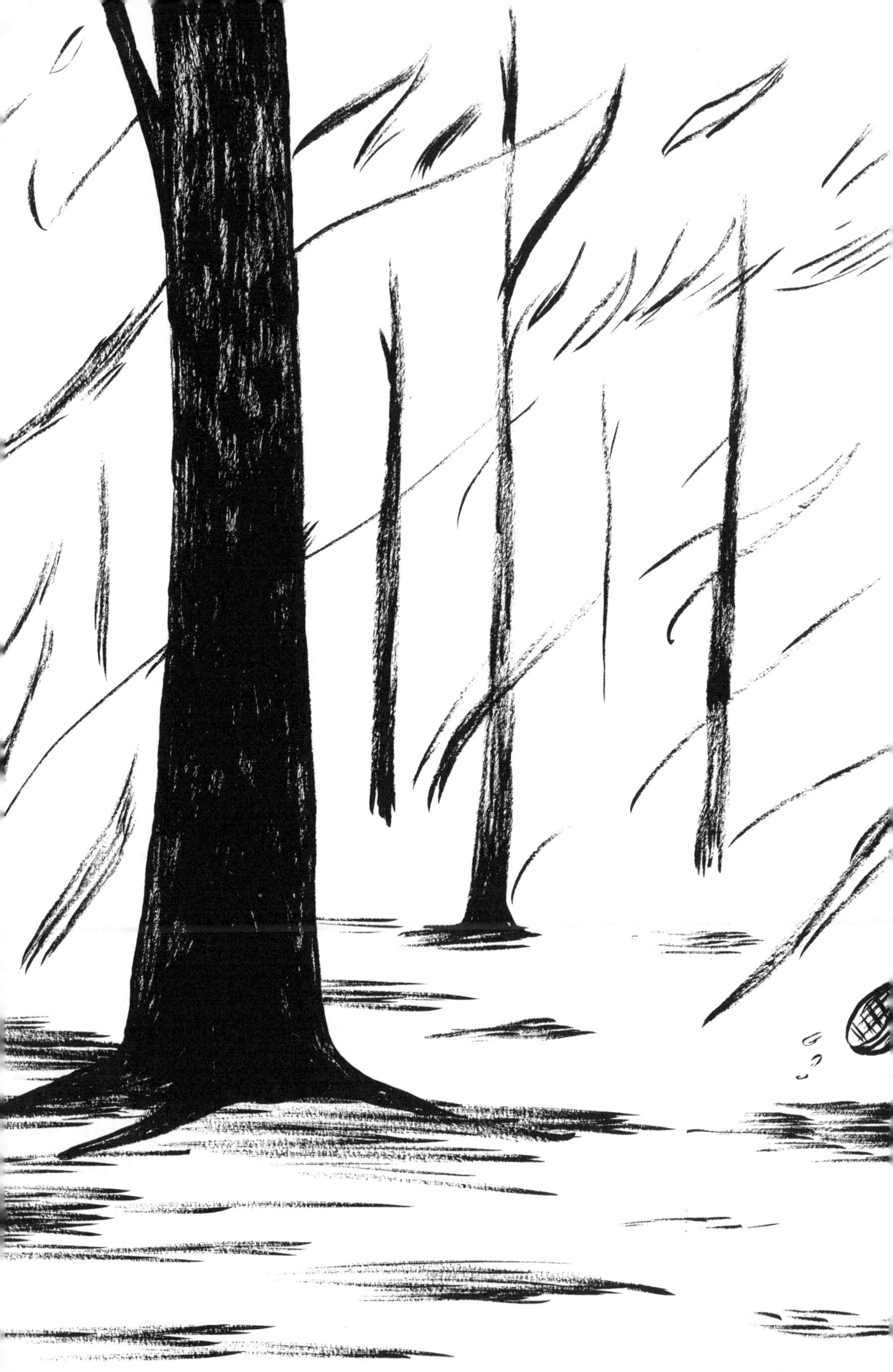

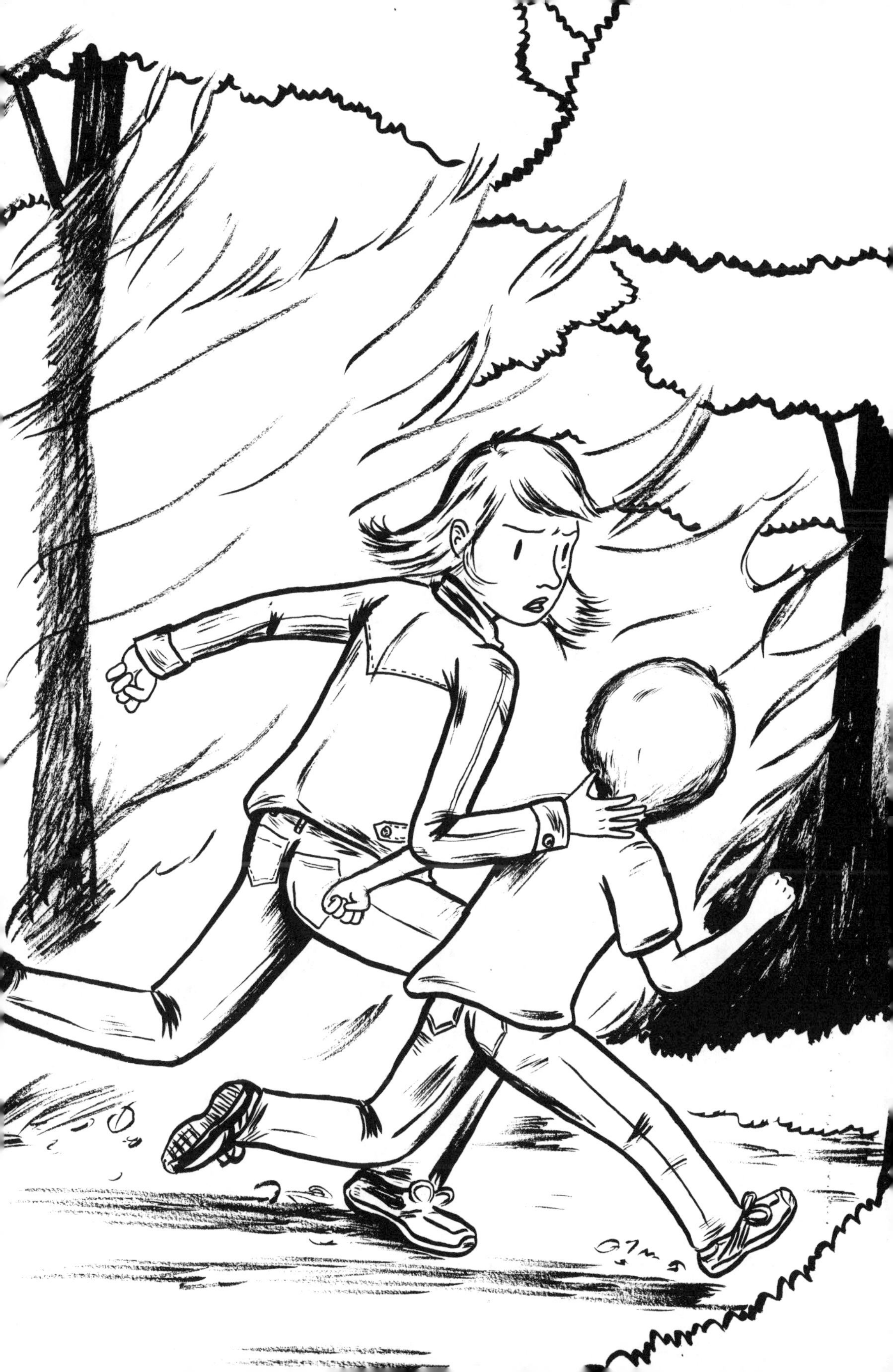

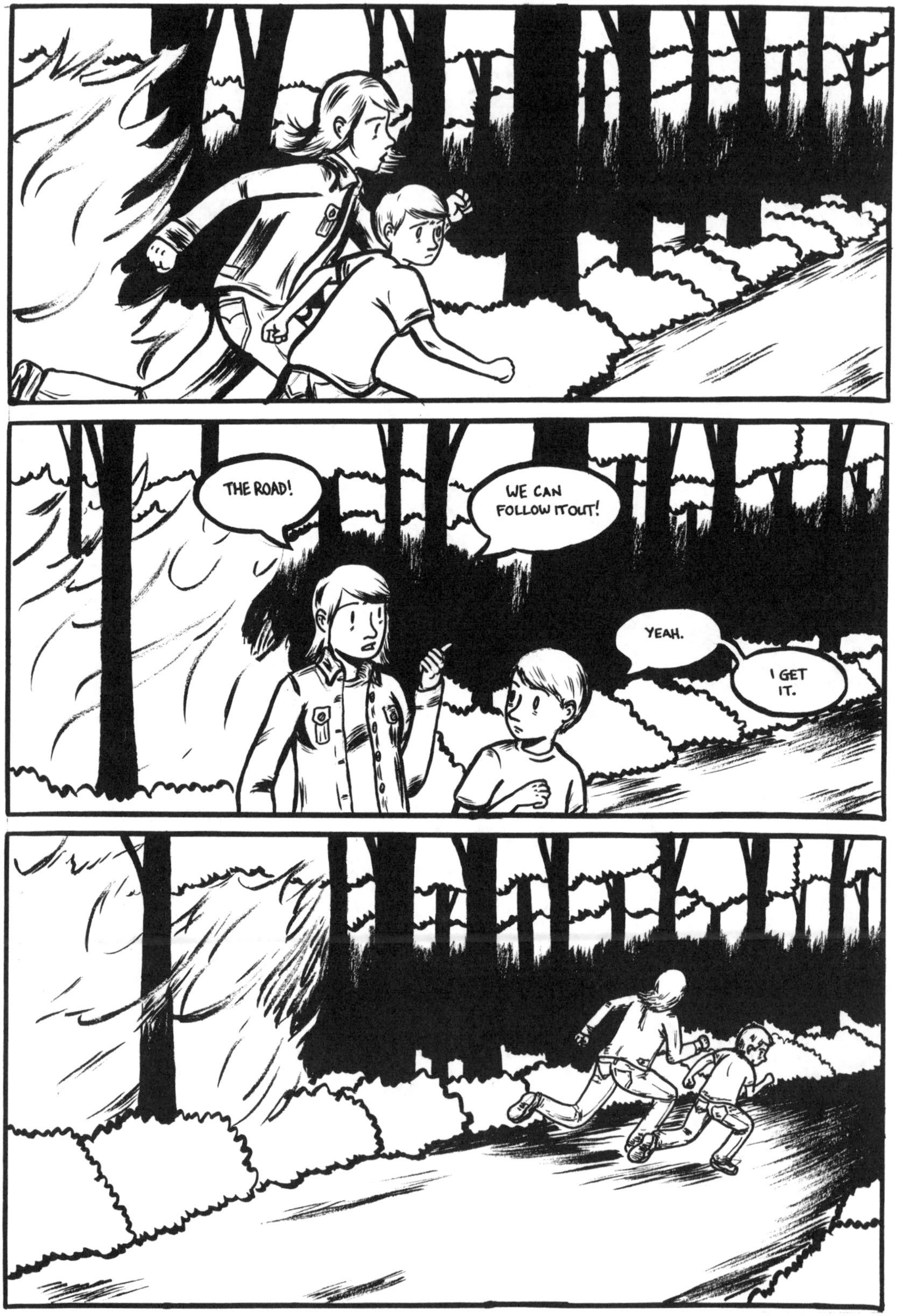
THE ROAD!
WE CAN FOLLOW IT OUT!
YEAH.
I GET IT.

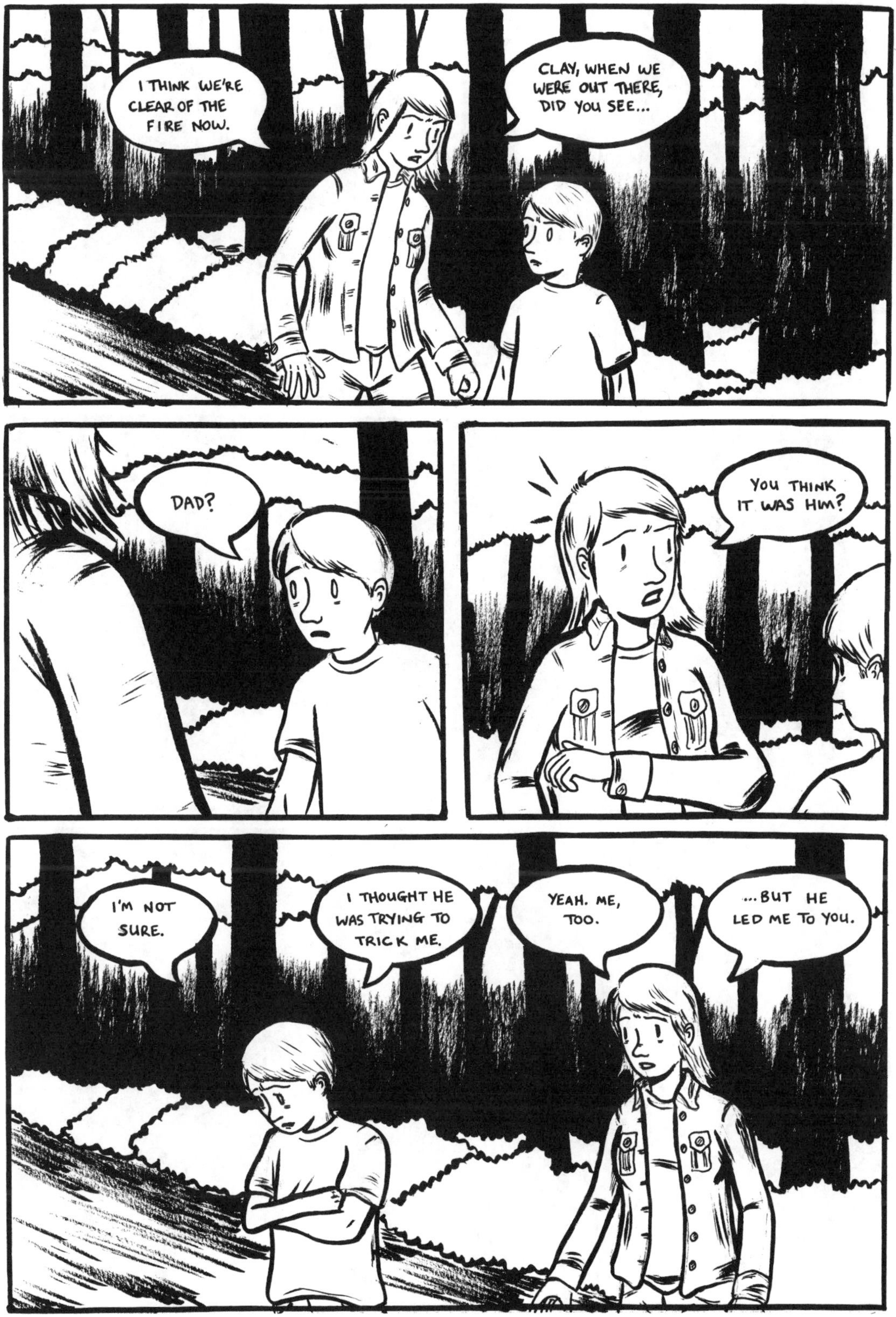
I THINK WE'RE CLEAR OF THE FIRE NOW.
CLAY, WHEN WE WERE OUT THERE, DID YOU SEE...
DAD?
YOU THINK IT WAS HIM?
I'M NOT SURE.
I THOUGHT HE WAS TRYING TO TRICK ME.
YEAH. ME, TOO.
...BUT HE LED ME TO YOU.

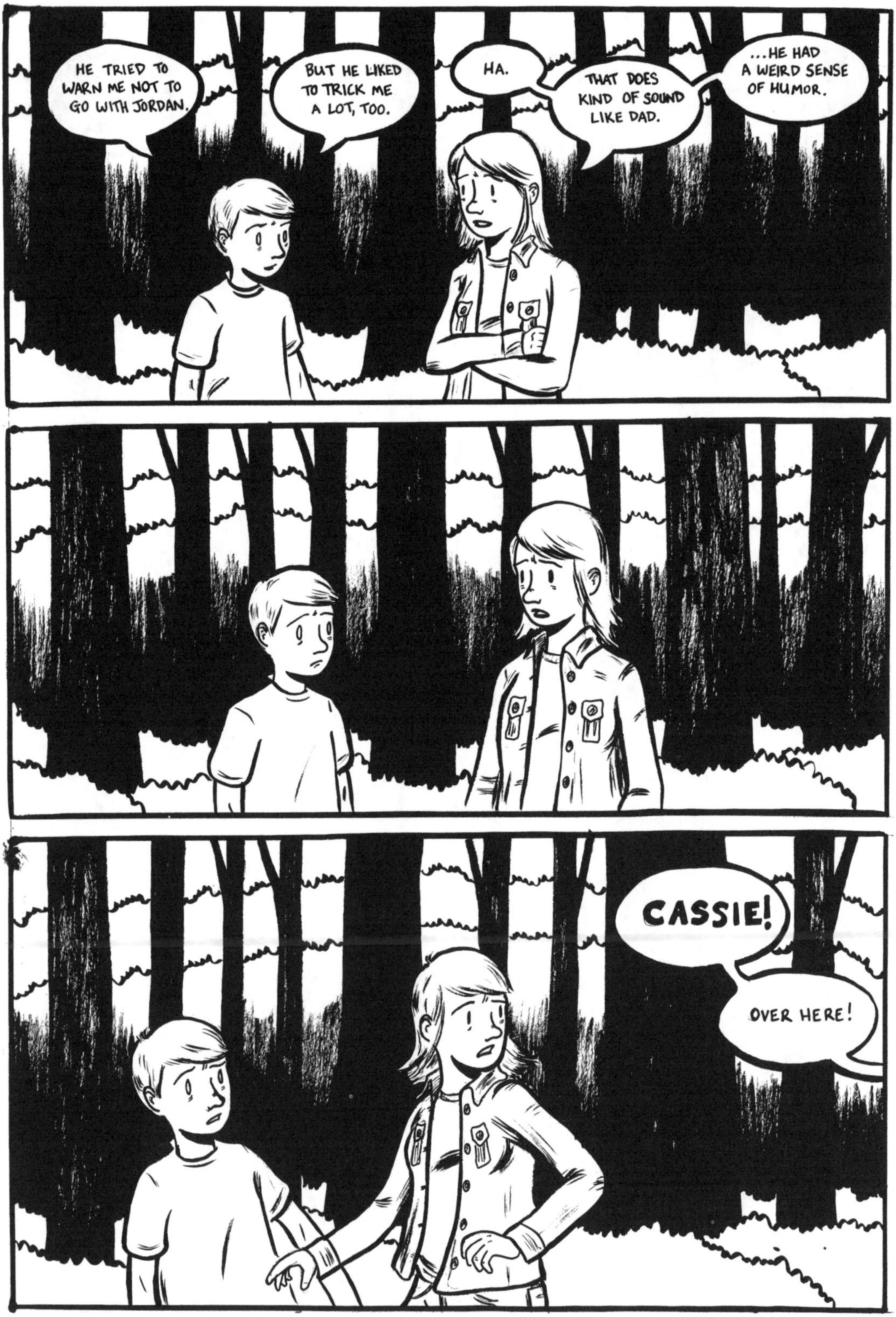
HE TRIED TO WARN ME NOT TO GO WITH JORDAN.
BUT HE LIKED TO TRICK ME A LOT, TOO.
HA.
THAT DOES KIND OF SOUND LIKE DAD.
...HE HAD A WEIRD SENSE OF HUMOR.
CASSIE!
OVER HERE!

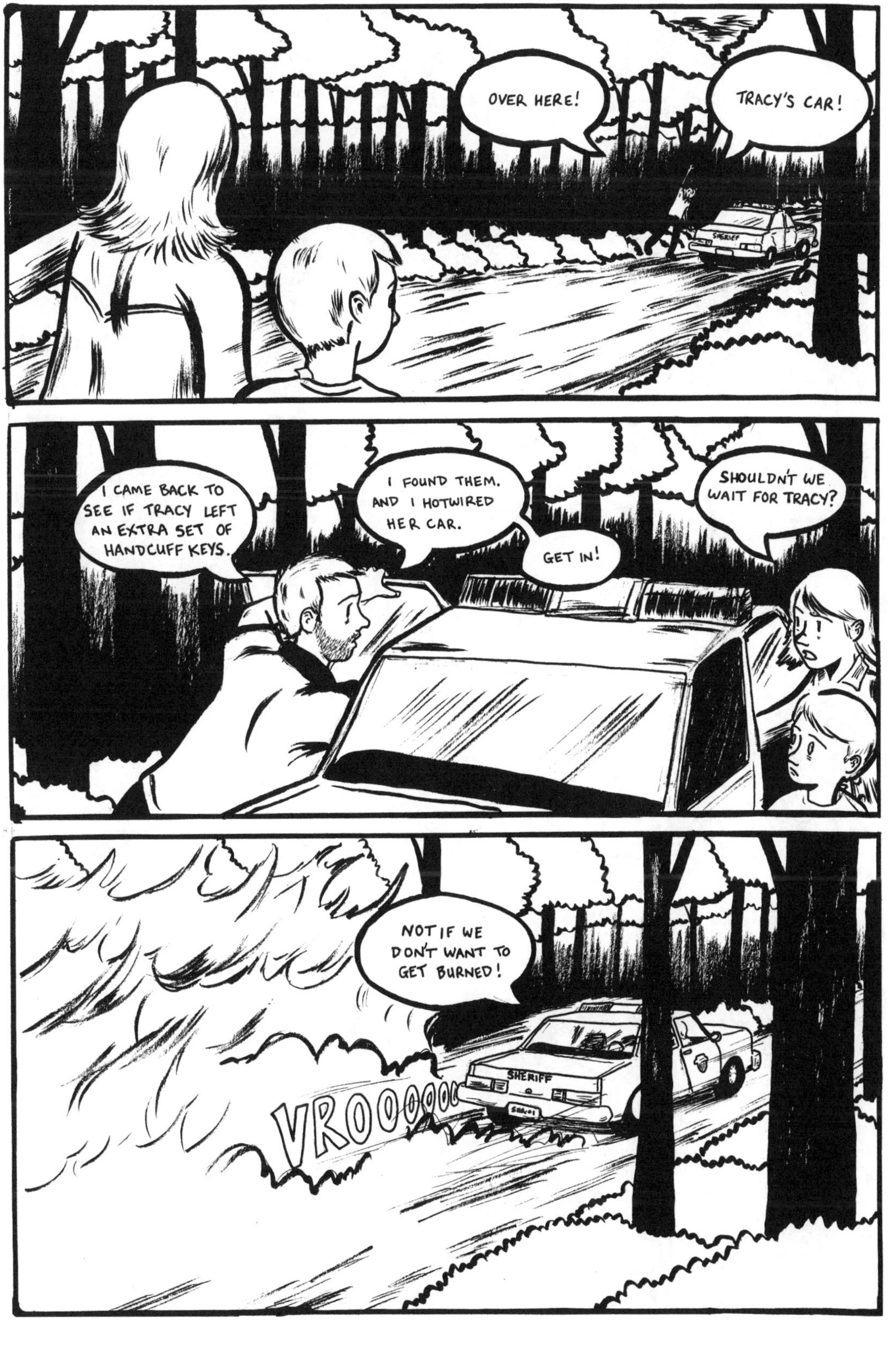
OVER HERE!
TRACY'S CAR!
SHERIFF
I CAME BACK TO SEE IF TRACY LEFT AN EXTRA SET OF HANDCUFF KEYS.
I FOUND THEM. AND I HOTWIRED HER CAR.
GET IN!
SHOULDN'T WE WAIT FOR TRACY?
NOT IF WE DON'T WANT TO GET BURNED!
SHERIFF
VROOOOO

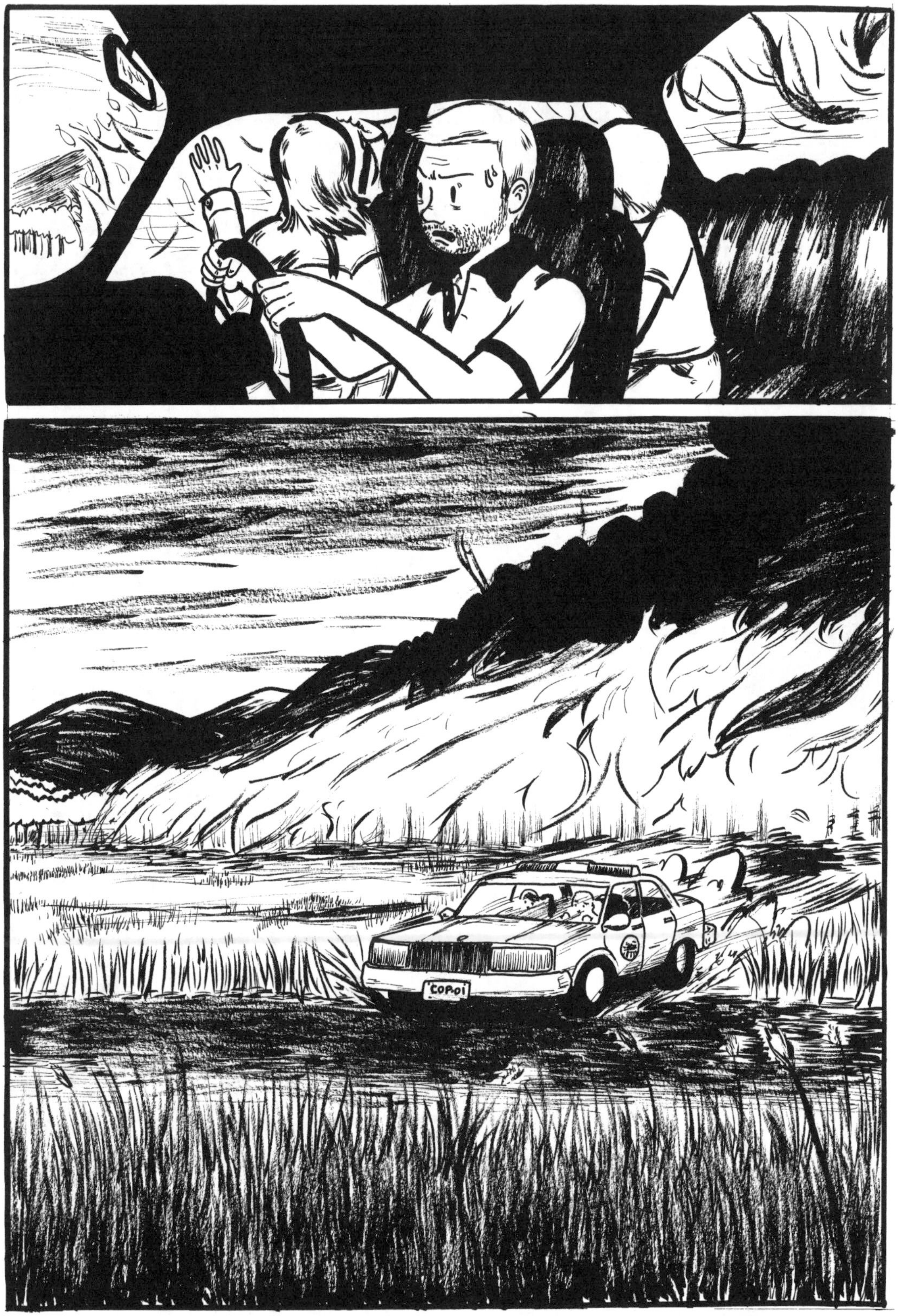
COP-01

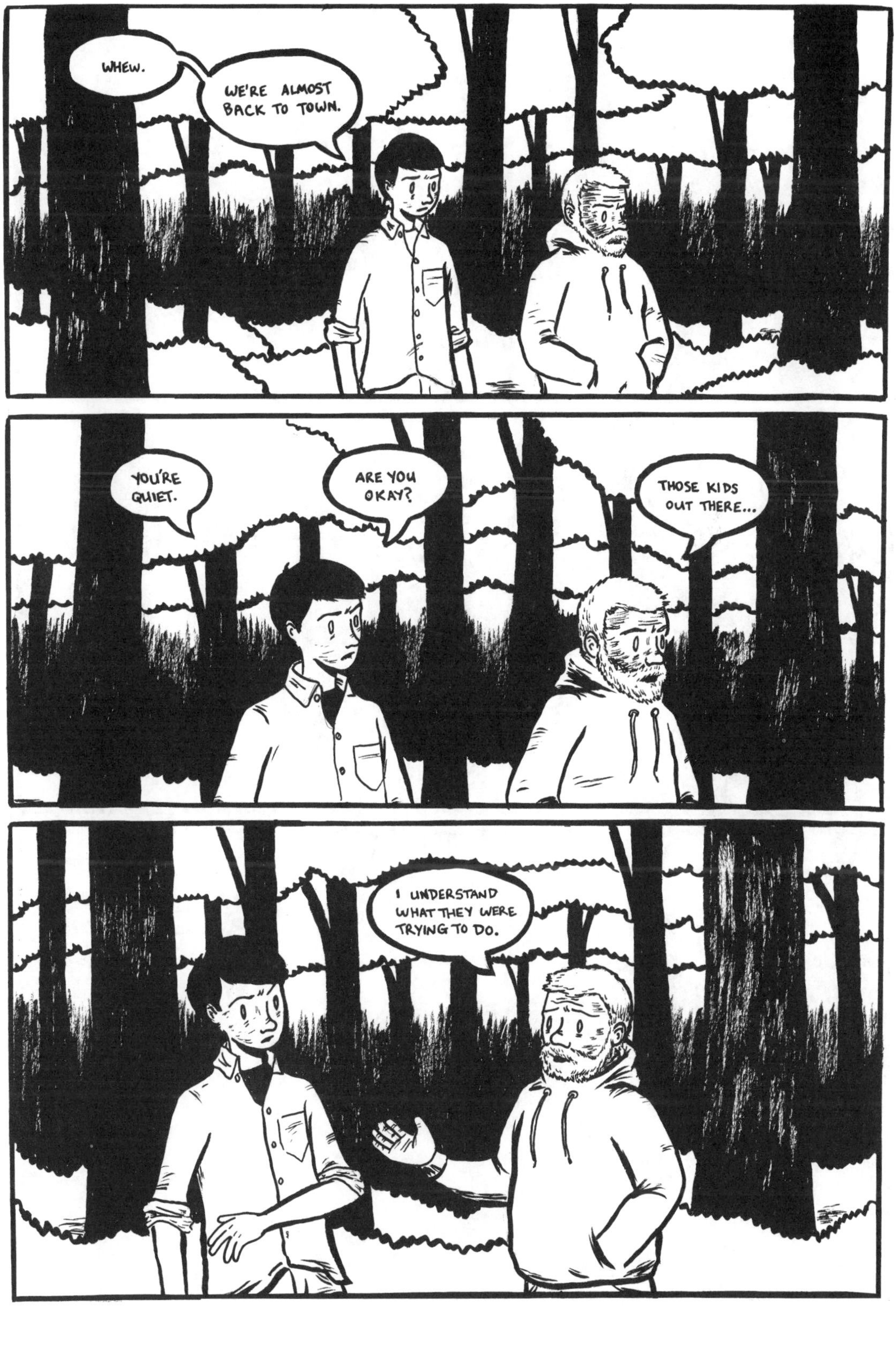
WHEW.
WE'RE ALMOST BACK TO TOWN.
YOU'RE QUIET.
ARE YOU OKAY?
THOSE KIDS OUT THERE...
I UNDERSTAND WHAT THEY WERE TRYING TO DO.

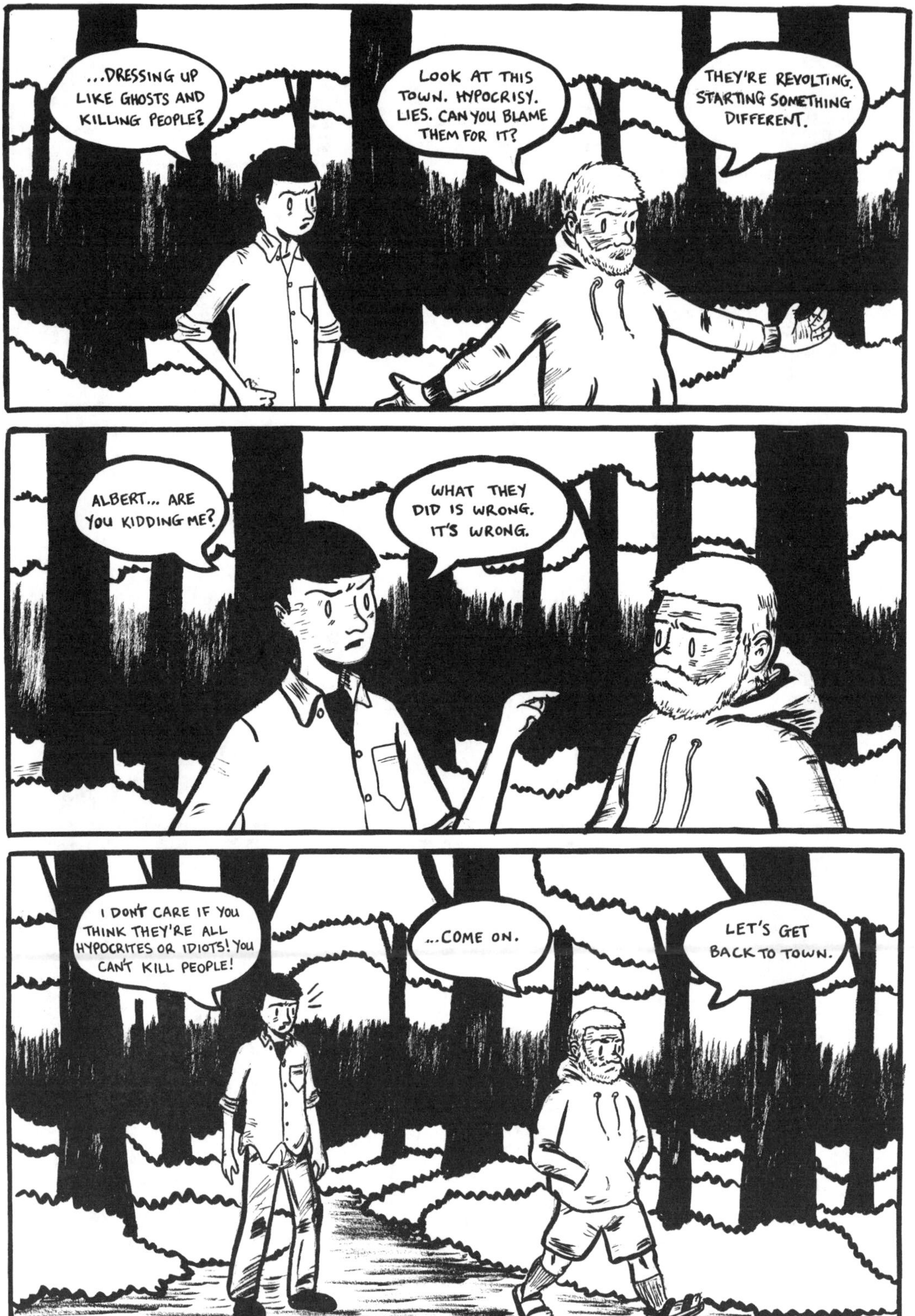
...DRESSING UP LIKE GHOSTS AND KILLING PEOPLE?
LOOK AT THIS TOWN. HYPOCRISY. LIES. CAN YOU BLAME THEM FOR IT?
THEY'RE REVOLTING. STARTING SOMETHING DIFFERENT.
ALBERT... ARE YOU KIDDING ME?
WHAT THEY DID IS WRONG. IT'S WRONG.
I DON'T CARE IF YOU THINK THEY'RE ALL HYPOCRITES OR IDIOTS! YOU CAN'T KILL PEOPLE!
...COME ON.
LET'S GET BACK TO TOWN.

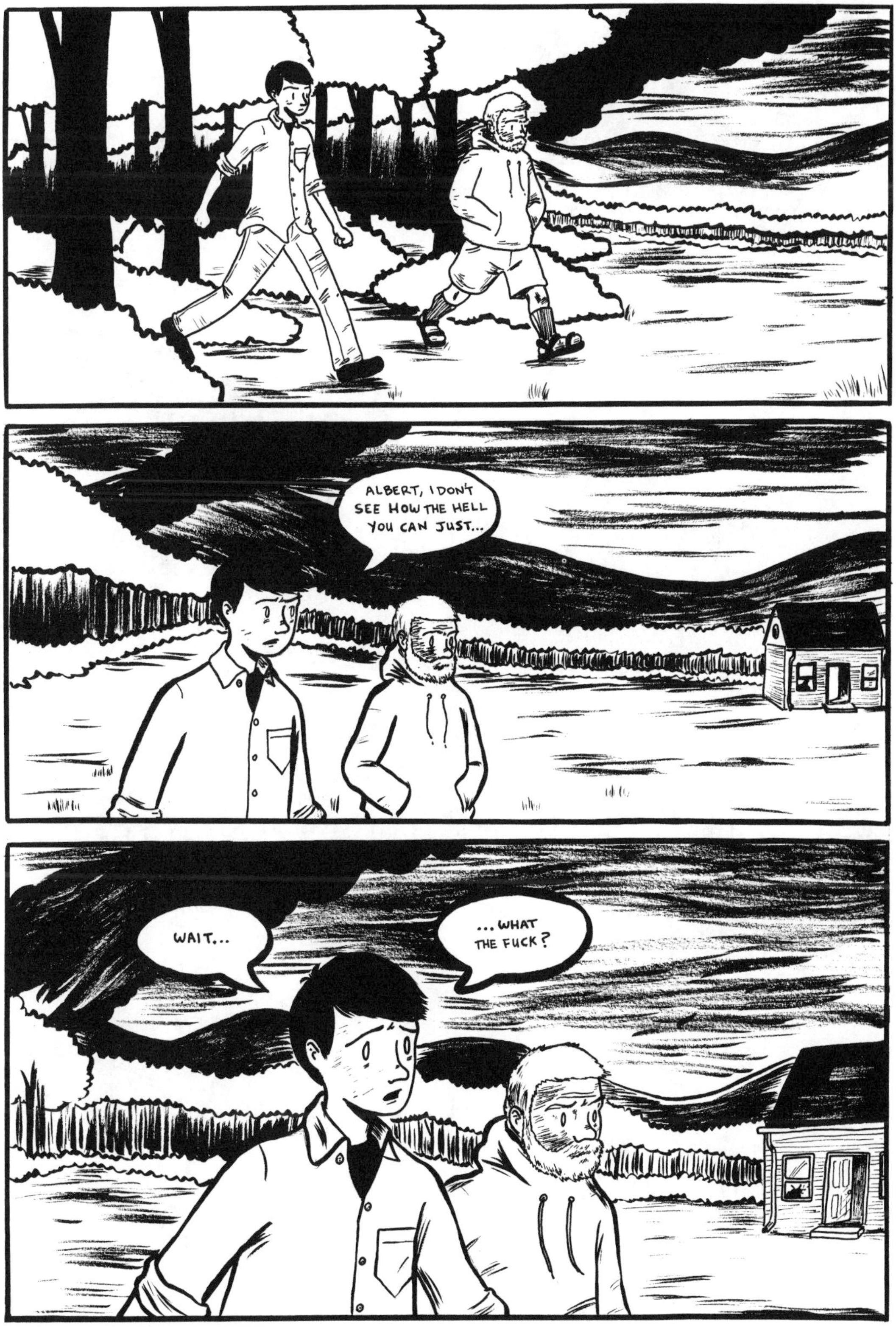
ALBERT, I DON'T SEE HOW THE HELL YOU CAN JUST...
WAIT...
...WHAT THE FUCK?

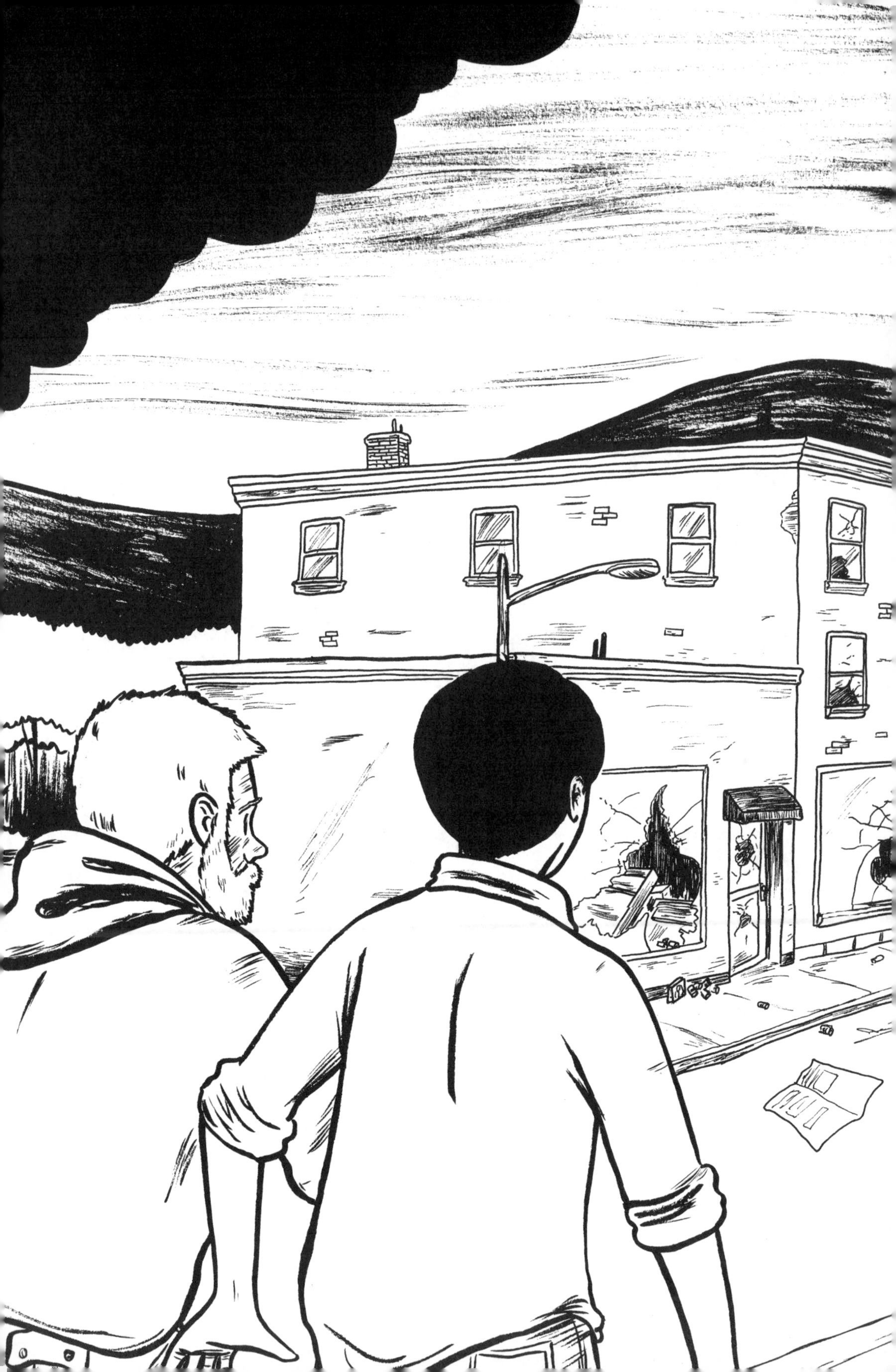

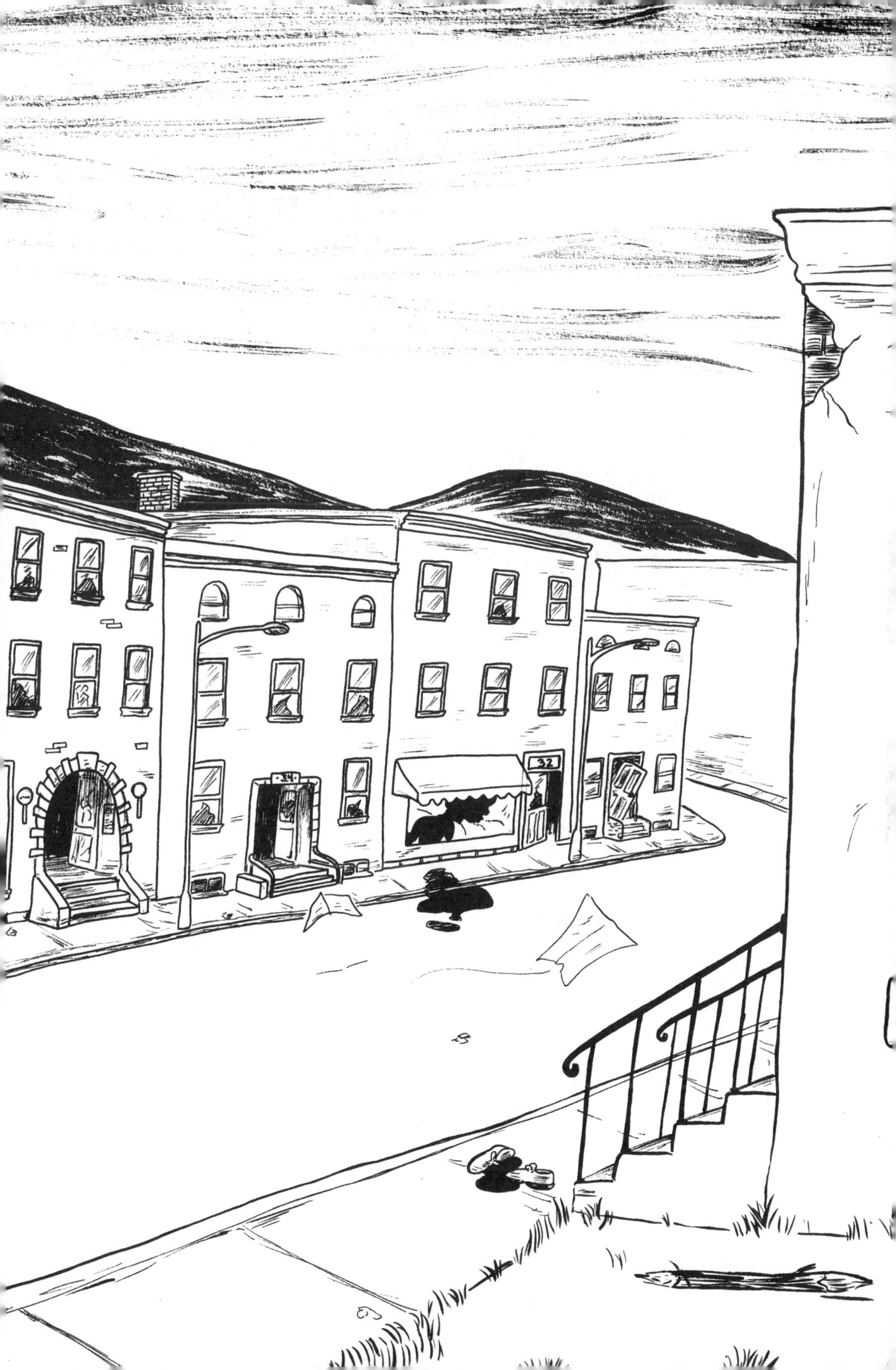
32

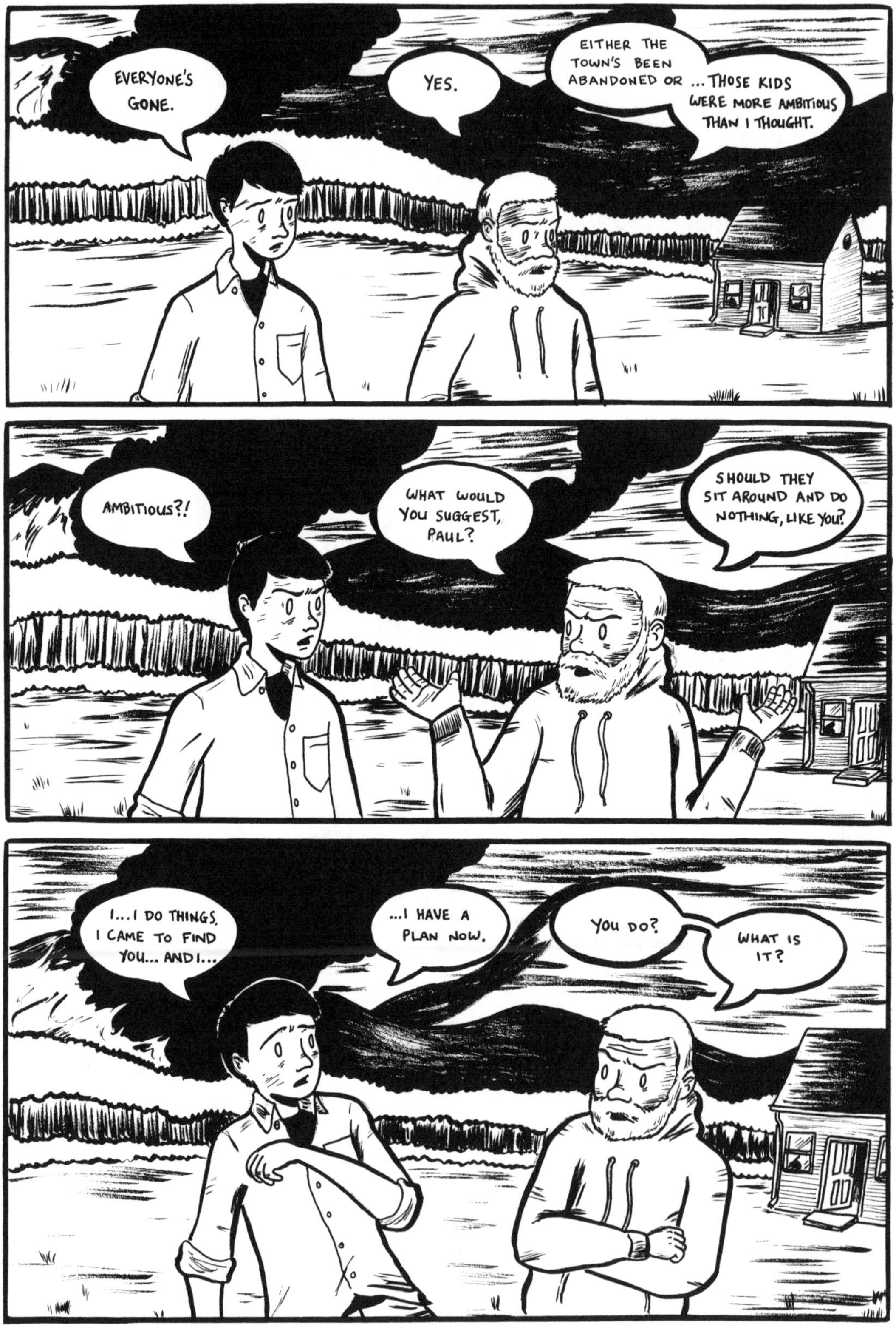
EVERYONE'S GONE.
YES.
EITHER THE TOWN'S BEEN ABANDONED OR
... THOSE KIDS WERE MORE AMBITIOUS THAN I THOUGHT.
AMBITIOUS?!
WHAT WOULD YOU SUGGEST, PAUL?
SHOULD THEY SIT AROUND AND DO NOTHING, LIKE YOU?
I...I DO THINGS. I CAME TO FIND YOU... AND I...
...I HAVE A PLAN NOW.
YOU DO?
WHAT IS IT?

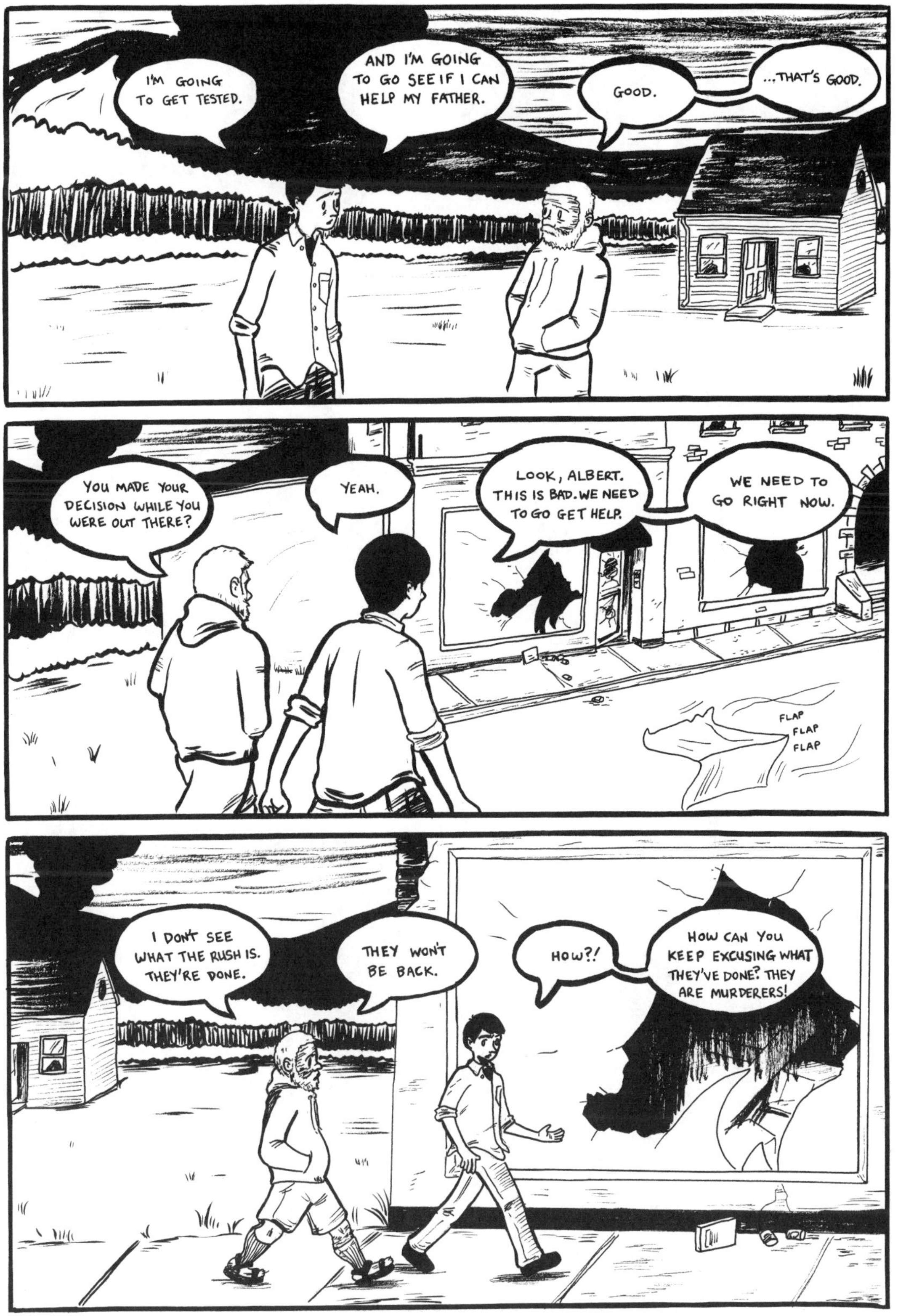

I'M GOING TO GET TESTED.
AND I'M GOING TO GO SEE IF I CAN HELP MY FATHER.
GOOD.
...THAT'S GOOD.
YOU MADE YOUR DECISION WHILE YOU WERE OUT THERE?
YEAH.
LOOK, ALBERT. THIS IS BAD. WE NEED TO GO GET HELP.
WE NEED TO GO RIGHT NOW.
FLAP
FLAP
FLAP
I DON'T SEE WHAT THE RUSH IS. THEY'RE DONE.
THEY WON'T BE BACK.
HOW?!
HOW CAN YOU KEEP EXCUSING WHAT THEY'VE DONE? THEY ARE MURDERERS!

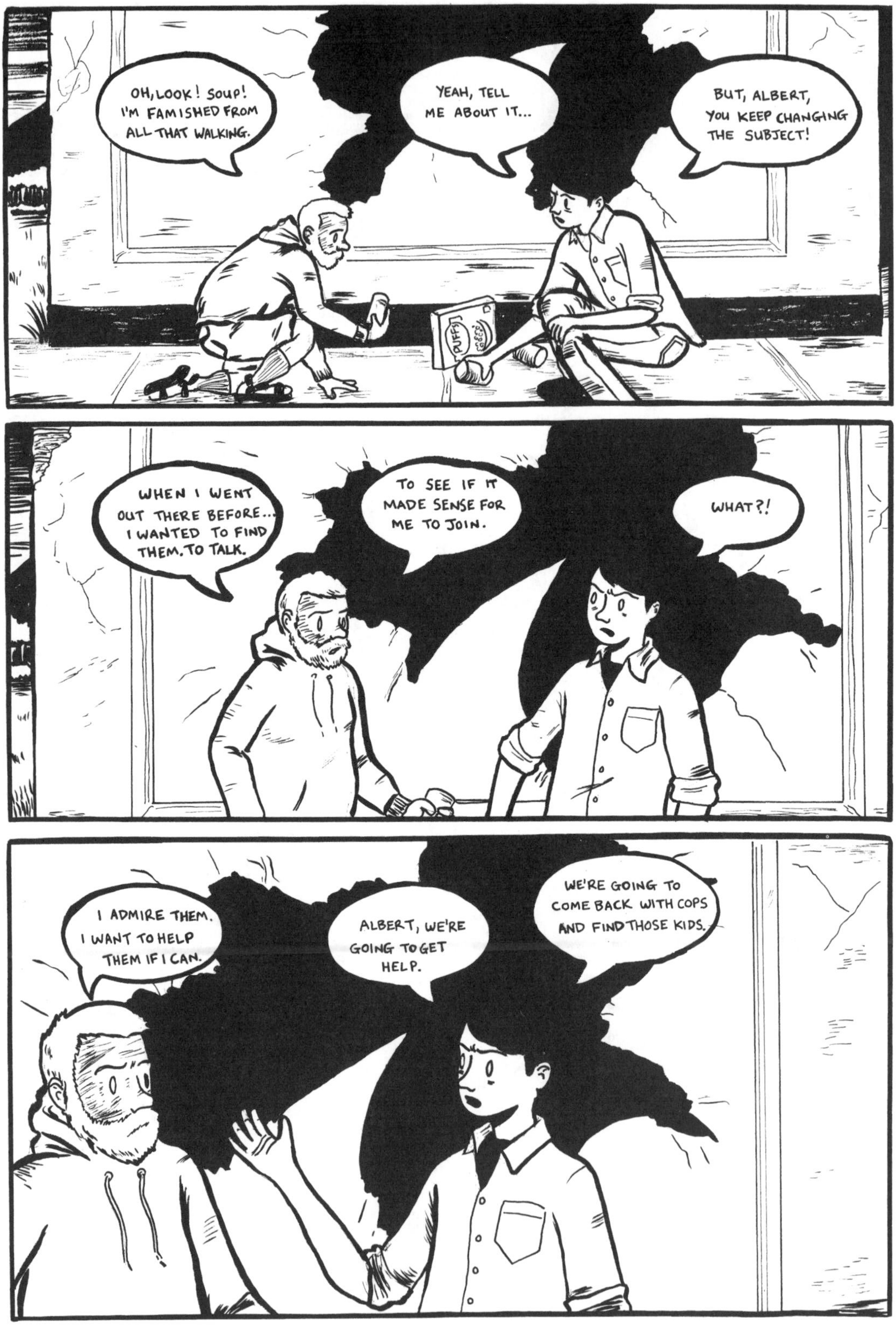
OH, LOOK! SOUP! I'M FAMISHED FROM ALL THAT WALKING.
YEAH, TELL ME ABOUT IT...
BUT, ALBERT, YOU KEEP CHANGING THE SUBJECT!
PUFFS
WHEN I WENT OUT THERE BEFORE... I WANTED TO FIND THEM. TO TALK.
TO SEE IF IT MADE SENSE FOR ME TO JOIN.
WHAT?!
I ADMIRE THEM. I WANT TO HELP THEM IF I CAN.
ALBERT, WE'RE GOING TO GET HELP.
WE'RE GOING TO COME BACK WITH COPS AND FIND THOSE KIDS.

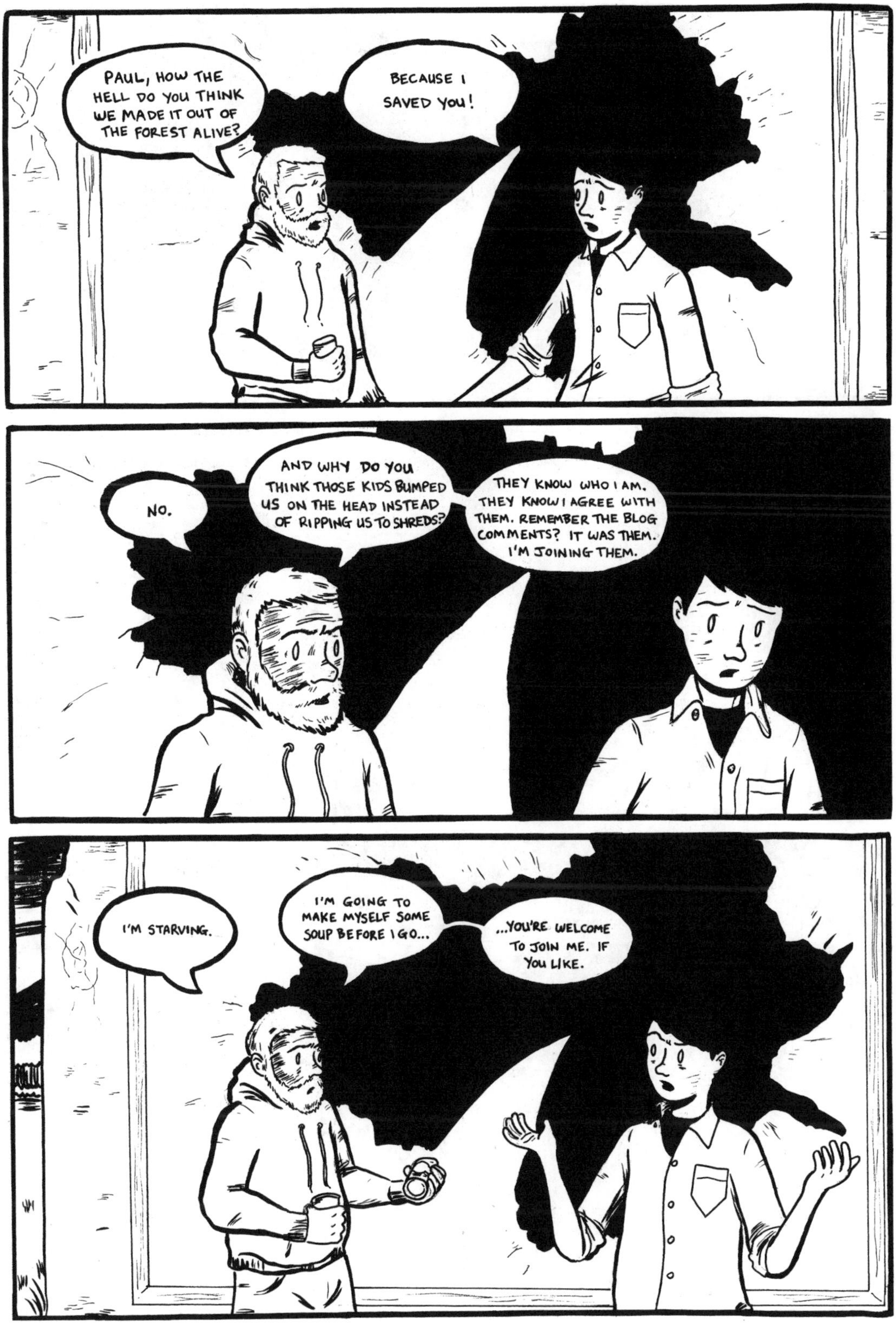
PAUL, HOW THE HELL DO YOU THINK WE MADE IT OUT OF THE FOREST ALIVE?
BECAUSE I SAVED YOU!
NO.
AND WHY DO YOU THINK THOSE KIDS BUMPED US ON THE HEAD INSTEAD OF RIPPING US TO SHREDS?
THEY KNOW WHO I AM. THEY KNOW I AGREE WITH THEM. REMEMBER THE BLOG COMMENTS? IT WAS THEM. I'M JOINING THEM.
I'M STARVING.
I'M GOING TO MAKE MYSELF SOME SOUP BEFORE I GO...
...YOU'RE WELCOME TO JOIN ME. IF YOU LIKE.

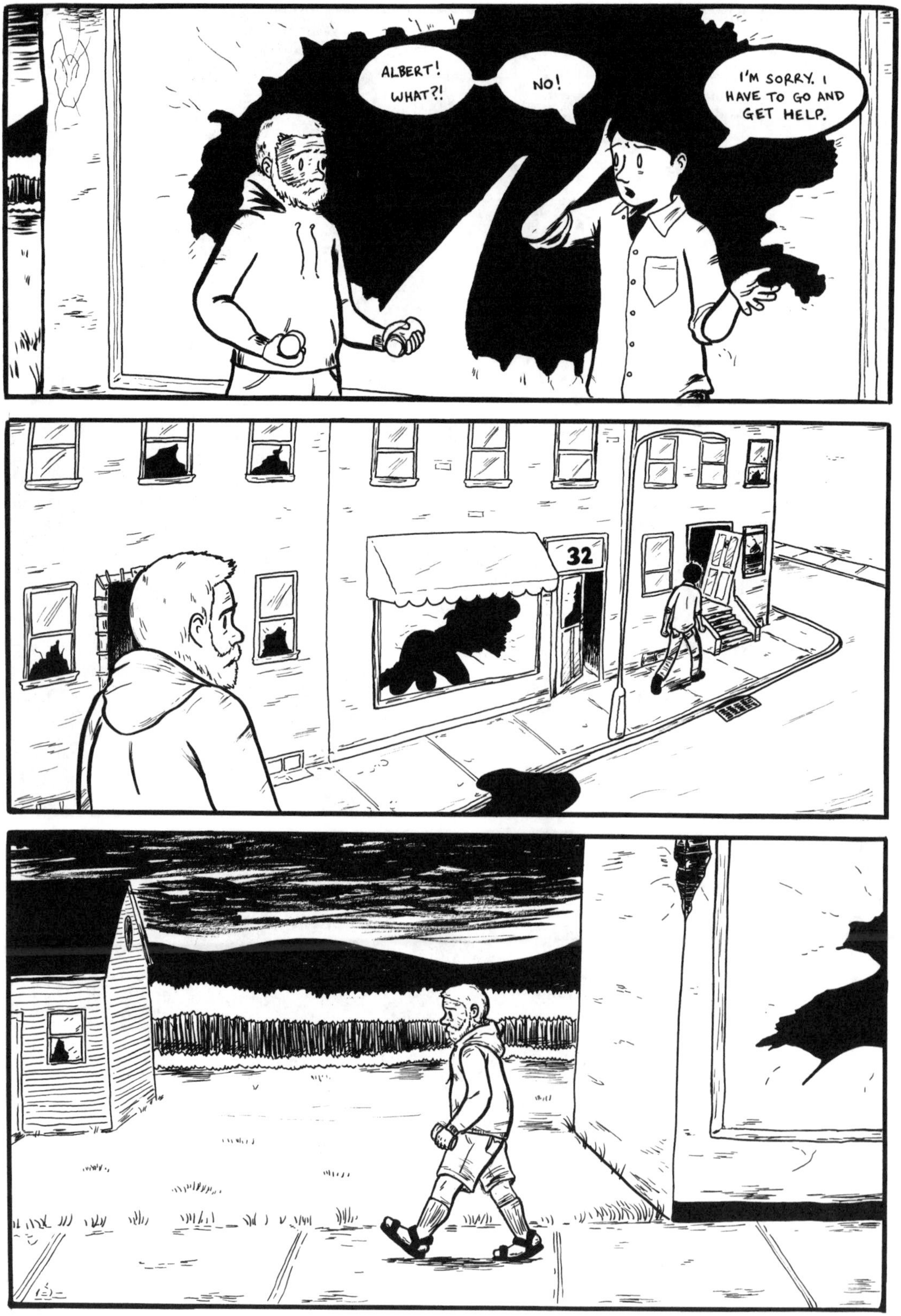
ALBERT! WHAT?!
NO!
I'M SORRY. I HAVE TO GO AND GET HELP.
32

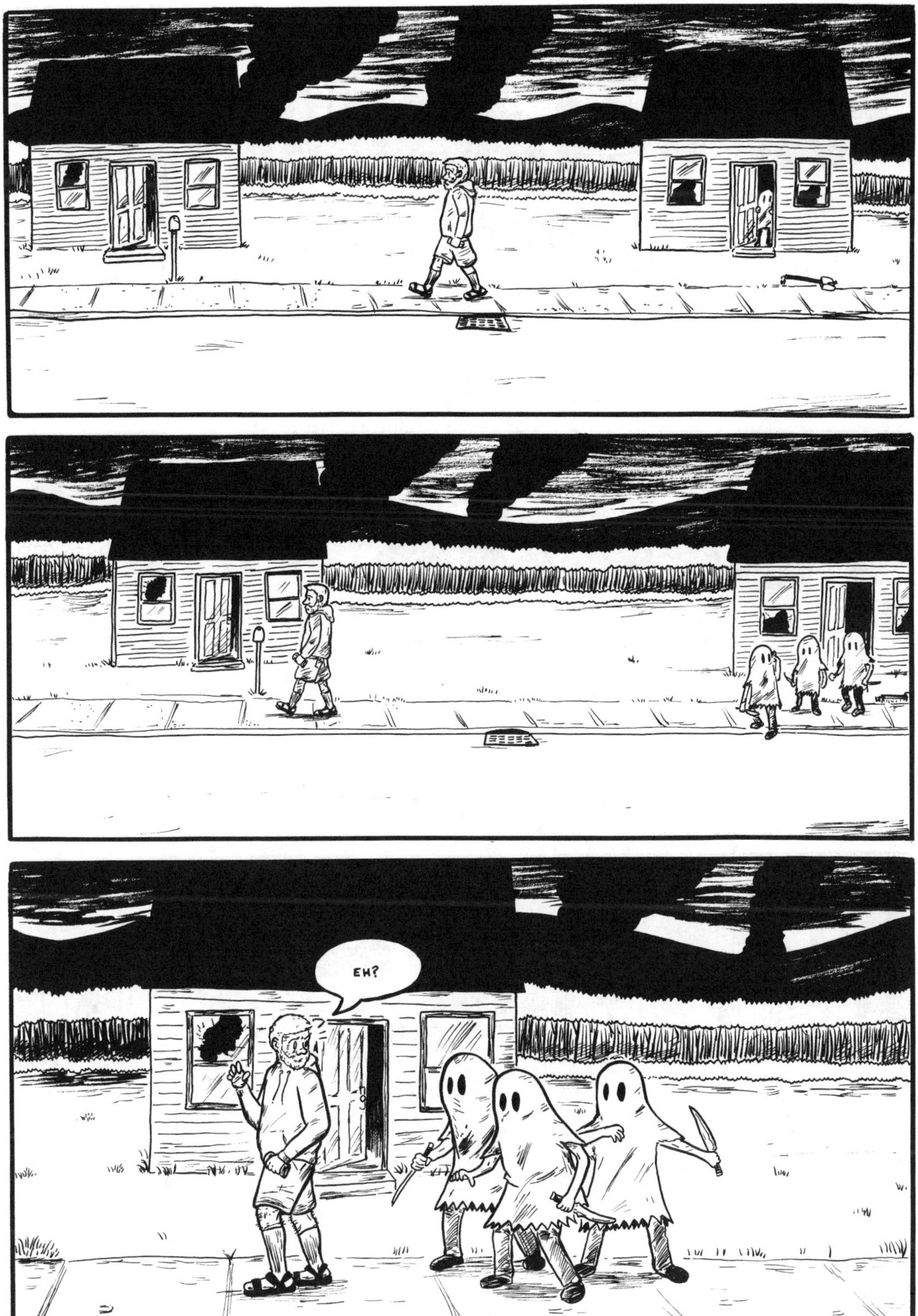
EH?

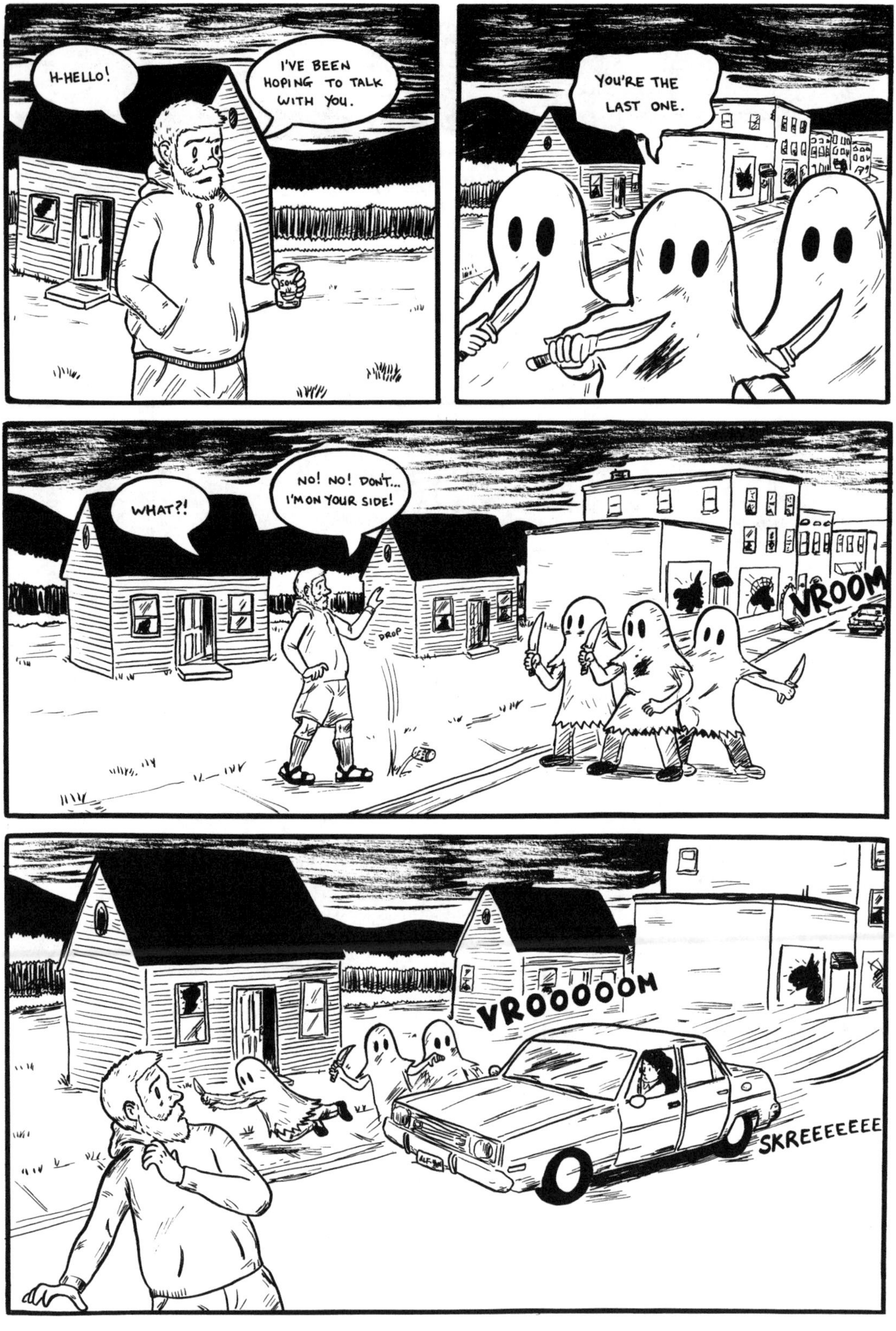
H-HELLO!
I'VE BEEN HOPING TO TALK WITH YOU.
YOU'RE THE LAST ONE.
WHAT?!
NO! NO! DON'T... I'M ON YOUR SIDE!
DROP
VROOM
VROOOOOM
SKREEEEEEE

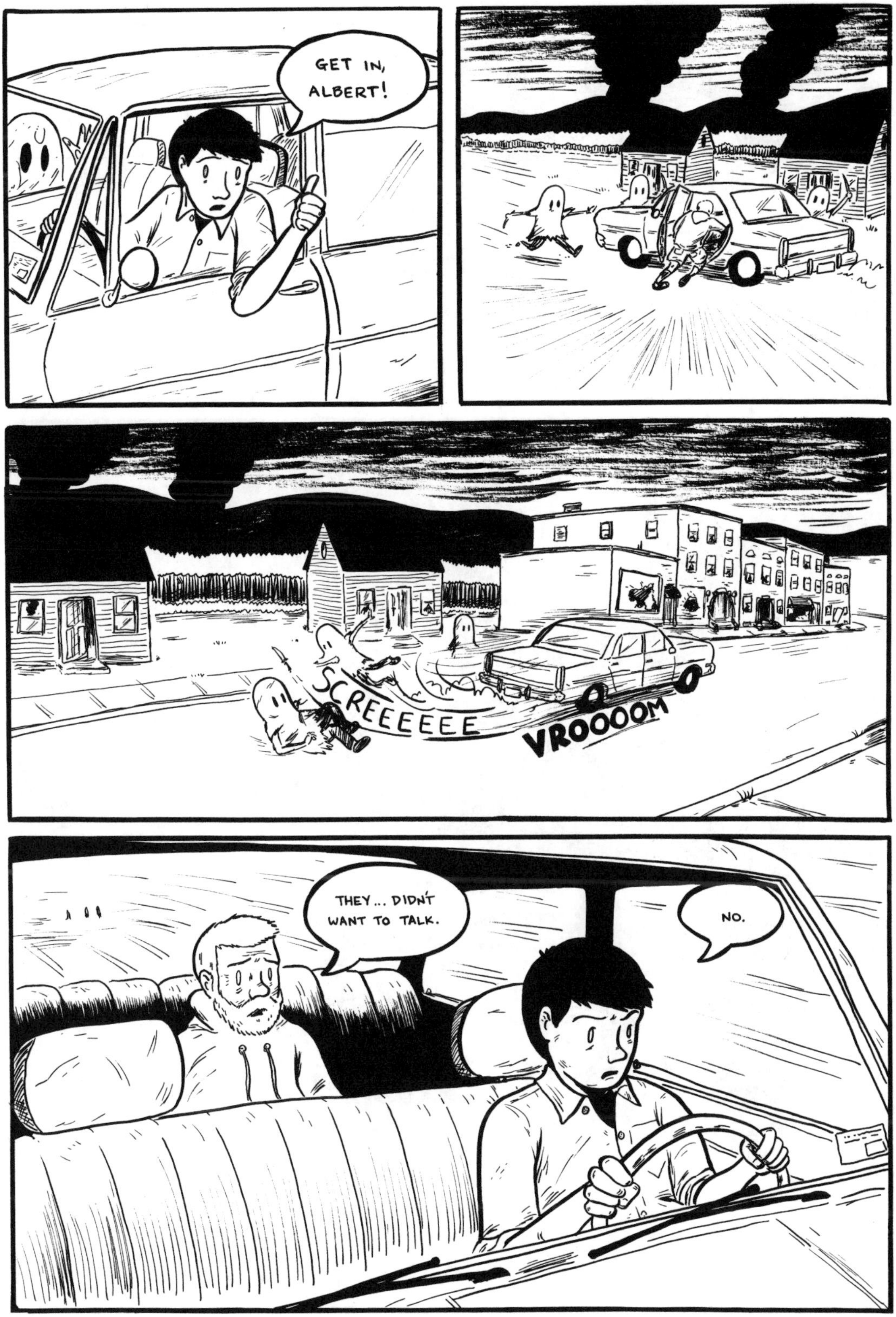
GET IN, ALBERT!
SCREEEEEEE
VROOOOM
...
THEY... DIDN'T WANT TO TALK.
NO.

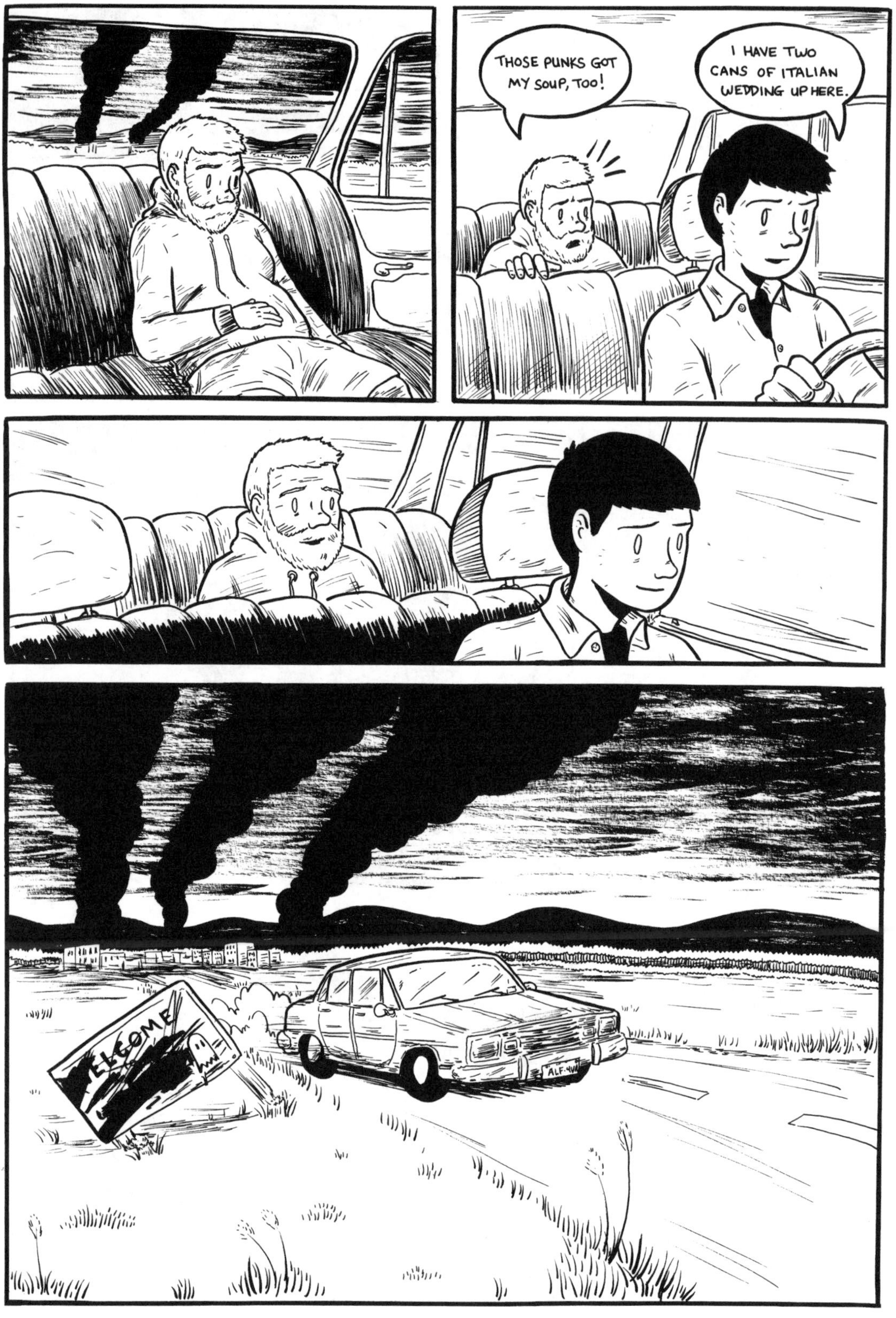
THOSE PUNKS GOT MY SOUP, TOO!
I HAVE TWO CANS OF ITALIAN WEDDING UP HERE.

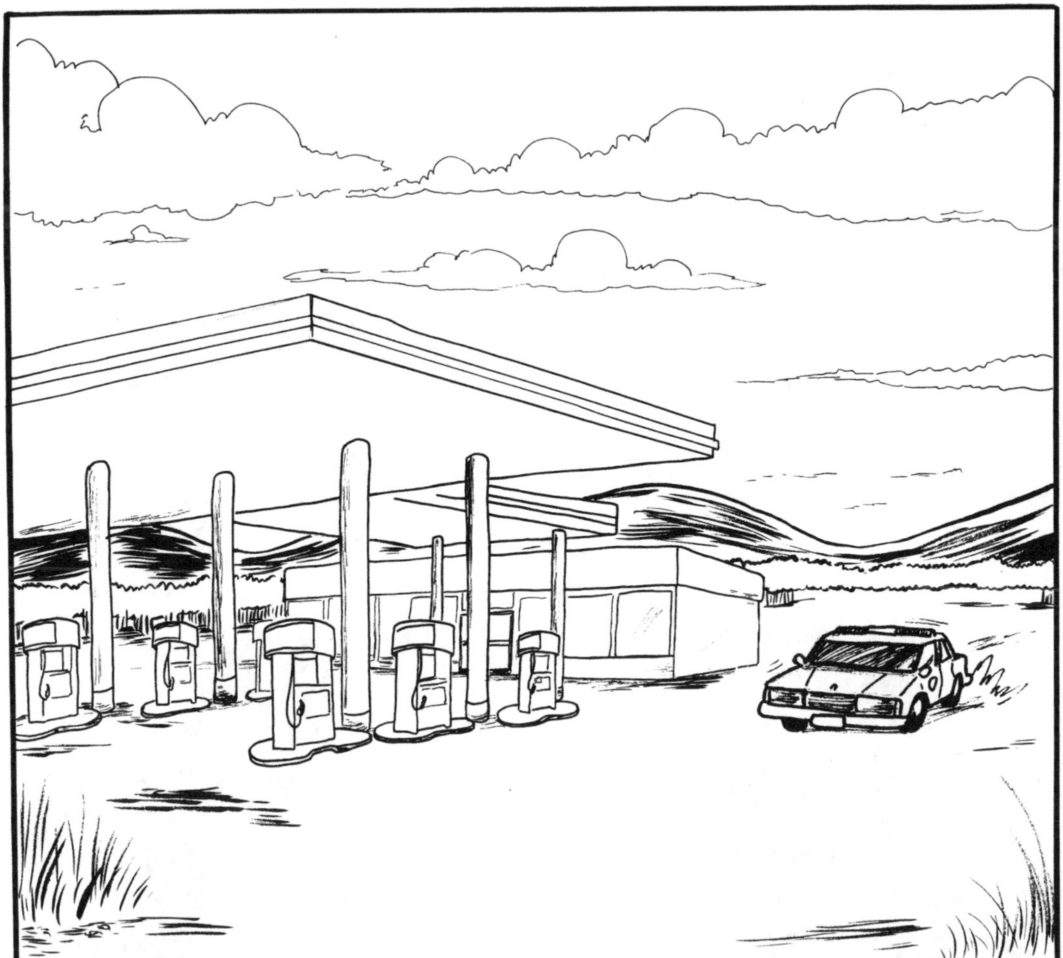

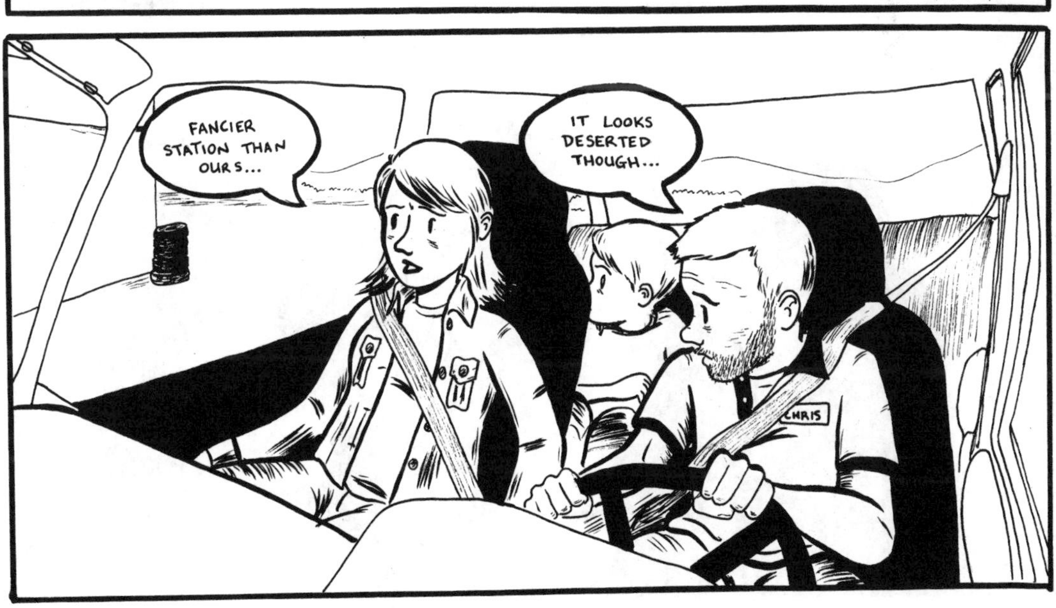
FANCIER STATION THAN OURS...
IT LOOKS DESERTED THOUGH...
CHRIS

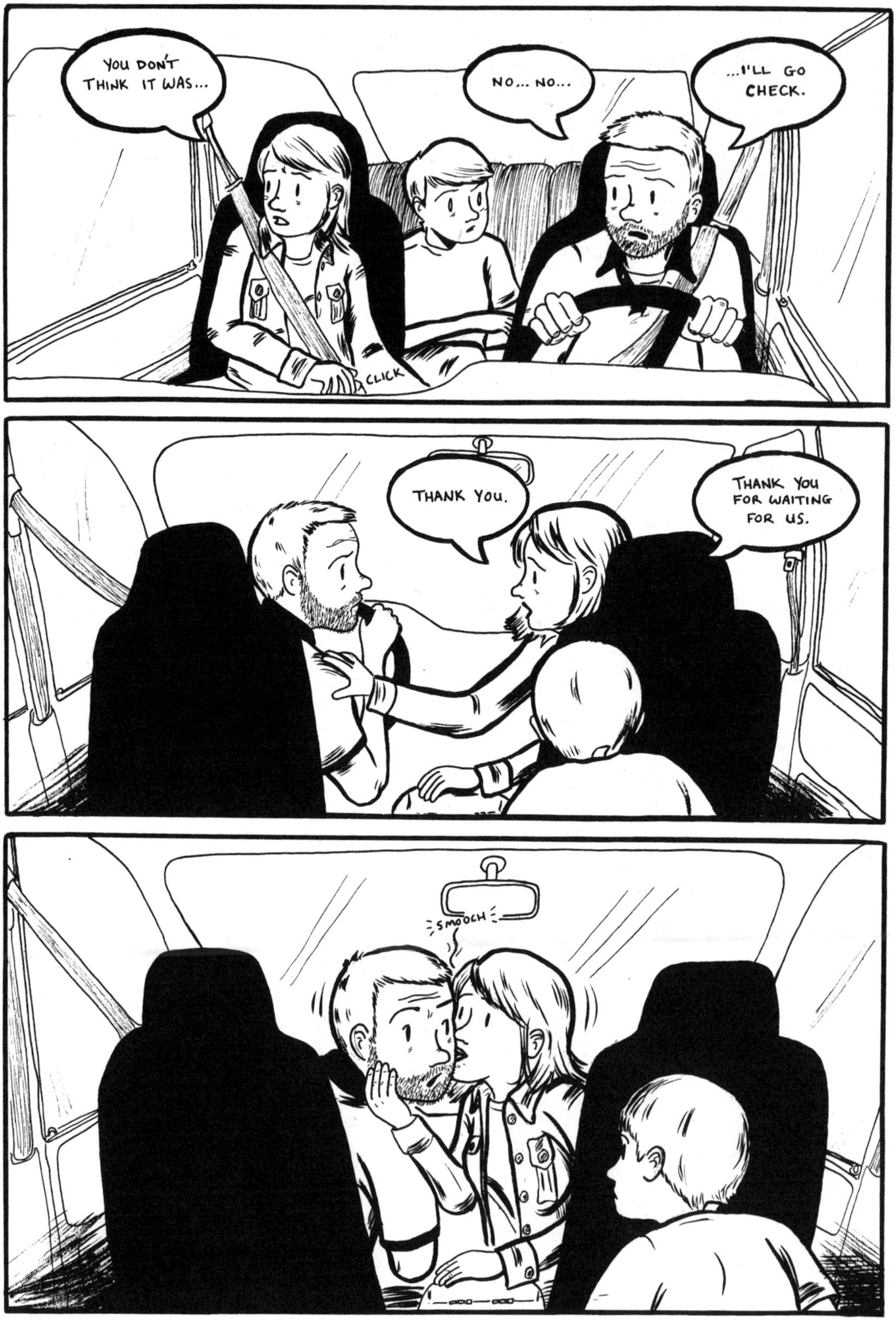
YOU DON'T THINK IT WAS...
NO... NO...
...I'LL GO CHECK.
CLICK
THANK YOU.
THANK YOU FOR WAITING FOR US.
SMOOCH

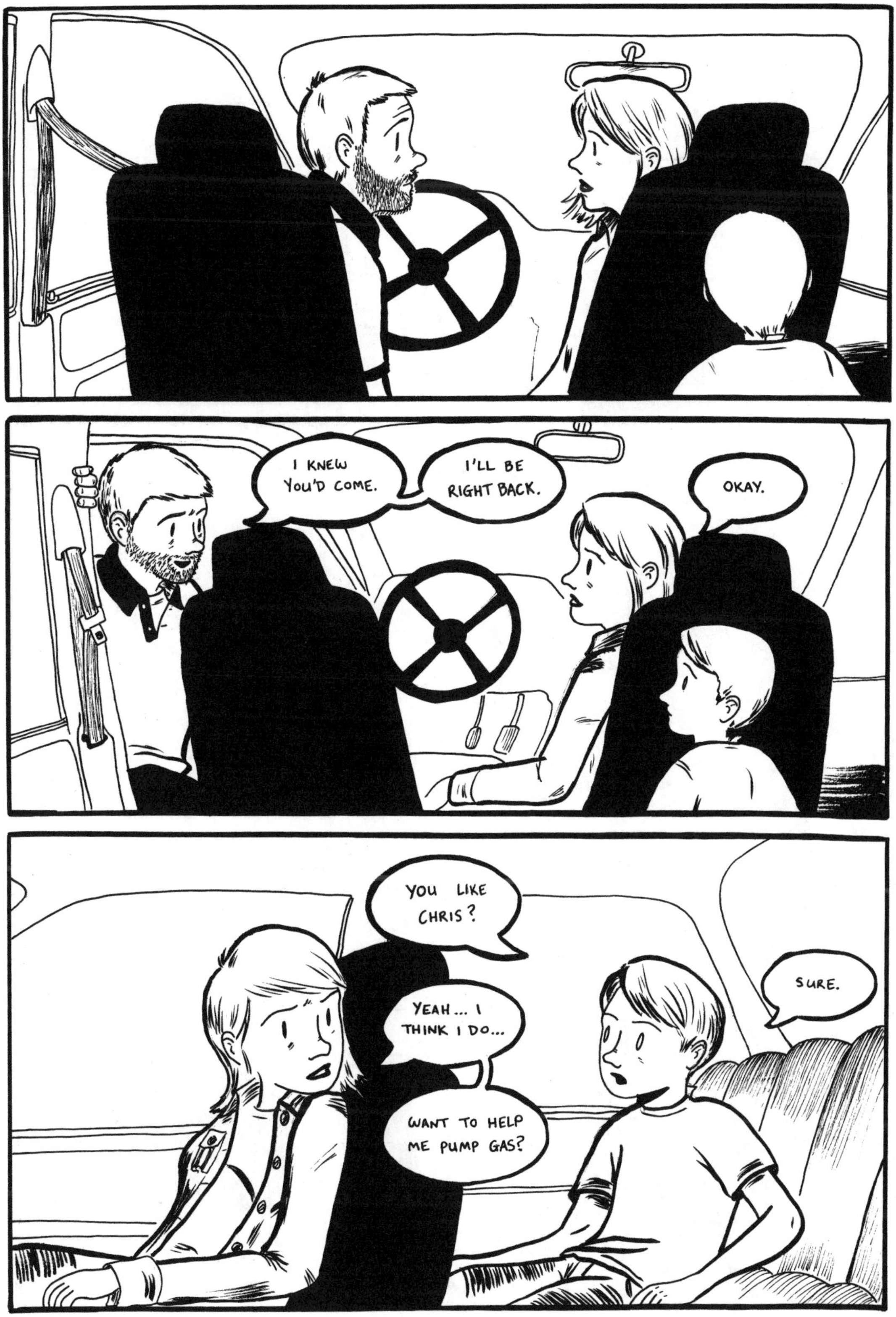
I KNEW YOU'D COME.
I'LL BE RIGHT BACK.
OKAY.
YOU LIKE CHRIS?
SURE.
YEAH... I THINK I DO...
WANT TO HELP ME PUMP GAS?

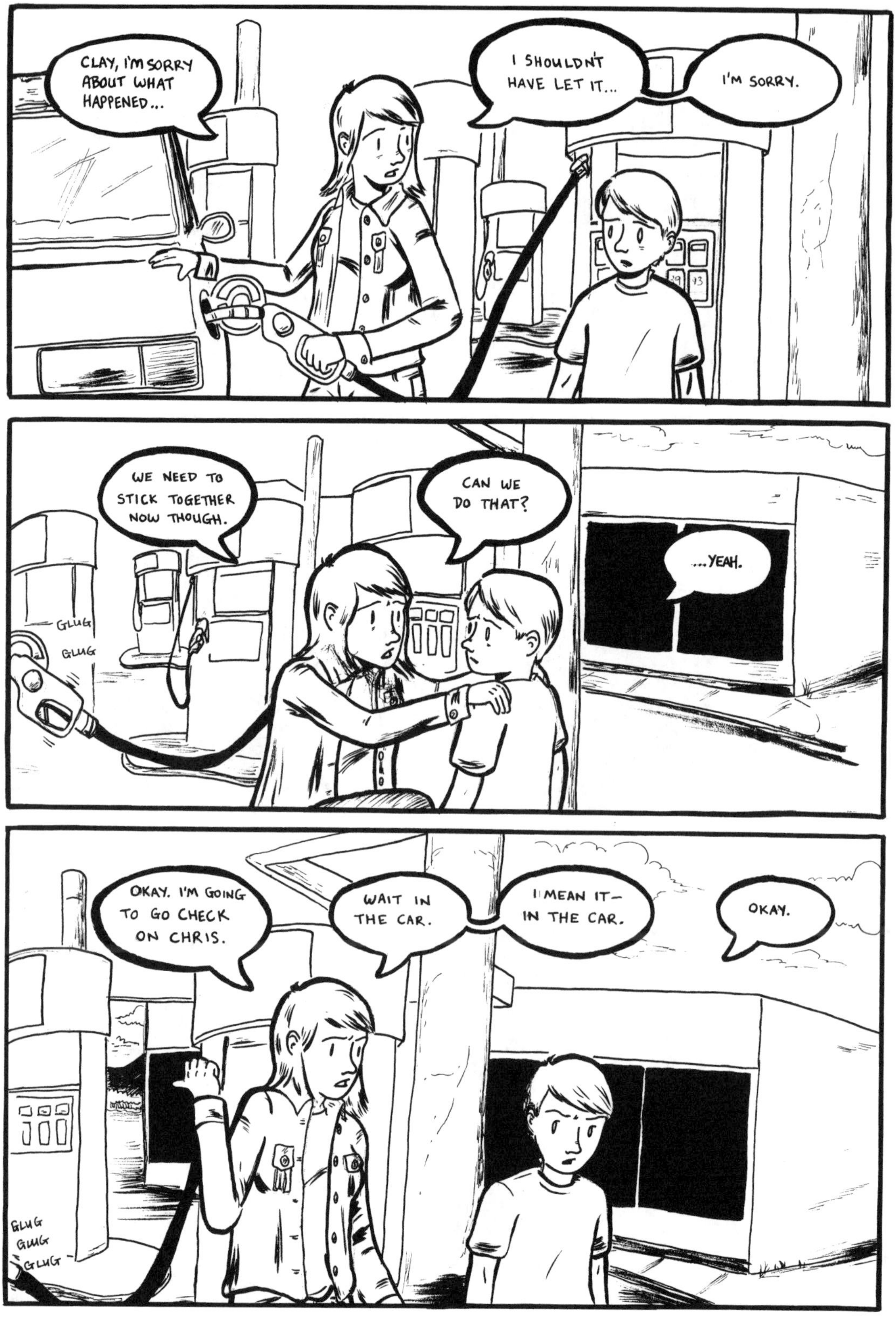
CLAY, I'M SORRY ABOUT WHAT HAPPENED...
I SHOULDN'T HAVE LET IT...
I'M SORRY.
WE NEED TO STICK TOGETHER NOW THOUGH.
CAN WE DO THAT?
GLUG
GLUG
...YEAH.
OKAY. I'M GOING TO GO CHECK ON CHRIS.
WAIT IN THE CAR.
I MEAN IT- IN THE CAR.
OKAY.
GLUG
GLUG
GLUG

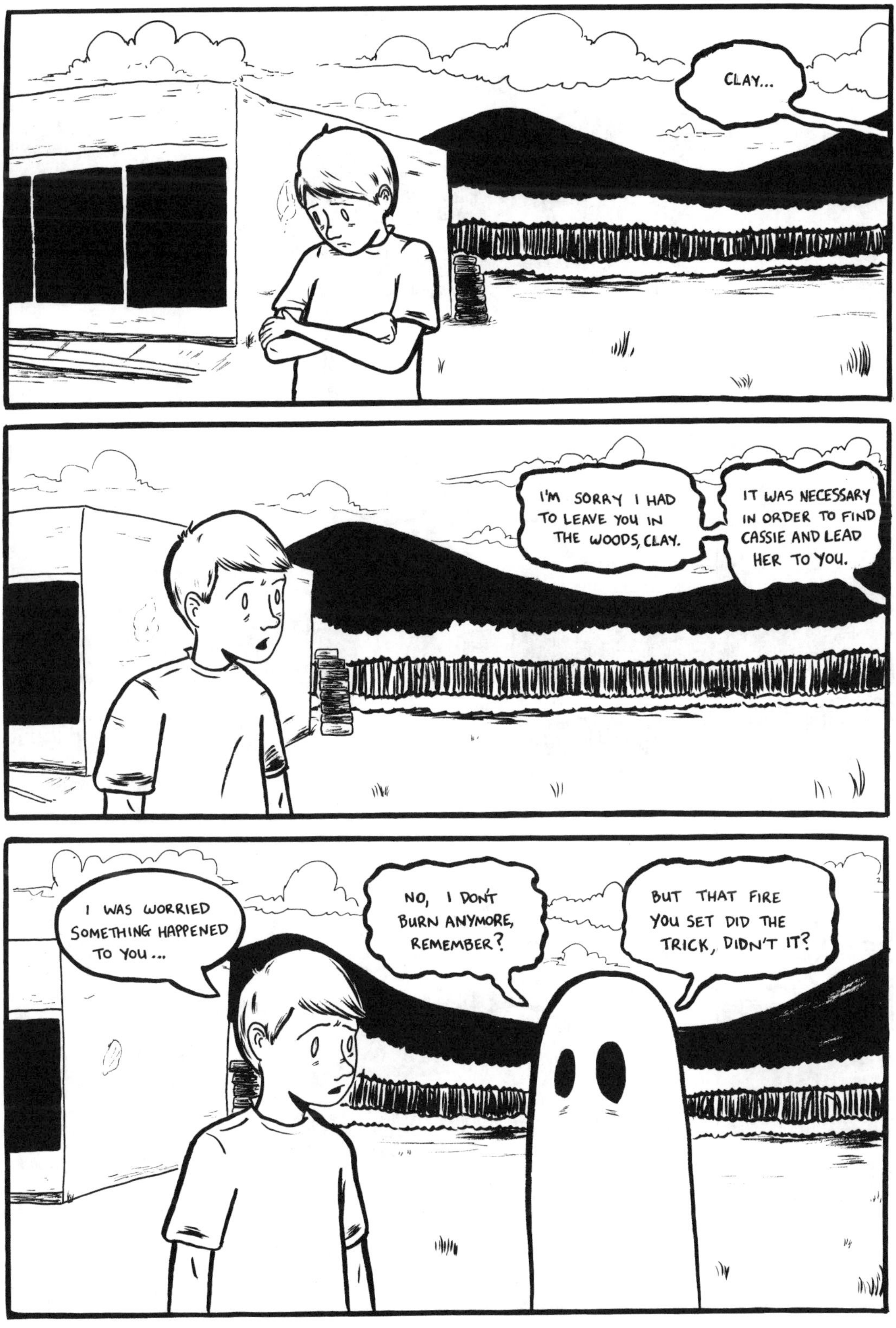
CLAY...
I'M SORRY I HAD TO LEAVE YOU IN THE WOODS, CLAY.
IT WAS NECESSARY IN ORDER TO FIND CASSIE AND LEAD HER TO YOU.
I WAS WORRIED SOMETHING HAPPENED TO YOU...
NO, I DON'T BURN ANYMORE, REMEMBER?
BUT THAT FIRE YOU SET DID THE TRICK, DIDN'T IT?

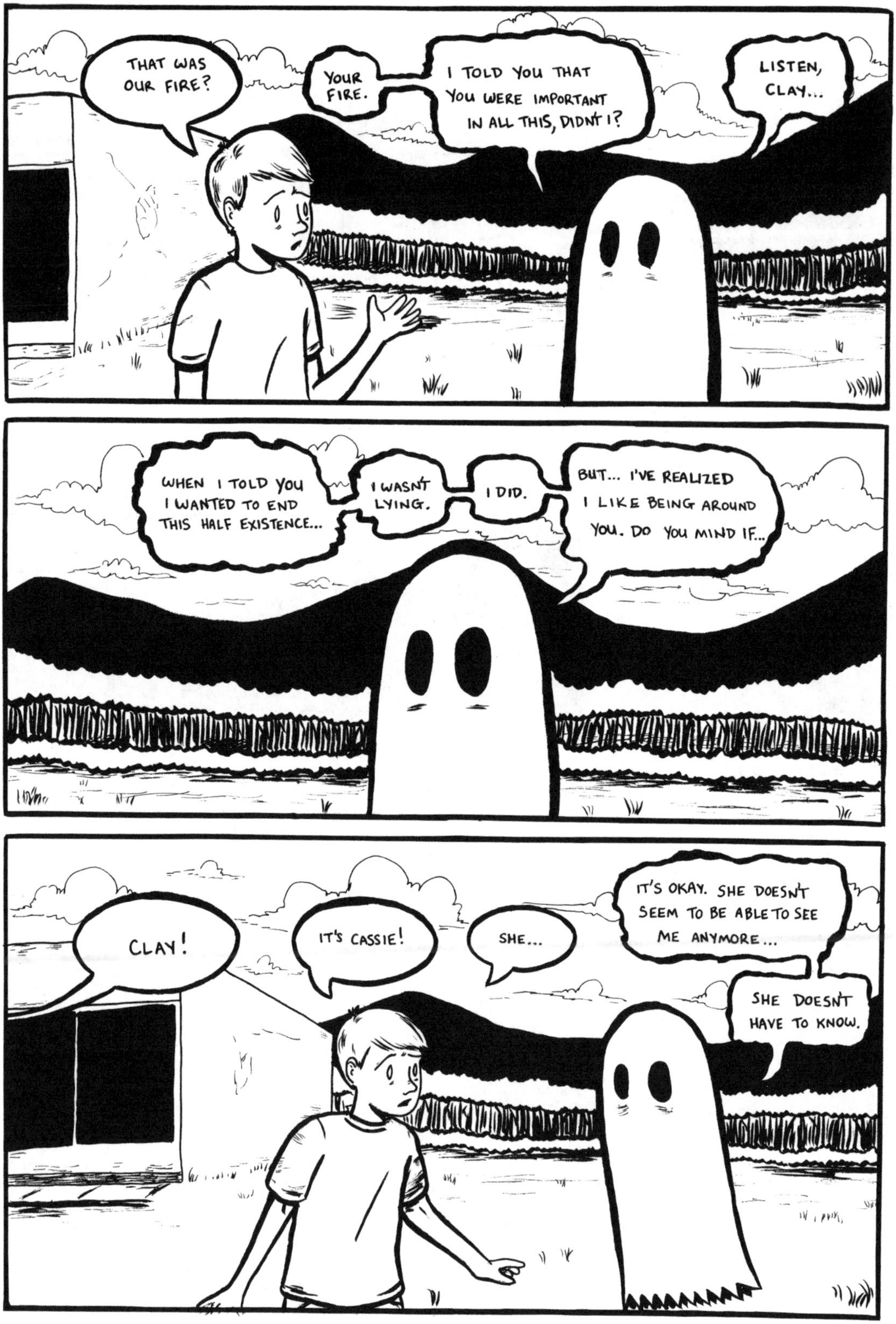
THAT WAS OUR FIRE?
YOUR FIRE.
I TOLD YOU THAT YOU WERE IMPORTANT IN ALL THIS, DIDN'T I?
LISTEN, CLAY...
WHEN I TOLD YOU I WANTED TO END THIS HALF EXISTENCE...
I WASN'T LYING.
I DID.
BUT... I'VE REALIZED I LIKE BEING AROUND YOU. DO YOU MIND IF...
CLAY!
IT'S CASSIE!
SHE...
IT'S OKAY. SHE DOESN'T SEEM TO BE ABLE TO SEE ME ANYMORE...
SHE DOESN'T HAVE TO KNOW.

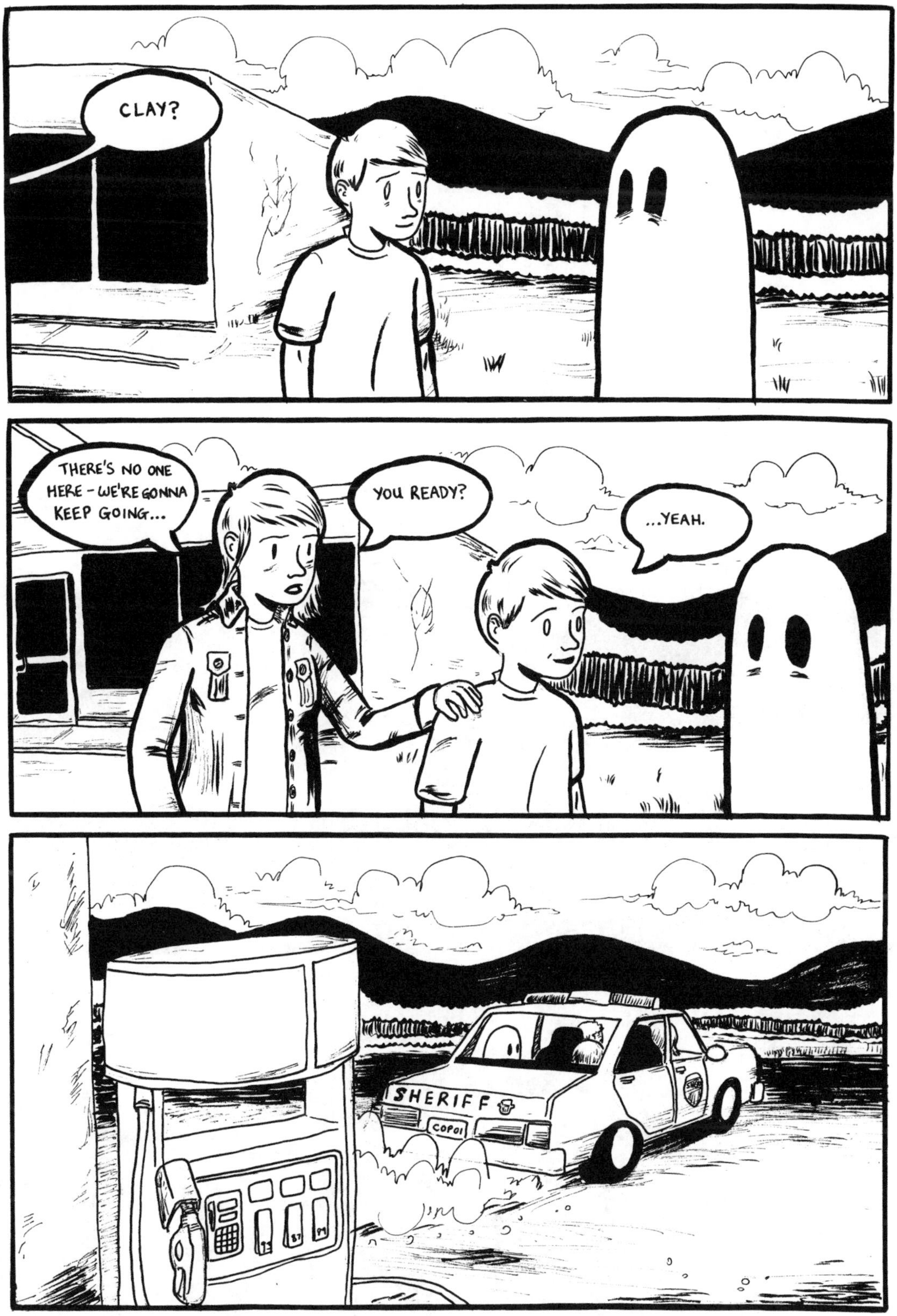
CLAY?
THERE'S NO ONE HERE - WE'RE GONNA KEEP GOING...
YOU READY?
...YEAH.
SHERIFF
COP01

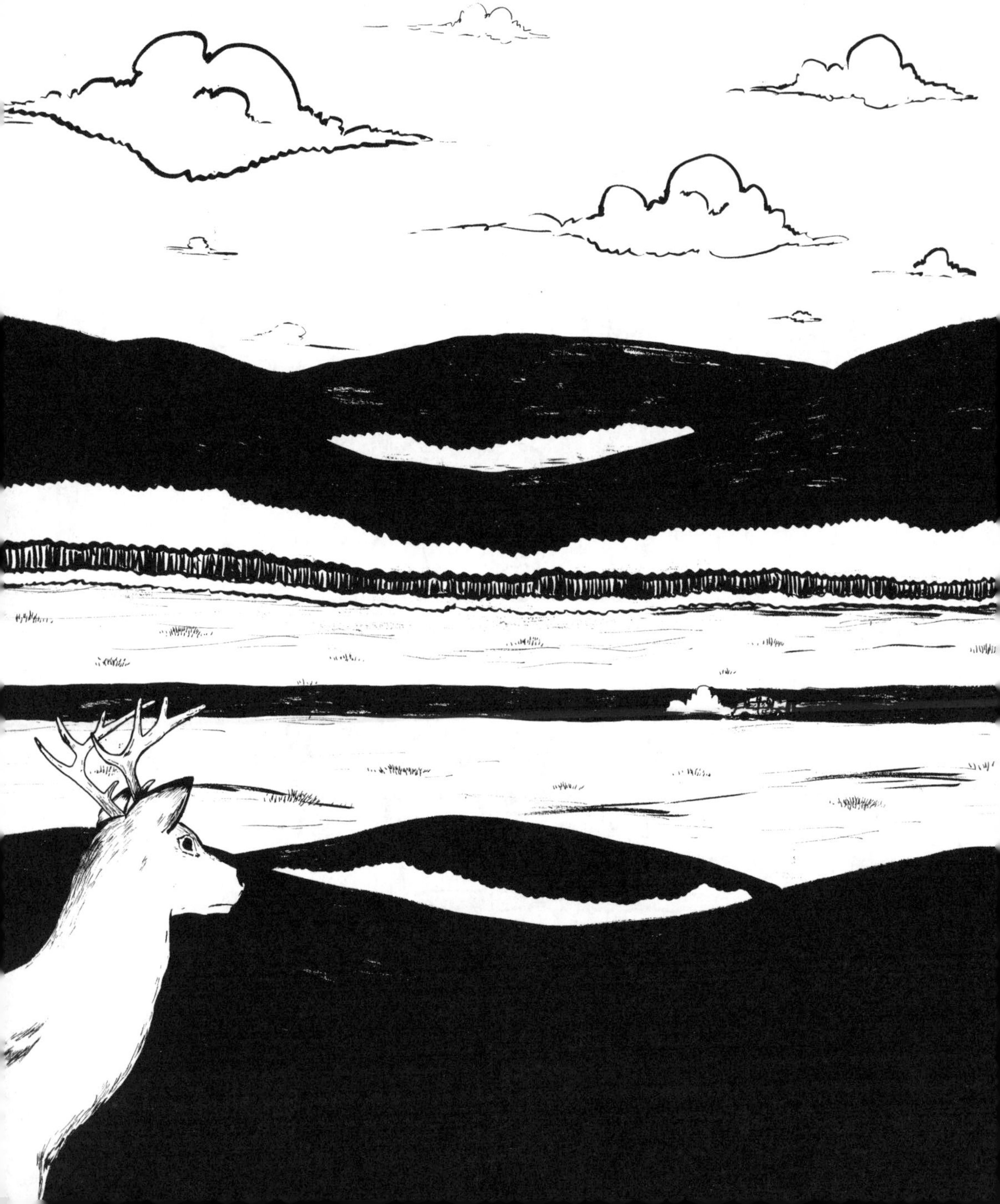

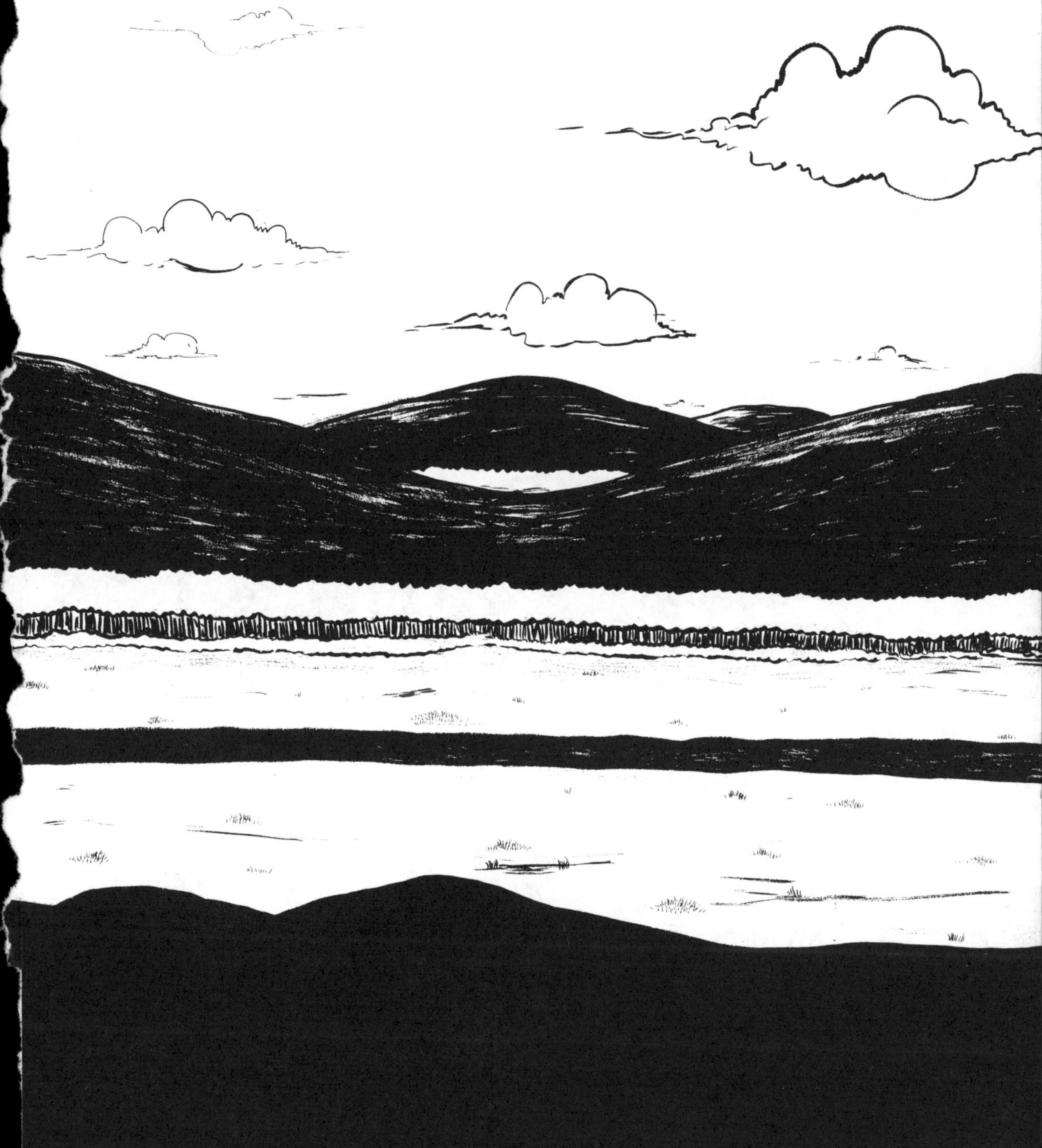

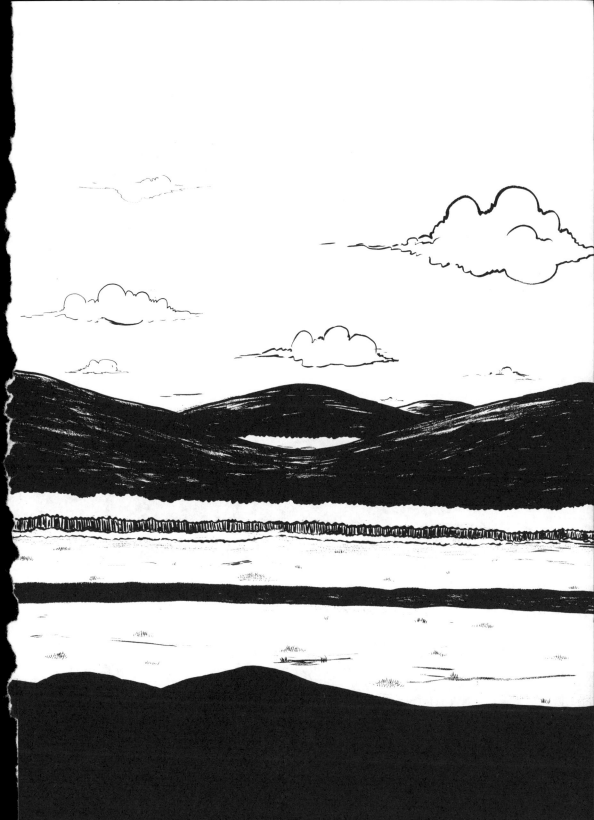

THIS BOOK WAS DRAWN BETWEEN 2007 AND 2012, IN VERMONT AND BROOKLYN. IT WOULD NOT HAVE BEEN POSSIBLE WITHOUT THE SUPPORT, ENCOURAGEMENT, AND LOVE OF MY GOOD FRIENDS AND FAMILY.

THANK YOU TO:

LEON AND BARRY, MOM AND DAD, RYAN, JACQUELINE, CHRIS, ANDREW, ALEX, JOE, CHUCK, MELISSA, GABBY, JERMAINE AND EVERYONE ELSE WHO TRICKED ME INTO NOT STOPPING. YOU ARE THE BEST.

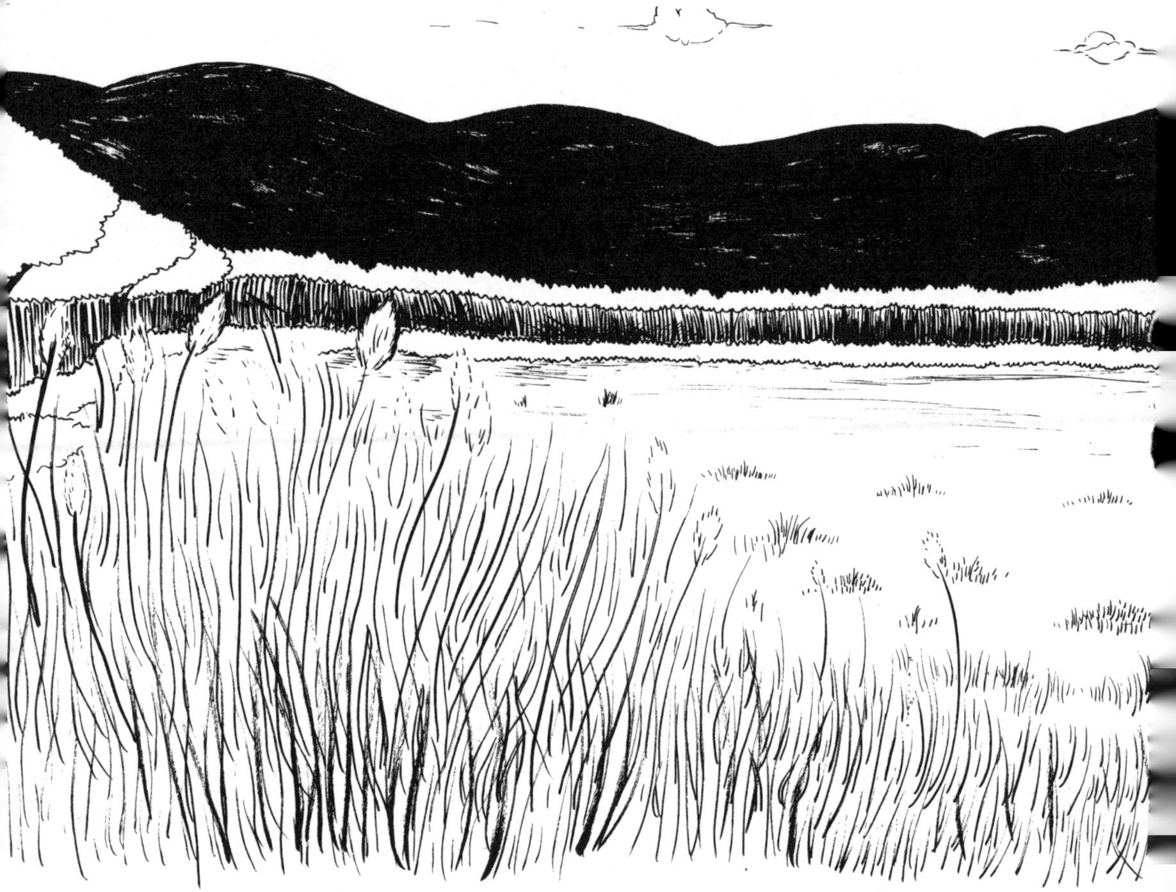